Dynasty of Light

Foundational Studies and Discourse in Color Theory

Alan Shijo McManus Burner

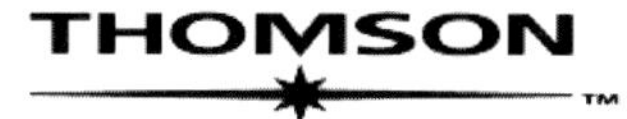

Dynasty of Light: Foundational Studies and Discourse in Color Theory

Alan Shijo McManus Burner

Editor:
Jason Fremder

Marketing Coordinators:
Lindsay Annett and Sara Mercurio

Production/Manufacturing Supervisor:
Donna M. Brown

Senior Project Coordinator:
Jennifer Flinchpaugh

Pre-Media Services Supervisor:
Dan Plofchan

Rights and Permissions Specialist:
Kalina Hintz

Senior Prepress Specialists:
Phil Beran, Kim Fry and Deanna Dixon

Cover Design:
Krista Pierson

Cover Image:
Alan Shijo McManus Burner

Cover Printer:
Coral Graphics

Compositor:
Ellie Moore

Printer:
Quebecor World Versailles

Printed in the United States of America
1 2 3 4 5 6 7 8 9 07 06 05

For more information, please contact Thomson Learning, 5191 Natorp Boulevard, Mason, OH 45040.

Or you can visit our Internet site at www.thomsonlearning.com

ISBN 0-759-34330-6

About the Author

Alan Burner is a graduate from the University of California, with an emphasis in fine arts as well as a humanities background in Japanese Language and Literature. In 1981 he earned his MFA degree, and has since been extensively involved in the art world. Alan has worked in various capacities as an artist, lecturer, educator and author. He has contributed his skills as an artist and educator in Johannesburg, South Africa, Paris, France, Yokohama, Japan and in Southern California. His art forms include mediums such as digital paint, acrylic painted constructions, photography, bronze sculpture, ceramics, and video performance. Most of his work in these media have also been represented in his set designs seen in previous televised presentations on PBS as well as in gallery exhibitions. He currently works as an artist/educator in the Los Angeles area, having taught at various universities and colleges. He currently conducts workshops within the same area and is a senior faculty member at the Art Institute of California-Orange County.

As an avid traveler and color enthusiast, he has been involved with critical investigations about the nature and character of color, various theories, realities and cultural perspectives. His primary research time is spent in Paris, France and Kyoto, Japan as well as occasional trips to the Hawaiian Islands. French Gothic architecture, Pacific Island imagery, and early Japanese literature and art are at the forefront of his varied pallet of interests, and frequently serve as some of his most passionate examples for discussions about the theory of color. His most recent artwork is a compilation of influence from the French, Japanese and Hawaiian cultures, with an emphasis on color mood contrasts.

Acknowledgements

To Brad Janis whom I owe so much, and to that extent is the first recipient of my gratitude. I would also like to extend my gratitude to those on the executive committee at the Art Institute of California-Orange County, for their gracious support in this endeavor. To my colleagues at the University of California, Irvine, Paris University, Paris, France, and at the Art Institute of California for their supportive advise and thoughtful dialogue during the course of constructing this text. Particular thanks to colleagues Denis Ribouillault for thoughtful conversations about historical European color perspectives, Melinda Lester for encouragement, Richard Ewing for caricature illustrations, to Michael Hanson for his enthusiasm about textbook content, Denise Kotler for physics advice and William Jaynes for his success in embracing this new approach to color theory education. A special thanks also to Kayo Suzuki for the *Colors of Japan,* and Christo and Jeanne-Claude for their counsel in respect to *Valley Curtain* and *The Umbrellas.*

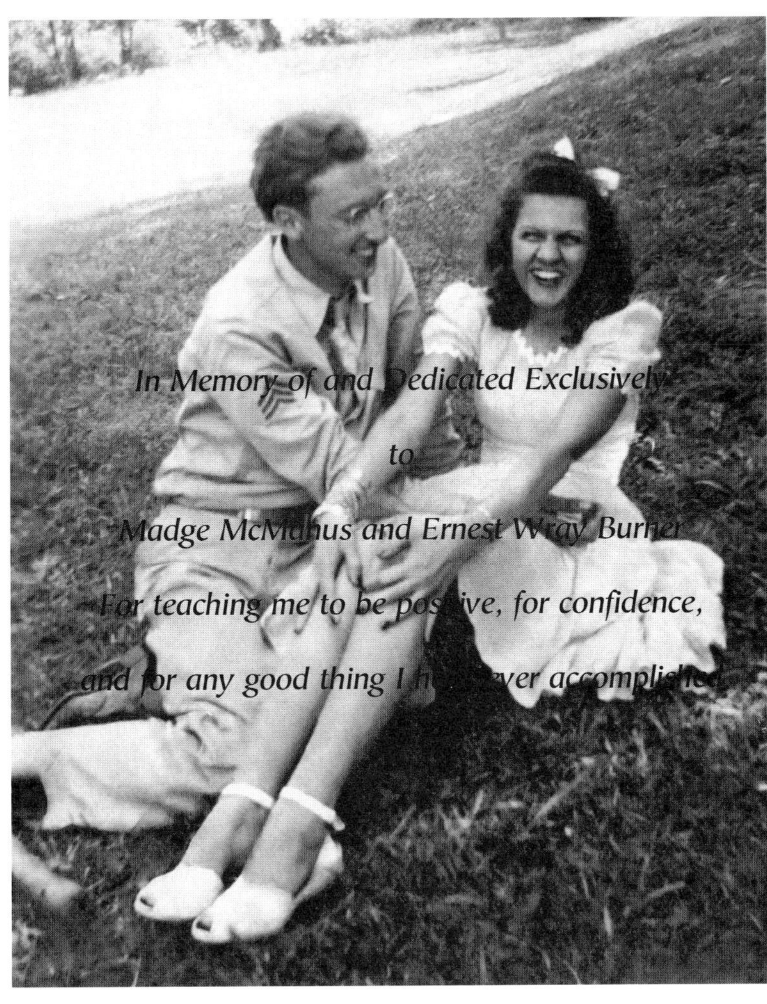

In Memory of and Dedicated Exclusively

to

Madge McManus and Ernest Wray Burner

For teaching me to be positive, for confidence,

and for any good thing I have ever accomplished.

Table of Contents

Preface

Color theory—in its presence in our lives from the sun to artificial lights—is the cornerstone element in design and painting development. The pedagogy of color training teaches formal relationships, pushing objects forward through saturation, contrast, and subdued or contrasted relationships, and combined through sharing similar value. The student is awakened to color. We are aware, superficially, of light and color, going blindly through life until the great awakening happens at age six from a sunset, in college, or at sixty. There is a moment where color and light become spiritual and aware in all of our moments, enveloping—even creating—the moods of our world from the bluish light in the early morning to the spectral color in the setting sun. Colored lights in dance clubs diffuse and change shadows from warm to cool, as hues shift in an evening of music and dancing, dictating our moods. Chromotherapy holistically heals while laser light shows and fireworks dazzle our senses and denote celebration. Color is our life, our waking perception in our eyes and mental process. Color dazzles our experiences from aurora borealis to the orange flash when struck with a sharp pain; it makes our memories, it touches our soul.

Color is the most basic element in painting. From our tubes or jars we mix and layer color to simulate the experience of living, whether it's conceptual and useable like the quark, or the archetype of consciousness—the human face. Without a strong understanding of the seven color contrasts, one cannot even begin to paint in a naturistic style, to move past the limitations of painting what we see to painting what we know, and in turn understanding what we see. When we study classicism, we understand that through anatomy and perspective, we can convincingly represent the forms of the world. Strong opinions about color strategies guide painting the body to achieve a fully three dimensional form through warm light and cool shadows.

Students need to think critically to ask basic questions about the ever-changing world around them. The study of color archetypes is important, for example, in reading Christian paintings. Understanding the Holy Mary figure is often clothed in red and blue is purely intuitive and subjective. But the choice of hue and saturation does more—it shows who her character is. Charity can be represented through red, sweetness through pink in her inner robes, and the serenity bestowed on her symbolized in her blue outer robe. In the study of the archetype, the student can begin to ask questions about corporate color use today, entirely contrived and manipulated to provoke a measured response: What is the meaning of green in today's cleaning products? These reasons are a few of the essential reasons why color is critical as a foundation course. As the student matures into specialty, color builds on other relationships to finish off interiors, web pages and paintings with splashes of color and value. Color can be an entire occupation, such as in textiles where color, value and shape decisions are critical to a tapestry designer or pattern maker.

Dynasty of Light offers an entire analysis of the color process from the scientific to the poetic. Its components stimulate the student's critical thinking skills through practical assignments and written work. The text is a comprehensive methodology to aid in the education of an art student. Art education today is not simply about hands-on projects but also about the intellectual activity of understanding the environment, history, and culture. The text stresses the science of color from studies on the properties of light to the molecular breakdown of minerals and vegetables. *Dynasty of Light* shows the student that art is an intellectual as well as intuitive endeavor.

While some may present their color classes with an emphasis on both additive and subtractive processes, my particular color classes are pigment intensive workshops where we examine harmony through the seven color contrasts, concentrating initially on saturation, value and extension, color archetypes, and the science of color. We see through the seven contrasts of color and their combined properties, and negate their intrinsic effects to find overall brown or grays in making color harmony-agreements. Color illustrations from *Dynasty of Light* provide me with examples from Robert Indiana through Van Eyck to illustrate color unity. The harmony fables from Japanese lore show the student a marked difference in East-West culture and yet also reinforce how important balance is in color, symbolically and visually, and that balance is a fundamental attribute in color usage in Eastern and Western culture.

The class also focuses heavily on color's verbal and poetic virtues, which are examined in *Dynasty of Light* with a section on exceptional observations about color's tendencies from Goethe to Newton. These instructional examples of studying color from waking life propel an important step in a student's development when they become conscious of color and analyze the everyday and the mundane. Alan's personal observations of color and its ingrained archetype on his own life shows the student that color is not something in which experiences are learned academically, but are instead reinforced in our lifelong acquaintance with color.

In the section "Light and the Eye" the student is immersed in the mechanics of the eye and properties of the rods and cones, and the mystery of the brain as a processor in which one third of its gray matter is dedicated to the complicated task of sight. From "Tints and Shades—Deep Space, Mass, and Volume" the student is taught from numerous color file examples how painters have used the observation of light and physical properties to make depth in artwork. Saturation and value changes mixed with observation about reflected and refracted light from "Sensations of Color" help the student to think in color systems. Passages on color blindness have inspired color assignments investigating red and green deficiencies in vision and painting those visual anomalies from theory.

Dynasty of Light is the instructional companion in my color classes. I have found that its poetic and intellectual tone creates a sincere sense of curiosity in my students. The color files show numerous examples of meaning, simulation of natural phenomenon, and skillful color use in painting. Its multicultural, East-West sensibilities are perfect for the cultural diversity in my Southern California classroom. When a student begins to master form relationships and drawing, color relationships become the next crucial step in learning to simulate and conceive nature, which is an essential skill to the painter and designer. This is a text that can be used several different ways. First it is a critical assessment of color usage throughout art history. Second, it is a scientific reading which addresses the origins of the universe, color's relationship to heat and energy, and the mechanics of the brain. Third it is an affirmation that written and oral skills are as essential as hands-on exercises in art education.

Michael Hanson

Definitions of Textbook Components—The Written Analysis

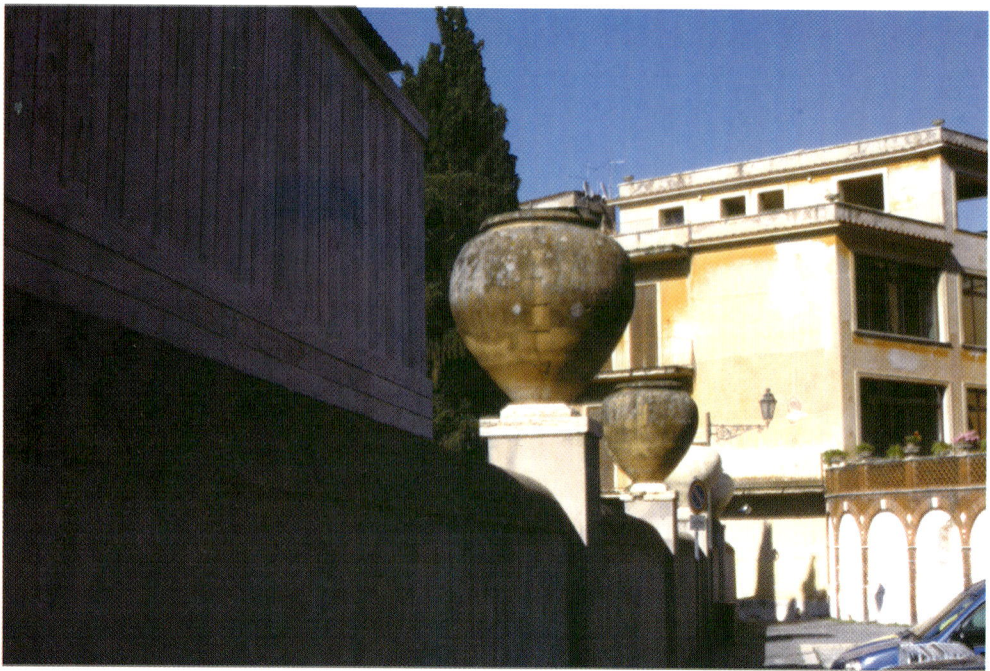

Street Scene, Tivoli, Italy.
Photo by Alan Burner.

Tivoli, with its typical small town "pottery village" atmosphere, creates an ambiance of beautiful simplicity and delicate color nuances. A subtle complementary color harmony of warm yellow-oranges and cool blue-violets dominate this street scene. The background apartment building bathes in the sun's intense light on a hot July summer day, while the foreground wall beckons the passer-by to a shady retreat from the heat of the day.

The plaza street's imagery, in a sense, becomes a painting, which is emphasized by high contrasting color, and graceful variations of tints and shades. The monolithic architecture with its hot radiant yellow-orange surface, is in direct opposition to the wall's cooling blue-violet shades. Values of violets and oranges exemplify the sense of mass and weight seen in the majestic vases on the wall. Their dull violet and deep orange patinas provide a transitional link of color gradations between the wall and the building.

The lack of saturated color on the architectural wall, as well as the dull shades of the concrete and wood partition, illustrates the extremes of high contrast with the more delicate transitions of value gradations, which are indicative of a hot summer day in Italy. The warm and cool contrasts of hue variations help to establish a certain power in the imagery itself. The chromatic value transitions of the large vases, the strong vertical thrust of the blue-violet textured wall, and the flat monolithic yellow-orange architecture controls the temperature of the space. As we feel the heat of the day, contrasted by a cooling shade, there is a very tranquil mood set specifically by the sedate sensibility on this quiet street in Tivoli.

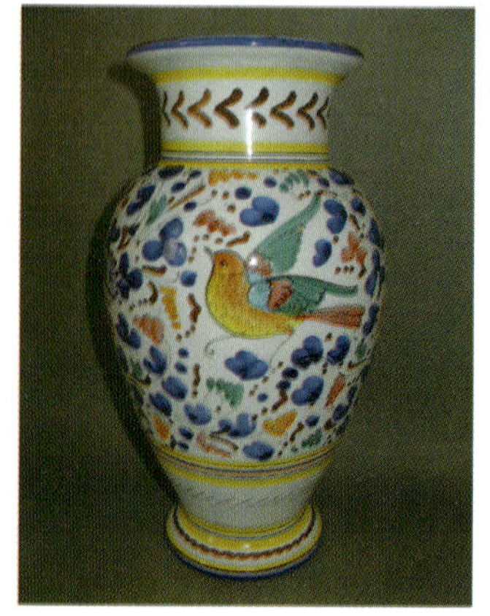

The typical colors of Italian ceramics reflect the spirited nature seen in its people, and are echoed in this vase from Tivoli.
Photo by Alan Burner.

A New Approach to Color Education

This textbook offers some new and challenging approaches, as well as traditional approaches, to the instruction of color theory, both in content and methodology. In reality, it is a collection of *color investigations,* which takes a serious look into the psychological, philosophical, and physiological effects of color. *Dynasty of Light* also covers conventional physics and the traditional characteristics of color. It is instructional discourse, which covers everything from the science of color to the emotional and spiritual nuances of color. The student will learn to integrate the visual and intellectual aspects of learning in a more comprehensive way through a series of *written analysis* and *color projects.*

The respected institution of color theory and those who preceded us—Aristotle, Sir Isaac Newton, Johannes Itten, and many others—have made critical color investigations, wrote extensively about their findings, and presented them to the world. In the case of Newton, certain key elements to the nature of light and color are the foundation stones for what we teach today. Out of these early findings emerged a conventional method for teaching color theory which we've subscribed to for many years. This foundation of color theory pioneered the discovery of color and its ramifications. We owe it eternal loyalty and great respect.

Since Newton's time, we have discovered new and exciting aspects about color and methods for teaching it . When this textbook was conceived, it was my intention not to create yet another color theory book for the sake of writing a text. We don't need another book on the subject repeating the same approach. As we reach into the 21st century, we have discovered and have put into action many new approaches to living our lives. Why then, shouldn't we make solid steps forward in the all-inclusive education of color theory?

Through the expertise of the color theory instructor, students will discover the mysteries of the color world. To enhance that discovery, this text book offers a comprehensive arrangement of color investigations and a story of color from the physical to the spiritual attributes.

One of the components of the text that departs from traditional books on the subjects is the suggested written analysis of color compositions, which is an important option in the student's education of color. Within any color theory course, as it is with this text, there are normally a collection of relevant hands-on projects. Accompanying these projects, whether selected from this text or the individual instructor's preferred repertoire of assignments, is written analysis for the sake of thoroughness. The student could, for example, write a summary or analysis on their finished project, or analyze an assigned color composition of the instructor's choice.

One of the problems of educating the serious student of color lies within the proper exercising of critical thinking skills. Certainly, the traditional approaches to color theory education are sound and encouraged in the conventional application of color project assignments. We have found, however, that incorporating the written analysis of various color compositions is a valuable tool in the deeper understanding and retention of color theory and science. This text encourages the development of critical color observation by project solutions, as well as written and oral analysis.

Studies show that a student's ability to absorb and retain information is most effective when writing, as opposed to merely listening to lectures. Therefore, *class lecture notes, written assignments* and *color analysis* serve to aid in a student's retention of what is taught. Preservation of learned material is typically 35–45% greater when putting the pen to paper in a lecture, or if writing about a particular research project. Writing helps not only to perfect the student's proclivity to retain information, but in the ability to efficiently *communicate* about the subject. Our goal then is to develop the capability to demonstrate color proficiency by both written work and project assignments.

The students are provided with an opportunity to illustrate their development in critical thinking skills, by researching selected artist's work and making a thorough written analysis. For the analysis, the student is first asked to study and write about important historical information (short biography) concerning an assigned artist, linking the purposes of the artist to the work. Secondly, the student presents an effective written color analysis about the artwork itself.

A Word about Mood and Emotion

Before we begin with the color analysis, it is probably a good thing to discuss the emotional issues of color briefly. Every color scheme or harmony elicits a particular emotion or mood. The component of mood is clearly one of the most important functions of color. Everything that incorporates the use of color, whether pigments on a canvass, designing on a computer monitor, or perhaps planning the interior of a room, has the end result of creating very specific moods. In reality it is mood, created by color, that reaches the soul, and stirs the emotions. It is therefore vital to develop an understanding of how color is part of that spiritual world—the inner being. During the course mood will become an issue which gains greater momentum as the student learns more about color and its various functions.

Here then is an explanation of the components of this text, beginning with the critical component of the *written analysis.* Consider the following works of George Inness and Frederic Leighton, as two color-mood analysis examples.

In the case of the American painter George Inness, we find that he made critical choices about the use of color in his artwork. These choices are directly responsible for the creation of specific moods. Let's look at the colors incorporated into George Inness' *Evening Landscape*.

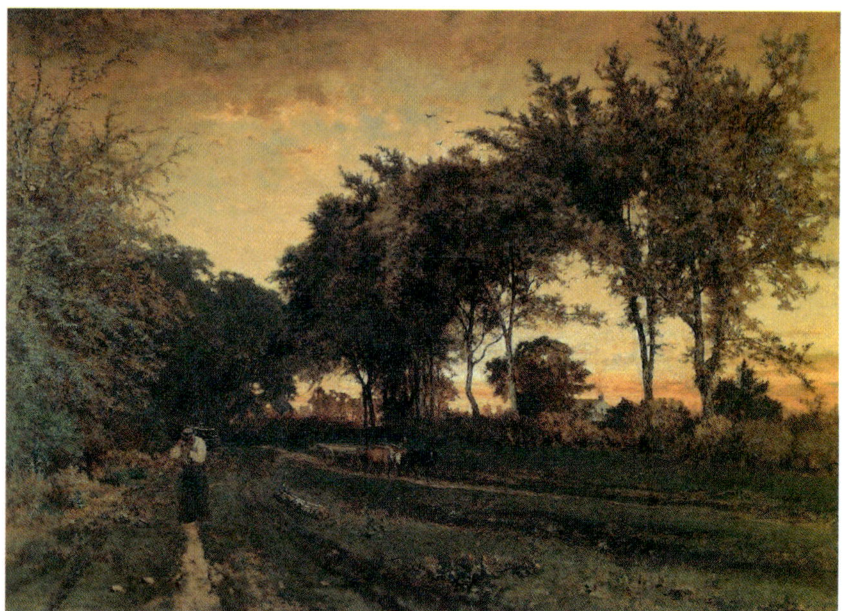

George Inness, *Evening Landscape,* 1862, gift of Dr. & Mrs. William E. Boeing, from the Permanent Collection, Museum of Art/Washington State University, Pullman, WA unframed, 48 1/2 × 66 1/4. From the permanent collection, Museum of Art/Washington State University, Pullman, Wa. Used by permission.

This painting sets up a striking contrast of complementary colors, or opposites, in terms of the *light, heavenly* red-orange sky, and the *weighty mass* of the blue-green terra firma. It is both complementary in terms of color and the representation of luminous space as opposed to solid heavy mass. The trees and the ground seem to consume the better part of the composition, with its dark and gloomy values.

It is the luminous, almost spiritual approach to painting the sky which focuses the eye on the earthiness of the environment and the toil of humankind. It is a revealing manifestation of color's effect on the human psyche. The mood is somber and respectful of both the human condition on earth and the earth itself. It speaks of the journey through life, both the bright spots and the burdens.

Inness shows us a world where God exists in a heavenly, spiritual realm, and humankind's existence is grounded and tangible. The mood and symbolic references are replete within the *Evening Landscape*.

> "The wisest and best way to know George Inness is to sit before his works, to search them to their depths, to study each item of composition, its bearing upon the great mass, to find, if one may, the law by which he constructed his proportions and placements, *to discover the reasons for color or tone choice, or that deeper significance,* the impulsive, artistic and religious, which created it"
>
> Elliott Daingerfield

Leighton's *Flaming June*, is one of the finest examples of 18th century Victorian art today. Intensely feminine, the mood of this painting replicates a *tranquil* slumber, and yet it conveys a sensuous *energy*. The *calmness of mood* is reflected by the image itself, yet the various hues of orange expose a sensually *energized* composition. The painting illustrates the fine and subtle nuances of chromatic value, which change through the elegantly sheer drapery.

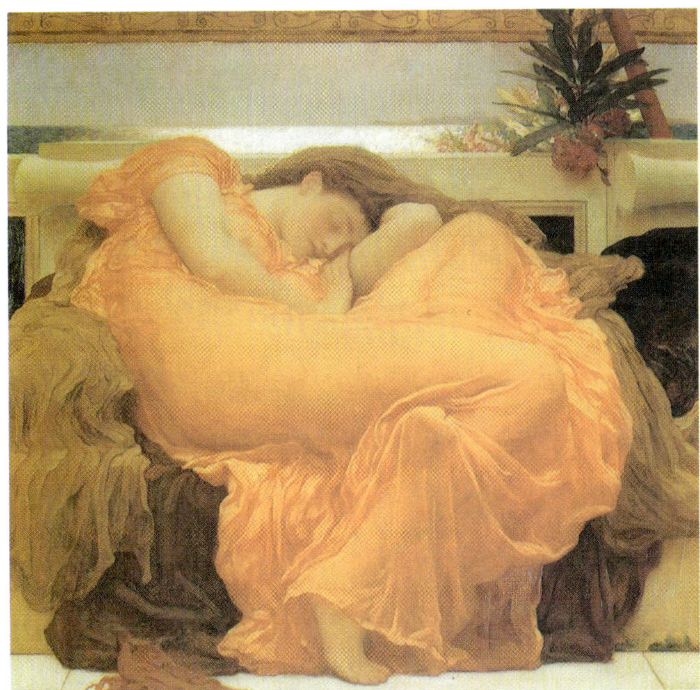

Flaming June by Frederic Leighton.
Museo de Arte, Ponce, Puerto Rico, U.S.A. © Art Resource, NY.

The delicate hues of orange seem to invite a type of erotic expectation, if not in a dream.

In Leighton's painting, we again see contrasts; the tangible and the intangible. June's physical body, the warm passionate hues in the composition, contrasted to her dream state or spiritual existence perhaps seen by the delicate luminescence of the composition itself.

Component One—The Written Analysis

I would like to take this opportunity to discuss just how important writing is by using specific examples of successful artists throughout history. If we can establish their success based on their need to write, then certainly we are beholden to consider the same for ourselves. Some of the greatest color artists throughout history understood that creative prowess cannot be achieved by simply responding to the medium, based on physical response alone, but by very careful observation and investigation. Each of the following artists used writing to achieve a specific result, albeit not the same one, but they all achieved one thing in common—successful art.

Leonardo da Vinci, of the high Renaissance knew something of the relationship between the written word and visual creation. Leonardo wrote extensively about art—in fact some thought that perhaps he wrote too much and painted too little. Certainly a great number of his journals contain both sketches and written observations. Da Vinci was a leader in the world of written investigations into art and color, as well as a *scientist* and inventor.

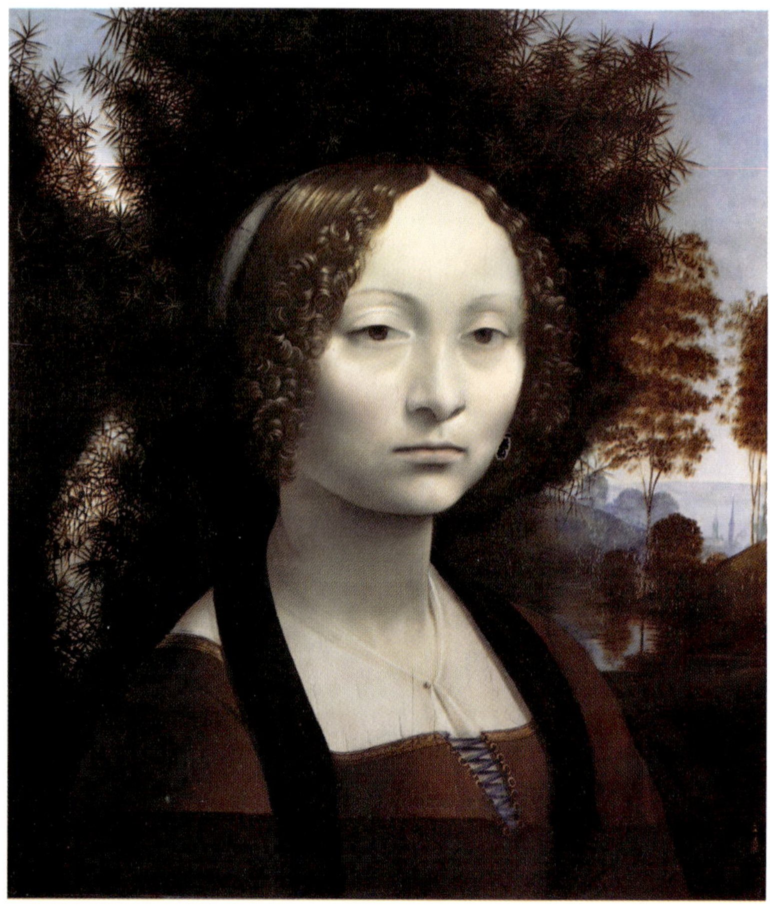

Ginevra de Benci by Leonardo da Vinci.
© 2004 Board of Trustees, National Gallery of Art, Washington, c. 1474.

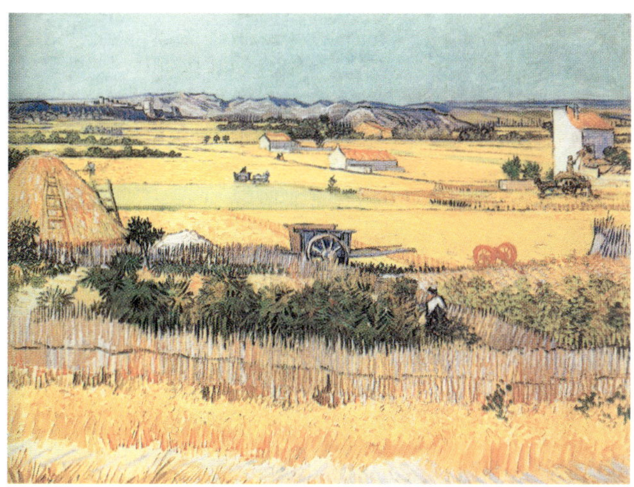

Harvest at La Crau, with Montmajour in the Background by Vincent van Gogh.
Amsterdam, Rijksmuseum Vincent van Gogh, Vincent van Gogh Foundation.

He was both a *philosopher* and *scientist* on the subject of color.

Da Vinci understood the development of critical thinking skills and color prowess attained by the persistent use of the pen. The more he observed, the more he wrote and the more he wrote, the more proficient he became with color. How could he remember so many critical observations about color, unless he were to record them? By doing so he developed an intimate understanding about the use of color.

His written scientific annotations served him well in clarifying his color formulas accurately, and his recorded philosophical arguments between the painter (himself), the poet and the musician also proved beneficial. His discourse on their debates, as to whose medium was the most "excellent" in the creative process, cemented in his own mind the validity of *his* opinion and therefore, the difference and superiority of painting. We realize that his philosophy concerning superiority is subjective, and serves more to the benefit of the artist.

It shouldn't be any wonder or secret then, after so many austere renderings and written observations about people and their sensibilities, that works such as the *Mona Lisa* and *Ginevra de Benci* are so accomplished. Da Vinci's strict execution of pigments is certainly due to his faithful records of observation. In this case, it would seem that observations from past records gave him the edge for the creation of *Lisa Gherardini,* since we have no records or notes about her specifically.

Vincent van Gogh was notorious for his written observations of life via his letters to his brother, Theo. It has been reported that there are at least 800 known letters in which Van Gogh discusses his personal needs and beliefs, hardships of life, his inability to work, and the reflections and memories that fill his "head and heart".

Van Gogh's approach to the recorded journal was decidedly different than the conventional, since he wrote in letter format, and yet they carried the tone of a diary read by his benefactor, Theo. Van Gogh worked through is observations about people—how they worked, labored and the difficulty of life for example—in his letters. Once he had reconciled their pains, he chose the subdued and shaded color schemes necessary to project that mood.

In his painting, the *Potato Eaters,* he was fascinated with the idea of back-breaking work: planting, cultivating, digging the potatoes out of the ground, and at last eating them. All this was a product of the laborers' own hands. There were times when he would write and produce paintings about *Arles,* where he had spent many a happy day in his earlier life. They were pleasant memories. Paintings such as the *Wheat Stacks with Reaper,* or *Vincent's House in Arles (The Yellow House)* are ablaze with rich and often saturated color. They are brilliant color fields of yellows and oranges, paintings that allowed him to vicariously live out his life, for the moment, in peace and tranquility.

Van Gogh's letters reveal a highly intelligent man, in spite of his psychological issues. There is no contention that Van Gogh was one of the greatest master color experts within the history of art. His vast luminescent color fields of emotion create the precise mood of the artist and help us to understand the mind of Van Gogh. Clearly, the success of his work depended on his evaluation of everyday life through writing letters to his one benevolent supporter, Theo.

Paul Gauguin, with his flat and often saturated color fields of paint, perceived the importance as an artist of keeping a journal of written observations.

In his Tahitian journals, he records many personal feelings and accounts of island life away from his native France. As Gauguin moved more towards the abstract use of color, he began to write more frequently about the validity of his color theories. In a lesson to one of his young apprentices, it is recorded "....How do you see these trees? They are yellow. Well then, put down yellow. And that shadow is rather blue. So, render it with pure ultramarine. Those red leaves? Use vermillion." He saw yellows in a tree and painted them with as much saturation as possible.

Often times painting *from memory*, he recorded the color exaggeration as he translated it in his mind. What he committed to the written page was then cemented in his mind. Gauguin wrote extensively about his art concerns as well, often validating, and sometimes inviting criticism. Like Van Gogh, who was occasionally a recipient of Gauguin's letters, Gauguin was a letter writer extraordinaire.

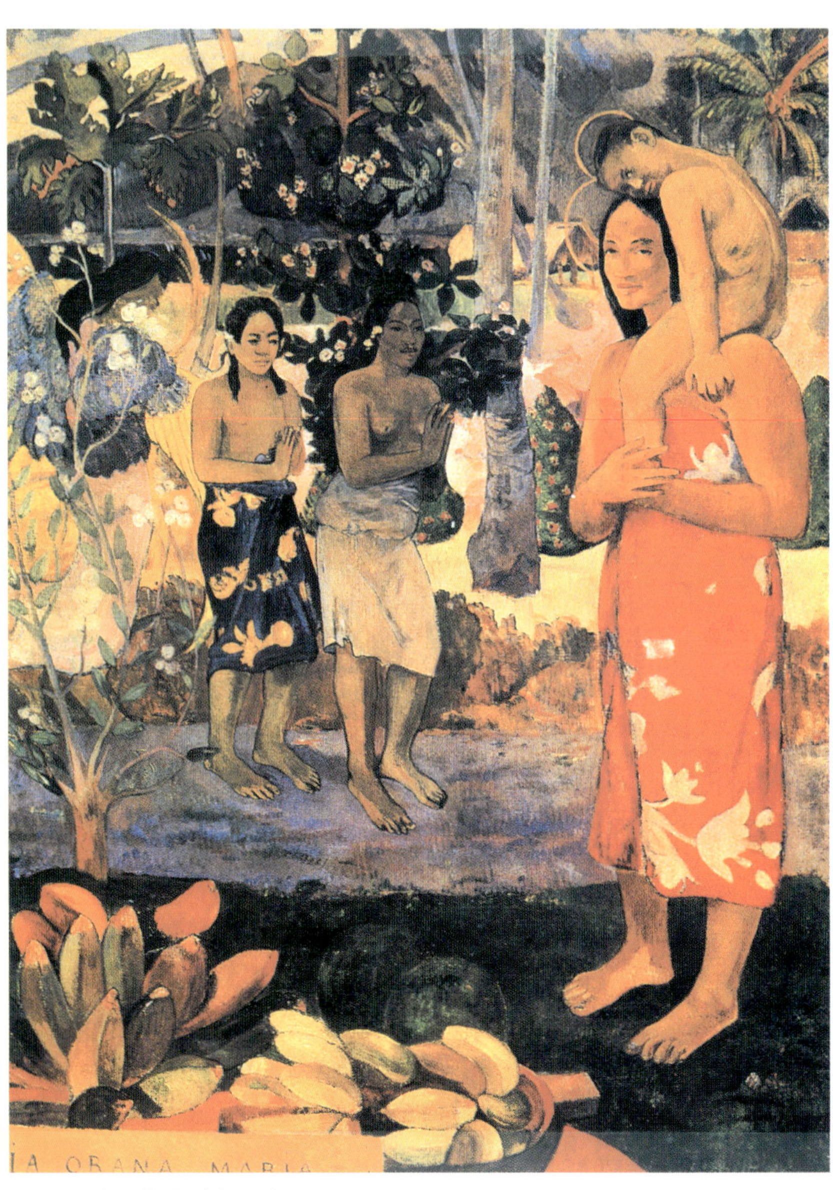

Iaorana Maria by Paul Gauguin.
New York, Metropolitan Museum of Art.

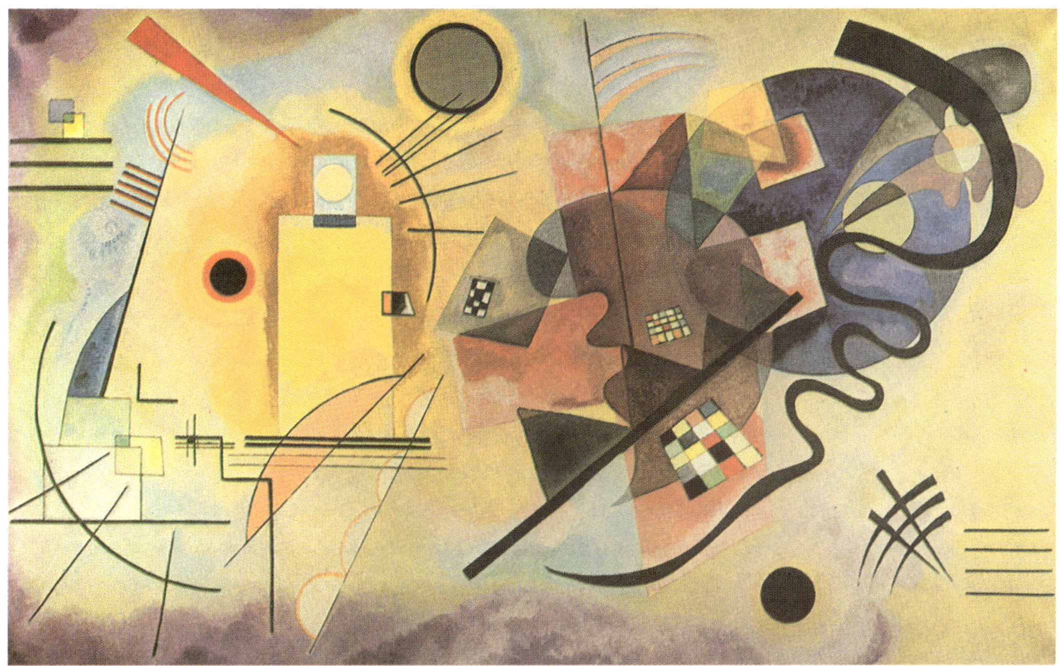

Yellow, Red and Blue by Wassily Kandinsky.

Wassily Kandinsky, the artist, intellectual and profound writer about art concerns in the twentieth century, revealed his prowess in the spiritual realm of art. His records about communicating the spiritual intangible into a physical concrete world are unparalleled. He presents his findings through the written word, a discourse on the subject few have managed to achieve. His has made critical observations about the ramifications of line and symbolism, and his revelations of exploratory missions in art take us deep into the spiritual world of color.

Kandinsky's precise and very meticulous observations give us a greater understanding of what he refers to as "external nature," expressed in linear color compositions, which are then contrasted to the "inner nature". Kandinsky declared that color in and of itself is capable of unfolding the spiritual realm if it is not assigned a certain predetermined shape or image.

Pablo Picasso, one of history's most successful artists, is replete of artwork but was seriously deficient when it came to writing skills. (His focus was singular to a fault, as he depleted his female com-

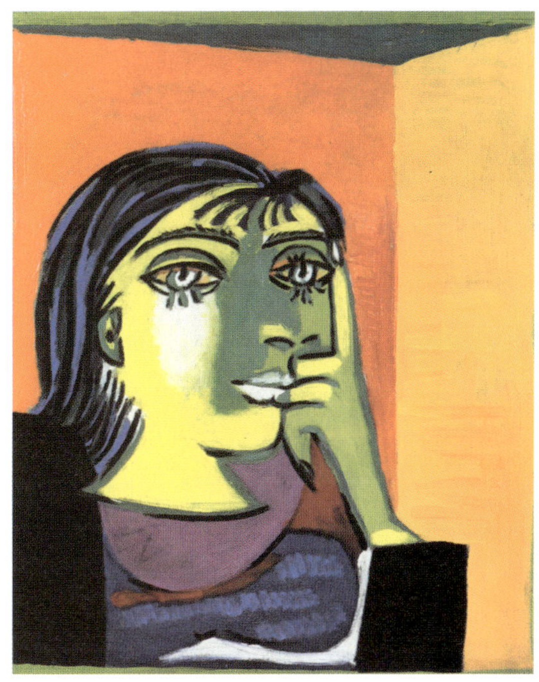

Portrait of Dora Maar by Pablo Picasso.

panions of their vigor.) He would use them for the soul purpose of art subjects, and discard them after the transfusion of their energies into his work—the finished painting. However, Picasso understood full well the necessity for the written journal regarding art and its evaluation, so he surrounded himself with poets and writers. Francoise, his young lover, writes that Picasso was able to discuss his artwork eloquently because of his friendships with poets and writers. After one of Pablo's gatherings with friends she writes; "Afterwards Pablo, who—for things like that—was an extremely adaptable, supple person, always talked very perceptively about his painting because of his intimacy with those who had been able to discover the right words." f/n (p.136 of *Life with Picasso*)

Even a non-writer like Picasso understood the extreme value of the written word. After all, how could he have been so articulate in his dialogs without some source that enabled him to clearly define what he accomplished in his work? Certainly, if he was unable to write for whatever reason, then his writer friends could. Here is an art form so full of expression and visual dynamic that it requires the descriptive force and sophistication only a writer can provide. Writers such as Max Jacob, Paul Eluard, Andre' Breton and Apollinaire were all key elements in his success.

How to begin a written analysis of color in a composition

Often, the student of color will be asked to fine tune critical thinking skills by the careful analysis of a composition (in this case a painting). Frequently, students are overwhelmed because they tend to look at the composite parts simultaneously, rather than singularly. The result is always "where do I start?" or "why can't I find much to write about?" Here's how to begin: since mood is the chief characteristic of color, and the final result of most color analysis, first try to isolate the mood, and then validate that decision. In the second composition, we will cite the mood of the colors lastly, which is normally a more accurate method. Finally, there should be three phases to the analyzing of color in any composition. Look at the two samples following, and notice how each area is observed and noted, piece by piece, section by section:

Example One

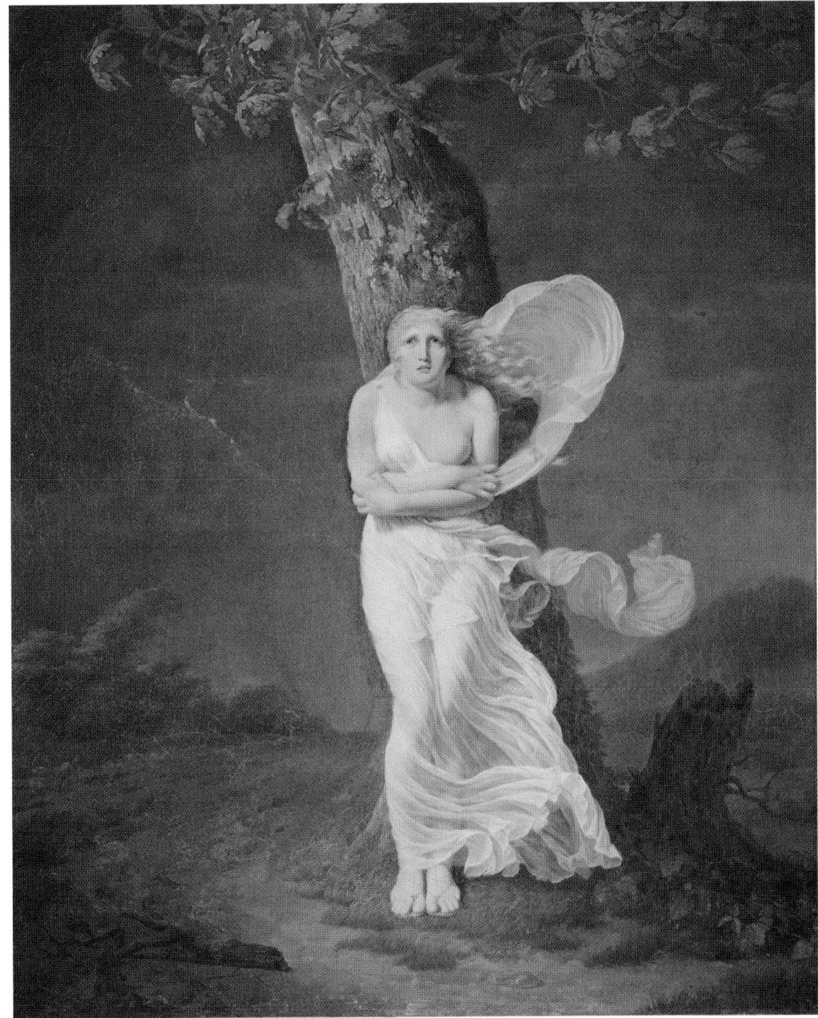

Painting of A Young Woman out in the Country Finds Herself Caught in a Storm by Fereole de Bonnemaison.
Erich Lessing/Art Resource, NY.

First Draft General Outline of Fereole de Bonnemaison's Painting

1. Mood: Background is dark and fearful. Blue tones.
2. Shaded blue gradations. Background values.
3. Tree is centered. Foreground. Greens and yellows, some red tones.
4. Different value changes in the composition.
5. Red-orange and yellow-green bark.
6. Tree contrast.
7. Tree's texture.
8. Figure of a young girl. Clothing blowing-off.
9. Intensity of the skin tones, seems luminous.
10. Contrast of figure with background.
11. Delicate vs. Harshness.
12. Earth/foreground.

Second Draft with Specific Outline of Fereole de Bonnemaison's Painting

1. Mood: Fearful, depressing, filled with gloom and despair. It is full of darkness contrasted by light.
2. Background: Beginning at the horizon and ascending to the top of the composition, the background of medium shaded blue to darkest blue, creates a smooth transition of chromatic values. It is the shaded blue gradations which seem to create the mystery, the darkness which overwhelms the center figure.
3. Large and slightly diagonal tree splits composition. Lighter shade of green foliage creates a marginal contrast between it and the darker background.
4. Tints and shades, or value changes from light to dark and back again, create the illusion of three-dimension, as is the case throughout the painting.
5. The underneath layer of tree's bark is composed of a red-orange, ranging from an intense red-orange area over her head, to a shaded red-orange. The outer layer of bark is a dull yellow-green.
6. The bark of the tree sets up a middle range contrast between it and the background.
7. The rapid transitions of values or light to dark gradations of yellow-green in the bark create the illusion of rough texture.
8. The foreground is occupied by a young girl, whose clothing is being ripped from her body by the force of the wind. The mood is now validated, as we sense dark stormy dismal weather. The girl's expression matches the mood created by the colors in the composition.
9. The texture of her skin seems very soft, as very intense lightest orange values make the subtlest value gradations.
10. The intensely light blue gown reveals the severity of the weather by its horizontal rippling. The resultant contrast of the lightest blue robe and the darkest blue background, creates the illusion of space in the composition. The lightest orange hue of her skin helps to push her further into the foreground.
11. There is a symbolic contrast between the delicacy of the light orange skin, the lightest blue gown in the foreground, and the sturdy and harsh darker blues of the stormy environment around her.
12. Finally, the shaded or dulled green and orange hues of the foreground on which the girl stands, lead the eye back to the horizon and up into the dark blue clouds.

Third and Final Draft of Fereole de Bonnemaison's Painting (no longer an outline)

Beginning with the mood of the painting, we are drawn to several aspects of the composition; the figure, tree and background. I want to site the mood aspects of color in the painting first, and show why it is color which creates mood, more than the expression of the figure's face itself.

I am drawn to the background hues of shaded blue and violet values. As they eye moves from the horizon, the lighter shaded blues make a smooth transition upward, gradating into an extremely dark blue, which is almost black in appearance. The background clouds create a darkness, a certain mystery about the weather and what is about to happen. The sky is depressing, the air heavy, as the intensity of the storm increases and begins to overwhelm the young girl.

The tree is particularly important because it sets up a gradual diagonal, splitting the composition and creating a tilt or certain instability about the composition. The light and dark values of dull green leaves blow with intensity, and seem to barely separate themselves from the dark sky. The value gradations in the green foliage seem to create a leaf which is forced into a cupped shape, further exaggerating the storm's ferocity. The leaves are convincingly three-dimensional, as is the entire composition, because of the variations of value changes.

The texture of the tree's bark is believably rough, thanks to a more severe or rapid change of value, or light to dark rendering. The underneath, newer bark exposing itself in selected patches, is shown by the red-orange to shaded red-orange hues, compared to the older higher intensity surface bark of yellow-greens. The bark now creates a middle-range contrast between the tree and the background. A definite depth of space is created as a result.

A young girl occupies the foreground, positioned close to the center of the composition, just ahead of the tree's trunk. Her clothing rippling violently in the wind is partially blown off of her body. The leaves on the tree seem to struggle to remain on the branches, as does her sheer gossamer robe to her body. At this point, we look up to her face, only to find the girl's expression validates the mood which the colors have already revealed.

The texture of her skin reflects a very intense lightest orange, making the most subtle of *sfumato* value gradations. Her skin is soft, delicate and contrasts against the harshness of the dull blues and violets in the background. Commensurately, the refined lightest blue fabric and darkest blue background creates the illusion of deep space by nature of the contrast itself. Her intense light orange skin assists to move her body into the foreground.

The shaded or dull green and orange hues of the foreground, by which the girl stands, leads the viewer's eye towards the background horizon again, and eventually ascends up into the darkness of the deep blue-violet clouds.

Finally, there is also a *symbolic contrast* between the delicacy of her light orange skin tones and her light blue gown, against the sturdy and harsh darker blues and blue-violets of the story environment around her. The red-oranges of the tree's bark and the red-orange hair draw the figure close to the tree, holding her safely against the trunk.

The emotion and energy of this painting in the totality of its composite parts combine with the subtle dyad harmonies (complements of blues and oranges) to create a dynamic composition reflecting the mood of terror in this impending storm.

Example Two

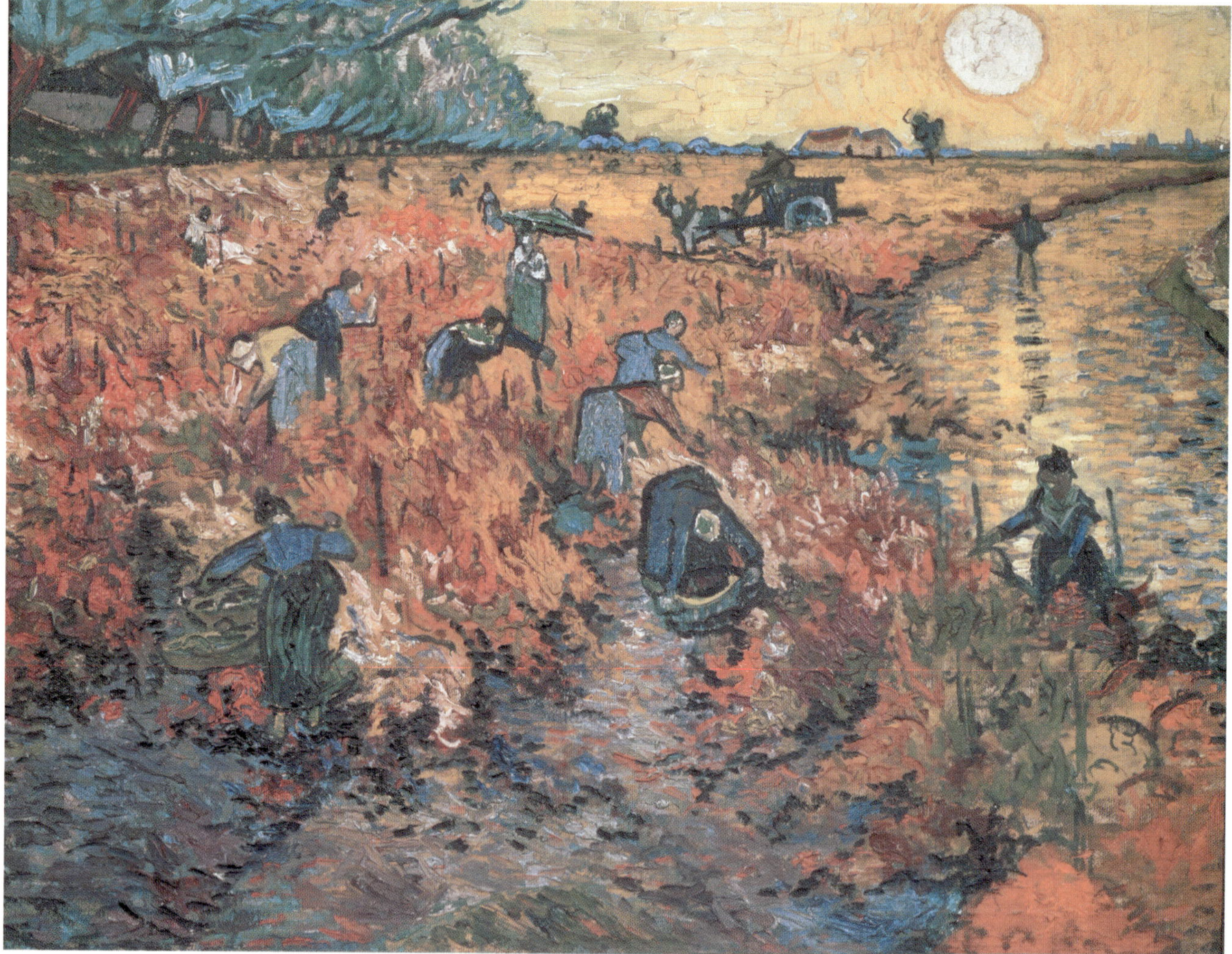

The Red Vineyard, Arles, November, 1888 by Vincent van Gogh.
Erich Lessing/Art Resource, NY.

First Draft General Outline of Vincent van Gogh's Painting

1. Background light yellow sun.
2. Sky/horizon occupies very little space. Intense sky.
3. Saturated orange—Background.
4. Saturated red/shaded red—middle-ground.
5. Dark foreground—Blue greens
6. Body of water: Blue-greens, yellow-oranges.
7. Grape pickers.
8. Perspective by line and color. Larger analogous areas.
9. Lesser blue-green areas.
10. Black shade and line.
11. Light violet hills, under trees.
12. Mood is somber.

Second Draft Specific Outline of Vincent van Gogh's Painting

1. Background focal point illuminated by a very intensely light yellow sun, surrounded by yellow-orange rays of light.
2. Horizon line to the top of the composition occupies only one-fifth of the uppermost composition. In that space the sun, a barn, and a row of blue-green trees exist. There is a green tint that radiates out from the trees, into the intensely lit, light yellow sky.
3. Just below the horizon, still in the extreme background, lays a patch of fairly saturated orange, which takes the eye to the stretches of the vineyard.
4. Middle-ground area consists of saturated red hues, which moves further into the forward to create a darker shaded red area of vines.
5. Foreground is perceived to be light shaded greens to very dark shaded green, interspersed with splashes of shaded red-orange.
6. The right-side of the composition consists of a body of water, reflecting blue-greens and yellow-oranges.
7. The vineyard itself is peppered with field hands, or grape pickers who are harvesting the crop. End of day and tired from hard labor.
8. Strong sense of perspective is created by line and color. Foreground is dark and becomes lighter, or more intense as we move into the background. Red, orange and yellow dominate, with red-orange and yellow-orange interspersed between those areas. A dominant *analogous* color harmony prevails throughout the largest part of the composition.
9. Blue-green dominates the remaining one-third of the painting.
10. Patches and lines of black accent the composition, creating shades under the trees as well as the floor of the vineyard and the grape stakes.
11. A slight amount of light violet shows up under the trees, the horizon's hills, and on fabrics worn by the workers.
12. Mood is somber, created not by the saturated colors, but by contrast of them to the very dull and shaded blue-greens. The darkness creates contrast to the saturation, and it seems as though the lesser area of that darkness is consuming the greater area of saturated space.

Third and Final Draft of Vincent van Gogh's Painting

The Red Vineyard exhibits a blazing light yellow sun setting near the horizon line. Yellow-orange lines surround the sun's perimeter and radiate out from its edge into a sky of intense yellow. The circular lines of yellow-orange mix with the intense yellow of the sky to produce a saturated yellow field of color. The area which occupies the sky is no more than one-fifth of the overall composition, and yet it dominates as a focal point, in contrast to the bulk of colors in the painting. A blue-green tint radiates into the yellow sky. Working from the background of the painting, the row of blue-green trees seems to pull the eye from the horizon into the vineyard itself.

The immediate area or field below the horizon emits soft glow of saturated orange, contrasting and drawing attention to the figure on the cart. Just below, in the middle-ground area, the vineyard becomes a very saturated red, which transforms it closer to the viewer's space, into a shaded red, or red-orange field. The foreground then becomes light shaded blue-greens and dark blue-greens, interspersed with splashes of shaded red-orange hues.

On the right side, middle-ground of the painting, a body of water glistens and reflects the blues of a darkening sky. The yellow-orange hues of the setting sun are mirrored as well, providing a cool quiet for the approaching sunset.

The vineyard is peppered with people picking the grape crop, as the horse drawn cart moves through the field to collect the harvest. They seem to be working slowly, as if to be weary at a days end of hard labor. Darkness is settling over the field, and the colors of red begin to darken in the first half of the composition, sedating the picture.

A strong sense of deep space is created by line and color perspective. As the eye focuses on the foreground, it slowly moves into the background space, as the hues become lighter, or more intense. Red, orange and yellow seem to control the predominately analogous composition, with hues of red-orange and yellow-orange interspersed between those areas. The remaining one-third of the painting is dominated by blue-greens, with black patches in the foreground field, grape sticks, lines and shadows under the trees. Additionally, there exists the smallest amount of light violet in the horizon's hills, and on some of the worker's clothing.

The mood is somber at this days end, created not by the saturated colors themselves, but by the very nature of their contrast to the darker, dull shaded blue-greens. The dullness of the blue-greens creates a type of saturated contrast with the more intense hues. It is as though the darkness of the lesser area is consumes the greater area of saturated space. The rapidly changing chromatic values bring about the night quickly, as workers hurriedly pick the last remaining fruit.

The work of Fereole de Bonnemaison and Vincent van Gogh are just two examples of breaking-down the component parts of a color composition and identifying their specific functions. There are various other techniques for the accomplishment of analyzing a color composition, but this methodology seems to produce the best results for the average student. Looking at the entire painting can be intimidating, but by describing each color area of the composition, we are more careful to see everything in that quadrant. A color theorist is not merely concerned with identifying visual components alone, but also about learning to see color correctly—how it functions and manipulates mood.

In the first example, we began by identifying the mood immediately. When we analyzed the second image, however, mood may have been more difficult to identify, and so the emotional issue was the last attribute to be cited. Often, the mood of a composition is apparent immediately, other times it is not. To validate why a color or a scheme of colors creates a particular mood, it's sometimes necessary to identify each compositional element first. Afterwards, the sum total of these components help us recognize the emotional factors. When we successfully analyze, we essentially transform our critical thinking into concrete knowledge. The results are in, and what we learn must be calculated in the written word. This process of analysis has lasting results that the student actually carries out of the class and commits to memory.

I hope that the student realizes the significance of written color analysis. Artists and designers from all disciplines must possess the ability to effectively communicate and use appropriate color vocabulary whether in written or oral form.

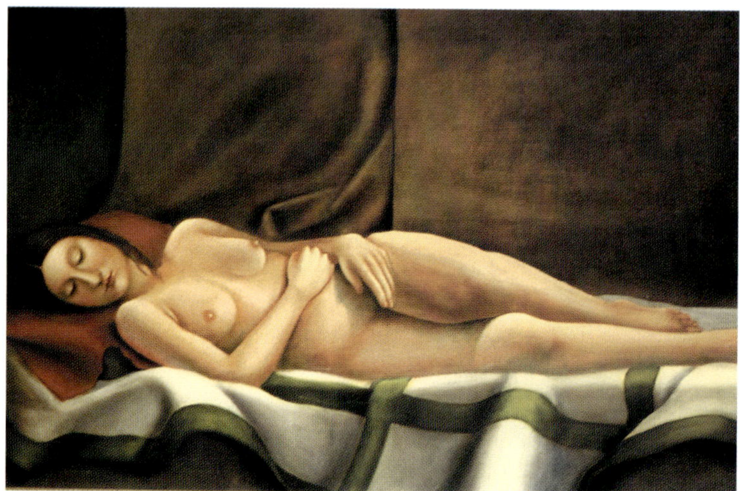

Student Artwork, *Reclining Nude.*

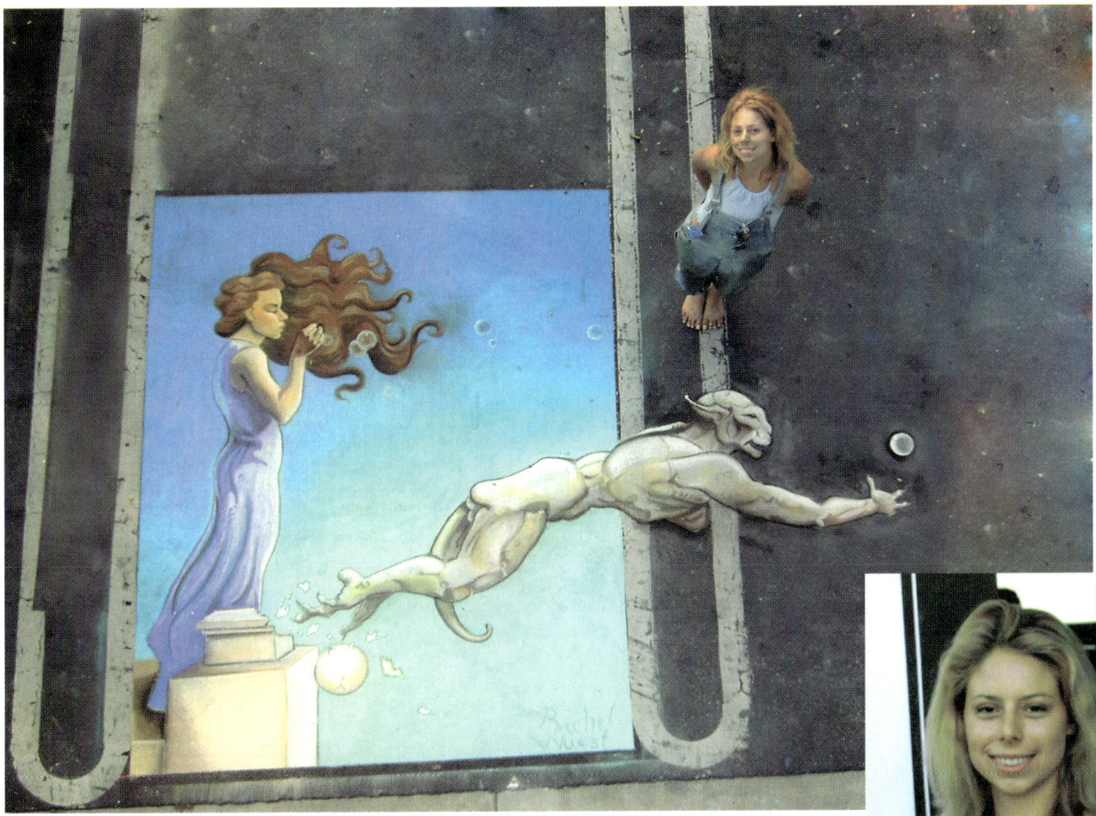

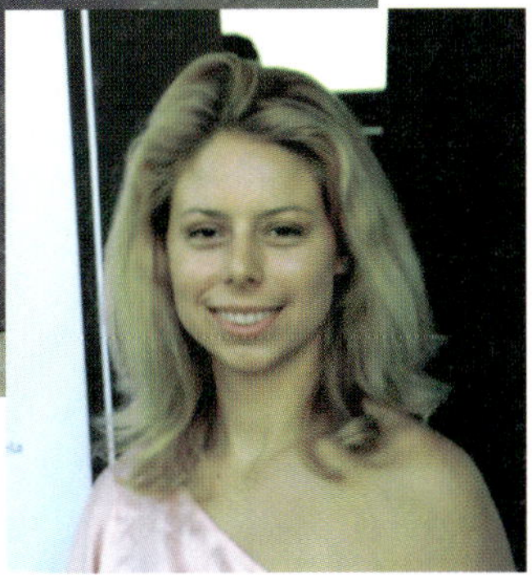

Rachael Wuest, *Chalk Drawing.*
This student understands the value of her ability to analyze compositional color. The drawing demonstrates her knowledge of saturation, intensity, value, tints and shades, contrast, harmony and emotional appeal.

Component Two—Project Proposals

Undertaking a project is an equally important task for the student of color. What we know intellectually we also must put into practice. The next step is to transform knowledge into a demonstrated product. The application of colored pigments to a surface, the creation of color fields on a computer monitor, or the three-dimensional application of color harmonies of a designed interior all rely on physically manipulating color.

In the first chapter, you will be introduced to *saturation, intensity* and *values*. In the next chapter we will continue our discussions about saturation and intensity issues, and then in the third and fourth chapters *contrast* and *tints* and *shades* will be explored through a variety of possible projects. Chapter Five will focus on *color harmony*, and chapters six

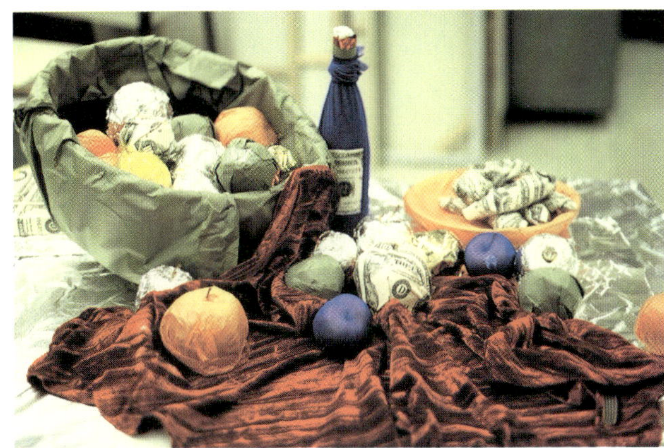

Student Work, *Three-Dimensional Colour Study.*
Ordinary objects are changed by color and texture differences. The emphasis was to analyze color mood transformations when altering the original colors.

and seven investigates emotional factors of *color expression* and the *spiritual dimension* of color.

All chapters include a developed project and written analysis in order to demonstrate knowledge in that area. *The purpose of the hands-on project is the physical manifestation of your understanding of color, just as the written analysis evaluates your intellectual comprehension of the topic.* Your assignment may come in various forms: the application of color pigments and various materials, arrangements of three-dimensional color objects, photographs, computer applications, and such, depending on the instructor's construction of the class.

It is important to note here that there are various suggested projects throughout the text. However, the instructor may select project assignments from their own repertoire of projects to better accommodate the structure of the particular class. The projects in this text are focused primarily on the hands-on approach, such as with pigments (paint) and film (photography). However, from time to time computer applications may become necessary as well.

There are many equally legitimate project methods and mediums for the instruction of color theory. Whatever the medium of choice, or selected project style, the basic information presented in this text is relevant for all applications of color theory education.

Component Three— Reading Complements

There are actually four segments of *guest lectures* (reading complements) throughout the book. Noted for exceptional prowess in the subject, these authors will be highlighted for their relevant and accomplished essays on the subject. These essays are not considered to be absolutely necessary in the education of color theory. Rather, they serve as an additional source to provide *supplementary research*, and to illuminate and clarify lecture topics in their respective chapters. Three of the four essays provide relevant scientific explanations, while the fourth deals with important historical documentation and valuable additional insight.

Component Four— Historical References

Historical figures (artists) whose artwork is considered relevant to any given topic in a particular chapter will be documented, which will serve as a complement to the lecture, as well as clarify specific color concerns. Artwork of each artist represented contains a relevant study of that chapter's special emphasis, which your instructor may choose to lec-

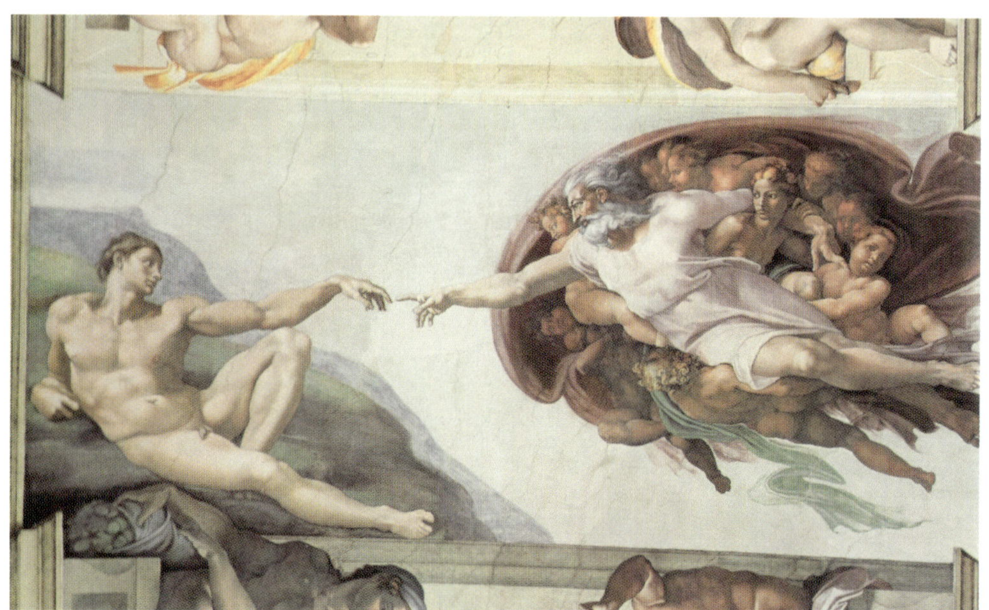

Michelangelo, *The creation of Adam* [Detail of vault fresco]. Sistine Chapel, Vatican—Rome. © Bettmann/CORBIS. This ceiling fresco is a small portion of a much larger rendition of Biblical stories, which many consider to be a visual record of events.

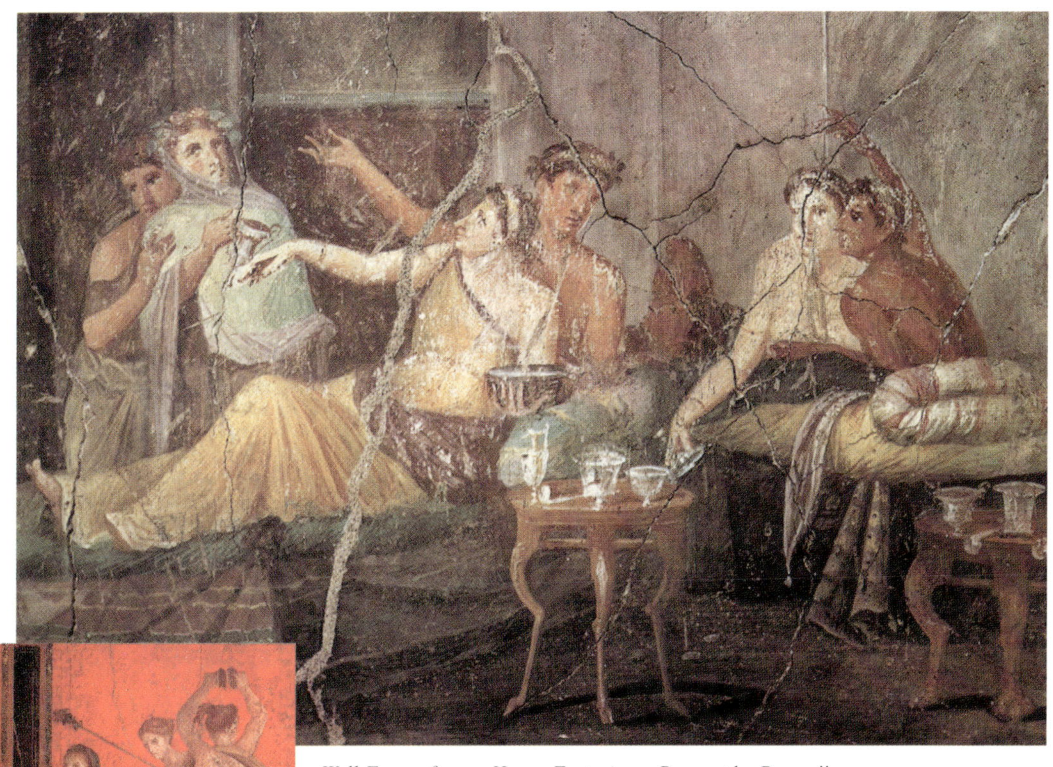

Wall Fresco from a House Featuring a Banquet by Pompeii.

(top) The triclinium, frescoed in the 3rd style, featured banqueting scenes in the centre of the walls; a complete glass table service resting on a three-legged wooden table is portrayed here, as if to flaunt the owner's standard of living. (left) In scene VIII, when the pleasure is over, the girl is whipped by a winged demon to the clash of cymbals played by two bacchantes.

ture about, in order to provide further clarification to the subject.

I would additionally like to make a case for the *study of artwork, or art history*. We now have artworks and writings of artists from past centuries, containing valuable information about the history of the world. History is about written records of past human events, art history concerns *visual* records of past human events. It is one thing to read about past civilizations, it is quite another to witness them through such things as pigmented frescos and painted compositions.

It is profound that we knew so little about ancient Rome and their habits until the excavation of Pompeii's ruins, a popular vacation spot and luxurious city south of Rome. The excavation of the city of Pompeii was begun in 1748, and continued for the next 247 years to the end of the 20th century (about 1995). These diggings proved to be one of the most significant discoveries in the history of art, revealing beautiful frescos, often wall to wall, within the homes of the city's inhabitants.

In 79 AD, after the area was plagued with a series of earthquakes, the nearby Mt. Vesuvius erupted, spewing tons of volcanic ash into the air over Pompeii. As the ash settled over the city, intermittent rain storms quickly cooled and hardened the ash layer falling over the city. For more than sixteen hundred years, Pompeii lay buried and forgotten. It was these layers of ash which sealed the city and protected it from nature's punishment of time. As a result, the well preserved pigmented walls of Pompeii have provided us with amazing detail and insight into the Roman culture (see wall frescos on next page). The frescos are in such good condition, we know exactly which *colors* were important to the Romans and the significance of particular color schemes and harmonies in that culture.

The case for the study of color is particularly relevant both then and now. Every artist should be concerned with the study of art history and how colors of any particular period in history functioned, and why. One example is seen in the red and blue color schemes that typify many of the gothic cathedral windows (see the Law Window). Long before the Roman empire, red was the predominant color of choice when dying fabrics. Red was plentiful, it came from an organic or plant (flora) based dye, and it was much more resistant to fading than other colors. Red certainly was more vivid, and seemed to posses a majestic ambiance not seen in the remaining spectrum.

Red was so popular in the Roman world, it actually reigned as the color supreme through the midpoint of the Medieval period. As time progressed far beyond the Roman empire, *blue* began to surface as the popular color, thanks to the availability of the woad plant, or leaf. Blue was no longer thought of as a commoner's color, and began to be worn and used more frequently during the 11th and 12th centuries. By the 13th century contrasting red and blue color schemes began to grace the Gothic cathedral windows. Soon enough, hues of blue became the color of choice over red, worn even by the highest of nobility.

Color choices throughout history have not been arbitrary. Color decisions incorporate symbolic, psychological and spiritual aspects into any given situation, as well as a host of other specific and well-designed color functions. Anyone who has a career associated with color is beholden, then, to the importance of color proficiency.

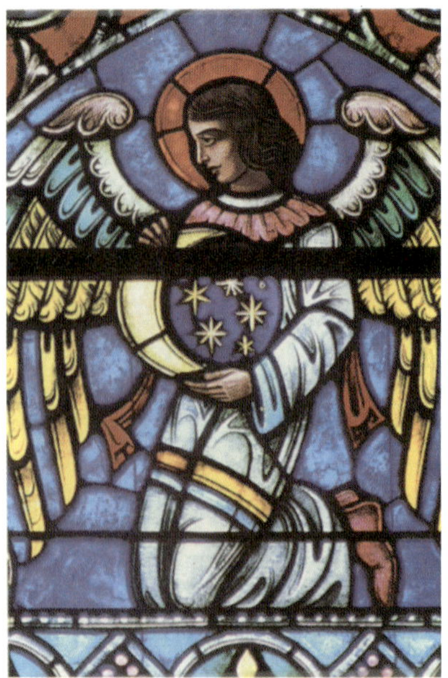

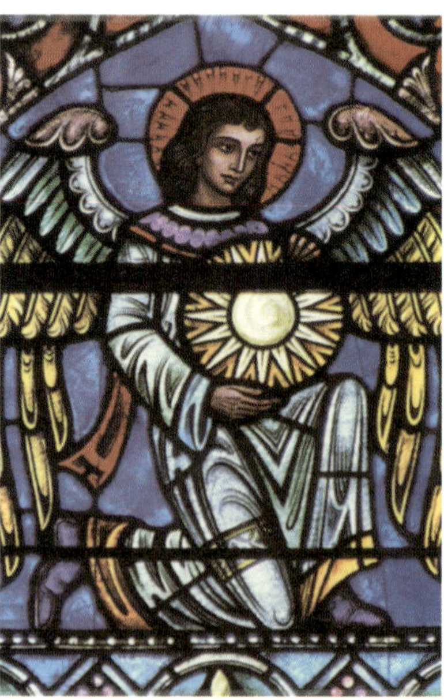

Details from the Law Window in the Nave—Washington National Cathedral.. Photo Courtesy of Washington National Cathedral.

Our brief studies of individual artists in the *lecture artists* section, therefore, will not be unlike the student's quest to color analyze a given work of art. The difference is that the lecture artist's section provides an opportunity for the student to see how the instructor methodically analyzes a color composition. The student is encouraged to take notes while the instructor discusses each composition. This will provide the student with an example of how the instructor wants the analysis to proceed.

Historically, colorists understood the importance of the *critical thinking* mind. Now, in the 21st century, the color savvy professional artist or designer needs critical thinking skills more than ever. The great art masters of centuries past were awesome because of their intensive investigations into the *Dynasty of Light*.

Note: Colors referred to in the text may occasionally differ from the originals due to differences in various printing process. Every effort is made to present colors as accurately as possible.

The Sovereignty of Light

Color Physics, Color Saturation, Intensity and Value

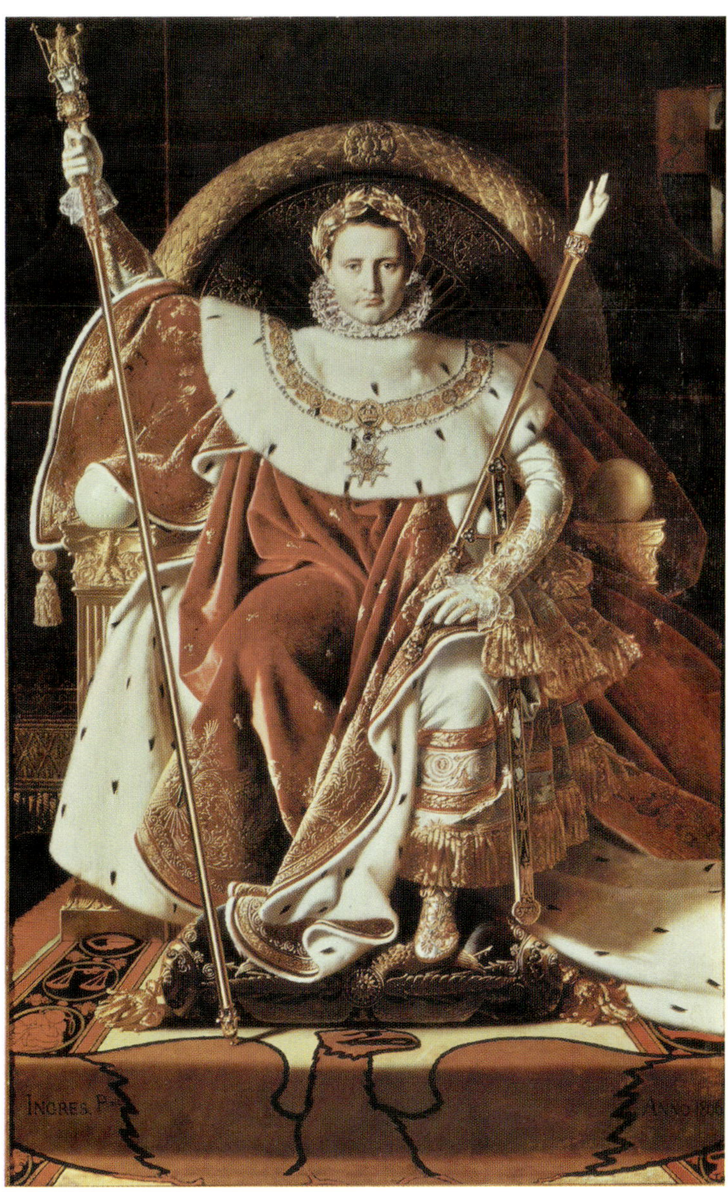

Napoleon I in Royal Garb, by Jean Auguste Dominique Ingres (1780–1867). © Giraudon/Art Resource, NY.

Chapter One

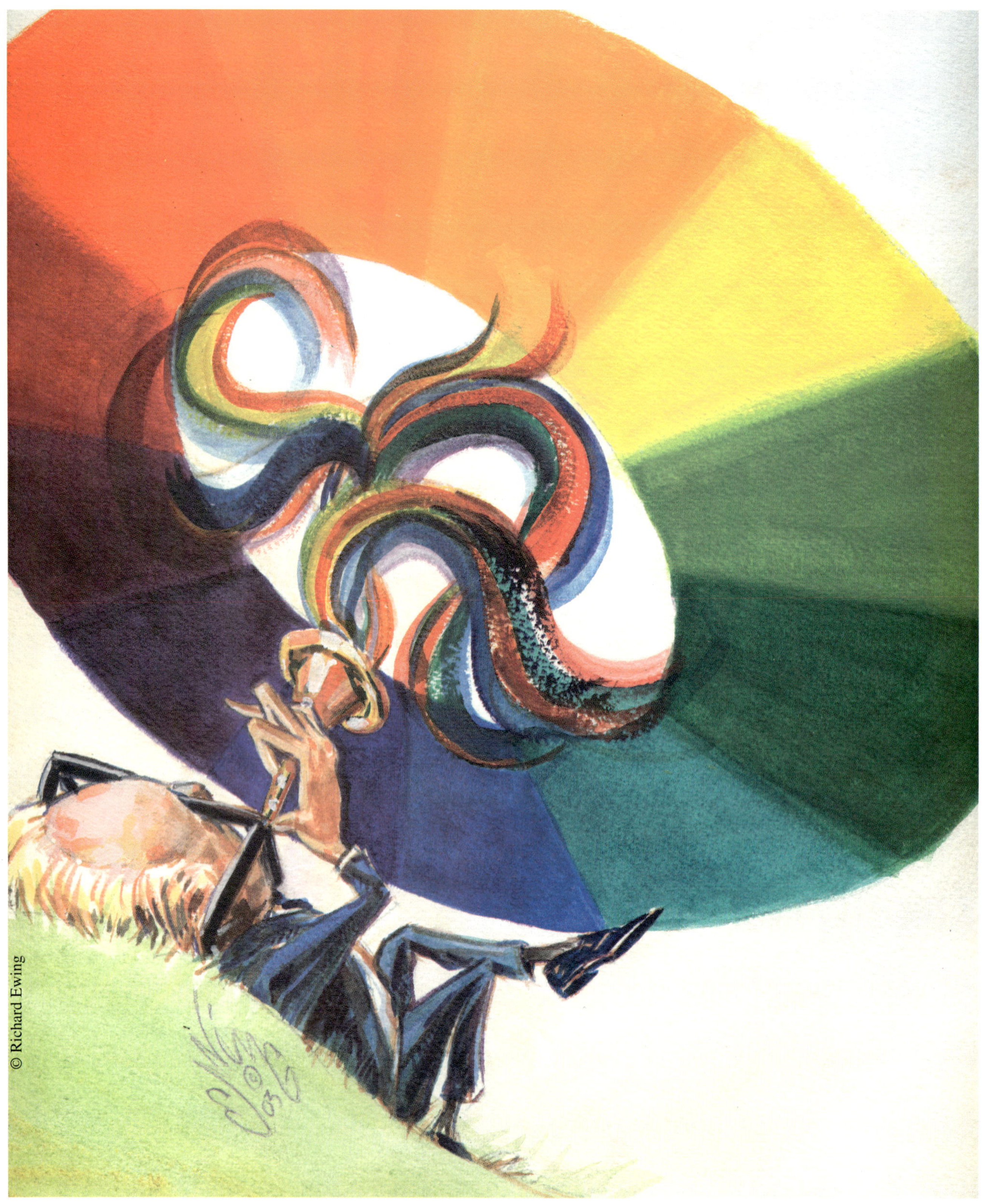

Color Wheel

The Twelve–Part Color Circle

There are many complexities and variations about the theory of color. The very reason for the designation *color theory* tells us something about the nature of the subject itself. During our discourse, we will discover aspects about color that are both factual and theoretical. That is to say some attributes of color are *written-in-stone* while others are interpretive in nature.

Let's begin with the very basics: the *twelve-part color circle.* We want to illustrate how the twelve–part color circle is developed from the triadic color harmony of red, yellow and blue. These three equilateral colors on the color circle are known as the *primary colors*. They exist in and of themselves and cannot be created by the mixing of other colors. Put another way, we can say that all other colors are produced by various mixtures of primaries. They are the foundational source of all other color amalgamations in the subtractive color world.

By separating a circle into twelve equal parts, we will first establish the *primaries* of yellow (top), red (lower right), and blue (lower left) into an equilateral triangle. Next, the *secondary* colors of orange, green and violet are established. They are located equilaterally as well, arranged with a space between each primary and secondary.

A secondary color is achieved by the mixing of two *primaries,* for example:

Red + Yellow = Orange
Red + Blue = Violet
Yellow + Blue = Green

Now that we have established the primary and secondary colors, we have one more set of colors to create *intermediate* colors (see tertiary explanation).*

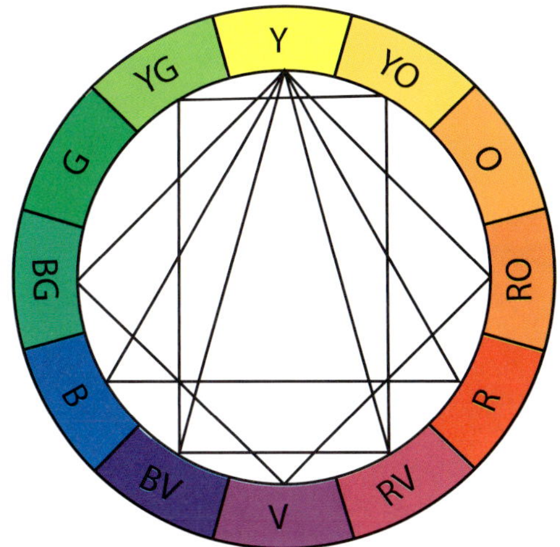

The intermediate (tertiary) colors are inserted between one primary and one secondary, and are made by mixing one primary and one secondary as follows:

Red + Orange = Red Orange
Red + Violet = Red Violet
Blue + Violet = Blue Violet
Blue + Green = Blue Green
Yellow + Green = Yellow Green
Yellow + Orange = Yellow Orange

This establishment of color with its own distinctive location within the color circle, is the same sequence of color as a natural rainbow, as well as the natural spectrum of colors seen through a clear prism.

Tertiary color is commonly referred to as the mixing of one primary and one secondary color. But we also know that the combination of those two colors are known as *intermediates* since the resultant color is located *intermediately* or between the primary and secondary colors. Officially the dictionary defines the word tertiary as being "of the third order, or rank," which would then infer that two colors are mixed to produce the one. That being the case, intermediate and tertiary color could be one in the same since there is no specific designation. Interestingly

*Here is where theory interjects itself. Speculation as to whether or not the term tertiary holds the same meaning as intermediate color occasionally arises. Today most artists use the word tertiary and intermediate interchangeably.

enough, the term tertiary has been known to refer to the *mixing of two secondary colors* as well.

What may better support the idea of the term *tertiary* is the dictionary definition. The definition above indicates a certain weakness on the part of the third color. For example, primary yellow is the purest yellow; it's created by no other combination of colors. A secondary orange is a blend of yellow and red, which results in yellow-orange. On the other hand, intermediates are just that—between, or in the middle of the primary and secondary color.

Normally, two secondary colors will create (depending on percentage of the mix) resultant brown hues (one example), which is more or less a range of shaded orange to red tones. This is very different than how we see the intermediate hue.

Additionally this should not be confused with the mixture of two *complements,* which produce a neutralized, or grayed effect (these issue will be discussed in greater detail later in the text). For the sake of continuity we will let the terms intermediate and tertiary remain as interchangeable at this point.

Lecture Summary:

The Visible Color Spectrum and Sir Isaac Newton

In Sir Isaac Newton's *Treatise of the Reflections, Refractions, Inflections and Colours of Light,* he investigates the origins of color by the careful observation of light. He began the analysis of light by focusing the source into a clear triangular prism.

A narrow slit was first cut into a flat surface with a beam of pure white sunlight directed through it, and then onto a prism. As the white light refracted through the prism, it dispersed into a visible color spectrum of red, orange, yellow, green, blue, indigo and violet. This white light to color process can be reversed by collecting the addition of those colors through a converging lens. This will transfer, or mix, color back to its original white light.

At this point it is prudent to define the process as *additive color.* When we mix colors of *light* it is referred to as *additive* color mixing. The principal colors of additive light are red, green, and blue often seen on your computer monitor. The opposite of additive would be the *subtractive* color mixing process, which would be the mixing of *pigments.* The principal colors of subtractive, or pigmented color are red, yellow, and blue. This subject will be dealt with in Chapter Two and Seven.

One way to more completely understand additive colors is to divide them into complementary groups such as green, blue and violet, and then red, orange and yellow. If we were to then converge the two groups of light equally the result would be white. But what happens should we isolate just one color from the spectrum, such as yellow? The remaining colors added together will be yellow's complement—violet. (Commensurately, any other color which is singularly separated, the remainder will become its complement.)

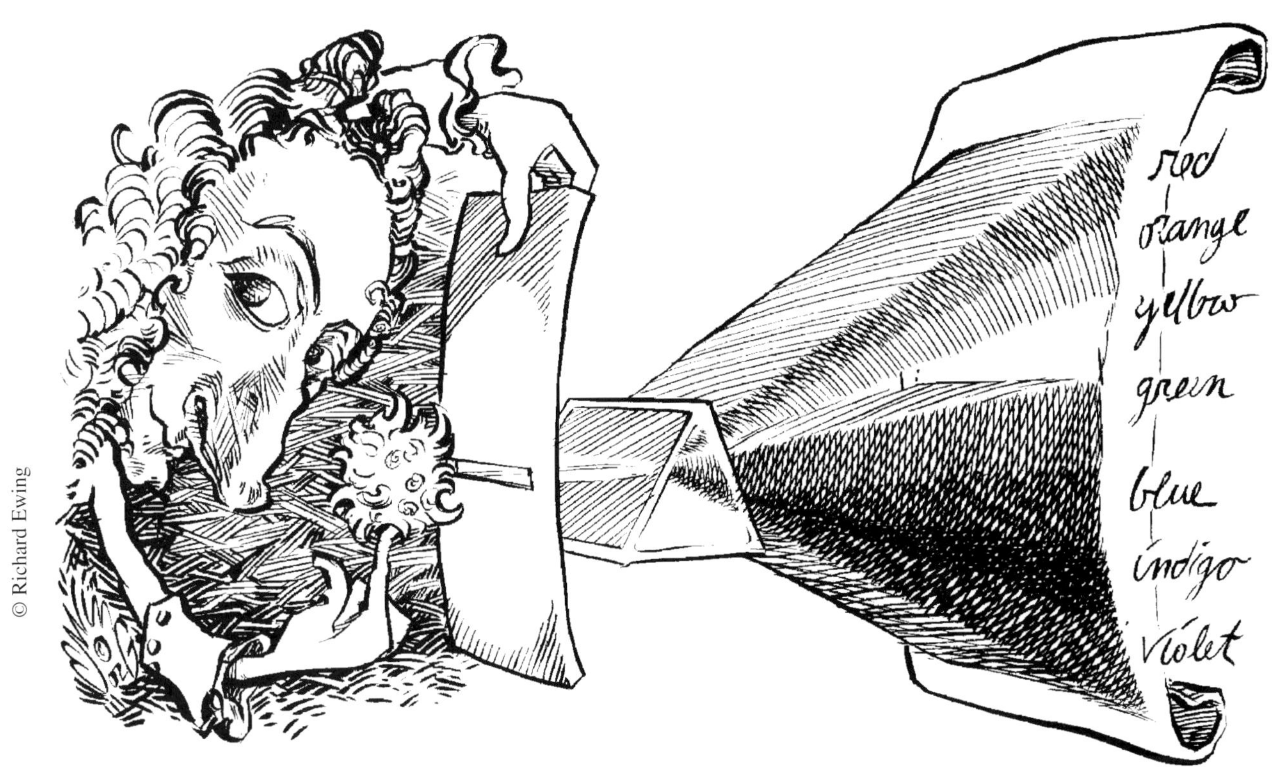

Lecture Summary:

Light

In 1873 James Clerk Maxell presented his formula known as "Maxell's Equation's," which brought forth the concept that electrical charges actually interacted via a force field. He proceeded to demonstrate that there could be a marriage between electricity and magnetism. In fact, he soon realized that the electromagnetic wave had the exact same speed as light (300,000 km/s), and that the joining of these two forces resulted in the actual creation of light. It was this new finding that opened our eyes to the world of light.

Soon came a profound realization that there were new kinds of light, which all had various and specific wavelengths, depending on the amount of energy emitted by a given wave. Basically, shorter wavelengths would equate to greater energy and longer waves generated a lower energy, yet all electromagnetic waves are actual energies that vibrate throughout the known universe.

As we can see from the chart, which measures light in terms of wavelengths, the gamma and X-rays are the *most energetic* and yet have very *short wave lengths*. Next, a very familiar form of radiation from the sun is ultraviolet, which is responsible for human maladies such as burns and skin cancer. All of the aforementioned lights emit the most harmful radiation to the human life form. The invisible ultraviolet is one step higher than the visible spectrum of violet, which can be seen.

Next, decreasing in energy, the *visible color spectrum* can be seen on the chart, and occupies just a very small area of the total spectrum of lights. This

The Electromagnetic Spectrum

On either side of the familiar (but tiny) visible rainbow of red, orange, yellow, green, blue, indigo, and violet lie vast bands of nonvisible radiation. The higher the energy of the radiation, the shorter its wavelength. The spectrum divisions between the different forms of radiation overlap because the names derive in part from how the radiation is generated and the technology used to detect it.

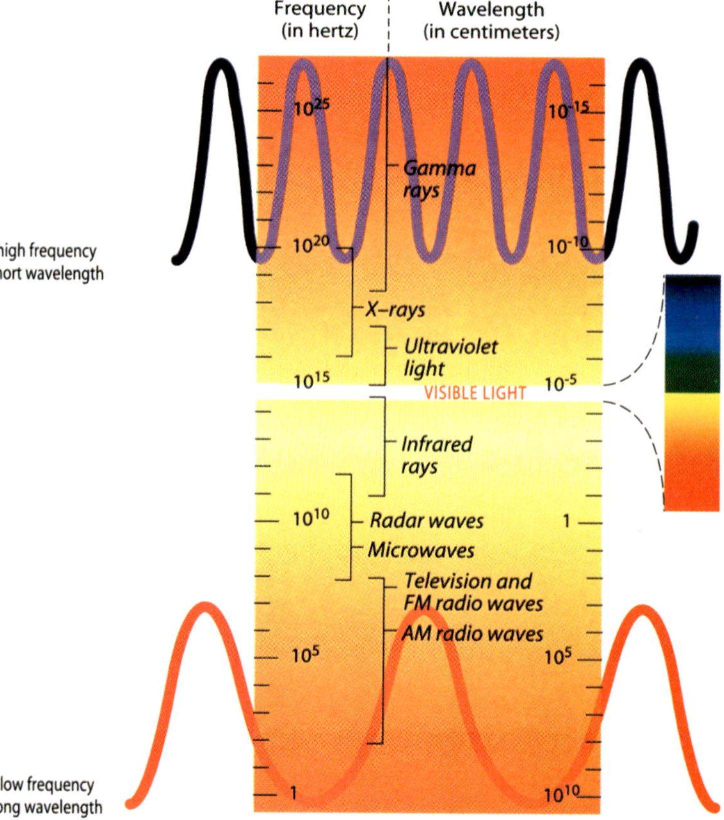

Earth's Atmospheric Shield

Electromagnetic radiation bombards Earth from all directions in the universe, the bulk of it from our own Sun. Only certain wavelengths of radiation get through to the surface because Earth's atmosphere reflects, absorbs, or scatters the rest. Oxygen and nitrogen atoms in the thermosphere absorb nearly all x-rays and gamma rays, the most energetic forms of light; the mesosphere and stratosphere screen the remainder. A significant portion of ultraviolet light entering the mesosphere and stratosphere is absorbed by ozone molecules, protecting us from lethal doses. At 10 miles, radiation of longer wavelengths—from visible through radio—enters the troposphere, where water vapor, trace gases, carbon dioxide, dust particles, and pollutants absorb the infrared. Long-wavelength radio waves slide right past these small particles, however, making the radio window one of the most transparent for astronomical observation.

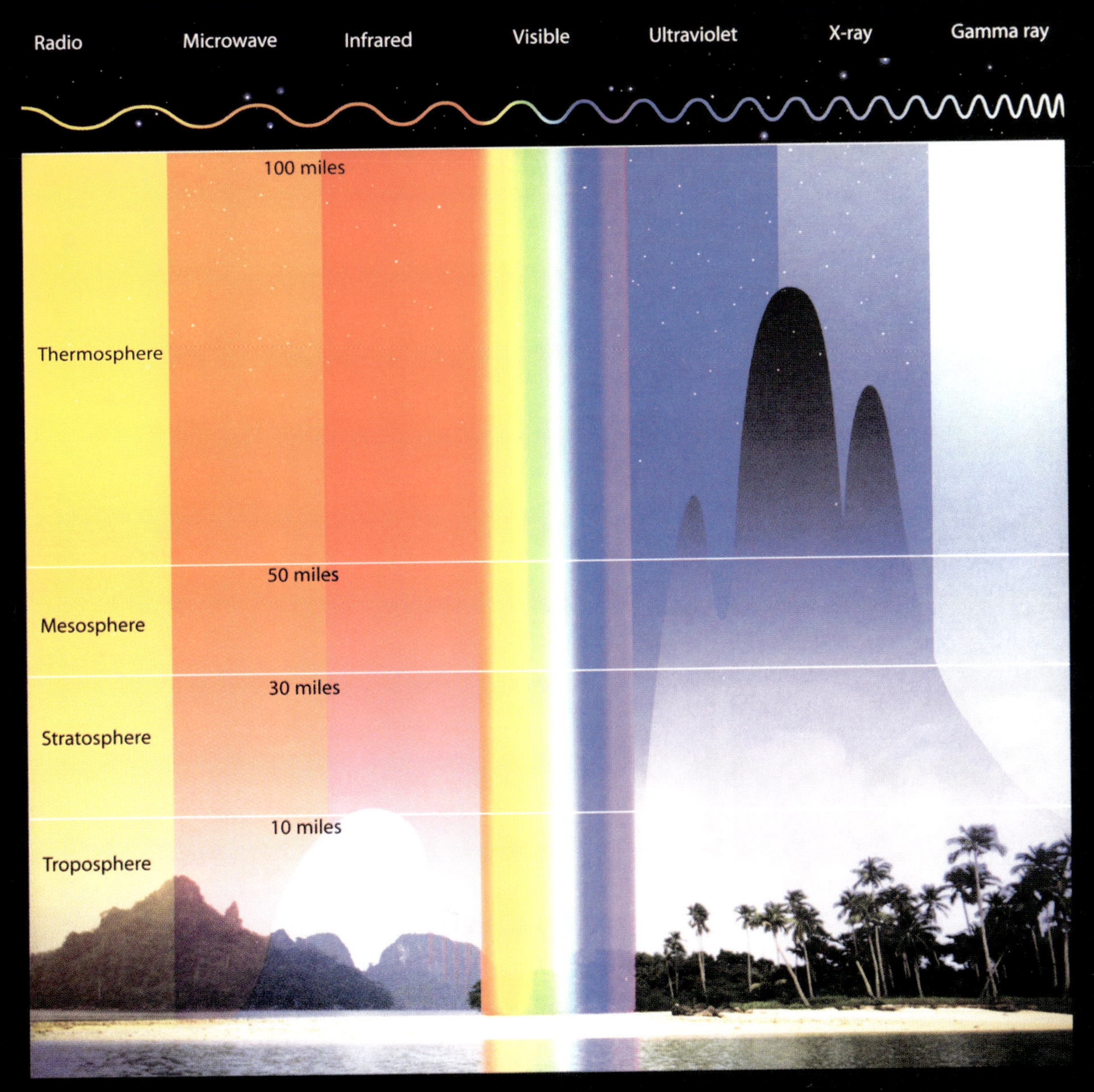

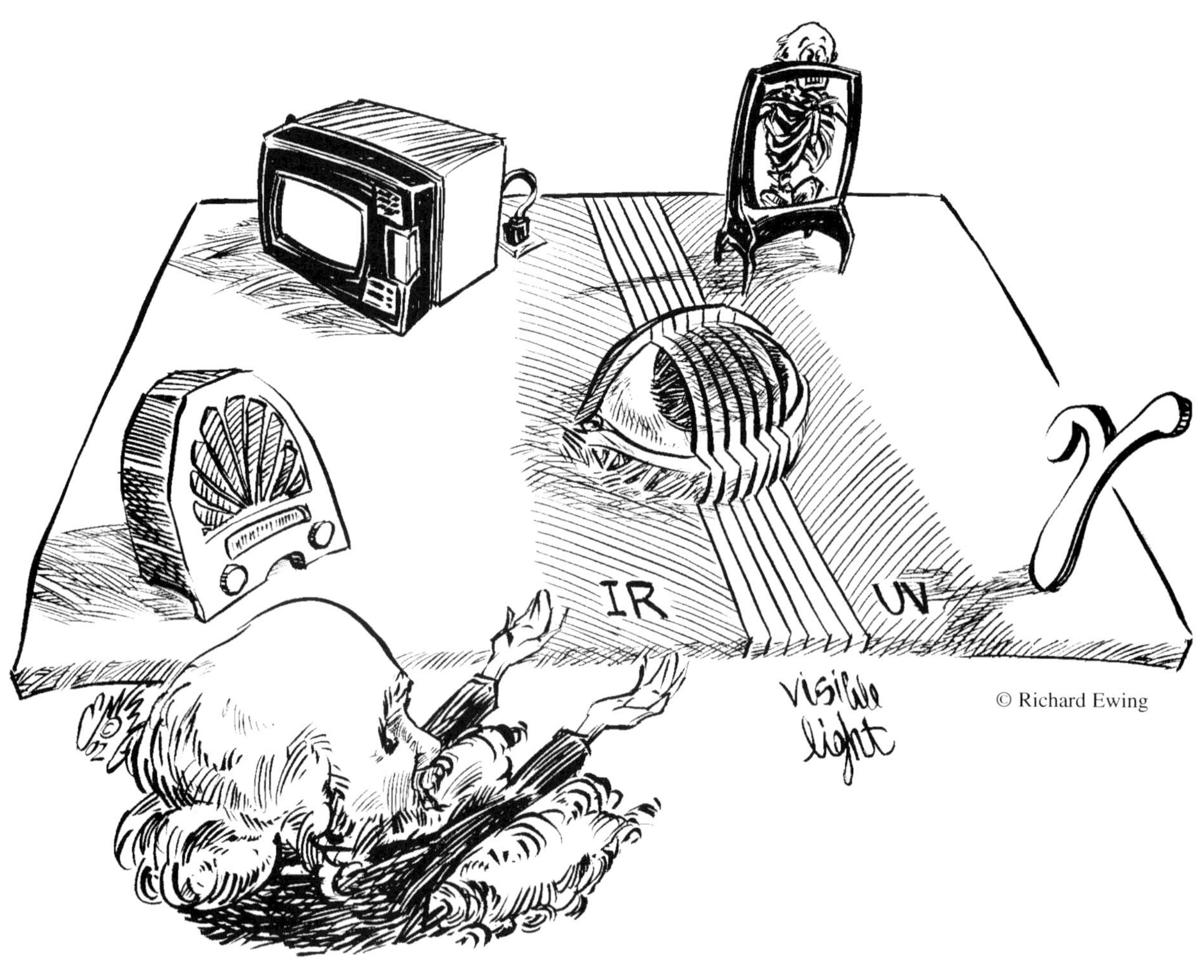

is the region of the most importance to us, since artists and designers rely on visible color.

The visible spectrum is bordered on the low side by infrared, which has wavelengths too long to see—basically beyond the color *red*. Of course, we have previously mentioned the other side of the color spectrum bounded by ultraviolet, which also is out of visible range from violet. The lowest energy levels with the *longest wavelengths* are naturally microwaves and radio waves. We now know that for the major part of the electromagnetic spectrum most lights cannot be seen, and in fact it is but a fraction of that light scale which is visible.

Each member of the visible spectrum of color also has a particular wavelength and energy level. Because red is closest to infra*red* light, it has the longest waves but the lowest energy level, whereas violet, which is closest to ultra*violet* has the highest energy level and the shortest waves (see chart: The Visible Spectrum—Wavelength Standard).

Additionally, colors with the longest wavelength not only have the lowest energy level, but are the least refracted colors as well. Violet, on the other hand, has the shortest wavelengths, highest energy level, and the greatest refraction of all the visible colors.

It is still a mystery in terms of how exactly the *eye to brain* function works, since we do not know how we actually discriminate wavelengths. We do, however, know about actual colors of physical *objects* themselves. When superimposing a green filter over a red filter and then placing them in front of white light the result will be black. These complements (red and green) cancel each other, since the green filter absorbs

The Visible Spectrum—Wavelength Standard

Color	Wavelength in Mill microns	Frequency in Cycles per Second
Red	800-650 (longest waves)	400-470 (lowest energy)
Orange	640-590	470-520
Yellow	580-550	520-590
Green	530-490	590-650
Blue	480-460	650-700
Indigo	450-440	700-760
Violet	430-390 (shortest waves)	760-800 (highest energy)

all other spectral colors except green. Commensurately, the red filter does the same. All of the color has been *stolen* and nothing is left but black.

The colors of physical objects, as well as pigments, are *subtractive* because their colors are the result of absorption. A red apple does not contain color in and of itself, but it is the light which is responsible for the production of red in the apple. It is the *molecular constitution* of the apple's surface that absorbs orange, yellow, green, blue and violet, reflecting *only red* back to the viewer's eye. The purer the white light source (sun), the redder the apple will appear. If we were, for example, to illuminate the apple with a green light, which is the complement of red, then the apple will appear black, thus canceling each other. Complements will complement each other side by side, and defeat each other when combined. The results are commensurable for all other complements, as well.

Earth's Atmosphere

Another interesting side note about light (color) wavelengths is to observe why the colors of the earth's atmosphere change throughout the day. During a sunrise or sunset the light rays from the sun hits the earth's surface at an angle, and therefore travel through greater distances, or larger volumes of atmosphere before reaching the earth's surface. The reason a sunrise has a reddish tone and sunsets change from yellow to orange to red is that the blue wavelengths are fragmented and dispersed, which then allow more of the red, red-orange and yellow wavelengths to reach the terrain.

Lecture Summary:

Color Anonymity and the Atom

A Word About Color Anonymity

Color theory itself possesses a certain ambiguity and mystery, as well as its particular fact-based representations. Occasionally, the student will observe what seems to be *ambiguity,* and yet what appears to be vague in reality is nothing more than subjectivity. From time to time, color does seem to be contradictory, and yet we learn to accept its two-sided character.

The fact-based characteristics of color are the observations that we can *visually see,* as well as evaluate, and are not subject to interpretation. They are what they are.

Other attributes of color anonymity are hidden within the *mysteries* that are *unseen by the naked eye.* Concrete knowledge about the science of color is derived from this aspect and helps to develop a clearer understanding about its function. It is here where we will briefly focus on the mysteries of the unseen and smallest unit of color.

The Atom

Originally, the idea that natural occurrences can be explained in terms of elementary ingredients was first recorded in the Greek town of Miletus of Ionia in the 6th century B.C. (ca. 625–547 B.C.). The initial concept of the atom, however, came about a century later by **Democritus** and **Leucippus** (ca. 480-ca. 420 B.C.). Their idea was that all matter was made up of indivisible and eternal particles. The Greek word *atomos,* which literally means "that

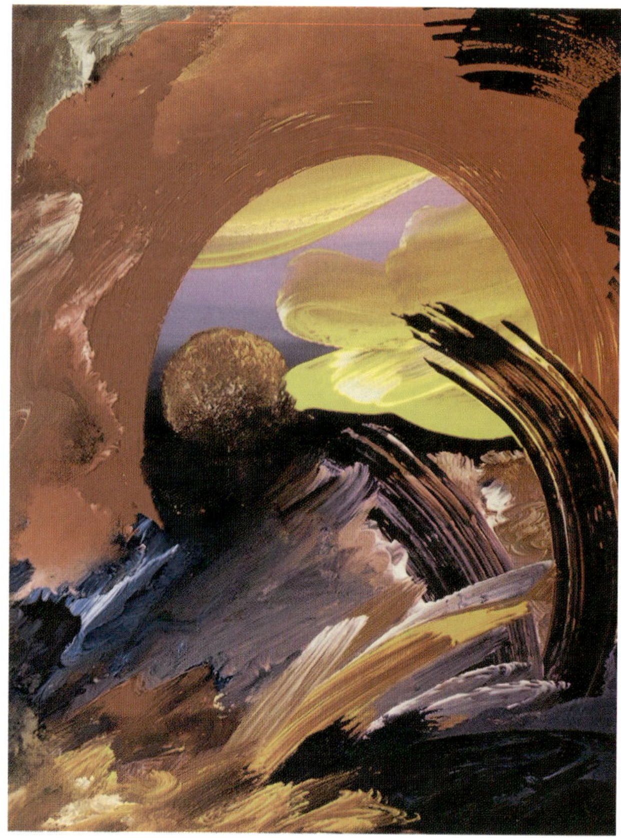

The Atom Revealed by Shijo. Symbolic Color Abstraction #1.

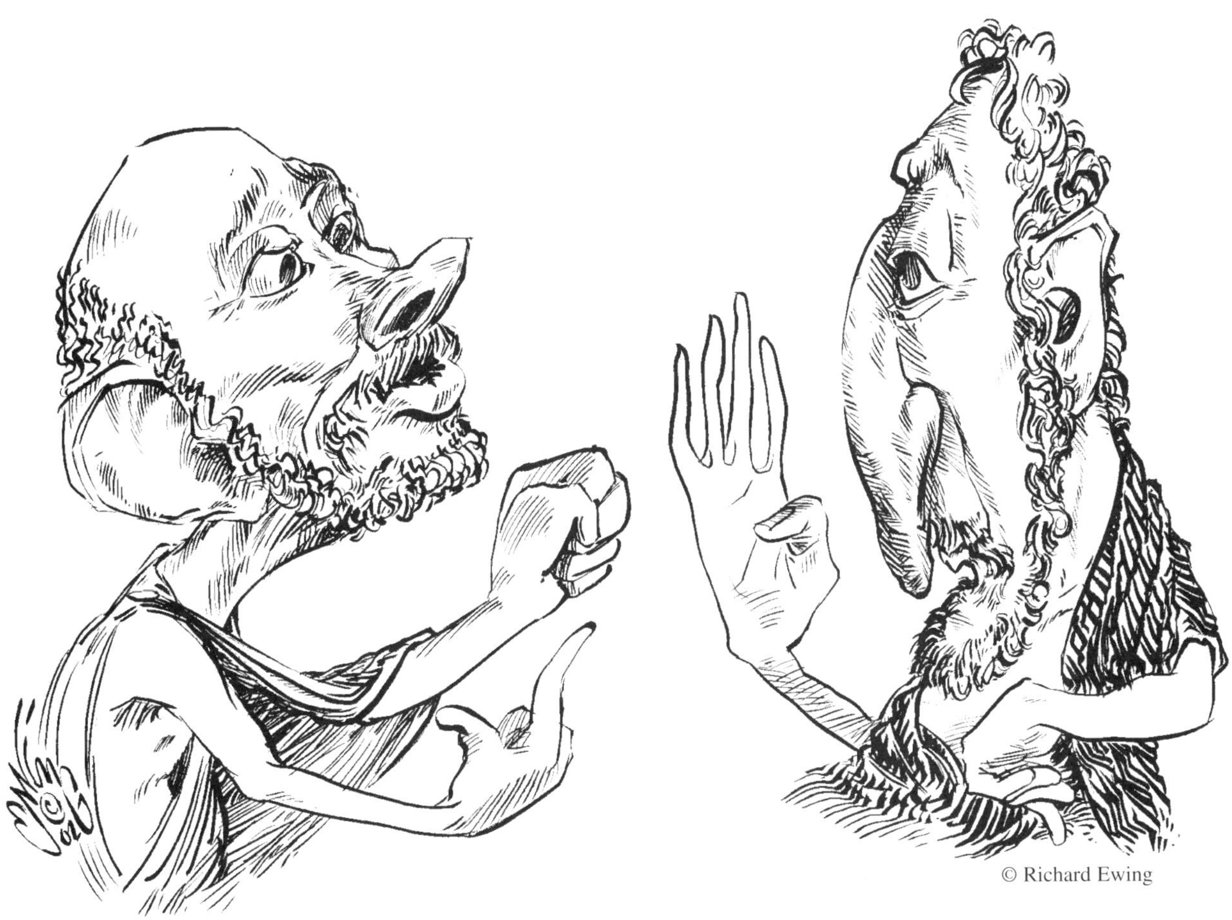
© Richard Ewing

Plato's approaches (philosophy) were always on a more spiritual plane, but it was Aristotle who was more connected to the earth with his scientific views.

which cannot be divided", seemed an appropriate name to describe the nature of their theory, thus the use of the name *atom* was first used.

Around the same time **Aristotle** and **Plato** were spending hours arguing their philosophical differences. Plato's approaches were always on a more spiritual plane, but it was Aristotle who was more connected to the earth with his scientific views.

Soon enough, Leucippus's idea about the atom was put to rest in favor of Aristotle's more popular notion that there were instead four fundamental substances: air, water, earth, and fire. At this point the atom was nothing more than a solid mass; unknown was the idea of a nucleus with even smaller particles. Of course, Aristotle was unable go much farther than to hypothesize about *matter* since his methods for turning theory into fact were limited, to say the least. The whole issue about the existence of the atom slowly died out and remained dormant for the next two millennia.

Over two thousand years later, in 1662, the atomic hypothesis awoke when Irish physicist **Robert Boyle** admitted that the only way to make sense of gasses being compressed was to acknowledge the atom itself. The slow discovery of this atomic premise continued when John Dalton proposed, in 1808, that all matter comprises atoms. Towards the dawn of the *atomos* years in Greece, it was thought that the atom itself was the basic building block of matter, but in 1897 **Joseph Thomson** gave us experimental proof that the atom actually had an internal structure, beginning with the electron.

The Discovery of the Atomic Structure: Color Quarks

The Electron and the Photon

It was **Joseph Thomson** who discovered the first particle, the ***electron,*** and its mass. The electron maintains an orbit inside of the atom around the nucleus at an enormous velocity of 186,000 mps (the speed of light). The energy variances between electron orbits determines the energy level of the light that is to be absorbed. When an electron changes the level of its orbit from higher to lower, it immediately emits a ***photon,*** which will carry borrowed energy (surplus) away from the original electron, only to be absorbed by another. The energy from the photon is actually the difference registered between the first and final orbit's state. It was **Albert Einstein** who realized in 1905 that light existed as small bundles of energy, swarming around the electron like bees on a hive. He referred to them as photons. It was Einstein who actually completed Max Planck's research on photoelectric effects and thus created the photon.

The Nucleus

Soon after, **Lord Ernest Rutherford** proposed and later proved that the atom had a heart, a very small area in the center of the atom, which he named the ***nucleus.*** In reality, the nucleus of the atom is so small that it has a ratio of a grain of rice to a football stadium—the stadium representing the atom and the

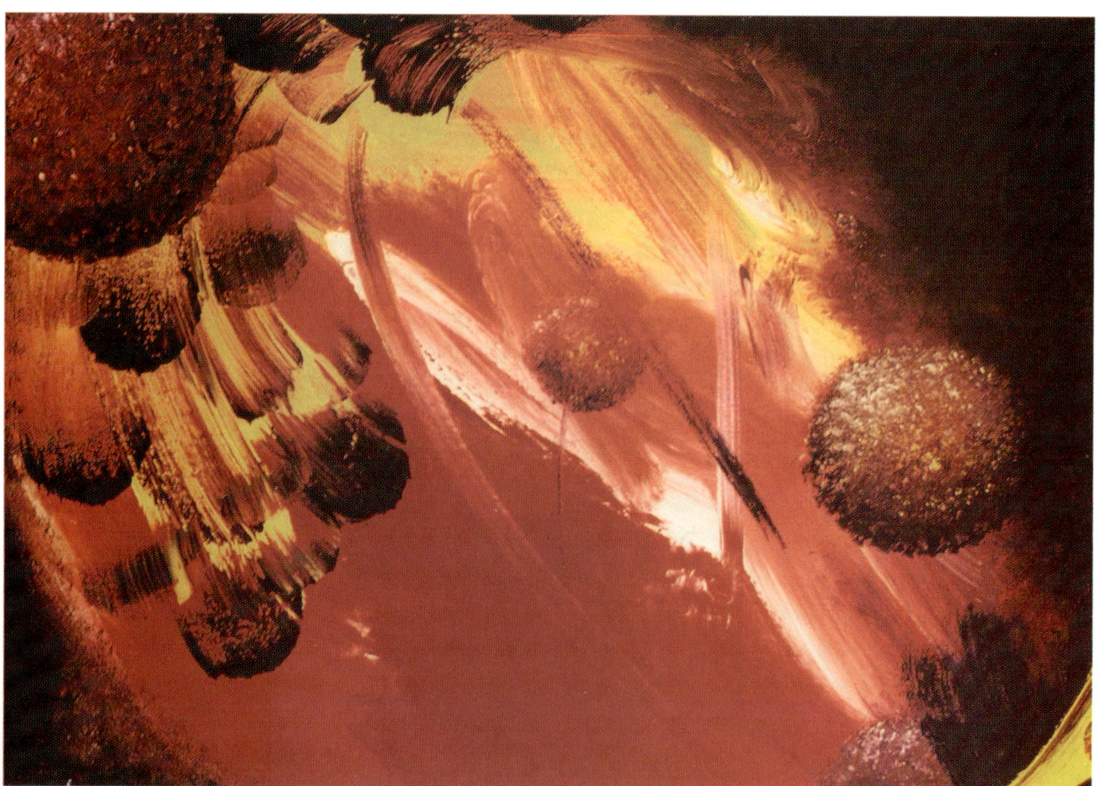

The Course of the Electron and Its Photons by Shijo.
Symbolic Color Abstraction #2.

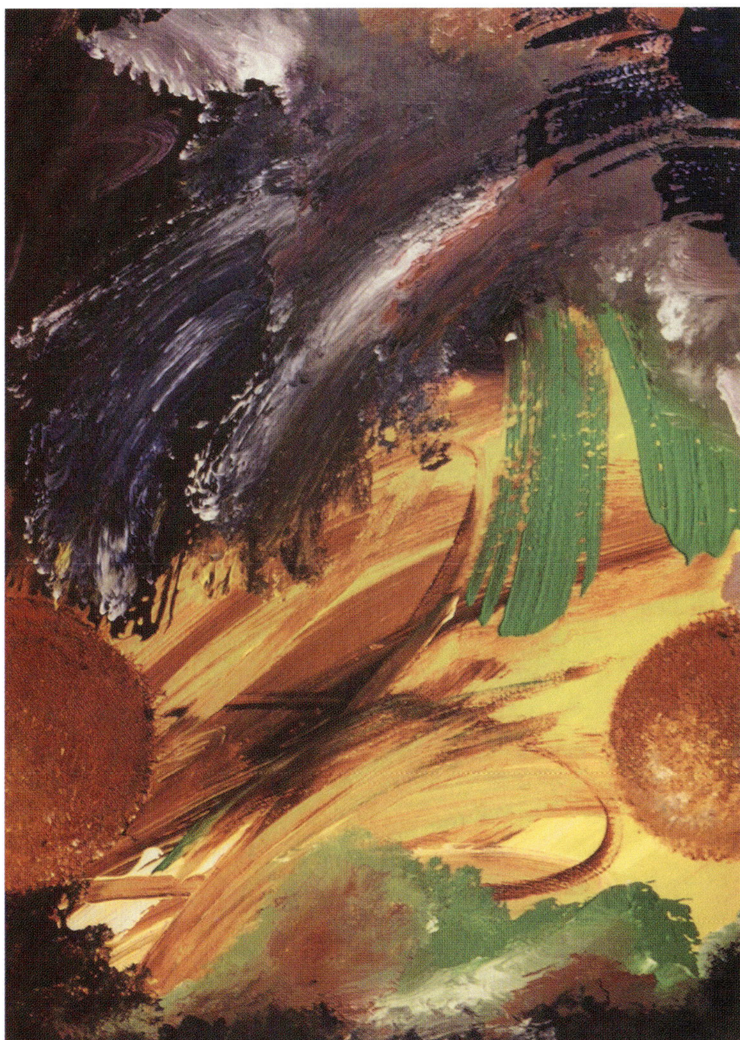

The Nucleus of the Atom by Shijo.
Symbolic Color Abstraction #3.

rice being the nucleus. Now, we can begin to assemble the atomic structure partially. So far, we have electrons simultaneously orbiting a nucleus and exchanging photons, which all exist inside of the atom.

The Proton

It was the uncovering of the nucleus and its structure which also led **Rutherford** to the detection of the ***proton*** in 1919. Protons contain an electrical charge. In fact, they all have the same type of charge, which causes them to repel one another. The atomic nucleus is partially composed of these protons.

The Neutron

The proton is companion to the ***neutron*** within the nuclei. The neutron also resides inside of the nucleus with the proton as revealed by **James Chadwick** twelve years later in 1932. Since neutrons are not identical to protons, and protons are all charged alike, it is the neutrons which help to separate protons from each other. Stable nuclei will typically contain an equal amount of protons and neutrons.

The Nucleons

When the proton and the neutron are referred to as a unit, they are called ***nucleons.*** A nucleus contains pairs of protons and neutrons held together by this nuclear glue.

The Quark

It seemed that the mysteries about the atom had all been uncovered. Then in 1963, the American physicist **Murry Gell-Mann** finally discovered the basic building block of all atomic nuclei throughout the universe, the ***quark.*** The quark has been a particularly important discovery about the atom, especially to color theorists. The *smallest* of all provable particles resides within the proton and neutron structure as bundles of quarks. Each bundle is referred to as a baryon (baryon wrapper), which contains one quark each of red, blue and green. Just as it is with the additive color primaries, the three quarks when combined together create white light. At last, the source of color is found in the smallest particle of the atom. These R-G-B bundles of primary colors of light are represented on your computer monitor, such as in Photoshop, etc.

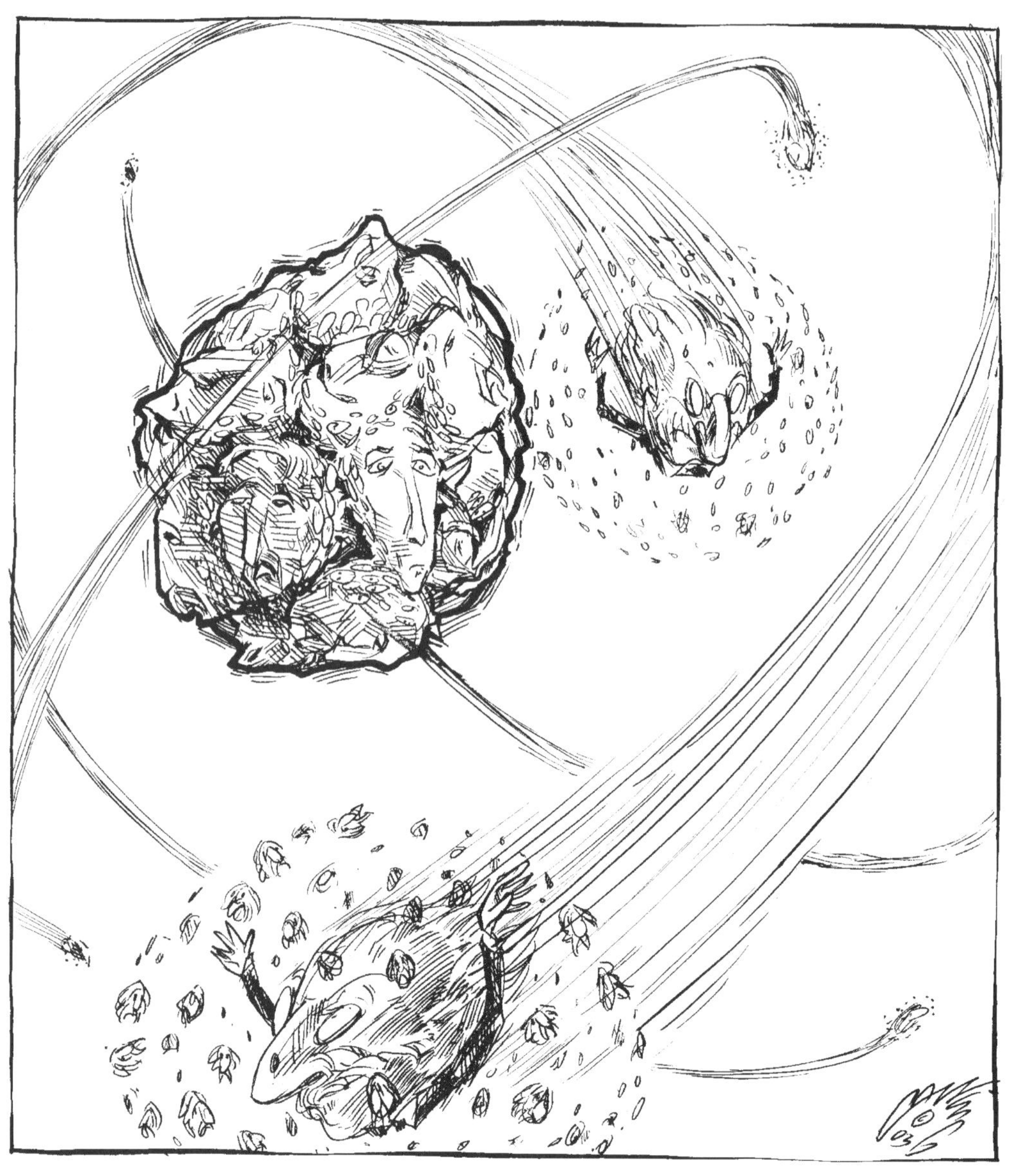

© Richard Ewing

The energy contained in a single atom causes one to stand in awe, as to how it is all held together

Smashing Marbles

The Origins of Color and Color Sightings

I really can't remember how many times my friend and I spent the night on top of a mountain when we were younger. At the ripe age of 15 we would lay under the warm summer stars, so many and so brilliant. The Milky Way, luminous and silent spread before us across the heavens, in a glorious array of sparkling jewels. We never ceased to be amazed about the boundaries of space and what mysteries lay beyond our ability to imagine.

Planets, stars, galaxies and the universe were truly a *dynasty of light* within their own right. All of humankind had looked upon, wondered, and studied through the centuries what was now ours to contemplate. Seldom has humanity had such case to wonder and imagine, as to look upon heaven's lights. What was actually out there and how far did the universe extend? These were questions we would ask ourselves each time we lay on the mountain.

"So, how far does the universe reach, before the end?" I inquired passively.

The answer was not what I was expecting, and snapped me into an obsession of inquiries.

"What? I know you are smarter than that ... what's the matter with you?" my friend exclaimed. "Surely you are joking?"

"What do you mean, what do I mean?" I replied indignantly. "It seems pretty obvious that there has to be an end to everything. After all, nothing can simply

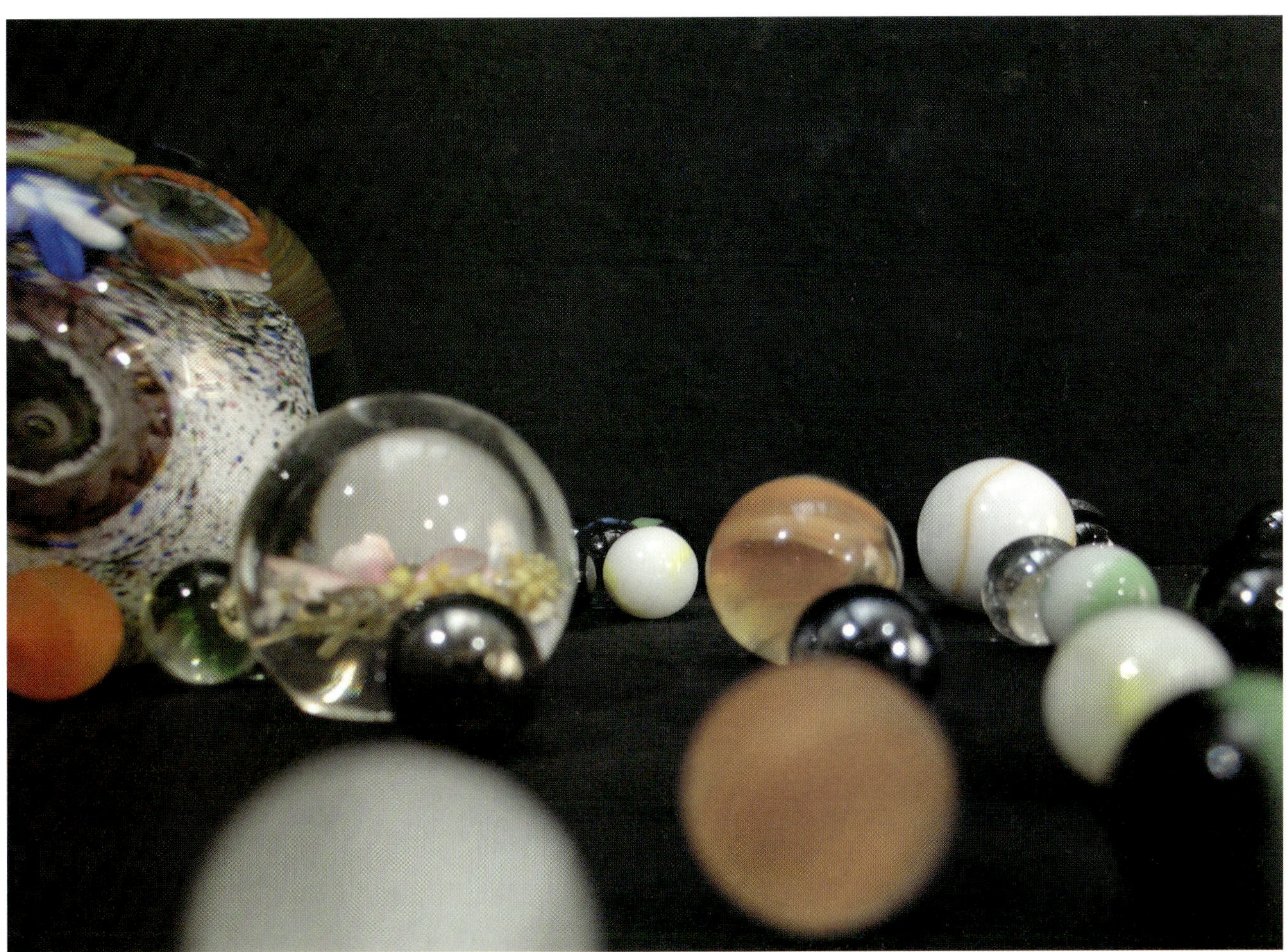

Photo by Alan Burner.

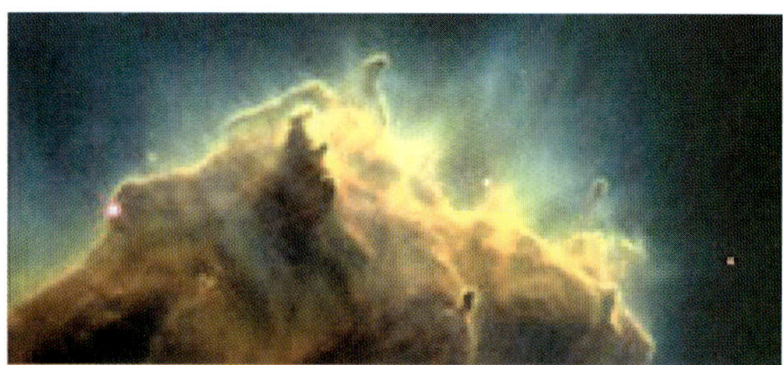

The Eagle Nebula from the Hubble Telescope.
Harry N. Abrams, Inc.

go on forever...especially nothing!" Void of any knowledge concerning Einstein's theories, I continued "You have to be able to prove that. How can you just say something that ridiculous?"

"That's it! You have found the answer. There must indeed be a *gigantic wall* out there with a big sign that says *The End,*" he said, becoming more obnoxious by the second.

"Yeah, that's it," I replied.

"So, what's behind the wall?" was his final question.

We lay out under that wonderful and warm summer sky thinking about our problem, until at last, we fell asleep with mental exhaustion.

We awoke determined to find the answer. We found ourselves in my dad's garage that afternoon. You should see the great stuff this man had in his little kingdom. I always loved that workshop, with the essence of everything that was my father. His collection of tools and.....hammers!

"That's it, the hammer!" my friend quipped. "You still have those great big boulder marbles?"

"Sure, right here! But why?"

"Just give me the marble, will ya?" I had no idea what a hammer had to do with marbles, but I always knew he was a little weird.

We sat down in the center of the concrete floor. It was a cold slab, and I wasn't happy at all about it, but my interest was sparked and so I endured.

"Put the marble on the floor and cover your eyes," he said.

Szwaaaack! The fragments of glass seemed to crackle through the air at enormous velocity. Eyes uncovered, we wondered where the marble had gone. The fragments were so small that what remained was a tiny mound of powdered glass fragments.

"Pick out a single piece of glass, and set it over here on the floor," he suggested. "Here, use these tweezers. You'll need them to isolate the fragment."

I had a tough time of it, getting that tiny piece of glass, but I finally segregated the piece.

Kaathud! Down came the hammer on the fragment. Absent were sounds of crackling glass fragments this time, only the cold thud of the hammers steel head on the floor. By this time, I was sure that my friend had some odd obsession about destroying things.

"What are you doing?"

"Never mind. Now get another piece of that marble," he demanded.

"There isn't another piece, look around!"

You guessed it . . . "wham" . . . the hammer came down on what was nothing more than a tiny powder fragment on the floor. He proceeded to elaborate on the continuous process of striking each smaller piece, until...

"Until there is nothing left, whatsoever," I burst out in self-righteous declaration. With a disappointed look on his face, he began to explain that I was as clueless about this demonstration as I was uninformed about the *infinite space* issue the night before. Soon enough, however, he began to reach me as he drew out illustrations on the back of sandpaper sheets, with my dad's favorite drafting pen. We got to the point where the molecule was smashed, and then the atom, the nuclei, and finally the smashing of the protons and neutrons within the nucleus. The only thing left to disintegrate was the smallest provable particle, the quark.

"Aha!" said I. "There you have it, there is nothing left to smash," thinking back to my end of the universe theory.

"No, you see, they hypothesize that there are smaller particles yet, something called *strings,* you see!" He continued as if to convince himself with every word.

It was then that I realized that matter could not be forced into nonexistence, anymore than you could say that there was an end of outer space.

Later, as I was contemplating color as a student at the university, I was at a certain quandary as to where color came from. I thought back to my childhood dilemma with my more enlightened friend, and realized that it was the quark that held the secret.

As I studied I found that quarks were bundled together as inseparable groups of three: one red, one green and one blue quark, which are also the primaries of additive color, or the R-G-B seen on my computer monitor. I learned that these *quarks* of red, green and blue combined together to produce *white light,* and therefore energy. The exact opposite is true of the subtractive primaries, or pigments, which combined create black.

Suddenly everything became clear. Even the Earth's solar system, with the planets in orbit around the Sun, seemed to strangely replicate the electrons and photons in orbit around atom's nucleus. In fact, when nuclei actually collide and then connect together, the result is nuclear fusion. The same is true of our Sun. As these nuclear forces are liberated they create massive amounts of energy. From the smallest particle to the largest bodies in space, from the quark to the super nova, we understand more about the source of color, the *Dynasty of Light.*

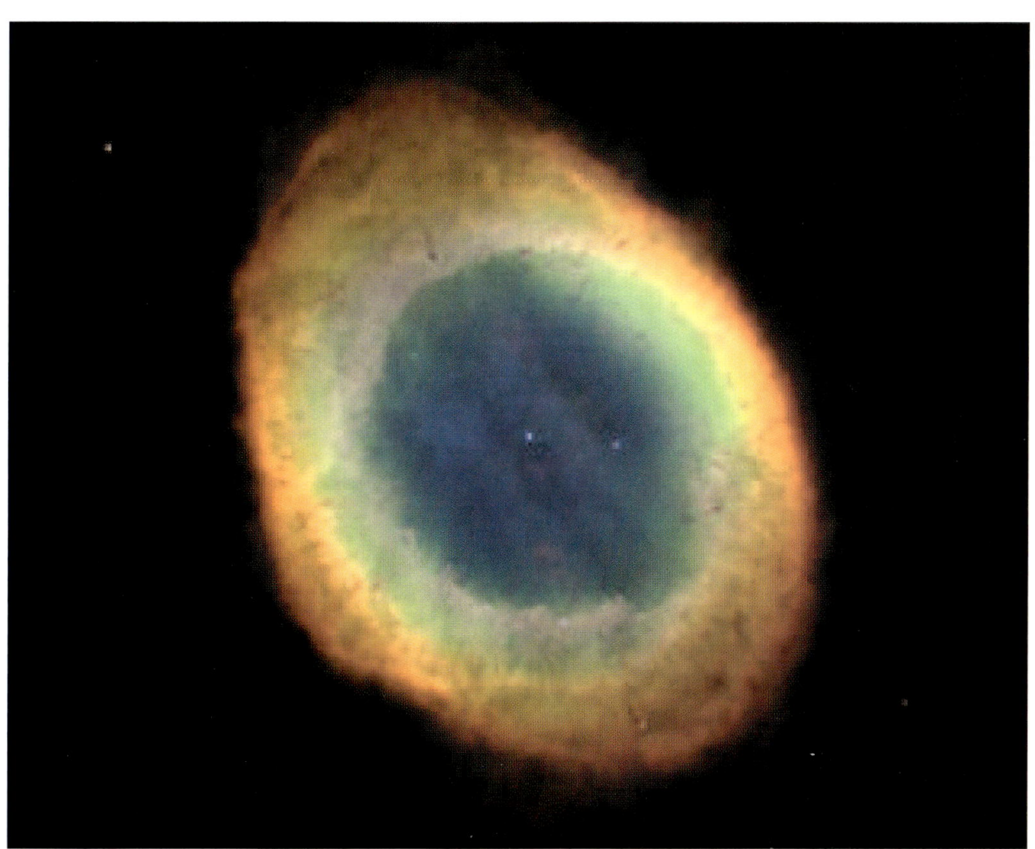

Ring Nebula (Planetary Nebulae—Dying Star).
Ring Nebula M57, photographed by Howard Bond, STScI, with the Hubble Space Telescope.

Lecture Summary:

The Carbon Atom—Crystals and Cathedrals

We have discussed both the purest (outer) source of color, which is produced by the sun's white light, as well as the *inner* resource of color, the atom's quark. Let us shift our focus a bit to one of the most dynamic examples of light and color, and to a subject which we are very familiar—the diamond. We will see that the *white diamond** is really one of the best examples for illustrating the effects of *additive* color. Also, colored diamonds will be used to create a better understanding for the nature of *subtractive* color. First, however, let us briefly discuss the nature of the diamond's *atomic structure.*

A diamond's molecular structure is comprised of five *carbon atoms* which form a *tetrahedron.* One atom is in the center with the other four surrounding it and equally spaced. Each tetrahedron arrangement is bonded at an equal distance from the other, creating the crystal structure of the stone. It takes four tetrahedrons in order to develop the interior, or core, of the diamond unit cell. The four corners of each unit cell are constructed of *carbon atom tetrahedrons* in their respective unit cells. Outer atoms of similar core tetrahedrons are in turn bonded to atoms, which are part of the other unit cells. This network of interconnected crystal structures creates the ultimate hardness by which the diamond is so well known.

The diamond is actually an excellent visual link between the unseen inner color quark and the very obvious spectrum often seen through a prism or in the form of a rainbow.

We know that the unseen color quarks are the smallest verifiable particle of the atom, and the outer evidence of color is produced by pure white light from the sun. When we direct a ray of white light at a clear prism the light is refracted through this triangular shaped crystal, which separates the beam of visible light into the component wavelengths, the seven spectrum colors. So the energy of pure white light is interpreted into color escaping from the prism, and colored quarks of red, green and blue are bound up within the atom, their energy also creating white light. The diamond, on the other hand, attracts the light. It is absorbed into the carbon crystal, and is then seen as color, trapped forever and eternally refracted within its many facets.

It wasn't until the 19th century that the crude uncut diamond was transformed into the ultimate source of color brilliance. A new cutting technique called *brillianteering* finally exploited the potential of radiant white light to reveal the uniqueness of a diamond's fire or its color dispersion. The *brillianteering* method gave way to the discovery of the *brilliant* cut. Basically, a brilliant cut diamond consists of 57 highly polished facets—28 facets at the bottom, 28 facets in the crown and one at the point of the pavilion (culet). These facets act as tiny mirrors. The 28 crown facets attract light into the diamond, which is then reflected by the 28 pavilion facets. In 1919 the ultimate brilliant cut was discovered by a 19-year-old math student by the name of Marcel Tolkowsky. He mathematically figured the appropriate ratio between facet angles opposite each other. This allowed the diamond to exhibit the *maximum refracted inner light without losing the essential reflected outer light.*

The round brilliant diamond has 56 exact symmetrical cuts (57 counting the culet), which is the ideal proportion for a round brilliant cut diamond. The diamond is uniquely beautiful because it is alive with ever-changing color (the fire) as one shifts from one viewing angle to another. This process of turning a crude, uncut diamond into the ultimate

*Note: A clear or transparent diamond is referred to as a white diamond in the industry.

form then reveals the captive spectrum of color sparkle, or fire, within.

We are certainly familiar with many forms of spectral manifestations as seen through rainbows, bevel cut glass, prisms and celestial displays (auroras), to name a few. The diamond stands in a uniquely different category. A perfectly faceted diamond will put on the greatest show on earth. Captive within, the *fire's* color spectrum (dispersion) constantly changes, and seems convincingly alive. The white diamond is the ultimate in clarity and sparkle. It dazzles, and almost mesmerizes the eye as the spectrum of colors dance within the mirrored facets. Deep within the colorless diamond there is a world of fantasy, alive with its alluring sparkle, as if to commune with the spiritual nature of humankind itself.

There is another type of diamond, which assumes a completely different characteristic than the traditional *colorless** or white stone. These are colored diamonds, or sometimes referred to as *fancies. Colored* diamonds have more of a mood association than do the colorless stones. Colored diamonds often times, however, create more of a deep, dark, mysterious mood. Some are dazzling with clear radiant color, while others are permeated with deep saturated mood.

On the following page is a sample list of colored diamonds in terms of *Saturation, Hue and Lightness* from the *Aurora* collection. In our lecture we will discuss the similarities that are shared between the colored diamond, and conventional color theories in subtractive and additive color applications. These similarities occur in hue, saturation and intensity (brightness/lightness). For example, pigmented hues possess a certain brightness (intensity) factor, in a similar way that diamonds reflect light (lightness factor). Of course *saturation,* whether in color theory applications or within the *Aurora* collection, refers commensurately to color purity, as does *hue* in its naming of a color.

Once you have looked over the *Saturation, Hue and Lightness* list, look at the *Colored Diamonds* chart from the *Aurora Collection,* and study saturation and lightness as it relates to the particular diamond. Try to determine the level of saturation first (weak, moderate or strong) without looking at the saturation information. You will notice that your judgment or recognition of saturated color may seem different than it is with pigmented methods of assessment.

Note: The white diamond is also referred to as colorless, as opposed to the colored diamonds seen on the following color charts.

Saturation and Intensity in Pure White Light

Here we see an actual photograph of intense pure white sunlight striking a five carat weight white diamond. The diamond itself is somewhat blurred as the intensity of light overwhelms the entire image. Notice the result of pure energy. We know that the atom and its component parts, such as the reaction found in photon [electron] exchanges and the R-G-B quark bundles, generates energy. Energy creates light, and light produces color. In this photo, we can see the results of that process in a very visual sense. Look at the discharge of color, as white light refracts through the ultimate prism of light. It is almost impossible to capture the true and complete colors within a diamond photographically, or otherwise. The colors are both saturated and intense, so much so, that it cannot normally be recorded precisely. The diamond refracts the most saturated light possible, while it also exemplifies the greatest possible intensity in color.

Allowing the diamond to refract its colors directly onto a white surface (extending out from the crown), permits us to see *indirectly* just how pure "saturation" can be in light. Seeing the diamond's color on that surface is the absolute saturation or pureness possible in light. Looking *directly* then at the diamond, allows one to see color in its ultimate "intensity".

On the following pages you'll find a simple diagram called *The Diamond's Composite Parts, a Diamond Color Circle Chart,* a sample of the *Aurora Diamond Collection,* and a chart listing *Saturation, Hue, and Lightness of Colored Diamonds.* Study the relationship between conventional saturation and intensity in pigments, and that of the same found in colored diamonds. This will help you to clarify the difference between saturation and intensity, as well as the very nature of color itself.

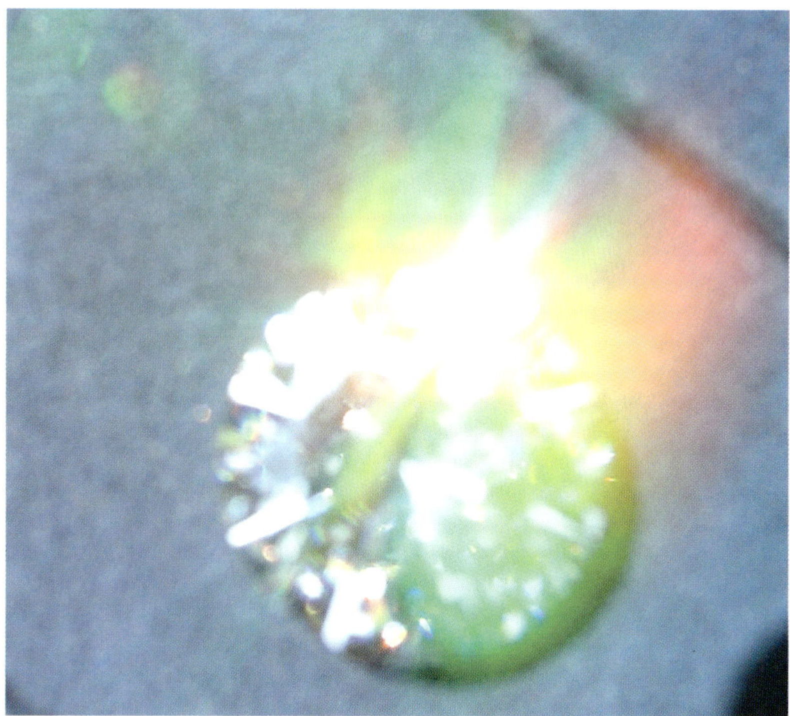

Five Carat Round Brilliant Diamond in White Sunlight.
Photo by Alan Burner.

Composite Parts of a Faceted Diamond—The Round Brilliant

Use this page to diagram the difference between *refraction* and *reflection.*

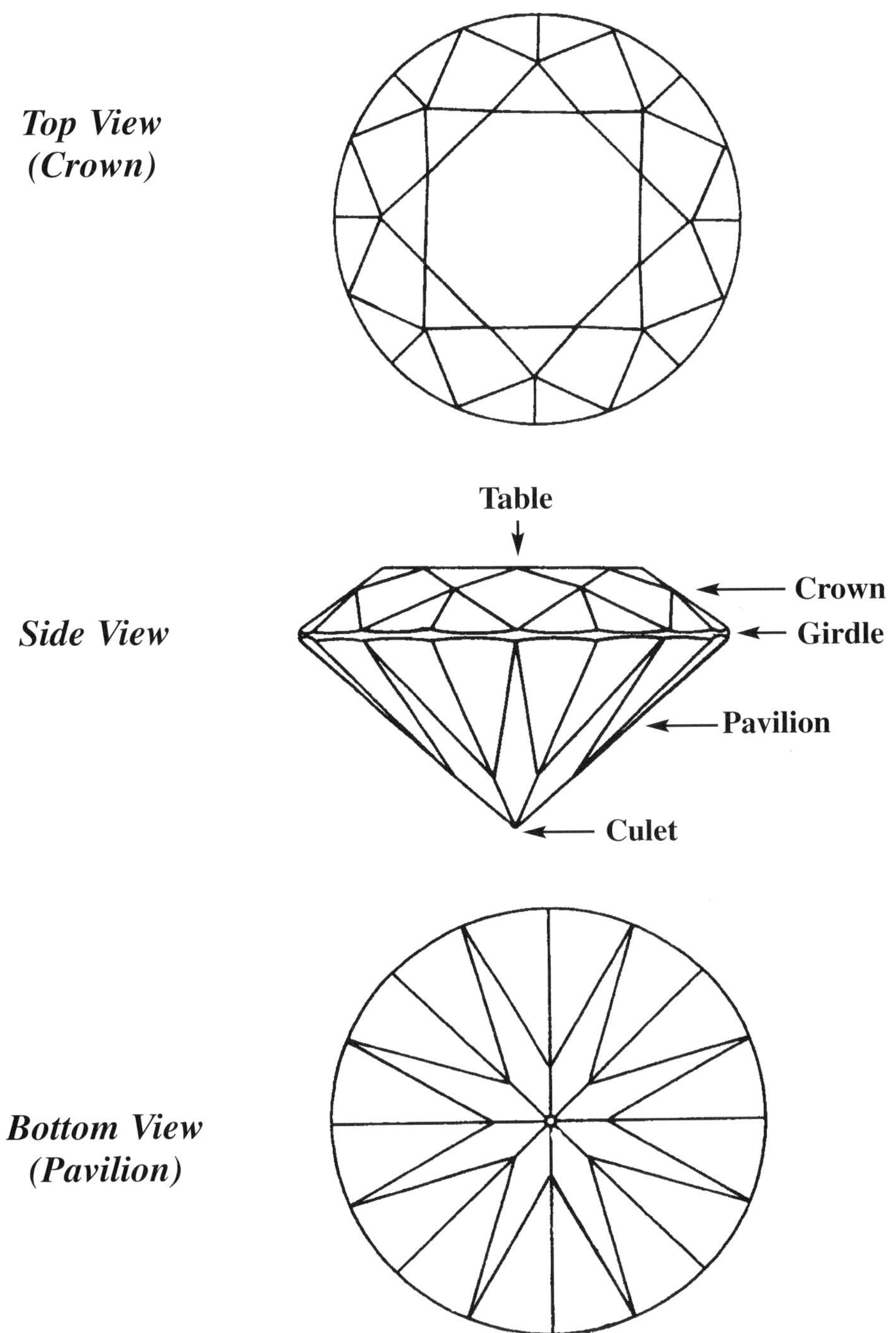

Diamond Color Chart (Color Circle)

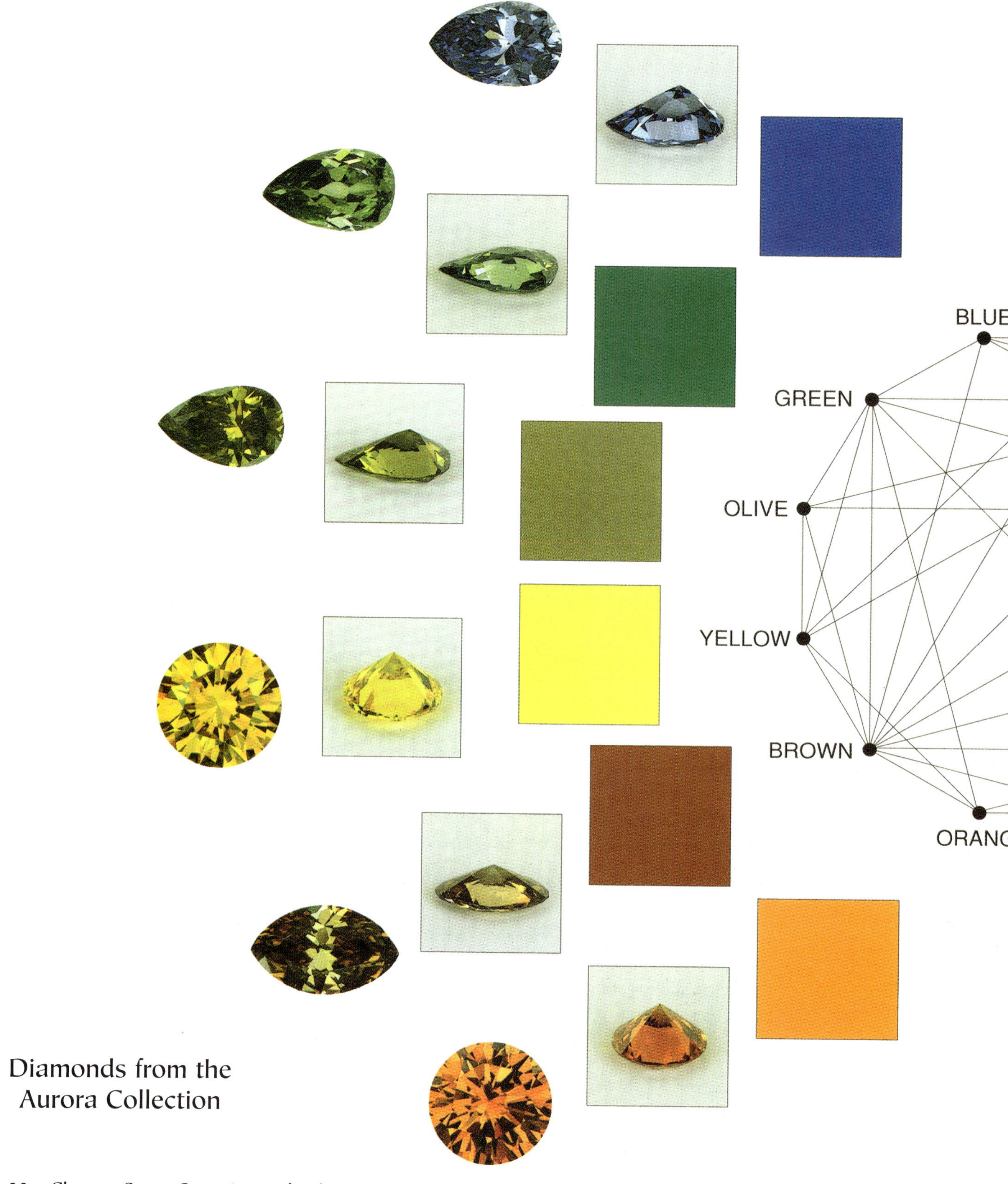

Diamonds from the Aurora Collection

Diamond Color Chart (Color Circle)

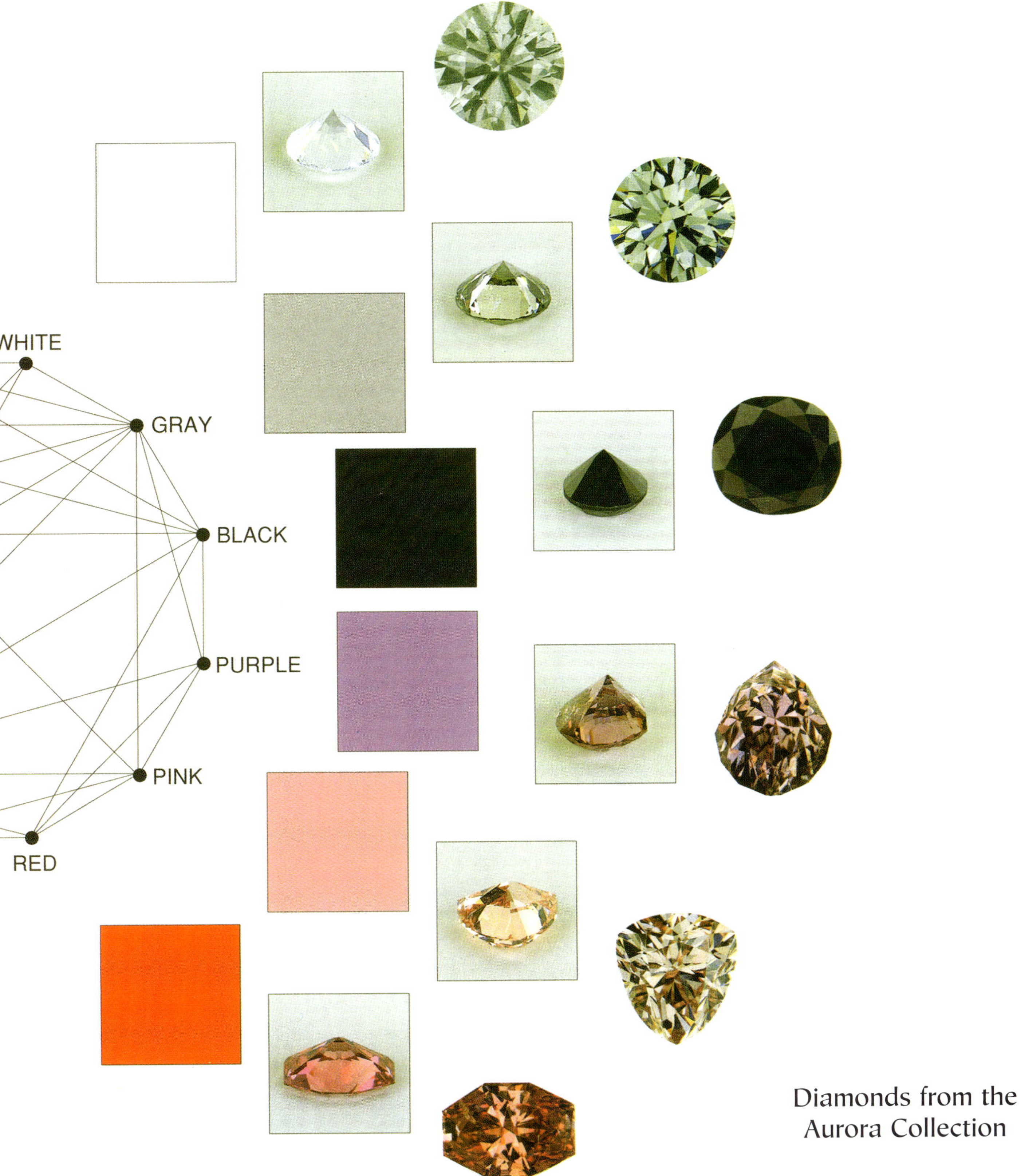

Diamonds from the Aurora Collection

Diamonds from the Aurora Collection

Number **45**
Weight .... 0.49 ct
Measurements .... 5.08 - 5.17 x 3.07 mm
Shape .... round
Cutting .... modern brilliant
Common Name .... **sapphire**
Hue (HUE) .... blue (B)
Lightness (LIT) .... dark (Dk)
Saturation (SAT) .... weak (Wk)

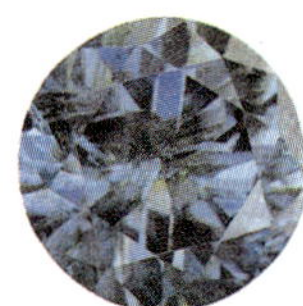

"... Diamonds of a faint bluish tinge are not unfrequently found... the rich deep blue diamond is of extreme rarity... although writers describe these stones as possessing in an eminent degree the beauty of fine sapphires, no comparison can really be instituted, their blue color being peculiar to themselves — dark, verging on indigo, possessing a characteristic intensity which differs materially from the mild, soft hue of the sapphire..."

E.W. Streeter 1884

"... The Jagersfontein mine is... characterized by... exquisite fancy stones of deep sapphire-blue colour."

P.A. Wagner 1914

Number **46**
Weight .... 0.49 ct
Measurements .... 5.11 - 5.14 x 3.07 mm
Shape .... round
Cutting .... modern brilliant
Common Name .... **ochre**
Hue (HUE) ....
.... brownish orangish yellow (br-o-Y)
Lightness (LIT) .... medium (Med)
Saturation (SAT) ... strong-very strong (St-VSt)

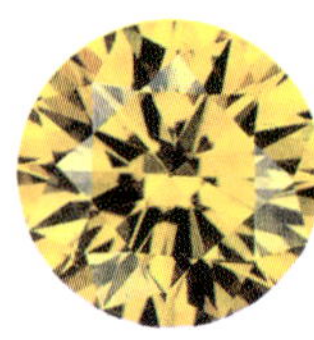

"... Coloured diamonds... fine deep golden yellow or canaries and pronounced fancy colours always find a ready market..."

M.D. Rothschild 1891

"... The deep yellow canary diamonds, the black, and brown, and many other shades are also unusual and desirable."

Marcus & Co. 1937

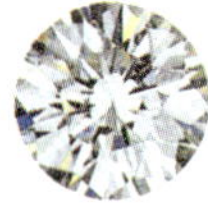

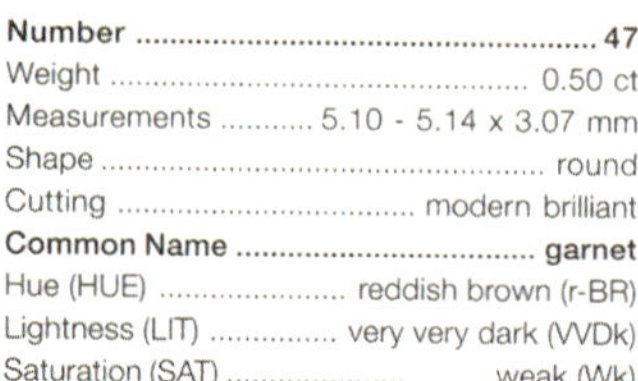

Number **47**
Weight .... 0.50 ct
Measurements .... 5.10 - 5.14 x 3.07 mm
Shape .... round
Cutting .... modern brilliant
Common Name .... **garnet**
Hue (HUE) .... reddish brown (r-BR)
Lightness (LIT) .... very very dark (VVDk)
Saturation (SAT) .... weak (Wk)

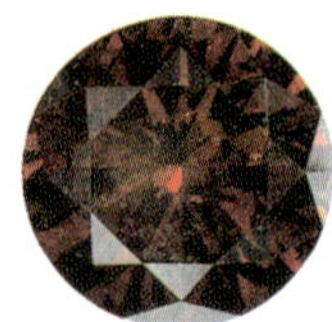

"... The princely collection of the late Mr. Hope possessed a diamond of a blood-red garnet shade..."

A.C. Hamlin 1884

"... diamonds of strong, rich, deep tints are extremely rare; so, too, are the garnet, hyacinth, rose, peach-blossom, and lilac colored specimens..."

G. Merrill 1922

Number **48**
Weight .... 0.50 ct
Measurements .... 6.04 x 4.39 x 2.77 mm
Shape .... pear
Cutting .... modern brilliant
Common Name .... **cinnamon**
Hue (HUE) ....
.... pinkish orangish brown (pk-o-BR)
Lightness (LIT) .... medium (Med)
Saturation (SAT) ...... weak-moderate (Wk-Md)

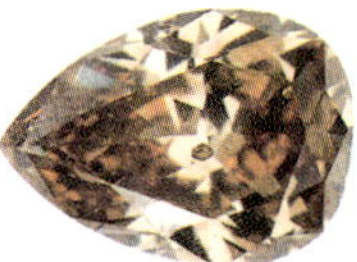

"... Diamonds occur in all shades, from deep yellow to pure white and jet black, from deep brown to light cinnamon, also green, blue, pink, yellow, orange, and opaque..."

W. Crookes 1909

"... the Kimberley Mine... characterized by yielding brown stones... a considerable percentage of smoky and... Diamonds of a peculiar pinkish brown colour."

P.A. Wagner 1914

Diamonds from the Aurora Collection

"... A large diamond... of a brown colour, with a reflection of a vinous [wine coloured] tinge."

J.L. Bournon 1815

"... 'Fancies' include all decided colors... various shades of blue, rose, copper... are included in this classification..."

W.R. Cattelle 1903

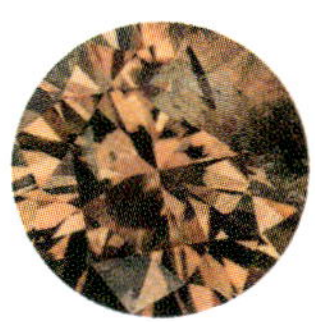

Number 49
Weight .... 0.51 ct
Measurements .... 5.15 - 5.17 x 3.14 mm
Shape .... round
Cutting .... modern brilliant
Common Name .... copper
Hue (HUE) ..... orangish pink-brown (o-PK-BR)
Lightness (LIT) .... medium-dark (Md-Dk)
Saturation (SAT) .... weak-moderate (Wk-Md)

"... However, brown-orange stones, 'burnt orange,' in trade terms, have increased in popularity in recent months..."

R. Shor 1987

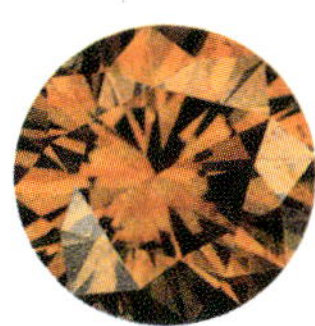

Number 50
Weight .... 0.51 ct
Measurements .... 5.08 - 5.20 x 3.09 mm
Shape .... round
Cutting .... modern brilliant
Common Name .... burnt
Hue (HUE) .... brown-orange (BR-O)
Lightness (LIT) .... dark (Dk)
Saturation (SAT) .... moderate (Mod)

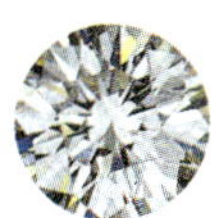

"... There are many different colors — red, green, and blue, probably being the rarest colors. Then there is pink, mauve, violet, orange, all the colors found in the spectrum and many others in combination with each other. Their rarity is such that collectors and connoisseurs are prepared to pay a very high price for these stones..."

J. Roux 1985

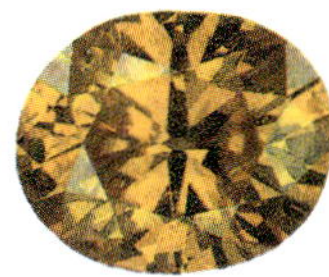

Number 51
Weight .... 0.51 ct
Measurements .... 5.61 x 4.63 x 2.78 mm
Shape .... oval
Cutting .... modern brilliant
Common Name .... marigold
Hue (HUE) .... brownish yellow-orange (br-Y-O)
Lightness (LIT) .... medium (Med)
Saturation (SAT) .... very strong (VSt)

"... Colors speak all languages..."

Joseph Addison 1714

"... 'Canaries' whose bright yellow is faintly highlighted by a hint of orange."

C. Crespin 1984

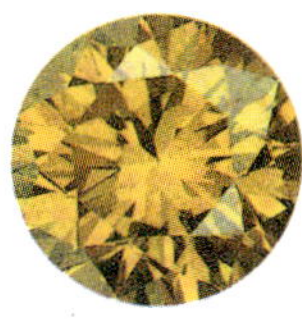

Number 52
Weight .... 0.51 ct
Measurements .... 5.04 - 5.08 x 3.26 mm
Shape .... round
Cutting .... modern brilliant
Common Name .... sunflower
Hue (HUE) .... orangish yellow (o-Y)
Lightness (LIT) .... medium (Med)
Saturation (SAT) ....
.... strong-very strong (St-VSt)

Saturation, Hue, and Lightness of Colored Diamonds

The following chart lists Hue (color name), Saturation, and Lightness definitions according to the appropriate institution.

Hue Name as per Standard Color Theory*	Formal Hue Name as per Aurora**	Common Hue Name as per Aurora	Saturation Strength as per Aurora	Lightness Reflected as per Aurora
Yellows:				
Saturated Yellow	Brownish Yellow	Banana	St to VSt	Lt to Med
Light Yellow	Yellow	Maize	St	Lt to Med
Dark Yellow	Org/Brown Yellow	Amber	Mod	Med
Blues:				
Blue Violet	Blue	Blueberry	Wk to Mod	Med to Dk
Light Blue	Blue	Sapphire	Wk	Dk
Saturated Blue	Blue	Navy	Wk to Md	Med to Dk
Reds:				
Dark Red	Reddish Org Brown	Chestnut	Wk	VDk
Light Red	Purplish Pink	Rose	Wk to Mod	Med
Dark Red Orange	Orangish Brown	Mahogany	Wk to Mod	VDk
Greens:				
Light Yellow Green	Greenish Yellow	Chartreuse	St	VLt
Yellow Green	Yellow Green	Grass	Mod	Lt to Med
Dark Green	Greenish Olive	Chameleon	Wk to Mod	Dk

Saturation Definitions:
Wk = Weak
Mod = Moderate
St = Strong
VSt = Very Strong

Lightness Definitions:
VLt = Very Light
Lt = Light
Med = Medium
Dk = Dark and VDk = Very Dark

Hue Definitions:
According to the respective conventions

*Standard Color Theory = Taught in Traditional Additive/Subtractive Applications
**Aurora = Aurora Collection by Alan Bronstein

Lecture Summary:

A Thousand Nights Fantasy and the Gothic Diamond: A Tribute to Light

In this short essay we will observe and discuss color in terms of its revealing source, which is white light. There are, of course, the many important traditional aspects for the study of light and color, especially from a physics standpoint. In this discussion, however, we shall take a more comparative approach to the subject, using the *gothic cathedral* and the *diamond* as the ultimate revealing source of light's substance, which is color. In this instance, we will take a closer look at the character or personality of color, its functional purposes, and its symbolic nature.

Recently, while in Paris we revisited Notre Dame, one of Europe's finest examples of medieval gothic cathedrals. So important is this cathedral that all signs in France that indicate the distance to Paris actually list the distance to Notre Dame. If you are

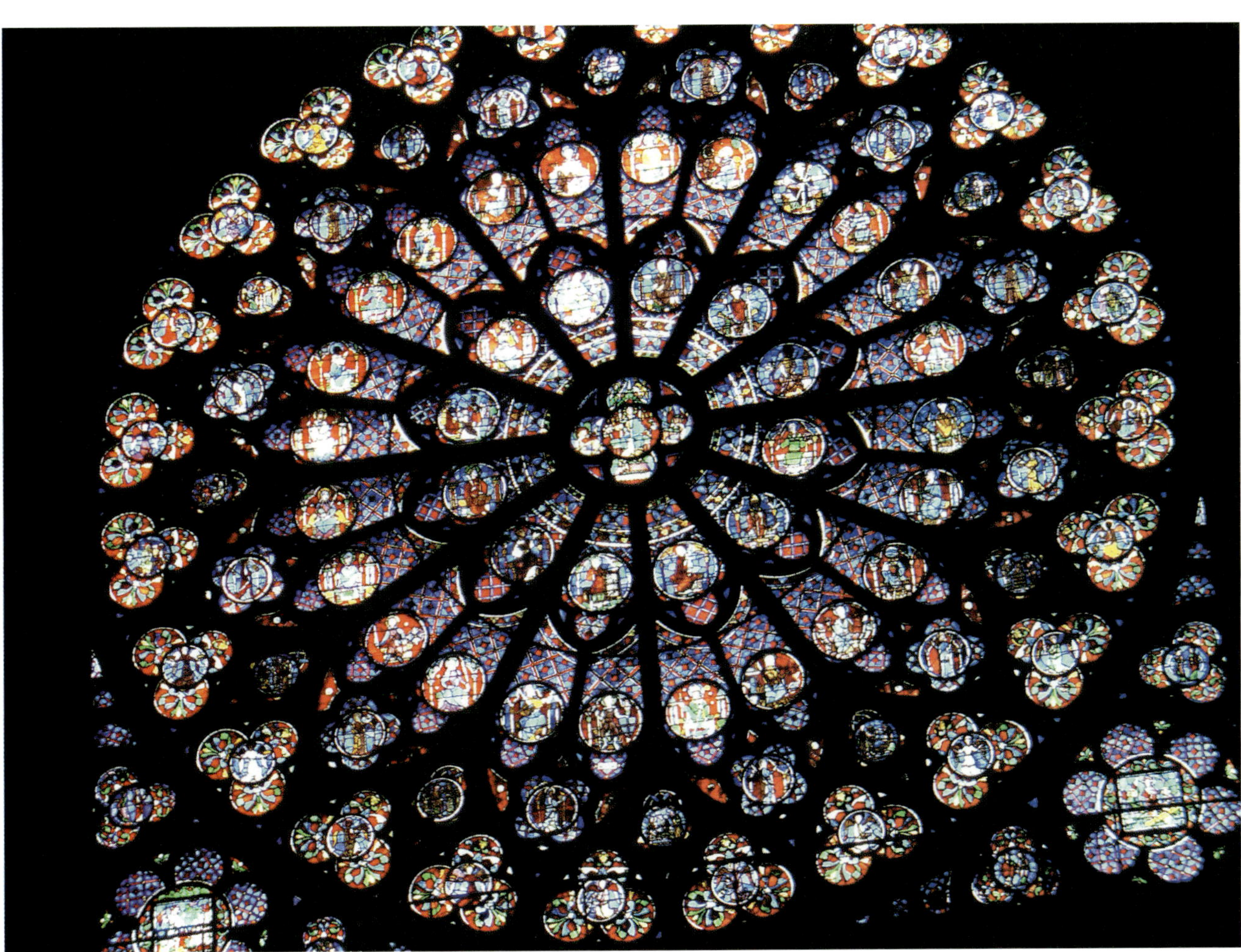

The Northern Rose Window of the Notre Dame Cathedral in Paris.
Photo by Alan Burner.

eight kilometers from Paris, you are, in reality, eight kilometers from the cathedral, rather than Paris' city limits.

Built in the 12th and 13th centuries, this glorious structure with its towering architectural vertical thrusts, immediately performs its task to draw one's eyes toward the heavens, and ultimately to the source of light. Through the Middle Ages in the Christian world, light has often been synonymous with God, or the light emanating from God. Therefore, to look heavenward was to see the light of God Himself. This was an extremely important aspect of the gothic cathedral, both seen on the massive exterior elements, as well as the interior volume spaces. On the outside, Notre Dame's exterior reaches 300 feet above ground and dominates the entire area, as the Seine River flows around it.

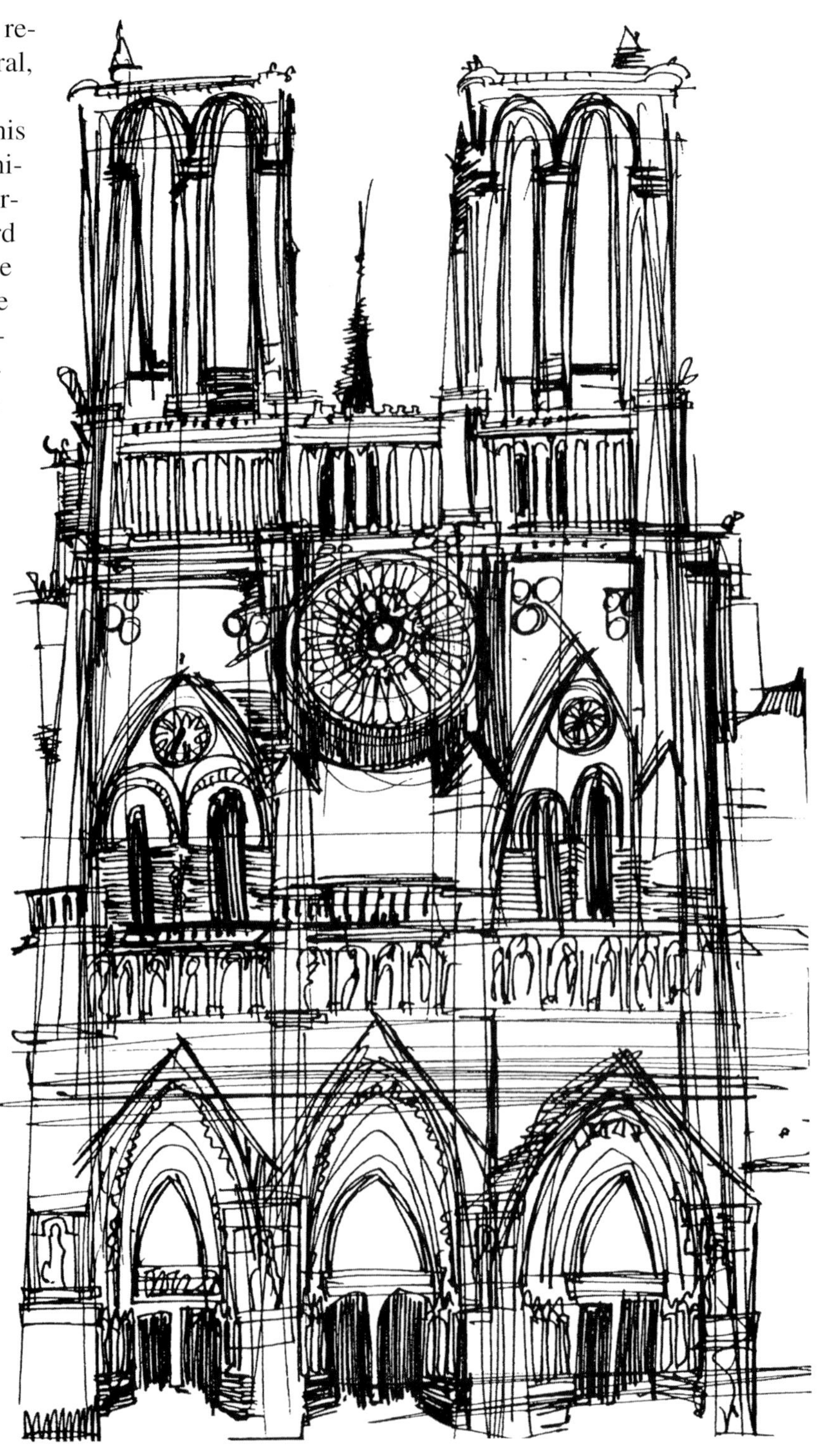

Approaching the cathedral from the front the second most noticeable aspect of the structure most noticeable are the multiple figurative sculptures and reliefs, which form a strong horizontal band under the Rose Window. Many of these figurative reliefs and sculptures depict the last judgment, Christ and the church, apostles, prophets, etc. Since many peoples of the medieval period were mostly illiterate, these figurative elements would perform an extremely valuable function. The Biblical accounts came alive to greet the church goer, as this sculptural building reminded them of the familiar Gospel (meaning: *good news*) stories.

The value of the Paris cathedral became particularly evident by this point in history. Still in its youth, Notre Dame was to become a sanctuary of God's light and forgiveness; a retreat for the community in a world rapidly plummeting into chaos. Those were the years when the infamous *Black Death* struck down fully one-third of the population, from Iceland to India. Death and destruction were all around. Wars broke out in continuous waves of devastation, flooding the landscape with immeasurable carnage. It was Europe that was at the forefront of it all, with France bearing one of the heaviest burdens. The cathedral became a temporal escape into a sanctuary of God's divine light; a small world of tranquility to experience a moment's safe haven.

Immediately upon entering Notre Dame, an overwhelming feeling of God's presence prevailed, as one's head would be immediately drawn upward 115 feet to the ceiling above.

A high ceiling was paramount in order for the gothic cathedral to function properly with its stunning height pulling the eye upward to stand in awe of heaven's majesty, searching for the mercy and grace of God.

One of the problems in the creation of these monumental ceilings was that of structural integrity. The ceiling itself, and more importantly the walls, which were in support of the entire roof structure, had to be properly reinforced. In the earlier Romanesque churches, massive walls were needed in order to support the barrel vault ceilings. The problem was in the massiveness of the walls. The actual wall mass restricted the number of windows, which in turn restricted the quality of light in the church. Basically, the fewer the openings the stronger the wall. At some point, a conflict arose as to the function of a cathedral. It was necessary for the walls to maintain proper support of the ceiling/roof structure, and yet walls needed to be lighter as larger portals would be required to illuminate the ceiling, as well as the remaining interior spaces. If one's eyes were meant to be lifted toward heaven, then the interior was too dark, the ceiling or height so undetectable, thereby minimizing the effectual presence of a heavenly host. The obvious resolve would then be to install larger windows to increase the amount of light needed to illuminate the cathedral properly.

The resultant outcome of this crisis for light was largely responsible for the concept of the gothic cathedral itself. It was characterized by the advent of several new architectural changes: the *rib vaulted* ceiling, the *flying buttress* system, and lighter walls with large stained-glass windows. *Rib vaulted* ceilings consisted of four-part vaults, which were built on *pointed-arch ribs.* These rib vaults were more self-supporting than were the old Romanesque barrel vaults, which was important, because suddenly massive walls were no longer required. To further enrich the process, an exoskeletal buttressing system was created known as *flying buttresses.* This new buttressing system was comprised of an arm or arched wing which stretched out from the exterior walls to an independent vertical buttress, allowing the builders to open-up large portals of light for *stained-glass windows.*

The gothic cathedral became the ultimate expression of heaven on earth. As one enters the massive structure of the church, it is impossible to continue the course of the journey without suddenly realizing the overwhelming presence of vertical space. Standing breathlessly, head lifted to the ceiling above, the windows suddenly burst into full view as if to declare the glory of heaven. As one enters the vast interior, the stained glass windows of Notre Dame seem to explode into an array of transformed heavenly light. This illumination from heaven suddenly becomes a vast color field resultant from facets of saturated hues.

Perhaps the windows of Notre Dame become even more noticeable, since it is one of the darkest of all gothic cathedrals. The second story gallery windows are fairly remote, and the massive honeycombed nature of the interior chambers restricts the free flow of light throughout the cathedral. In most cathedrals the light floods the interior spaces, turning them into luminous jewels of color, as opposed to Notre Dame, which suffers from its darkness. An amazing thing happens however, because of the absence of light: the north and south transept rose windows actually become much more radiant and spectacular.

Certainly it is because of the dark and light contrast that causes us to see such an extreme sensation of brilliance. The fact is that Notre Dame's Rose Windows, especially the north window are of the most highly regarded of all gothic cathedrals. The radiating bars of tracery on the northern Rose extend out to an immense thirty-one and a half feet in diameter from the center oculus. The Rose Windows tell a story, specifically Biblical truths about Jesus

Christ and His church. Beginning with the northern transept window we observe the Virgin Mary with Jesus at the center, surrounded by concentric rings of Old Testament prophets, judges and clerics. The south transept Rose window features Christ on the throne, which is surrounded by rings of apostles and church martyrs.

The use of light in gothic windows was very important to the church because of its symbolical purposes. The light entering through the windows into the church was as though the divine light came from heaven, or God Himself, and was flooding the interior of the church. From the highest to the lowest, from God to humankind, the colors of heavenly light came down and bathed all within the House of the Lord.

(The church, by its beauty alone, acts as a Sacrament. . . . . . like the plain and forest, the cathedral has its atmosphere, its fragrance, its light and shadow, its chiaroscuro. The great rose with the setting sun behind it seems, in the hours of the evening, to be the sun itself, on the point of disappearing at the edge of a marvelous forest. But this is a transfigured world, Where light is more dazzling than in ordinary life, and shadow more mysterious.)

—Emile Male, Religious Art, *1949*

The world of the gothic cathedral is indeed transfigured by these enormous windows of light. An interesting note at this juncture would be to mention the existence of an authentic gothic cathedral built in the 20th century in our very own Washington D.C. Begun in 1907, the Washington National Cathedral was completed 83 years later in 1990, and is exemplary of the gothic cathedral in every aspect, including the interior light.

It is also interesting to note here that the light of the interior spaces seem to replicate the hues of certain colored diamonds, found in the famous *Aurora Collection* of colored diamonds. Several diamonds have variations on the same color, but there is a diamond in that collection possessing a particular "burnt" orange color. The National Cathedral's larger inner spaces are a similar color of orange as seen in the diamond's interior, which in turn may be similar to how we would perceive the light from heaven itself. The windows and interior spaces are built to allow the maximum amount of light into the church interiors, similar to the diamond's construction. Of course, gothic cathedrals vary in their effective light depending on the

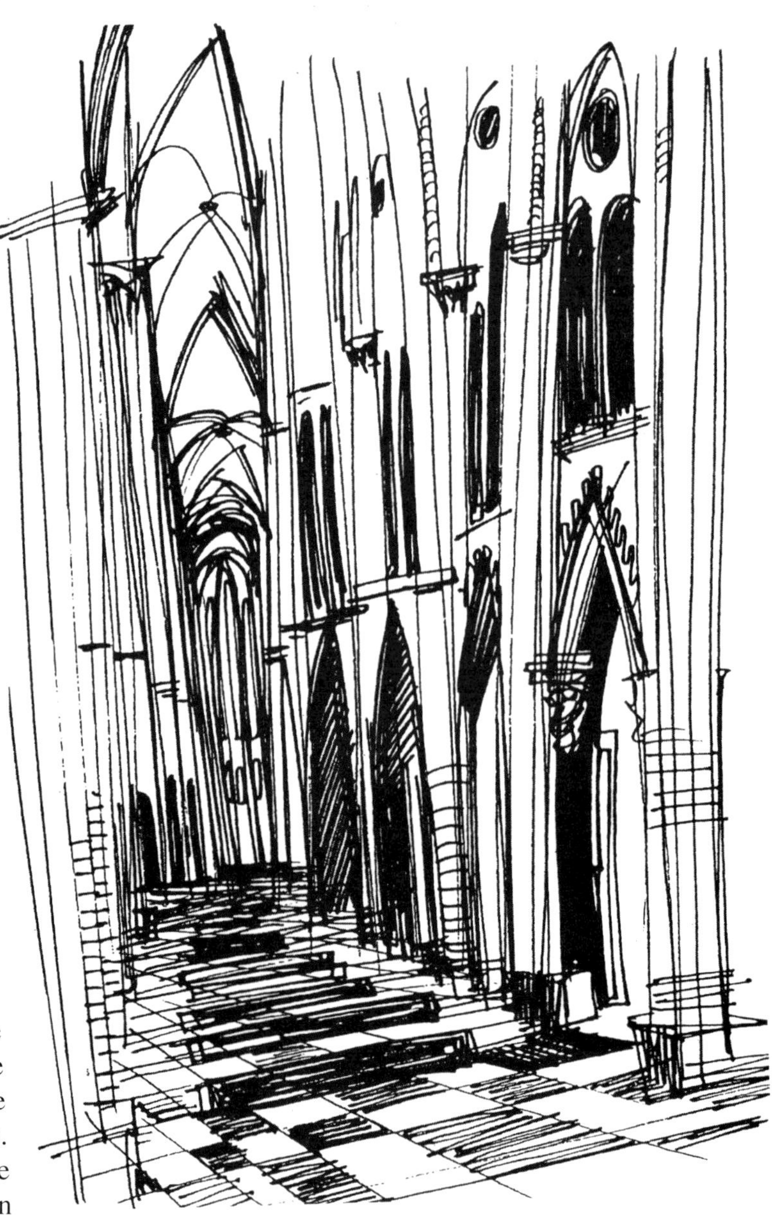

time of the year (Sun's direction) and whether it is cloudy or sunny on any given day.

As we mentioned, the intensity of the north and south Rose Windows are significantly noticeable, as one notices the contrast of extreme saturated light seen in the window as opposed to the darkness of the interior spaces. Not because of any intention by the church builders, the darkness in the church became synonymous with the Biblical principle concerning the darkness in "man's heart." The windows then reveal their contrasting light, which then symbolize the divine light from heaven illuminating humankind's *dark heart.*

These huge windows often seem like gigantic colored jewels, capturing not only the essence of perceived heavenly light, but of one's own imagination. As we compare light, we have looked briefly at the gothic cathedral window but we would also like to call attention to its sequel—the diamond.

The diamond is about romance. It is permanent, mysterious, and most definitely the "stuff" by which fantasies and dreams are made. What is it about fantasy that holds such intrigue? Certainly as human beings we occasionally nurture fantasies—filled with never ending possibilities and imaginations, one is often compelled to ponder the effects of illusion becoming reality. We know that fantasies are often developed from fragments of actual experience constructed by the many facets of our lives. The fantasy is assembled like many mirrors from the past. As the light of imagination reflects from each mirror, or memory, it reveals an exaggeration or fantasy, a total fabrication from our memories and desires. We may daydream or become so mesmerized that for a moment we live in that dream, only to be yanked back into reality moments later. They are *stolen moments* in time, revisited.

It seems as though our minds can create a thousand fantasies. Our imaginations take us far away—yet only for the *moment.* My most coveted fantasies many times reveal themselves in the form of daydreaming—visions filled with light and brilliant colors, as though those elements somehow helped to enhance the fantasy, or perhaps make it more credible. The colorful environment within my fantasies was always exciting and energetic, adding fuel to my imagination. Because of these *illuminations,* I have observed that light and color are essential elements in creating the emotion and mood of my dream world.

It is the absolute nature of light to expose its component of color. There are many demonstrations of color in the world: the tranquil blues within the ocean and in the skies, the passion felt in the color orange, the sensuousness of red, the celebration of yellow, or the peaceful rest of green meadows and forests. We can experience color through thunderous and explosive volcanoes, or the radiant translucency of a rainbow. All create an emotional response of one sort or another. How then, would it be if we could experience the moods and emotions of all colors simultaneously? One of fantasy's greatest attributes is the ability to create intense emotional responses. Imagine then, all emotions experienced at one time.

Perhaps there is a symbolic reference for these combined moods. I am reminded of a particular warm and breezy late October night, as the fragrance of autumn flowed over the terrace, stirring the air in the room. The intensely moonlit evening conspired with the fall breezes to keep me awake. The warm temperatures that night did not correspond to the typical autumn colors in my mind. As I lay on my bed desperately trying to sleep, colors of summer—blues, greens and violets—dashed through my head, even though I knew the colors identified with that season should be variations of orange and red.

Unable to discern the season of my existence, I finally rose out of my sleep-deprived state to see for myself. Just then, an intense flash of blue and green light suddenly invaded my eyes, drawing me to my mother's heirloom diamond sitting just beneath the lamp. I soon became mesmerized as I began to contemplate the color of this rather large, five carat diamond. As if to fall in and out of consciousness, I continued to stare closer into this all too familiar arrangement of carbon atoms, until I realized what was actually happening.

The diamond had in fact cast a spell over me with its bursts of radiating energy and ever changing spectrum of hues. The ultimate performance of light and color had claimed its victim. The white light of the lamp was continuously being lured into the crystal, held captive and then dispersed into sparkling displays of color as the dream continued. My spirit remained captive as did the color in this crystal, and I danced within the facets until the spell was broken. There I stood in front of yet another Rose Window.

Nothing exhibits the attributes of light as does a perfect diamond, so brilliant and alive with clarity and fire. It creates dancing colors, moods of celebration, of hot summer nights, cool tropical breezes, and dazzling romantic holidays. It's hypnotic whisper pulls you into a *Thousand-Nights fantasy.*

Diamonds are not revered simply because they sparkle with color, or because they are mere shiny bobbles. They are spellbinding jewels, symbolic of fantasy fulfilled, of hopes and dreams, which finally captivate and romance the viewer. A diamond can be the fantasy, as well as a sophisticated charm of eternal elegance, or a symbol for good fortune and happiness. In a sense, we desire to enter the fantasy perhaps through the diamond's interior itself. To get inside is to live the fantasy and to experience the color and its power over us.

Since we cannot enter the diamond physically, or experience an affinity with it, we can only imagine how it could be instead by entering the gothic cathedral itself. It is different in many ways and yet fundamentally the same.

The Gothic style architecture with massive colored windows was crucial in bringing light into its space, and into the soul of humankind. The two important aspects about the construction of the cathedral were *space* and *light.* The first was to create an enormity of space by means of the cathedrals towering *vertical thrust,* with its high ceilings. The next step then would be to satisfy the light requirement by incorporating the use of external flying buttress systems. This in turn opened up wall space, allowing for the installation of larger colored windows to emit greater amounts of *light.* These new portals thereby were responsible for filling the space with the radiant color of the heavenly *New Jerusalem,* referred to in the Book of Revelation. Diamonds and cathedrals both require accuracy and symmetry in their construction. They are both required to capture the optimum light, which in turn creates the color mood by which we derive inspiration and dare to dream.

It is one thing to imagine or create a *fantasy* through observing a diamond's color, but it is quite another to experience the *reality* and power of God himself through the interior spaces of the cathedral.

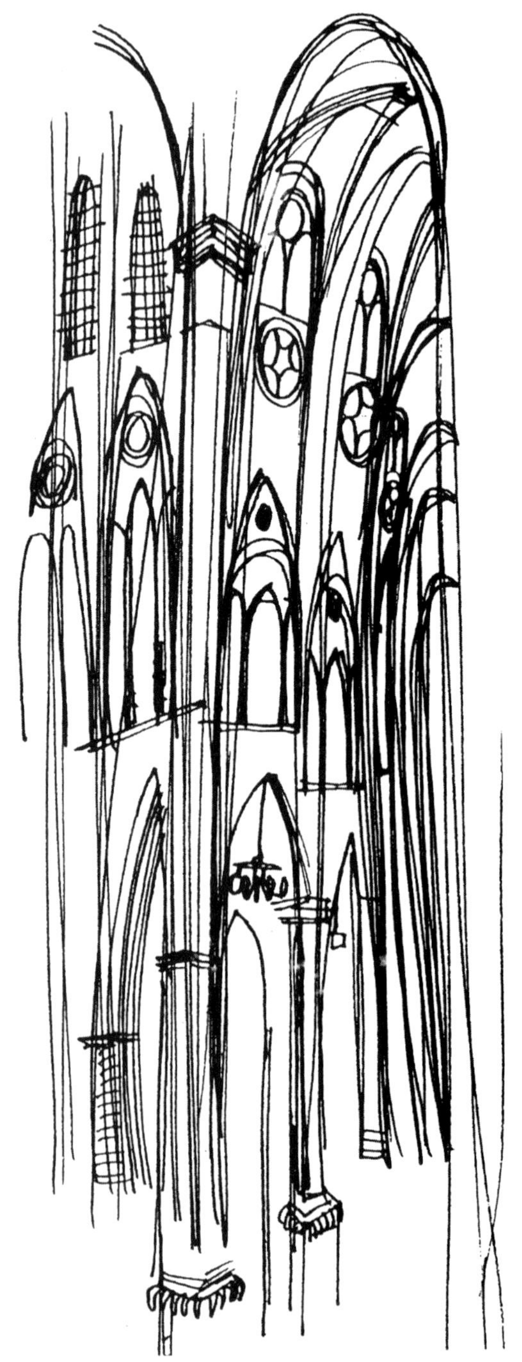

When walking through the National Cathedral in Washington D.C., an amazing phenomena seems to often happen. As you experience the mood of this building, you become aware of color immediately, as if walking through the *spectrum,* grandiose style. People who have not walked close to God or for that matter have not known Him, often leave the cathedral in awe of God's presence. It is quite a spectacle to observe.

The one-hundred foot high, vaulted ceiling creates a startling and extreme space, one which leaves the observer without adequate words. Additionally, the presence of pure sunlight from heaven, which passes dramatically through the colored glass facets, can perhaps simulate the essence of a diamond for the participant. Is the cathedral a type of surrogate diamond? Certainly the original idea of the cathedral was that one could experience God's presence by His light, which is translated through the glass into pure saturated color. His light therefore, was the source of color, which illuminated the chapel and further revealed the nature of God.

Through this brief study we have covered the components of light through both the diamond and the gothic cathedral. The diamond can only be entered through a color fantasy world, one which stimulates our *imagination* and allows us to escape reality. The cathedral, on the other hand, can be experienced on a more physical and spiritual level, causing us to contemplate issues more *realistically.*

Diamond Characteristics

- Brilliance and Clarity: Quality of light (white light)
- Fire: The flashes of color refracted in the facets
- Light: Reveals color
- Saturation of colored diamonds

Cathedral Window Characteristics

- Purity or quality of light: Light from God Himself
- Intensity of warm and cool colors
  reflected from the windows
- Transforms light: specific radiant color
- Saturated stained-glass

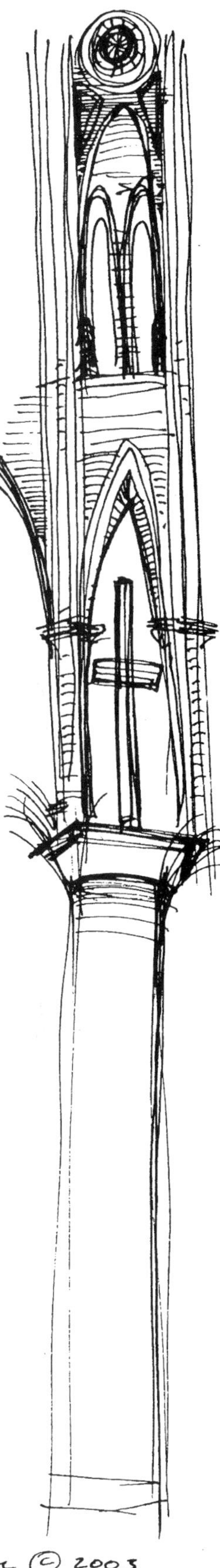

The Gothic Diamond

The Notre Dame Rose
Gothic petals transformed;
Facets for a portal of heaven's glory.
A rose window splashes
Translucent, illuminated color,
Over opposing vaulted walls.
Within a community's spiritual fortress,
The Rose endures, blossoming
And revealing
The "dynasty of light."

We understand, therefore
The diamond.
Not unlike Heaven's majesty,
It reveals
Faceted windows of
Sparkle and celebration.
Dazzling flashes of color
In a moment of time.
It is then a perfect choreography
Of color.
A fire that reveals
A "dynasty of light."

Shijo,
Notre Dame de Paris
Paris, 2003

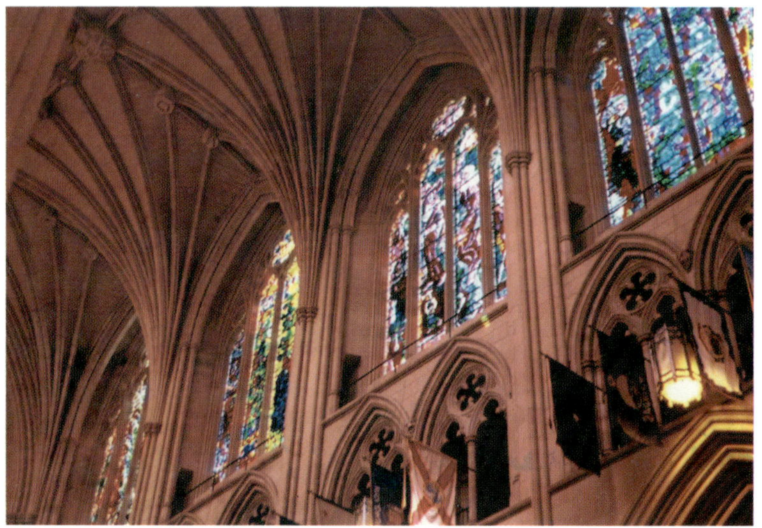

Interior of the Washington (D.C.) National Cathedral.
Photo by Alan Burner.

Saturation and Intensity

For many years it has been said that saturation and intensity are one in the same. In one respect this is possible, depending on how the subject is approached. First let's examine the true nature of saturation, and then intensity.

Our first task is to examine saturation in terms of its traditional definition. This is somewhat difficult in itself since definitions vary from text to text. Let's see if we can sort this out logically.

A general term for saturation:

Pigmented (subtractive color) saturation is the absolute purity of a hue. It is completely free from the influence of black, gray or white; it is the pure intensity of a given hue. In colors of light (additive color), or prismatic hues, it is the color spectrum, which possesses the maximum saturation or intensity of hue.

The problem that arises is with the term *intensity,* used twice within the paragraph. This is why we think that saturation and intensity are the same. In reality, there is a fairly distinct difference, even though there are some similarities. This is one of the "anonymity" issues that we can perhaps resolve by this brief discourse.

Saturation

Saturation refers to the absolute purest state of a color and to primary or secondary colors in particular. In this example we will use yellow. In the color bar below, we see a saturated yellow patch on the left, after which various degrees of yellow's complement (violet) are added. The addition of violet changes the intensity of the yellow to a dull, lifeless

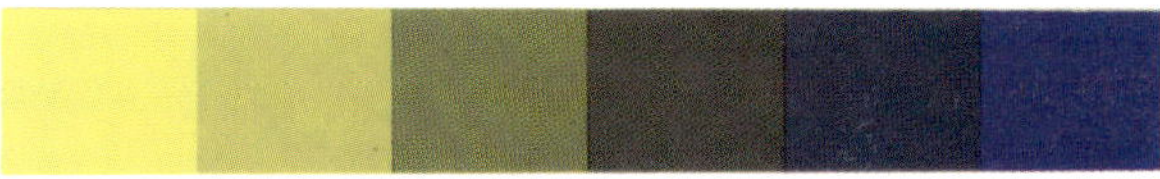

Intensity Scale with Additions of Violet

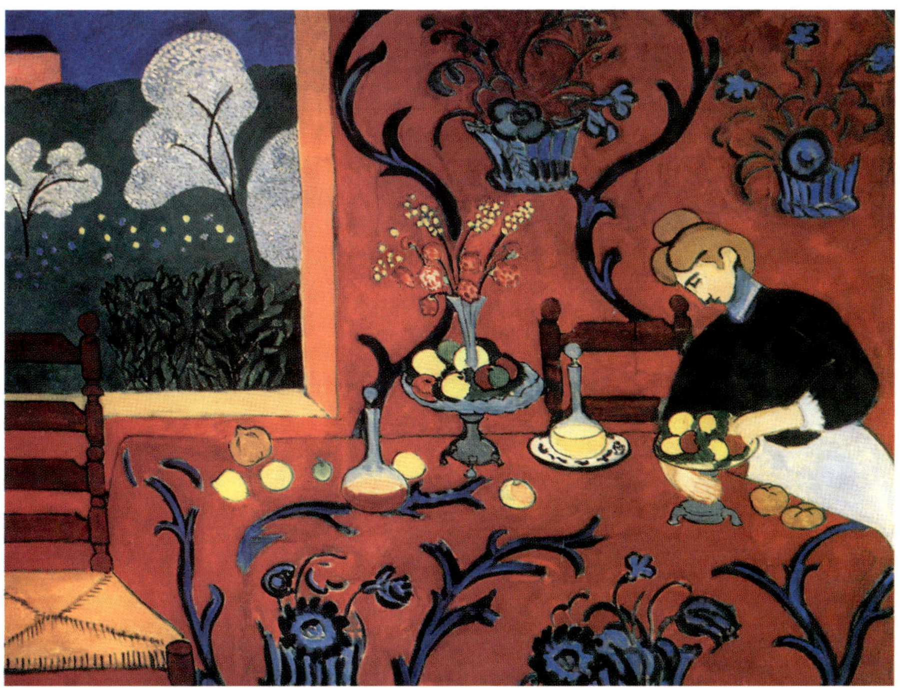

Harmony in Red by Henri Matisse.

Saturated red dominate this composition to create a very specific mood response.

hue. Just a small amount of violet has changed the character of yellow from celebration to an unhealthy pale hue. Its purity has been compromised, and eventually the yellow (weakest of all colors), is overcome by the violet (strongest of all colors).

The following is an exercise, which begins the process of critical thinking.

When you are in the process of learning a subject, it is often important to find out *why* it is so, or *if* it is the truth. Settling issues from your own research will help to build a solid base for your education in art. Please consider the argument about the similarities and dissimilarities between saturation and intensity:

Saturation and intensity, it can be said, are *superficially* the same, but *fundamentally* different. Intensity is the degree of chromatic value changes, which lead toward or away from saturation. It is, for example, the degree of brightness of yellow moving toward or away from its saturated state. Basic differences are that *saturation refers to purity of a color and intensity addresses brightness.* Yellow, in reality, becomes more intensified as white is added, and is therefore brighter than its saturated condition.

Traditionally we have said that the highest form of intensity is the saturated state of the color. That would be true if we say that *intensity* makes reference to *concentration,* yet we know that intensity also refers to *brightness,* which is not necessarily saturation.

Let's consider a different approach. If brightness equates to intensity, we could say that lightest yellow is the most intense (white additions) and the dullest yellow is the least (black additions), with *purity, or saturation* residing between the two (see yellow intensity scale on the following page). The problem with the two terms is that *brightness* itself can refer to either *intensity* (concentration) or *vividness* (saturation). The argument should best be resolved then at this point by stating that full intensity (concentration) would be the purest or saturated state, and *brightness* would then be better referred to as the *lightness* of a given color.

"All painting is composed of line and color. Line and color are the essence of painting. Hence they must be freed from their bondage to the imitation of nature and allowed to exist for themselves. Painting occupies a plane surface. The plane surface is integral with the physical and psychological being of the painting. Hence the plane surface must be respected, must be allowed to declare itself, must not be falsified by imitations of volume. Painting must be as flat as the surface it is painted on."

Piet Mondrian

In Mondrian's composition, saturated red, yellow and blue are presented as pure color extraordinaire. Saturated color here is presented in all of its glory: full, rich and passionate. Saturation is strong and powerful, and eludes to an entirely different course of feelings than does intensity.

An example is shown on the *cover page* of this chapter. Napoleon sits on his throne after being crowned Emperor of France in the Notre Dame de Paris. The warm saturated red robe speaks about authority and strength; it is the *power* of red. The high contrast created between the red robe and the dark

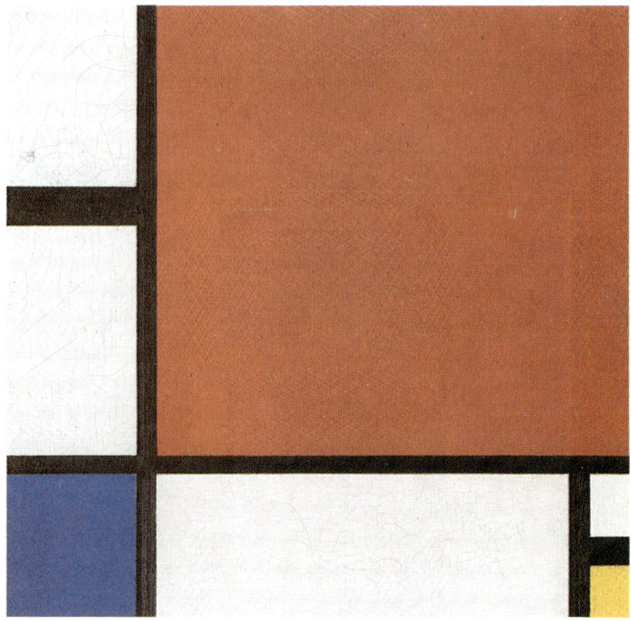

Composition with Red, Yellow and Blue by Piet Beeldrecht Mondrian. © 2003 Mondrian/Holtzman Trust/Artists Rights Society (ARS), New York.

background creates an even more commanding image, as we focus entirely on the Emperor. The white collar and inner robe lining is the highest possible *intensity* there is, which is contrasted against the most *saturated* of grays, or the black background.

Intensity

One of intensity's scenarios can be seen in the *Portrait of a Lady* (detail). In this detail there is of course a total lack of saturation. Instead, her face illustrates intensities within a range of light red-oranges, giving her face a radiance and subtle luminosity. Intensity has a much wider range of possibilities than saturation does. It creates tints and shades (chromatic values), mass and believable illusion of space all of which are observed in the *Portrait of a Lady*. Here, the mellifluous nuances of the skin's tone is created by the harmonious surface of intensity changes. Intensity differences normally begin with the minor addition of another color or a complement, whereas values are accomplished by the addition of black or white to a color. As opposed to intensity, saturation has but one state or condition that it can exist, and instead creates powerful moods and symbols to manipulate the viewers psyche. Saturation then, becomes much more mood specific as a lone hue.

Bartolome Esteban Murillo's, *The Immaculate Conception of Soult* illustrates that intensity is the dominant force of the painting. There is no evidence of saturation in this composition, since the orange tones make a transition from lightest orange to darkest orange to red-orange. The range of intensities produced in this piece creates a very translucent heavenly atmosphere.

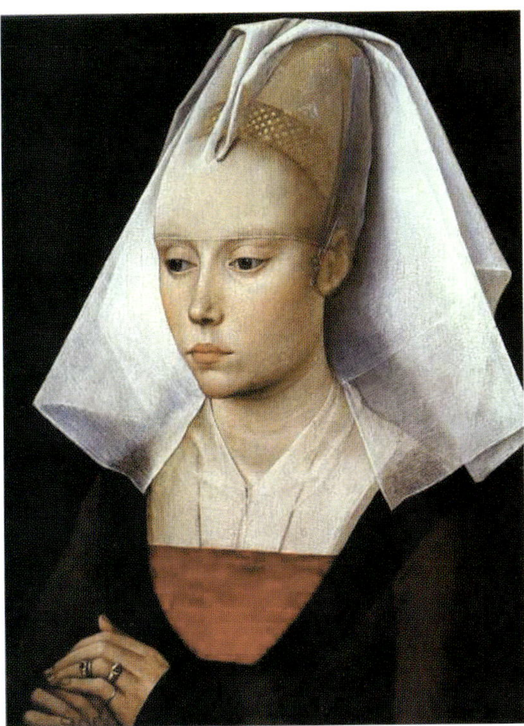

Portrait of a Lady (detail) by Rogier Van der Weyden.

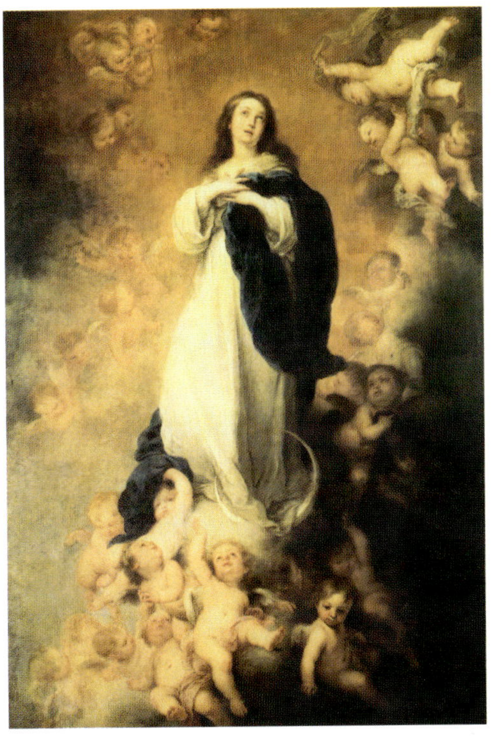

The Immaculate Conception of Soult by Bartolome Esteban Murillo.

Value

The word value in and of itself refers to achromatic (absence of color) conditions, such as black, gray and white. It also refers to producing a lighter color by the addition of white, or making a color darker by adding black, and all gradations between.

Below, the center patch is just as yellow as it can possibly get and is therefore saturated. The varying degrees of brightness of white (left side) involved with each yellow patch, are all leading towards saturation. As soon as saturation has been reached (fourth yellow section from the left), black is then added and its results seen in the fifth section. The slight black addition has robbed the yellow of its liveliness, taking yellow away from its saturated state, into dullness.

Yellow Intensity Scale

Michelangelo's *Creation of Adam* also shows gradations of values. Both intensity and value changes are evident in the Sistine Chapel ceiling at Vatican City in Rome. This work is the artist's claim to fame, in part due to his exquisite use of value systems. A section of that ceiling is seen (opposite page), in the form of the *Libyan Sibyl* (1508–12) illustrating quite well his prowess with values.

During the high renaissance in Italy, it was the Pope who dictated an artist's destiny. Michelangelo desperately wanted to sculpt, and considered his focus to be in the realm of sculpture. A conflict arose when the Pope demanded that Michelangelo paint frescos, rather than to follow his heart's desire, which was to sculpt. Really there was an enormous amount of blank wall space, and if you were ever desirous of an art career in Italy, then one was beholden to work in the Church's medium of choice. So Michelangelo became painter by day and sculptor by night.

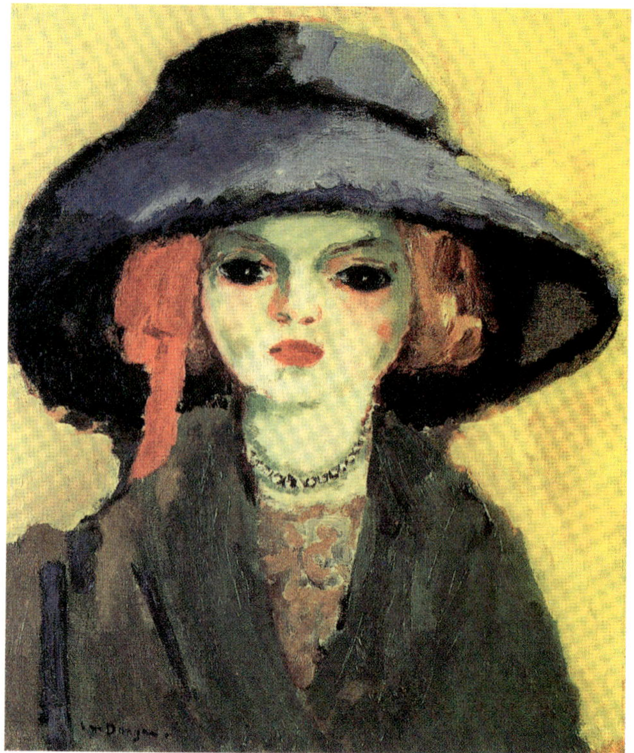

Portrait of Dolly by Kees Van Dongen.
©2003 Artists Rights Society (ARS), New York/ADAGP, Paris.

Dongen's *Portrait of Dolly* exemplifies the results of shading with small amounts of black added to yellow. Notice that (as is with the yellow value bar example) yellow begins to exhibit a degree of greenness when there are additions of black. Also of interest are the effects of value, intensity and saturation on the composition. The near saturation of the yellow background affects the *violet* in that it seems more intense, and the shaded green jacket seems much duller than it actually is. In the same manner, the yellow seems brighter because of the lack of saturation and intensity in the jacket, as well as certain violet hues seen in the hat.

Michelangelo's *Libyan Sibyl,* is an excellent study in value gradations. This artwork is a small section of a larger whole seen on the Sistine Chapel ceiling at the Vatican in Rome. The artist's frescos suddenly seem to

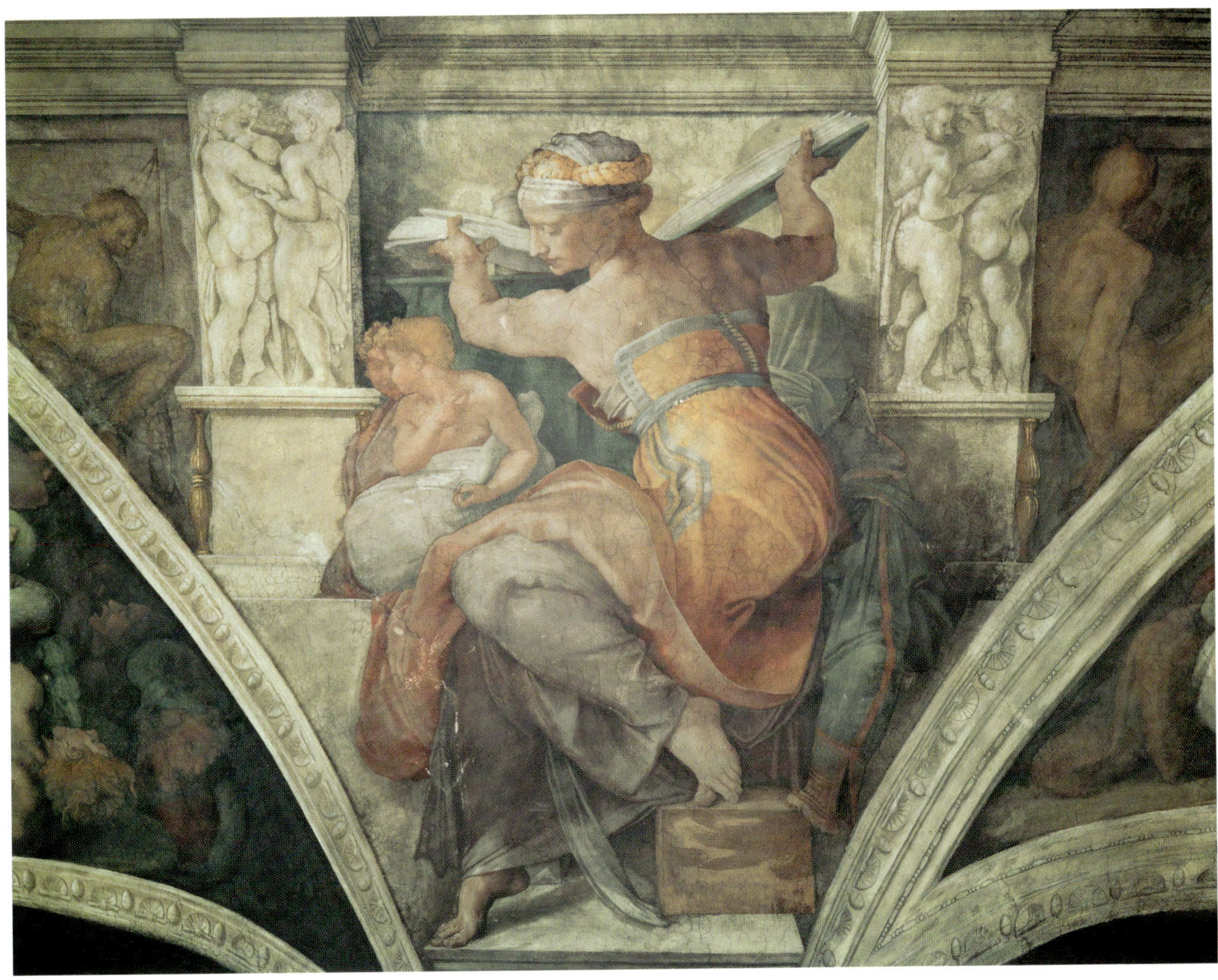

The Libyan Sibyl by Michelangelo.
Scala/Art Resource, NY.

"pop" away from the wall into three-dimensional space. His ability to create value systems had become highly accurate. The artist himself, always revered sculpture more than painting a flat surface, but the Papal powers that be pressured him to paint frescos, since there was an abundance of empty wall space. That being the case, Michelangelo lived-out much of his sculptural experiences vicariously through his painted frescos. He was so inclined toward sculptural forms in space, that he became one of the most renowned three-dimensional painters of all time.

We can see just after this short discussion that there are differences between saturation and intensity. Very simply, saturation exists in only one state, whereas intensity can exist, increasing or decreasing in various stages, creating a range of three-dimensional possibilities.

A more subtle illustration of saturation, with intensity and value gradations, can be seen in the video still by Shijo (next page). The most evident illustration is on the surface of the arms and legs of Aiko's Warrior, particularly her left arm forward.

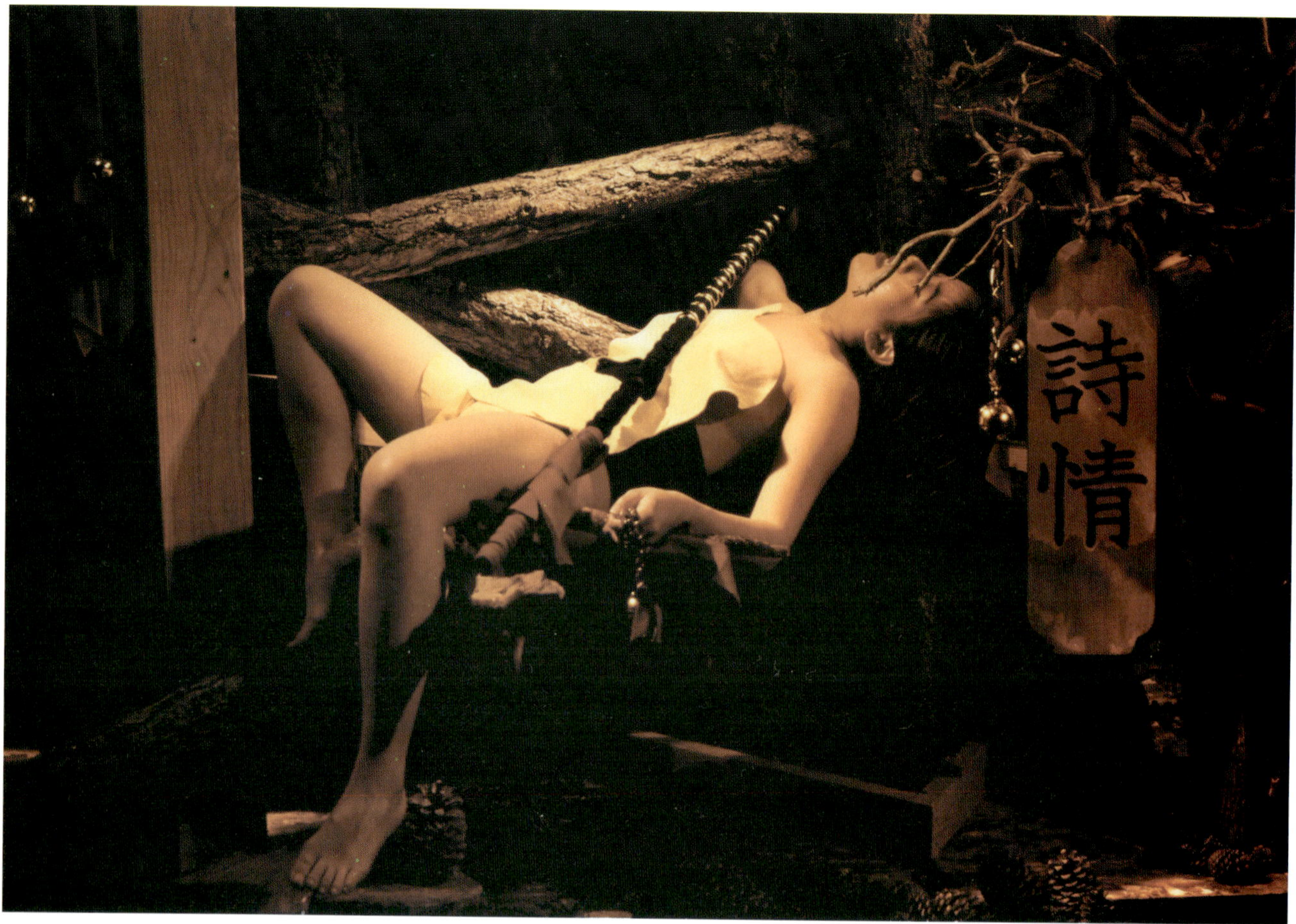

Aiko's Warrior Sleeps; A Thousand-Nights Fantasy, by Shijo.

Exactly in the center of her arm we see the most saturation, that is the orangeness of her skin. As the shades move to the back of the arm, there is a quick change to a very dark value, after which we observe the fairly rapid change of the lightest intensity of orange on the top portion of the arm.

The entire photographic composition is comprised of darkest to lightest oranges, which are indicative of a monochromatic color harmony.

Finally, it is important to take a look at color from a different angle. The intensity of a color often relates to the intensity of the subject matter itself. We can take an ordinary subject, without the intensity of action, and turn it into a vibrant and brilliant display of color intensities, transforming the object into a theatrical performance.

Bernini's *The Ecstasy of St. Teresa,* for example, translates mood and emotion quite well, without the

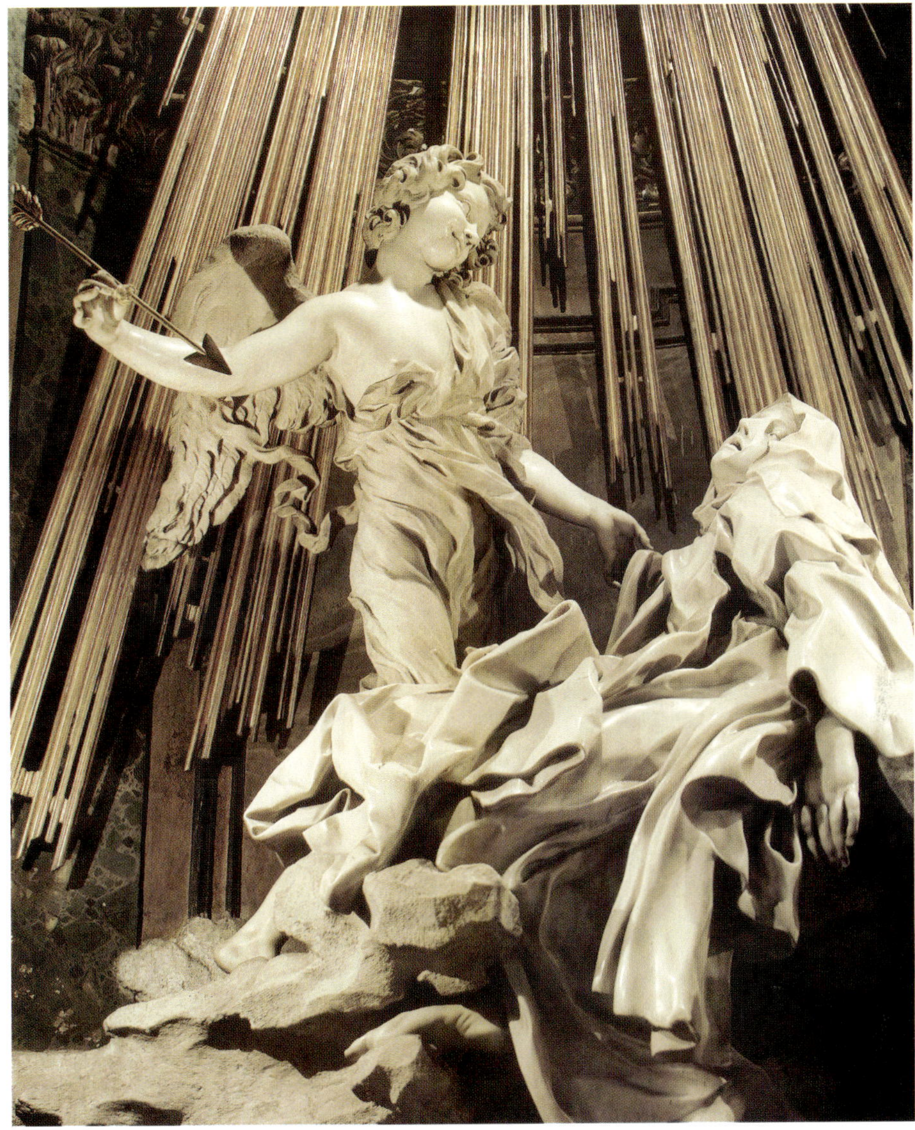

The Ecstasy of St. Teresa by Gian Lorenzo Bernini.
Santa Maria della Vittoria, Coronado Chapel, Rome © Gianni Dagli Orti/CORBIS.

aid of color. It is the function of color to create emotion and mood through saturation, intensity and value, just as this sculpture does through visual theatrics.

As we refer back to Mondrian's *Composition with Red, Yellow and Blue,* we understand that the use of non-objective (no recognizable form) color must create the mood on it's own merits, without the help of any recognizable or objective form such as that seen in Bernini's *The Ecstasy of St. Teresa.*

Sovereignty of Light

The celebrated father of French impressionism, Claude Monet, knew full well about the *dynasty of light.* He thought well beyond the scope of color visuals, but lived for the imminent opportunity to catch light at its optimal time during any given day. Monet worshipped the omnipotence of light. He was the master of seeing color, for observing the hues that were actually seen by the human eye, as opposed to preconceived notions of color. First and foremost this painter knew that the *authority of color* (Chapter Two), was first dependant on the *sovereignty of light.*

A brief study of Monet's paintings of the Rouen Cathedral will introduce the student of color to his prowess in light observation.

Monet was a student of light as well as color. To be able to see color clearly and understand it, one must first know something about the properties of light. The artist set aside several years of his life to make a thorough study of the Rouen Cathedral. In fact, he persuaded the landlord of an apartment building across the street from the cathedral to allow him to use a second floor apartment directly across the street. With a commanding view of the cathedral's façade, he began his acute studies of the play of light across its surface. He illustrated conspicuous distinctions between light in the morning and light at dawn.

In the early morning light the top half of the cathedral is bathed in cool blues and violets. Monet layers the cool composition with the blue's complement of orange, which further enhances the richness of light on the blue surface. The overall surface then

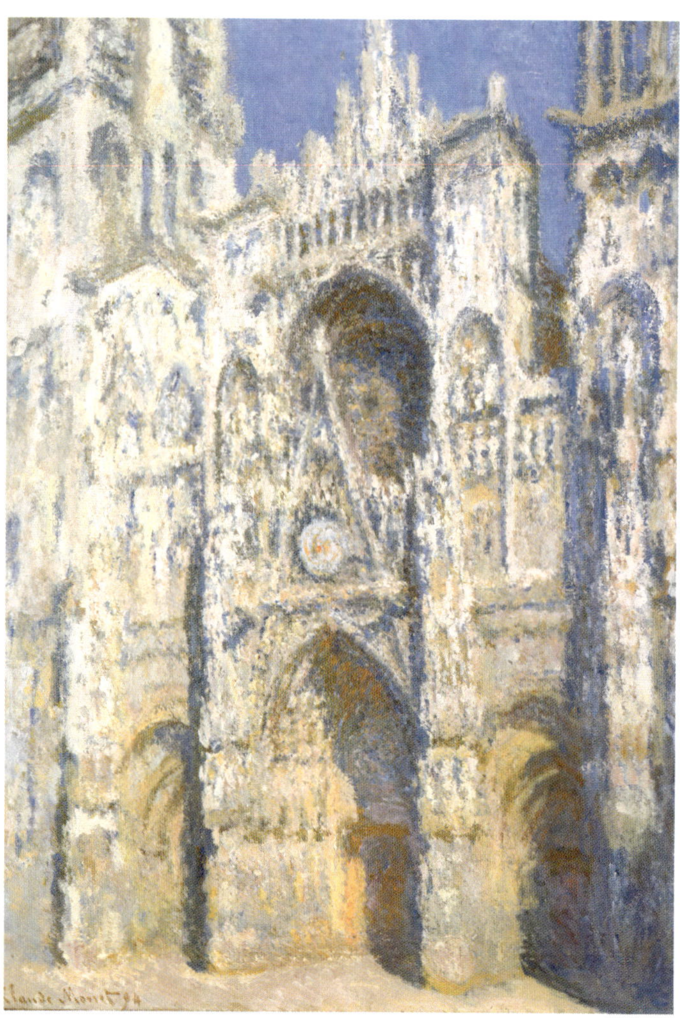

The Portal and the Tour d'Albane (Morning Effect) by Claude Monet.
© Burstein Collection/CORBIS.

is interpreted as light to dark violets. The portal itself is actually the emphasis, as the ever lightening deep violet tones begin to expose the front doors and the entire portal itself. The viewer anticipates the approaching light, as it will soon immerse the entire structure. The intensity of the light on the top half of the building causes us to focus on the façade itself, since the bell tower seems to merge into the atmosphere, and reach into heaven.

Now in the approaching night sky, we see the opposite, as the cathedral is immersed in warm orange light, with just the slightest amount of blue and violet tones. Everything is the opposite; what was cool blues in the morning, is now its complement of orange at the reverse time of the day. The sun is going down rather than coming up, and the cathedral's light is being *consumed by the darkness,* as opposed to the morning *light overwhelming* the darkness. One might be tempted to think there was no difference, but Monet had become intensely aware that the early morning light is not the same as the late afternoon light. The mood content is radically different.

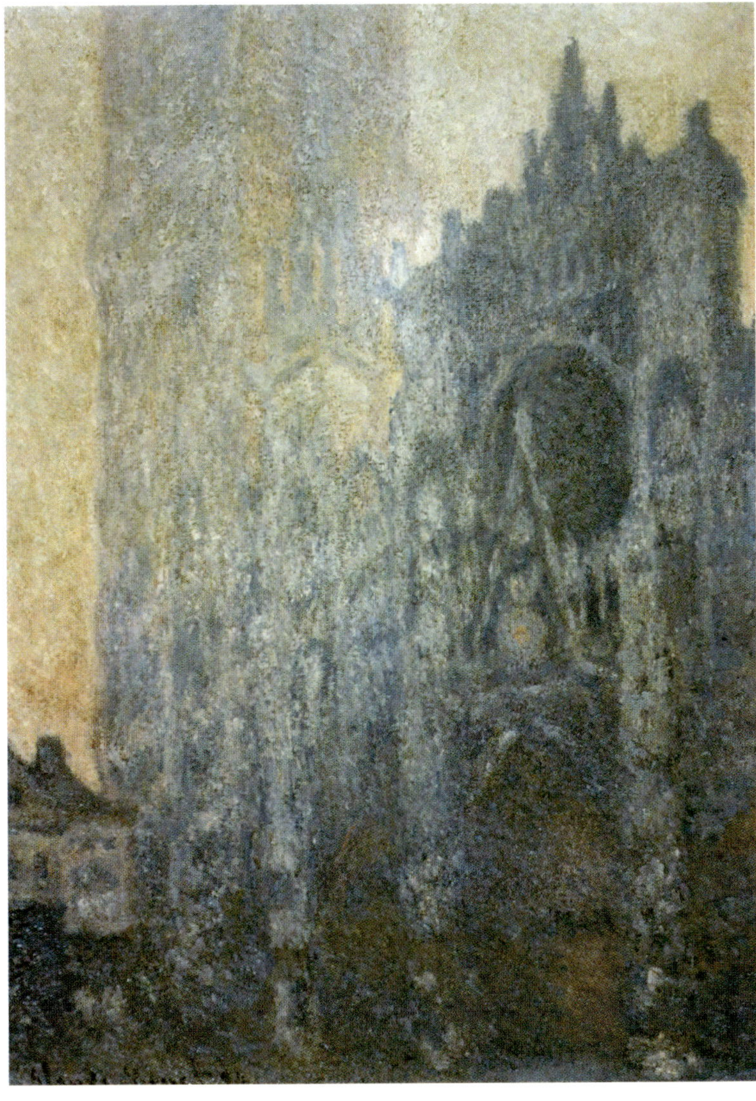

The Portal and the Tour d'Albane at Dawn by Claude Monet.

"I am worn out, I give up, and what's more, something that never happens to me, I couldn't sleep for nightmares. The cathedral was coming down on top of me, it was blue, or pink, or yellow," Monet records in a letter. His studies of the light's affect on the Rouen Cathedral had exhausted him to the point of despair. This was his commitment to the study of light and its component of color.

Light was so important to Monet that he once claimed that the only truly acceptable time to paint the façade of the cathedral was between 12:00 and 2:00, when the light began to fall across the surface front from right to left. The strange thing about Monet's obsession with light is that he missed the most important aspect of light concerning a gothic cathedral: the interior light:

> *"I was interrupted today, and instead of working on 12 canvasses, as I had hoped, I only worked on ten. There was a great celebration at the cathedral, the inauguration of the moment to the former Archbishop Bonnechose. A sung Mass performed by 300 who had come from Paris...bref, since this morning the portal was draped in black, which greatly hindered me; so I wanted to go to this Mass, but the seats at five francs had been sold out the day before; luckily, Madame Monier was able to obtain an invitation for me and I was wonderfully placed. It was marvelously beautiful and I saw some superb things that could be done inside, which I very much regret not having seen earlier."*

For a painter of light, this could mean only one thing: he was overwhelmed by the capture and transformation of heavenly light, which burst through a multitude of stained glass windows. An artist who had spent his life focusing almost exclusively on the effects of light on painting in the *out-of-doors* now could see another entire world of possibilities for light effects. Indoors was a place, which from outward appearances, would seem void of any serious potential study of light. So massive, so visually heavy and so intimidating, why would one think to study light on its interior? Yet as we can see in this chapter, the *interior* of the gothic cathedral is most certainly a fortress for the majesty and *sovereignty of light.*

Chapter One
Project Proposal

The Project–Color Mixing: Saturation, Intensity and Value Chart

We have chosen a somewhat restricted pallet of primary colors for this particular exercise (see Special Note) illustrating the effects of mixing pairs of colors. (L) and then (R) refers to color placement on the *left* and on the *right*. For example, in Group One (top left corner of the composition) Quinacridone Red is applied full saturation in the left square, and Ultramarine Blue is applied full saturation, to the opposite right-hand square, with gradient intensities in between:

- Quinacridone Red (L), Ultramarine Blue (R)
  [Top Left Quadrant] **Group 1**
- Hansa Yellow Light (L), Cerulean Blue (R)
  [Center Left Quadrant] **Group 2**
- Cadmium Yellow Light (L), Cadmium Red Light (R)
  [Bottom Left Quadrant] **Group 3**
- Cadmium Red Light (L), Ultramarine Blue (R)
  [Top Right Quadrant] **Group 4**
- Quinachridone Red (L), Cerulean Blue (R)
  [Center Right Quadrant] **Group 5**
- Cadmium Red Light (L), Cerulean Blue (R)
  [Bottom Right Quadrant] **Group 6**

Chart Layout:

There will be six groups of color patches, each group will contain 30 color patches. Lines one, two

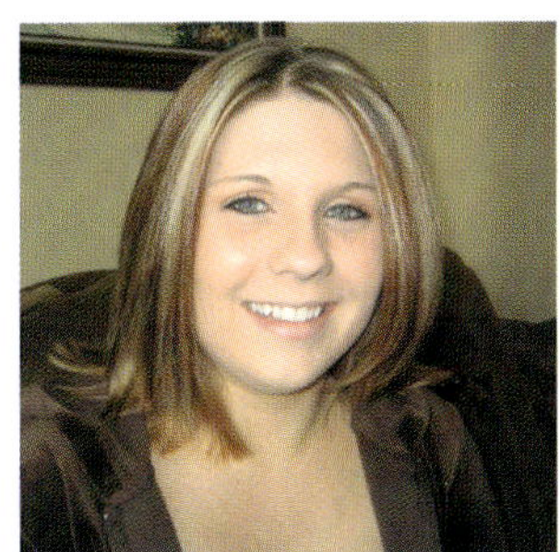

Janessa Roberts

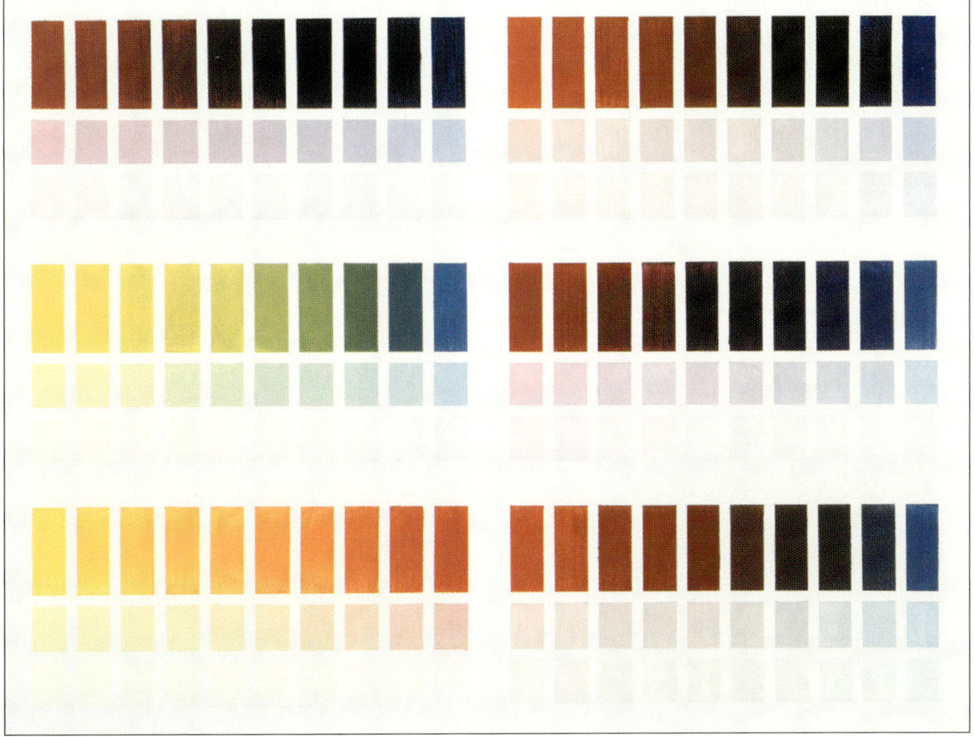

Student Color Chart by Janessa Roberts.

and three are nine patches across. The top row of horizontal patches indicates color intensity changes in saturation. The center and bottom rows of horizontal patches will illustrate value changes.

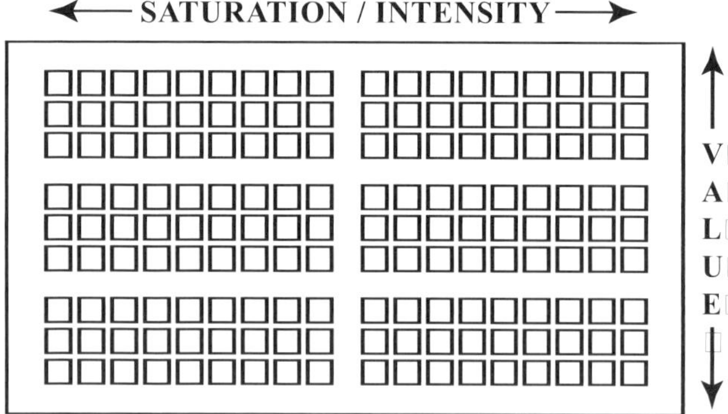

Method:

Begin first by taping off the color patch grid system with 1/4" wide artist's tape, according to the specification measurements below. Using the top left group as an example, we are changing intensities by working our way across the saturation/intensity patches, from left to right. The student will be changing the intensity of quinacridone red (1st left side square) to violet (5th and 6th center squares), and ultimately back to ultramarine blue (10th right side square). We will use *Group One* as the example as follows:

- To start with, saturated *quinacridone red* should be painted in the first upper left corner patch in column one.
- Then in the upper right corner of that same group, paint in the ninth patch with saturated *ultramarine blue.*
- Pour a puddle of quinachridone red onto a dedicated mixing surface.
- Next, separate a small puddle of quinacridone red from the larger puddle, and add enough white to that smaller puddle in order to produce a lighter red value. Paint this on the patch directly under the saturated patch which is above.
- Now, add white again to the same smaller tinted puddle, to increase the lightness of the existing light red value all the more. Discard the remaining portion when finished.
- Next, add a very small amount of ultramarine blue to the larger original red puddle to produce a slightly darker red intensity, and paint this onto the second patch on the horizontal top row, next to the first saturated red patch.
- Again, separate a very small puddle from the large darker red puddle, and add enough white to produce a lighter value of that mixture. Apply to the second horizontal patch.
- Now, add white again to lighten that mixture and paint it in the next patch down.
- One more time, add even more white again, to get the lightest value on the last patch vertically.
- Repeat the process until you have completed all nine color bars across.

Hint: When adding white to the red puddle, instead think about adding a small amount of the red portion to a small white puddle. This helps to conserve the paint, so that you won't use as much white. It is easier to darken a color than to lighten it.

Remember that as acrylic paint dries it will transform into a darker tint. When you begin the value color patches, you must mix more white into the *intensity-modified* pigment than you may first think. This is a common problem, and if you do not develop your sensibility about pigments drying darker, you will always struggle when creating contrasts.

Project Specifications:

- All color patches are 1" × 1"
- The vertical space between groups should be one inch
- Space between all color patches vertical and horizontal is 1/4" wide
- 1 1/2" space between each group horizontally, except for the bottom, which would be 2 1/2"
- Center the six groups on the 18" × 24" horizontal composition (140 lb watercolor paper)
- Acrylic paints are suggested.

Neatness Factor:

We want to stress quality. Please be sure to present a clean, well-organized and hard-edged presentation of your color chart. The crisp, neatly organized project is always more effectual when the student demonstrates a concern about every detail.

Special Note About Primary Colors and Hue Selections:

- **Phthalo Blue, Hansa Yellow, and Quinacridone Magenta** are three of the more traditionally used, in order to achieve optimal results. However, a somewhat more **restricted palette of primary colors** has been selected in order to develop greater sensitivity about changing intensities and values in hue.

For example cadmium red light is the lightest possible red, before considering it to be orange. Most students tend to see it as orange or red-orange. Since this particular red is often mistaken for orange, it therefore, demands greater skill and sensitivity when mixing yellow and red to produce the orange, and so on.

Project Proposal

R-G-B and Depth of Field
By Michael Hanson

This assignment functions with the RGB, that is the red, green and blue found in additive color, and seen in the quark in this chapter. The lecture asserts in relation to the cones in our eyes (rods and cones-Rossotti), more red, less green, and even less blue, which correlate to long depth-of-field painting or compositions.

The assignment is to paint on top of a black and white photocopy. Separate the picture plane of a landscape into predominantly blues and light values in the background, greens in the middle ground, and primarily reds in the foreground. This assertion of separating these planes is illustrated in the compositions below:

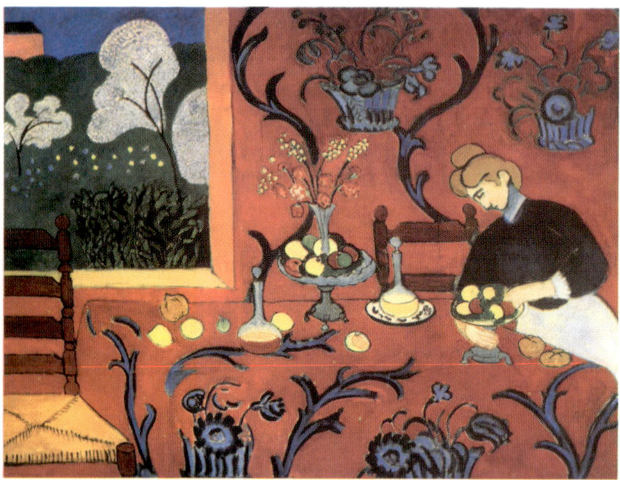

Harmony in Red by Henri Matisse.
© 2003 Succession H. Hatisse, Paris/Artists Rights Society (ARS), New York.

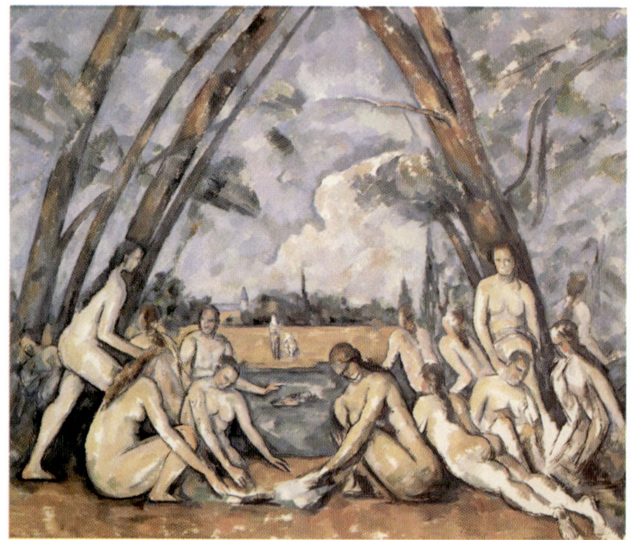

The Large Bathers by Paul Cezanne.
© Philadelphia Museum of Art/CORBIS.

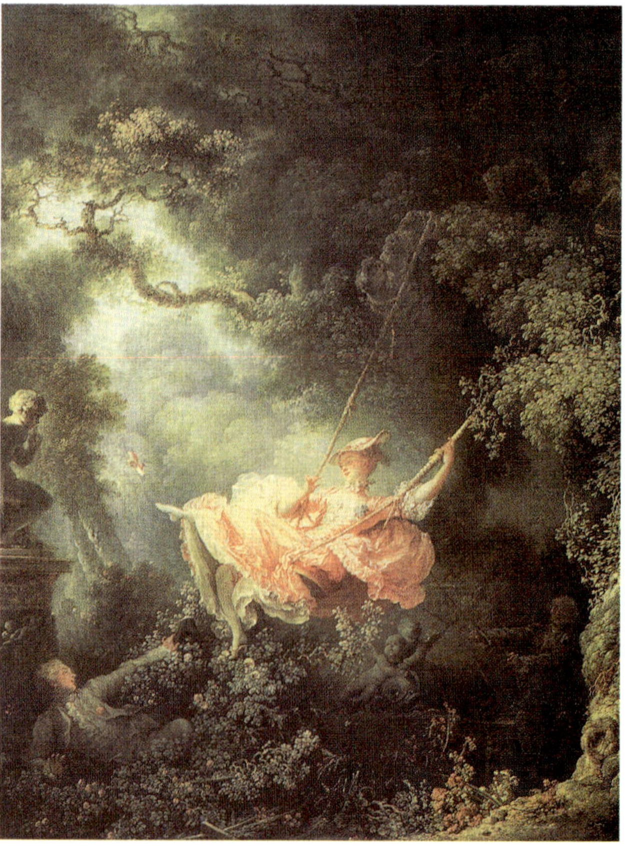

The Swing by Jean Honoré Fragnard.
By the kind permission of the Trustees of the Wallace Collection, London.

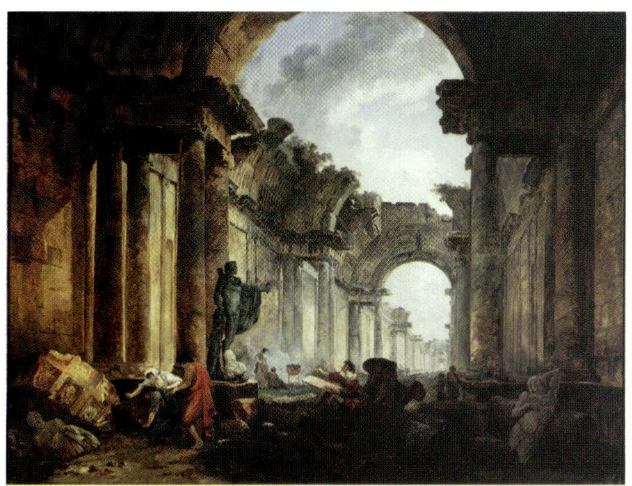

Fantastical View of the Grande Gallery of the Louvre by Hubert Robert.

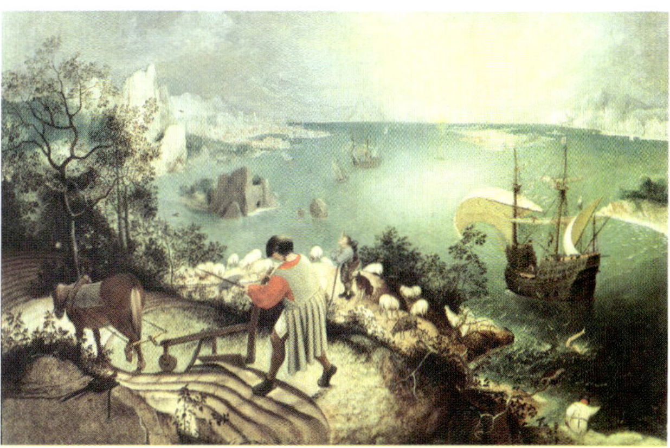

Landscape with Fall of Icarus by Pieter Brueghel.

The reverse is true in the following:

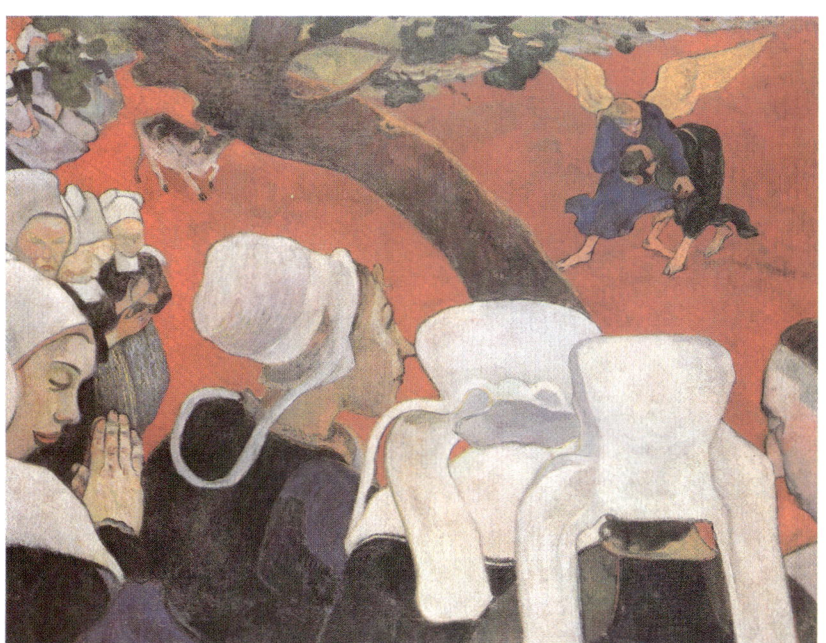

Vision After the Sermon, Jacob Wrestling with the Angel by Paul Gauguin.

Please study the student results below as examples:

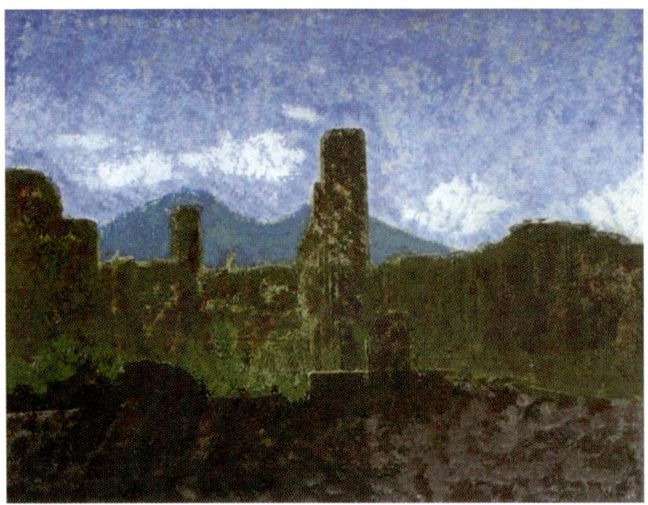

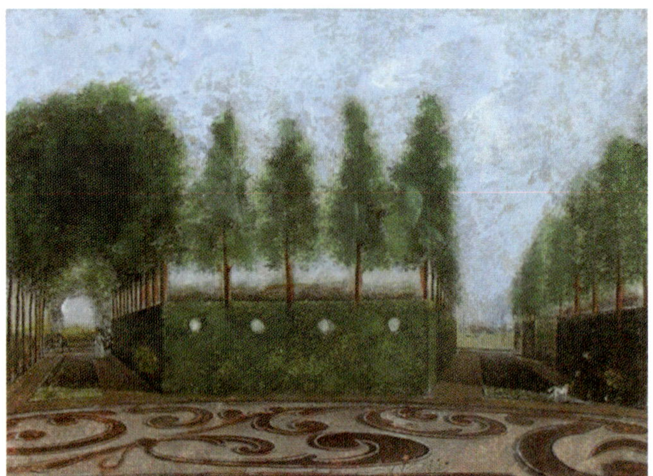

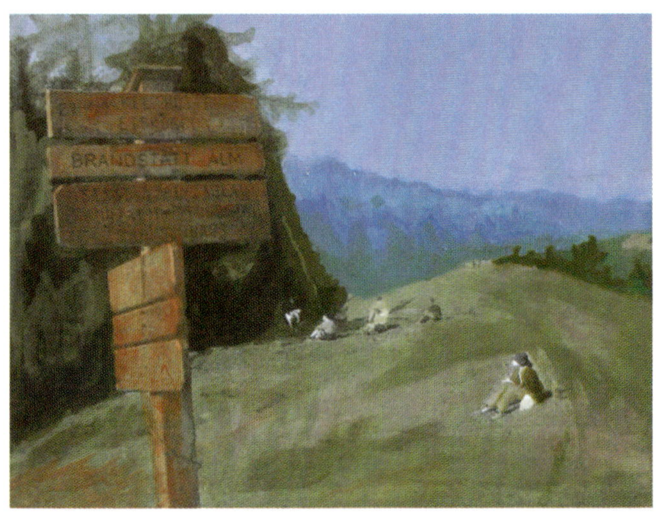

Project Proposal

The Color Star of Johannes Itten
By William Jaynes

Objective:

This project will provide the student with an understanding of the three-dimensional relationship of color, which is more thoroughly expressed as a *sphere* than by a color circle. Johannes Itten's color star is nothing more than a three-dimensional color sphere that has been interpreted onto a two-dimensional flat plane. The star contains the relationship of *hue, value and saturation.* Additionally, the student will gain a clearer understanding of the inherent *light and dark* value aspects of hue.

Project:

Color Star: The student will create two well-crafted stars. The first will be a color star, which is the pure hue relationship derived from the traditional color wheel. This part will contain the subtractive primaries of yellow, red and blue, with secondary colors of orange, violet and green. Additionally, the intermediate colors of yellow-orange, red-orange, red-violet, blue-violet, blue-green and yellow-green. Once the color wheel of the star is painted, the student will tint (pure color plus white) two steps towards the center, with the center resulting in pure white. Next, shade (pure color plus black) two steps outward, resulting with the star tips becoming black.

Value Star: After the color star is completed, the student will translate the star into a *value* star. The value star will be painted next to the color star. Think of the value component as color, which has

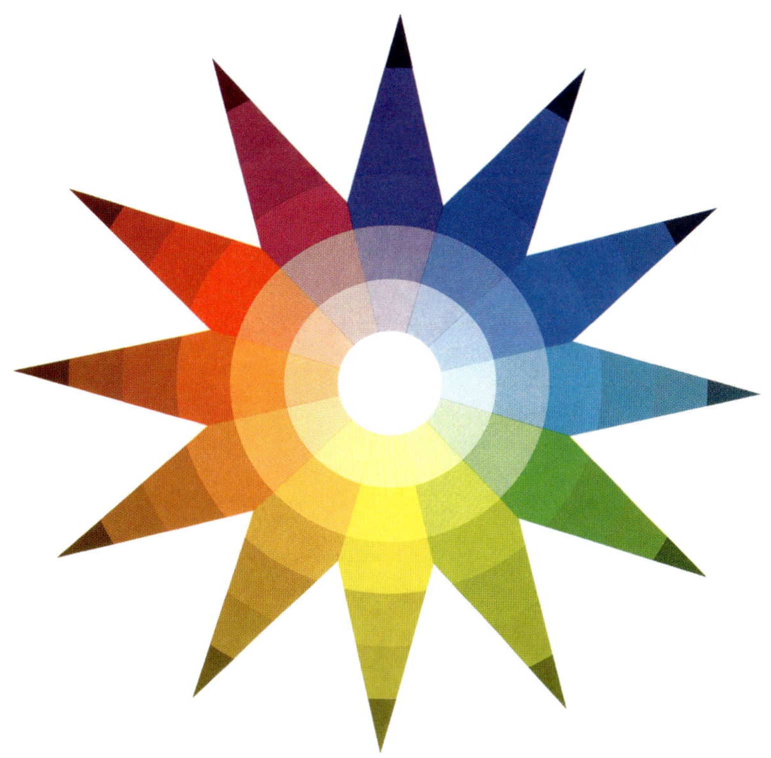

Johannes Itten's Color Star

been drained of its hue, or think in terms of the computer, which is able to translate a true color image into a gray scale mode. In successful translation, the value star will contain the same value weight as the color star.

Test the value translation by photocopying the color star on a color copy machine, but be sure that you set it to *gray scale mode.* The black and white photocopy of the color star should closely match the painted value star.

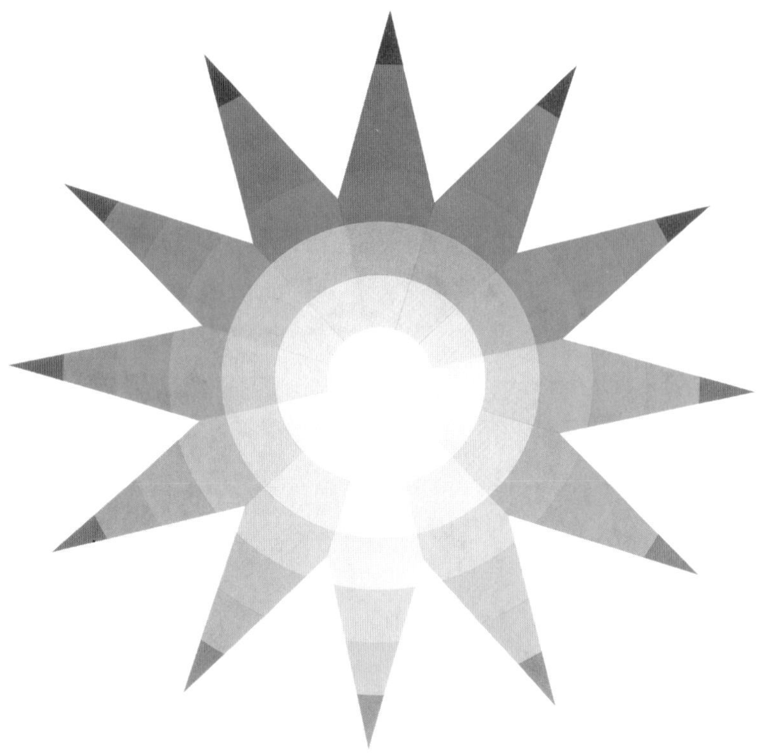

Johannes Itten's Color Star (achromatic)

The Properties of Light and Color Authority

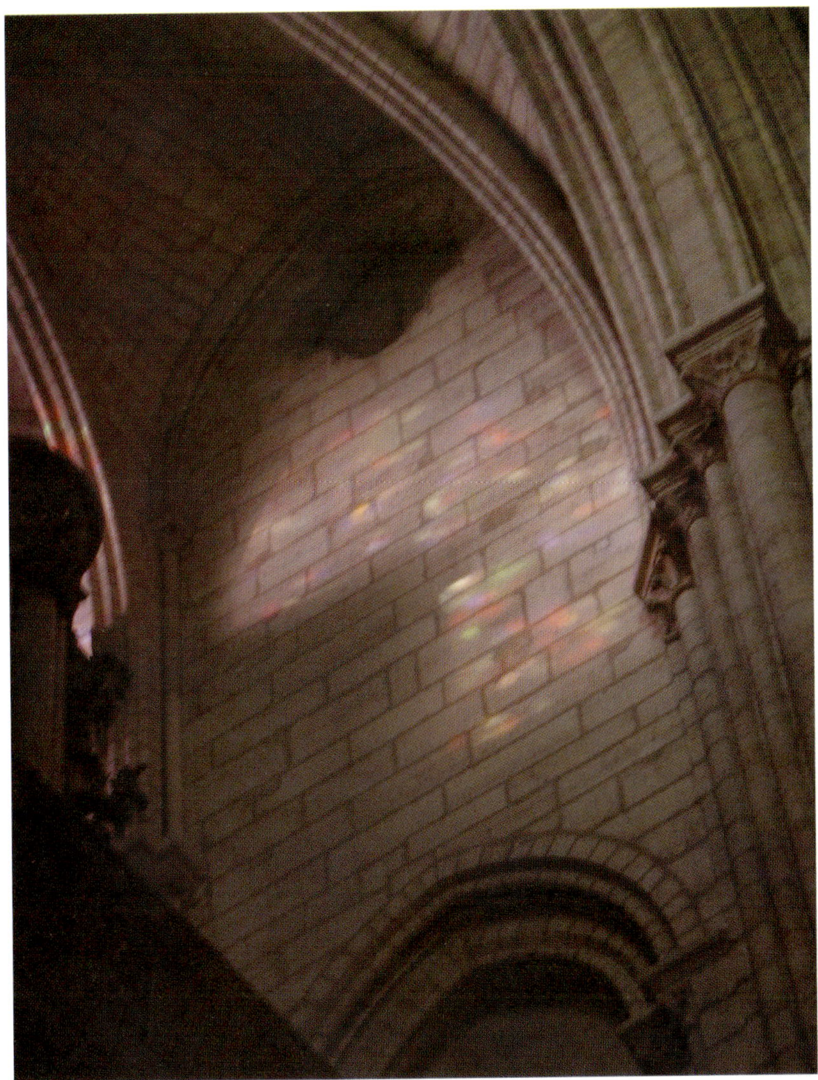

Interior of Notre Dame de Paris: Light Transformed Through Colored Windows.
Photo by Alan Burner.

Chapter Two

Introduction to Chapter Two

In the previous chapter we discussed the Sovereignty of Light, and its endowment of color over the world. Our emphasis was primarily on the interior of the cathedral's inner qualities of light, transformed into its seven component parts or colors. Often we focused on the atmospheric color conditions on the inside of the gothic cathedral, because of its overtness, yet at that point we had not discussed the more subtle exterior surface colors as they change over the period of a day.

It is vital to create the most careful observations in order to create a greater sensitivity to the more restrained color surfaces. Consider how Notre Dame de Paris changes in color (see following two pages) as the day progresses. It is not merely an achromatic cathedral created by a darkening sky; it is the transformation of the surface color from an advancing sun.

Notre Dame de Paris (Image One) is observed late in the afternoon on the south side. Note that the surface is a *very light and radiant yellow*. The sun is just about at its highest here during the spring, and creates the brightest radiance of light in a 24-hour period. This is the peak of the Cathedral's most intense color.

Notre Dame de Paris (Image Two) is a bit later in the afternoon, and we can now see a substantial change in the exterior surface. The radiant light yellow surface has lost some of its intensity, and has been reduced. The *yellow has dulled* considerably, with the slightest indicator of a *violet tinge* on the lower shaded area.

Notre Dame de Paris (Image Three) has now completely lost its yellowness, the intensity level has greatly reduced to the point where the lightest surface is now *lightest red-orange*, with more prominent *violet* tones appearing in the shaded regions.

Notre Dame de Paris (Image Four) has now lost much of its *red-orangeness*, and reflects a *dull orange* with slightest *violet* hues. What began as a very *light yellow* intense surface, has now become a very dull *red-orange* to *violet* cathedral. The architecture has taken on the *yellow's complement* at sunset. As the sun's white light diminishes from the surface, the sunset itself becomes more *orange to red-orange*.

These are some of the light and color issues that critical thinking colorists learn to discover. Gaining a greater visual sensitivity to the colors of light on a surface is paramount in the learning process. Claude Monet struggled with the subtle nuances of color in his paintings of the Reims Cathedral for several years. We realize after our eyes have become sensitized to color, that our brain often tells us that the cathedral is nothing more than colorless, while our eyes actually see yellows, oranges, red-orange, violets and indigos. What we think we see and what we actually see are often two different things. The secret, then, is to learn to question what we think we see through critical and often lengthy observation of a surface's color.

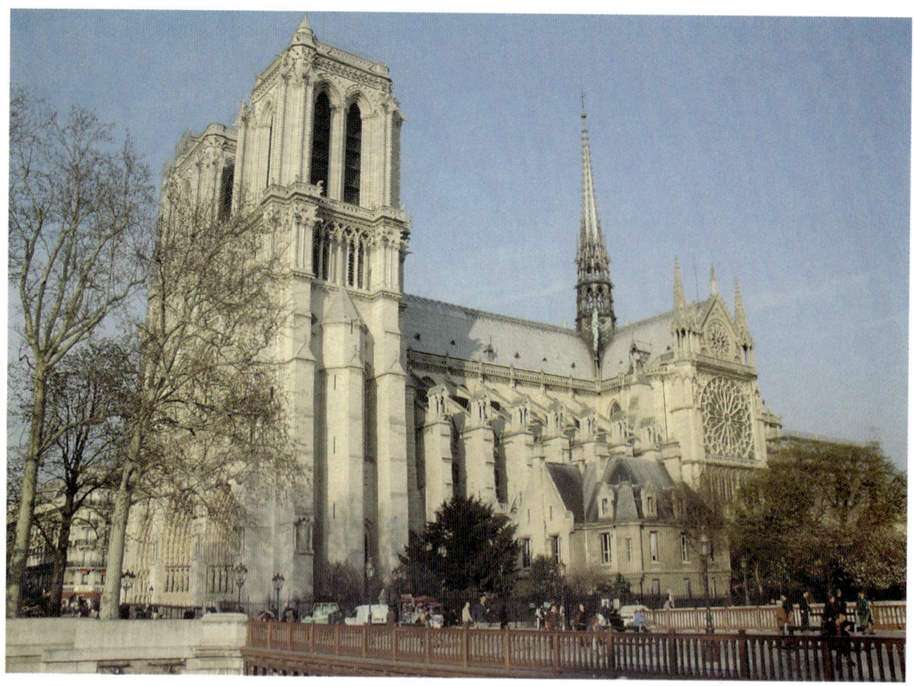

Image One. Notre Dame de Paris.
Photo by Alan Burner.

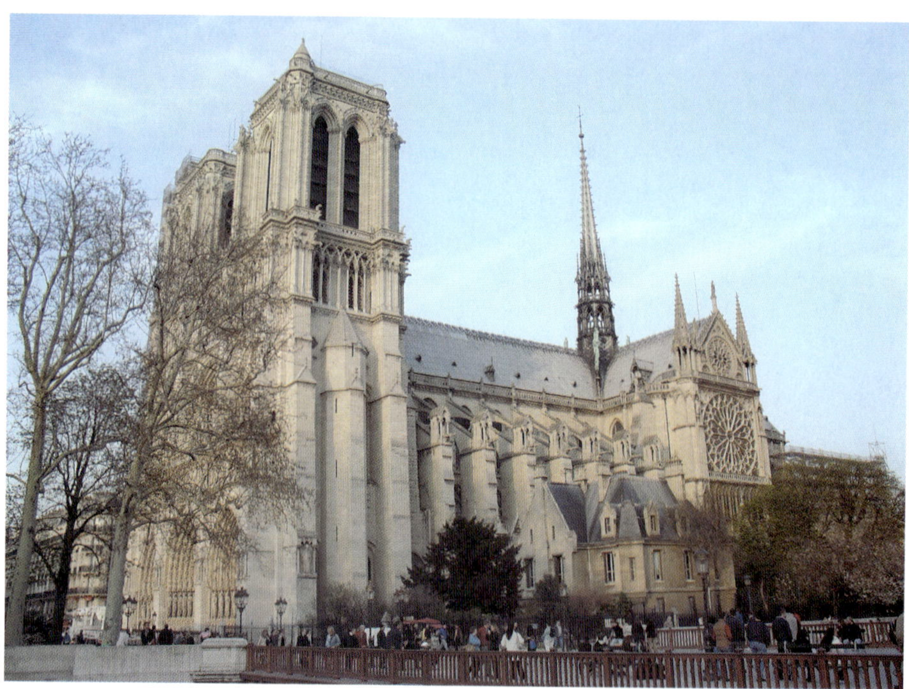

Image Two. Notre Dame de Paris.
Photo by Alan Burner.

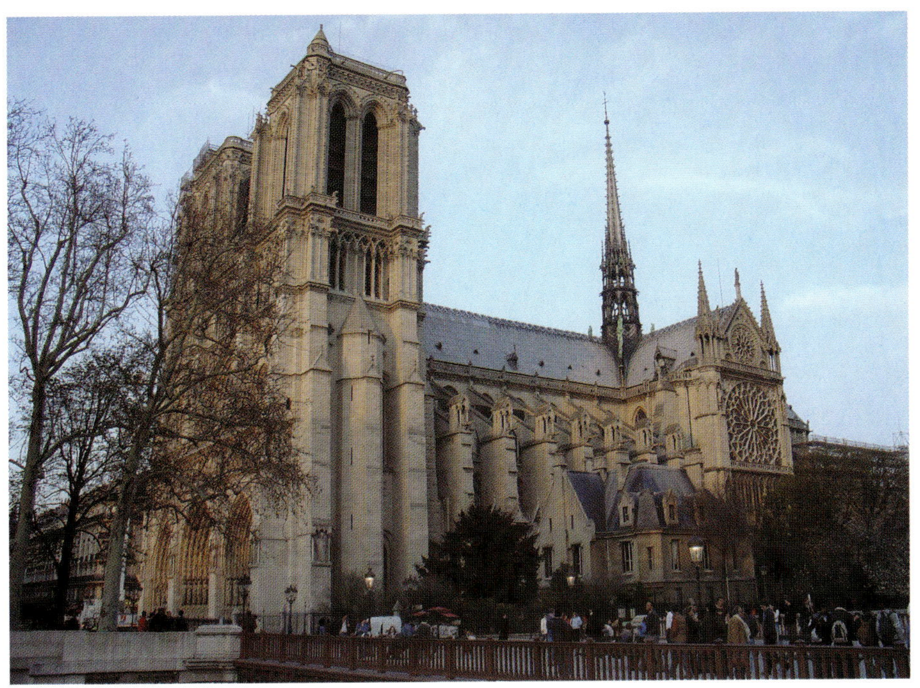

Image Three. Notre Dame de Paris.
Photo by Alan Burner.

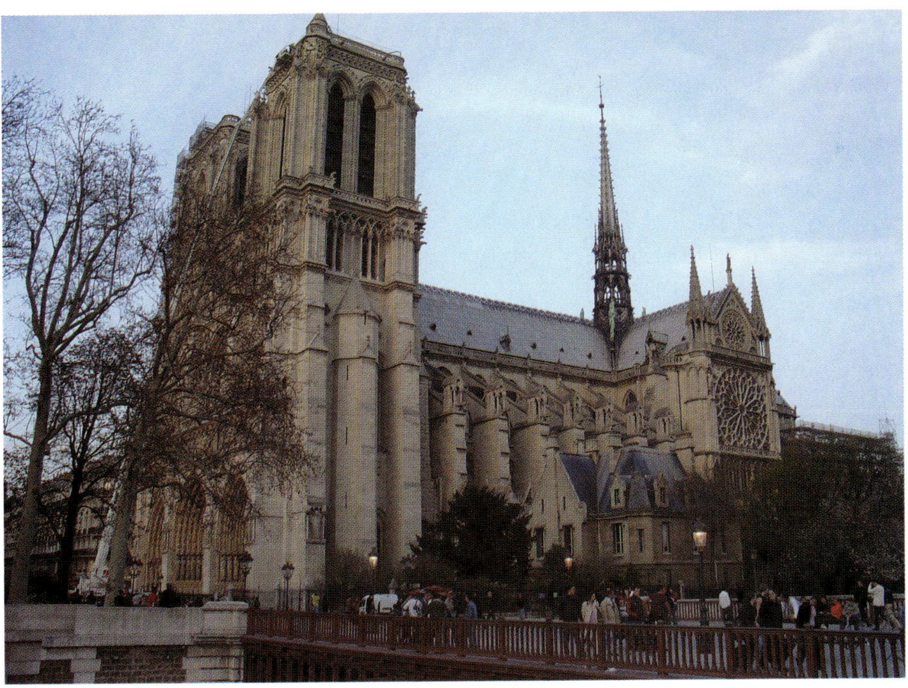

Image Four. Notre Dame de Paris.
Photo by Alan Burner.

Also in the previous chapter, we discussed saturation, intensity and value and produced a color chart exhibiting these three aspects of color. We also talked about the largest or most prevalent sources of color, which is light emanating from the sun, to the smallest provable particle, such as the quark. We studied generally the Gothic cathedral and its role with light and color, the diamond, the carbon atom and the electromagnetic spectrum—all within their relationships to light.

In this section we want to pursue more specifics about light and color, especially as it pertains to what we refer to as the *Authority of Color.* Essentially, color has the influence and command of establishing focal points, depth of space, and so forth. Its chief function even more so is the psychological ramifications, that is, the establishment of the emotional appeal, the mood control of the viewer/patron.

Additionally, we will take a more critical look at color mixing by using a more sensitive collection of colors. As you have noticed by now, colors such as *cadmium red light* are more difficult to maneuver in the direction of orange. This red hue is often interpreted as orange itself, since it is so far from the conventionally used red of *quinacridone magenta*, for example. Cadmium red light is the lightest official red on the market and is often interpreted by the viewer as orange rather than red.

The color mixing project proposal for this chapter deals with yellow exclusively, since yellow is the most intense, and yet weakest color. We have learned that yellow is the most easily influenced of all colors, by the addition of the slightest amount of black for example. Using these very sensitive colors for our next suggested project will help to develop a greater sensitivity about the process of color mixing. As indicated before, we are eliminating the conventional primaries, and substituting them for a more minimal palette, in order to *fine tune* the colorists sensitivity for optimal desired results and the recognition of subtle nuances.

Conventional Primary Mixing Colors	**Project Proposal Choices**
Quinacridone Magenta Cadmium Red Light	Quinacridone Red
Hansa Yellow Cadmium Yellow Light	Hansa Yellow
Phthalo Blue Cerulean Blue	Ultramarine Blue

Even though the conventional primaries are more easily controlled and achieve the more "expected" result, the project proposal primaries are designed to create a more diverse experience in color mixing. Certainly it is appropriate to experience all of the primary triad possibilities, and it is encouraged as your color education continues.

Before moving into your next project proposal or an alternative project, please take the time to read the following essay written by Isaac Asimov.

We most certainly know of Asimov's prowess as a *science fiction writer*, but many are not aware that he was also a *scholar of atomic science.*

It was his profound understanding of the science of atoms which gave his fiction additional credibility (not to mention the added creative potential). You will find his essay an effective tool in the further study of the nature of light, the source of all color.

This chapter begins with further observations of light and color at two Gothic cathedrals, one Gothic chapel, pigmented illustrations (paintings), and a *real-life* observation as to the influence and authority of color.

The Authority of Color

Notre Dame de Paris

We return back to Notre Dame de Paris, in order to begin our discussion about the *authority of color*. More specifically, we take our pilgrimage directly to the south Rose Window; the *Gothic Diamond*. One need only attend a Sunday service at the cathedral to fully understand the symbolic and spiritual ramifications of the cathedral's colored windows, as well as the interior ambiance of the church. The cathedral was built and used during the middle ages, a period from approximately 400 to 1400 A.D, that was marked by Christianity's central role. The cathedral was used as a spiritual and community center; it was in fact the focal point of the city, where people of the community went for encouragement and spiritual strength. Of course, now it remains a spiritual and community center. Parisians today still gather together for worship at the cathedral, as well as on the common gathering grounds at Notre Dame. Eight hundred years later, people are still coming, if for nothing more than to enjoy an afternoon of "people watching," as the cathedral remains the focal point of Paris. As we discussed in Chapter One, it is ground zero for all distances measured to Paris. Notre Dame is of the foremost examples of light and color, and a superb illustration of the authority of color, and indeed light itself.

There are some points of interest that should be discussed briefly, before we discuss color authority itself. When we look at the floor plan of Notre Dame de Paris, we can see that the basic interior plan of the cathedral replicates a cross, that is the cross by which Jesus Christ was crucified, as told by the scriptures. Actually, the transept illustrates the horizontal of the cross, while the altar (seen in the following floor plan, as well as the following image of the Ambulatory Altar), chancel, choir, Crossing, and center aisle represents the vertical post of the crucifix. There are, of course, many cathedrals throughout France built in the crucifix form, some even more obvious as a cross than others. The transept of the cathedral is the horizontal representation of the cross, which has on its left end the South Rose Window, and on its right end the North Rose Window. The left hand of Christ, then, was nailed where the South Rose Window would be, and the right hand on the side of the North Rose Window. The north window is predominantly cool greens and blues while the south window, with its reds and blues, appears as a enormous warm violet jewel.

The Narthex and West Rose Window would be at the impaled feet of Christ, while the Chancel and Altar indicate the Head of Christ; above this are five radial chapels with 13 colored-glass arched windows. The Rose Windows, then, represent the three initial major wounds.

A Rose Window does not exist at the head of Christ. Rather, there is the chancel and altar, and behind that radiating chapels joined in a half circle at the east end, all referred to as the ambulatory. These chapels are adorned with elegant stained glass arched windows throughout (seen in the radial chapels behind the altar—next page), and exist where the Head of Christ would be on the cross. As we discussed in the chapter one essay, *A Thousand Nights Fantasy and the Gothic Diamond; A Tribute to Light, light* becomes a symbol of God's eternal light. A light coming into a world of darkness, or the darkness in the human heart, exemplified especially in the middle-ages.

Historians often refer to Notre Dame de Paris as being the darkest of all major high gothic cathedrals. This at first would seem to be a serious problem, since the cathedrals were redesigned with flying buttresses (Chapter One) or an exoskeletal system in order to allow more light into the inner space. Much of the light that enters the smaller chapels along the side aisles is absorbed or transformed by the time it reaches the actual side aisles of the church. Also, much of the light is absorbed by the areas in the cathedral with deep niches where few windows exist. However, it is precisely the fact that this is an extremely dark cathedral that we are encouraged to use it as an example of light and color. Let's find out why.

As we indicated, the darkness of Notre Dame also symbolically represents the dark and light contrasts of the human struggle, or condition. The dark

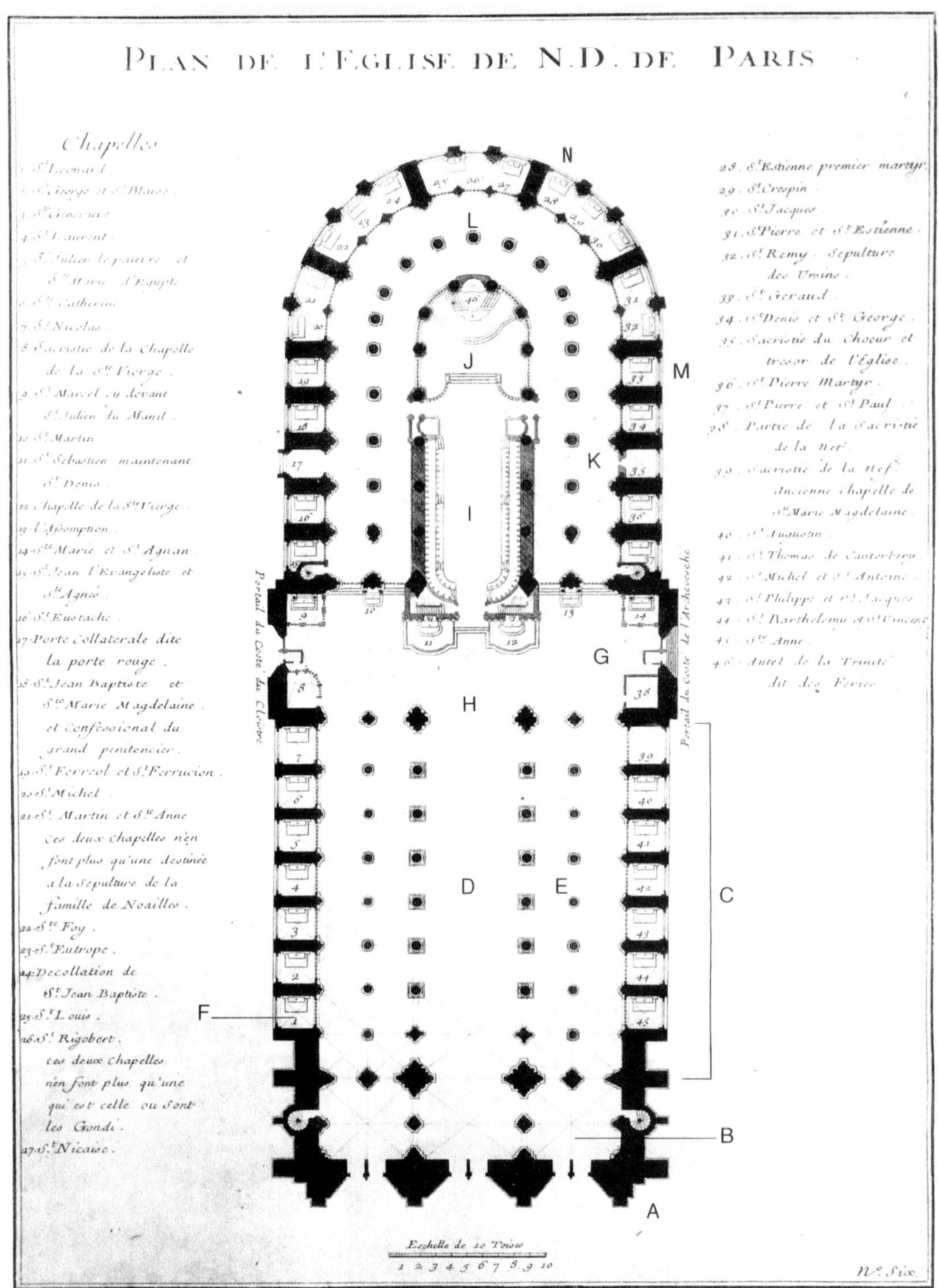

A	Facade
B	Narthex
C	Nave
D	Center aisle
E	Side aisles
F	Chapel
G	Transept
H	Crossing
I	Choir
J	Chancel
K	Straight side aisles of the choir
L	Ambulatory
M	Chapels of the side aisles of the choir
N	Radial chapels of the ambulatory

Plan specifying the dedications of each chapel, from François-Philippe Charpentier, *Description historique et chronologique de l'église métropolitaine de Paris* (Paris, 1767).

Floor Plan—Notre Dame de Paris. Used by permission.

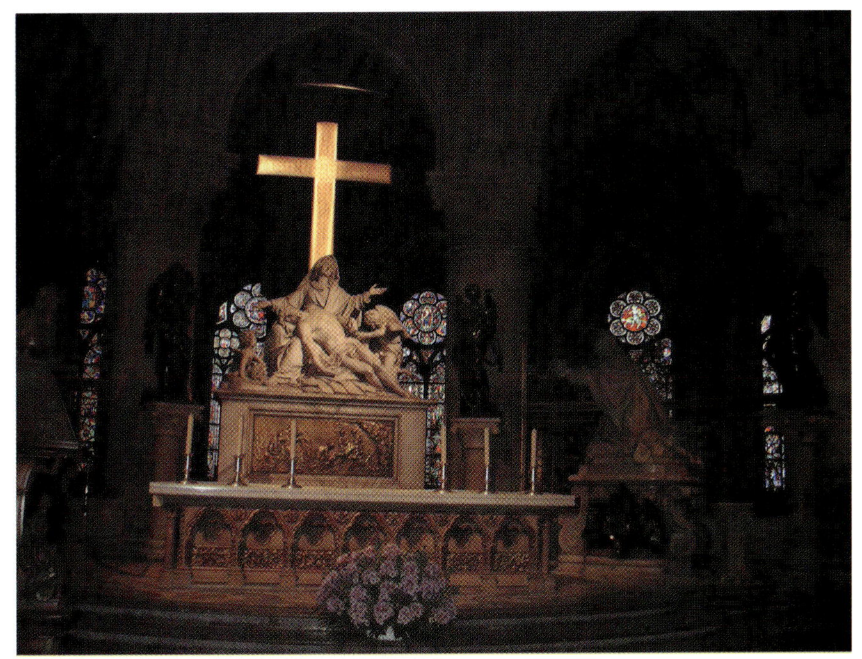

Ambulatory Altar of Notre Dame de Paris.
Photo by Alan Burner.

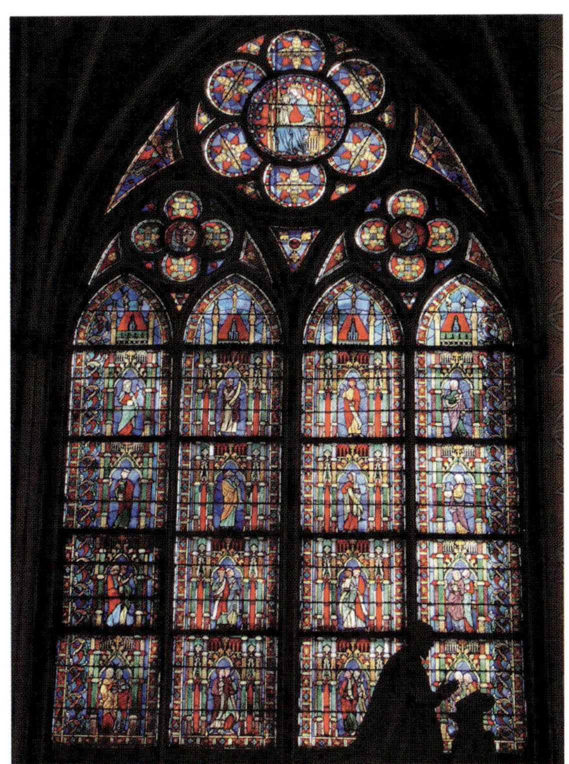

Notre Dame de Paris—Chapel Window—Notre Dame de Paris.
Photo by Alan Burner.

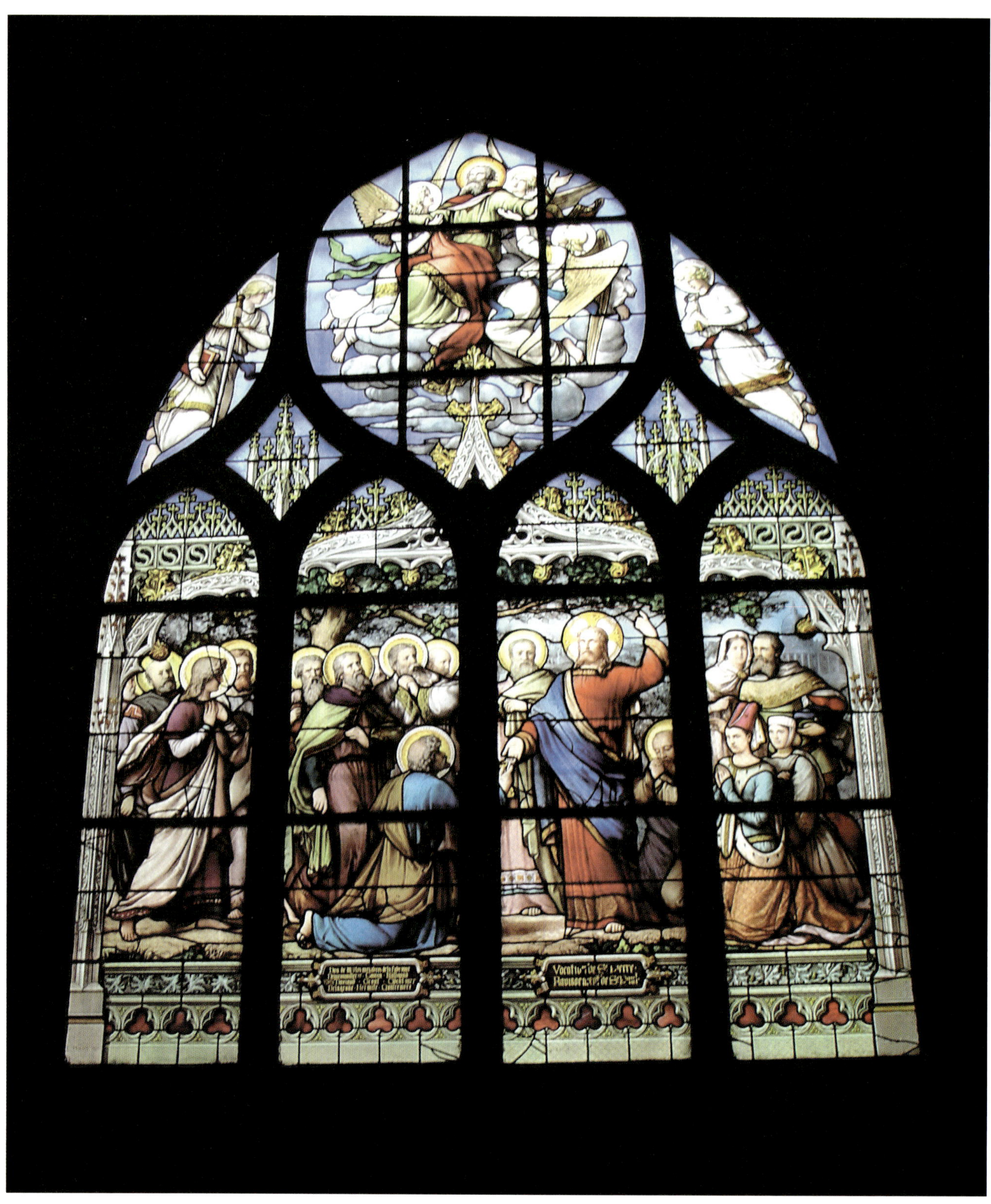

Cathedral Chapel Window.
Photo by Alan Burner.

side of humankind as opposed to the light side of a loving and caring God. Good and evil, love and hate, celebration and agony, light and dark—these always provide contrast and emphasis when paired together. That being the case, we observe that the brilliance of saturated colored windows are surrounded by the darkness within each chapel*.

The contrast of dark space against an illuminated color panel is striking, and it is the dark areas which emphasize color all the more. We have a symbolic match then—the darkness of the human heart, and the Light of Heaven illuminating the soul. A building constructed in dark times with the hope of salvation, the Light of the Kingdom of Heaven enters every colored portal. Of course, the nave (sanctuary) is always lighter because it is at the Heart of God.

We are first tempted to think that the darkness will be the all powerful and consuming force, but soon enough we discover that the lighting of a single candle demands the darkness to flee. One single candle illuminates, if only slightly, that which is in the darkness.

As more candles are lit, greater amounts of energy are created and, therefore, more light is generated which reveals and creates color. Once this sovereignty of light has established the authority of color, the commanding role of color begins to manipulate the human senses.

As we look to the South Rose Window, it is in a very real sense what we would hope a diamond to be. This huge circular window reveals the ultimate in color authority—saturated color developed by pure white light. The window is faceted color brilliance, and its fire cannot be compared, written about, or photographed with any degree of adequacy. The only possible way to comprehend the fire and brilliance of this window is to experience it, to stand before its beauty and eloquence. It is the Eye of God; the Jewel of Heaven. The color presentation seen in the Rose Window authoritatively captivates one's imaginations, and visually holds the participant in what seems to be a spell of sorts. This window really commands the attention of the viewer, and seems equally difficult to walk away from.

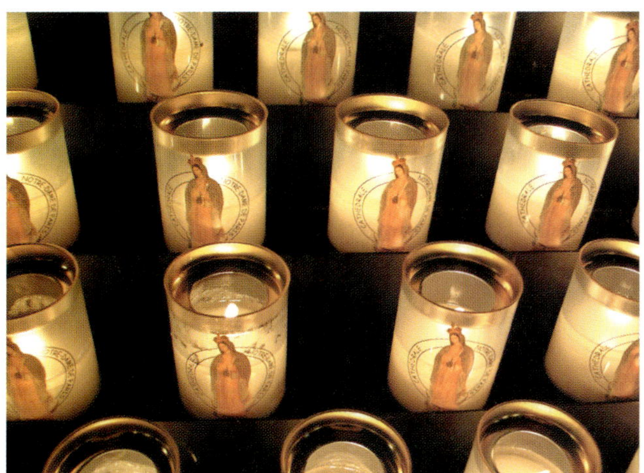

Candles in Notre Dame's *Transept* Section of the Cathedral.
Photos by Alan Burner.

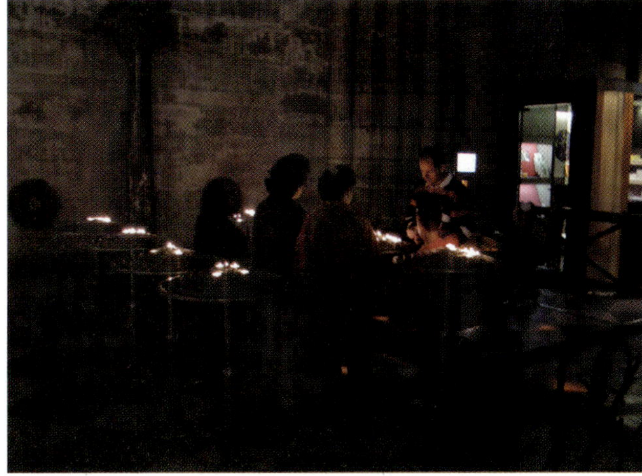

A Family Lights Candles on Easter Sunday in Notre Dame's *Nave* Section.
Photos by Alan Burner.

*Windows on the south side tend to illuminate the chapels on that side much more adequately, during the sun's most advantageous time of day, as opposed to the north side windows that are quite dark by comparison. The optimal illumination period for the south side is in the late winter and early fall for the south-side, whereas, the north's best time is mid-summer. These would be the exceptions to an otherwise darker period of the year for chapels within the cathedral.

Sainte Severin Cathedral

An interesting question was presented to me while standing under the southern Rose Window one day. As I was remarking as to the importance of light concerning Notre Dame's *Gothic Diamond* (The window; Chap. One) a student quipped, "If light were so important, then why didn't the builders assemble more tracery of clear or white glass into the windows, which would allow a greater amount of light to enter the nave, and perhaps the chapel areas?"

The question had validity, certainly after all, why not simply install clear glass windows? As I considered the inquiry, I suddenly realized that the answer was simple, and yet somewhat complex, in another sense. Knowing that I couldn't ignore the more complex issues forever, I chose the uncomplicated response for the moment. The simple and most obvious answer is, that white light is thought of by most, as purely a light source for illumination purposes only. Light in this case can be the illuminator, or the "revealer" of truth. It is a literal "revelation." However, in and of itself white light does not always inspire. We must remember that light is color, and color is authoritative. Light cannot create mood by itself, but in its white form needs to be transformed into its component parts to influence the observer's emotions more concretely. To illustrate with an example, we shall take a walk across the river Seine to the St. Severin Cathedral.

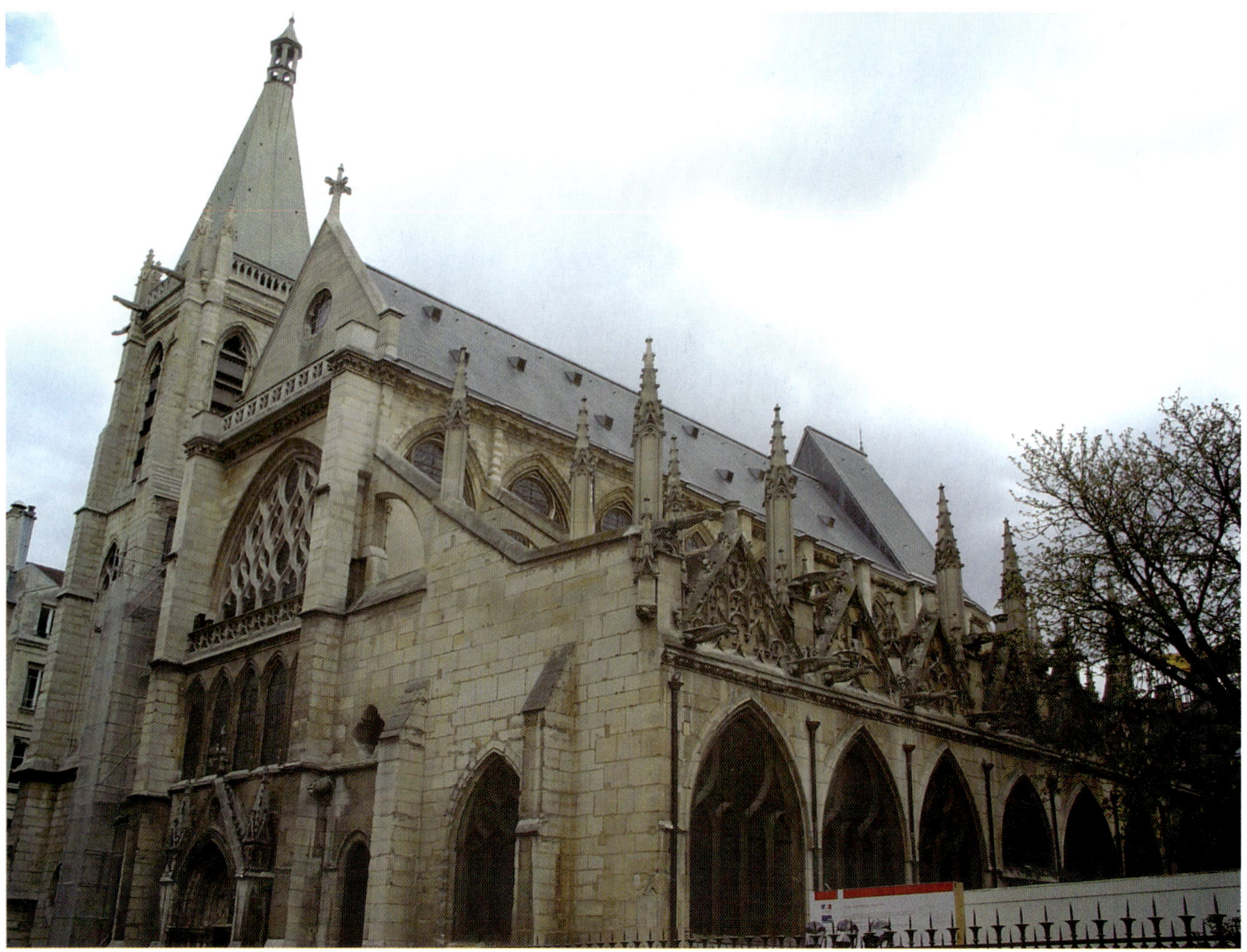

South Exterior View of St. Severin.
Photo by Alan Burner.

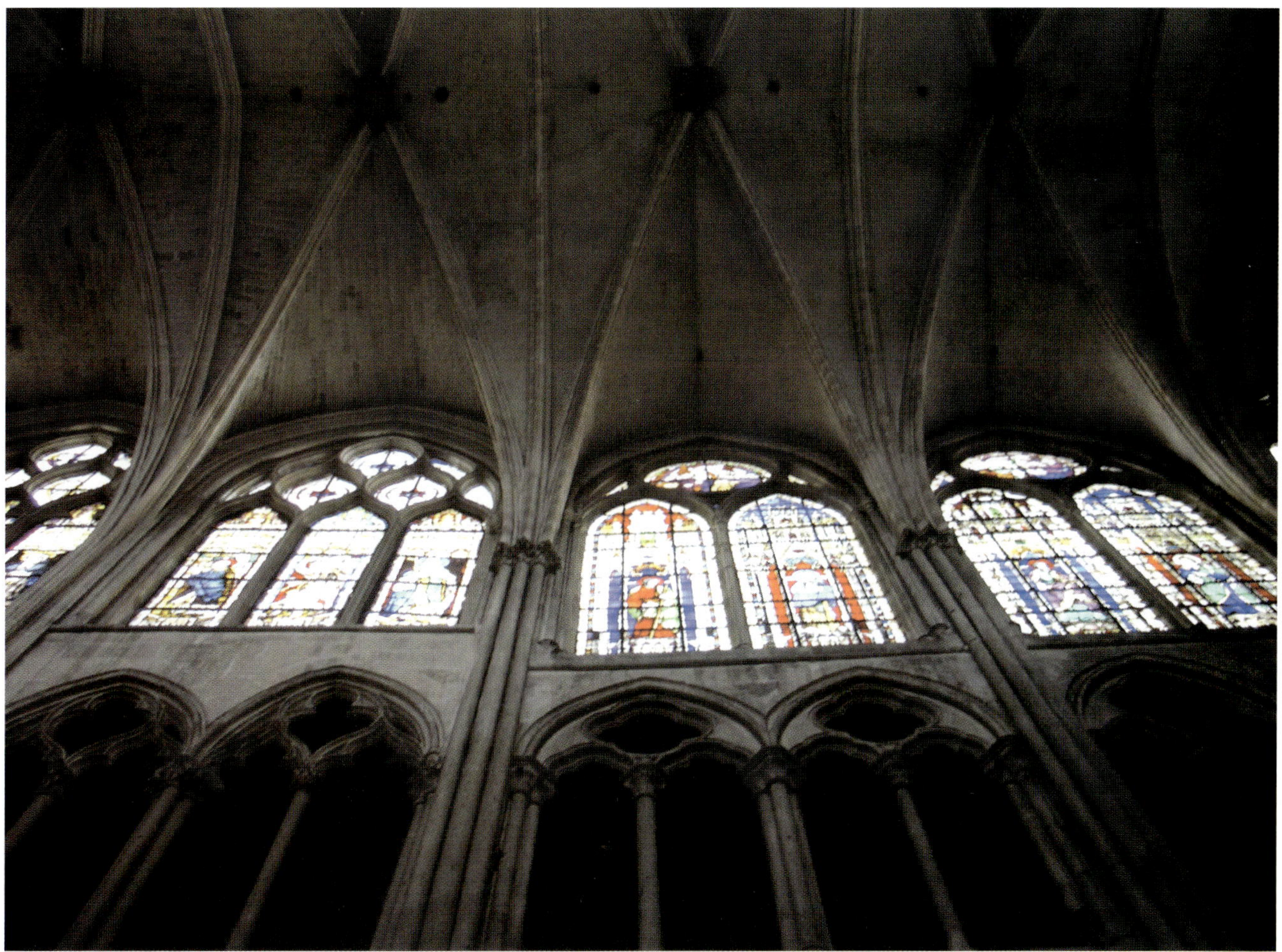

Interior Groin Vaults and Windows of St. Severin.
Photo by Alan Burner.

When we enter the cathedral, we get a better idea of what happens in the interior nave when a certain amount of white light is not intercepted by colored glass windows.

The entire quadrant of upper windows are endowed with substantial clear glass traceries, as well as colored pieces of glass. This departs somewhat from the typical Gothic window, which is normally laden with colored glass. Notice in the photograph how much light floods the interior, as opposed to Notre Dame. The ambiance is quite different than many Gothic cathedrals, as the entire main sanctuary is radiant with white light as opposed to absolute color. Color is not overt by any stretch of the imagination. We see minimal color and the absence of serious color ambiance is quite unexpected. Of course, as one views the entire nave, every quiet and subdued hue of color can be observed on the walls and floor as well as on the chairs themselves. The interior nave of the church has an environment of subtle color and intense pure light.

It is intriguing to realize that the nave area gathers such an enormous quantity of light while surrounded by various extremely dark smaller chapels. Unlike the main sanctuary, the adjacent chapels are each enhanced by a colored window. It is the darkness of these lower chapels which enhances the colors of each chapel window.

Two aspects about light and color in this cathedral are important. First, the chapels are recessed far back from the actual sanctuary, where the main

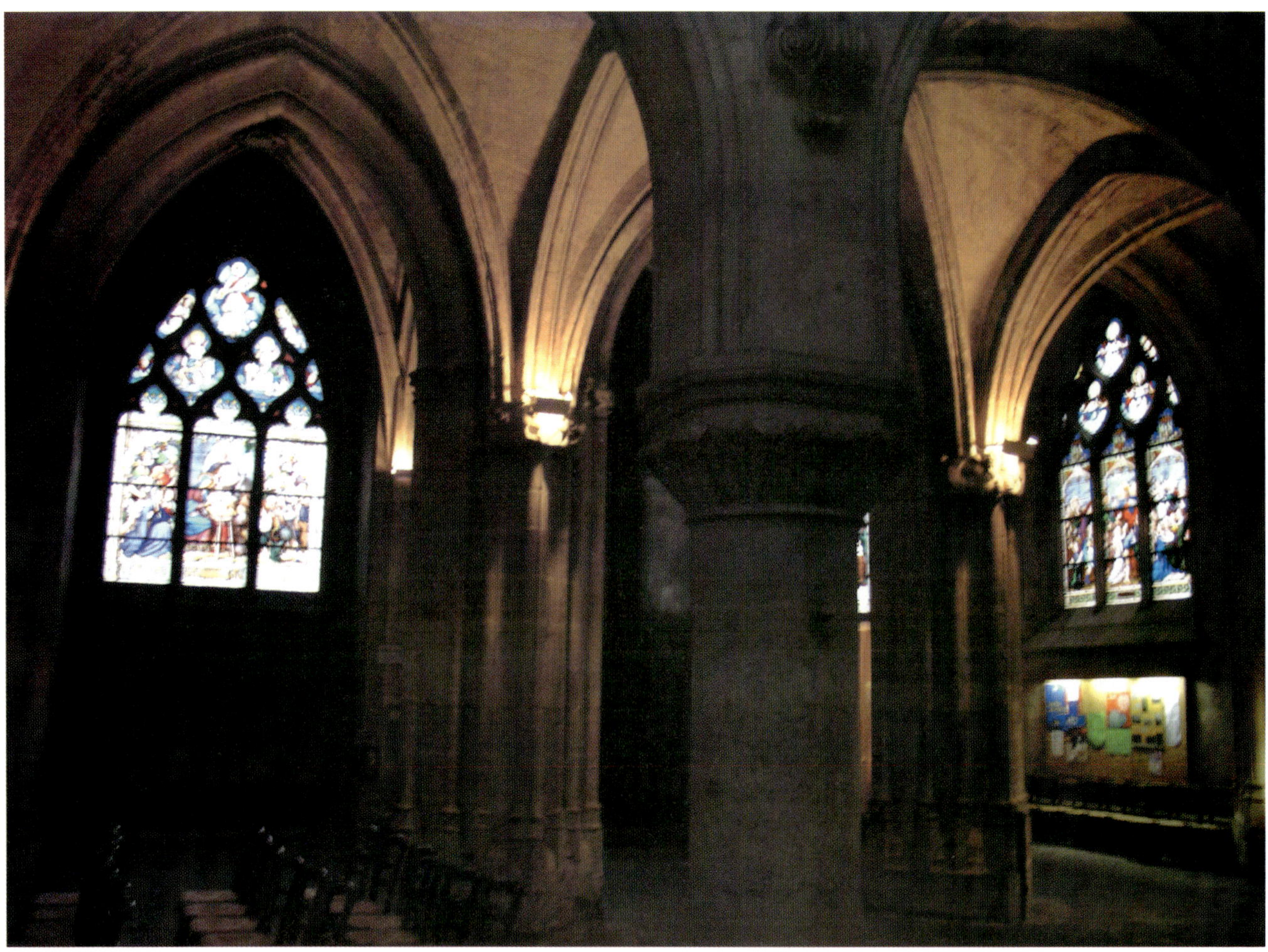

Interior View of St. Severin's Interior Chapels Viewed From the Nave Through the Side Aisle.
Photo by Alan Burner.

source of light prevails. This effect contrasts with the small chapels that are minimally illuminated, facilitating the creation of very dark chapels. Secondly, though the chapels are dark, they actually display exquisitely beautiful colored windows, thanks to the darkness in each chapel. It is the dark quality of the chapel which creates a full spectacle of elegant and saturated color. This symbolically matches the spiritual teachings of the age, which identified "mankind" as lost in darkness, which was then contrasted to the Holy Light of God.

St. Severin chapels each create a mood of their own. One could say that symbolically, the center nave (sanctuary) exposed the worshipper to God's pure light and the Heart of God and therefore exposed the worshipper to the nature of their individual sins. After bathing in God's Holy light, one could confess one's sin in the chapel, after which God would receive the rejuvenated worshipper back into the arms of salvation, fully forgiven.

The more complex issues about the colored widows, as opposed to clear windows, lies within the churches two dimensional images of color, and how they relate to the exterior three dimensional images. Color makes historical references, symbolic gestures, and strong visual scenarios, all designed to instruct and manipulate the senses. The matter becomes so complex that it cannot be adequately discussed at this point in its entirety, but will be addressed occasionally through the text. We will allow the subject to surface from time to time, in order that we may have a selection of various examples.

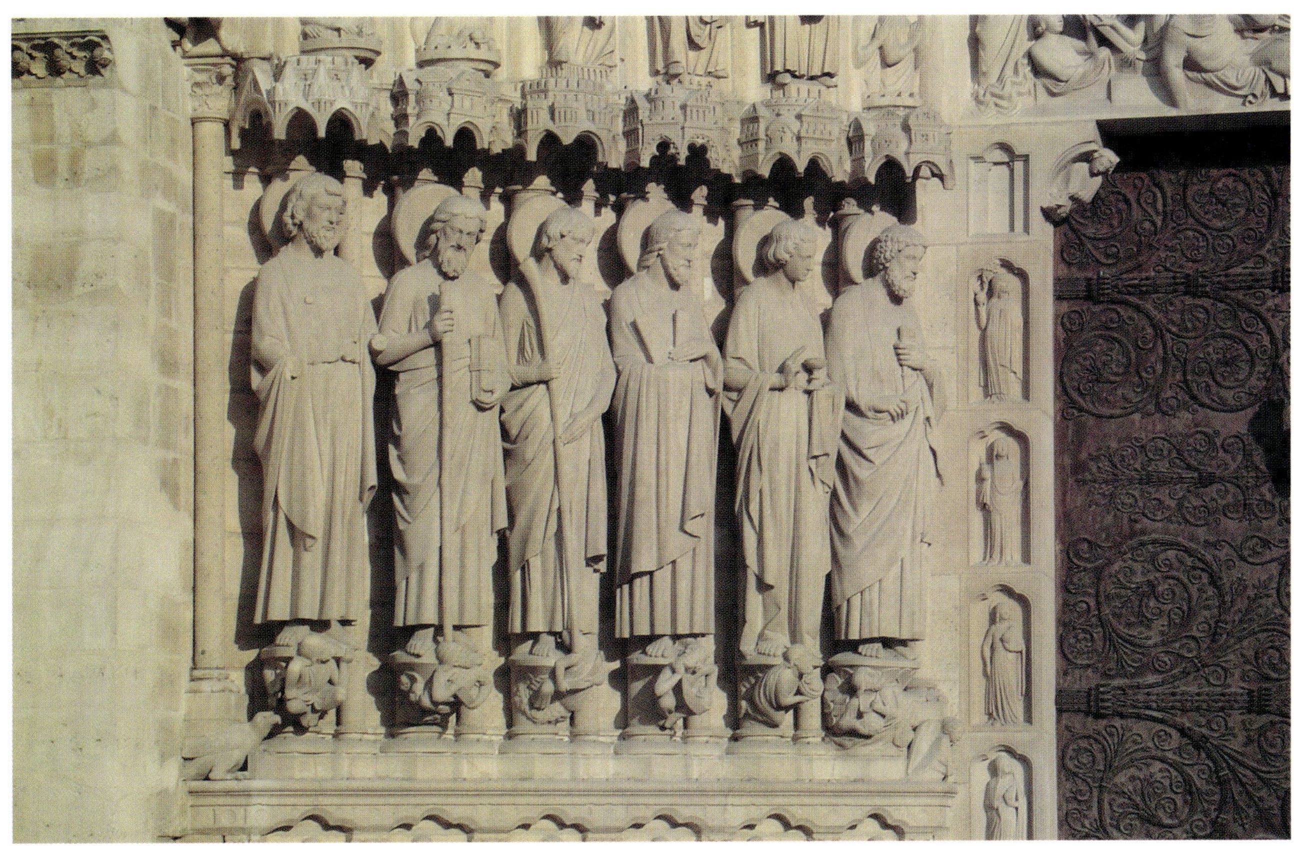

Central Portal of Notre Dame's West Façade: Left Jamb Depicting St. Peter, St. John, St. Andrew, St. James, St. Simeon and St. Bartholomew. Photo by Alan Burner.

A more immediate and obvious contrast can be seen between the cathedral's exterior and interior. The exterior statuary relates to the interior ambiance both in symbolism seen in the windows and the message preached from the pulpit. A slightly more complex relationship has to be seen symbolically, between the seemingly colorless or perhaps monochromatic nature of the statuary, and the color which is represented spiritually through the figurative sculptures.

Let's examine exactly the nature of the color represented by the exterior figures, though unseen. We understand by now that color is expressive, just as the faces on the sculptures above are communicative. Take a look at the figures from left to right, and see whether or not you can identify the subtle differences of their facial expressions. The first figure seems stern and very somber, and if we were to assign color to it, perhaps we would say deep blue. The second figure is peaceful or content, perhaps a lighter blue or even yellow. The third figure seems somewhat sad, the weight of a true violet may indicate that mood. The fourth stands calmly, the fifth is perhaps inquisitive, and the last stands humbly before the Lord (unseen in this photo). There are many scenarios by which color can relate here. Bible verse, when compared with the cathedral, could indicate that the exterior, or outer shell of humankind is a façade, yet the inner person is the genuine article, so to speak. It is the condition of the heart of the person that can be filled with the joys of a God-centered life, which then translates from a rather colorless* void into a life of light and vibrant colors.

*Of course, to color theory students, the exterior is not colorless, but by the average definition and to the common person, it does seem to be colorless.

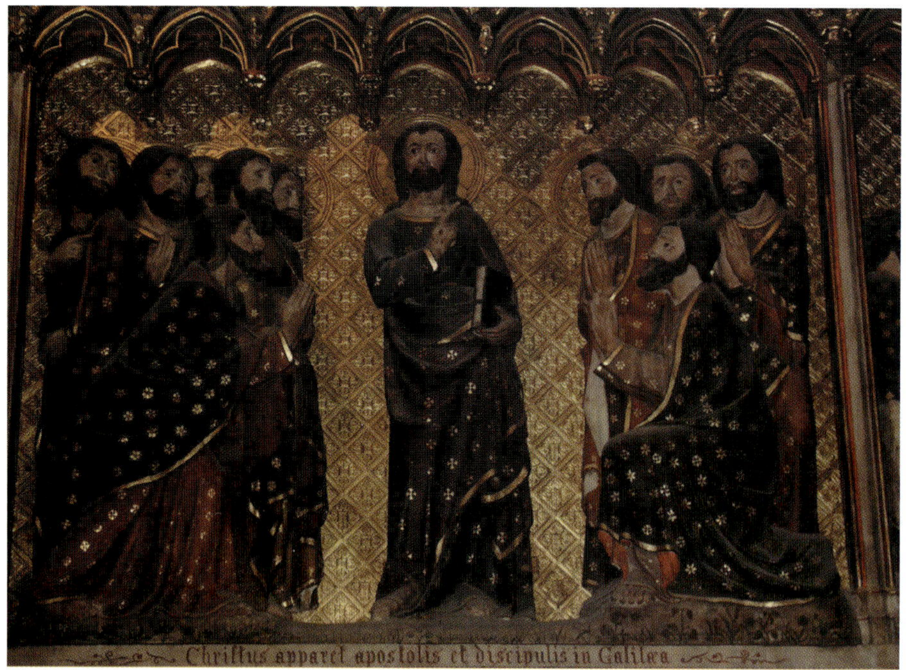

Back side of the Notre Dame Choir: The Risen Christ with His Disciples.
Photo by Alan Burner.

The figurative sculptures on the cathedral's façade, beckon the sinner to come in, and hear the message of salvation. Once inside the peace of God's love radiates from the windows of colorful glass figures, filling the chamber with the spiritual atmosphere of it's color. This was the message of the church during the middle-ages, and the principle motivation behind its construction.

Once inside, one can observe beautiful figurative wall reliefs in full color. These are actually scenes created in a full narrative of the life of Christ, just behind the choir walls. The interior of the cathedral begins to have a very galleried effect; it is a type of visual music, an orchestrated ambiance of color.

When we return to the outside of the structure, the windows are all but lifeless, in terms of color. The exterior stained glass windows vary from light blue-green, deep blue-gray, or deepest gray-violet, depending on the time of day. The exterior is so radically different that it is almost shocking to realize it is the same window. The interior window illuminates into a *translucent* portal of Heaven's glory, while the outside demonstrates a very *opaque* and forbidden, or closed-off surface. The windows are so dependant on the transfusion of light, that the difference between the outside surface and interior is striking.

As a child, I attended a church with my parents (much smaller of course), that was much that way, or

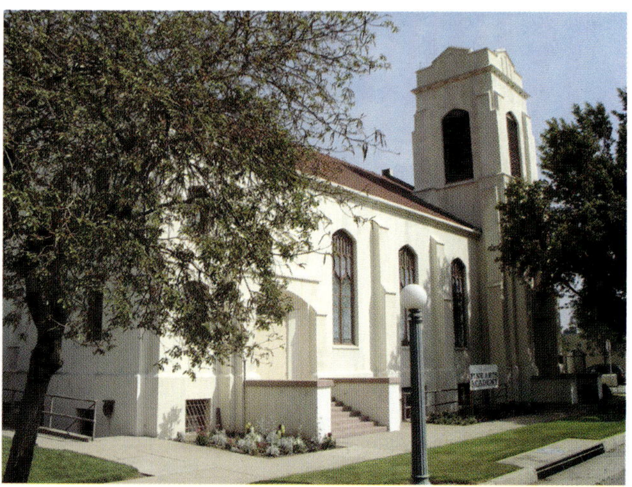

Author's Childhood Church.
Photo by Alan Burner.

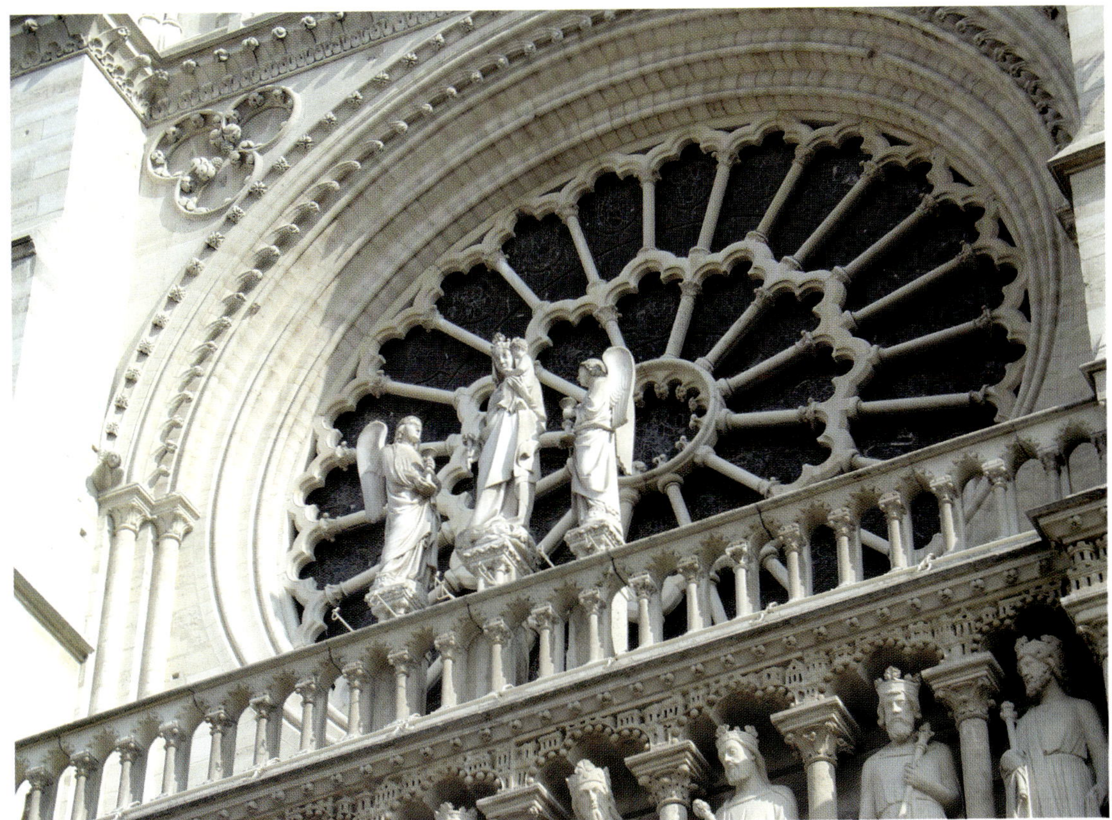

West Rose Window, Notre Dame de Paris.
Photo by Alan Burner.

at least in terms of the windows. I remember specifically thinking how "ugly" the windows were every Sunday, as I approached from outside the church. They were dull and lifeless. How could they build something so completely unattractive? Once inside, I couldn't understand where the ugly windows had gone. All I could see were beautiful arrays of colors, in what oddly enough seemed to be in the same location as the unsightly windows. I would run out repeatedly, trying to believe that they were really the same windows. I never really said much to my parents, I just thought my eyes were weird.

At Notre Dame de Paris, the exterior walls, as well as the interior are much the same in terms of the building materials and surface quality. A very light orange and absorbent textured surface, the material seems as ordinary as one could expect. However, in the absence of color stimulation, the statuary makes-up for the difference. The exterior is the elegant expression of High Gothic, with its multitudes of figurative works (above). It seems more a case for mass than volume, as the overwhelming sculptural sense of the building dominates the area. The color stimulus, which is minimal on the exterior, is more than compensated for by the beauty of the stained glass tracery and three-dimensional forms. Once inside the intensely lit exterior, saturated windows of color, sculptural reliefs, and sedately colored walls create a volume of color spectacle hard to imagine.

The minimal representation of three-dimensional figures in the interior is subtlety transformed by color softly splashing over the wall surfaces, particularly notable in the south chapels.

The authority of color establishes its own interior mood through the saturated windows. It transforms the walls, often splashing elegant displays of color over the wall surface, which changes constantly as the day progresses.

Rainy days present a window of richly saturated colors and deep shades. The deep reds are luscious

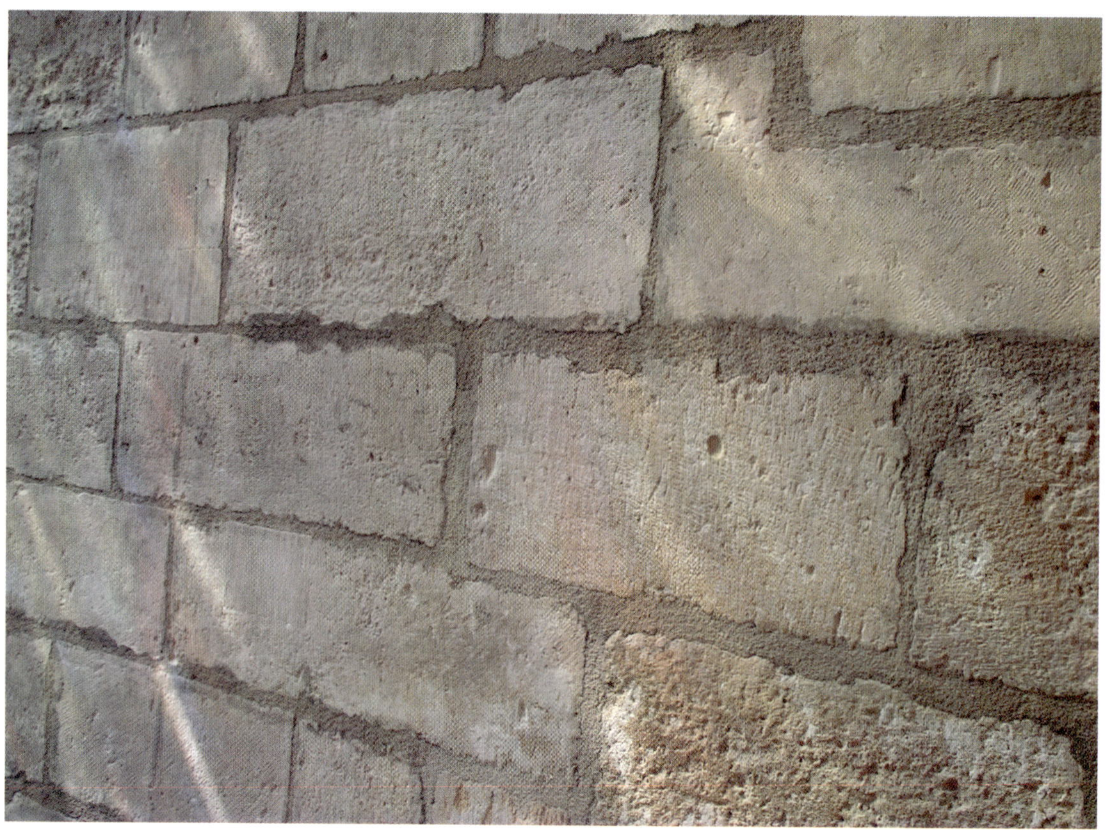

Interior Chapel Wall.
Photo by Alan Burner.

and full, and mysterious ultramarine blues immerse the mind in fantasy. It is a truly beautiful and quite different experience. Even while the brilliance of the windows are diminished from low light, the colors are still evident and inspirational. The interior of the church has also changed accordingly. The mood is very somber, so much so that the interior relies on sources other than the sun itself. Lamps and candles must be lit to recreate the atmosphere once again. Whether the sun fully illuminates the interior or partially, color transforms the interior space in such a way that ultimately *our emotional state* is seriously affected. This is just one example of the power and *authority of color*.

So it is now clear that the colors in the individual facets of glass found in the tracery on any given stained glass window function to evoke an emotional response. To create the appropriate mood is always at the forefront of any color application. The windows, such as the Rose Window, were most assuredly no exception. The stories that are told in each window often correspond to the energy expressed by the colors, increasing the mood complement—that is of the story and it's emotional state. Second, and more importantly, it is the combined ambiance of colors created within the actual atmosphere, or space of the cathedral, that produces a very somber and respectful environment. There is no doubt concerning the suggestion of a heavenly environment existing for those who would enter these Gates of Heaven. The Cathedral is open to all of its citizens, a hope of protection and salvation in a troubled time. Still today, we can observe people wandering into Notre Dame and watch as the psychological effect of colors in light help to deliver in them a moment's peace and quiet.

The reader may have noticed by this point that the windows dominant colors are usually blues and reds. The typical basic four colors are red and green, blue and yellow, with red and blue dominating the window plane. In most all cases, these hues are very saturated color. Since saturated color is the purest form of a color, it is therefore the most authoritative. In every case saturated color is used almost exclusively throughout the high gothic cathedrals in France. Red exhibits its warm, passionate and energized moods, and the coolness of blue keeps it calm and reflects a certain quietness. They rule with great authority throughout the composition. *Saturation is authoritative*.

St. Chapelle

We have discussed Notre Dame de Paris as it pertains to color authority, focusing mostly on color saturation, and then St. Severin, which indicates high intensity color contrasted to saturated color. Now let us take a look at another very different example of a Gothic structure: St. Chapelle. It is situated just a few blocks away from Notre Dame.

St. Chapelle, a late Gothic architectural chapel, was consecrated in 1248 A.D., and originally was not simply a religious icon, but had political ramifications as well. It is reported that Louis IX purchased the *Crown of Thorns* and a fragment of the *True Cross* from the Crucifixion of Christ, and had them enshrined at St. Chapelle. The cost of the relics were actually quite a bit more than was the initial cost of the building itself.

Even though the chapel windows depict more than 1,100 Biblical stories, it is very difficult to decipher them, because of the intensity of light and color that fills the room. This royal chapel was the example of what may perhaps be waiting in paradise, or at least the simplistic version or earthly vision of it, especially for the king and his family. It was a type of connection or symbolic confirmation of the king's authority over the people, given by God himself.

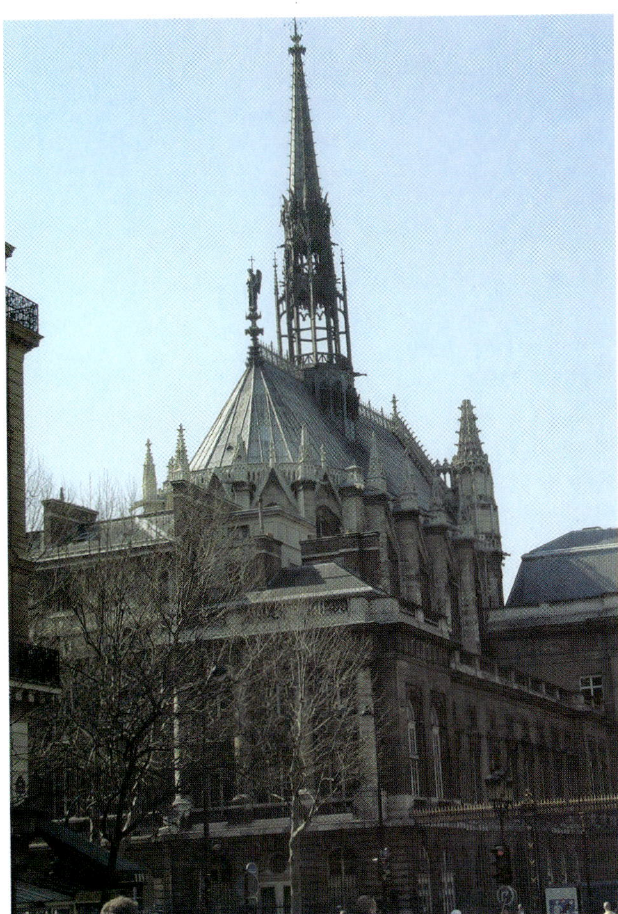

North Side Exterior View of Sainte Chapelle.
Photo by Alan Burner.

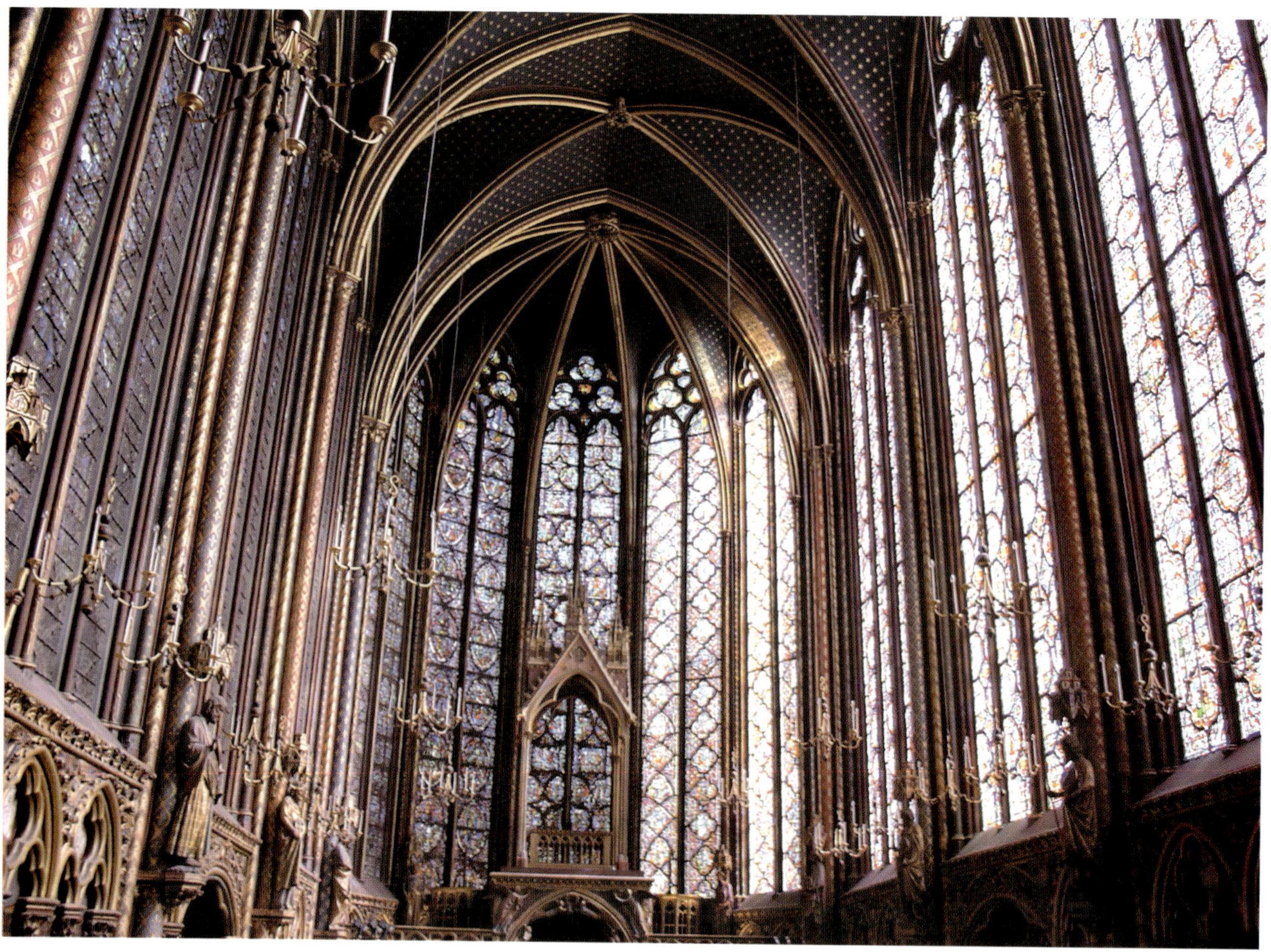

Interior of Sainte Chapelle.
Photo by Alan Burner.

The composite parts are simple. One enters through the west end narthex area directly into the nave. There is but one room featuring a gilded alter at the opposite end. There are no side aisles, only one huge space surrounded with stunning vertical colored glass windows, reaching to the very top of its groin vaulted ceiling.

The ribs of the vaults, as well as the colonnades, are primarily of gilded gold, creating an even stronger vertical thrust toward heaven. It is impossible not to look upward when one first enters the structure. Integrated with the gold surfaces are intricate designs of saturated blue and red, which also correspond to the blue and red hues in the stained glass windows. All create a perfect harmony of illuminated color through the entire interior space.

Let us say that if the South Rose Window is the diamond of Notre Dame de Paris, then St. Chapelle is the diamond of Paris. Of course St. Chapelle differs greatly from Notre Dame in size as well as color effects. Notre Dame is, of course, an oversized church (cathedral), whereas St. Chapelle is really a huge chapel. St. Chapelle no doubt accomplishes what we would hope a cathedral would, in that it is the *ultimate depository* of light and color. It summarizes both Chapters One and Two, in that it epitomizes both the *sovereignty of light* and *the authority of color.*

To enter St. Chapelle is to walk through a fantasy created by color and light. It is neither about saturated color or intensity specifically, but it is each individual piece of colored glass combining together, mixing colors in the atmosphere itself to create an unparalleled heavenly ambiance. The brilliance of color is overwhelming, as it seeks to illuminate the very soul of every person who enters. In reality, it seems almost impossible to absorb the composite aesthetic effect of St. Chapelle. It is as if to feel an array of multiple moods and emotions. It visually dazzles, it is color and light supreme. It is the authority of color to control all who enter.

Authority of Color

Jean-Auguste Dominique Ingres

At this point, we turn our attention from mineral pigmented glass, to oil pigmented paint on canvas. Let us observe the function of colors by examining a painting by Jean-Auguste Dominique Ingres, in a different approach to the authority of color.

In his preliminary drawing of *Odalisque with Slave*, the work resolves the figurative decisions of placement, position, proportion and gesture, as well as the determination of values, etc. Many times artists use drawing as a preview for what later becomes a painting, dealing with all of the other compositional elements first, before resolving the most important element of color.

The drawing, effective as it may be, is severely limited in its emotional appeal. What we do see in terms of emotion is realized by facial expression alone. Perhaps body positioning may enhance the mood to a degree, but the drawing remains minimally charged with emotion without color. Fundamentally, a certain degree of emotion is ex-

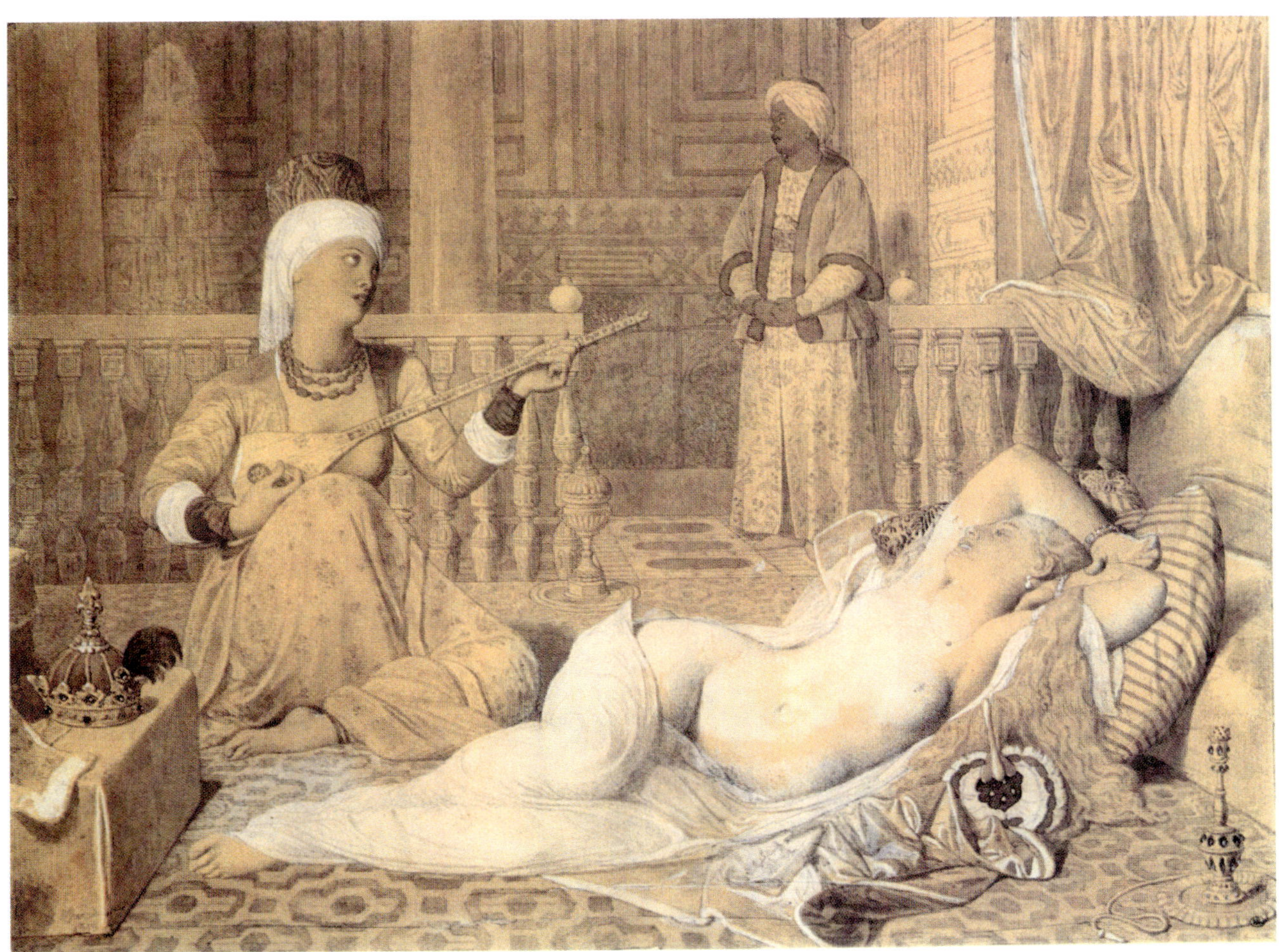

Odalisque With Slave by Jean-Auguste Dominique Ingres—Drawing.

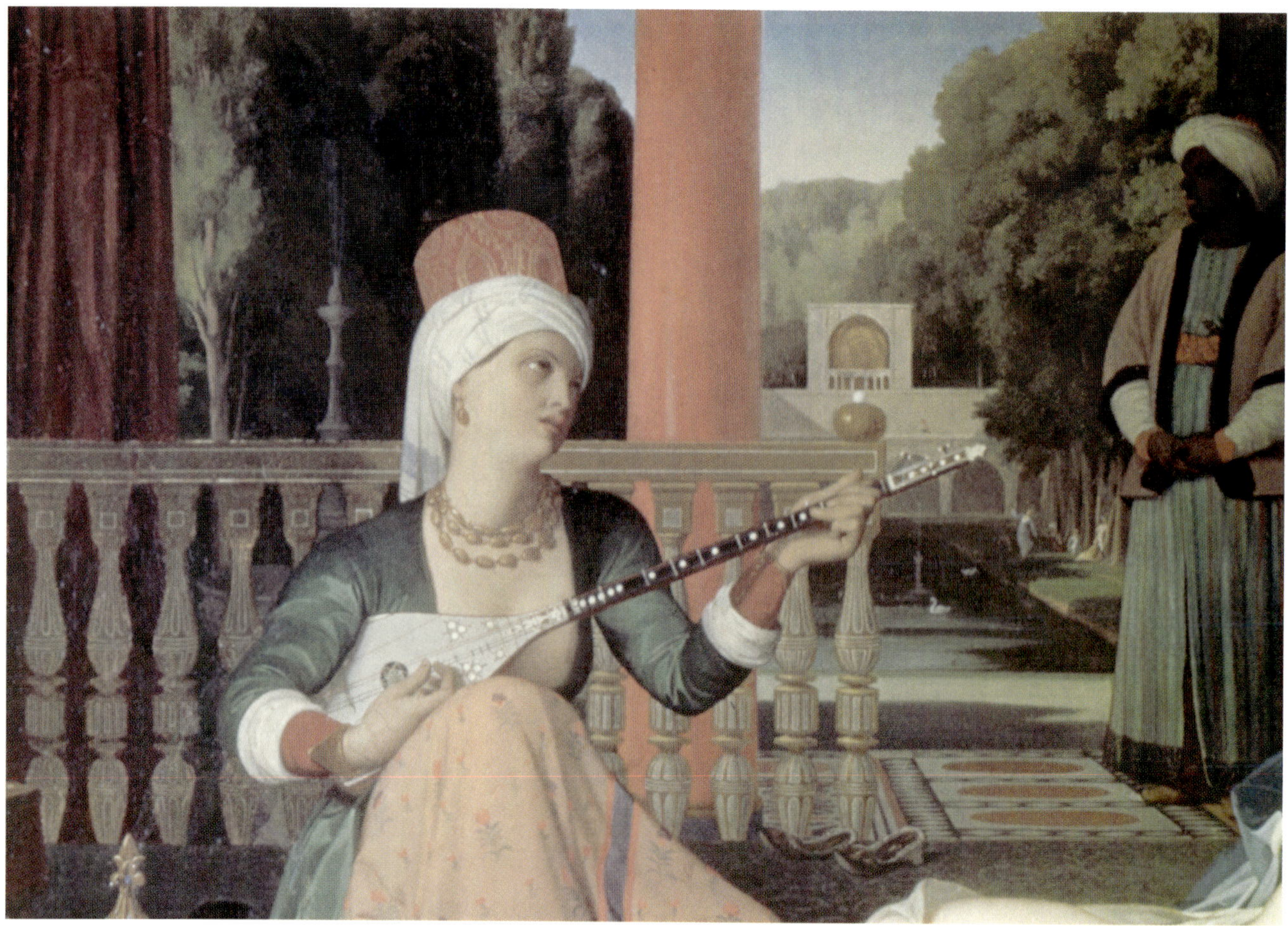

Odalisque With Slave by Jean-Auguste Dominique Ingres—Painting.

pressed, but it is somewhat deplete of mood. We cannot imagine the mood fully without it's source, which is color.

Once color is added, the picture changes from a mere drawing to an elegant, sophisticated composition, complete with emotional richness. Suddenly the authority of color becomes evident. As color is developed, we see the painting emerge as a living document, complete with warm sensuous reds and passionate oranges, complemented by stable and calming green hues. The contrast of her light orange skin makes reference to the more saturated orange skirt of the musician, which in turn connects to the saturated red hues in the remaining composition. The painting then makes a transition from saturated reds in the background to orange in the immediate middle ground, and then to the lightest orange hues observed in the foreground figure. The saturation of red and orange, in unison with the intensity of lightest orange, dominate and direct the eye exactly where the painter wants the viewer to focus. The authority of color controls the viewer's emotions, and dictates our mood. The color now enhances the expression of emotion on the figures' faces to complete the total emotional scenario.

In order to make a stronger point about saturation and the authority of color, we will make a comparison

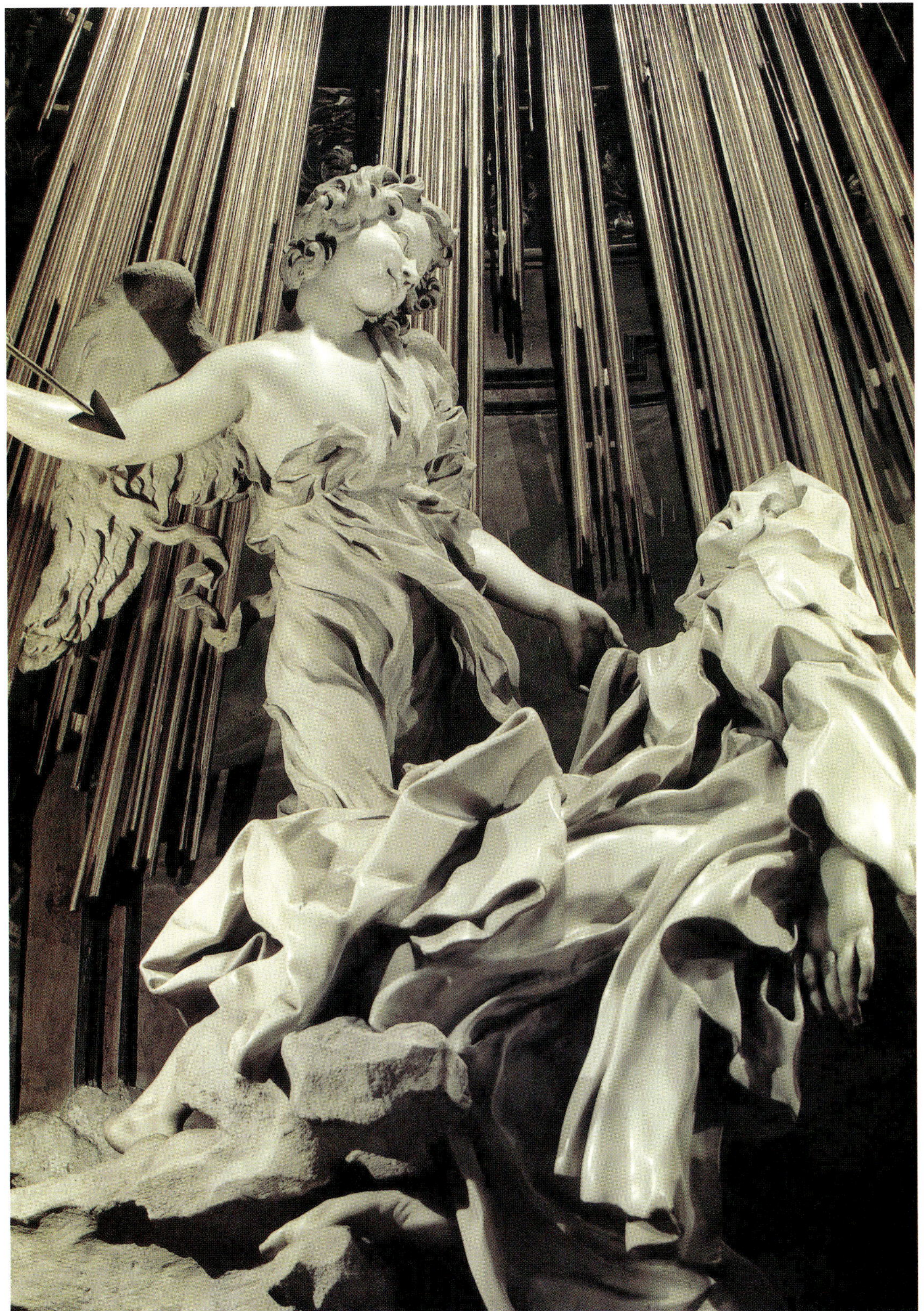

The Ecstasy of St. Teresa, by Gian Lorenzo Bernini.
Santa Maria della Vittoria, Coronado Chapel, Rome © Gianni Dagli Orti/CORBIS.

between Ingres' *Odalisque With Slave* and Bernini's *The Ecstasy of St. Teresa*.

As it is with the artworks of Bernini, *The Ecstasy of St. Teresa* translates mood and emotion through recognizable images. The realistic and dramatic body positions and facial expressions create a body language that convinces us that there is a high degree of emotion. In this case, it is the familiarity of subject matter that helps the viewer to clearly understand the mood of the artwork. The mood and emotional content is obvious without any color representation and there is very little that color could do to greatly expound on that in this particular artwork. In Bernini's *The Ecstasy of St. Teresa* the flowing drapery and the soft and sensuous expression of St. Teresa's face contrast against the background's stark vertical light rays.

Odalisque with Slave also demonstrates a sensuous position, as we observe the nude's soft curves, contrasted against a harsh geometry of architecture. Ingres, however, presents us with a painting lush in saturated color, especially noticeable in the red columns and drapery, which contrast against her tinted light red skin and suggesting a greater degree of sensuality. Here, saturation plays one of its finest roles through the *authority of color*.

Ask yourself if "*The Ecstasy of St. Teresa* were to be a color composition or painting, what colors would I use?" Considering that color does create mood, what colors would we use to empower the figures to their maximum desired effect? Consider the theatrics of the piece, and then ask yourself if you would use reds and oranges. Perhaps, perhaps not! After all, the reds may be too extreme coupled with the drama of the figures.

In any case, our summary concludes that in Bernini's work, it is the *dramatic and theatrical* effects of the sculpture which convey the emotion. It is clearly *color authority* that dictates mood in Ingres' work. Both works are equally effective, it is simply a difference of figurative gestures.

Fairfield Porter, Katie and Anne

Finally, we want to examine the work of American painter Fairfield Porter (see following image). One thing we know about effective design or artwork is that it seeks to capture one's attention and then effectively plots a way by which the viewer will be held hostage, long enough to create the appropriate mood. It may be by means of subject matter, texture, figurative expression, proportional extremes, scale, spatial uniqueness, or variations thereof. It is, however, the controlling factors of color which are responsible generally for the impact of a work. The use of intensity, saturation and value will always dominate color compositions or objects. The authority of color seems to have a certain majesty.

The painting, *Katie and Anne* has the initial impact that light is somehow flooding in from the outside. In fact, the room seems to be lighted with an impossible deluge of color and light. Yet the interior is much lighter than the out-of-doors itself. The painting attracts our attention first and foremost by the saturated hues of the carpet, the blouse on the woman, and the long stemmed flowers in the background vase, all a very saturated yellow. Though the yellow does not spatially dominate the composition, it does overwhelm the painting by virtue of its saturated condition. Of all the colors, yellow is most certainly the brightest.

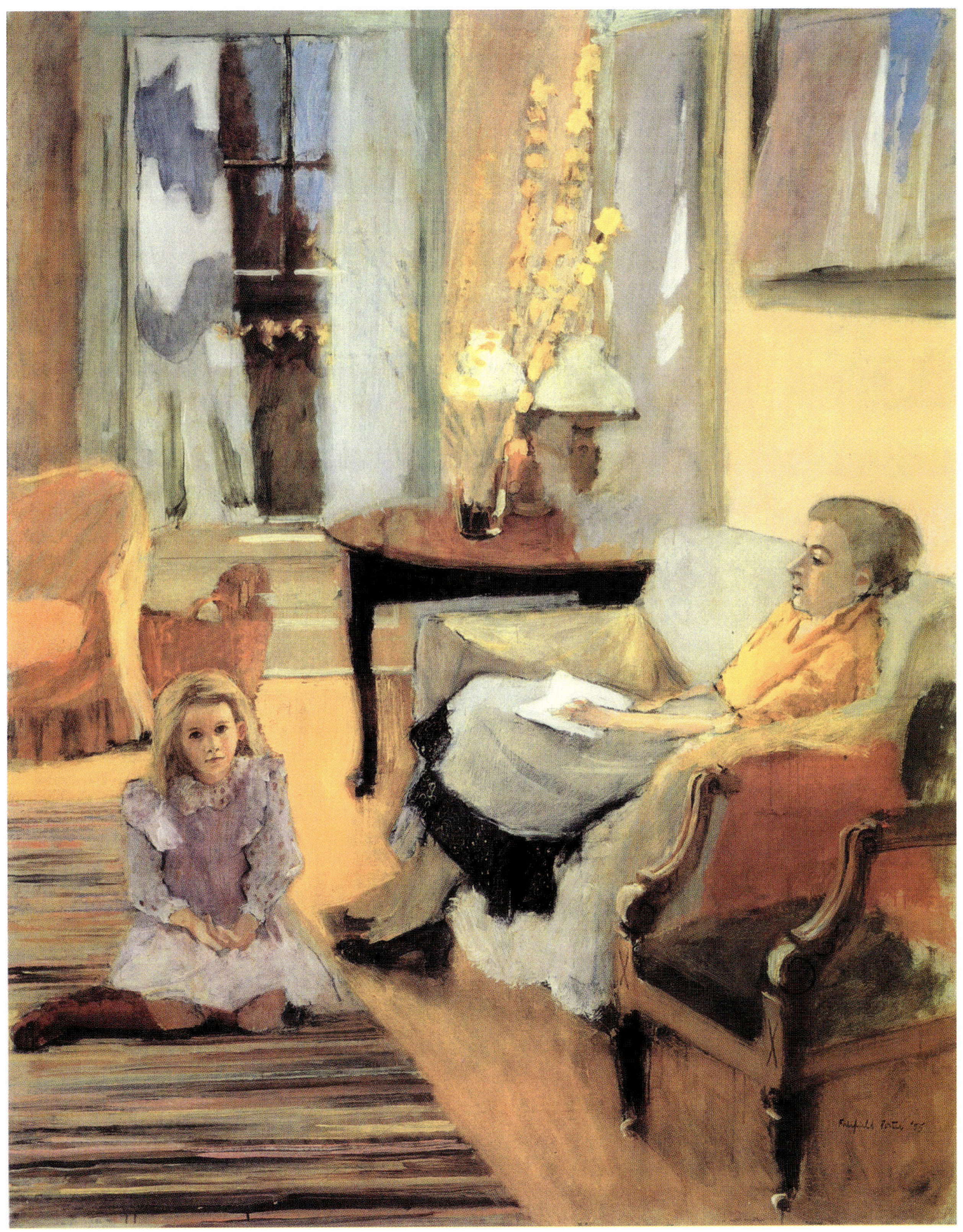

Katie and Anne by Fairfield Porter.

Side Notes

Two Androids and a Baby

I had a very interesting and rather humorous incident on a recent return trip from Paris.

It begins on the initial journey to that great city. On that plane, there was a young couple sitting on the other side of the isle with an infant, perhaps six months old. The situation remains vivid in my mind, since the child complained intermittently for half of the trip. At some point the entire passenger population seemed to be on edge, in various degrees; myself included. How absolutely lovely it was to arrive in Europe. As much as I love children, I couldn't wait to get off of that plane!

Finally, as the day arrived for my return back to the states, I was blissful to say the least. My research had gone very well. After all, it was springtime in Paris, and my work was productive and inspirational beyond my expectations. My mood was definitely as good as it gets.

As we began to board the aircraft, I was already looking forward to refining my notes on the return trip. As was settling into my seat, I began to do my usual scan of who my neighbors would be for the next 12 hours. Amazing! Who should I see perched across the aisle from me...that's right, *the* baby!

What are the odds that I would be sitting in the exact same seat, and the same three people in their respective seats, on the return home? Hard to believe. My joy turned to somber trepidation, as I glared at the sweet little bundle of innocence. Wondering when "baby" would fire himself up again, I leaned over to give him a smile. He was an adorable child, full of smiles, and of course loved the attention of other people.

As soon as the wheels left the ground, the baby began his proclamations.....he was bored to tears, as expected. The parents began their usual routine of bouncing, an occasional gentle shake (always made him smile) and then a quick feeding. Bounce, shake and feed, that was it.

After an hour of repeated fussing from the baby, I finally gave up trying to do any creative writing. The parents themselves sat quietly hour after hour, smiling at the fussy baby and completely unbothered by the whole adventure. It was as if they were almost without feeling. These two parents, even though loving and caring, were clueless as to the solution. At the exact moment I closed the lid to my computer, *the light went on!* Here I was doing research on color theory, when I suddenly realized that the environment around the baby was almost completely colorless in the dim light. As the baby was being bounced, he was facing a muted light blue bulkhead, looking at absolutely nothing but a blank wall. The parents both wore light blue, and the seats were of comparable hues; it was a monochromatic dull environment.

What parents would not bring one single colorful toy on a 12 hour flight? They were...*androids*, that's it! Two androids and a human baby.....completely without emotion. Everyone in the aircraft was irritated but the parents. *Bounce, shake and feed, bounce, shake and feed....shake that baby....somebody stop the madness!*

Eureka! I suddenly realized the answer. I think sometimes that I am perhaps a bit slow myself, since it took me two trips across the Atlantic to figure it out. I reached up to my overhead compartment, where I had a large bag of specialized pigments purchased in Paris; red, orange, yellow, green, blue and violet, fist-sized jars perfect for the baby.

My parents generation had a saying, "silence is golden." That term never made more sense than it did that day. For the duration of the remaining trip, the baby required no more than a little stimulus. He was completely under the domination of color. We live in a world of color. Color entices, lures and captivates the subconscious, as one falls under the power of *color authority.*

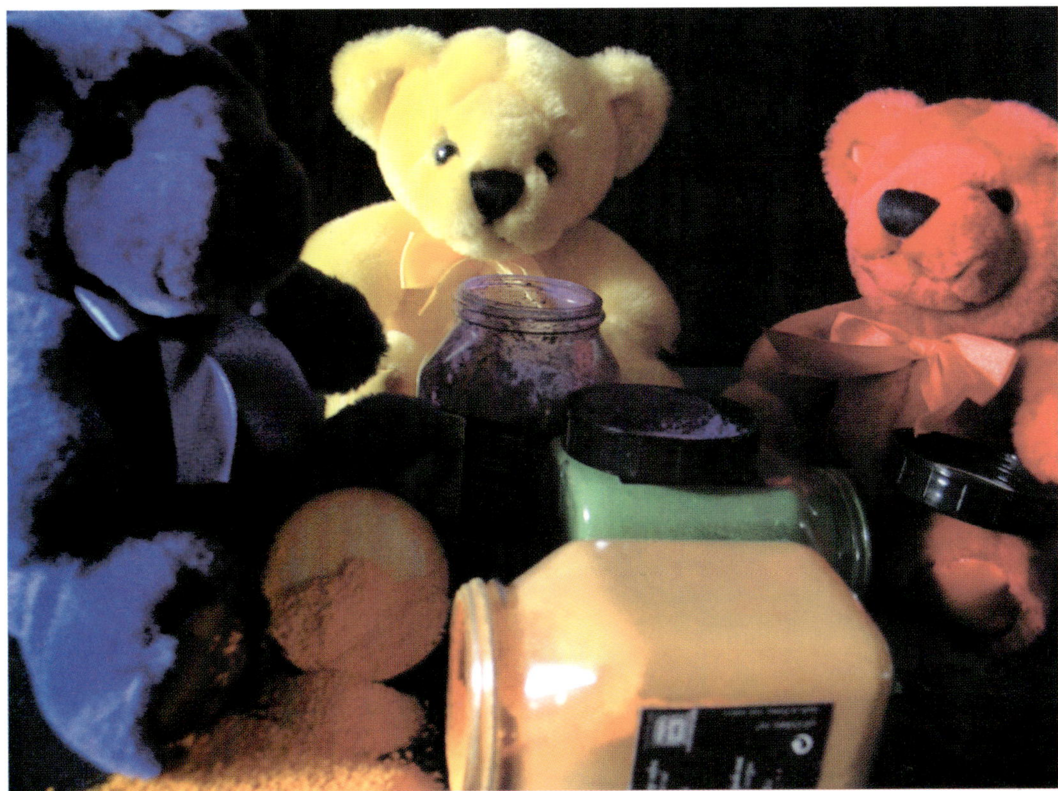

Photo by Alan Burner.

The Subtractive Colors of Pigments and Their Properties

The following pages list color pigments manufactured in France by *Sennelier.* Here is a description of their properties, as well as a chemical composition list. After that, you will find a color chart of the pigments that they produce. This information can be effectively used in your studies of color, such as saturation, transparency, and opaqueness.

Whites

Flake White

Basic lead carbonate, or lead white.
This white is well known since antiquity - the Romans called it "ceruse". Sennelier still prepares it following the same ancient methods. Opaque and dense, it creates a highly durable film, and is best used in an oil binder. Avoid mixtures with cadmiums and ultramarine blues. Suitable for fresco, but prepare it with caution, due to its toxic nature. Not recommended for water-based techniques.

Lithopone White

Zinc sulfide and barium sulfate. Dense opaque white invented in 1860 by the French chemist de Romanange. Creates tints with exceptional luminosity. Frequently used in grounds.

Blanc de Meudon or Marly White

Natural chalk carbonate. Delicate white with good covering capabilities, generally used in water-based paints. Often used in conjunction with Lithopone white.

Titanium White

Titanium dioxide (rutile variety). Very lightfast. An opaque, very dense white that mixes well with all colors. An excellent all-around white appropriate for both oil- and water-based colours. The most recent of the white pigments to be developed, this pigment, which dates to about 1915, occupies an important position in the white family.

Zinc White

Zinc oxide, which dates back to 18th century painting, was first manufactured by the French chemist Courtois. A stable, non-toxic semi-transparent pigment that mixes well with all colours. Use it in thin layers, or in combination with titanium white. Used most frequently in oil, gouache, and watercolour. Suitable for fresco.

Blacks

In its pure state, black literally does not exist. In fact, all substances that appear black actually have the capacity to absorb the entire range of colours found in white light.

Ivory Black

Carbon from animal bones calcified in a vase, rather than ivory tusks as was in the past. A warm, intense black that turns brownish when mixed with white. Very good lightfastness. In oil painting, requires large amounts of binder. Does not dry well. Suitable for all techniques, but in fresco, Black for Fresco is preferable.

Black for Fresco

Carbon smoke soot. This black works especially well for fresco, for which it is primarily used, but is entirely suitable for all techniques. Very lightfast.

Mars Black

Iron oxide. This synthetic black is durable and very lightfast. Creates cool gray shades. Suitable for all techniques including fresco.

Ochres

Ochres have been in use since prehistory. These coloured clays, which contain iron oxide found in the earth, generally come from France and Italy. These natural pigments are perfectly lightfast and suitable for all techniques, especially for fresco (with the exception of brown ochre).

Yellow Ochre

Natural, clay-base yellow. A warm, slightly transparent colour.

Red Ochre

Calcified yellow ochre.

Brown Ochre

Rich, dark brown formulated from natural clays and synthetic pigments. Not recommended for fresco.

Browns

Madder Brown

Transparent "azo" pigment and extenders. Very intense, transparent, reddish brown with high tinting strength. Suitable for all techniques, except fresco.

Red Brown

Iron oxide. Good covering brown, very lightfast and stable in mixtures. Recommended for all techniques including fresco.

Van Dyck Brown

Iron oxide. Purple brown. Very lightfast and stable in mixtures. Suitable for all techniques, including fresco.

Earths

Natural earths

(Raw Sienna, Burnt Sienna, Raw Umber, Burnt Umber, Green Earth).

All the siennas, umbers, and green earths are entirely natural and come from Italian soil. They are all natural iron oxides. The natural earth colours are completely lightfast and stable in mixtures. Colours referred to as "burnt" come from calcified native earth. Siennas and umbers require a great amount of oil in grinding. Since earths naturally have excellent drying properties, avoid adding drying agents.

Earth pigments are suitable for all techniques, and are recommended for fresco.

Reds

Cadmium Red Substitutes

(Light, Deep, Purple, and Orange).

Nitrogenous "azo" pigments, zinc oxide, extenders. As with cadmium yellow substitutes, cadmium red substitutes are composed of several pigments reproducing the genuine cadmium shade. These colours offer:

- good lightfastness.
- stability in mixtures in any binder.

Suitable for oil, gouache, watercolour, and acrylic, but not recommended for fresco.

Cadmium Red Genuine

(Light, Purple, Orange and Deep).

Sulfoselenide of cadmium. Opaque mineral pigment with excellent covering power. Completely lightfast and stable in mixtures in any binder. Suitable for all techniques, including fresco. Do not mix with flake white.

Permanent Red Deep

Calcium lake and extenders. Synthetic organic red that imparts bright, intense carmine red shades. Good tinting strength, average lightfastness. Used mainly for decorative purposes. Not suitable for fresco.

Helios Red

Toluidine red. A brilliant organic red, extremely intense and luminous. High tinting strength, average lightfastness. Suitable for all techniques, including oil, gouache, watercolour, tempera and acrylic. Not suitable for fresco.

Mars Red

Iron oxide. Dark, rich brownish red. Provides a transparent film with excellent tinting strength. Very lightfast and stable in mixtures. Suitable for all techniques, including fresco.

Venetian Red

Iron oxide. Vibrant brown with excellent colouring capacity. Very lightfast and stable in mixtures. Suitable for all techniques, especially fresco.

Quinacridone Red

Organic pigment with very high tinting strength; very lightfast. An intense, vibrant red that is transparent and therefore outstanding for glazing. In mixtures with white, provides a luminous, delicate pink.

French Vermilion Substitute

The mineral known as Cinnabar dates back to antiquity; the Romans called it minium. In 1687, Schulte used mercury to create the Vermilion pigment, named after "Vermeil" (bright red). As a result of its toxicity and its poor stability (notably in mixtures with flake white) artists since the early 20th century have increasingly replaced it with this substitute, made from nitrogenous "azo" and extenders. Bright, luminous orange-red with high tinting strength. Good lightfastness. Suitable for all techniques except fresco.

Chinese Vermilion Substitute

Toluidine red and extenders. Deep, lake-like red. Average lightfastness. Suitable for all techniques except fresco.

Yellows

Bright Yellow

A mixture of zinc oxide, mononitrogenous "azo" yellow, and modified arylide. A warm yellow with a good lightfastness, compatible with any binder except fresco.

Cadmium Yellow Substitute

Cadmium colours, discovered in Germany in 1817 by Stromeyer, were quickly adopted by artists, who appreciated their intensity and high tinting strength.

All dry pigments designated as substitutes are made from a combination of synthetic organic pigments that reproduce the genuine pigment colour, but at a much lower price. Cadmium yellow substitute is a stable compound of inert, mononitrogenous "azo" pigments and extenders. Very lightfast, it is stable in all binders: oil acrylic, watercolour, gouache. For fresco use only genuine cadmium colours.

Cadmium Yellow

Cadmium sulfide. Mineral pigment providing an opaque intense yellow with good tinting strength and lightfastness. Suitable for all techniques. Do not mix with flake white or chrome yellows.

Chrome Yellow

Lead chromate. This pigment, predecessor of the cadmiums, provides excellent tinting strength and a solid, durable film. However, these pigments present certain negative aspects: in addition to their toxicity and poor lightfastness, they tend to darken over time. Unsuitable for fresco. Still used primarily because of its reasonable price, and as part of painting tradition. When used to mix greens, provides very deep, dense shades.

Lemon Yellow

Formerly used in the form of zinc yellow, whose weaknesses led to the formulation of lemon yellow from synthetic organic mononitrogenous "azo" pigments. Very good lightfastness. Suitable for use in all binders, and provides very stable mixtures. Good tinting strength. Not recommended for fresco.

Indian Yellow Substitute

Composition of nitrogenous "azo" pigments that reproduce the genuine Indian Yellow shade.

Luminous, very lightfast, transparent pigment. Frequently employed for warming up hues. Suitable for all techniques except fresco.

Mars Yellow

Nitrogenous "azo" pigment and natural earth. At one time, this pigment was obtained from a concentrate of animal urine from India, but for more than 50 years, it has been reproduced with modern pigments. Transparent, very lightfast pigment. High tinting strength. Suitable for all techniques except fresco.

Naples Yellow Substitute

Documented by Cennino Cennini, the appearance of Naples Yellow has not been clearly established. True Naples Yellow is a lead antimonate that was frequently employed in past centuries. Its properties have now been rediscovered. Since genuine Naples Yellow is toxic, this colour is a substitute based on zinc oxide, titanium dioxide, and mononitrogenous "azo" yellow. A luminous, very lightfast colour, this yellow yields a rich, beautiful, dense paste. Suitable in all binders, including oil, watercolour, tempera and acrylic. Not suitable for fresco.

Nickel Yellow

Nickel-titanate yellow. A vibrant yellow with a slight greenish hue. Very good tinting strength, excellent lightfastness in mixtures and shades. Can be mixed with all pigments and suitable in any binder, including fresco.

Greens

English Green Light

Nitrogenous "azo" and Phthalocyanine. Provides a softly luminous green. High tinting strength. Good lightfastness and stability in mixtures. Not recommended for fresco.

English Green Deep

Nitrogenous "azo" and Phthalocyanine. Deep bluish green. Powerful tinting strength. Good lightfastness, stable in mixtures. Not recommended for fresco.

Baryte Green

Chromate of baryte, Phthalocyanine, and strontium chromate. Pale, luminous green with excellent covering capacity. Average lightfastness. Because it is classified as toxic, this pigment should not be used in powdered form. Good drying properties when used in oil. Suitable for all techniques. Not recommended for fresco.

Cobalt Green Light

Combination of zinc and cobalt green. Cold, pale green with a lovely tonality, pulling toward turquoise. A pure colour with good covering power, low tinting strength. Very lightfast and stable in mixture. Suitable for all techniques, including fresco.

Emerald Green Substitute

Phthalocyanine and extenders. Close in appearance to genuine emerald green, but at a much more reasonable price. Luminous green with high tinting strength. Good lightfastness and stability in mixtures. Not recommended for fresco.

Emerald Green

In the 19th century, Pannetier created this transparent shade, which was rapidly adopted by painters for its remarkable properties, especially for glazing. "Hydrated" chromium oxide. Deep, intense green. Very good lightfastness, stable in mixture. Especially well-suited to oil glazes. Less vibrant, and with a lower tinting strength than Emerald Green Substitute. Suitable for all techniques and with all binders, especially fresco. Avoid applying it in very thick layers.

Chromium Oxide Green

Anhydrous Chromium Oxide. Dull green hue. Excellent tinting strength and covering power. Very good lightfastness and stability in mixtures. When used in oil, provides a very buttery, east-to-use paste. Recommended for fresco.

Veronese Green

Genuine Veronese Green, which is a copper arsenate, is quite toxic. This bright, luminous hue reproduces the original with modern pigments-mononitrogenous "azo," Phthalocyanine, and extenders. Pale green tone. Luminous, good covering power, low tinting strength. Very lightfast. Suitable in all binders, except fresco.

Phthalocyanine Green

Synthetic organic pigment. Its characteristics are identical to those of Phthalocyanine Blue, but in a brilliant rich green hue.

Blues

Cerulean Blue Substitute

Cerulean Blue Substitute is based on barium sulfate and Phthalocyanine blue. This hue, an imitation of genuine cerulean blue, provides remarkable lightfastness. Very high tinting strength. Suitable for all techniques.

Cerulean Blue

Cobalt stannate. Invented around 1850, under the name celestial blue. Derived from cobalt blue, in a harmonious, blue-green hue. Opaque, very lightfast, stable in mixtures. Suitable for all techniques. Very precious pigment.

Cobalt Blue

Cobalt aluminate. In the 19th century, the French chemist Thenard successfully obtained this pigment from a natural mineral. A very pure blue shade. Excellent lightfastness, very stable in mixtures. Suitable for all techniques.

Ultramarine Blue Light

Silico aluminate of sodium polysulfides. In 1828, the chemist Guillemet synthetically reproduced the natural colour of Lapis Lazuli, which had been in use since antiquity. Variations in the hue result from the size of its microparticles. The preparation of ultramarine blue is quite complex, and varies according to the desired individual shade. Luminous, intense blue that approaches the appearance of cobalt blue, and provides bright, pleasant effects in shading. Mixes well with other pigments, but, since it contains sulfur, should not be mixed with flake White or chrome based pigments. Suitable for all techniques.

Ultramarine Blue Deep

Silico aluminate of sodium polysulfides. Preparation identical to that of Ultramarine Blue light. A deep, very intense shade, more purple than Ultramarine Blue light. Very lightfast. An important colour on most artists' palettes. Suitable for fresco.

Prussian Blue

Ferric ferrocyanide. Discovered in Prussia at the beginning of the 18th century. Difficult to grind and moisten. Very high tinting strength. Good lightfastness (contrary to its reputation) except in oil colours, where it tends to darken. Strong, transparent tone. Dries out oily binders. Not suitable for fresco.

Indigo Blue

Indanthrone blue. Synthetic organic pigment. Reproduction of true indigo, which comes from an Indian plant. Very high tinting strength. Remarkable lightfastness. Provides a semi-opaque film. A deep, intense blue suitable for all binders, except fresco.

Azure (Hue)

Formerly produced in the form of Manganese Blue. Genuine until the dangers of its manufacture led to its disappearance. Azure is made from synthetic organic pigments phthalocyanine blue and barium sulfate. Very lightfast. Suitable for all techniques, except fresco. Provides a bright, luminous, turquoise blue shade.

Cobalt Blue Deep

Cobalt aluminate. The varying temperatures at which it is calcinated (cooked) accounts for the many different shade of Cobalt Blue. Bright, deep blue with excellent lightfast properties that mixes very well with other pigments. Suitable for all techniques.

Cobalt Turquoise

Cobalt aluminate. A unique turquoise hue whose brightness cannot be matched in other mixtures. Excellent lightfastness. To retain its unique vividness in oil painting, use it with a non-yellowing oil (safflower).

Phthalocyanine Blue

Pure synthetic organic pigment with exceptionally high tinting strength. Very good lightfastness. Suitable for all techniques (except fresco). Because of its powerful tinting strength, use it with discretion. A transparent hue well-suited to glazing techniques. Provides a blue palette ranging from pale sky blue to dark, somber tones similar to Prussian blue. In mixtures, use it to create an infinite range of greens.

Violets

Cobalt Violet Deep

Cobalt phosphate. Dark purple hue, very lightfast and stable in mixtures. Low tinting strength but good covering power. Recommended for fresco.

Mineral Violet

Manganese phosphate. Red-purple hue. Good covering power, average tinting strength, good lightfastness. Suitable for all mediums except fresco and water-based techniques.

Ultramarine Violet

Silico aluminate of sodium. Mineral pigment. Suitable for all techniques including fresco. Low tinting strength. Provides a transparent, muted, red-violet film. Very lightfast.

Lakes

Synthetic alizarin was formulated from tar in 1868 by Groebe and Libermann. It perfectly reproduces Madder (Garance), traditionally extracted from the ground root "Rubian tinctorium."

Alizarin Scarlet Lake

Nitrogenous "azo" lake. Bright, extremely luminous, transparent red. Principally used in oil, watercolour, tempera and acrylic. Average lightfastness. In oil, used primarily in glazes because when applied in thick pastes, it is prone to cracking. Not recommended for fresco.

Alizarin Red Lake

Alizarin lake on aluminum hydrate base. Deep, transparent red with a carmine hue. Average lightfastness. High tinting strength. When used in oil, has a tendency to crack. Slow drying. Suitable for all techniques, except fresco.

Black Lake

Synthetic aniline black that is velvety and intense. In tints, takes on a slightly bluish hue. Average lightfastness. Not recommended for fresco.

Solferino Lake (Tyrian Rose)

Calcified aluminum hydrate base lake. Very bright pink. Poor lightfastness, excellent tinting strength. Because of its fugitive nature, use with discretion. Not suitable for fresco.

Iridescent Pigments

Titanium dioxide. Iridescent pigments undergo surface treatment with mica; their level of iridescence varies according to the mica content. As a result of reflections and light interference, they may take on very different colours. Extremely lightfast, excellent covering power, non-toxic. Used for a wide range of applications, including cosmetics. Suitable in all binders, including oils, vinyl paints, resins, etc.

Avoid grinding iridescent pigments; grinding may destroy their "mother of pearl" effect.

Primary Colors

This unique range of primaries was especially developed for the Sennelier range of dry pigments. Each of these hues was formulated to offer exactly the same tinting strength, so in mixtures, they allow you to create medium hue secondary colours:

1 part yellow + 1 part red = medium orange hue
1 part red + 1 part blue = medium purple hue
1 part yellow + 1 part blue = medium green hue

As a result of the equal intensity of these three primaries, the progressive mixtures of hues, mixed, remain distinct. Therefore, it is not necessary to add white to maintain the purity of these mixtures. All three have excellent lightfastness.

Primary Blue

Phthalocyanine pigment and extenders. Very lightfast. Good tinting strength. Suitable for all techniques, including oil, gouache, watercolour, tempera and acrylic.

Primary Yellow

Nitrogenous "azo" pigment and extenders. Very lightfast. Good tinting strength. Can be used in all techniques: oil, gouache, watercolour, tempera and acrylic.

Primary Red

Quinacridone pigment and extenders. Very lightfast. Good tinting strength. Suitable for all techniques, including oil, gouache, watercolour, tempera and acrylic.

Metallics: Copper, Yellow Gold, Red Gold

Metallic pigments produced from metal alloy powders that have undergone surface treatment. Suitable for all oil and water-based binders except acrylic and fresco. Apply a varnish over metallic colours to prevent oxidation.

Fluorescent Pigments

Fluorescence, which results from the pigments' ability to transform light, provides unique tonalities that only exist outside nature. These pigments are extremely unstable, and are recommended only for temporary artworks. Very poor lightfastness. Not recommended for fresco.

Phosphorescent Pigments: Yellow-green

Inorganic, phosphorescent Zinc sulfide powders. Recommended for use with water-based binders (except fresco). Since excessive grinding weakens their phosphorescent qualities, pigments should be mixed gently with a binder, or ground lightly.

Humidity and ultraviolet rays can darken these pigments. If the colours are exposed to direct light, keep the humidity of the environment under 50%. Applied in favourable conditions, the special properties of these pigments can last for years.

L.F.: Lightfastness
***: Very good lightfastness
**: Good lightfastness
*: Average lightfastness
o : Poor lightfastness

O: Opaque
T: Transparent
S/O: Semi-opaque

Name	N°	Pigments	L.F.	O/T	Chemical Composition	F.	O.M..	N.G.	R.
Flake White	108	PW1	★★	S/O	Basic Lead Carbonate	Y	Y	Y	N
Lithopone White	128	PW5	★★★	S/O	Zinc Sulfide, Barium Sulfate	Y	Y	Y	Y
Marly White	131	PW18	★★★	S/O	Natural Chalk Carbonate	Y	Y	Y	Y
Titanium White	116	PW6	★★★	O	Titanium Oxide	Y	Y	Y	Y
Zinc White	119	PW4	★★★	S/O	Zinc Oxide	N	Y	Y	Y
Primary Blue	385	PB15	★★★	S/O	Phthalocyanine Blue, Minerals	N	Y	Y	Y
Azur (Hue)	320	PB15	★★★	S/O	Phthalocyanine Blue, Minerals	N	Y	Y	Y
Cerulean Blue Sub.	323	PB15	★★★	S/O	Phthalocyanine Blue, Minerals	N	Y	Y	Y
Cerulean Blue	305	PB35	★★★	O	Cobalt Stannate	Y	Y	Y	Y
Cobalt Blue	307	PB72	★★★	T	Cobalt Aluminate	Y	Y	Y	Y
Indigo Blue	308	PB60	★★★	S/O	Indanthrone Blue	N	Y	Y	Y
Cobalt Blue Deep	309	PB74	★★★	S/O	Cobalt Aluminate	Y	Y	Y	Y
Cobalt Blue Turquoise	341	PB36	★★★	S/O	Cobalt Stannate	Y	Y	Y	Y
Phthalocyanine Blue	387	PB15	★★★	T	Phthalocyanine Blue	N	Y	Y	Y
Ultramarine Blue Light	312	PB29	★★★	T	Silico aluminate of Sodium Polysulfides	Y	Y	Y	Y
Ultramarine Blue Deep	315	PB29	★★★	T	Silico aluminateof Sodium Polysuflides	Y	Y	Y	Y
Prussian Blue	318	PB27	★★★	T	Ferric ferrocyanide	N	Y	Y	Y
Primary Yellow	574	PY1, PY3	★★	S/O	Mononitrogenous "azo"pigments, extenders	N	Y	Y	Y
Bright Yellow	511	PY1, PR4	★★	S/O	Mononitrogenous "azo" pigments, extenders	N	Y	Y	Y
Cadmium Yellow Light Sub	539	PY1, PY3	★★	S/O	Mononitrogenous "azo" pigments, extenders	N	Y	Y	Y
Cadmium Yellow Deep Sub.	543	PY1	★★	S/O	Mononitrogenous "azo" pigments, extenders	N	Y	Y	Y
Cadmium Lemon Yellow Sub.	545	PY1, PY3	★★	S/O	Mononitrogenous "azo" pigments, extenders	N	Y	Y	Y
Cadmium Yellow Medium Sub.	541	PY1	★★	S/O	Mononitrogenous "azo" pigments, extenders	N	Y	Y	Y
Cadmium Orange Yellow Sub.	547	PY1, PR4	★★	S/O	Mononitrogenous "azo" pigments, extenders	N	Y	Y	Y
Cadmium Lemon Yellow	535	PY35	★★★	O	Cadmium Sulfide	Y	Y	Y	Y
Cadmium Yellow Light	529	PY35	★★★	O	Cadmium Sulfide	Y	Y	Y	Y
Cadmium Yellow Deep	533	PY35	★★★	O	Cadmium Sulfide	Y	Y	Y	Y
Cadmium Yellow Medium	531	PY35	★★★	O	Cadmium Sulfide	Y	Y	Y	Y
Cadmium Orange Yellow	537	PO20	★★★	O	Cadmium Sulfide, Cadmium Selenide	Y	Y	Y	Y
Chrome Yellow Light	549	PY34	★★	O	Lead Chromate	N	Y	Y	N
Chrome Yellow Deep	551	PY34	★★	O	Lead Chromate	N	Y	Y	N
Lemon Yellow	501	PY3	★★	T	Mononitrogenous "azo" pigments, extenders	N	Y	Y	Y
Indian Yellow Sub.	517	PY1, PY83	★★	T	Mononitrogenous "azo" pigments, extenders	N	Y	Y	Y
Mars Yellow	505	PY1, PBr7	★★	T	Mononitrogenous "azo" pigments, extenders	N	Y	Y	Y
Naples Yellow Sub.	567	PY1	★★	O	Mononitrogenous "azo" pigments, extenders	N	Y	Y	Y
Nickel Yellow	576	PY53	★★★	O	Nickel Titanate	Y	Y	Y	Y
Alizarin Scarlet Lake	694	PR48:2, PY83	★★	T	Mononitrogenous "azo" pigments, extenders	N	Y	Y	Y
Alizarin Red Lake	696	PR83	★★	T	Anthraquinone	N	Y	Y	Y
Solferino Lake (Tyrian Rose)	697	PR173	o	T	Xanthene Lake	N	Y	Y	Y
Black Lake	763	PBk1	★	T	Black Aniline	N	Y	Y	a.
Ivory Black	755	PBk9	★★★	O	Bone Black	N	Y	Y	Y
Black for Fresco	761	PBk6/7	★★★	S/O	Carbon Black	Y	Y	Y	Y
Mars Black	759	PBk11	★★★	O	Synthetic Iron Oxide	Y	Y	Y	Y
Yellow Ochre	252	PY43	★★★	T	Natural Earth	Y	Y	Y	Y
Red Ochre	259	PR102	★★★	O	Natural Earth	Y	Y	Y	Y
Brown Ochre	255	PBr7, PB7	★★★	S/O	Natural Earth, Phthalocyanine Green	N	Y	Y	Y
Primary Red	686	PV19	★★★	S/O	Quinacridone Violet	N	Y	Y	Y

F : Suitable for Fresco
O.M. : Suitable for oil binders (oils, alkyds, resins...)
: Suitable for natural gums (water)
R. : Suitable for acrylic resins, vinyls (water)

N : No
Y : Yes
a. : Avoid
n.a. : not applicable

Name	N°	Pigments	L.F.	O/T	Chemical Composition	F.	O.M..	N.G.	R.
Cadmium Red Light Sub.	613	PR4	★★	S/O	Mononitrogenous "azo" pigments, extenders	N	Y	Y	Y
Cadmium Red Orange Light Sub.	615	PR4, PY1	★★	S/O	Mononitrogenous "azo" pigments, extenders	N	Y	Y	Y
Cadmium Red Purple Light Sub.	617	PR3	★★	S/O	Mononitrogenous "azo" pigments, extenders	N	Y	Y	Y
Cadmium Red Light	605	PR108	★★★	O	Cadmium Sulfide, Cadmium Selenide	Y	Y	Y	Y
Cadmium Red Deep	606	PR108	★★★	O	Cadmium Sulfide, Cadmium Selenide	Y	Y	Y	Y
Cadmium Red Orange	609	PO20	★★★	O	Cadmium Sulfide, Cadmium Selenide	Y	Y	Y	Y
Cadmium Red Purple	611	PR108	★★★	O	Cadmium Sulfide, Cadmium Selenide	Y	Y	Y	Y
Permanent Red Deep	603	PR3, PR48:2	★★	T	Mononitrogenous "azo" pigments, extenders	N	Y	Y	Y
Helios Red	619	PR3	★★	T	Mononitrogenous "azo" pigments, extenders	N	Y	Y	Y
Mars Red	631	PR101	★★★	S/O	Synthetic Iron Oxide	Y	Y	Y	Y
Venetian Red	623	PR101	★★★	O	Synthetic Iron Oxide	Y	Y	Y	Y
Quinacridone Red	679	PR122	★★★	T	Quinacridone Red	N	Y	Y	Y
Chinese Vermilion Sub.	677	PR3	★★	O	Mononitrogenous "azo" pigments, extenders	N	Y	Y	Y
French Vermilion Sub.	675	PR4, PY1	★★	O	Mononitrogenous "azo" pigments, extenders	N	Y	Y	Y
Brown Madder	471	PBr23, PY42	★★★	S/O	Mononitrogenous "azo" pigments, iron oxide, extenders	N	Y	Y	Y
Red Brown	405	PR101, PBr7	★★★	O	Iron Oxide	Y	Y	Y	Y
Van Dyck Brown	407	PBr8	★★	O	Manganese Brown	Y	Y	Y	a.
Raw Umber	205	PBr7	★★★	S/O	Natural Earth	Y	Y	Y	Y
Burnt Umber	202	PBr7	★★★	S/O	Natural Earth	Y	Y	Y	Y
Raw Sienna	208	PBr7	★★★	T	Natural Earth	Y	Y	Y	Y
Burnt Sienna	211	PBr7	★★★	T	Natural Earth	Y	Y	Y	Y
Green Earth	213	PG23	★★★	T	Natural Earth	Y	Y	Y	Y
English Green Light	805	PY74, PG7	★★★	S/O	Mononitrogenous "azo" pigments Phtalocyanine green	N	Y	Y	Y
English Green Deep	807	PG36	★★★	S/O	Phtalocyanine green, extenders	N	Y	Y	Y
Baryte Green	821	PY32, PY31	★★★	O	Barium Chromate, strontium	N	Y	a.	a.
Cobalt Green Light	833	PG19	★★★	O	Cobalt Oxide, Zinc	Y	Y	Y	a.
Cobalt Green Deep	835	PG19	★★★	O	Cobalt Oxide, Zinc	Y	Y	Y	a.
Emerald Green Sub.	869	PG7	★★★	S/O	Phtalocyanine Green, extenders	N	Y	Y	Y
Emerald Green	837	PG18	★★★	T	Chromium Oxide (hydrated)	Y	Y	Y	Y
Chromium Oxide Green	815	PG17	★★★	O	Chromium Oxide	Y	Y	Y	Y
Veronese Green	847	PG36, PY3	★★★	T	Phtalocyanine Green, Monoazo yellow pigments, extenders	N	Y	Y	Y
Phtalocyanine Green	896	PG7	★★★	T	Phtalocyanine Green	N	Y	Y	Y
Cobalt Violet Deep	909	PV14	★★★	O	Cobalt Phosphate	Y	Y	a.	a.
Mineral Violet	915	PV16	★★★	T	Manganese Phosphate	N	Y	a.	a.
Ultramarine Violet	916	PV15	★★★	T	Silico aluminate of Sodium	Y	Y	Y	Y
Copper	36	None	★★	N.A.	Powdered Metal Alloys	N	Y	a.	Y
Red Gold	40	None	★★	N.A.	Powdered Metal Alloys	N	Y	a.	Y
Yellow Gold	30	None	★★	N.A.	Powdered Metal Alloys	N	Y	a.	Y
Iridescent	20	None	★★★	N.A.	Mica, Titanium dioxide	N	Y	Y	Y
Phosphorescent	10	None	N.A.	N.A.	Phosphorescent Pigments	N	Y	Y	Y
Fluorescent Yellow	502	None	o	N.A.	Fluorescent Pigment	N	Y	Y	Y
Fluorescent Orange	648	None	o	N.A.	Fluorescent Pigment	N	Y	Y	Y
Fluorescent Red	604	None	o	N.A.	Fluorescent Pigment	N	Y	Y	Y
Fluorescent Pink	654	None	o	N.A.	Fluorescent Pigment	N	Y	Y	Y
Fluorescent Green	895	None	o	N.A.	Fluorescent Pigment	N	Y	Y	Y
Fluorescent Blue	304	None	o	N.A.	Fluorescent Pigment	N	Y	Y	Y
These descriptions are merely suggestions; Sennelier cannot be held responsible for results obtained									

Sennelier Dry Pigments

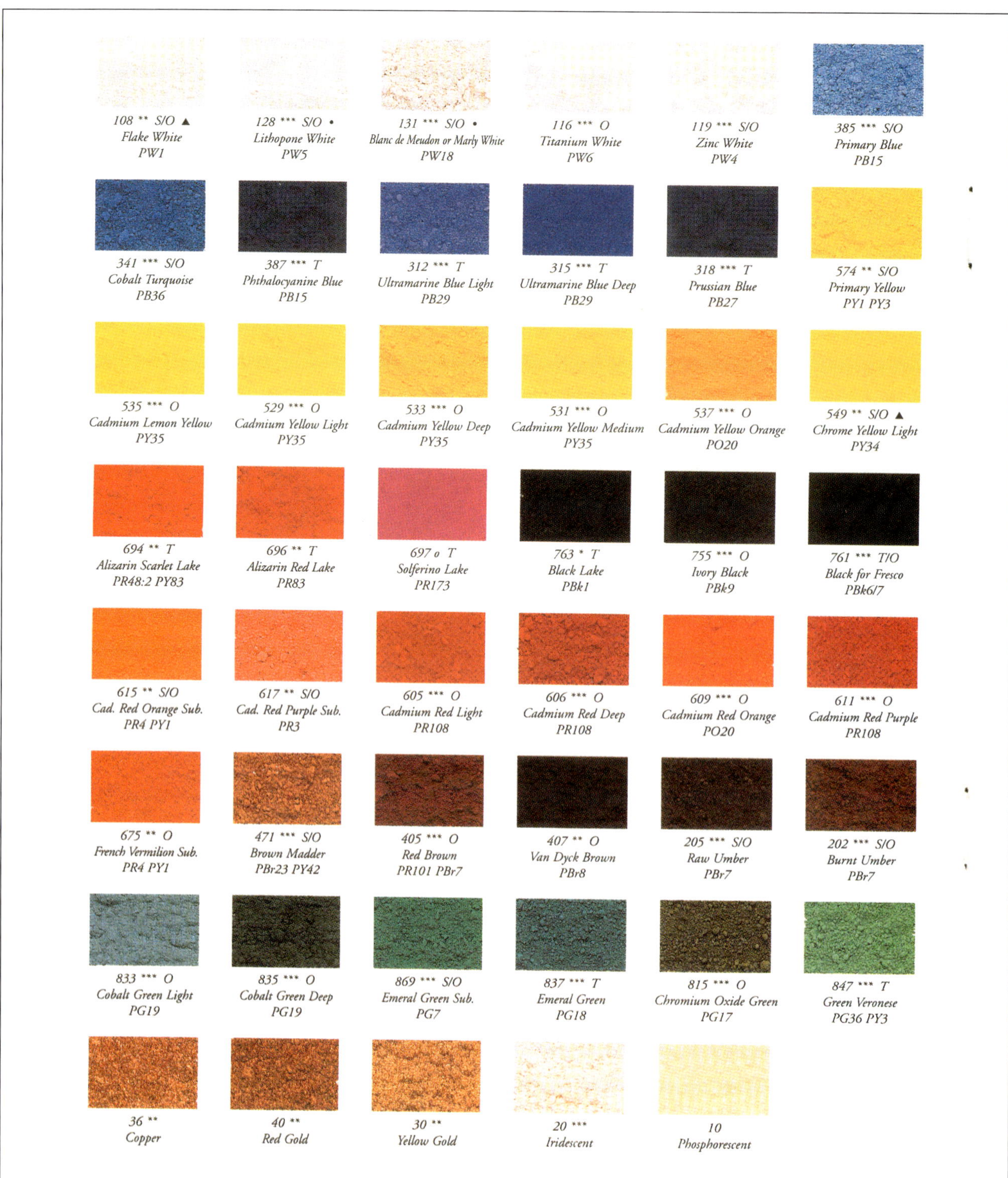

*** : *Very good lightfastness*
** : *Good lightfastness*
* : *Average lightfastness*
o : *Poor lightfastness*

O : *Opaque*
T : *Transparent*
S/T : *Semi-opaque*

▲ : *Jars with safety caps*

*320 *** S/O*
Azure (Hue)
PB15

*323 *** S/O*
Cerulean Blue Sub.
PB15

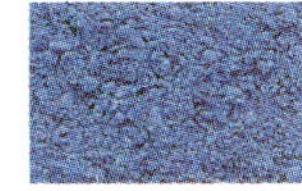

*305 *** O*
Cerulean Blue
PB35

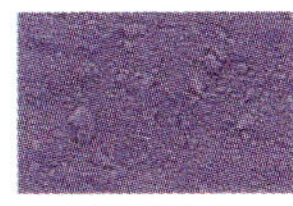

*307 *** T*
Cobalt Blue
PB72

*308 *** S/O*
Indigo Blue
PB60

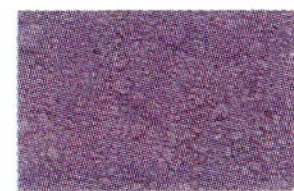

*309 *** S/O*
Cobalt Blue Deep
PB74

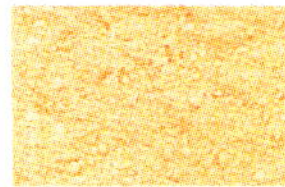

*511 ** S/O*
Bright Yellow
PY1 PR4

*539 ** S/O*
Cad. Yellow Light Sub.
PY1 PY3

*543 ** S/O*
Cad. Yellow Deep Sub..
PY1

*545 ** S/O*
Cad. Lemon Yellow Sub.
PY1 PY3

*541 ** S/O*
Cad. Yellow Medium Sub.
PY1

*547 ** S/O*
Cad. Yellow Orange Sub.
PY1 PR4

*551 ** O ▲*
Chrome Yellow Deep
PY34

*501 ** T*
Lemon Yellow
PY3

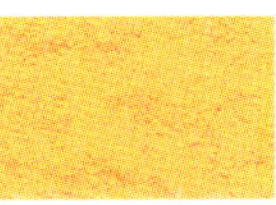

*517 ** T*
Indian Yellow Sub.
PY1 PY83

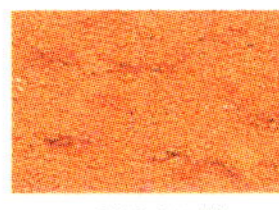

*505 ** T*
Mars Yellow
PY1 PBr7

*567 ** O*
Naples Yellow Sub.
PY1

*576 *** O*
Nickel Yellow
PY53

*759 *** O*
Mars Black
PBk11

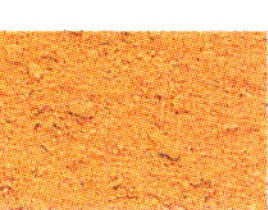

*252 *** T*
Yellow Ochre
PY43

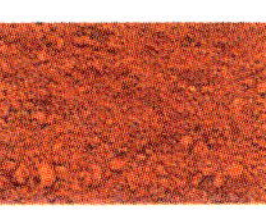

*259 *** O*
Red Ochre
PR102

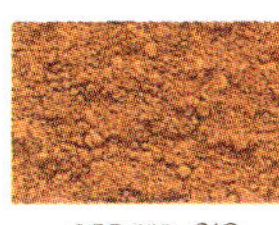

*255 *** S/O*
Brown Ochre
PBr7 PG7

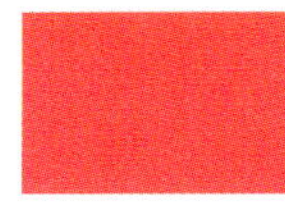

*686 *** S/O*
Primary Red
PV19

*613 ** S/O*
Cad. Red Light Sub.
PR4

*603 ** T*
Permanent Red Deep
PR3 PR48:2

*619 ** T*
Helios Red
PR3

*631 *** S/O*
Mars Red
PR101

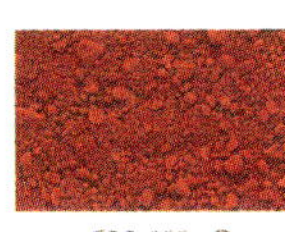

*623 *** O*
Venetian Red
PR101

*679 *** T*
Quinacridone Red
PR122

*677 ** O*
Chinese Vermilion Sub.
PR3

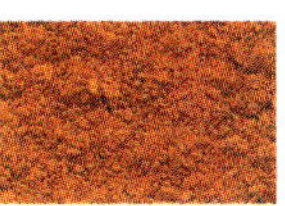

*208 *** T*
Raw Sienna
PBr7

*211 *** T*
Burnt Sienna
PBr7

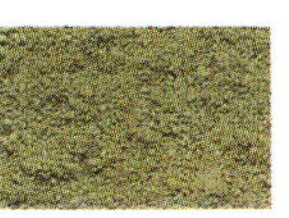

*213 *** T*
Green Earth
PG23

*805 *** S/O*
English Green Light
PY74 PG7

*807 *** S/O*
English Green Deep
PG36

*821 *** O ▲*
Baryte Green
PY32 PY31

*896 *** T*
Phthalocyanine Green
PG7

*909 *** O*
Cobalt Violet Deep
PV14

*915 *** T*
Mineral Violet
PV16

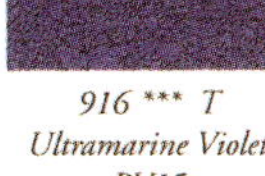

*916 *** T*
Ultramarine Violet
PV15

The shades on these swatches approximate the actual colours as closely as possible, but are limited by reproduction techniques.
These shades should only by used as approximate versions of the actual hues.

502 o
Fluorescent Yellow

648 o
Fluorescent Orange

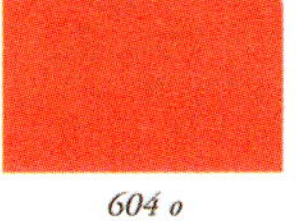

604 o
Fluorescent Red

654 o
Fluorescent Pink

895 o
Fluorescent Green

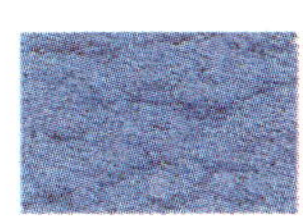

304 o
Fluorescent Blue

Reading Complement

Light

by Isaac Asimov

Particles and Waves

If we are prepared to admit that all matter is composed of atoms, then it is reasonable to ask if there is anything in the world that isn't matter and, therefore, isn't composed of atoms. The first possibility that might spring to mind is light.

It has always seemed obvious that light is immaterial. Solids and liquids can be touched, have mass, and therefore weight, and take up space. Gases cannot be felt in the same way that solids and liquids can, but a moving gas can be felt. We have all experienced high winds and we well know what a tornado can do. Then, too, air will take up room so that if an "empty" beaker (actually full of air) is plunged, open end down, into a tank of water, the water does not fill the beaker unless, somehow, the air is allowed to escape. In 1643, the Italian physicist Evangelista Torricelli (1608–1647) showed that air had weight and that this weight could support a column of mercury 76 centimeters (30 inches) high.

Light, however, has none of these properties. It cannot be felt, even though the heat it might produce can. It has never been found to have perceptible mass or weight, and it does not appear to take up space.

This doesn't mean that light was dismissed as unimportant because it was insubstantial, however. The first words of God, as given in the Bible, are: "Let there be light." What's more, under the name of fire, it was the fourth of the ancient Earthly elements, on a par with the three material ones of air, water, and earth.

Sunlight was naturally considered to be light at its purest. It was white light, unchanging and eternal. If sunlight were made to pass through colored glass, it would pick up the color of the glass, but that would be an earthly impurity. Again, when objects burned on earth and gave off light, that light might be yellow, orange, or red. In some cases, if certain powders were cast into the fire, it might even burn green or blue. But again, these were earthly impurities that gave rise to color.

The one colored object that seemed to be divorced from anything earthly was the rainbow, which was sufficiently awe-inspiring to give rise to myths and legends. It was thought to be the bridge between Heaven and Earth, used by divine messengers. (The Greek messenger of the gods is given the name Iris, which is Greek for "rainbow.") It was also a divine guarantee that the world would never again be destroyed by flood, so that it appears at the end of rainstorms, indicating that God has remembered and stopped the rain.

In 1665, however, the English scientist Isaac Newton (1642–1727) produced his own rainbow. In a darkened room, he allowed a beam of sunlight to enter through a hole in a shutter, and passed that beam through a three-dimensional triangular wedge of glass called a prism. The beam of light spread out and produced a band of colors on the white wall beyond, the colors being red, orange, yellow, green, blue, and violet, in that order—just the order in which they occur in the rainbow.

A rainbow, we now know, is caused by sunlight passing through the innumerable droplets of rain still in the air after a rainshower. These droplets have the same effect on light rays as a glass prism.

Apparently, then, sunlight is not "pure" light, after all. Its whiteness is merely the effect produced on the eye by a mixture of all of these colors. By having the light pass through a prism and then pass through another prism held in the reverse position, the separated colors will rejoin and form white light again.

In that these colors are thoroughly immaterial, Newton called the rainbow band a spectrum, from the Latin word for "ghost." Newton's spectrum created a problem, however. For the colors to be separated on passing through the prism Newton believed each one must have its ordinary straight-line path bent (refracted) as it passed into and out of the glass—each color bent to a different extent (red the least and violet the most), so that they were separated and seen each by itself when the beam hit the wall. What, then, could light be made of that would account for the separation of light into a spectrum?

Newton was an atomist and so it naturally occurred to him that light was made up of tiny particles, like the atoms of matter, except that the particles of light did not have mass. He had no clear notion, however, as to how the particles of colored light might differ among themselves, and why some should be refracted by a prism to a greater extent than others.

Furthermore, when two beams of light crossed each other, one remained unaffected by the other. If both consisted of particles, should not those particles collide and bounce off one another randomly so that the beam would grow fuzzy and spread outward after collision?

The Dutch physicist Christiaan Huygens (1629–1695) had an alternate suggestion. He thought light consisted of tiny waves. In 1678 he advanced arguments for showing that an entire series of waves might advance in what looked like a straight line, just as a beam of particles would, and that two beams, each made up of waves, would cross each other without either being, in the end, disturbed.

The trouble with the wave suggestion was that people thought of the types of waves produced in water, such as when a pebble is dropped into a still pond. As those water waves expand, they tend to move around an obstruction such as a piece of wood (diffraction) and join again on the other side. In that case, wouldn't light waves curve around an obstruction and cast no shadows, or at least fuzzy ones? Instead, as is well known, light casts sharp shadows if the light source is small and steady. Such sharp shadows are exactly what you would expect if light were a beam of minute particles, and this was considered a strong argument against waves.

It is interesting to note that the Italian physicist Francesco Maria Grimaldi (ca. 1618–1663) had noticed that a beam of light passing through two narrow openings, one behind the other, widened a little bit, indicating it had diffracted outward very slightly as it passed through the openings. His observation was published in 1665, two years after his death, but some how it didn't attract attention. (In science, as in many other types of human endeavor, important discoveries or events sometime get lost in the shuffle.)

Huygens, nevertheless, showed that light, if composed of waves, might well have waves of different lengths. Those portions of light with the longest waves would be least refracted. The shorter the waves, the greater the refraction. In this way, one could explain the spectrum, in that it might be that red had the longest waves and that orange, yellow, green, and blue were made up of successively shorter waves, while violet was made up of the shortest.

On the whole, as we look back on it, Huygens had the better of the argument, but Newton's reputation was growing rapidly (he was undoubtedly the greatest scientist who had ever lived) and it was hard to take up a position against him. (Scientists, in that they are as human as anyone else, are sometimes swayed by personalities as well as by logic.)

Throughout the 1700s then, most scientists accepted the fact that light consisted of little particles. This might have helped the growth of atomism in connection with matter, and as atomism gained, that in turn strengthened the particle view of light.

In 1801, however, the English physicist Thomas Young (1773–1829) performed a crucial experiment. He let light fall upon a surface containing two closely adjacent slits. Each slit served as the source of a cone of light, and the two cones overlapped before falling on a screen.

If light were composed of particles, the overlapping region should receive particles from both slits and be brighter than the outlying regions that received particles from only one slit or the other. This was not so. What Young found was that the overlapping portions consisted of stripes—bright bands and dim bands alternating.

There seemed no way of explaining this phenomenon by the particle hypothesis. With waves, however, there was no problem. If the waves from one slit were in phase with those from the other slit, both keeping perfect step, then the ups and downs of one set of waves (or the ins and outs) would be reinforced by those of the other set, and the oscillation of the two combined would be stronger than of either separately. Brightness would increase.

On the other hand, if the waves from one slit were out of phase with those from the other slit—if one set of waves went up while the other went down (or one went in while the other went out)—then the two waves would cancel each other, at least in part, and the two combined would be weaker than either separately. Brightness would decrease.

Young was able to show that, under the conditions of his experiment, the two sets of waves would be in phase in one region, out of phase in the next, in phase again in the next, and so on, alternately. The bright and dim bands that were observed would be expected of waves.

Because one set of waves interferes with, and cancels, the other set in specific places, these bands are called interference patterns. Such interference patterns are observed when one set of waves on a calm water surface overlaps another. They are also observed when two beams of sound (known to consist of waves) intersect each other. The wave nature of light thus appeared to be demonstrated by Young's experiment (although, as we might expect, that didn't mean that those who believed in the particle view surrendered easily—because they didn't).

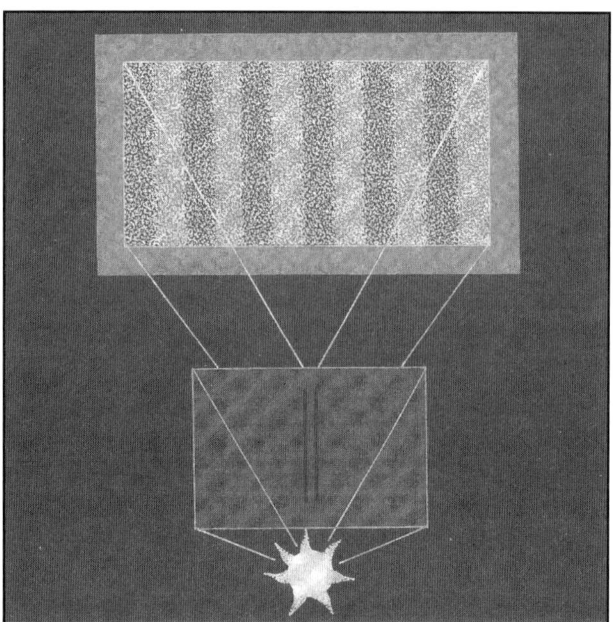

In 1801, Thomas Young let light fall on a surface containing two closely adjacent slits. The wedge of light from each slit fell on a screen and overlapped, resulting in a pattern of stripes—bright bands and dim bands alternating. There seemed no way of explaining this phenomenon by the particle hypothesis.

It was even possible, from the width of the interference bands, to calculate the length of a single wave of light (wavelength). It turned out that light waves had lengths in the neighborhood of 1/20,000 of a centimeter (or 1/50,000 of an inch). The wavelength of red light was a little longer than that, while the wavelength of violet light was a little shorter. This means that a ray of light an inch long will have, more or less, 50,000 waves, end to end, along the ray. It also means that about fifty atoms can be placed end to end along a single wavelength of light.

That explained why light cast sharp shadows despite being made of waves. Waves bend around obstacles only when the obstacles are not much longer than the wave in question. A wave would not bend around anything substantially longer than itself. Sound waves are very long and can move around most ordinary obstacles.

Almost anything we can easily see, however, is much, much longer than a light wave, so there's virtually no turning for them, and the shadows they cast are sharp. There is a very *slight* turning effect, however, and where the objects are quite small, the shadow's edge is inclined to be slightly fuzzy. That explains the diffraction effect that Grimaldi had discovered 130 years before Young's time.

The issue wasn't settled, however. People knew of two types of waves. There were water waves, in which the wave spread outward, but the particles of water moved up and down in a direction at right angles to the direction in which the wave progressed. This is called a transverse wave. There were also sound waves, in which the wave also spread outward, but the particles of air moved in and out, in a direction parallel to the direction in which the wave progressed. This is called a longitudinal wave.

Which of these two describes light waves? Huygens, when he first elaborated the wave hy-

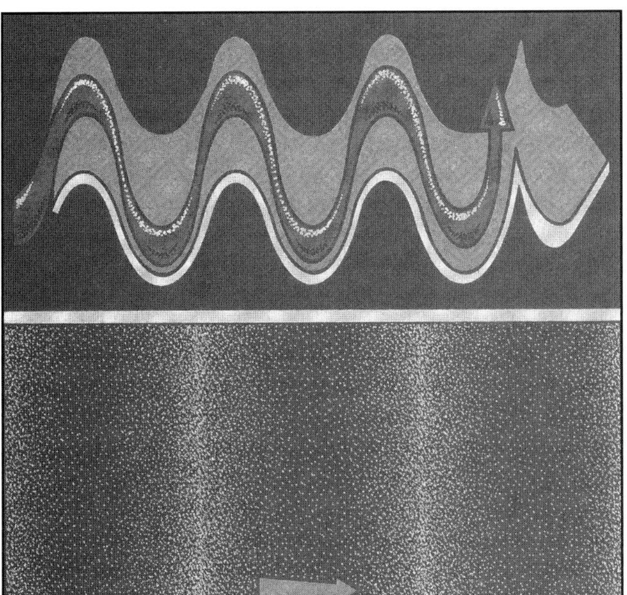

1. Water waves spread outward, and the particles of water move up and down in a direction at right angles to the direction in which the wave progresses. This type of wave is called a transverse wave.

2. Sound waves also spread outward, but the particles of air move in and out in a direction parallel to the direction in which the wave progresses. This type is called a longitudinal wave.

pothesis, might have felt that light and sound, both being the cause of sense perceptions, should be similar in nature. Sound was known to be a longitudinal wave, so he suggested that light was a longitudinal wave, too. Young, when he demonstrated the wave nature of light, also thought so.

Earlier, in 1669, however, the Danish scholar Erasmus Bartholin (1625–1698) received a transparent crystal from Iceland, of a type now called Iceland spar. He noted that objects viewed through the crystal were seen double. He assumed that light passing through the crystal was refracted at two different angles, so that some emerged in one place and the rest in a slightly different place, producing a double image.

Bartholin could not explain why this should be, and neither could Newton or Huygens. The phenomenon was therefore pushed to one side as temporarily inexplicable. (Not everything can be explained at some particular stage of knowledge. The only sensible thing to do is to explain what you can and hope that, as knowledge advances, the time will come when the temporarily unexplainable can also be explained.)

In 1817, Young realize that double refraction could not be easily explained if light consisted of particles or of longitudinal waves. It could be explained quite easily, however, if light consisted of transverse waves.

The French physicist Augustin Jean Fresnel (1788–1827) adopted this point of view and worked out a careful theoretical study of light as transverse waves, one that explained all that was known about the behavior of light at that time. That settled it. For the next eighty years, physicists were quite satisfied that light was made up of tiny transverse waves and that this was the whole of the answer.

The Four Phenomena

It is a rare answer that is *completely* satisfactory, and this seems especially true in science, where every answer seems to uncover a more subtle question. If we grant that light exists in waves, as sound and a disturbed pond surface do, then there remains the problem that light waves travel easily through a vacuum, whereas sound waves and water waves do not.

Water waves exist because water molecules move up and down regularly. If water did not exist, then neither would water waves. Sound waves exist because air molecules (or the molecules of any medium through which sound travels) move in and out regularly. If air or any other medium did not exist, sound waves would not exist either.

In the case of light waves, however, what is it that is moving up and down? It can't be any type of ordinary matter, for light waves can pass through a vacuum where, apparently, there is no matter.

Newton had a similar problem when he worked out the law of universal gravitation in 1687. The Sun held the Earth in its gravitational grip across 150 million kilometer (93 million miles) of vacuum. How could the gravitational effect, whatever it was, travel across a vacuum?

Newtown wondered if, perhaps, vacuum was not really *nothing* but consisted of a type of matter more subtle than ordinary matter and therefore not easily detectable. This vacuum matter came to be called ether, in homage to the "aether" Aristotle imagined as making up the heavenly bodies. The gravitational attraction pulled at the ether, and this pull was conducted from one bit of ether to the next until, finally, the Sun was pulling at the Earth.

Perhaps it was this ether (or another type) that waved up and down as light passed through. It had to fill all of space because we could see even the most distant stars. What's more, it had to be so fine and rarefied a type of matter that it did not in any way interfere with the passage of the Earth, or any other heavenly body, however light, as it progressed through space. Fresnel suggested that ether permeated the very body of the Earth and of all other heavenly bodies.

The particles of ether, however, when moved up, must experience a restoring force that moves them down, past the equilibrium point, then up again. The more rigid a medium, the more rapidly it vibrates up and down, and the more rapidly a wave progresses through it.

Light travels at a speed of 299,792 kilometers (186,290 miles) per second. This was first determined, very approximately, by the Danish astronomer Olaus Roemer (1644–1710) in 1676. To allow light to travel at such a speed, the ether must be more rigid than steel.

To have the vacuum made of something so fine that it allowed bodies to pass through it freely and without measurable interference, and at the same time so stiff as to be more rigid than steel, was rather puzzling, but scientists didn't seem to have any choice but to suppose that this was the case.

In addition to light and gravity, two other phenomena were known that could make themselves felt across a vacuum. They were electricity and magnetism. Both were first studied, according to tradition, by Thales. He studied a certain piece of iron ore, first found near the town of Magnesia on the eastern shore of the Aegean Sea. It had the property of attracting pieces of iron and he is supposed to have called it *ho magnetes lithos* ("the Magnesian Rock"). Objects with the property of attracting iron have been called magnets ever since.

Thales also found that lumps of amber (a fossilized resin), if rubbed, attracted not iron particularly, but *any* light object. This difference in behavior meant the attraction was not that of magnetism. The Greek word for amber is elektron and, eventually, this phenomenon came to be called electricity as a consequence.

Sometime in the eleventh century, in China—but exactly where and by whom and under what circumstances is unknown—it was discovered that if a needle made of magnetic ore, or of steel that had been magnetized by being stroked by magnetic ore, was allowed to turn freely, it would align itself north and south. In addition, if the ends were marked in some way, it would be seen that the same end always turned north.

That end was called the Magnetic North Pole, and the other the Magnetic South Pole. In 1269, the French scholar Petrus Peregrinus (1240–?) experimented with such needles and found that the Magnetic North Pole of one would be attracted to the Magnetic South Pole of the other. On the other hand, the Magnetic North Pole of two magnetized needles would repel each other, as would the Magnetic South Poles of the two needles. In short, like magnetic poles repelled each other while unlike magnetic poles attracted each other.

In 1785, the French physicist Charles Augustin de Coulomb (1736–1806) measured the strength of the force by which a Magnetic North Pole attracted a Magnetic South Pole, or repelled another Magnetic North Pole. He found that the attraction or repulsion declined as the square of the distance (the inverse square law). That is, if you increased the distance to x times what it was before, the force between the poles became $1/x \times 1/x$, or $1/x^2$, what it was before. When Newton dealt with gravitational attraction what followed was to become the inverse square law.

Thus, the Moon is sixty times as far from the Earth's center as the Earth's surface is. The Earth's gravitational pull at the distance of the Moon is only $1/60 \times 1/60$, or 1/3600 of what it is on the Earth's surface. Nevertheless, this pull is proportional to the product of the two masses involved, and the Earth and Moon are so massive that the Earth's gravitational pull is still large enough at the distance of the Moon to hold the Moon in orbit.

For that matter, the Sun can hold the Earth in orbit across a distance nearly 400 times that between the Earth and the Moon. Indeed, huge clusters of galaxies, stretching across millions of light-years of space are held together by gravitational pulls.

Yet as it turns out, the *magnetic* attraction between two magnetized needles is trillions of trillions of trillions of times as strong as the *gravitational* attraction between those same two magnetized needles. Why is it, then, that we are so aware of gravitational pulls and hardly at all aware of magnetic pulls? Why are astronomical bodies held together by gravitation, while we never hear of two bodies held together by some magnetic force?

The answer is that magnetism involves both an attraction and a repulsion, both of equal intensity.

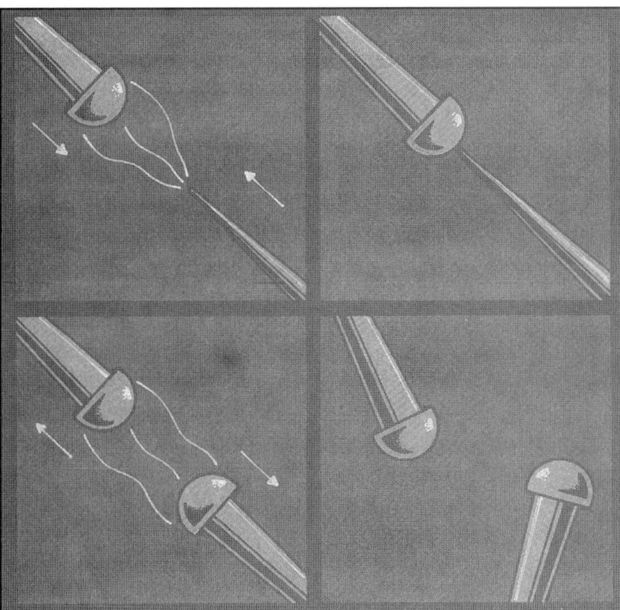

1. and 2. An unmagnetized iron needle will be attracted to either the North or the South pole of a magnet. Once magnetized, however, one end will be repelled, while the other will attract.

3. Unlike poles (N, S) attract.

4. Like poles (N, N or S, S) repel.

Gravitation involves *only* an attraction. There is no such thing as gravitational repulsion.

The world is full of magnets. As we shall see, every atom is a tiny magnet. The magnets of the Universe are turned every which way, however, and there is as much chance of repulsions here and there as attractions. On the whole, the two cancel each other and, by and large, we are left with a Universe in which there is not much magnetic attraction or repulsion overall.

Gravitation, however, involving only an attraction simply piles up, so to speak. Although the effect of gravitational pull is so small as to be unnoticeable for ordinary objects, or even for mountains, by the time you have objects the size of the Earth or the Sun the gravitational pull is enormous.

Still, magnetism does play its part. Suppose you place a piece of stiff paper over a magnetized steel bar. Scatter some iron filings upon the paper and tap it. The tapping allows the filings to move and to take up some natural position with respect to the magnet. When this is done, the filings arrange themselves in a group of curved lines extending from one pole of the magnet to the other. Peregrinus had noticed this, and, in 1831, the English scientist Michael Faraday (1791–1867) considered the subject.

To Faraday it seemed that the influence of the magnet stretched out through space in all directions in a magnetic field that weakened with distance according to the inverse square law. Through the field one could draw a vast number of lines (magnetic lines of force) that marked out regions where the strength of the magnetic field was the same. Such lines were followed by the iron filings and were thus made visible.

That is why magnetic needles in a compass point north and south. The Earth itself is a magnet, and the needles line up with the magnetic lines of force that go from one of Earth's magnetic poles to the other. (Earth's magnetic poles are located in the far north and the far south, but are a considerable distance from the geographic poles of rotation.) A great many other facts about magnets can be explained by the concept of the magnetic field and its lines of force, and Faraday's notion has remained valid ever since. (There are also gravitational and electric fields, and lines of force there, too.)

What about electricity, by the way? The English physicist William Gilbert (ca. 1544–1603) extended Thales's work on electrified substances. He explained in a book he published in 1600 that substances other than amber would also attract light objects if rubbed. Gilbert called all such objects electrics.

In 1733, the French chemist Charles François de Cisternay Dufay (1698–1739) experimented with rods of glass and of resin, both of which could be "electrified" when rubbed, and made capable of attracting light objects. Both would then attract small bits of cork, which were in turn, electrified.

A piece of cork electrified by glass would attract a piece of cork electrified by resin. Two pieces of cork, each electrified by glass, would however, repel each other—as would two pieces of cork, each electrified by resin. Dufay concluded, therefore, that there were two types of electricity. Each repelled itself, but attracted the other, as in the case of the two types of magnetic poles.

The American scholar Benjamin Franklin (1706–1790) took this one step further. He suggested, in 1747, that there was but one type of electricity, which all matter contained a normal amount of and which was undetectable. If certain objects were rubbed, however, then some of the electricity was removed, while if other objects were rubbed, some was added. Those objects that had an excess might be considered positively charged, those with a deficiency were negatively charged.

In such a case a positively charged object would attract a negatively charged one because contact would allow the excess charge in the first to flow into the second and make up the deficiency there. The two would cancel each other and leave two uncharged objects behind. (This was actually observed by Franklin in his experiments.) On the other hand, two positively charged objects would repel each other as would two negatively charged objects because in neither case was there a chance of charge flowing from one to the other.

It only remained for Franklin to decide which of the two types of electrically charged bodies had the excess and which the deficiency. There was no way of telling at the time, so Franklin chose arbitrarily. He decided that rubbed glass had an excess and should be considered positive (+), while rubbed resins had a deficiency and should be considered negative (–).

Ever since, people working with electric currents have assumed that current flows from positive to negative. Unfortunately, Franklin had a fifty-fifty chance of guessing right, and lost. It was the rod of resin that actually had the excess, so that the current really flows from negative to positive. That doesn't matter in electrical engineering, however. The results are the same whichever direction you imagine the current flowing, provided you stick by your decision and don't change your mind in midcourse.

Combining the Phenomena

There are, then, four phenomena that can make themselves felt across a vacuum: light, electricity, magnetism, and gravitation. All four might be pictured as making use of ether, but are they making use of the same ether, or does each one have an ether of its own? There was no way of telling, but sometimes light was pictured as waves in the luminiferous ether, from a Latin expression meaning "light carrying." Might there also turn out to be an "electriferous," a "magnetiferous," and a "gravitigerous" ether?

To be sure, the differences among the four were not equally great. Light did not seem either to attract or repel. Gravitation only attracted. Electricity and magnetism, however, each both attracted and repelled, and did so in much the same way with likes repelling and unlikes attracting. Of these last two, one seemed to arise out of the other.

In 1819, the Danish physicist Hans Christian Oersted (1777–1851) was lecturing on the electric current, and as a demonstration (it is not clear what he was trying to show), he brought a compass near a wire through which an electric current was flowing. To his own profound surprise, the compass needle reacted at once, pointing in a direction at right angles to the flow of current. When Oersted reversed the flow of current, the compass needle veered and pointed in the opposite direction, still at right angles to the current flow.

Oersted was the first to demonstrate an intimate connection between electricity and magnetism, but did not proceed in his investigations. Others who heard of the demonstration did, however, and at once.

In 1820, the French physicist Dominique François Arago (1786–1853) showed that a wire carrying an electric current acted as a magnet and could attract iron filings, something it would no longer do when the current ceased flowing. Because the wire was copper, this showed that magnetism was not necessarily an attribute of iron only, but might exist in any matter. Scientists began to speak of electromagnetism.

That same year, another French physicist, André Marie Ampère (1775–1836), showed that if two parallel wires had current flowing through each in the same direction, they attracted each other; if in opposite directions, they repelled each other.

If you twist a wire into a helix (the shape of a bedspring) and send a current through it, the current travels through each curve in the helix in the same direction. All of the curves attract one another and each sets up a magnetic field, every one reinforcing all of the others. The solenoid (coil of wire) then acts like a bar magnet with a North Magnetic Pole at one end and a South Magnetic Pole at the other.

In 1823, the British physicist William Sturgeon (1783–1850) wrapped wire about a U-shaped iron bar. The iron tended to intensity the magnetic field, and when the electric current was turned on, it became a surprisingly strong electromagnet.

In 1829, the American physicist Joseph Henry (1797–1878) used insulated wire (to prevent short-circuits), wrapping hundreds of turns of it about an iron bar, to produce an electromagnet that could lift phenomenal weights of iron when a current was passed through it.

Faraday then considered the reverse. If electricity could create magnetism, might not magnetism create electricity? He inserted an ordinary bar magnet into a helix of wire that was not connected to any battery that could start an electric current flowing in it. The magnet, nevertheless, experienced such a current when the magnet was pushed in, or pulled out. There was no current when the magnet was motionless at any point inside the helix. Apparently, the current flowed through the wire only when the wire cut across the magnetic lines of force, flowing in one direction as the magnet went in and in the other direction as it came out.

In 1831, Faraday worked out a system whereby a copper disc was turned between the poles of a magnet. An electric current was set up in the disc and flowed continually as long as the disc turned. It was an effort to keep it turning because it took work to push the disc across the magnetic lines of force. As long as this was done, however, by human or animal muscle, or by falling water, or by the force of steam produced by burning fuel, mechanical work was turned into electricity.

This time, it was Henry who reversed the situation. That same year, he invented the electric motor, in which the flow of electricity caused a wheel to turn.

All of these discoveries served to electrify the world (in a literal as well as a figurative sense) and to alter human society enormously. To scientists, however, the importance of these discoveries was that they increasingly demonstrated the close relationship between electricity and magnetism.

Indeed, there were those who began to think that there was a single electromagnetic field, one that at times, showed its electrical face to the world, and at times, its magnetic face. This reached its climax with the work of Maxwell. Between 1864 and 1873, he worked out the mathematical implications of Faraday's notions of fields and lines of force, and of the apparent connection of electric and magnetic fields. Maxwell ended by devising four comparatively simple equations (simple to mathematicians, at any rate) that described all known electrical and magnetic behavior. They have been known ever since as Maxwell's Equations.

Maxwell's Equations (whose validity is confirmed by all observations made since) show that electric fields and magnetic fields cannot exist separately. There is, indeed, only a combined electromagnetic field with an electric component and a magnetic component at right angles to each other.

If electric behavior and magnetic behavior were similar in all respects, the four equations would be symmetrical; they would exist in two mirror-image pairs. In one respect, however, the two phenomena do not match each other. An object can be either positively charged or negatively charged. In magnetic phenomena, on the other hand, the magnetic poles do not exist separately. Every object that shows magnetic properties has a North Magnetic Pole at one location and a South Magnetic Pole at another location. If a long magnetized needle, with a North Magnetic Pole at one end and a South Magnetic Pole at the other, is broken in the middle, the poles are *not* isolated. The end with the North Magnetic Pole instantly develops a South Magnetic Pole at the break, while the end with the South Magnetic Pole develops a North Magnetic Pole at the break.

Maxwell included this fact in his equations, which introduced a note of asymmetry. This has always bothered scientists, in whom there is a strong drive for simplicity and symmetry. This "flaw" in Maxwell's equations is something we'll return to later.

Maxwell showed that from his equations you can demonstrate that an oscillating electric field will produce, inevitably, and oscillating magnetic field, and so on indefinitely. This is the equivalent of an electromagnetic radiation moving outward, in wave form, at a constant speed. The speed of this radiation can be calculated by taking the ratio of certain units expressing magnetic phenomena to other units expressing electrical phenomena. This ratio works out to nearly 300,000 kilometers (186,290 miles) per second, which is the speed of light.

This could not be a coincidence. Light, it appeared, was an electromagnetic radiation. Maxwell's equations thus served to unify three of the four phenomena known to pass through a vacuum: electricity, magnetism, and light.

Only gravitation remained outside this unification. It seemed to have nothing to do with the unified three. Albert Einstein, in 1916, worked out his general theory of relativity, which improved on Newton's concept of gravitation. In Einstein's interpretation of gravity, which is now widely accepted as essentially correct, there should be gravitational radiation in the form of waves, analogous to electromagnetic radiation. Such gravitational waves, however, are much more subtle and feeble, and much more difficult to detect, than are electromagnetic waves. Despite some false alarms, they have not yet been detected at this moment of writing, although virtually no scientist in the field doubts that they exist.

Extending the Spectrum

Maxwell's Equations set no limitations on the period of oscillations of the field. There could be one oscillation per second or less, so that each wave would be 300,000 kilometers long, or more. There could also be a decillion oscillations per second or more, so that each wave would be a trillionth of a trillionth of a centimeter long. And there could be anything in between.

Light waves, however, represent only a tiny fraction of these possibilities. The longest wavelengths of visible light are 0.0007 millimeters long, and the shortest wavelengths of visible light are just about half this length. Does this mean there is electromagnetic radiation we don't see?

Through most of human history, the question as to whether light existed that could not be seen would have been considered a contradiction in terms. Light, by definition, was something that could be seen.

The German-British astronomer William Herschel (1738–1822) was, in 1800, the first to show this was not a contradiction after all. At that time it was thought that the light and heat one obtained from the Sun might be two separate phenomena. Herschel wondered if heat might be spread out in a spectrum just as light was.

Instead of studying the spectrum by eye, which noted only the light, Herschel studied it by thermometer, which measured the heat. He placed the thermometer at various places in the spectrum and noted the temperature. He expected that the temperature would be highest in the middle of the spectrum and that it would fall off at either end.

That did not happen. The temperature rose steadily as one progressed away from the violet, and reached its highest point at the extreme red.

Astonished, Herschel wondered what would happen if he placed the thermometer bulb *beyond* the red. He found, to his even greater astonishment, that the temperature rose to a higher figure there than anywhere in the visible spectrum. Herschel thought he had detected heat waves.

In a few years, however, the wave theory of light was established and a better interpretation became possible. Sunlight has a range of wavelengths that are spread out by a prism. Our retina reacts to wavelengths of light within certain limits, but sunlight has some waves that are longer than that of the visible red, and is therefore to be found beyond the red end of the spectrum. Our retina won't respond to such long waves, so we don't see them, but they are there anyway. They are called infrared rays, the prefix coming from a Latin word meaning "below," for you might view the spectrum as going from violet on the top to red on the bottom.

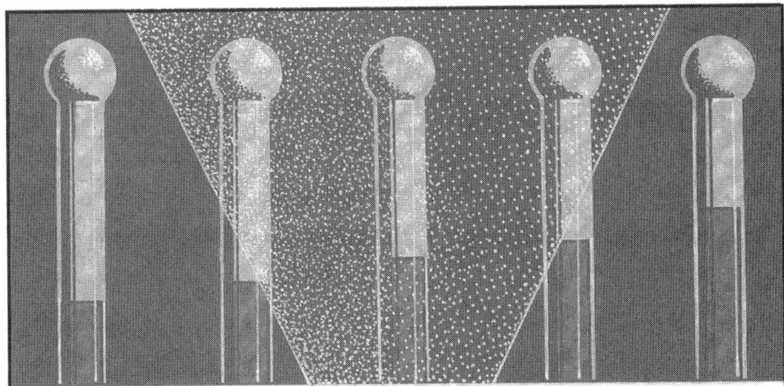

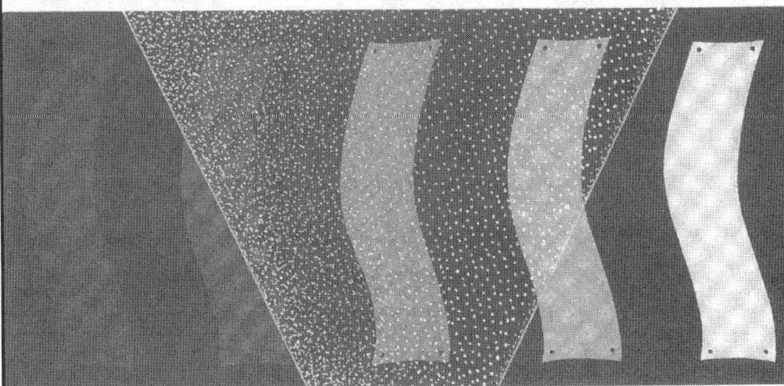

1. Infrared Light. In 1800, when William Herschel placed his thermometer in the dark area beyond the red end of the spectrum, he was surprised to record the highest temperature.

2. Ultraviolet Light. In 1770, Karl Wilhelm Scheele found that paper soaked in silver nitrate solution darkened most quickly when exposed to violet light. In 1801, John Wilhelm Ritter exposed the paper in the dark area beyond the violet and the paper darkened even more rapidly.

All light, when it strikes the skin, is either reflected or absorbed. When absorbed, its energy speeds up the motion of the molecules in our skin and this makes itself felt as heat. The longer the wavelength, the deeper it penetrates the skin and the more easily absorbed it is. Hence, although we can't see the infrared, we can feel it as heat, and the thermometer, for similar reasons, can record it as such.

It would help, of course, if it could be shown that infrared rays were actually made up of waves like those of light, but with longer wavelengths. One might allow two beams of infrared rays to overlap and produce interference fringes, but no one would be able to see them. Perhaps they could be detected by thermometer, with the temperature going up each time the instrument passed through a "brighter" area, and going down each time it passed through a "dimmer" one.

In 1830 the Italian physicist Leopoldo Nobili (1784–1835) invented a thermometer that would do the job. One of his co-workers was the Italian physicist Macedonio Melloni (1798–1854). Because glass would absorb a great deal of the infrared rays, Melloni made use of prisms formed of rock salt, which is transparent to infrared rays. As a result, interference fringes were set up and Mobili's thermometer showed that they existed. By 1850 Melloni had demonstrated that infrared rays showed all of the properties of light without exception—except that they could not be seen with the naked eye.

What about the other end of the spectrum, where violet light deepens into darkness? That story began in 1614, when the Italian chemist Angelo Sala (1576–1637) noticed that silver nitrate, a perfectly white compound, darkened on exposure to sunlight. We now know this happens because light contains energy and can force apart the molecule of silver nitrate, producing finely divided silver, which appears black.

About 1770 the Swedish chemist Karl Wilhelm Scheele (1742–1768) went into the subject in more detail, making use of the solar spectrum, which wasn't known in Sala's time. He soaked thin strips of white paper in solutions of silver nitrate, let them dry, and placed them in various parts of the spectrum. He found that the strips of paper darkened least quickly in the red, more quickly as one went farther and farther from the red, and most quickly in the violet. This happens (as we now know for reasons that will be explained later) because light increases in energy as one goes from red to violet.

Once Herschel discovered infrared rays in 1810, however, it occurred to the German chemist Johann Wilhelm Ritter (1776–1810) to check the other end of the spectrum. In 1801, he soaked strips of paper in silver nitrate solution and repeated Scheele's experiment except that he placed strips of paper *beyond* the violet, where no light was visible. As he suspected they might, the strips of paper darkened in this lightless region even more rapidly than they would in violet light. This represented the discovery of ultraviolet rays, where the prefix is from the Latin for "beyond."

Infrared and ultraviolet radiation existed just at the borders of the visible spectrum. Maxwell's Equations made it seem that there could be radiation far beyond the borders. If such radiation could be found, then Maxwell's Equations would be supported very strongly, for without them no one would have suspected such radiation might exist.

In 1888 the German physicist Heinrich Rudolf Hertz (1857–1894) made use of a rectangular wire, with a gap in it, as a detecting device. He set up an oscillating electric current in his laboratory. As the electric current oscillated, moving first this way, then that, it should emit electromagnetic radiation, with the radiation wave moving up while the current is going one way and then down when it is moving the other way. Such an electromagnetic wave should have a very long wavelength because, even if the oscillating electric current changes direction every small fraction of a second, light can move quite far between changes.

Hertz's rectangular wire would gain an electric current if the electromagnetic wave crossed it, and there would be a spark across the gap. Hertz got his spark. In addition, as he moved his rectangular wire here and there in the room, he got a spark where the wave was very high or very low, but no spark where it was in between. In this way, he could map the wave and determine its length.

Hertz had discovered what came to be called radio waves, which lay far beyond the infrared radiation and could have wavelengths of anywhere from centimeters to kilometers.

No one questioned Maxwell's equations after that. If there was a luminiferous ether, it carried electricity and magnetism also. If there was another ether, it existed only for gravitation.

In 1895, by the way, electromagnetic radiation was discovered far beyond the ultraviolet, with wavelengths exceedingly small. We will get to that later, after we consider a few other matters.

Dividing Energy

Electricity, magnetism, light, and gravitation are all forms of energy, where energy is anything that can be made to do work. These forms of energy certainly seem different from one another, but one can be turned into another. As we have already seen, electricity can be turned into magnetism, and vice versa, and a vibrating electromagnetic field can produce light. Gravitation can cause water to fall, with the falling water turning a turbine that can force a conductor through magnetic lines of force to produce electricity. Interconversions of energy and work represent the field of thermodynamics.

Such conversions are never completely efficient. Some energy is always lost in the process. The lost energy does not, however, disappear but makes it appearance as heat, which is still another form of energy. If heat is taken into account, then no energy is ever totally lost, nor does any energy ever appear out of nowhere. In other words, the total amount of energy in the Universe seems to be constant.

This is the Law of Conservation of Energy, or the first law of thermodynamics, which was finally placed in compelling terms in 1847 by the German physicist Hermann Ludwig Ferdinand von Helmholtz (1821–1894).

In a way, heat is the most fundamental form of energy, for any other form of energy can be converted *completely* into heat, while heat cannot be converted completely into nonheat energy. For this reason, heat is the most convenient phenomenon through which to study thermodynamics, a word, by the way, which is from the Greek for "movement of heat."

Heat had been closely studied by scientists ever since the first truly practical steam engine had been invented, in 1769, by the British engineer James Watt (1736–1819). Once the Law of Conservation of Energy was understood, the study of heat became even more intense.

After the advent of the steam engine there were two theories of the nature of heat. Some scientists thought of it as a type of subtle fluid that could travel from one piece of matter to another. Others thought of heat as a form of motion, of atoms and molecules moving or vibrating.

The latter suggestion, or the kinetic theory of heat (where kinetic is from a Greek word for "motion"), was finally established in the 1860s as the correct one when Maxwell and the Austrian physicist Ludwig Eduard Boltzmann (1844–1906) worked it out mathematically. They showed that everything that was known about heat could be interpreted satisfactorily by dealing with atoms and molecules that were moving or vibrating. As in the case of gases, the average speed ("velocity") of motion or vibration of the atoms and molecules making up *anything* is the measure of its temperature if the mass of the atoms and molecules is also taken into account. The total kinetic energy (which takes into account both mass and velocity) of all of those moving particles is the total heat of the substance.

Naturally then, the colder an object gets, the slower the motion of its atoms and molecules. If it gets cold enough, the kinetic energy of the particles reaches a minimum. It can then get no colder, and the temperature is at absolute zero. This notion was first proposed and made clear in 1848 by the British mathematician William Thomson (1824–1907), better known by his later title of Lord Kelvin. The number of Celsius degrees above absolute zero is the absolute temperature of a substance. If absolute zero is equal to –273.15° C, 0° C is equal to 273.15° K (for Kelvin) or 273.15° A (for absolute).

Any body at a temperature higher than that of its surroundings tends to lose heat as electromagnetic radiation. The higher the temperature, the more intense the radiation. In 1879, the Austrian physicist Joseph Stefan (1835–1893) worked this out exactly. He showed that the total radiation increased as the fourth power of the absolute temperature. Thus, if the absolute temperature was increased two times, say from 300° K to 600° K (that is, from 27° C to 327° C), then the total radiation would be increased $2 \times 2 \times 2 \times 2$, or 16 times.

Formerly, about 1860, the German physicist Gustav Robert Kirchhoff (1824–1887) had established the fact that any substance at a temperature lower than that of its surroundings would absorb light of particular wavelengths, and would then emit those same wavelengths when its temperature rose above that of its surroundings. It follows that if a substance absorbs *all* wavelengths of light (a "black body," in that it reflects none of them), it will emit all wavelengths when heated.

No object actually absorbs all wavelengths of light, in the usual sense of the word, but an object with a small hole in it does so after a fashion. Any radiation that finds its way into the hole is not likely to find its way out again and is finally absorbed in the interior. Therefore, when such an object is heated, black-body radiation—all of the wavelengths—should come pouring out of the hole.

This notion was first advanced by the German physicist Wilhelm Wien (1864–1928) in the 1890s. When he studied such black-body radiation, he found that a wide range of wavelengths was emitted, as was to be expected, and that the very long and very short wavelengths were low in quantity, with a peak somewhere in between. As the temperature rose, Wien found that the peak moved steadily in the direction of shorter wavelength. He announced this in 1895.

Stefan's Law and Wien's Law fit our experience. Suppose an object is at a temperature a little higher than that of our own body. If we put our hands near that object, we can feel a little warmth radiating from it. As the temperature of the object rises, the radiation becomes more noticeable and the peak radiation is at a shorter wavelength. A kettle of boiling water will deliver considerable warmth if our hand is placed near it. If the temperature is raised still higher, an object will eventually give off perceptible radiation at wavelengths short enough to be recognized by our retina as light. We first see red light because that is the light with the longest wavelength, and is the first to be emitted. The object is then red-hot. Naturally, most of the radiation is still in the infrared, but the tiny fraction that comes off in the visible portion of the spectrum is what we notice.

As the object continues to rise in temperature, it glows more and more bright. The color changes, too, as more and more of the shorter-wave light is emitted. As the object continues to grow still hotter, it becomes even brighter and the color undergoes another change as more, and shorter, wavelengths of light are emitted. The glow becomes more orange, and then yellow. Eventually, when something is as hot as the Sun's surface, it is white-hot, and the peak of the radiation is actually in the visible light region. If it grows still hotter, it becomes blue-white, and eventually, although it is brighter than ever (assuming we can look at it without destroying our eyes in the same instant), the peak is in the ultraviolet.

This heat/light progression created a problem for nineteenth-century scientists because it was difficult to make sense out of the pattern of black-body radiation. Toward the end of the 1890s, the British physicist John William Strutt, Lord Rayleigh (1842–1919), assumed that every wavelength had an equal chance of being radiated in black-body radiation. On that assumption, he worked out an equation that showed quite well how the radiation would increase in intensity as one went from very long wavelengths to shorter wavelengths. This equation, however, didn't provide for a peak wavelength, to be followed by a decline, as one approached still shorter wavelengths.

Instead the equation implied that the intensity would continue going up without limit as the wavelengths got shorter. This meant that any body should radiate chiefly in the short wavelengths, getting rid of all of its heat in a blast of violet, ultraviolet, and beyond. This is sometimes called the Violet Catastrophe. But the Violet Catastrophe does not take pace, so there must be something wrong with Rayleigh's reasoning. Wien himself worked out an equation that would fit the distribution of short wavelengths of black-body radiation, but it wouldn't fit the long wavelengths. It seemed as though physicists could explain either half of the radiation range, but not the whole.

The problem was taken up by the German physicist Max Karl Ernst Ludwig Planck (1858–1947). He thought there might be something wrong with Rayleigh's assumption that every wavelength had an equal chance of being radiated in black-body radiation. What if the shorter the wavelength, the less the chance of its being radiated?

One way of making this seem plausible is to suppose that energy is not continuous and can't be broken up into smaller and smaller pieces forever. (Until Planck's time, the continuity of energy had been taken for granted by physicists. No one had wondered if energy, like matter, might consist of tiny particles that couldn't be divided further.)

Planck assumed that the fundamental bit of energy was larger and larger as the wavelength grew smaller and smaller. This meant that for a given temperature, the radiation would rise in intensity as wavelengths grew shorter, just as the Rayleigh equation indicated. Eventually though, for wavelengths shorter still, the mounting size of the energy unit would increase the difficulty of getting enough energy into one place in order to radiate it. There would be a peak, and as the wavelengths continued to decrease, the radiation would actually decline.

As the temperature went up and the heat grew more intense, it would be easier to radiate the larger energy units and the peak would move in the direction of shorter wavelengths, just as Wien's Law would require. In short, the use of the energy units that Planck postulated completely solved the problem of black-body radiation.

Planck called these energy units quanta (quantum in the singular), which is a Latin word meaning "how much?" What counted, after all, in the answer to the black-body radiation puzzle was how much energy there is in the quanta of different wavelengths of radiation.

Planck advanced his quantum theory, and the equation it made possible for black-body radiation (which agreed with the actual observations both for long wavelengths and short wavelengths), in 1900. This theory proved so important—far more important than Planck at the time could possibly imagine—that all of physics prior to 1900 are called classical physics, and all of physics after 1900 are called modern physics. For his work on black-body radiation, Wien received a Nobel prize in 1911, and Planck received one in 1918.

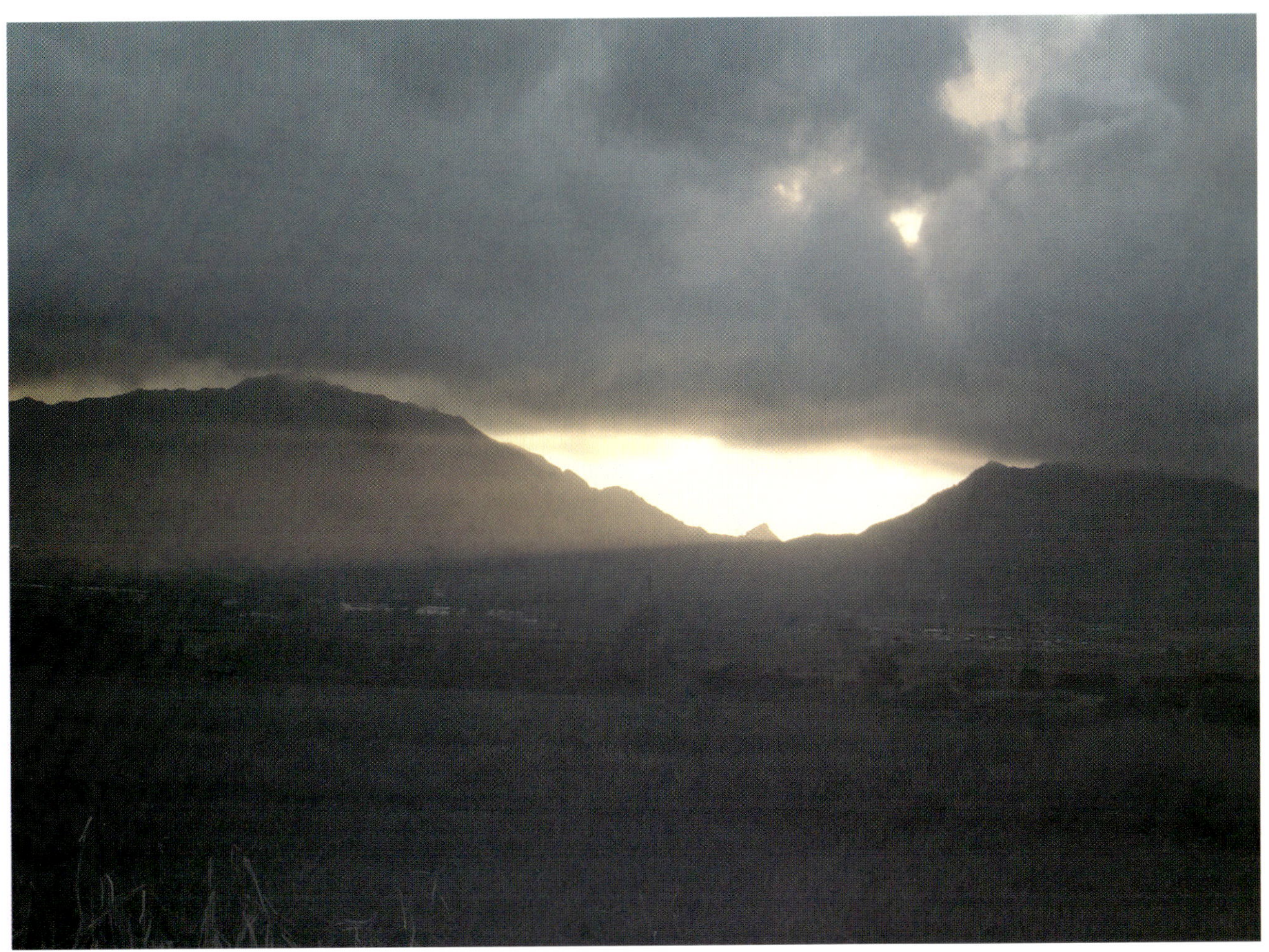

Mountains above the Dole Pineapple Plantation in Hawaii. A highway of pure white light finds its way through a rainy afternoon cloud burst. Photo by Alan Burner.

Chapter Two Project Proposal

The Project—Color Mixing: Saturation, Intensity and Value Chart

We have chosen a somewhat restricted pallet of primary colors for this particular exercise (see Special Note) illustrating the effects of mixing pairs of colors. (L) and then (R) refers to color placement on the *left* and on the *right*. For example: in Group One (top left corner of the composition) Hansa Yellow is applied full saturation in the left square, and Ultramarine Blue is applied full saturation, to the opposite right-hand square, with gradient intensities in between:

- Hansa Yellow (L), Ultramarine Blue (R)[Top Left Quadrant] **Group 1**
- Cadmium Yellow Light (L), Cerulean Blue(R)[Center Left Quadrant] **Group 2**
- Cadmium Yellow Light (L), Ultramarine Blue(R) [Bottom Left Quadrant] **Group 3**
- Cadmium Yellow Light (L), Quinachridone Red(R) [Top Right Quadrant] **Group 4**
- Hansa Yellow Light (L), Cadmium Red Light(R) [Center Right Quadrant] **Group 5**
- Hansa Yellow Light (L), Quinachridone Red(R) [Bottom Right Quadrant] **Group 6**

Chart Layout (see student color chart on last page of the project proposal):

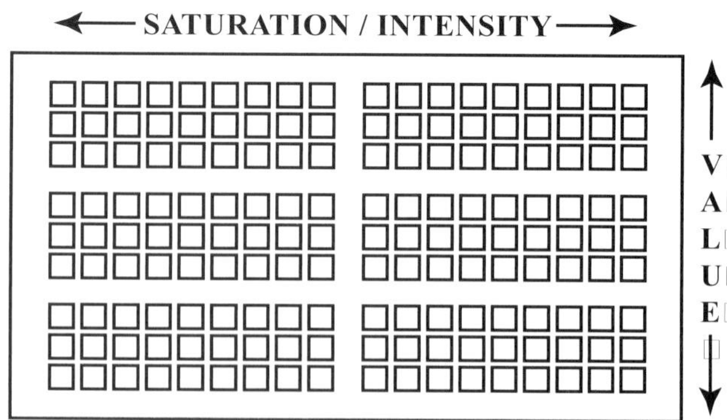

There will be six groups of color patches, each group will contain 27 color patches. Line one, two and three are nine patches across. The top row of horizontal patches indicates color intensity changes in saturation. The center and bottom row of horizontal patches will illustrate value changes.

Method:

Begin first by taping off the color patch grid system with 1/4" wide artist's tape or drafting tape, according to the specification measurements below. Using the top left group as an example, we are changing intensities by working our way across the saturation/intensity patches, from left to right. The student will be changing the intensity of Hansa Yellow (1st left side square) to green (5th center square), and ultimately back to ultramarine blue (9th right side square). We will use *Group One* as the example as follows:

- To start with, saturated Hansa Yellow should be painted in the first upper left corner patch in column one.
- Then in the upper right corner of that same group, paint in the ninth patch with saturated *ultramarine blue.*

- Pour a puddle of Hansa Yellow onto a dedicated mixing surface.
- Next, separate a small puddle of Hansa Yellow from the larger puddle, and add enough white to that smaller puddle in order to produce a lighter yellow value. Paint this on the patch directly under the saturated patch which is above.
- Now, add white again to the same smaller tinted puddle, to increase the lightness of the existing light yellow value, all the more. Discard the remaining portion when finished.
- Next, add a very small amount of ultramarine blue to the larger original Hansa Yellow puddle to produce a slightly darker Yellow intensity, and paint this onto the second patch on the horizontal top row, next to the first saturated yellow patch.
- Again, separate a very small puddle from the large darker yellow puddle, and add enough white to produce a lighter value of that mixture. Apply to the second horizontal patch.
- Now, add white again to lighten that mixture and paint it in the next patch down.
- One more time, add even more white again to get the lightest value on the last patch vertically.
- Repeat the process until you have completed all nine color bars across.

Hint: When adding white to the Hansa Yellow puddle, instead think about adding a small amount of the yellow portion to a small white puddle. This helps to conserve the paint, so that you won't use as much white. It is easier to darken a color, than to lighten it.

Remember, as acrylic paint dries it will transform into a darker tint. When you begin the value color patches, you must mix more white into the *intensity-modified* pigment than you may first think. This is a common problem, and if you do not develop your sensibility about pigments drying darker, you will always struggle when creating contrasts.

Project Specifications:

- All color patches are 1" x 1"
- The vertical space between groups should be one inch
- Space between all color patches vertical and horizontal is 1/4" wide
- One inch spacing between each group horizontally, as well as the center space between groups 1, 2, 3 and 4, 5, 6.
- Center the six groups on the 18" x 24" horizontal composition (140 lb watercolor paper)
- Acrylic paints are suggested.

Neatness Factor:

We want to stress quality. Please be sure to present a clean, well organized and hard-edged presentation of your color chart. The crisp, neatly organized project is always more effectual when the student demonstrates a concern about every detail.

Special Note About Primary Colors and Hue Selections:

- **Phthalo Blue, Hansa Yellow,** and **Quinacridone Magenta** are three of the more traditionally used, in order to achieve optimal results. However, a somewhat more *limited palette of primary colors* has been selected in order to develop greater sensitivity about changing intensities and values in hue.

  For example, cadmium red light is the lightest possible red, before considering it to be orange. Most students tend to see it as orange or red-orange. Since this particular red is often mistaken for orange, it therefore demands greater skill and sensitivity when mixing yellow and red to produce the orange, and so on.

Sample Student Color Chart:

In Chapter One, we mixed mostly darker, stronger colors, with less intensity, with the exception of two groups of yellow. The first color chart is normally easier, in respect to achieving the appropriate gradations of intensity changes. This second chart will offer a greater challenge, in that we are dealing with all yellow variations. Remembering that yellow is the most intense and yet weakest of the spectrum colors, we then know that yellow is more susceptible to intensity and value changes. The slightest invasion of another color changes the character of yellow severely, in most cases.

This new problem will enhance your sensitivity in color mixing, because of the color's delicate nature.

Note: There is often a struggle with intensity gradation. Group One seems to be reasonably accomplished, yet on color patches seven and eight, there is too much of a transition, which affects the ninth patch of Ultramarine blue.

Group Two, exhibits a slight problem in that there is too much transition between color patch six and seven. By the time the student has reached the orange section, their competency level has risen. Working down the values in white tints we see an increasingly lighter row of color patches. Often the yellows in the third row cannot be photographed because of their lightness in value.

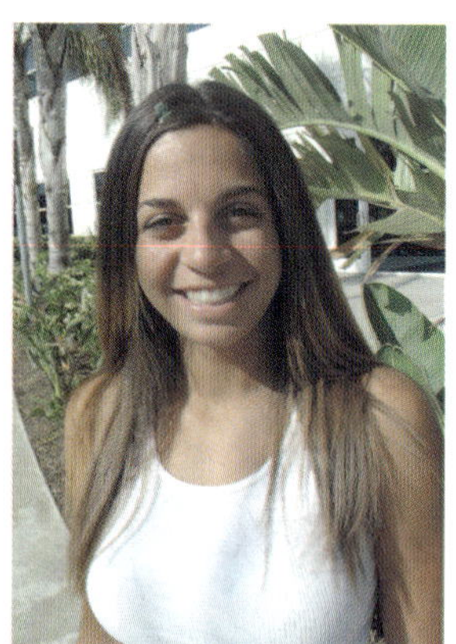

Mary Redaelli

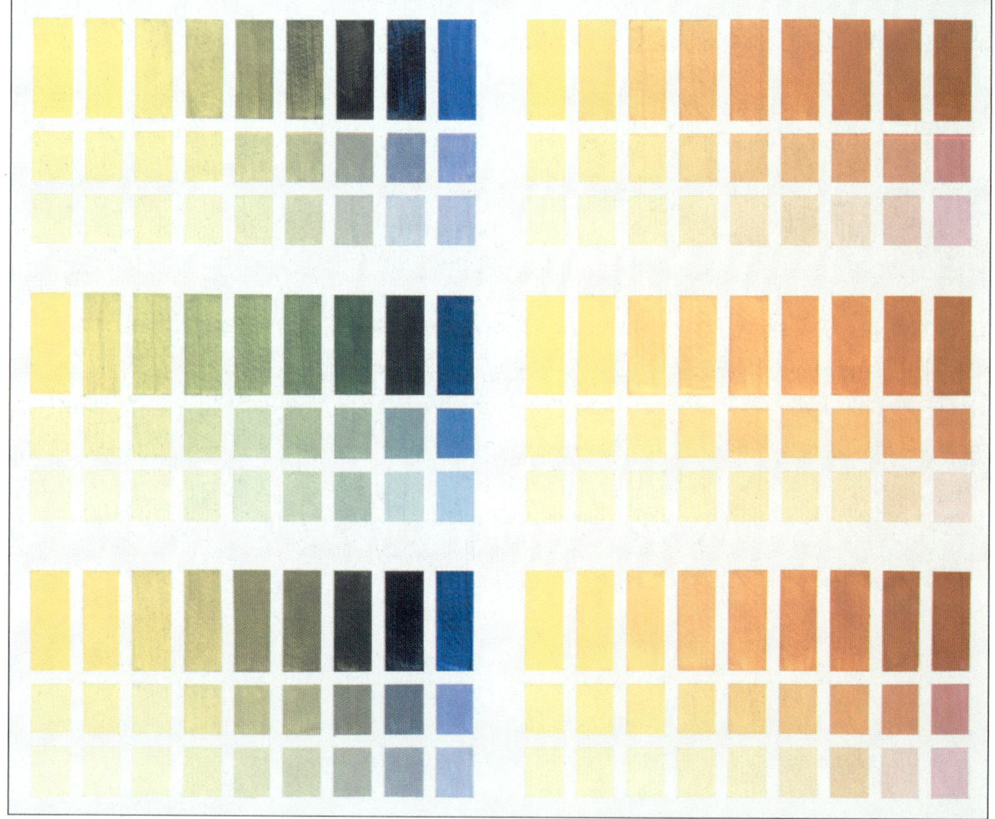

Student Color Chart by Mary Redaelli.

CONTRAST

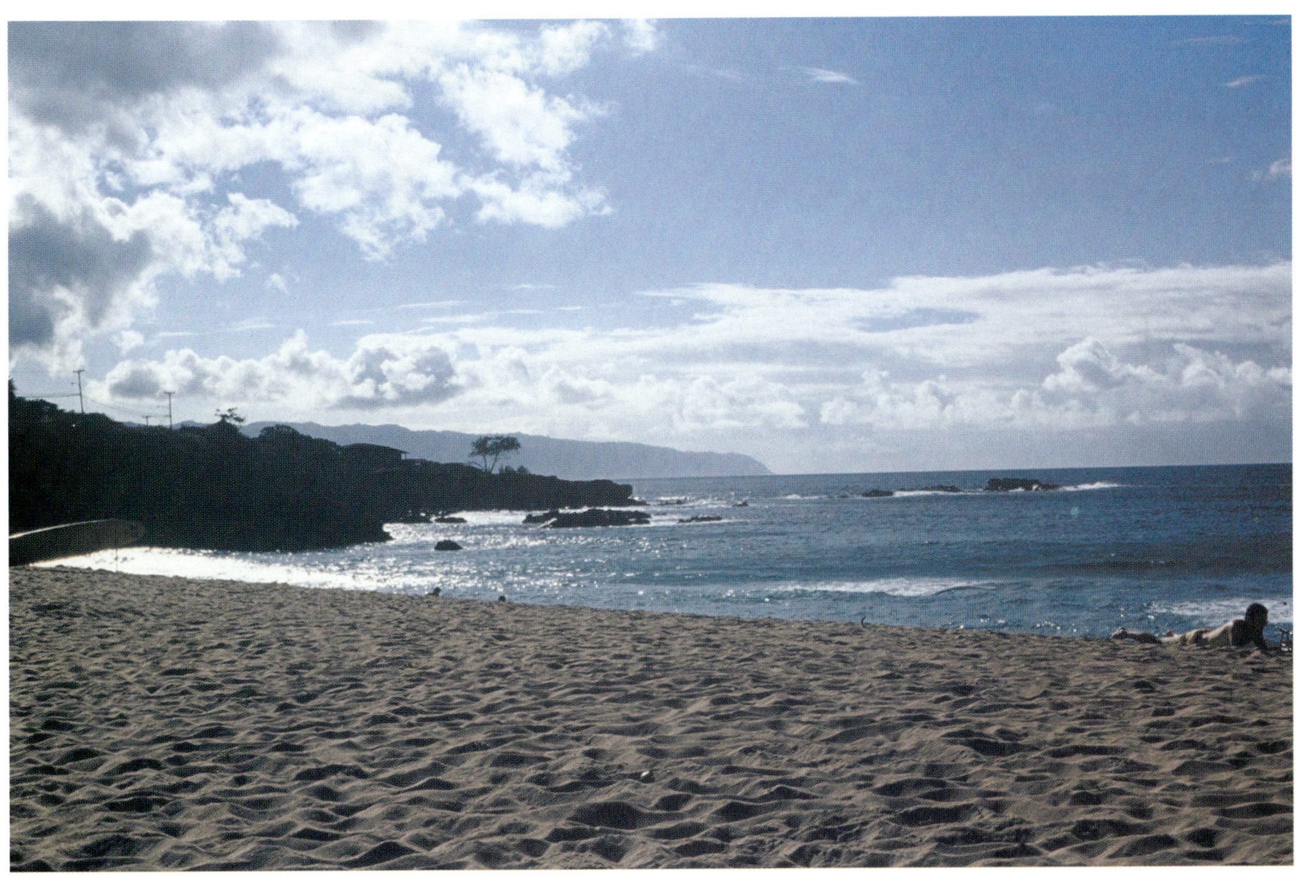

Complementary Contrasting Composition of Orange and Blue, Waimea Bay, Oahu, Hawaii.
Photo by Alan Burner.

CHAPTER THREE

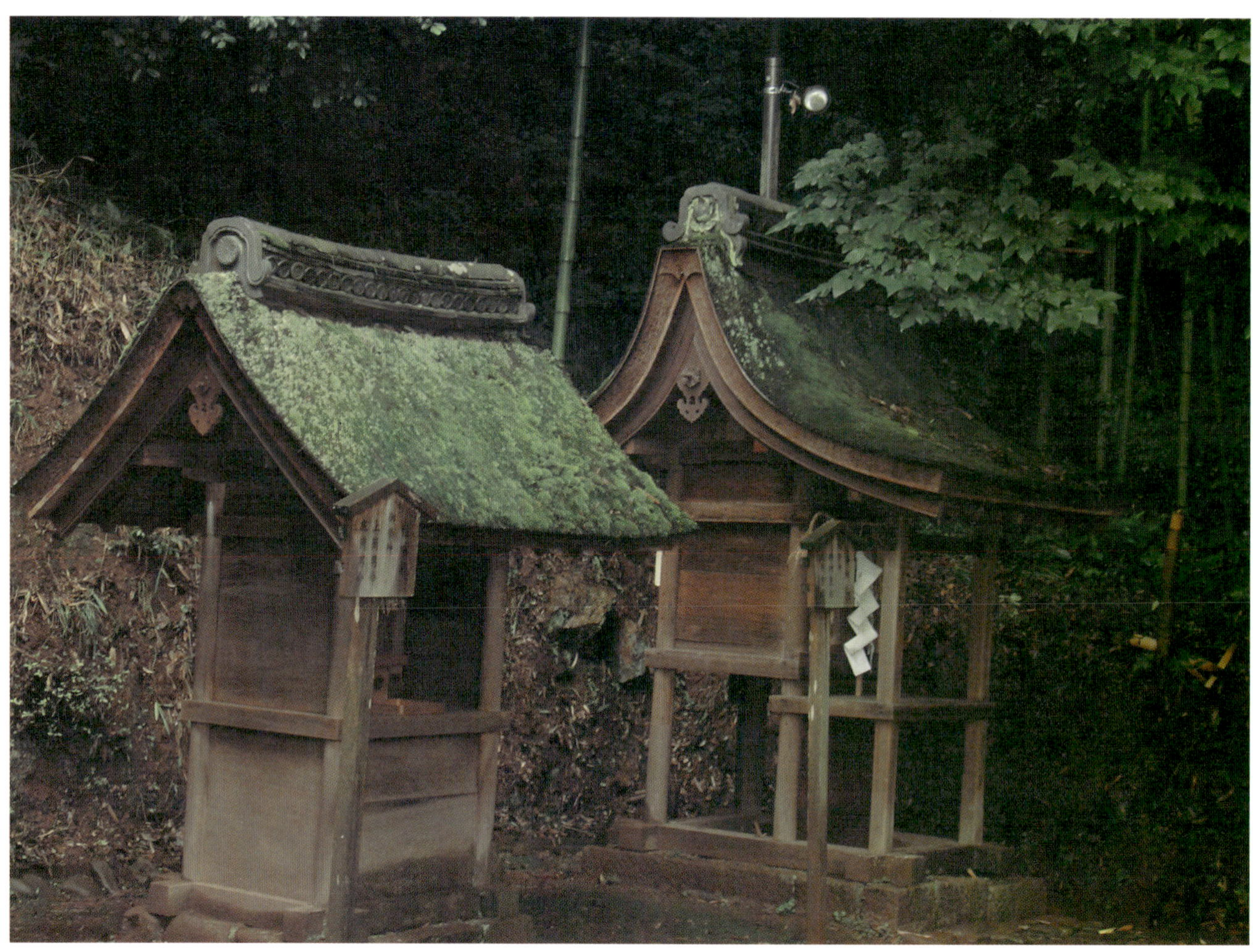

Red and green complementary contrast creates a serene and respectful mood setting for these two small shrines in Kyoto, Japan. Unlike dark and light contrast, it is a more subtle contrast, which nurtures the quiet beauty of the composition.
Photo by Alan Burner.

Introduction to Contrast

Understanding the functions of color contrast is vital as we learn about creating the illusion of compositional depth and distance (or the lack of it) as well as the forming of three-dimensional mass and focal points. Color contrast is also one of the chief components when we create emotional responses and mood contrasts.

Our primary focus, of course, will be on color contrast investigations. The very nature of contrast varies from high to low, depending on the degree of dissimilarity between values. Usually, when we refer to the maximum amount of difference in contrast, we are referring to *polar* or *diametrical* contrast. Color contrasts are very efficient at leading the viewer's eye to a desired location within a given composition or area.

As we study contrast through various projects and written assignments, it is important to remember the significance of contrast's character. We live

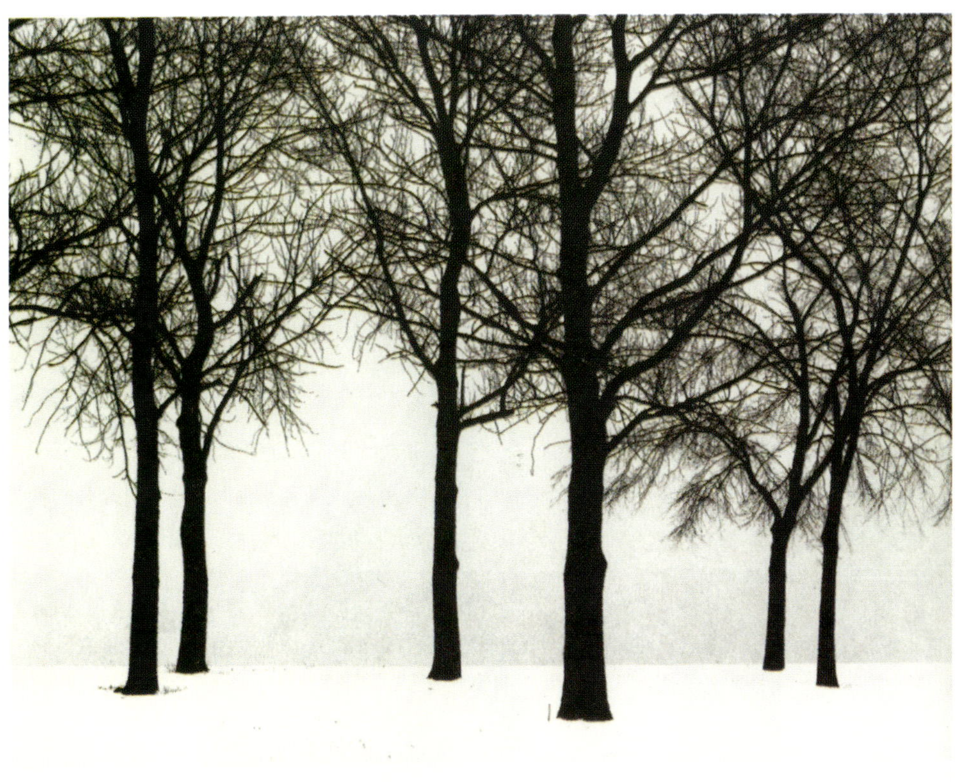

Gelatin Silver Print by Harry M. Callahan. The extreme light and dark contrast of the foreground trees and the background create powerful imagery, as well as a very lonely composition on a cold icy day. PaceWildensteinMacGill, New York, N.Y.

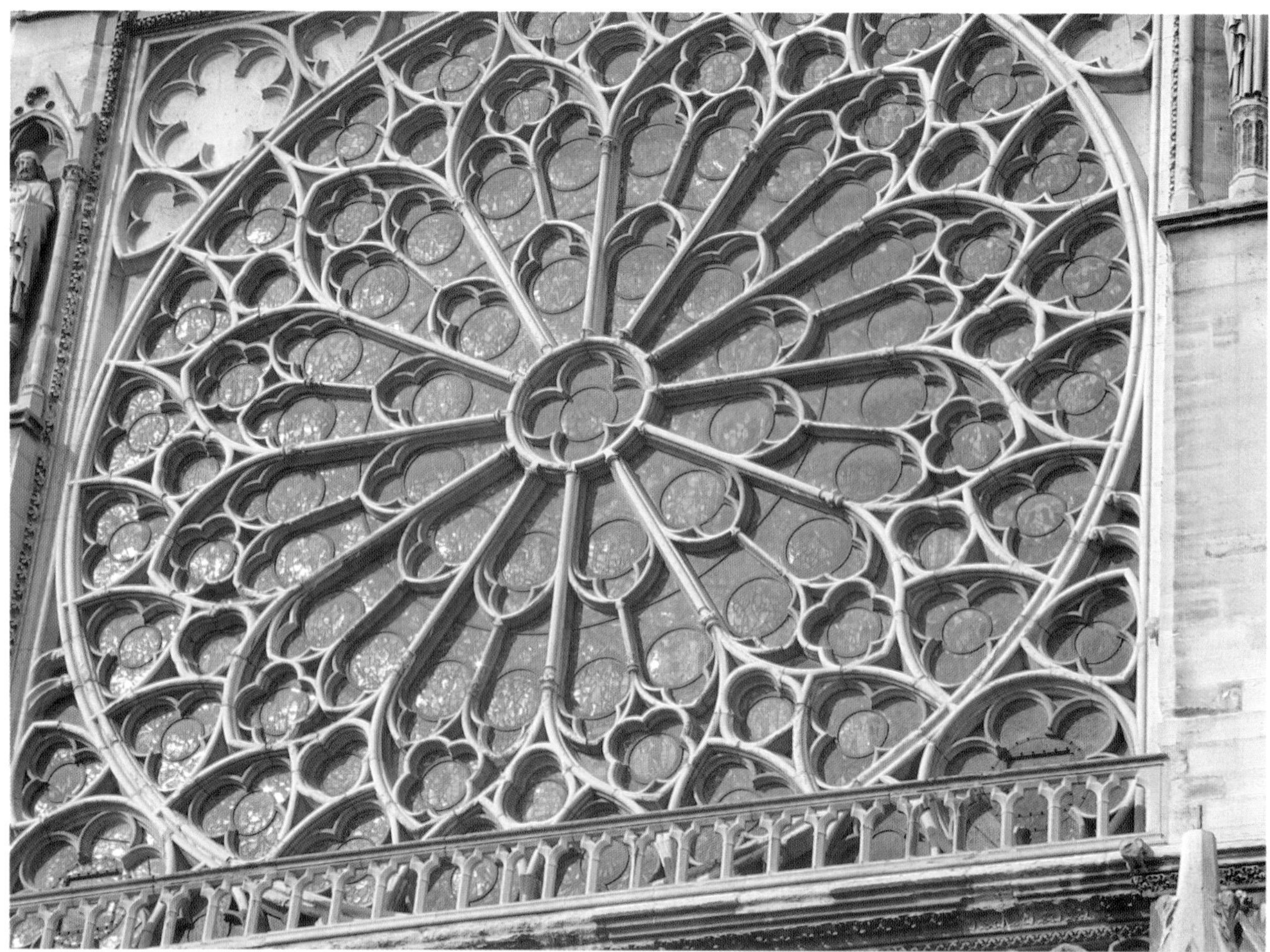

Exterior view of the South Rose Window, Notre Dame de Paris.
Photo by Alan Burner.

in a world of contrast—good and evil, love and hate, happy and sad, winners and losers, rich and poor, peace and war—not to mention the various cultural contrasts in our communities and around the world. Some of these contrasts are about choice, while others are predetermined. Since the world itself is made up of these variables, it then becomes more logical and obvious why color contrasts are significant. We must remember that *color's most valued asset is mood,* as we continue through the text, which is commensurate with the character of contrast, which also produces an abundance of mood variables, but by different means. We know as artists and designers that emotional responses are at the heart of the matter, and it is contrast that provides one of the keys to such response. Let's take a look now at the diversity of contrasts available to us.

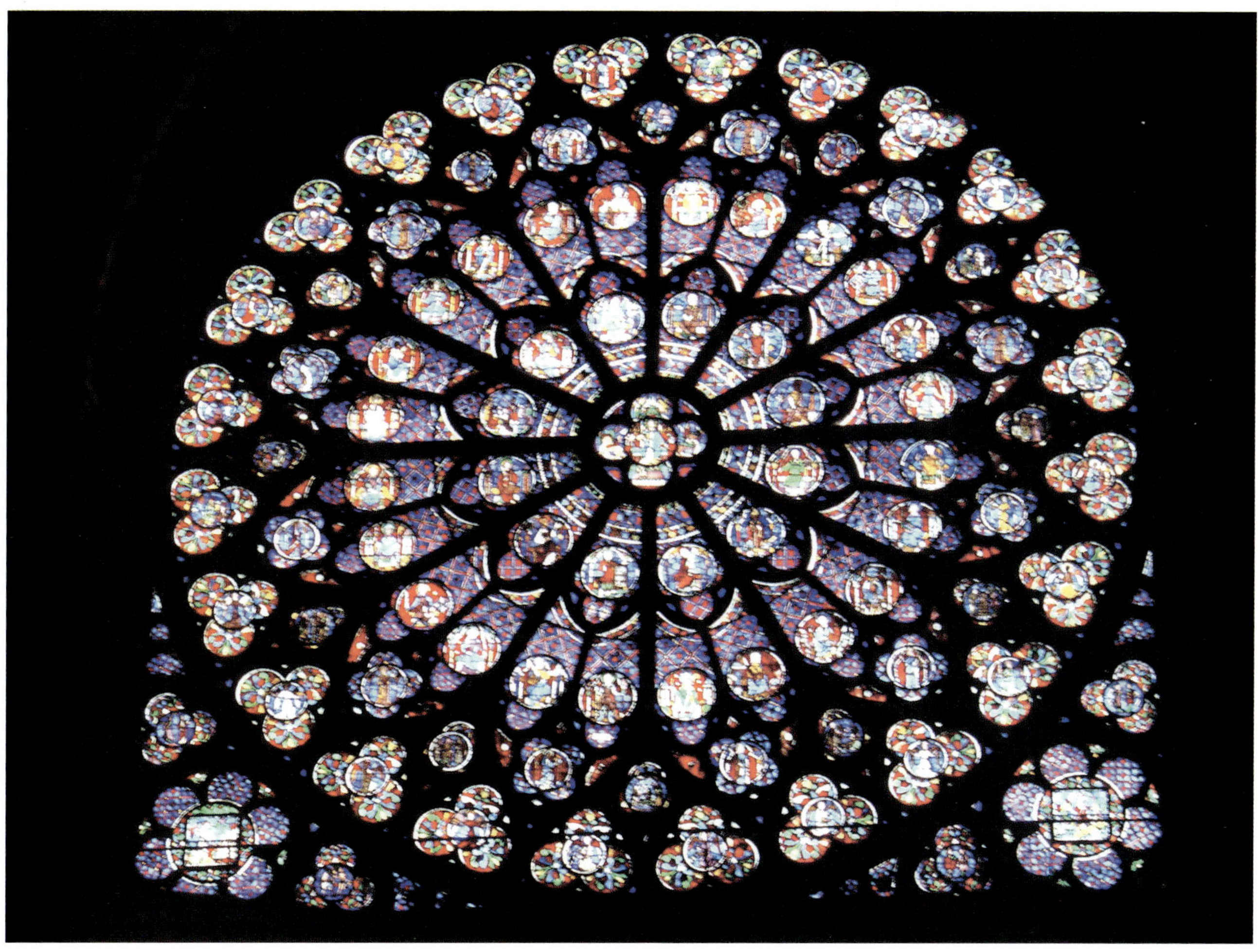

Interior view of the South Rose Window, Notre Dame de Paris.
Photo by Alan Burner.

The exterior of the South Rose Window of Notre Dame de Paris (opposite page) is flooded with spring sunlight, constantly bombarding it with the full spectrum of colors. The window, with its enormous size and Gothic elegance remains significant because of its beautiful tracery, structural integrity and actual function to translate light into color.

The interior of the South Rose Window of Notre Dame de Paris is quite another view. The high contrast of the solid Gothic tracery against the translucent colored glass radiates the sun's light throughout the Cathedral. It is the effect of *dark and light contrast* that truly transforms this colored diamond into heaven's gate, or the Eye of God.

On the following pages we will discuss the various types of contrasts and their importance.

Dark and Light Contrast

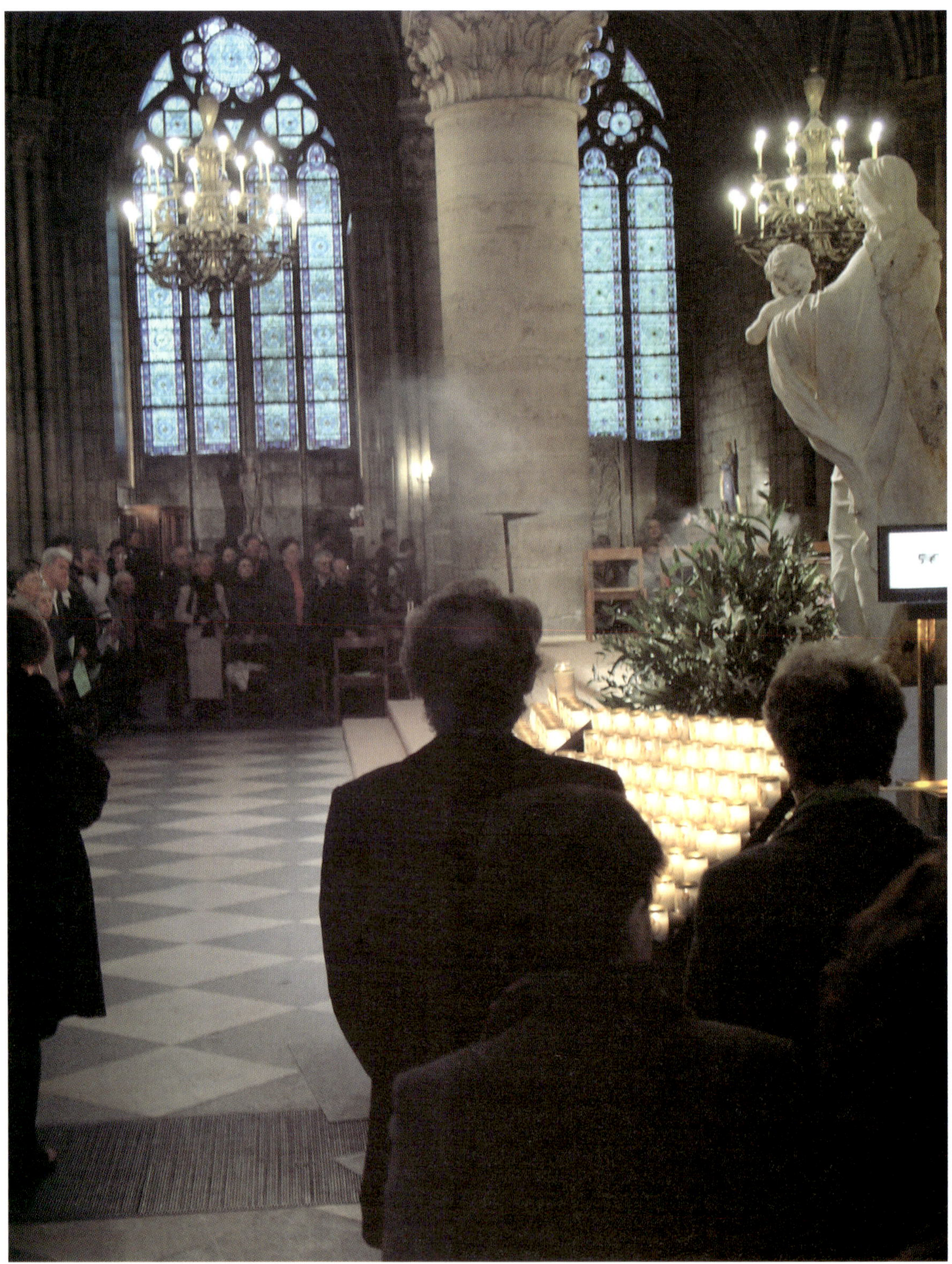

Sunday Morning Mass, Notre Dame de Paris, March 28th 2004. The dynamics of dark and light contrasts affect the interior of cathedral, which helps to create the dynamics commensurate with the mood of this Catholic Mass.
Photo by Alan Burner.

Dark and Light Contrast

The most extreme contrast is required for dark and light contrast. Therefore, it is optimally demonstrated in achromatic black and white and chromatically in violet and yellow. Extreme contrast always creates the most commanding statements. Certain essential functions are defined with the use of contrast, but before we look at the various examples of that, let's look at Picasso's *Charnel House* as an example of extreme contrast.

We notice that there are not only extremes of light and dark, but the weight of the painting is light to dark (or light to *heavy*), from top to bottom. The top one-third of the *Charnel House* is contour line, which causes the viewer's eyes to immediately shift downward to where the heavier, more weighted area of the composition remains. This weightier area is created by the employment of extreme black and white contrasts, juxtaposed with gray fragmented shapes. The dark areas dominate, pulling the figures of this disaster scene down to the floor. The contrast also aids to create a fragmented house of destruction, adding to the chaos illustrated by the linear elements, as well.

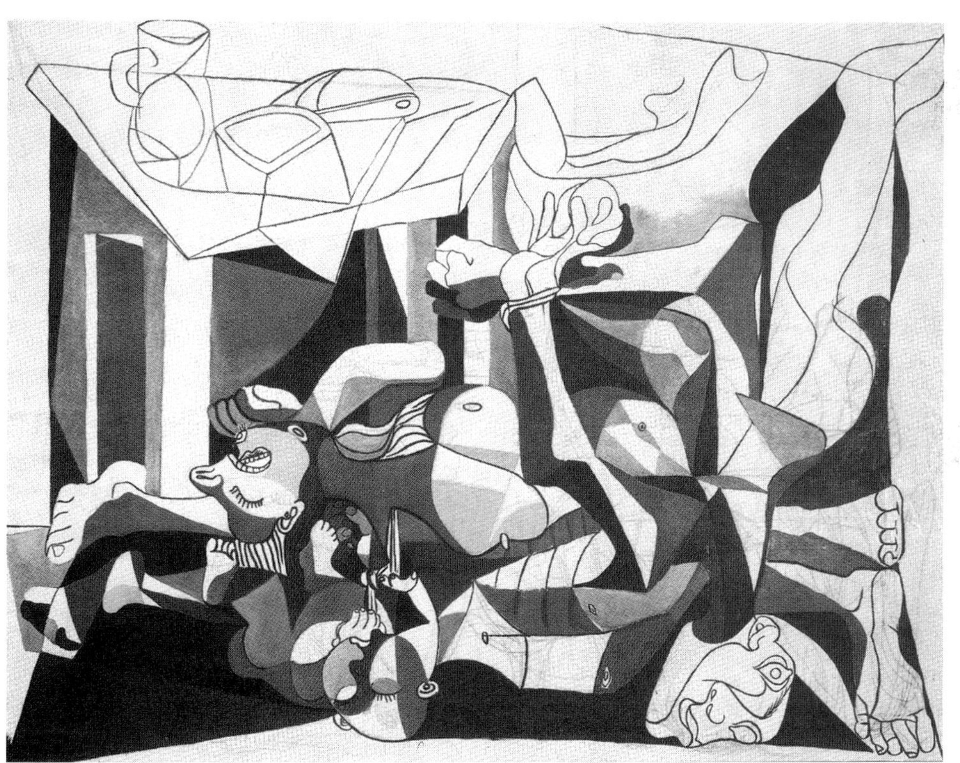

Pablo Picasso's achromatic painting *The Charnel House* 1944–45.

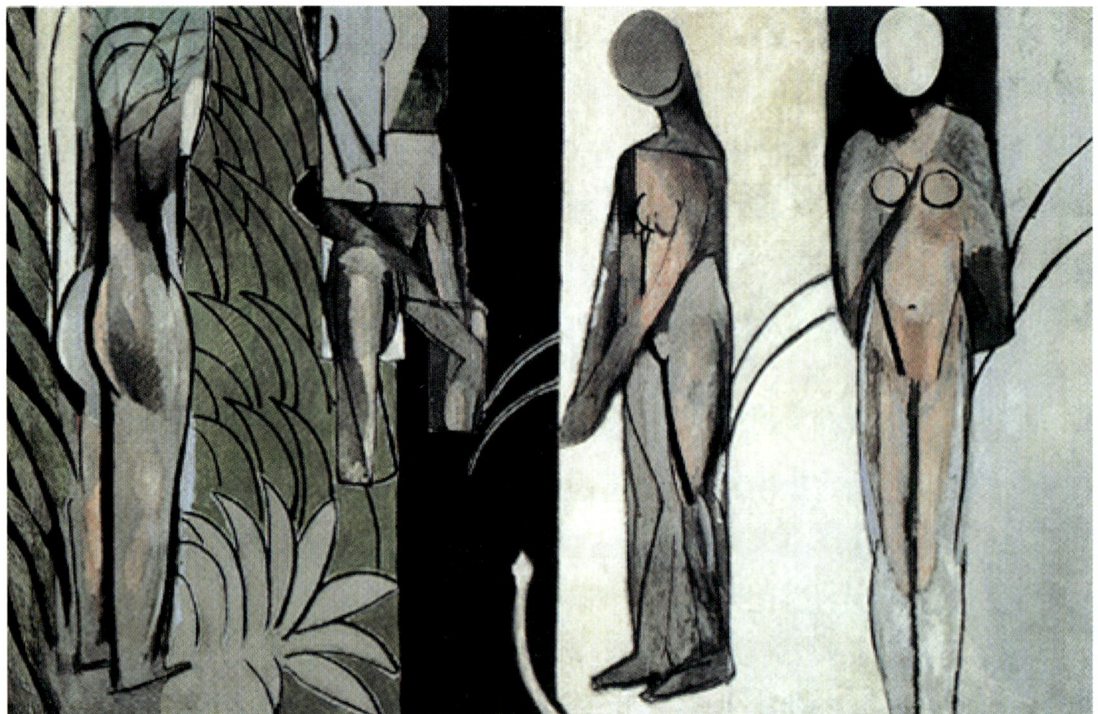

Bathers by the River by Matisee.

In Matisse's *Bathers by a River* we see a spatial division brought on in a different way by dark and light contrasts. The right side of the composition demonstrates high contrast between the background light green and the foreground figures of shaded green and orange tones. The right side, however, is weighted with a background of green, which relates to the dark orange values of the figures. Clearly there is contrast between the right side and the left of the composition, as well as between the background and foreground figures of the right, but minimal contrast is created on the left, between the background and foreground figures. The black vertical bar acts as sharp contrast on both sides, both dividing and helping the figures to make a transition from one side to the other. This particular contrast also acts as a transitional balance to one side or the other.

In *Artist and Goldfish* (opposite page) dark and light contrast is complemented by the introduction of limited areas of color. The composition is divided by quadrants of dark verticals, with a white lower ground that moves up to create a horizontal line against the gray-violet wall. The middle ground black vertical contrasted against the white lower horizontal creates a visual impact, which all leads the eye to focus on the goldfish bowl, also contrasted against the black ground. The yellow fruit helps to draw and hold the visual focus. The yellow fruit indirectly contrasts with its complement of violet in the upper background.

Let's take a closer look at the character of violet and yellow. We know that in the case of these complements, the maximum possibility of chromatic contrast can be achieved. Yellow has the most *intensity* of the spectral colors, it emits the high degree of brightness possible in color. Yellow is also, however, the *weakest* of all colors. The addition of the slightest amount of its complement violet, for example, will severely change the character of yellow, so much so that it will create an almost sickly, dulled response to the viewer. It is very susceptible to any outside invader.

Violet is the extreme opposite of yellow because it is the *least intense* of all spectral colors. If yellow

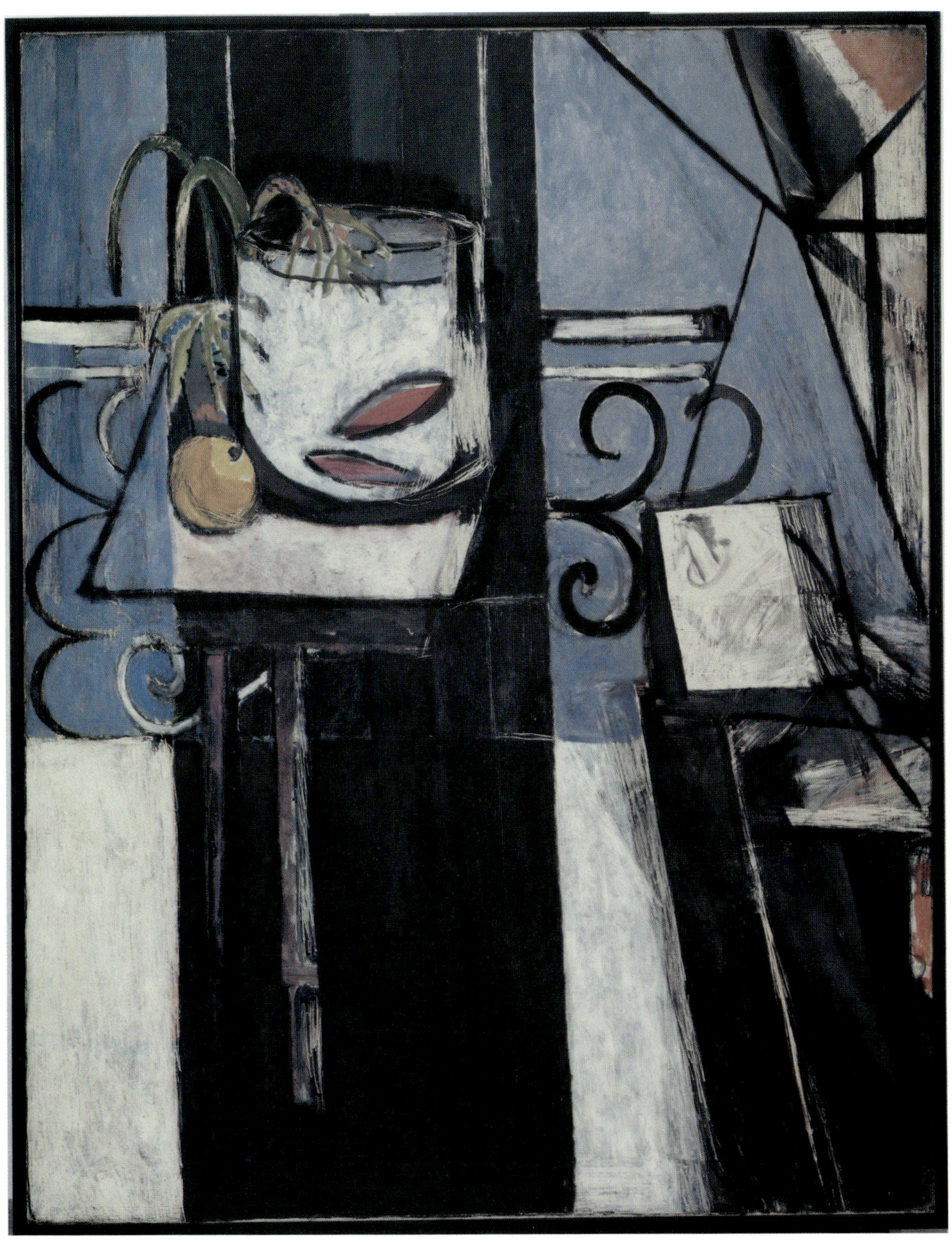

Artist and Goldfish by Henri Matisse.

possesses the maximum brightness possible, then violet has the most *dullness,* and is therefore the strongest. If we are to add the commensurable amount of yellow to violet, as we did violet to yellow, the result would be of no consequence. In fact, if we were to triple the amount of yellow to violet, we would still be unable to discern the difference. Violet, because of its strength, simply "eats" the yellow. Since yellow is so weak, it will then take a considerable amount of yellow to allow our eye to see the change.

In Helen Frankenthaler's *The Other Side of the Moon,* we can see a reasonable demonstration of the two weak and strong complements. First, look at the character of yellow. It is translucent and intense, almost as if we are experiencing the effects of an atmospheric condition, which allows us to travel infinitely into its deep space. It is only interrupted by the dark and opaque nature of the violet on the upper and right side of the composition, which then seems to absorb the translucent yellow into its darkness. The violet perimeter seems to pull the yellow into it's equally infinite, but mysterious, space never to be seen again.

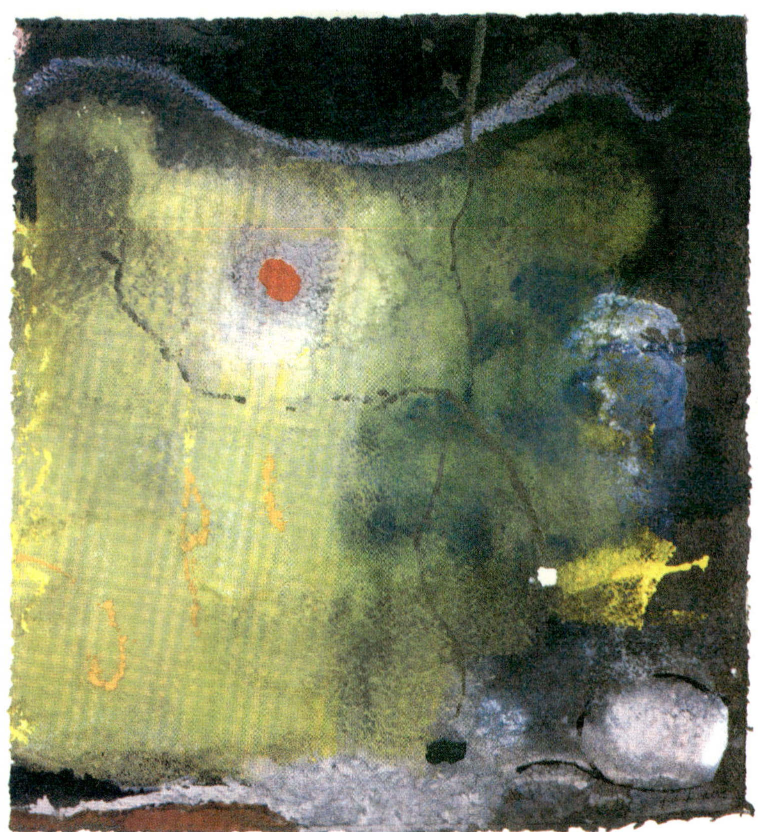

The Other Side of the Moon by Helen Frankenthaler.
Source: Knoedler & Company.

The Nature and Function of Dark and Light Contrast

Generally, it has been agreed upon that light advances in a composition and dark recedes. We will discuss why most agree that this is true in a general sense, but also point out that specifically there are many exceptions to that conclusion.

Let's begin with the general notion that light, or light colors, advance into the viewer's space. If we were to look at a simple sphere, we would immediately understand that if light is illuminating its surface, then the light would first make contact with the closest point on that surface, which means that light does advance, since it is closest to our eye. Anywhere there is an illuminated object, the light will advance, and the darker areas will recede. We are identifying specific objects *(object light)*, to lend credibility to this rule. Similarly, a portrait is the same, in that the areas that receive light first are the closer points to the viewer's vision, and so obviously light advances again, and so on. The rule of *object light* is therefore steadfast in that light advances and dark recedes.

However, in a composition of objects of form, the rule of *object light* can be quite different. *Compositional light*, or the entirety of a colored surface such as a painting, can do both. Dark also advances, while light recedes.

We will begin the discussion first by using the most easily understood concept of dark advancing, using Robert Motherwell's work. Immediately there is a sense that the dark image is in the foreground and the white is the established background. This, of course, is a very simplistic notion and does not support the notion in itself that dark advances, as does light. In this case it is simply the dominance of a large black form, which travels from one side of the composition to the other.

Now let us discuss several compositions with light and dark. Often students are confused over this issue when we simply state that, "light advances and dark recedes." We know this is true in terms of light which strikes a single image, but with *compositional light* there are many variations on that issue. Let's examine the two following compositions for further clarification.

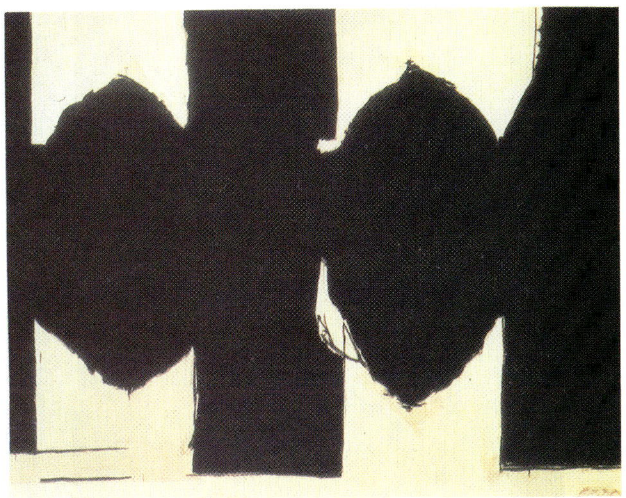

Elegy to the Spanish Republic No. 34 by Robert Motherwell.

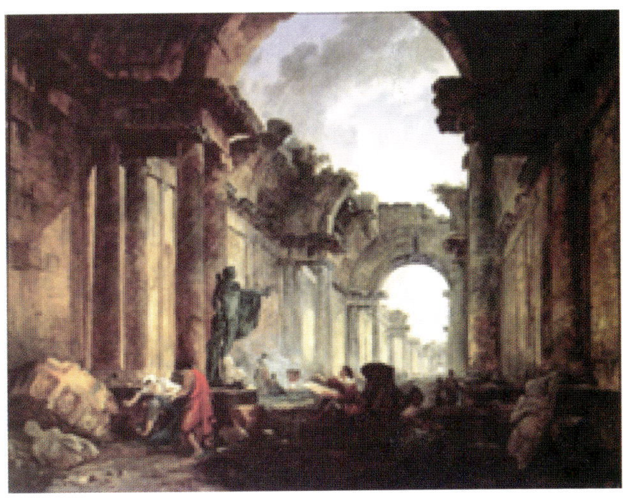

Fantastical View of the Grande Gallery of the Louvre by Hubert Robert.

The light in the *Grande Gallery* recedes into what seems to be infinite space, as perspective and light lead the eye into the distance. It is also the contrast of the light against the dark that helps to emphasize and push the first gallery of columns and its arch forward into the viewer's space. We see that the darkness from the long gallery hall diminishes rapidly, leaving an ominous and depressing dark foreground. Dark colors are clearly advancing while light recedes.

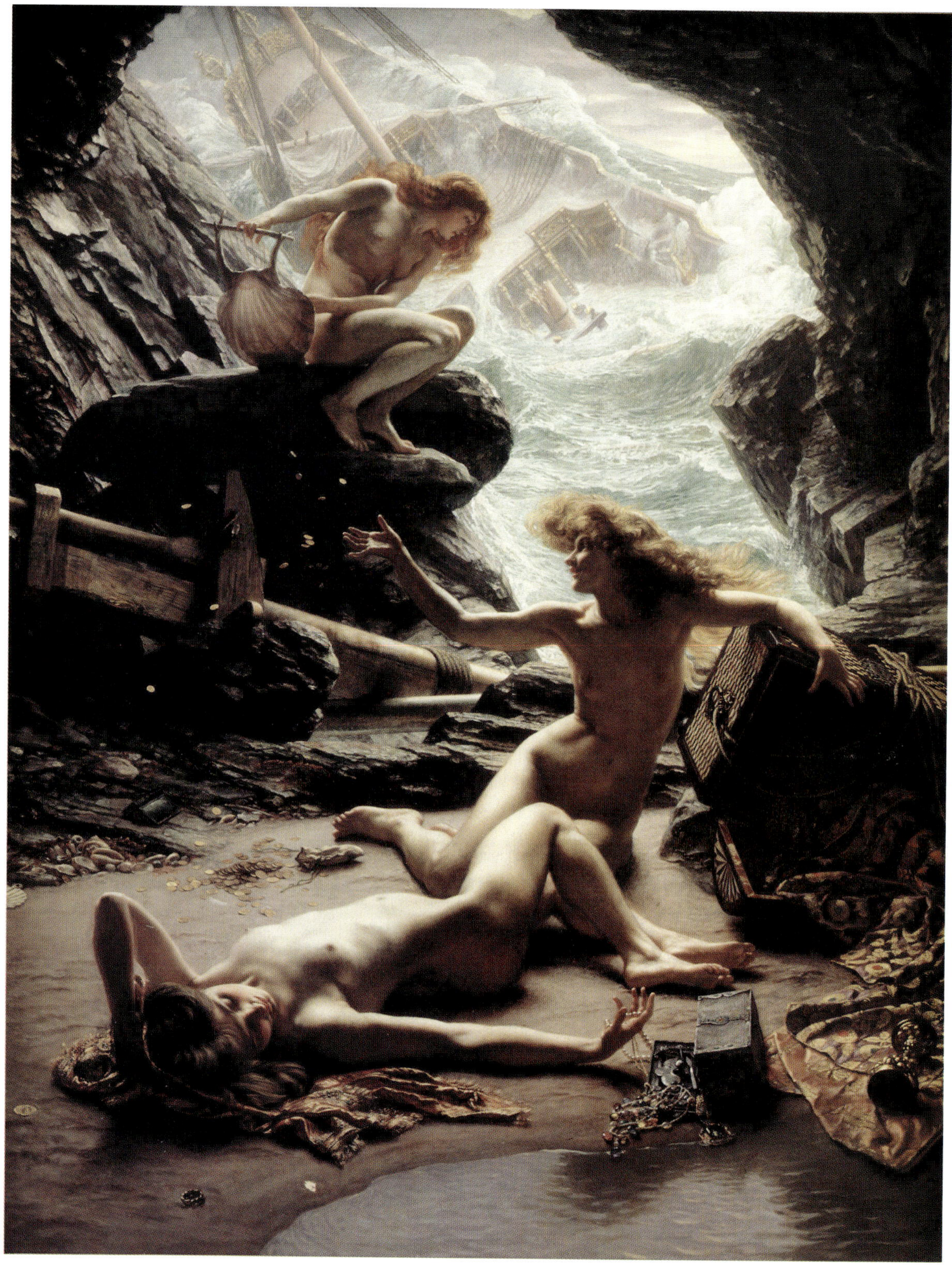

The Cave of the Storm Nymphs by Edward Poynter.

Edward Poynter's magnificent painting of *The Cave of the Storm Nymphs* illustrates the nature of dark and light at its best. It is an issue of background, middle-ground, and foreground contrasts that creates depth of space, as well as the dramatic effects of the composition. The background light contrasts against the middle-ground rocks, or opening to the cave, which brings the dark portal forward. The foreground then becomes somewhat lighter as the figures come closer into our space.

The picture has an intensely lit scene of a sinking ship in a turbulent ocean. The middle-ground dark contrast brings stability to the situation in that it provides a solid defense against the storm. Those two factors of dark and light contrast are important, because the viewer needs to feel the contrasts between the chaos and peace and the turbulence and calm of the situation. Finally, the foreground is neither dark or light, emphasizing the delicate nature of the predicament between the Nymphs themselves, and the brutal fury from where they came. Light and dark contrasts are seen especially emphasized on the immediate foreground figure. The three nymphs almost seem to be the same person, slowly progressing her way forward into a lighter and safer area of the cave. Each figure gets progressively lighter as she comes forward into space, and finally, light floods the foreground form, emphasizing that she is the first of the three to have solice from the storm.

It is *compositional light* that is creating spatial depth by the dark and light contrasts between the background, middle-ground and foreground. *Object light,* on the other hand, is creating extreme light and dark values, emphasizing the bodies of the nymphs, which enhances the drama of the disaster. The fear created in this work relies heavily on the light and dark contrasts of the color pallet.

The same effect, in a complete reversal of mood, can been seen in Frederick George Cotman's *One of the Family.* Again, we have the light background, (especially noted is the intensity of light through the window), dark middle-ground and the fairly well lit foreground. This time, however, the dark wall of the background emphasizes the environment of the horse, as opposed to the atmosphere of the people inside.

We know by now that dark and light contrast also functions as an emphasis element. Focal points

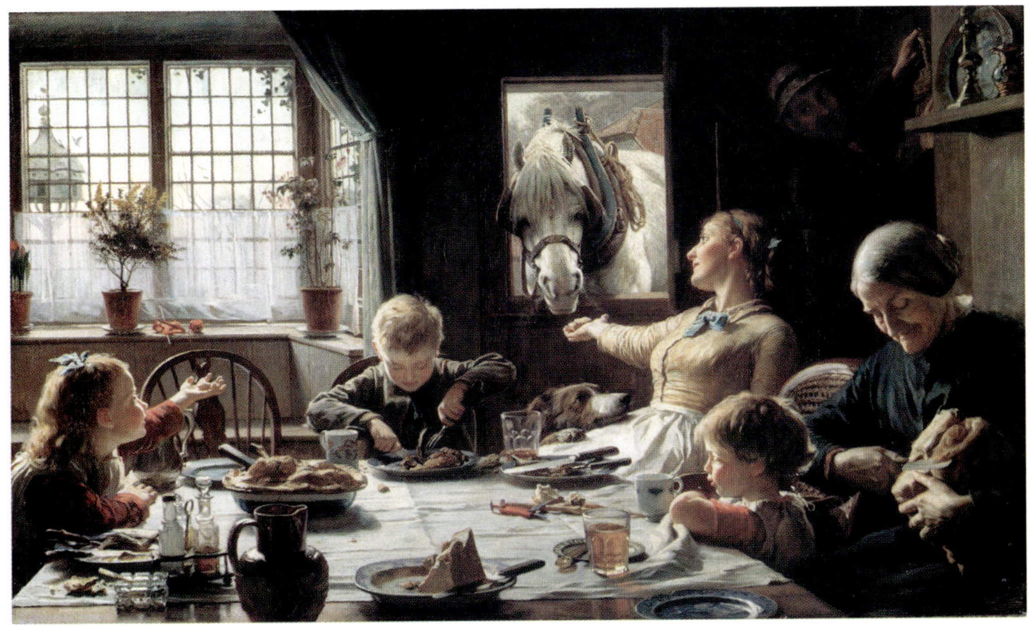

One of the Family 1880 by George Cotman.
National Museums Liverpool (The Walker).

are often generated by the use of dark and light contrasts. In David Roberts *The Israelites Leaving Egypt,* we see a reversal of the previous examples. Rather than a dark middle-ground, we instead see a well lighted middle-ground.

Here, even though the dark advances into our space, the emphasis is clearly on the middle-ground. The focus is on the thousands of Jews enslaved in Egypt who have finally been set free by Pharaoh, because of God's persistent plagues on the land. They are seen both preparing and leaving Egypt. Notice the extreme contrast of dark in the foreground and the right side of the composition. One cannot help but focus one's attention on the center lighted area.

A number of examples can be seen throughout the text, in terms of dark foreground and light backgrounds. Please take the time to locate and study these effects, in terms of how exactly dark and light functions.

In *Aiko's Determination* (opposite page), light objects advance into the viewer's space, while dark objects recede progressively towards the background. It is the intensity of light that casts a greater focus on Aiko in the foreground, pushing her further into the revealing space of the audience. The foreground light advances into the viewer's space, the middle ground objects linger in a quiet light, and the background slips quickly away into a secretive void.

The light and dark extremes create a very *tenebristic* composition, which in this performance instills the idea of mystery, as well as conflict within the story. Aiko searches tirelessly throughout her

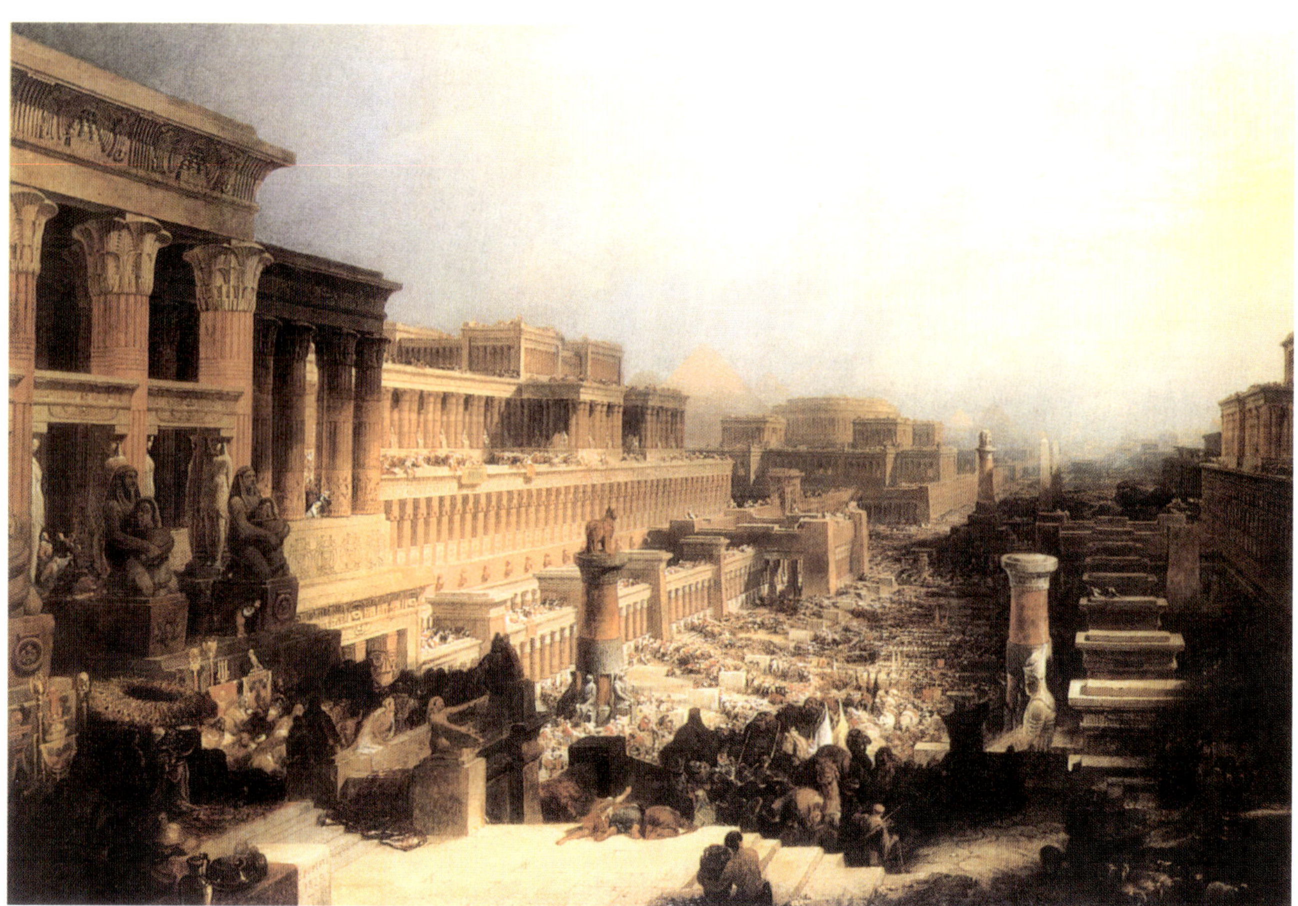

The Israelites Leaving Egypt by David Roberts.

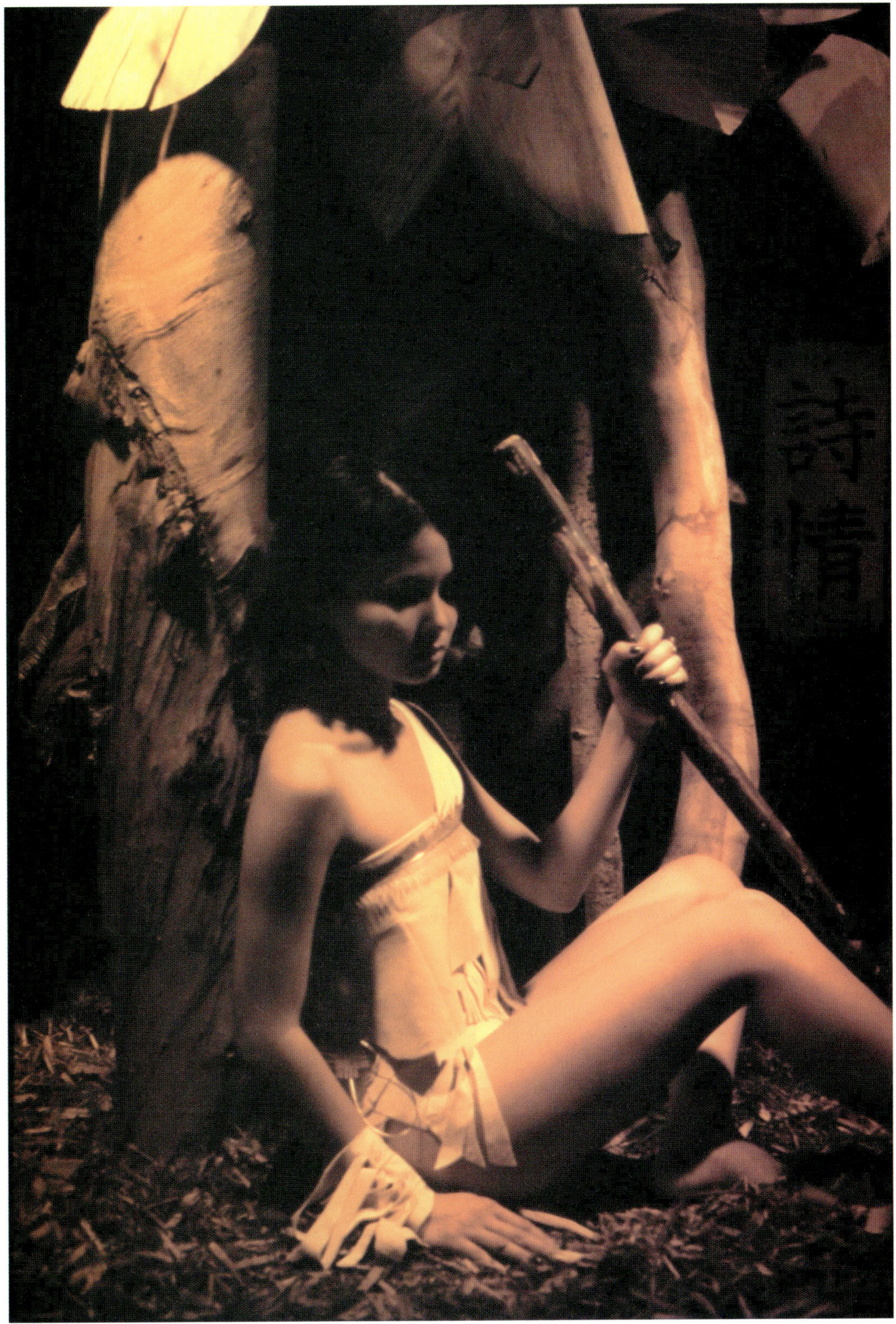

Shijo's *Aiko's Determination—Video Still.*
Alan Burner.

kingdom for her lover, Akihiko. Having stopped in dismay, she rests as the light source both puts emphasis on the figure, and beckons her to pursue. Light and darks constantly shift throughout the composition, forward and backward to create a seemingly endless depth of space. If it were not for the signage in the background, the depth of space would no doubt have limitless implications. It is the harshness of extreme contrast which produces the dynamic and causes the viewer to perceive the mystery, as well as the desperate mood of the composition. The dominant warm hues further enhance that emotional implication.

The *Third-Class Carriage* exemplifies the importance of dark and light contrast, and the relevance of *light advancing*. As these working class people pack together in the cramped space of the train, the obvious focus is on the two foreground figures. It is important for the artist to portray the life and hardships of these working class people. Not one single person in the train is wearing a smile, but it is especially true of the two ladies in the foreground. The people in the background seem to be less important to the artist, since they are obscured by the receding darkness in the back of the carriage. The two women illustrate one of the most revered paintings of the French Realist movement in the

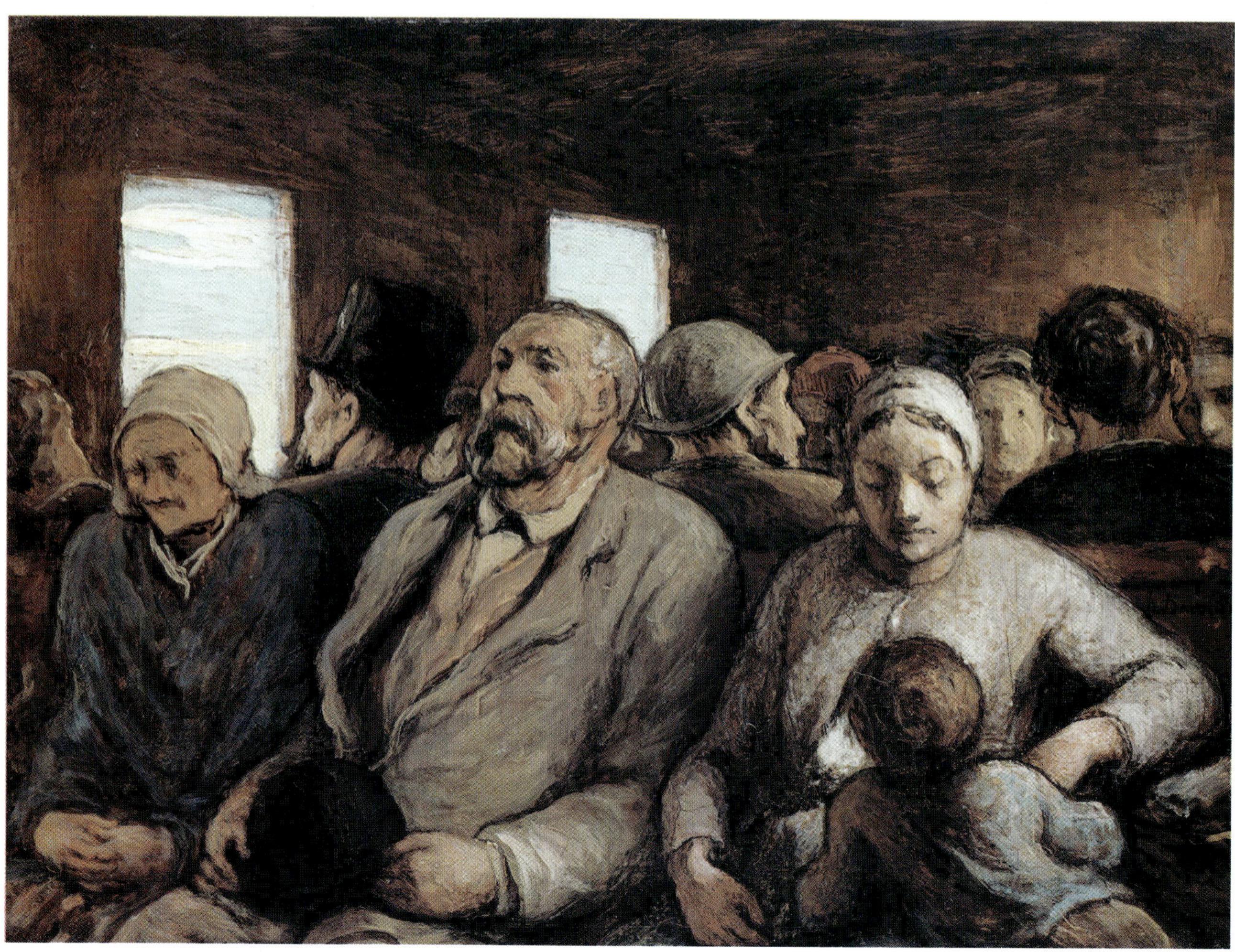

Third-Class Carriage by Honoré Daumier.
© Burstein Collection/CORBIS.

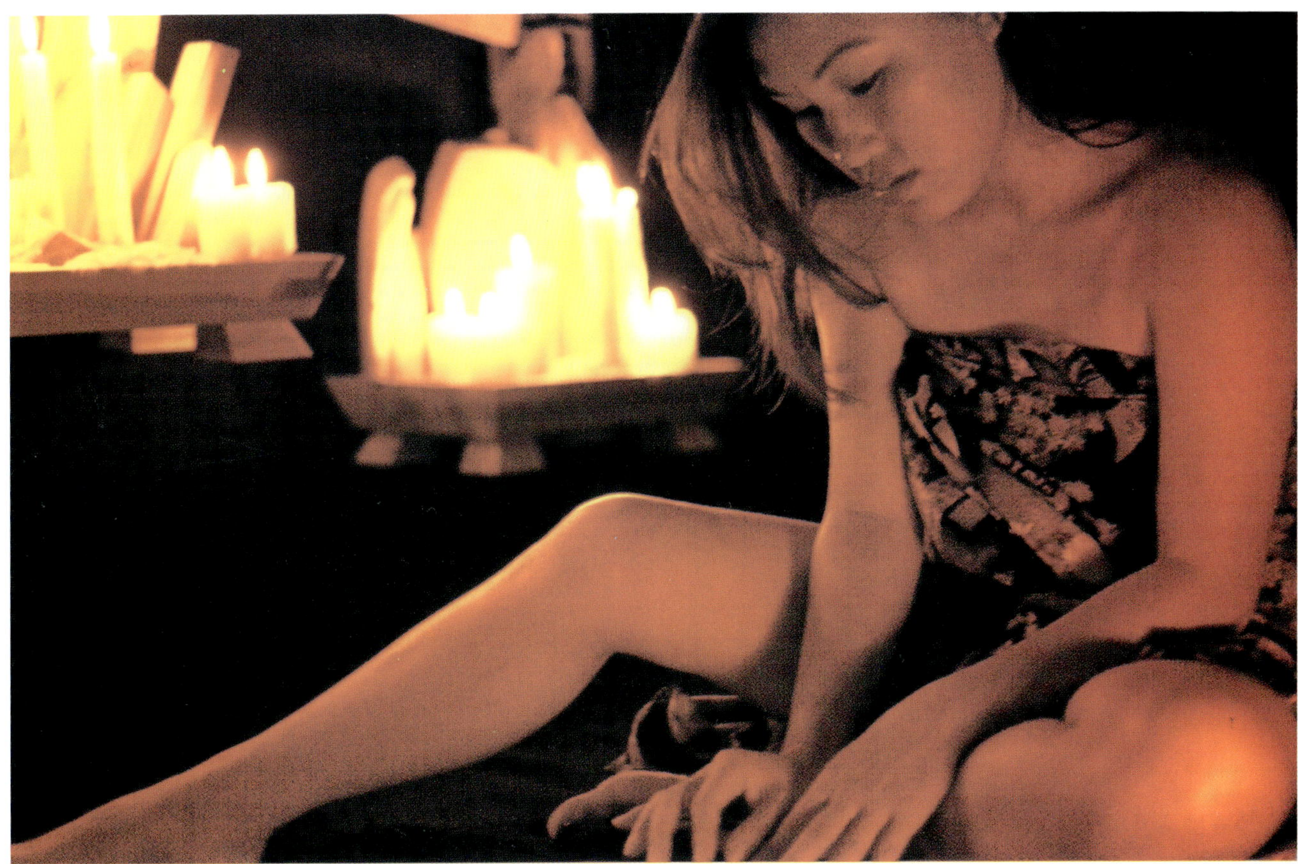

Shijo *Akihiko's Muse.*
Photo by Alan Burner.

19th century. Because of the contrasting advancing light, we are able understand exactly what the artist intends. We can easily read their faces, as they demonstrate the realistic hardships of physical work.

Akihiko's Muse is a classic light and dark scenario. In this case, it is neither black and white or yellow and violet, yet it exemplifies the power of light and dark contrast. It is important to point-out that even though black and white and yellow and violet are normally the best contrast opposites, other colors often demonstrate that quality as well. Here there is a sharp contrast of light and dark between the foreground and the background. The almost luminous red-orange figure of the muse makes a serious contrast against the dark ground behind her. One of the keys to this division of space is the luminosity of the figure, which actually contrasts against the more opaque background.

Also, the depth of space is enhanced by the luminous reflection of the candle's light on the upper portion of her extended leg, reinforcing the depth of space. Our immediate logical reaction would be to think that the brightness of the candles are diminishing the illusion of depth, but it is the diagonal line of the luminous leg against the dark background which helps to effectively split the composition.

Hue Contrast

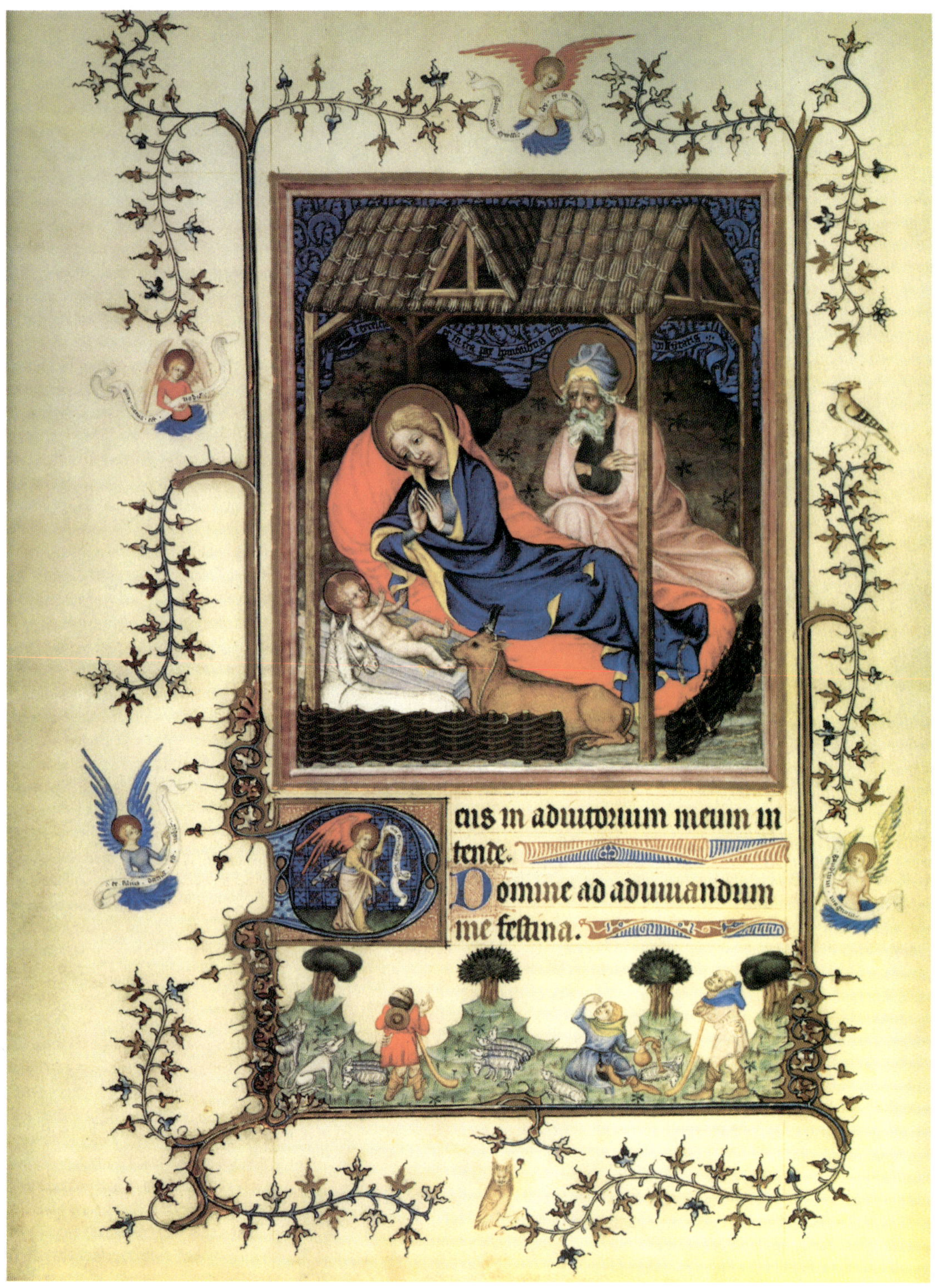

Illuminated Manuscripts Les Trés Belles Heures de Notre Dame du Duc de Berry, Miniature from the Illuminated Manuscripts of the Nativity and Annunciation to the Shepard.
Bibliothèque Nationale de France.
Hue contrast is evident in this illuminated manuscript. Whether we concentrate our attention towards the focal point of red, yellow and blue or the entire composition itself, with the addition of green, we can't help but notice the very evident contrasts of hue.

Hue Contrast

In dark and light contrast, we discussed the two most extreme contrasts, that is to say both black and white and violet and yellow. Contrast of hue is actually the most simple form of contrast that we will be discussing. It is easy to understand, and there are no complex issues regarding hue contrast.

Hue contrast must incorporate no less than three colors in order to be effective. These hues, however, must be clearly distinct from one another such as the three primaries. Red, yellow and blue are the most clearly defined hue contrasts, and far enough away from each other to provide the ultimate contrast. While these colors can be changed in value and intensity, the further away they are from the saturated primaries, the less effective the contrast.

Some possibilities are:
Yellow, Red and Blue
Yellow, Green, Blue and Red
Green, Blue, Orange and Black
Red, White and Blue

The possibilities are seemingly endless, as long as there is a reasonably distinguishable contrast between

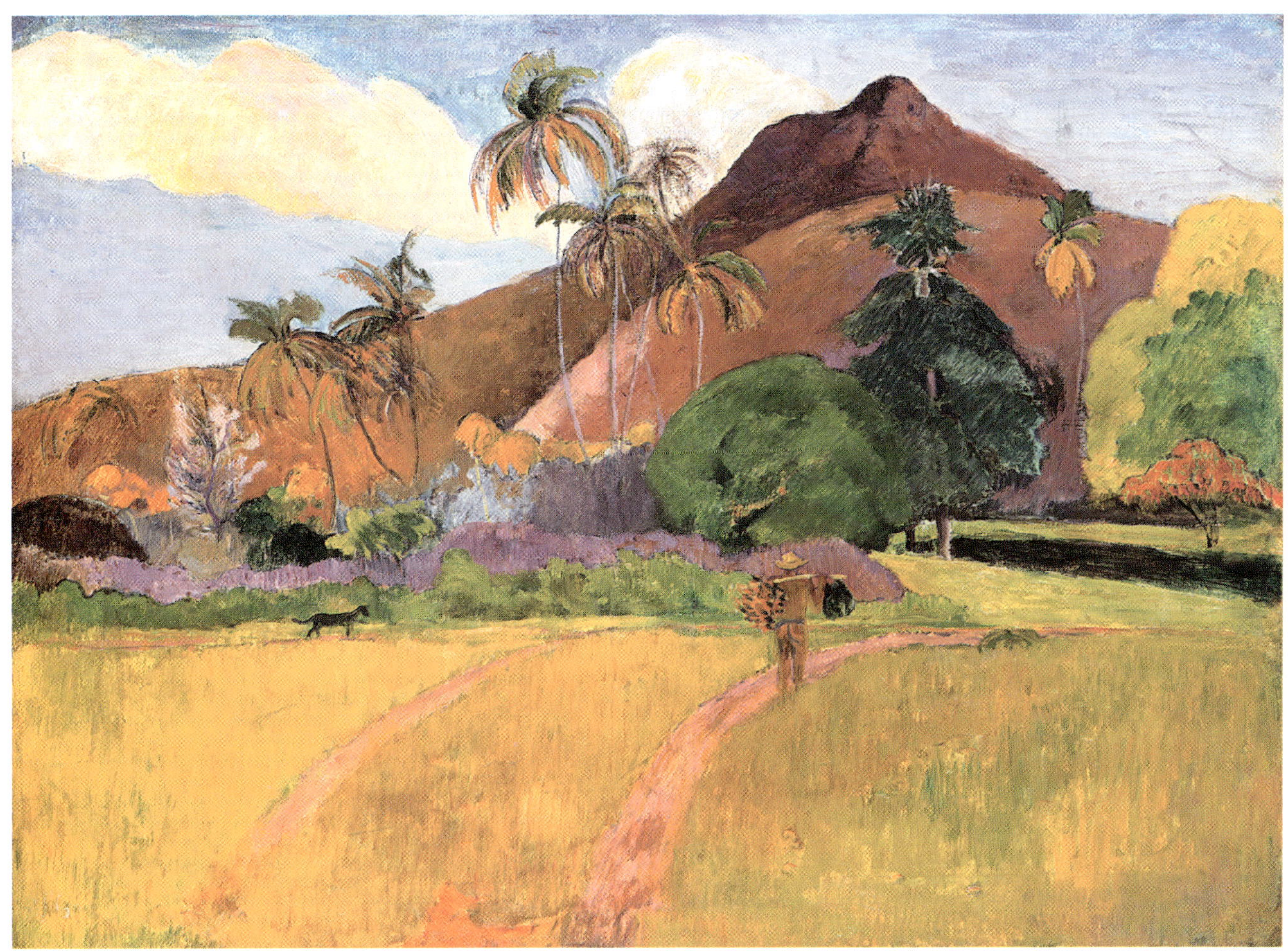

Tahitian Landscape by Paul Gauguin.
Minneapolis Institute of Arts.

the hues. Proportions of the primaries can be altered by nominal value changes, such as the addition of white (tinting) for greater brightness (intensity), or adding black (shading) for less intensity, or dullness. A shaded red then will still provide high contrast between itself and saturated yellow, or a tinted violet against blue will do the same. Of course, two shaded or two tinted hues will offer less contrast, and will eventually lose any significant contrast.

The effects of hue contrast offer many possibilities for the expressive nature of color. The contrast of these hues can be significant to form emotional responses such as a burst of joy, celebration, or sudden grief and despair. This type of contrast is such that it is obligated to produce a response.

In early 1891, Paul Gauguin methodically packed his bags and said farewell to his wife and children forever. His desperation to escape the complications of city life, such as it was in Paris, filled him with the hope that he could find solace in Tahiti, where he could paint his abstract color fields undisturbed.

In Paul Gauguin's *Tahitian Landscape* (previous page), we see an exemplary composition based on hue contrast. Yellow, green, violet and red (red-orange) control the mood of this warm composition. Gauguin's passionate response to the island world was his last stand. The landscape is one of his most emotional gestures yet. His love for the primitive, for the simple and uncomplicated world, and the sensuality discovered in his new Polynesian wife burst out onto this canvas. This painting is intensely rich with emotional responses, which hue contrast is famous for accomplishing.

Another compelling example of hue contrast can be found in the work of Henry Matisse's *Harmony in Red.*

Harmony in Red is at its optimal effectiveness because of the saturation balance throughout the composition. Red, yellow, green and blue are all in their saturated state, which provides sharp contrast and ultimately enhances the emotional level of impact. The level of energy that is created by this arrangement of

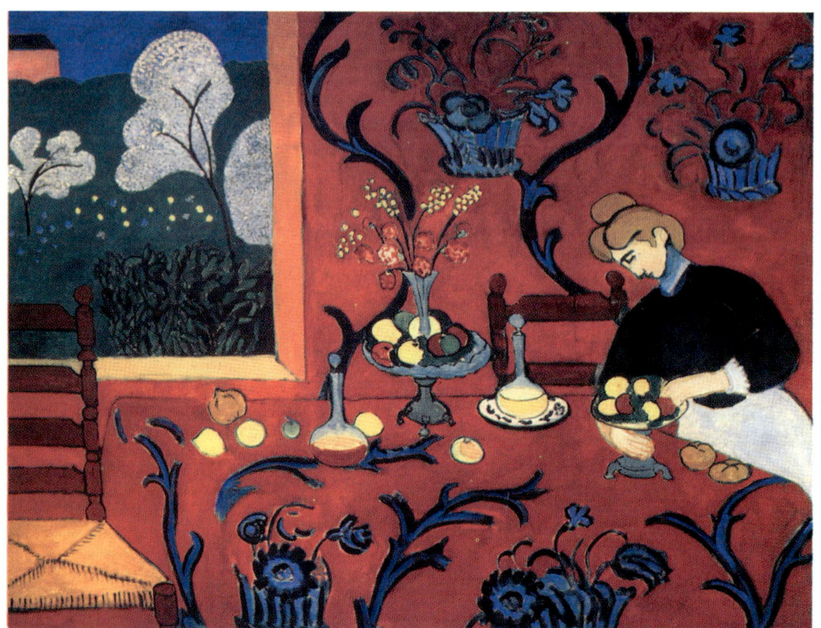

Harmony in Red by Henri Matisse

hue contrast cannot be understated. The energetic and passionate execution of pigments creates a harmony of colors, which actually radiate or pulsate with pure, saturated red. Red is barely held in control and is kept from overpowering the composition by the remaining fragmented colors of yellow and blue. The green area of the picture plane seems to calm the primary triad of colors inside of the room.

Roy Lichtenstein's *Forget It! Forget Me!* illustrates yet another aspect of hue contrast. We already know that the construction of hue contrast in a composition is capable of setting up a range of emotions or moods. The placement of one color next to another is critical in the creation of the appropriate mood. We understand that a moderately shaded red next to a yellow can change the character of one over the other. Color placement in hue contrast can either complement the other, or steal away the attention of the other. One may exert power over the other, while another will totally destroy its partner, and thereby gain all of the attention.

Forget It! Forget Me! serves to illustrate the effects of hue contrast and its varying moods. The dominant and controlling color in the picture is obvious, as this very saturated red separates the two couples in their dispute. The placement of red in the center, between the man and the woman, acts as a barrier, symbolizing their dispute. Red is a dynamic color and has contrasting characters within itself. Red can be angry and hateful, or it can be sensuous and passionate. Yellow, on the other hand, can be quite jovial or celebratory by nature, as blue can be rather stable or calming. Also, it is permissible to introduce black or white to the composition of hue

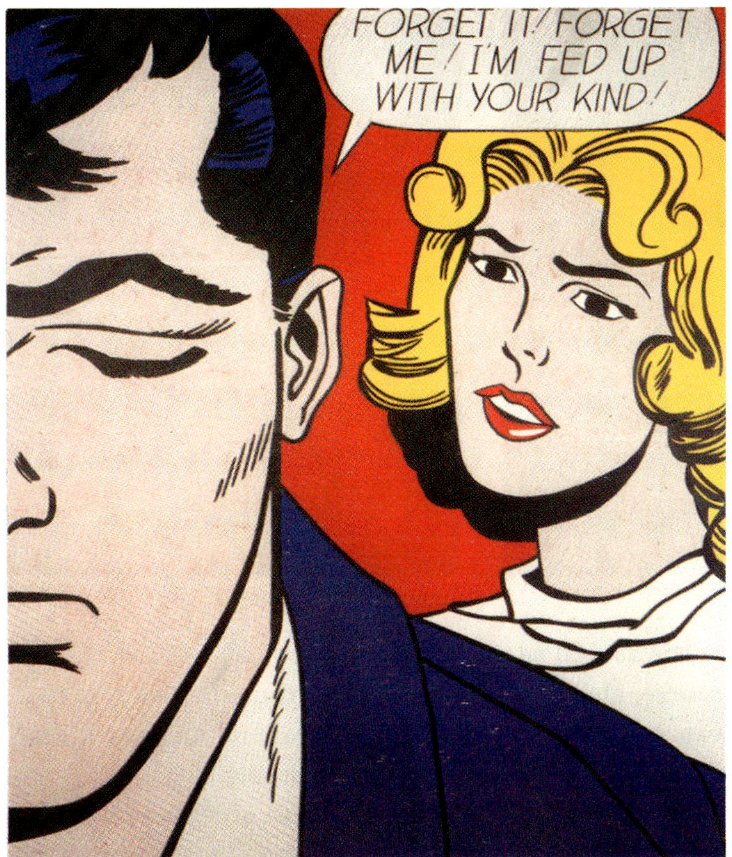

Forget It! Forget Me! by Roy Lichtenstein.
© Estate of Roy Lichtenstein.

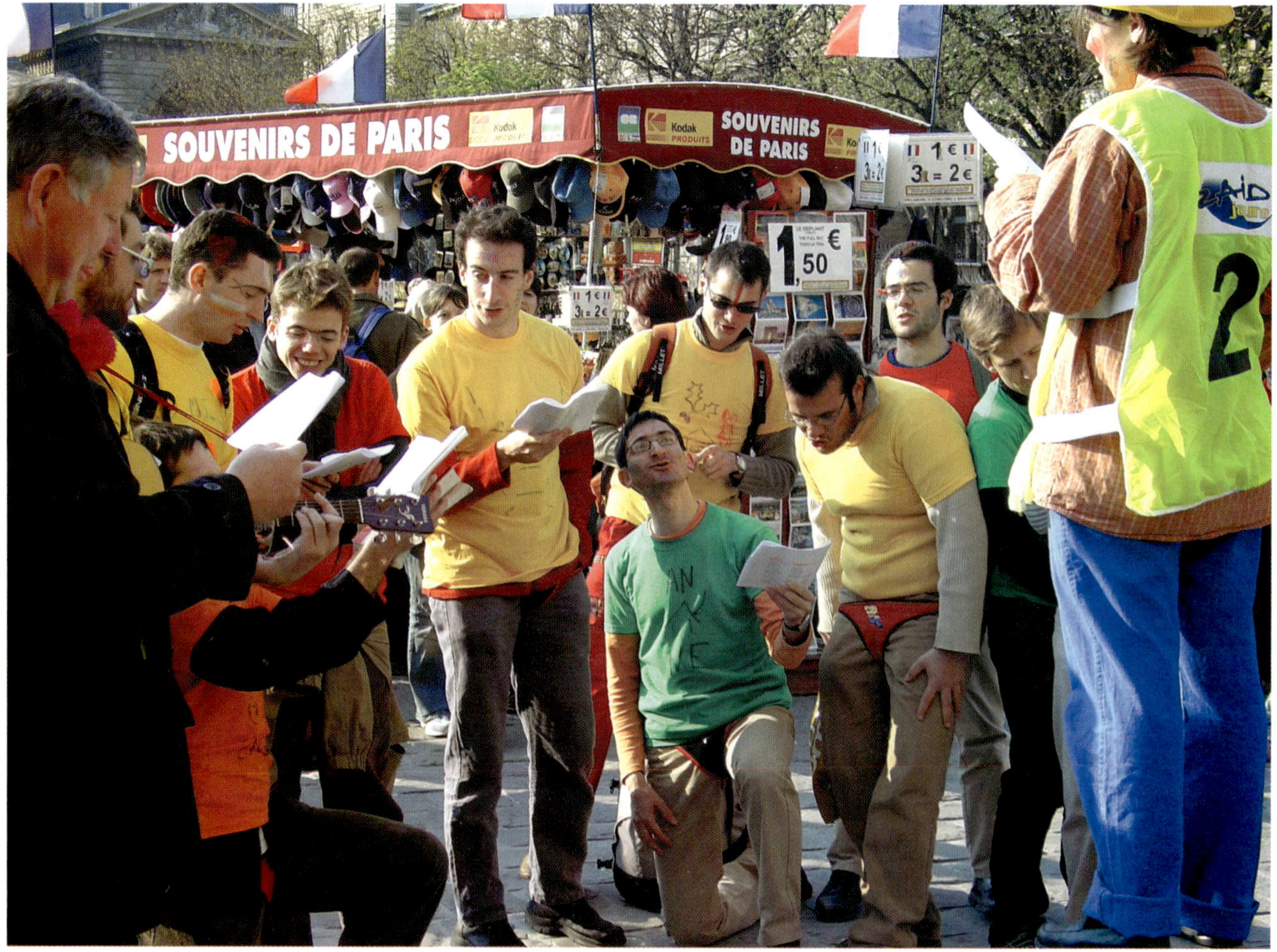

A Group of Impromptu Performers in Paris.
Photo by Alan Burner.

contrast. A white space in contrast to a blue or indigo patch will cause the blue/indigo area to appear to be darker and more mysterious. White next to yellow, however, can rob the color of some of its brilliance, and white next to red can take away a portion of the color's saturation. The addition of black next to red or yellow will cause the same hues to appear lighter and more intense. The defining element here is the black outlining of the characters, which provides a greater definition and contrast between the contrast of hues.

Hue contrast is not unlike certain aspects of the atom that we studied in Chapter One, which is a bit like harmony and chaos at the same time. The effects of hue contrast, because of their striking differences in color, often create a certain harmonious chaos of moods and emotional responses. If Picasso had been a colorist rather than a form artist, he most certainly would have often employed the use of hue contrast—for as he said, "a painting is first of all, a sum total of destructions."

Lastly, a familiar association of hue contrast would be found in the various tribal cultures of the world, such as the Native American Indian. With saturated hue contrasts, beautiful costumes of dyed fabrics, bracelets and necklaces of colored stones, ceramic beads and colorful feathers emulate the energy expressed in the tribal dance.

Even within a situation such as an impromtu performance on the streets of Paris (see facing page), the performers seem to understand the "attention-grabbing" necessity for color stimulus. In this case hue contrast dominates the scene. Saturated red, green and yellow dominate the composition with contrasts of hue, and even though they are not consciously orchestrating intentional hue contrasts, there is often a subconscious understanding about saturation and contrast in the novice of color. The performance takes place in the square in front of Notre Dame de Paris, where thousands of people come out during a weekend day to enjoy the warm sun and listen to the bell tower chime on Sunday. With all of the diversions simultaneously occurring that day, these young people drew the attention of the majority of people in the square with their pure colors and equally intense music.

Complementary Contrast

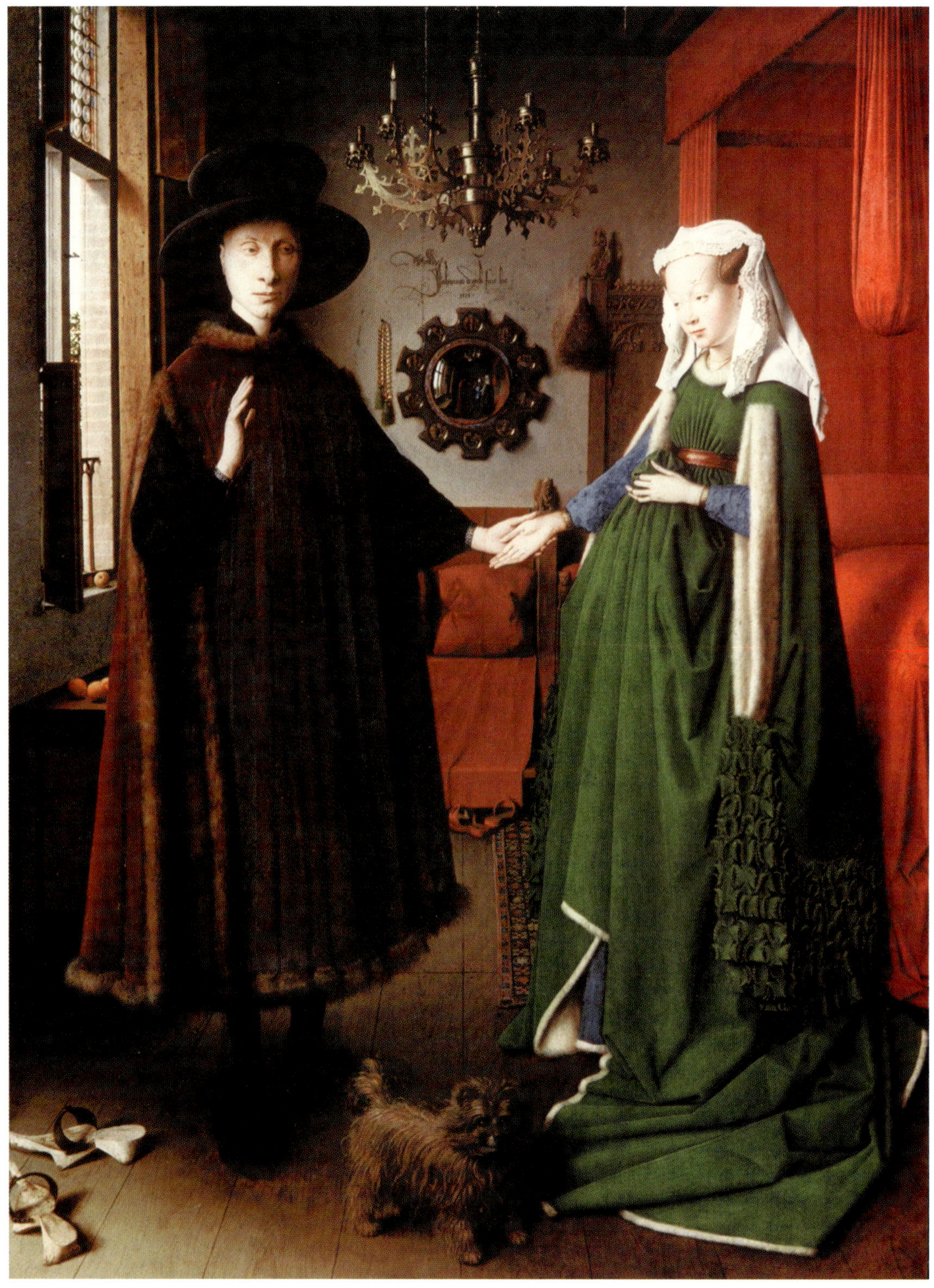

Giovanni Arnolfini and His Bride by Jan van Eyck.

Complementary Contrast

Complementary color is just that—two colors which complement each other. They are colors that exist directly opposite of each other on the color circle. Complements harmonize and balance one another, causing the other to appear even better, or sometimes more saturated than they actually are. Such is the case between Arnofini's bride's green dress and the red fabrics of the bed. The bed seems saturated, when, in fact, it is not fully saturated. When we look at the color circle, we understand that the primary colors are always present in complementary pairs consisting of one primary and one secondary color. These complements are: red and green, orange and blue and yellow and violet.

Complementary colors also possess a contradictory character. They not only complement one another, but they can also destroy or cancel each other. There is a very destructive nature about their relationship, and is unusually similar to human behavior.

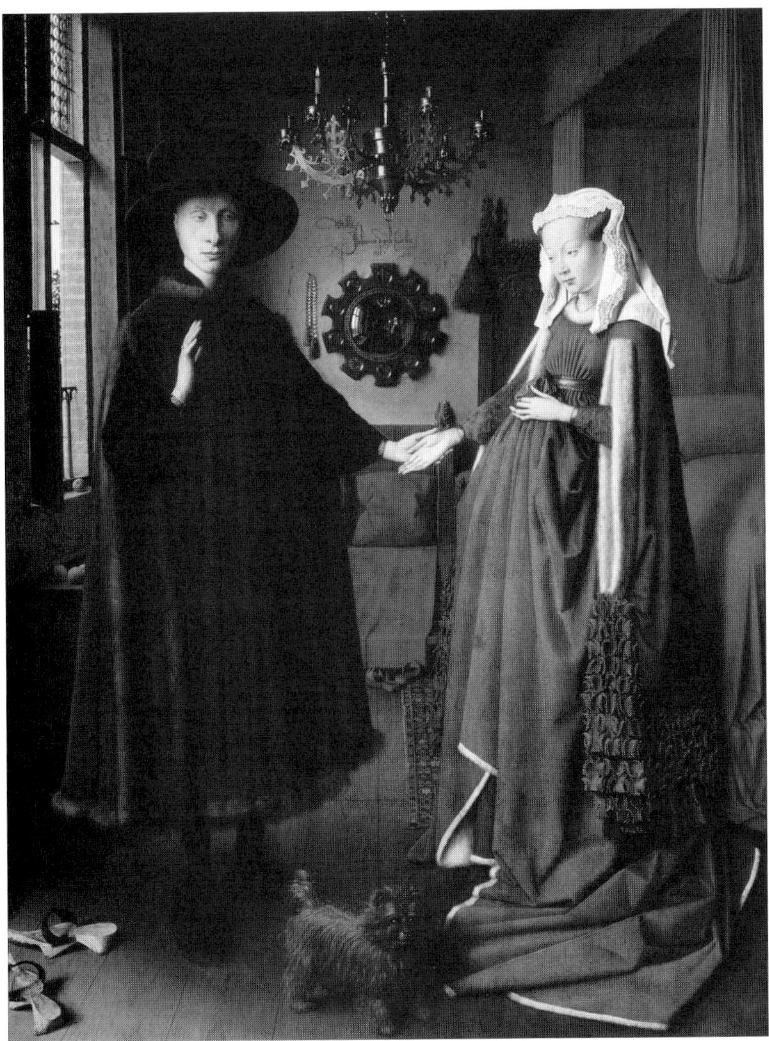

Giovanni Arnolfini and His Bride by Jan van Eyck. Achromatic.
© Archivo Iconografico, S.A./CORBIS.

Make a comparison study of this achromatic version of van Eyck's painting on the facing page, in order to determine how saturation and intensity convert to light and dark values. One composition is *achromatic,* while the other is *chromatic* value.

If they get too close to one another, they automatically eradicate each other. Complementary colors are in fact mutual enemies, as well as lovers. The mixing of two complements will always cancel chroma, and neutralize their ability to be effective. The mixing of two complements then create gray. So both complements possess strong chromatic powers, when linked side by side they complement and become more powerful, yet when they get too close they become enemies and are transformed into achromatic values.

An even more peculiar aspect of complements is that if you were to remove eleven of the twelve colors of light on the color circle, mixing the removed eleven colors would result in the complement of the color left behind. For every color on the circle, regardless of which color is segregated, the other eleven colors will mix to be its complement. This very peculiar phenomenon creates a visual after-image that a camera cannot record, even though the eye is able to see it: the eye requires a color to be balanced. When the color is absent, the eye will the compensate, or spontaneously manufacture the complement.

Jan van Eyck's painting is certainly one of the finest examples of complementary color and its effects. It uses both complements of yellow and violet (seen more subtly), and green and red (more obvious). The red and green complements are dominate, because the violet is of course a stronger and duller hue, as is the yellow more intensified, or less saturated.

The main event of complementary effects in Jan van Eyck's painting on the previous page is on the side of the bride. (Although she seems pregnant, her dress is merely gathered in front.) Many say that the bed chamber itself is saturated red, but if we look at the very center of the composition, we will see true saturated red. The bed chamber appears at first to be saturated, when it is actually tinted somewhat with white. The reason for this miscalculation is that the green dress *complements* the red and thereby causes it to look more red, or saturated than it really is.

The bride is the focal point. Some say that their joined hands are the focal point, but that is a compositional focal point, not a color directive. While the hands are indeed important, both compositionally and symbolically, it is rather the face of the bride that continues to pull our attention away from the hands. There is an extreme contrast set-up between the face and head piece, and the near saturation of the green and the red. Her head radiates, or is luminous, far more than their hands or the face of the groom. Compare the achromatic version (previous page) next to the chromatic version (facing page) and you will see that this bears out to be true. The values are darker everywhere in the composition than is her face and head piece.

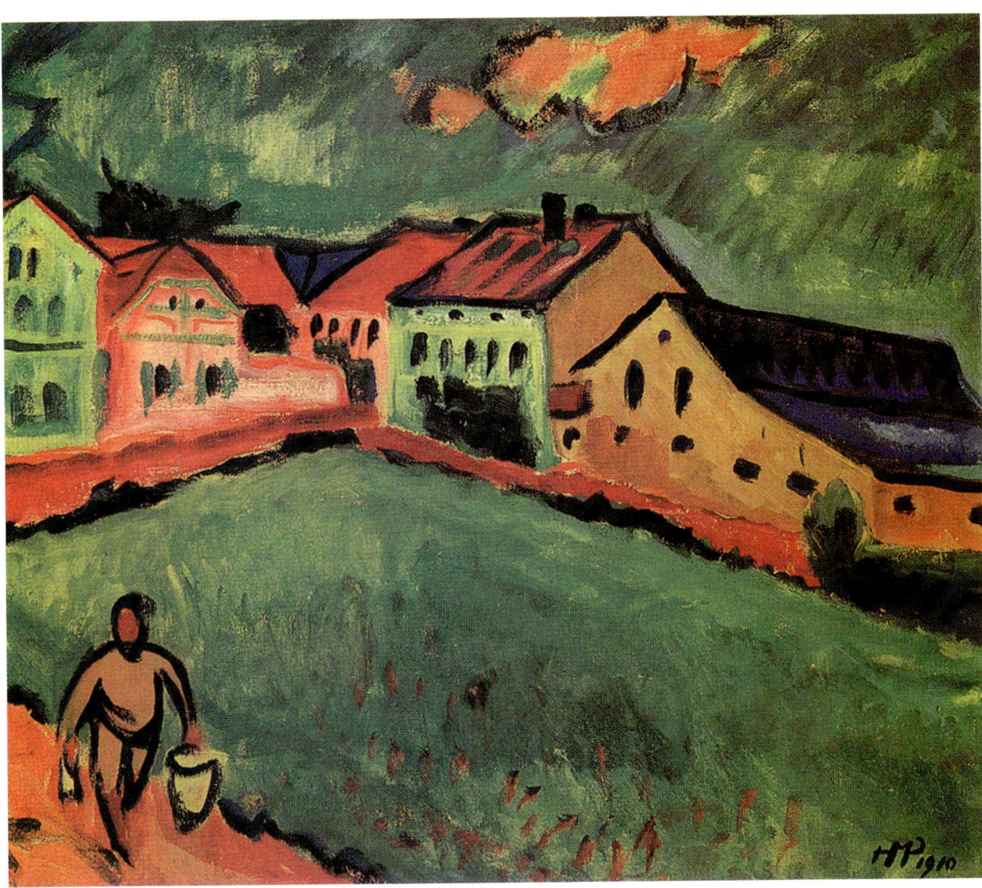

Meadow at Moritzburg by Max Hermann Pechstein.

Meadow at Moritzburg is a classic in terms of what complementary color harmonies can produce emotionally. The vibrant and emotional quality of this expressionistic painting is evident in this composition. Even though red and green complements are equal in color balance, it is sometimes the case where the two become too static, or predictable, and so it is sometimes necessary to introduce another color, or in this case a different complementary scheme. The complementary orange and violet structure in the foreground of structures, removes the static from the otherwise obvious approach to complements.

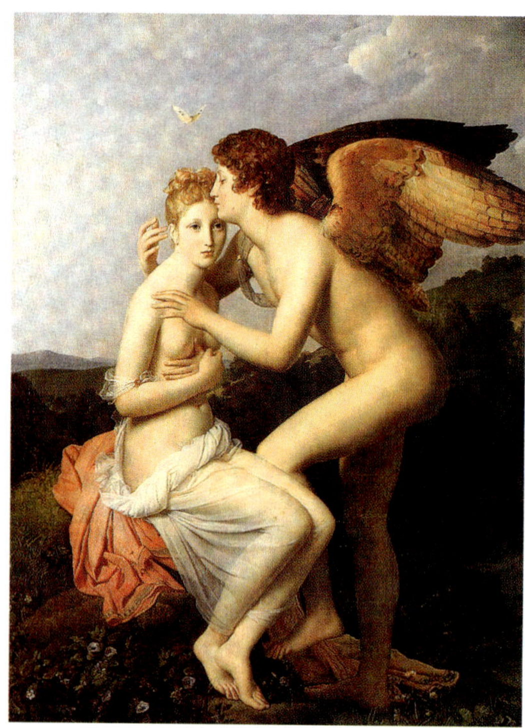

Cupid and Psyche by François Gérard, 1798.

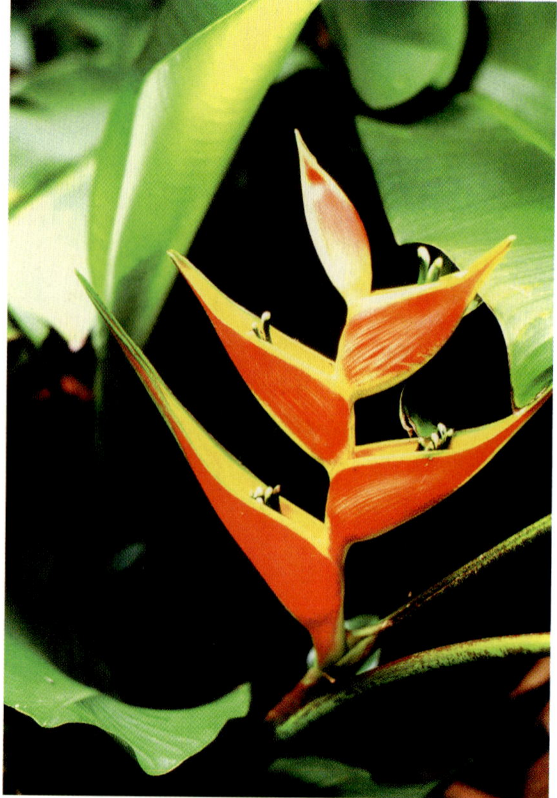

Hawaiian Flower Exemplifies a Complementary Contrast of Red and Green.
Photo by Alan Burner.

Gerard's *Cupid and Psyche* present a much subtler approach to complementary contrast. In fact the contrast doesn't even seem to quite fit, since we think of contrast as being more evident. Here is where the student must become more critical in their approach to the art of seeing. Split the composition diagonally from the lower right corner to the upper left corner. In the right upper diagonal side of the composition we see complements of light oranges and light blues. Cupid's body is a very light orange tone, his wings are darker orange and the sky presents itself as a fairly light blue. The lower left diagonal, where Psyche sits, imparts complements of red and green. The red drapery on which she sits quietly, helps the eye to see the slightest light red tones in her body. The green further enhances, or creates, a visual response with the viewer seeing more red in his skin than is perhaps there. The effects of complements here are the extreme opposite of *Arnolfini and His Bride,* where van Eyck paints an overt complementary harmony, as opposed to Gerard's very restrained or quiet set of complements.

This flower and its foliage are complementary, one to the other. The red seems redder than it is, because of the green background. In fact, the red is actually not a saturated red, but it is the dark contrast directly behind the flower as well as the surrounding green, which gives us the notion that it is very saturated. Conversely, the yellow border of the flower's cup prevents the red and green from forming the best possible contrast, as it becomes a type of buffer zone.

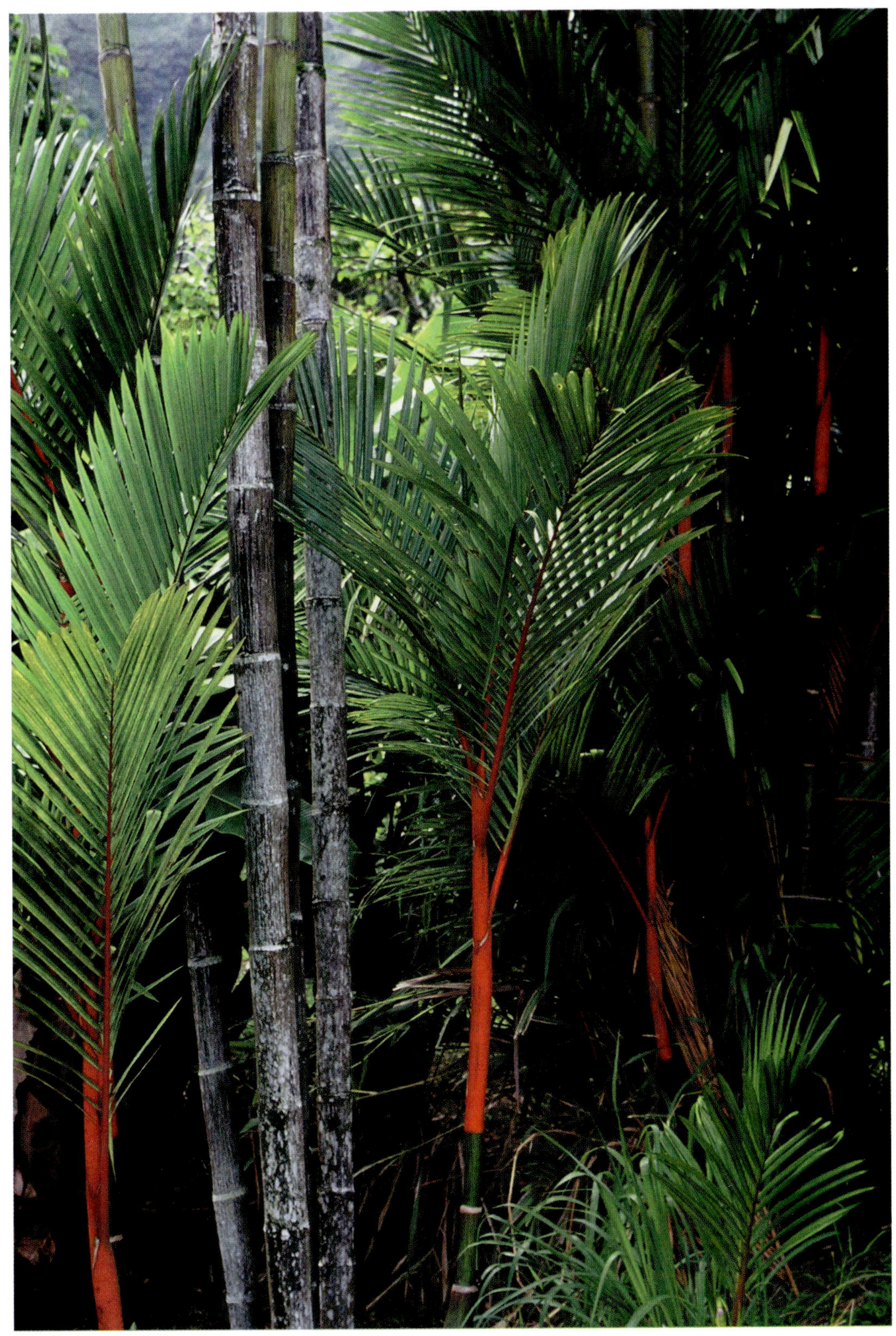

Hawaiian palms flourish on the north shore of Oahu's Botanical Gardens, which displays an abundant variety of complementary color flora and fauna.
Photo by Alan Burner.

Warm and Cool Contrast

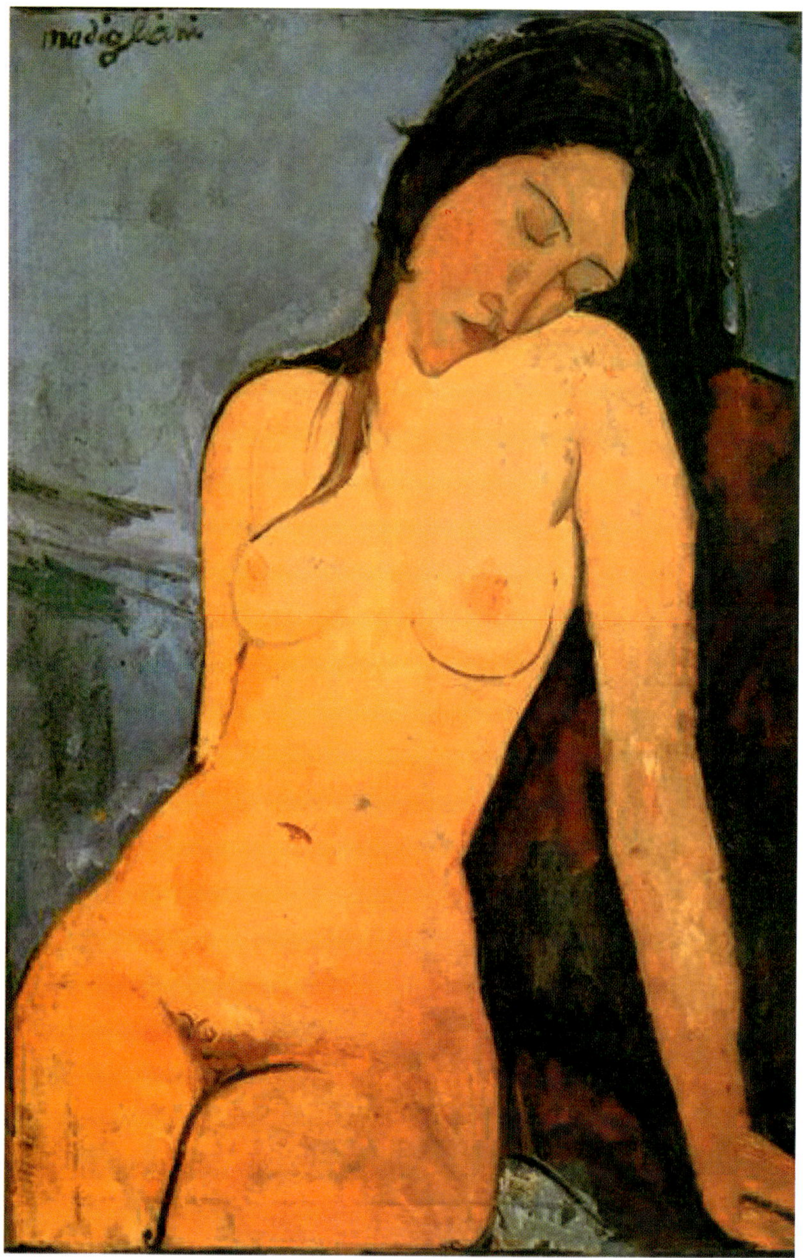

Seated Nude by Amedeo Modigliani.
The Samuel Courtland Trust, Courtland Institute of Art Gallery, London.
The contrasting cool blues and violets with warm reds and oranges in the seated nude composition, commensurately creates a mood of both tranquility and sensuality.

Warm and Cool Contrast

Warm colors are identified as red, orange and yellow, while cool colors are green, blue and violet. Warm and cool colors can be identified as having an actual warmth or coolness to them respectively. Red, orange and yellow visually warm and cool colors are equally cold or cool. To be more specific, the totality of warm colors are identified as yellow, yellow-orange, orange, red-orange, red, and red-violet. Specific cool colors are yellow-green, green, blue-green, blue, blue-violet and violet.* In terms of opposites or complements, the *strongest* (not highest contrast) would be red-orange and blue-green.

When referring to *color temperature*, we can imagine warm colors generated from an orange fire, or imagine the warmth of the sun's yellow heat, in contrast to a blue sky with its cooling breezes, or the chilling deep waters of blue-greens in the ocean. Temperature opposites are also responsible for the viewer's mood response. Consider for a moment some of the differing scenarios that warm and cool are similar to:

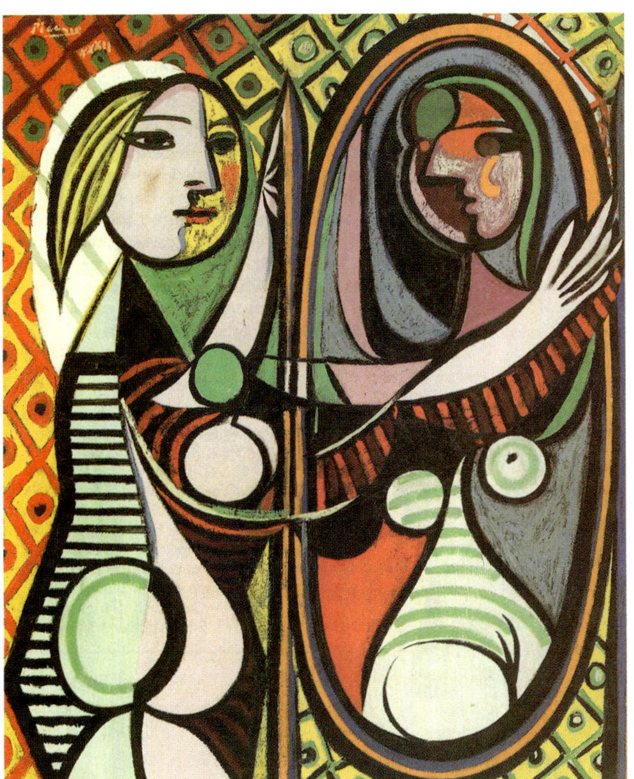

Girl Before a Mirror by Pablo Picasso.

Warm and Cool *Properties* Could Express:

Warm and Cool	Rare and Common
Transparent and Opaque	Light and Heavy
Wet and Dry	Deep and Shallow
Sun and Shade	

Warm and Cool *Personalities* Could Express:

Excitement and Calm	Peace and Chaos
Contentment and Depression	Hope and Despair
Brilliance and Gloom	

The contrast of saturated color contrasts normally demand a more powerful emotional response. Picasso's *Girl Before a Mirror* sets up strong alliances of warm and cool saturated and high intensity contrasts. The emotions of the artist seem be linked to the *Girl Before a Mirror* by his response to warm and cool contrasts. The color associations are commanding as this painting makes a case for the warm and cool nature of color, as well as serving as an example of hue contrast from our previous discussion.

Picasso's color schemes reflect the energy associated with the artist's life, as we will discuss in Chapter Six of this text.

Warm and cool contrast creates dynamic compositions of majesty and glory as we see in Murillo's *Immaculate Conception* seen on the following page. This composition lies in serious contrast to Picasso's saturated colors, hard edges and flat space. Murillo creates a subtle gradation of warm and cool contrasts. Especially noted is the absence of harsh contrast, rather we observe the careful variations of orange values which assist to create depth of space. The figure's blue robe contrasts against the misty red-orange background, which helps to push the figure into the foreground. Even without the saturated color as seen in Picasso's work, the painting of Murillo's surges with majesty and authority.

One of the periods of art in which light and warm and cool contrasts were important can be seen in the work of the Impressionists. Previously, we briefly studied the work of Claude Monet, particularly the Rouen Cathedral and the changes of color on it's surface during the day, or during the year, respectively.

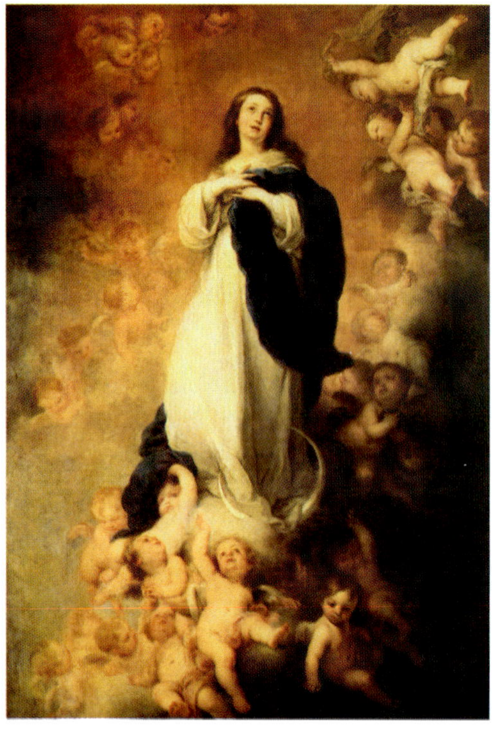

The Immaculate Conception of Soult by Bartolome Esteban Murillo.
© Archivo Iconografico, S.A./CORBIS

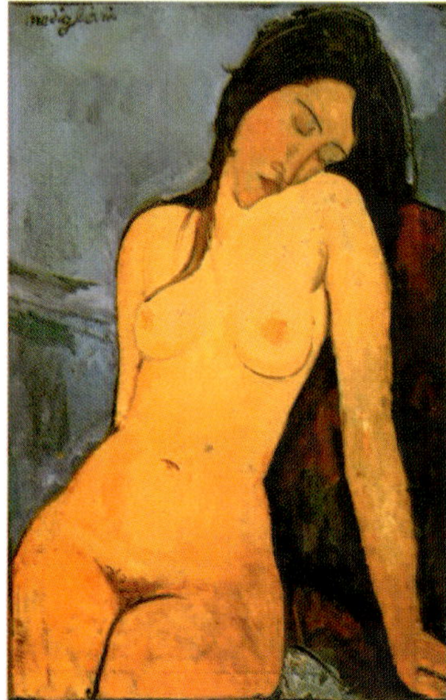

Seated Nude by Amedeo Modigliani.
The Samuel Courtland Trust, Courtland Institute of Art Gallery, London.

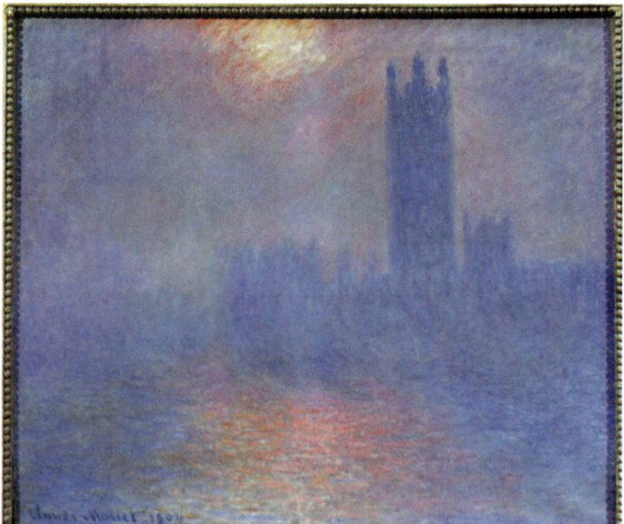

Houses of Parliament, effects of Sunlight in the Fog (London) by Claude Monet.
© Archivo Iconografico, S.A./CORBIS.

In Claude Monet's *Houses of Parliament*, the entire composition is dominated by cool blues and violets. The cold blueness of the water, as well as the atmosphere, can be sensed by the viewer, in contrast to the faint warmness of the red-orange sunlight struggling to break through the icy fog veil. In this frigid environment, the contrast of the warm red-orange against the prevailing cool blues, further acts to accentuate the coldness of the atmosphere.

Amedeo Modigliani's *"Seated Nude"* illustrates the force of warm and cool contrasts in a subtly more sensuous color scheme. Cool blues caress the right side of her body, while a warm shaded red supports her left side. The composition is diagonally split by the figure's light red-orange body, which ultimately creates a very relaxed and yet sensually energized painting. The blue is calm, the red is passionate, and the light red-orange unifies the two emotions of warm and cool colors.

Warm and cool colors can apply to a single color as well. For example, warm violets and cool violets may be produced by the addition of red or blue respectively. The warm violet will actually have a slight red tinge and the cool violet will possess a bluish tone. The student may not immediately recognize a warm violet to be such when confronted with the color, since it does take a little practice seeing the red in the violet. The same holds true when recognizing blue in a cool violet. Other variations exist, such as warm and cool black.

The greater the intensity, the less possible it is to change warm and cool components. Yellow, for example, turns yellow-green or yellow-orange, rather than becoming a warm or a cool yellow. Violet is able to become either warm or cool, as we remember that violet is the strongest (least intense) color, and therefore is not easily changed by the addition of blue or red. Yellow, conversely is the weakest (most intense) color, and so it is too easily influenced by additions of another color, and therefore changes to another color.

Vision After the Sermon is an interesting study because of its high contrast between saturation and intensity. Rather than creating spatial differences, such as depth, it is actually responsible, in part, for generating flat space. The saturation of the red background is no competition for the white* capped nuns in the foreground. We know that the *implication* of deep space is evident because of the perspective— large to smaller images, from foreground to background. We especially understand the implication of space because of the foreground. The nuns are not simply in the foreground, they are *in* the viewer's space.

In terms of illusion, however, the space is flat and so we do not feel a sense of depth whatsoever. The saturated red background is actually racing forward, while the white of the caps is receding into the composition, or the background. The more extreme the contrast between these two entities, the flatter the composition becomes. Contrast directs attention toward the two wrestling figures in the background. Gauguin wasn't really interested in portraying realistic space or figures, as much as he was concerned with registering the emotions of the conflict. In this Biblical account of Jacob wrestling the Angel, the color and contrast affiliation is the key component in achieving the appropriate intensity of mood.

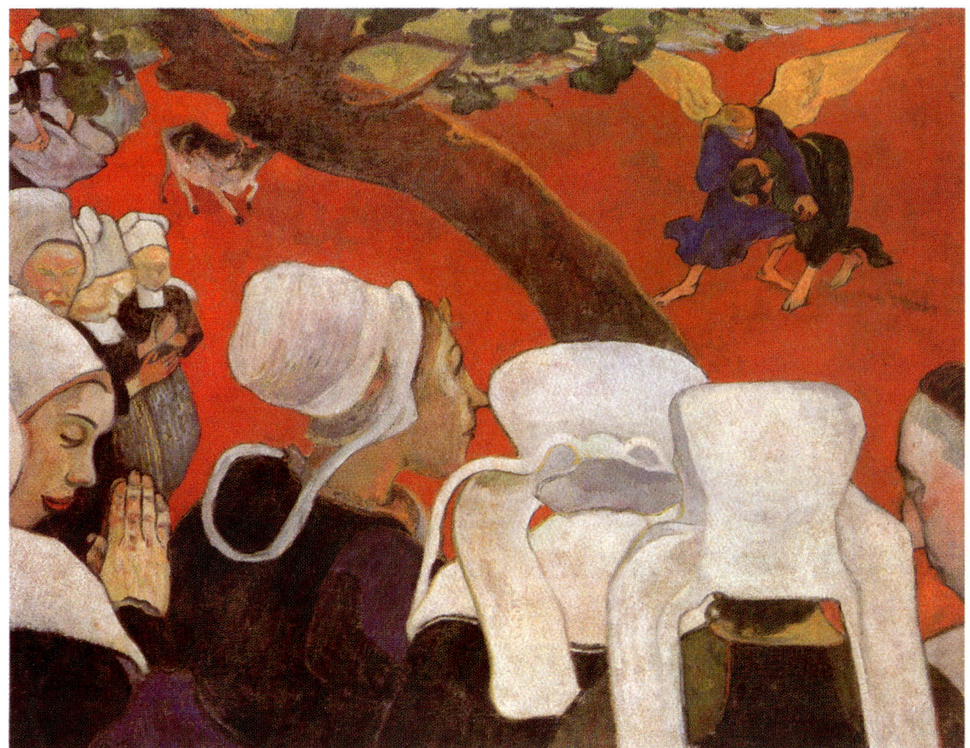

Vision After the Sermon, Jacob Wrestling with the Angel by Paul Gauguin.

*Actual colors vary, depending on printing. Caps are actually light indigo to blues.

Saturation Contrast

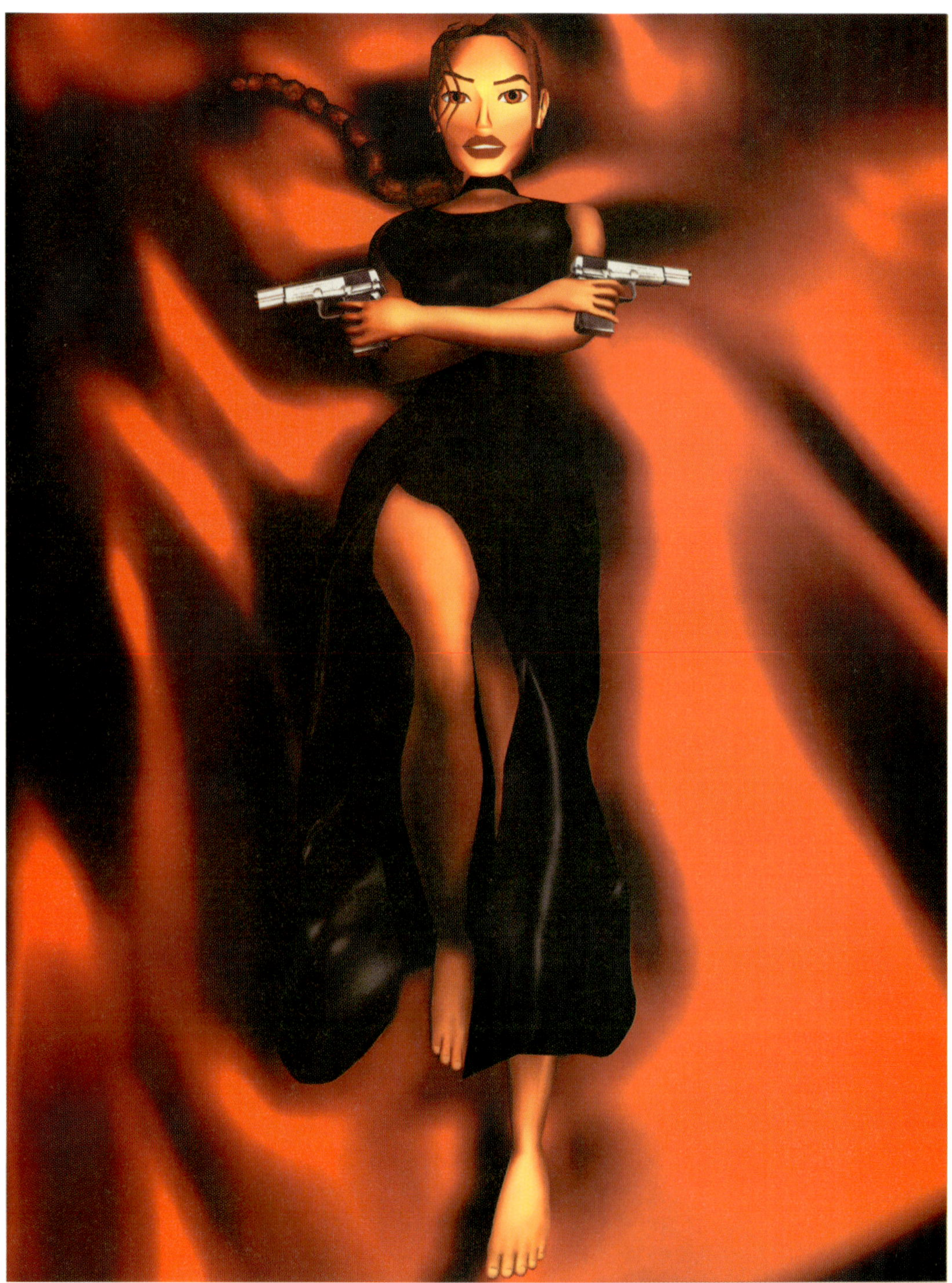

Lara Croft: Tomb Raider, PlayStation.
Used by permission of Eidos Inc.
The saturated red background sets the stage for the characteristics of *saturated contrast.* Subtle nuances of saturated contrast in this composition occur when the values change from red to dark red seen in the background, as well as, contrast between the saturated red and skin tones of Lara Croft.

Saturation Contrast

The Character of Saturation

Before we discuss saturation contrast, let us take a brief look at what the term saturation actually means. Previously we discussed the properties of saturation in Chapter One, but it bears repeating at this juncture. We know that the general description of saturation is the absolute purity of a hue, which is to say, its freedom from black, white or gray. First, we'll explore the *general* definition in the pure *technical* terms. Second, we will look at the term saturation in a more *specific* sense, as it relates to color "purity."

To do this we must explore the term *intensity*, as well. Many have espoused that saturation and intensity are one in the same. In fact this has been the popular language of this past century. We want to see why that is, and then propose a different approach to the two words. The general agreed definition among the majority of theorists is that *saturation is the degree of the purity of a color (and it's freedom from black or white) or hue as it is measured by intensity or brightness factors*. The well known color theorist of the 20th century, Johannes Itten, said that saturation "indicates the intensity or purity of a color."

This formal or *general* definition of saturation refers to any given hue in its most saturated state. Whether a primary, secondary or intermediate hue, it would then be whatever the most *pure state* of that hue could possibly be. We already understand that to intensify yellow, we add white. White is the vehicle that causes that yellow to become brighter, or more intense. This is where the problem arises. Does a color become more intense (or brighter) as it moves away from the saturated state, or towards it? If intensity relates to brightness, then we would have to say that greater intensity is moving away from the saturated condition. So, how do we then interpret intensity? Intensity is identified in most circles as *the degree or amount of saturation, strength or purity of any particular hue. A vivid or brilliant color is high intensity, a dull color is low intensity.* This supports the notion that intensity moves *away from* the saturated state, as does dullness. But if intensity were the same as saturation, then would it not make more sense that greater intensity is working its way *toward* saturation, rather than away from it?

Intensity is certainly saturation's companion, if not the exact same family. To say that they are the same then requires some explanation. As we examine the evolving debate over this complicated definition, these are the types of questions we need to ask ourselves,. We must be willing to give a deductive answer when the question arises, and then it is up to the individual to discern the differences between intensity and saturation.

To further explore what saturation is then, would be to offer the specific argument about the word *purity*, which is *commensurate to saturation.* Let's take *purity* to the extreme and precise. Purity relates to color in the following ways:

- Primary colors exist in and of themselves. We cannot mix any other combination of colors to come up with yellow, blue and red. They are the foundation colors for all others.
- Secondary colors are produced by mixing two primary colors.
- Intermediate colors (some say tertiary) are made by combining one primary and one secondary color.
- All of these colors have a saturated or pure state.

A common question is, "In concrete terms, if we were to subscribe the term *purity* to saturation, wouldn't we actually only refer to the primaries as truly the saturated colors?" One could say that purity has been violated when any other color has been introduced into another. It would not simply be the case of *freedom from black or white* to keep it saturated, but any color would rob the purity. However, to understand the word purity, we need to look to another word under purity's definitions, for better understanding. If we substitute the word *clarity* of a given hue or color, that reveals that only black or white truly eliminates purity, since they intensify or dull down a color. Black and white additions prevent clarity of color and opacify the true character of the color.

Nothing has really changed. All we have done in this case is prove to ourselves how saturation/purity functions, and confirm why it is that only black and white additions prevent saturation. We have basically done so by changing the word from *purity* to *clarity*. Now we know why the primaries are not solely relegated to purity. So then purity is not in the sense that color be *untouched*, or virgin color, so to speak. Rather it is a state of *visual clarity*, which then quenches the argument that it would be any color that compromises the purity or saturation of a color.*

Saturation Contrast

Saturation contrast is the difference between the *purity* of colors and the lighter or darker less pure colors. Saturation contrast is sometime very obvious, and other times it takes a very close look to determine whether or not it is indeed the difference in intensity or darkness.

This bouquet is an example of saturation contrast. The dried flowers that surround the saturated red flowers were at one time the same hue. Now that they have dried, there is an extreme contrast of saturation, which is easy to see. The bouquet is not necessarily the best example, but it serves as the concept behind saturation contrast.

There are a number of methods to demonstrate saturation contrast.

1. A color may be changed or diluted by the addition of black. Black actually dispossesses a color of its light characteristics, as to construct a type of filter in order to screen out a portion of the light itself.

   As we consider *The Penitent Magdalene* (page 145) the primary color red seen on the figure's dress has been diluted or shaded with black to create darkness in the room. The addition of black creates a very deep and dark muted red-orange in a large part of the background, which has developed a focused and mysteriously quiet composition. In terms of

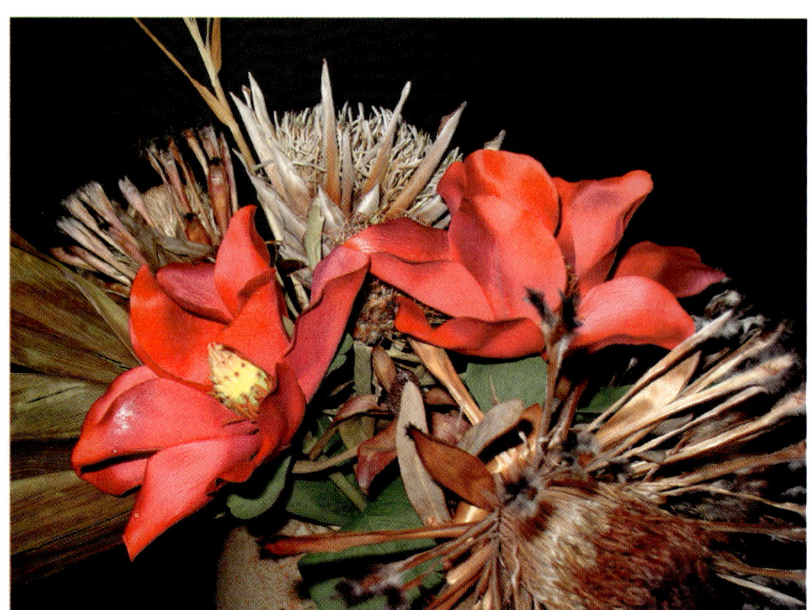

Dried arrangement of Hawaiian flowers.
Photo by Alan Burner.

* Note: An emphasis of this text is to use and develop a student's critical thinking skills to indicate why such theory is true. Rather than always assuming everything you hear is gospel, why not investigate to see why it is true, or in some cases, questionable?

high contrasts of light to dark color, La Tour was a master at the use of saturated contrasts.

2. A color may be changed or diluted by the addition of white. The effect of white additions are rather varied. Generally, white will cause the character of a pure color to become somewhat cooler, even if it is a warm color.

   Rosenquist's painting for the *Study of Marilyn* (below right) demonstrates how saturation contrast functions when white is added, intensifying the composition. The saturated red of the lipstick and fingernails has been extended into a very light tinted red throughout the rest of the composition. There is a wide variety of lightest red, to darker red, to the saturated red.

3. A saturated color may be changed or diluted with black and white (gray). The addition of gray will always cause a given color to have a certain neutrality or dullness.

   In O'Keeffe's *Black Iris,* what was originally blue and violets has the appearance of having been shaded, or neutralized by black and white additions. What we normally expect to see is more intense color in an Iris, but instead we see an iris which demonstrates a very mysterious, almost depressed mood. The color of the flower has been drastically dulled , so as to completely change the character of it's original color.

4. A saturated color may be changed or diluted with it's complement. The addition of green to red, for example, dulls the red progressively until the red seems almost black (depending on the hue of red).

   Notice the green tints and shades on the sides of the mountains and in the clouds themselves in the painting *The Great Day of*

The Penitent Magdalene by Georges de La Tour. © Réunion des Musées Nationaux/Art Resource, NY.

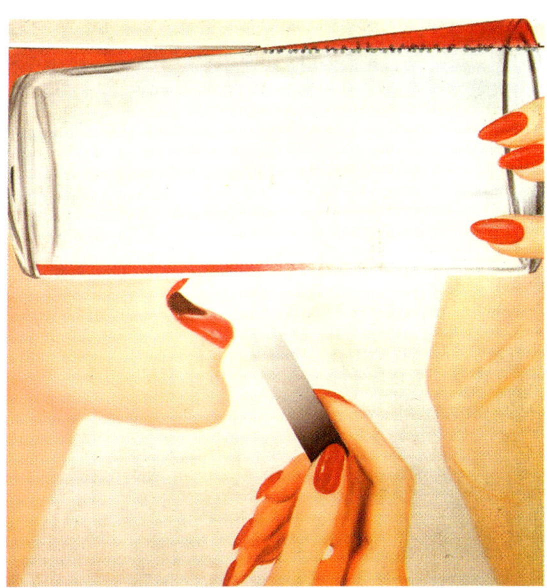

STUDY FOR MARILYN by James Rosenquist. 1962, 37.5 × 36 in., Oil on canvas. © James Rosenquist/Licensed by VAGA, New York, NY.

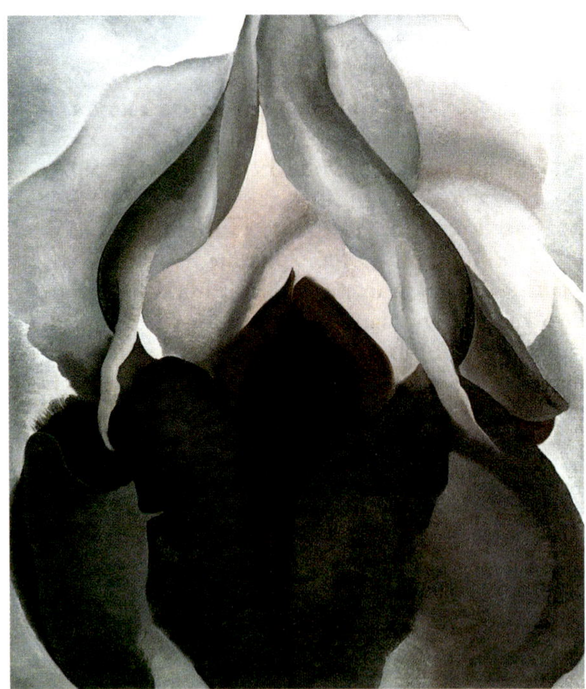

Black Iris by Georgia O'Keeffe.

His Wrath by John Martin. As the slopes of the cliffside progress downward and blend with the red, the area becomes darker and darker, creating an enormous contrast with the saturated red areas. Adding white to this dull red/green complementary mix, will lighten the mixture to produce some very unusual tints and shades (see middle ground clouds, with lighter dull reds and greens).

John Martin's painting (below) illustrates the power of saturated contrast. The center of the composition is a very saturated red-orange, in what appears to be an approaching smoky sunset. Below, the earth opens to reveal a lighter red-orange glow, which contrasts heavily against the darkest red-orange foreground. Fully half of the composition consists of a deep shaded red, which appears to have been dulled down by its complement of green.

Saturated contrast comes in many versions. A good example would be to present a complementary contrast, one which would be saturated and the other dulled. Saturated red next to the dulled green complement is one method. The green would be dulled by adding its complement of red to the mix, creating a very dull green next to the saturated red. Complementary colors always *complement* one another, but when one is dulled, the contrast is even greater, as well as the complement.

Saturated contrast can also produce provocative emotional effects. Black added to violet seems to change the color to sudden dreariness. Such may be the case with O'Keeffe's *Black Iris*. The sudden in-

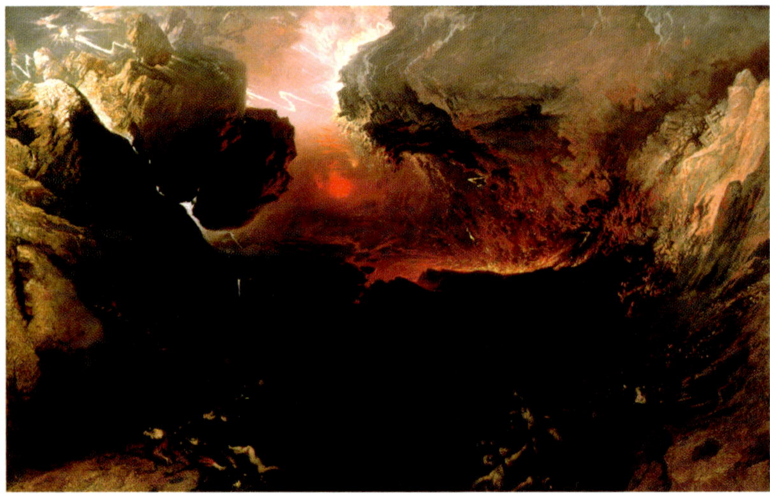

The Great Day of His Wrath by John Martin.

troduction of black into yellow by small degrees extinguishes the light, as this dulled hue's personality begins to change into a more noxious or unsavory mood. Even though yellow is normally a very vibrant and jubilant color, small amounts of black or violet, for example, can change yellow into a very harsh and disparaging color.

The animated character of *Shenmue, Virtua Fighter IV, Playstation 2* is probably one of the most overt examples of saturation contrast (below).

Her earrings display a very saturated red, while her cloak is a very shaded red and her inner suit a tinted light red. The earrings and her inner suit are the focus of this saturation contrast example. Shenmue would not be considered as the most effective example, however, of saturation contrast, since there is so little actual saturation in the composition. In fact, Shenmue will serve as a better example of *tints and shades*, which we cover in the next chapter.

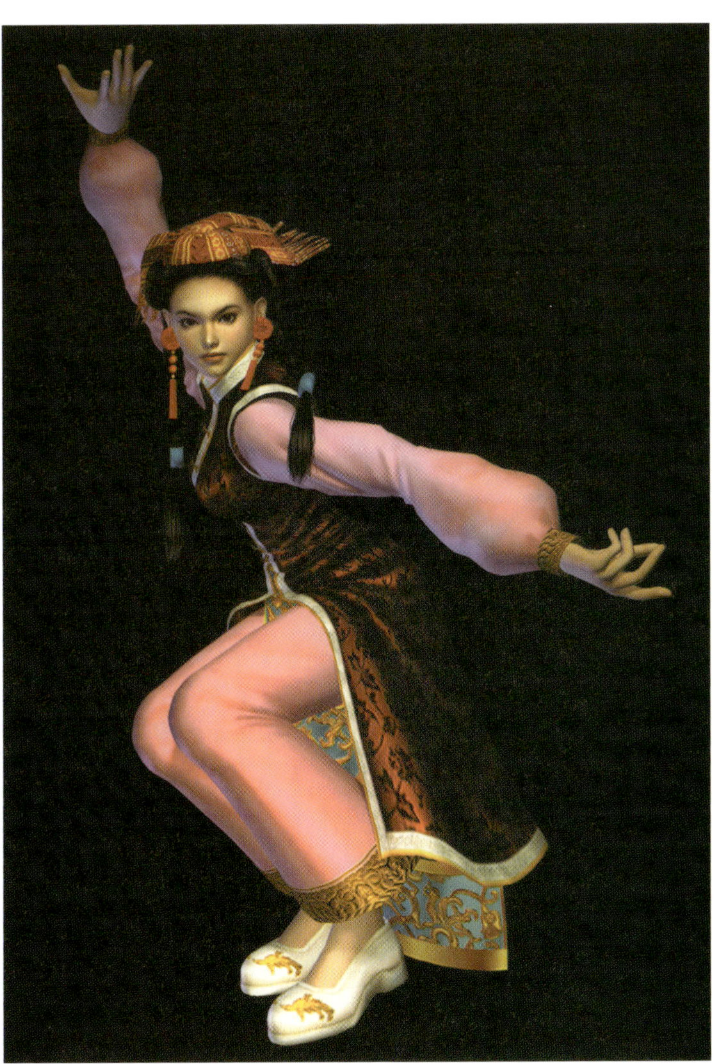

Shenmue, Virtua Fighter IV, Playstation 2.
Used by permission of Eidos Inc.

Simultaneous Contrast

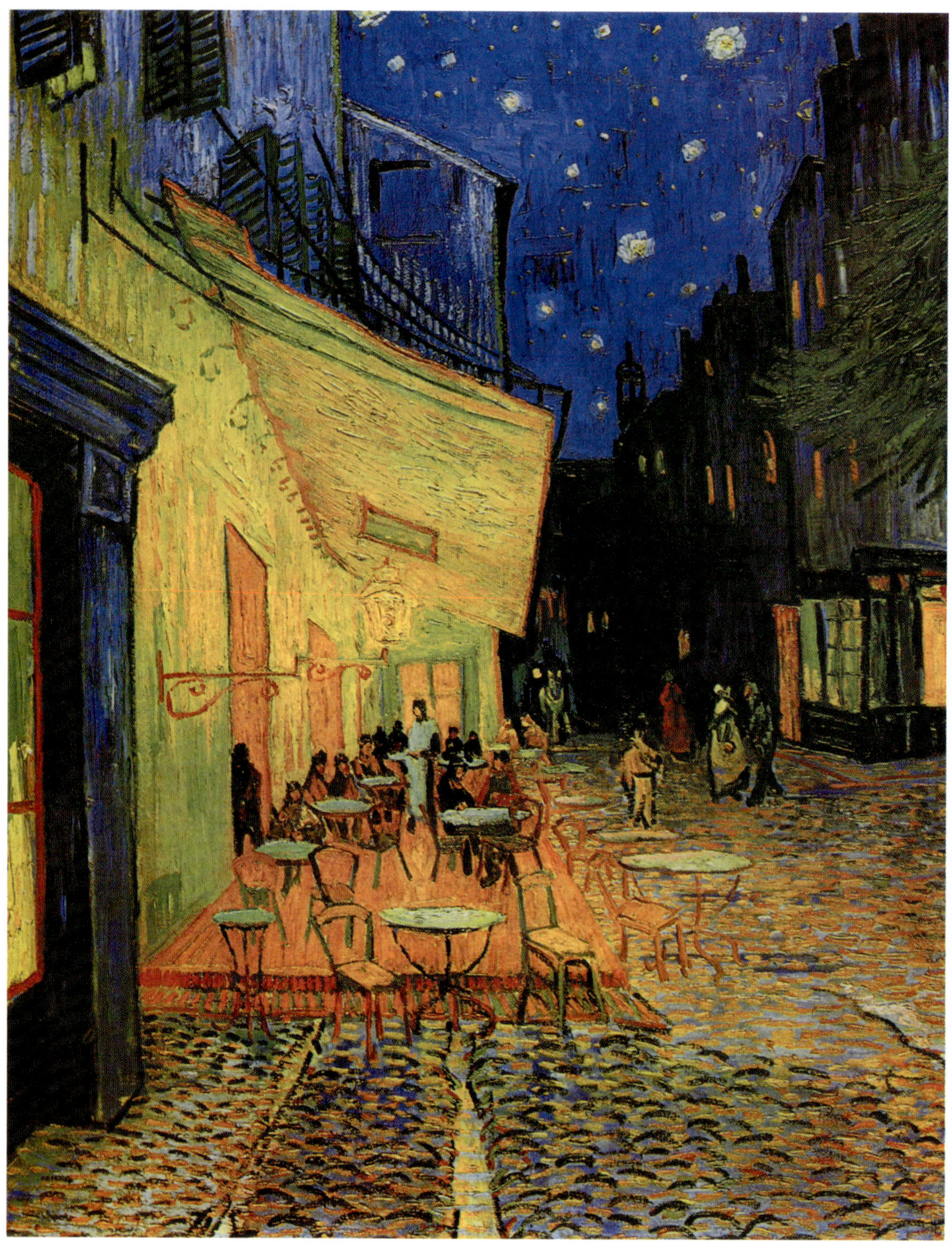

Café Terrace at Night by Vincent van Gogh, exemplifies just one of many excellent examples of Simultaneous Contrast.

Simultaneous Contrast

Simultaneous contrast basically refers to the manipulation of one color by placing it next to another. When placing a specified color next to another, one color will visually influence the character of the other hue in terms of value and intensity. Simultaneous contrast has an odd sort of similarity to that of complementary contrast in terms of psychological effects. Just as complements need each other, so do simultaneous contrasts when it pairs with opposites.

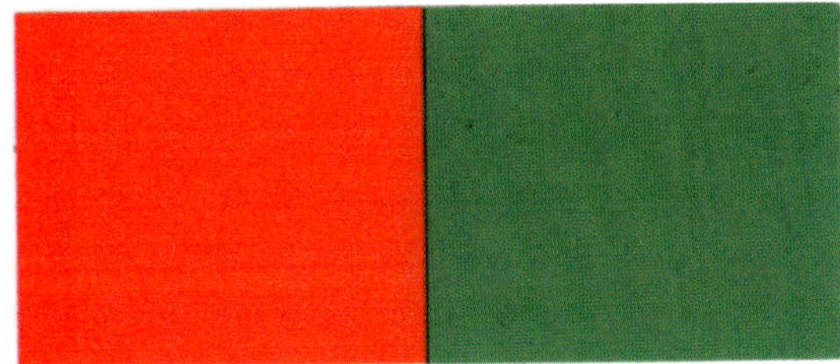

Red and Green Complements—Simultaneous Contrast

One way simultaneous contrast functions is the pairing of two complements, especially red and green, since they are of equal value. One should be able to see a thin gray line where the red and green meet in the center. This phenomenon has to do with mixing two complements. We mentioned earlier in the text that the mixing of two pigmented complements would result in the cancellation of the two colors. Basically, they physically cancel each other out. In simultaneous contrast, the eye mixes those two colors psychologically. Between the red and the green our eye produces gray.

Simultaneous contrast can be created by contrasting achromatic values, chromatic and achromatic pairs, or by contrasting *near complements* of chroma. For reasons that we do not entirely understand, the human eye simultaneously requires the complement of any given color, and as we discussed in the previous chapter, the eye instinctively produces the complement in its physical absence. Needless to say, this effect enters into the psychological realm, since the actual complement does not have a physical existence, and cannot be recorded effectively. This experiment works best two-dimensionally. Place two flat objects, or pieces of paper, in complementary colors together. Three dimensional surfaces will create a gray shadow, which becomes a false substitute for the gray line that should be there instead.

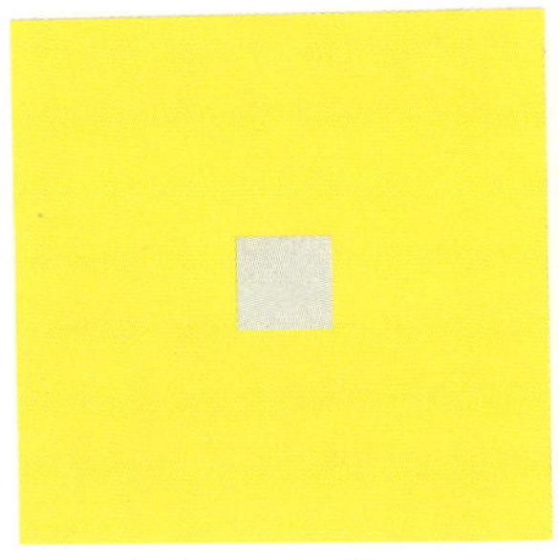

Yellow influence on Gray

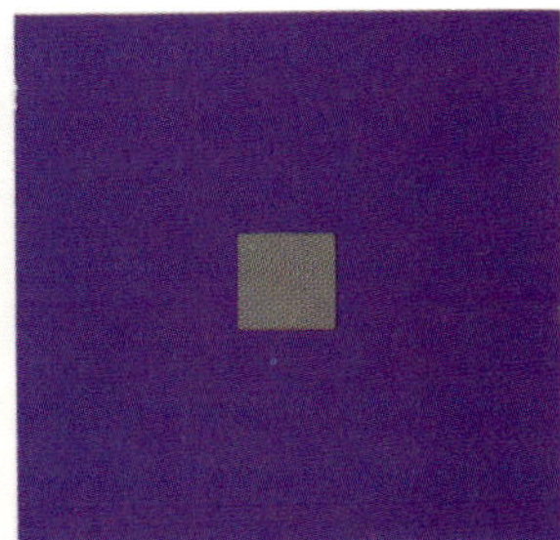

Violet Influence on Gray

Another way to achieve simultaneous contrast results can be observed in the above two examples. The gray squares are of the same value, but it is the influence of the saturated color which causes the gray squares to appear darker and lighter than the other respectively. The gray square seems very much more intense because the intensity of the yellow is causing the gray to lighten. The gray square also has a slight yellow tinge to it. The violet square influences its gray square, but in opposite fashion. The gray square is much darker, because it is taking on the attributes of violet, which is the least intense, or darkest color. The gray square here clearly has violet tones. Needless to say, the remaining colors of red, orange, green and blue will produce their own separate and commensurable influence over the same gray square.

The gray line effect can be measured in paintings, as well as bar samples. The gray line effect diminishes when the hard-edged complements become less distinct.

The reproduction of Robert Indian's *Love* composition (next page), exhibits a reasonable example of *simultaneous contrast.* Both the saturation levels of the green and the red trick the eye into seeing that gray zone. In lesser effect, the *near complements* of the red and blue will often produce a weaker version of that gray line.

Additionally, near complements (excluding the chromatic effect of gray seen above) produce

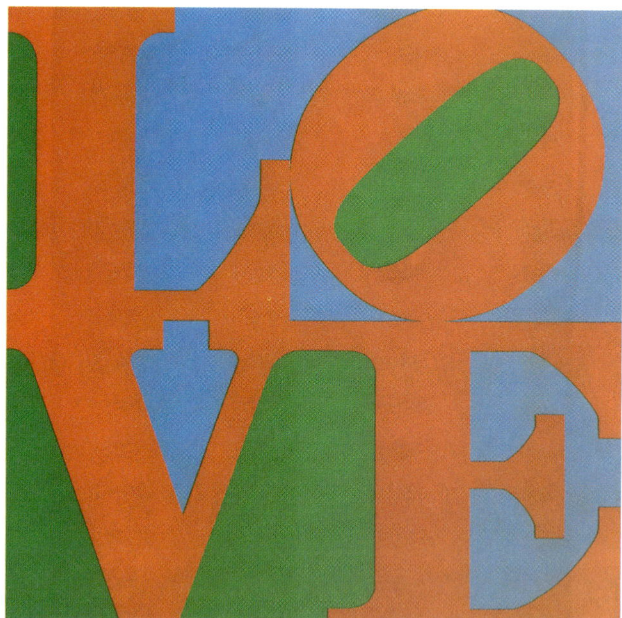

Love by Robert Indiana. This painting exhibits one version of simultaneous contrast. In the actual painting, the complements create a gray or neutral zone (line) between the green and the red letters. "Love" 1966 Robert Indiana © 1999 Morgan Art Foundation/Artists Rights Society (ARS), New York.

chromatic contrasts, such as with yellow and blue, orange and violet and red and blue. These all produce a variable gray zone, enhancing its neighboring color. In the case of orange and violet, for example, violet should cause the complement of orange, which is blue, to reflect back to itself. Orange in turn, would cause the complement of violet, which is yellow, to be pushed back to itself as well.

The results will yield an orange and a blue that have had the inherent natures altered, so that the near complements will be tinged with their own complement. Therefore, a certain change of intensity will occur. This may take a bit of practice to get accustomed to seeing these more subtle effects.

Van Gogh's *Café Terrace by Night* on page 148 is an excellent example of the effects of near complements in simultaneous contrast of yellow and blue. A certain shimmer can be detected in the yellow, and there is a richness about the deep blue night sky. Needless to say, the emphasis is on the café and it is the simultaneous contrast, or effect of it that intensifies the café to such an extreme. Van Gogh paints a blue to blue-violet sky, which creates a type of pulsating environment,. This dreamy atmosphere becomes almost another world, or a different time zone. The radiant café scene seems invitingly surreal, providing a place of evening solace from the dark night.

Van Gogh created other compositions with a similar attitude. Even though *Starry Night* is not a perfect or true example of simultaneous contrast, we can see analogous attributes built into the painting. The vast expanse of blue sky is illuminated by the radiant yellow stars. The dark blue sky against the yellow stars gives greater intensity to the stars themselves. One of the reasons that we cannot truly identify this painting as simultaneous contrast is because of the deep blue sky, which merges gradually with the luminous light from the stars, creating turbulence. This effect is the problem with connecting this painting to simultaneous contrast. What would be needed is a stronger contrast of blue against the yellow in order to create the optimal effect of the blue upon the stars.

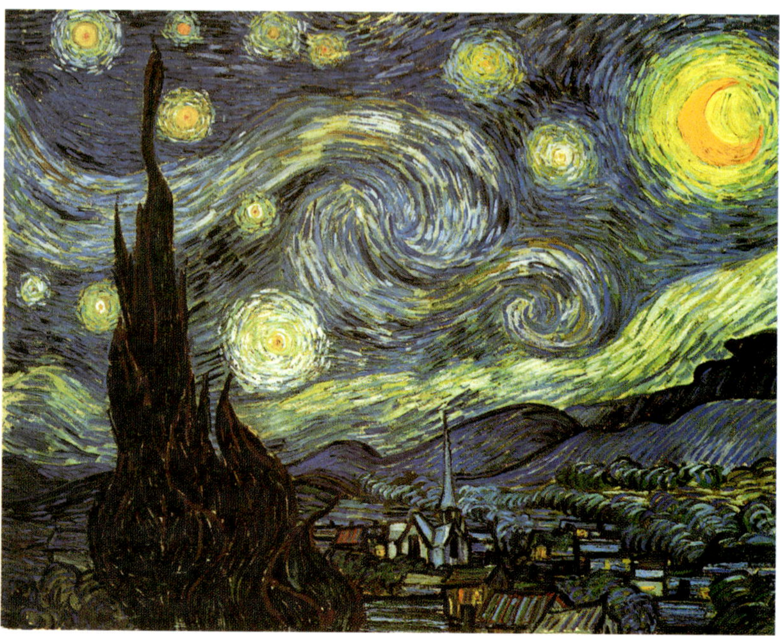

The Starry Night by Vincent van Gogh.
© The Museum of Modern Art/Licensed by SCALA/Art Resource, NY.

Color Balance and Extension Contrast

Color Balance

Before we present *extension contrast,* it is first important to understand *color balance.* Color balance is visually balancing color saturations and intensities. Every color combination, such as a complementary pair, must be visually balanced. Color harmonies must be balanced, whether they are dyads (two colors), triads (three colors), tetrads (four colors), or hexads (six colors). They all must be color balanced according to their degree of intensity, as shown in the following color bars:

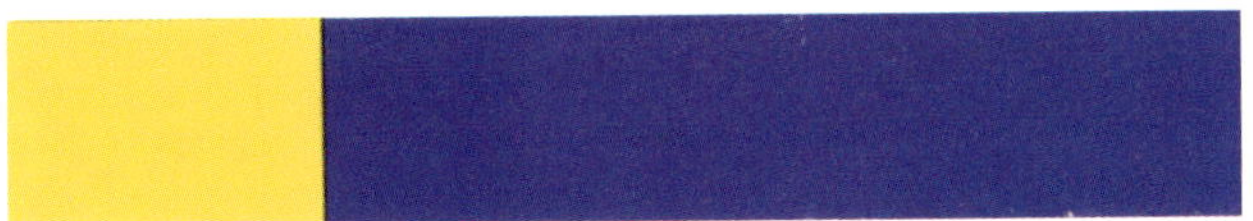

Yellow and Violet: 25% and 75%

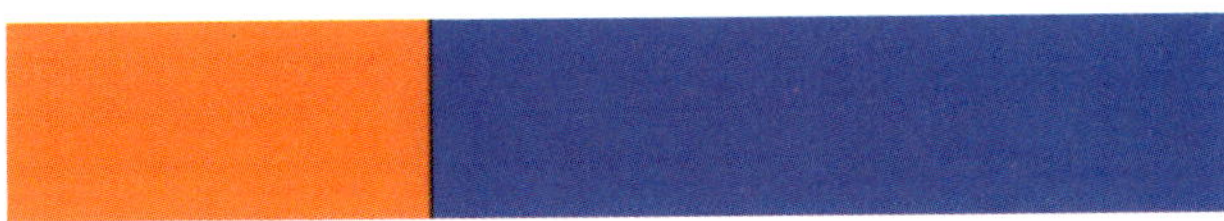

Orange and Blue: 33 1/3% and 66 2/3%

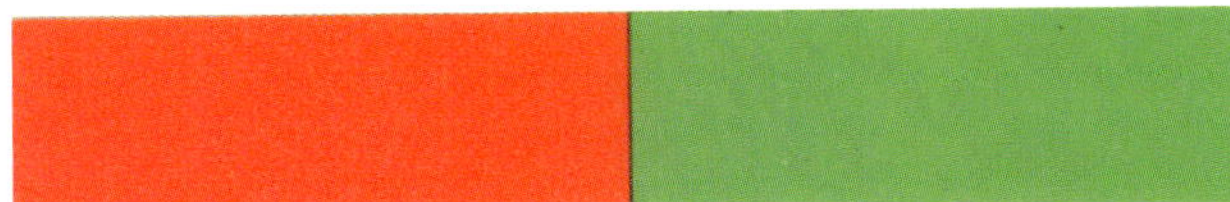

Red and Green: 50% and 50%

It is clear why color balance is important as we look at these examples. Yellow and violet complements require the greatest degree of difference in their percentage balance, and they are the most extreme of the color pairs. As we already know, yellow is the most intense of all colors and violet is the least intense. It therefore takes the greatest percentage of a color, which is violet, to control yellow's brilliance. The twenty five-seventy five percent ratio is needed, so that the eye does not focus on either of the two.

The same is true with the complements of orange and blue and red and green. The difference is the percentage between the two complements. The brighter, or more intense the color is, the less of that color is needed to balance the color complement of lesser intensity. When balancing more than two colors, such as a tetrad or hexad harmony, all colors will need to be balanced in order to create the optimal balance so that one does not draw attention to itself, more than another.

Helen Frankenthaler (below) incorporates color balance perfectly in her painting *The Other Side of the Moon.* Here the translucence of the yellow gradually disperses into the violet. The first inclination about the painting is that violet seems to slowly consume the yellow mist around the perimeter of the composition. On closer inspection, however, it is quite the opposite as the yellow slowly consumes the violet. It is, after all, the nature of light to disperse the dark. We know this from our discussions about the Gothic cathedral, and the effects of one single candle in a dark room, which is somewhat commensurate with this painting.

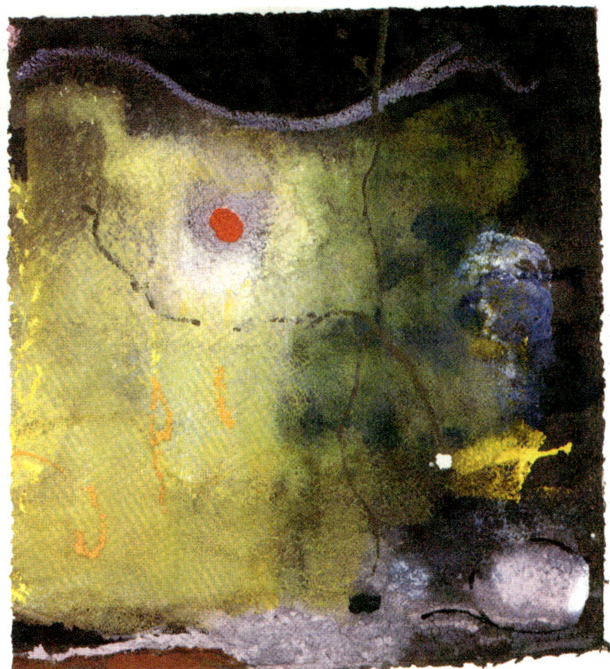

The Other Side of the Moon by Helen Frankenthaler
Source: Knoedler & Company

Extension Contrast

Extension contrast incorporates the same idea in terms of balance of color, but it is the *extreme* of the color balance system. The percentages are not constant as are those of color balance. There are color contrast compositions, which incorporate percentage extreme ratios of as little as three to five percent, depending on the color, saturation and intensity levels, plus imagery and emotional or mood concerns.

Of course we know that mood content is polar as well, since saturated yellow has more upbeat qualities, as opposed to the heavy and oppressing character of violet. Orange, while being fairly intense, does not have the equal brilliance to yellow. Because orange is much less intense, it is allowed more freedom within the percentage space. Blue is also less oppressive than violet, and commensurately does not require as great of a percentage of space. This means that red and green are the perfect couple, since neither one requires more or less percentage space than the other. These ratios are only valid when the colors stated remain in their saturated form. Should any of these be tainted in any way, the stability or balance of contrast changes as well.

These are the basics of harmonious proportions. The term extension contrast then, is allowing one color in the composition to dominate.

The warning flag at Waimea State Beach is a common site on the North Shore. It is a warning sign for those to think twice about going into the very dangerous surf. The red flag, in the lower center of the composition, is the first thing that the viewer notices. The saturated red flag controls the composition by virtue of its contrast extension. The vast expanse of blue is needed to balance the small amount of saturated red in the center. It actually takes that much blue in order to balance the small red flag in the picture. This is quite different from our standard color balance model, yet it does relate in an extreme sense. The smallest amount of red is balanced by the surrounding blues and or-

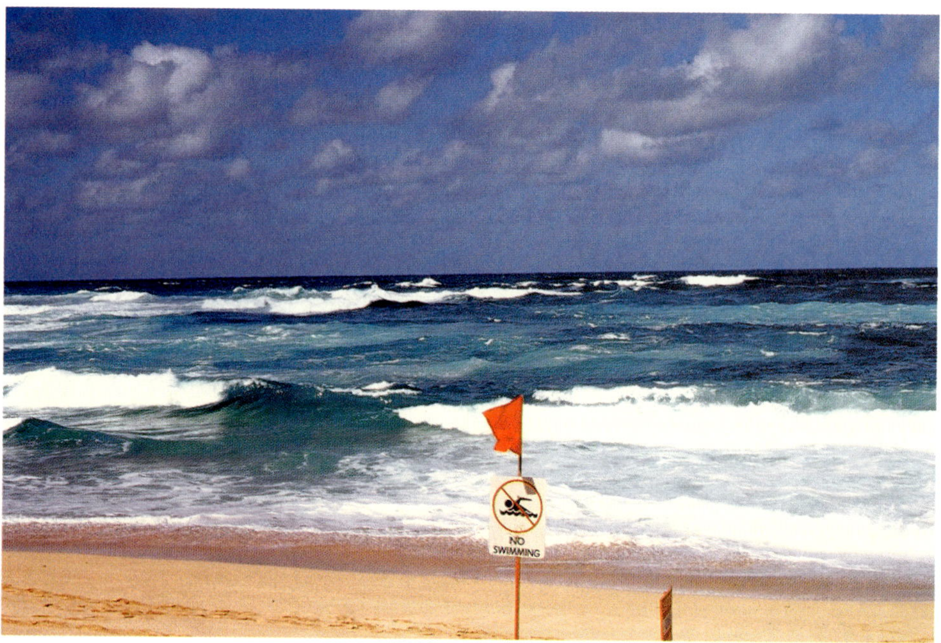

Warning Flag at Waimea State Beach, North Shore, Oahu, Hawaii.
Photo by Alan Burner.

ange sand, yet the flag clearly dominates for attention. It takes a full extension of other colors out into the picture plane in order to balance the minor amount of red.

Another example of extension contrast can be seen in Pieter Brueghl's painting *Landscape with Fall of Icarus*.

The red shirt of the plowman in the center of the composition seems to perform brilliantly, as if to fight for attention in a vast expanse of green, blue, blue-green and dark orange tones. Because the character of red is so aggressive, it holds credibility within the composition. The saturated red shirt of the plowman is not lost in the picture plane, as the tints and shades of dark oranges and light greens are not authoritative enough to keep the viewers eye from the red shirt for any length of time. In one sense, the green and orange tints and shades are struggling to overcome the saturated red, while the red itself seems to be putting on a type of performance, trying to draw attention away from the other colors, to itself.

In essence, extension contrast performs as an extreme version of color balance. Color balance is about specific percentages of complementary colors in harmony with one another, while extension is the competition of complements in a given space, or composition.

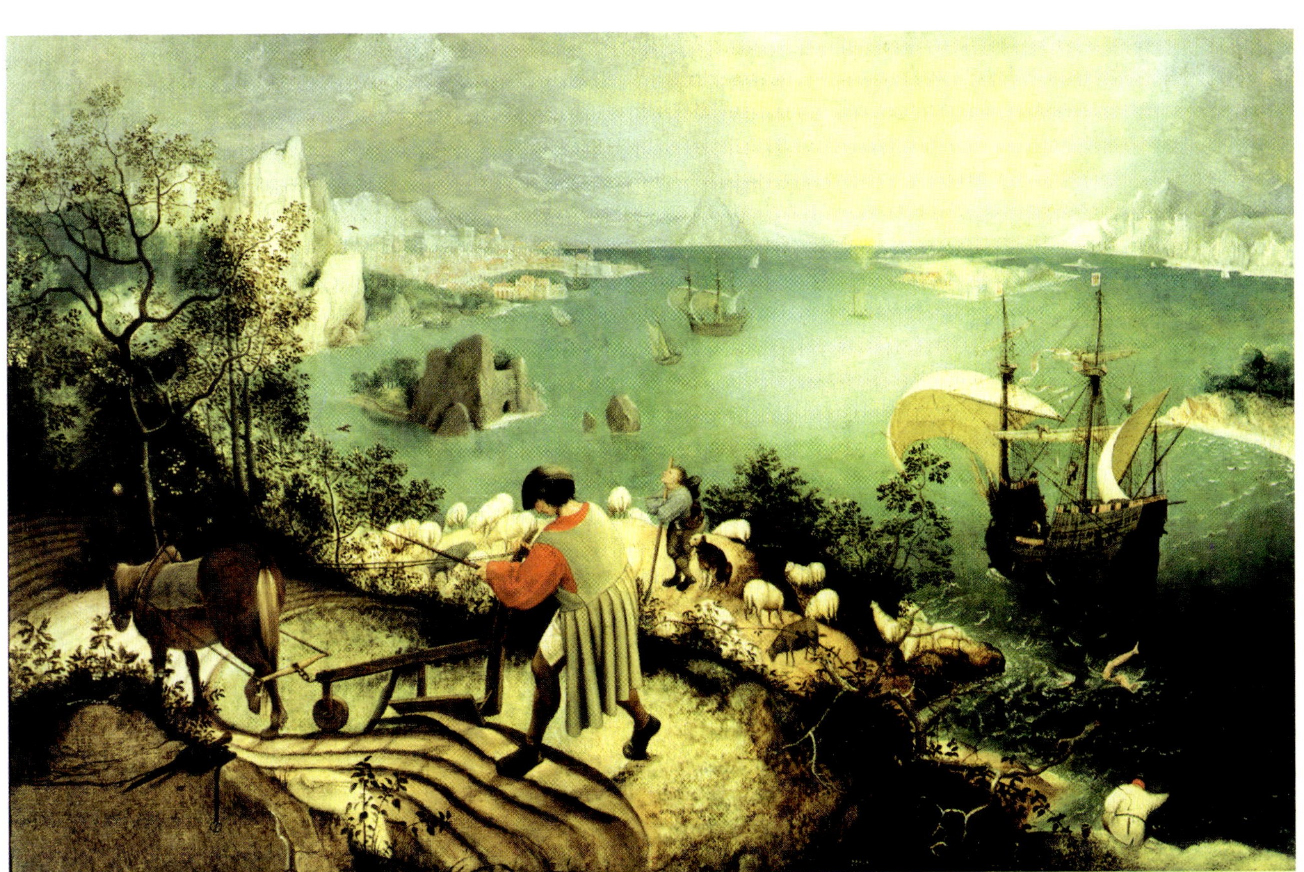

Landscape with Fall of Icarus by Pieter Brueghel.

Extension contrast is captured in this photograph, which is a result of a two hour traffic "snarl" in Southern California. At first glance, one is tempted to see the balance of complementary colors, yet the overall picture makes a better demonstration of *extension contrast*. The saturated orange shirt remains steadfastly in the center of the composition, while saturated blue pulls the eye out in every direction to see the entire picture. The greater part of the composition is neutral colors of gray values, excepting the very background colors. Of course, this is not a perfect example, as is Brueghel's work, but it does serve to illustrate the *concept* of extension.

In the following essay, we will continue our studies of light and color. This time, we will begin to focus more closely on the functional components of light, the colors that are produced and why. We will again look at the atomic structure, more specifically in relationship to colors produced by the particular elements in the outside natural environment.

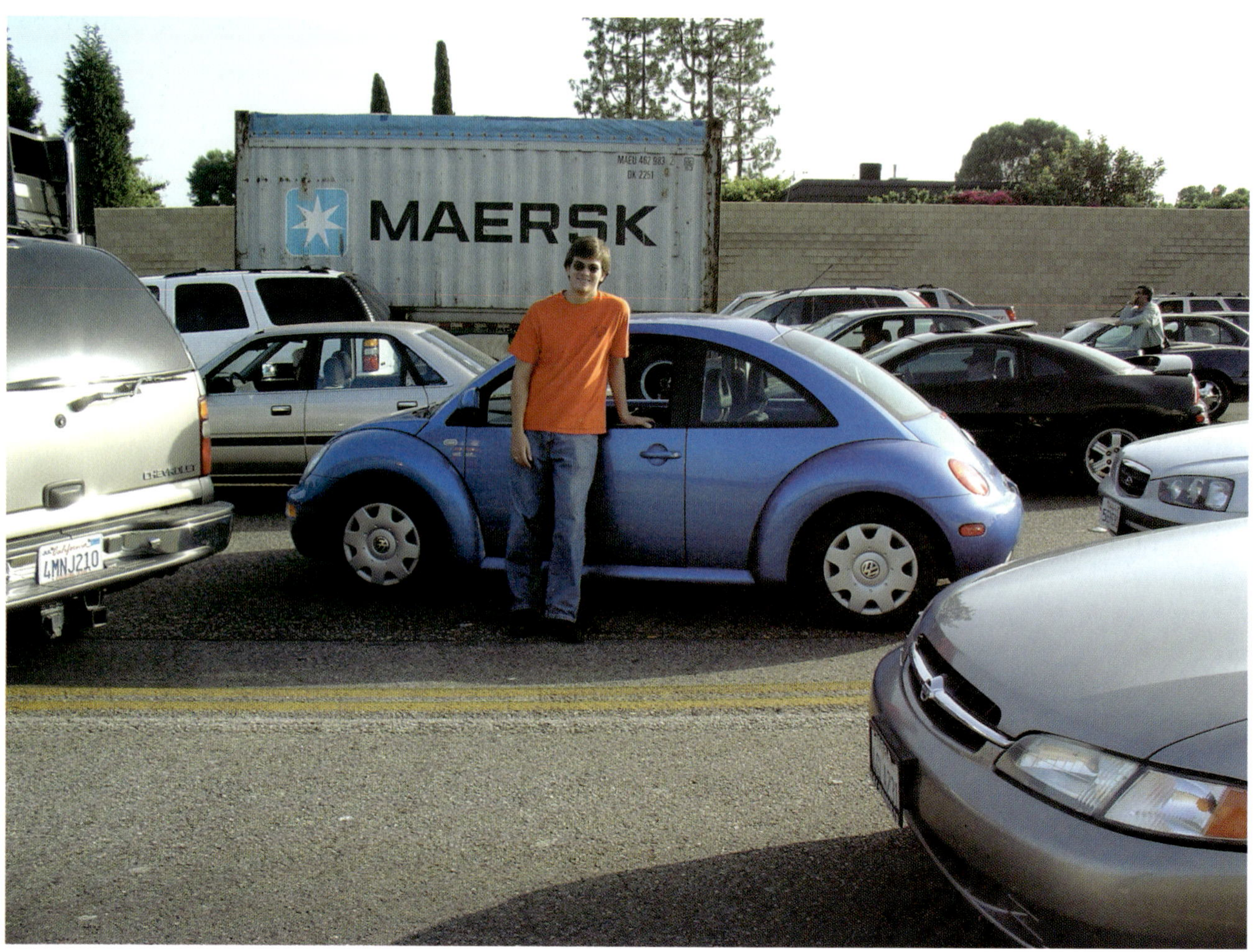

LA Gridlock.
Photo by Alan Burner.

Reading Complement

Sensations of Color Air and Water

By Hazel Rossotti

On this fine summer morning, the English Channel is almost turquoise, trimmed with white. Westwards, successive grassy headlands recede from green, through lovat, to smoky blue. The sky is not unrelievedly azure, for this is England, but the clouds are few, small and mostly white.

Looking westwards in the morning, we should have the sun behind us, so any light we can see must have bounced off something ahead of us. The colours which we see naturally depend on exactly what this 'something' is; on its composition, of course, but also on its size. Most of the 'invisible' particles in our atmosphere are tiny groups containing only two, sometimes three, atoms. They are many trillion, trillion times smaller than the smallest water droplet which we can actually see. But we can see water also as a skein of foam and as the ocean, extending to the horizon. Sunlight, of all visible wavelengths, stimulates oscillations in the tiny, widely separated particles in the air; but these oscillations re-emit mainly high-energy, short-wavelength *blue* light (see Figure 22). Blue light is also preferentially and more strongly scattered by those small particles of bulk matter, such as dust and germs, which, although they contain a large number of atoms, are appreciably larger than the wavelength of light. This blue light is responsible for the colour of fine smoke and distant landscapes.

A grassy headland looks green in sunlight because it absorbs most of the visible spectrum except for the green light, which is scattered in all directions from the surface. En route to the observer, it is scattered again, by molecules in air, and so its intensity is slightly decreased. The light which reaches the observer comprises this green light and the predominantly blue light which has been scattered off these same particles. So the green light we see from a distant headland is slightly less intense than from a near one, and it is mixed with considerable more

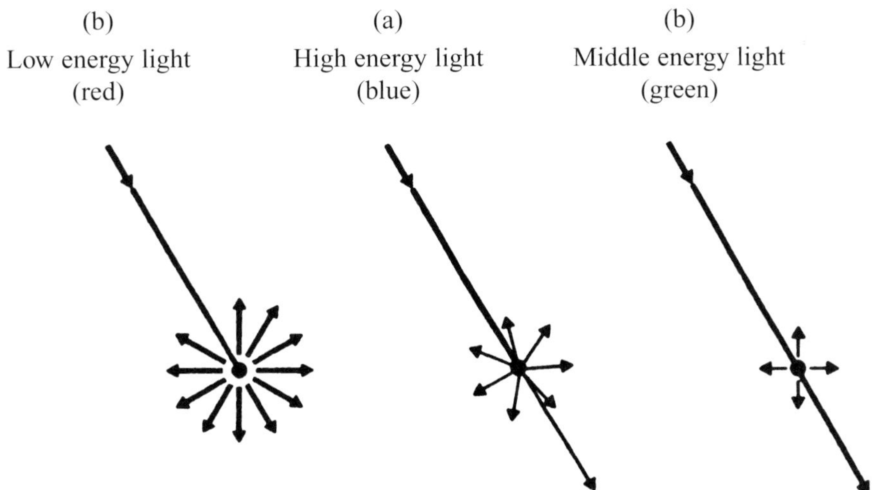

Figure 22. White light and tiny particles. *When light meets particles of size comparable to its wavelength, the high-energy light is preferentially scattered (a). As the energy decreases, the proportion of light transmitted increases (b), so that, for red light (c), very little scattering occurs.*

blue (see Figure 23); hence the colour gradation of aerial perspective by which painters endow their landscapes with a sense of depth.

Particles which are large compared to the wavelength of visible light do not scatter colours selectively. When white light falls on water droplets, therefore, that part of the light which is re-emitted, or scattered, is also white (see Figure 24). The smaller the droplets, the greater the surface between them and the air, and the higher the intensity of the scattered white light. Some clouds, which contain a high concentration of droplets, look sculpted rather than wispy. The dazzlingly white, fully illuminated regions of a bank of cumulus may cast shadows on the further parts, which in contrast seem grey.

If a cloud floats very low in the atmosphere, light scattered on to it from the Earth's surface may account for an appreciable fraction of its total illumination, and the cloud will then reflect some of the colour of the land, or water, over which it is passing. The low clouds which are all too common over the west coast of Scotland show heather-coloured tints in late summer (see Figure 25).

The sea, of course, reflects the sky. Water is the traditional mirror in mythology, from Greece to China. 'Narcissus joins his image in the lake' and 'the peasant drowns reaching for the moon.' But the sea is not a faithful mirror. It is always darker than the sky because it does not reflect 100 percent of the light that reaches it; and it is also greener. The light that falls on the sea will be a mixture of white light radiating from the sun, white light scattered from clouds, blue light from the sky and maybe a little light from the land. The light that travels from the sea to the observer comes by two routes. Some of it is reflected from the surface of the sea, and the colour of this is the same as the colour of the light shining on it. Other light may be reflected off the bottom of the sea; the colour of this light obviously depends on the colour of the sea bed. If this were

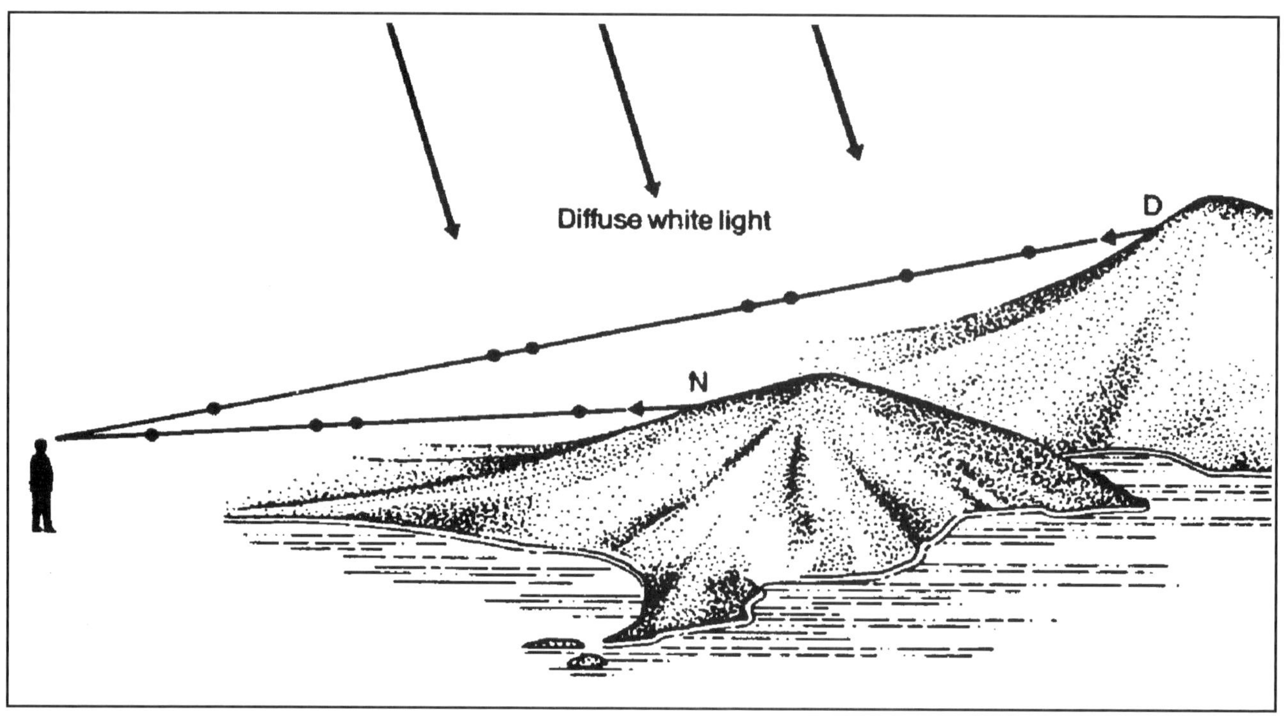

Figure 23. Distant blue. *The green light scattered from the distant grassy headland, D, is much the same as that from the nearer one, N. But, on its way to an observer, it meets more particles, which scatter away some green light (cf. Figure 22 (b)) and add some blue light (cf. Figure 22 (a)).*

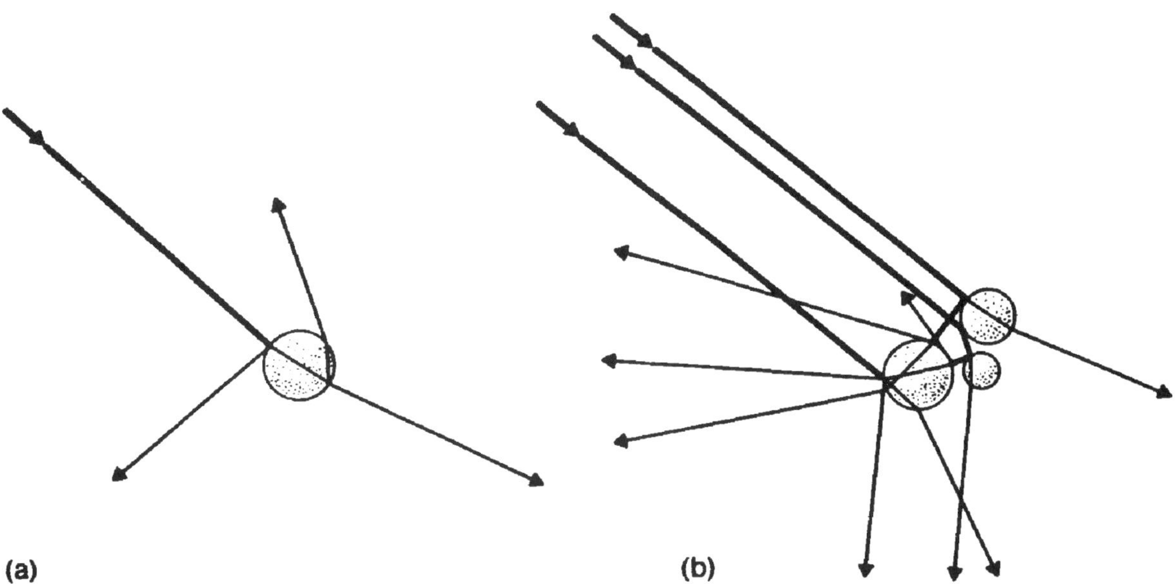

Figure 24. White light and droplets *(a) The reflection and transmission of white light by a single drop of water. (b) With a 'cloud' of three droplets, light emerges almost at random (even ignoring internal reflections).*

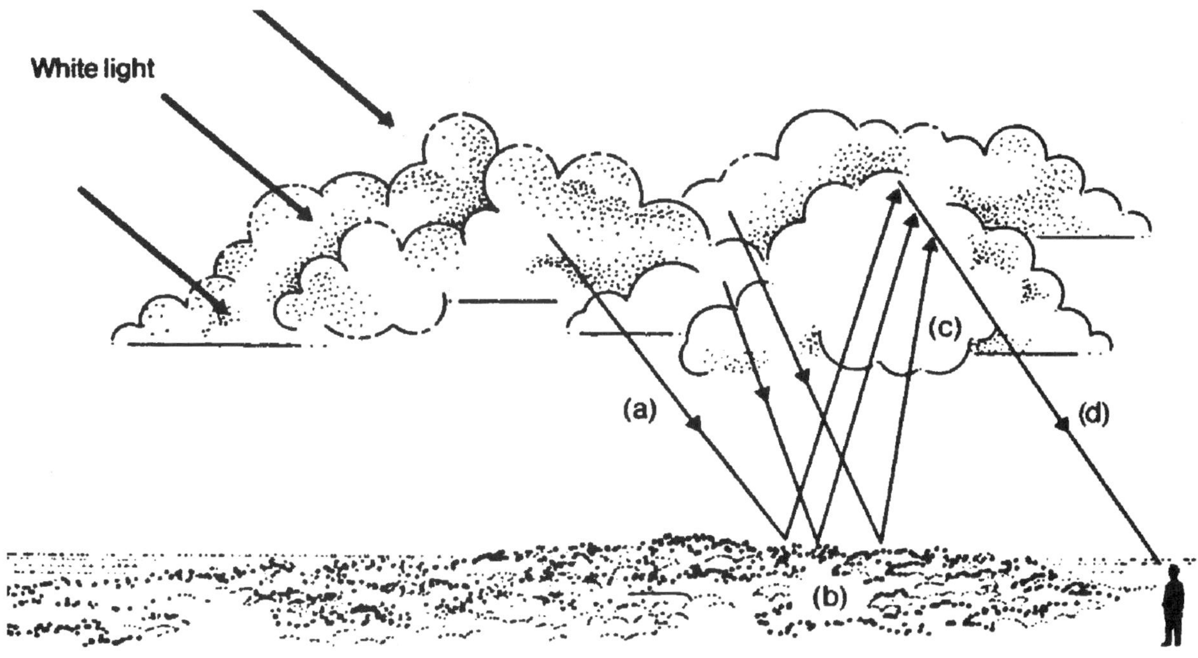

Figure 25. Reflected colour in clouds. *White sunlight (a) is scattered from cloud to hilltop. Flowering heather (b) absorbs green light preferentially, so blue and red are scattered preferentially (c) from the earth to water droplet and (d) back again. The cloud looks tinged with purple from the heather.*

covered with red coral, which absorbs all colours except red, the light reflected from the sea bed would be red. The sea would be magenta, as the observer would receive a mixture of blue and red light. But even if the sea bed were silver sand, the light reflected from the bottom would differ from the surface reflection because the water itself is very weakly coloured. It absorbs red light and so looks bluish green. The depth of the colour naturally increases with the water's depth; the red component of sunlight is almost totally absorbed by a hundred feet of water. Looking down from a cliff, or from an aeroplane, on to the coastline of a calm sea, we find the shallows charted in pale aquamarine, which darkens with depth, through clear blue-greens to sapphire.

The absorption of red light by water is dramatically illustrated by the Blue Grotto in Capri. This cave is connected to the open sea through a semi-circular hole only about 2.5 metres in diameter. Almost all the light which enters the eye of an observer inside the grotto has been reflected off the very pale sea bed about seven metres below the surface. As the sunlight therefore passes through at least 14 metres of water, an appreciable proportion of its red component is absorbed. So the water looks gleaming azure (see Figure 26).

As waves break, the water is flung into the air in a myriad of drops, and at each surface between air and water, sunlight is scattered, irrespective of wavelength, as from a cloud. So flying surf looks white, as does the foam at the sea's edge where air is momentarily encapsulated in bubbles of sea.

We return some twelve hours later to see the sun sinking behind black headlands in a blaze of red. The sunlight which reaches us has traveled through a much greater thickness of atmosphere at this late hour than it did around noon. Most of the blue light has been scattered away, as has much of the green and yellow; but the red and orange reaches us (see

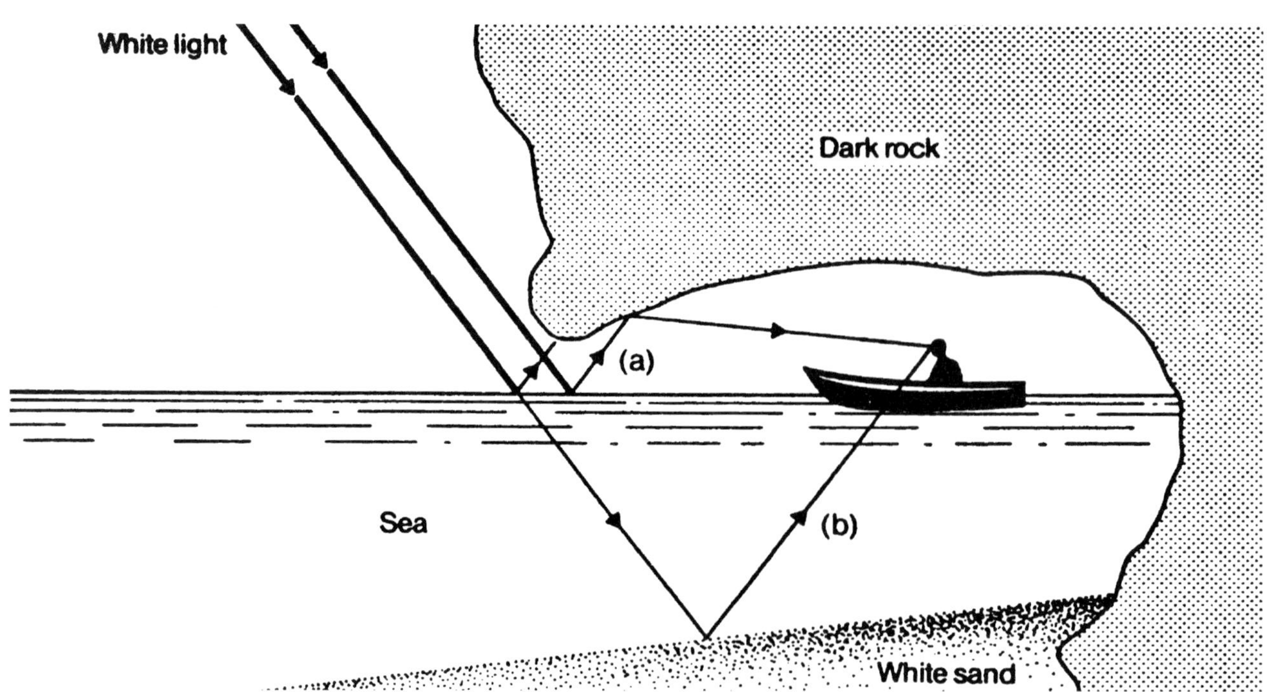

Figure 26. The Blue Grotto. *Of the little white light which enters the grotto by path (a), much is absorbed by the rock. Most of the light reaching the boatman has traveled along route (b), passing twice through a 7-metre layer of seawater, which absorbs most of the red light.*

Figure 27). As the sky to the east is dark blue, shading to emerald, a little blue light must have got through, and is being scattered back, together with light of the next highest energy, green. In an hour or so the only sunlight reaching us will be that reflected off the moon; and in moonlight we see no colour.

Sunsets are much influenced by the number and size of water droplets and solid particles in the air and are particularly spectacular after volcanic explosions which throw large quantities of very fine dust into the atmosphere. The scattering of light can also give rise to a range of less garish colours which can be seen when snorkeling on a sunny day in a calm sea. A swimmer who looks horizontally towards the sun, just under the surface of the water, sees the sea as almost as golden green. Much of the blue and violet has been scattered away, and some of the red has been absorbed. An about-turn sometimes produces a transformation scene in which the colour of the sea passes from green-grape and turquoise to a rich, though soft, blue-violet. When we are looking away from the sun, much of the light which reaches us is of short wavelength, scattered from particles which are too small either to sink or to make the sea look cloudy.

Of all the visual beauties of sea and sky, it is surely the rainbow which has most captured man's imagination. Symbol of God's pledge and man's hope, synonym for the infinitely varied richness of colour, no wonder that Wordsworth's heart leapt up when he beheld one. Although the rainbow is only one of a number of celestial arcs, it is perhaps the most spectacular. It is certainly one of the most familiar, at least to those who live in temperate zones with changeable weather. All we need is simultaneous rain and sunshine, with the sun behind the observer and not too high in the sky. Each drop of rain acts as a prism separating the sunlight into colours. If light of one particular wavelength meets a raindrop, some will be reflected back into the air and some will enter the drop. When the light within the drop reaches the surface, some will emerge back into the air and some will be reflected again within the drop. When the light enters or leaves the drop, its direction changes to an extent which depends on its

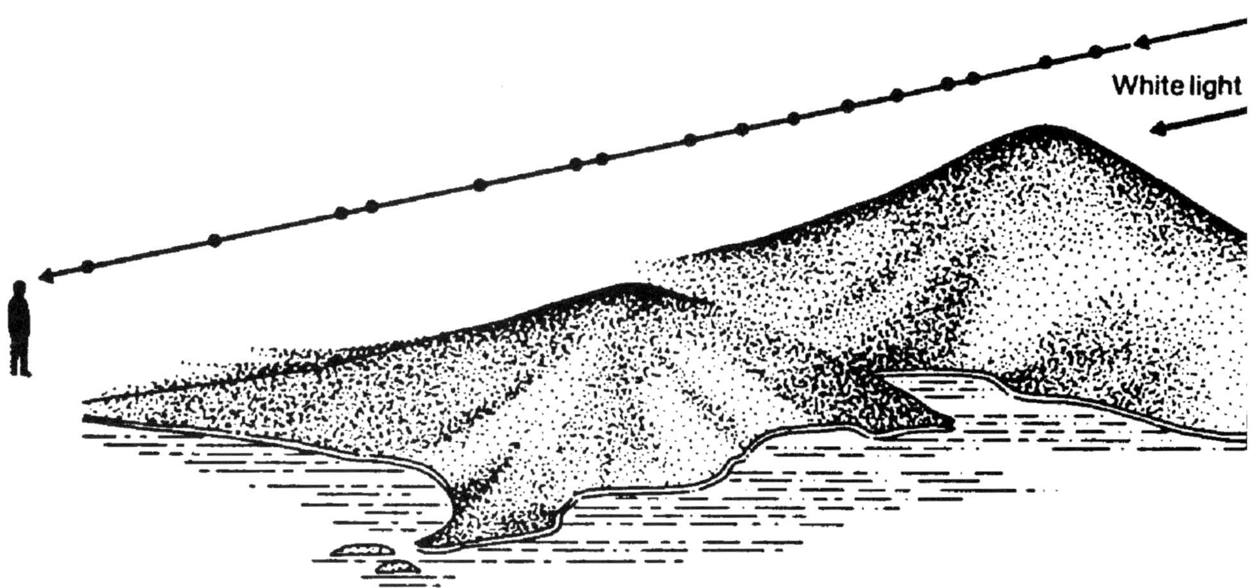

Figure 27. Sunset. *No light is scattered towards the observer from the headlands, which now look black. The low rays of the sun encounter many particles before they reach the observer. Almost all of the blue, and much of the green, has been scattered from them; the sun sets golden flame.*

wavelength. We can see this prismatic effect quite easily in a dew-drop early on a sunny morning when the light is still low enough to make the dew sparkle. If you focus your attention on a single drop and move your head gradually, you can see in turn each colour of the spectrum (see Figure 28).

When the sun shines on rain, we have a three-diamond dimensional mass of drops, all acting as prisms. After one reflection from an inner surface, each drop will re-radiate blue light at one angle to the sun, red at another and other colours at angles in between. We are not aware of all this, since we see only the light which falls on the very small area of our own pupils. We have to *scan* the emerging light from a single dew-drop in order to see the different colours. But when we stand and face sunlit rain, we receive blue light from some drops, green from others and so on. These drops, which supply an observer with light of a particular wavelength, all lie on the curved surface of a cone of which the axis runs through the observer (at the apex) towards the sun. The angle between the axis and the curved surface depends on wavelength. It is 40.6° for blue light, and 42° for red light. Other colours lie on cones of intermediate angle. The rainbow is that part of the bases of the set of cones which is visible above the skyline. The blue arc lies on the inside, as the blue cone has the sharpest apex (see Figure 29). As the sun rises in the sky, less of the rainbow protrudes over the horizon, and when the sun is more than 42° above the horizon, no rainbow will be visible (except from an airplane). A weaker, outer rainbow may be formed by light which has been reflected twice from the inner surface of drops. The cones of light are less than those formed after one reflection and the angle for red (50.4°) is less than that for blue (53.6°). Thus, although the red band is on the outside of the main rainbow, it is on the inside of the secondary one (see Figure 30). The water drops need not, of course, be rain. Spray from a boat, a waterfall or a lawn sprinkler can also split up sunlight into a spectrum of colour. But spray does not usually cover an area large enough to produce noticeably curved arcs. It can give a vivid strip of rainbow colours, but seldom an actual blow.

The band of colours in a rainbow is not exactly the same as the spectrum of sunlight obtained from a single triangular prism, and indeed, no two rainbows are identical. For light of only one wavelength, rays from the sun may enter the drop at slightly different angles, so they will travel at slightly different distances within the drop and emerge out of step with each other. As the angle of viewing them is gradually varied, the rays will alternately reinforce and cancel each other, to give a series of concentric bright and dark rings, of that particular colour, superimposed on the main rainbow.

The radii of these roundels depend on both the wavelength of the light and the size of the rain drops. From the discussion in Part Four of the effect

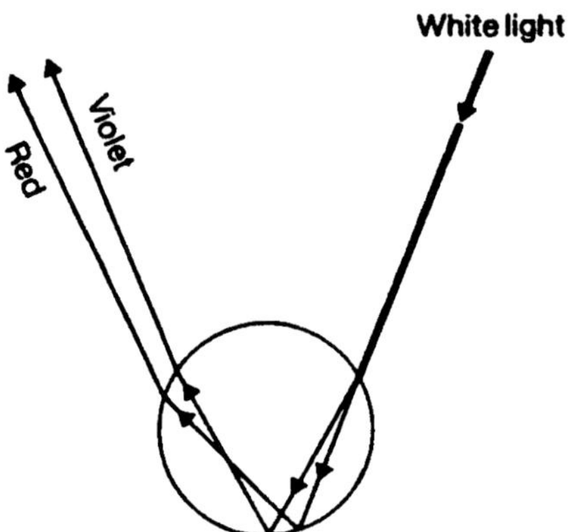

Figure 28. Colours from a dewdrop.

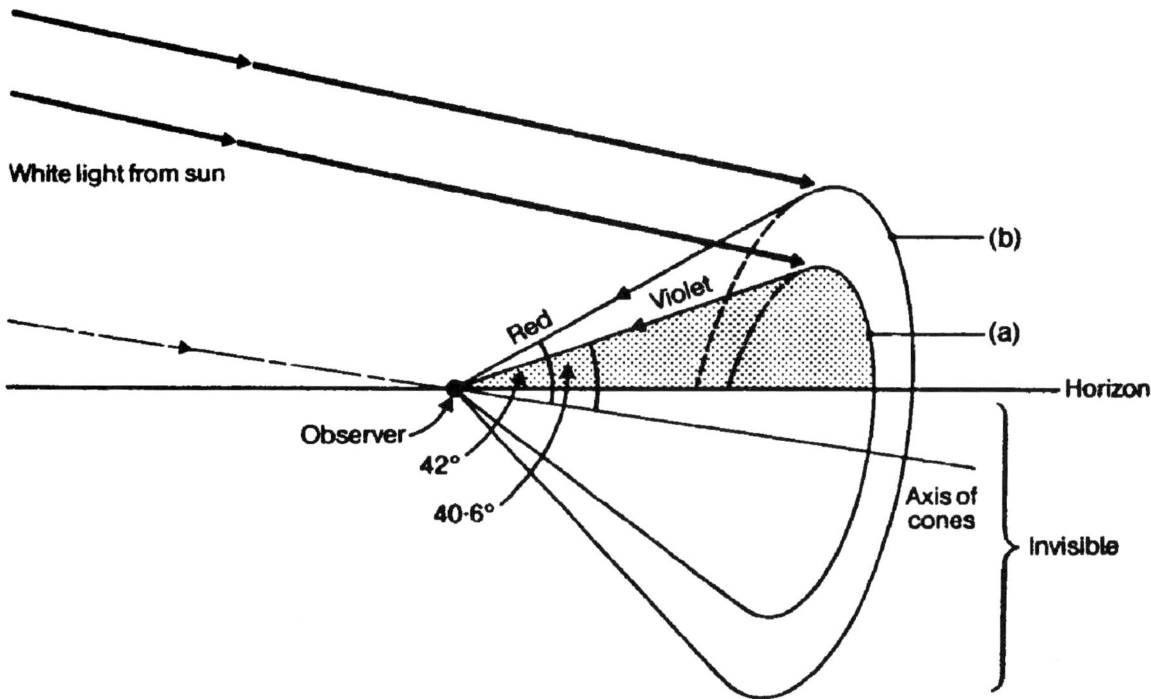

Figure 29. A primary rainbow. *The observer receives violet light from all drops on the shaded outer surface (a), and red from those on the unshaded outer surface (b). As the sun gets higher in the sky, that fraction of each cone which lies above the horizon decreases.*

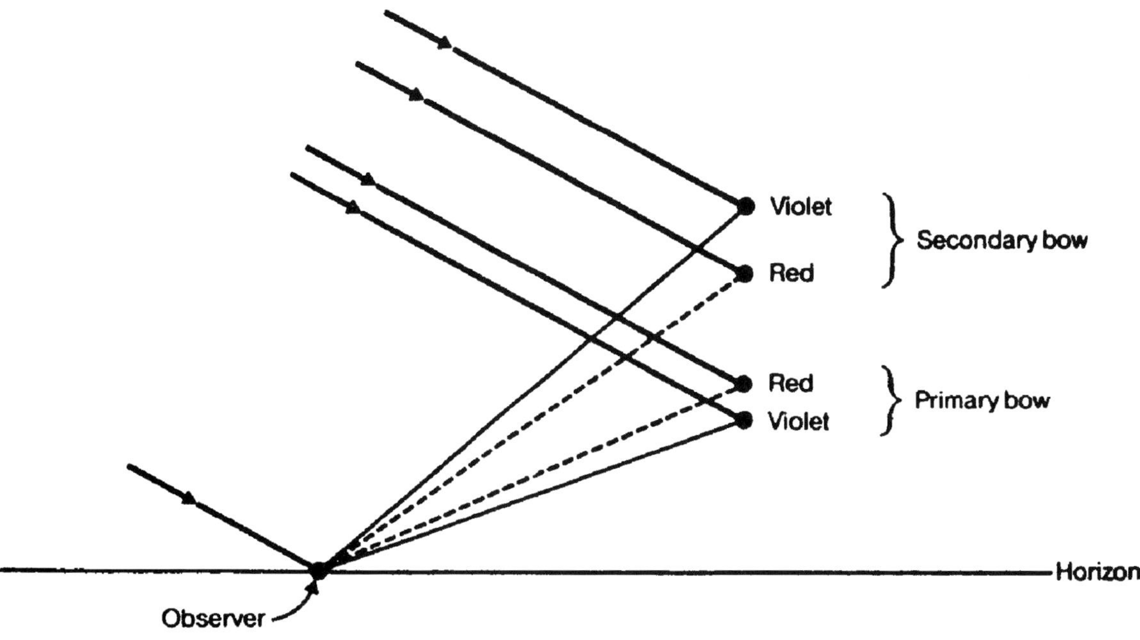

Figure 30. A double rainbow.

of mixing lights of two colours, we shall see that this effect accounts for the variation of the brightness, width and even the order of colours in a rainbow. Skilled viewers can use such observations to estimate the size of the drops. When the drops are extremely small, as in fog, the concentric rings of different colours are of closely similar radius. So, except at the extreme edges, the colours overlap. A fog bow is a white band, with a bluish inner edge and a reddish outer one.

Ice crystals, as well as raindrops, can act as prisms and produce circles of bright light. These can be seen around the sun, and quite a distance away from it (the radius of the smallest gives an angle of about 22° at the observer). Although predominantly white, these 'haloes' are coloured at the edges. Ice-crystals, which are usually hexagonal, can also exist as either long needles or flat plates, and since they are randomly orientated, they can produce a complex series of internal reflections. The various emergent beams may result, not only in circles of light, but in a complicated system of bright patches ("mock suns" or "sun dogs"), ellipses, pillars and even crosses. Interference of light passing through a cloud of droplets or ice crystals accounts for the coloured roundels, or coronae, to be seen around the moon when it is covered by light cloud, or round street lamps on a misty night. The exact colours of the

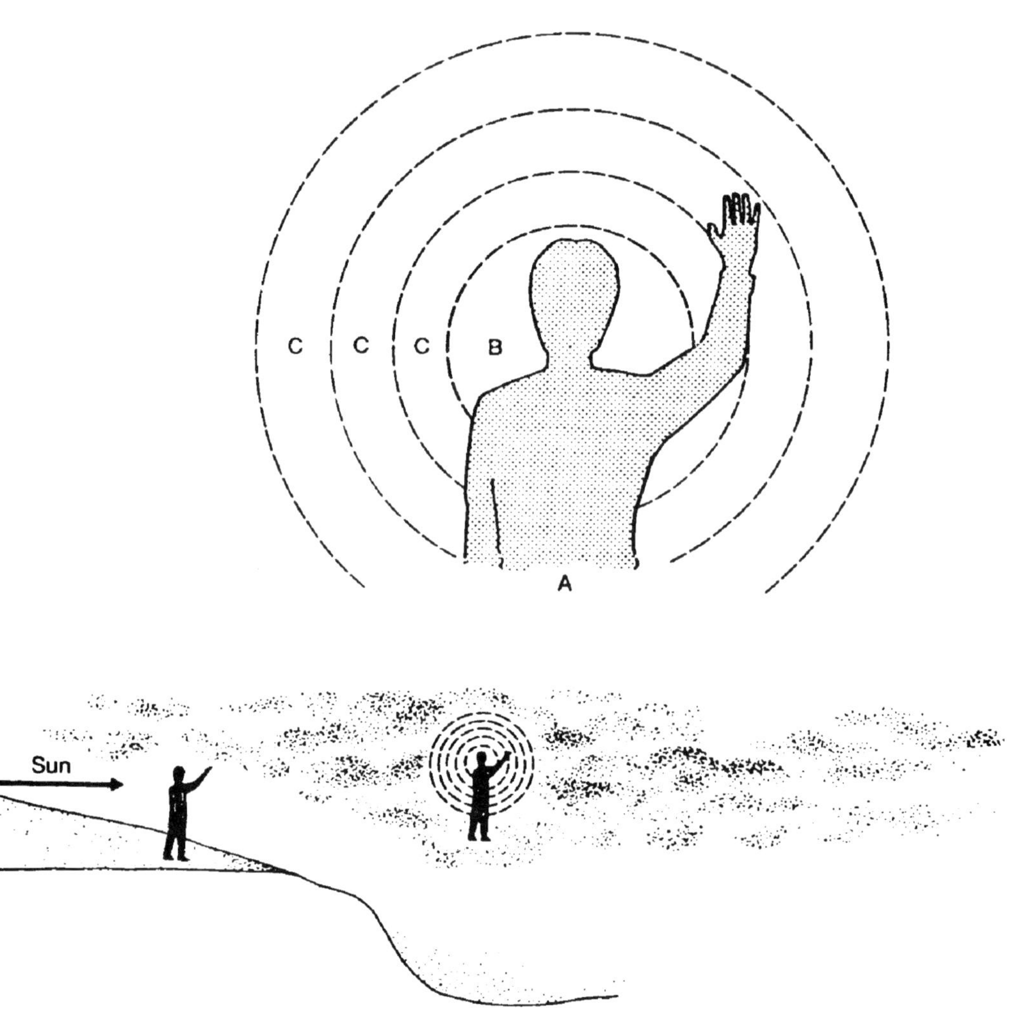

Figure 31. The Brocken spectre. *The head of the shadow, A, appears on a bright patch, B, surrounded by coloured rings, C.*

roundels again depend on the size of the crystal or drop. "Glories", too, are formed by overlapping rings of light of different wavelength. Like rainbows, they are seen when the observer is facing away from the sun, but for a glory to appear, the observer's shadow must fall on a cloud of small droplets of uniform size. This may happen quite often to the airborne, and occasionally to mountain walkers. The light seen by the observer originates directly behind him and is reflected straight back from the rim of the drop. The colours arise through interference between light reflected from different points on the rim. At the center of the rings, all shadow falls, around it lie a number of brightly coloured rings (see Figures 31 and 32). Since this apparition requires a shadow to be cast onto a cloud, it is likely to be seen by those

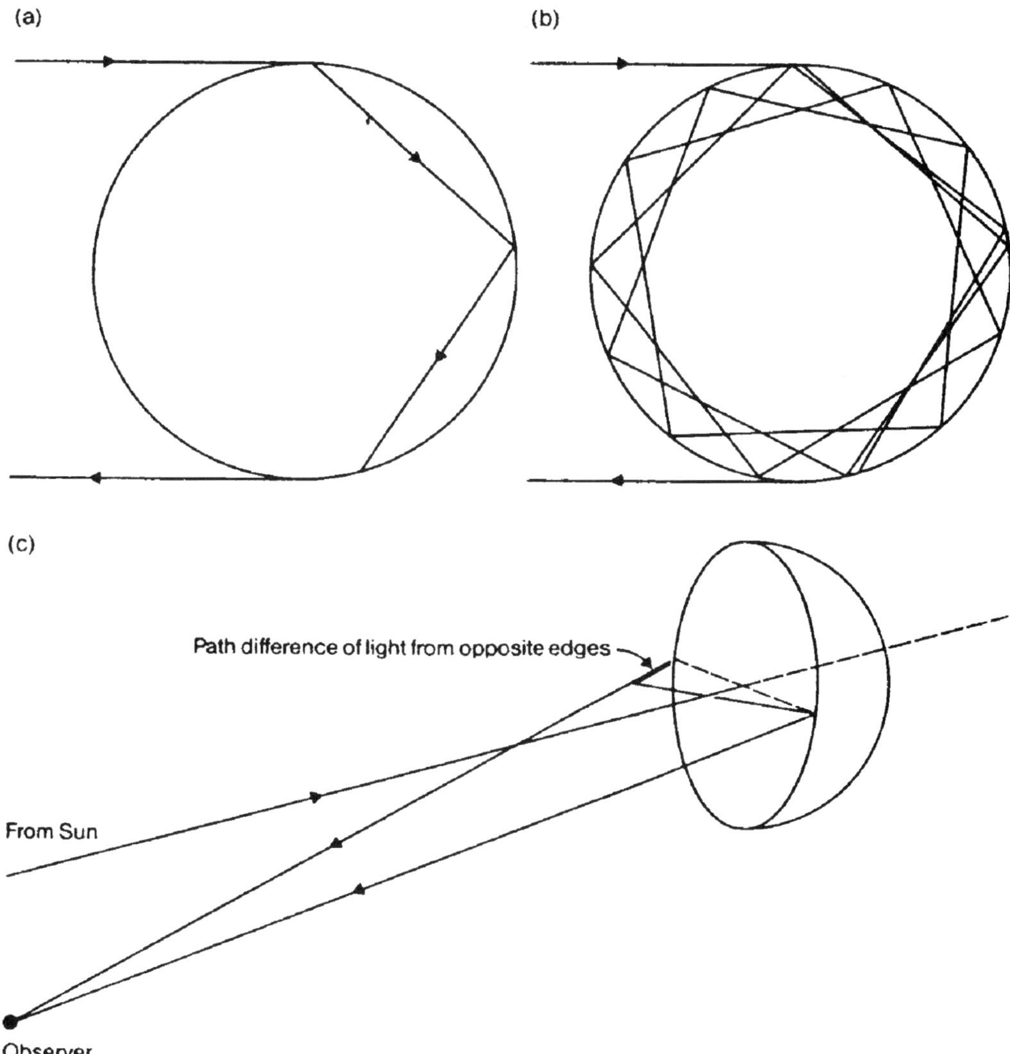

Figure 32. How a glory occurs. *Light entering a drop at its edge is reflected back in the same direction, after reflection (a) once, or (b) fifteen times from the inner surface. For drops straight ahead of the observer, all points on the edge are the same distance away, and no interference occurs. But from drops at an angle (c), the outer edge is farther from the observer, and interference may occur, giving bright and dark rings, at different angles for different colours. (Adapted, with permission, from H.C. Bryant and N. Jarmie,* Scientific American, *vol. 231, July 1974, p. 60.)*

standing on the brink of chasms and precipices at early morning. If the observer waves his arm, the apparition waves in reply. The experience is unnerving to a cold, tired hillwalker unfamiliar with the phenomenon of the Brockenspectre, or Broken Bow, and it is all too easy to see why Eastern mystics, thinking Buddha beckoned them, leaped off to join him. The analogous Pilot's Bow, which surrounds a small shadow of a plane on a cloud below, lacks the supernatural appeal of a halo around one's own head. Since the random scattering of white light from the cloud is likely to be brighter, the colours of the roundel are probably more dilute. A Pilot's Bow, although a diverting sight, scarcely seems to merit the term "glory."

The colours we have so far discussed all originate in sunlight. Energy of a multitude of visible wavelengths arrives at our planet, and a variety of interactions with the atmospheres and with the surface of the earth alters the proportions so that the mixture which is available at any particular point may not be 'white.' Sometimes, however, Earth may be lit from other sources. During a thunderstorm, clouds become electrically charged through friction. Electrons are transferred from one mass of droplets, hailstones or ice crystals to another in much the same way as nylon clothing becomes electrically charged in a rotary drier. When the excess, or deficiency, of electrons is large enough, there will be an electric discharge in which the electrical balance will be restored. There is a massive increase in temperature (up to 25,000°C). The air expands violently, and there is much reshuffling of particles and emission of energy as the air returns to its original, stable state.

In the visual region, energy of over two hundred different wavelengths is emitted, much of it in the high-energy region. So lightning, like the sparks from electric trains and faulty electrical connections, is white with a tinge of bluish-green. (Seen from an airplane flying above a distant storm, lightning can have a faintly pink look, presumably because, if the flash occurs below the plane, some of the higher-energy light is scattered back towards the ground.)

A somewhat similar electrical discharge occurs during the aurora, which is powered by the bombardment of air by electrons and other small, electrically charged particles which stream in from the sun, sometimes in great quantity and at great speed (about ten million per square centimeter per second at several thousand kilometers per second). The particles are attracted to the Earth's magnetic poles, and it is in these regions that auroral displays are the most spectacular. The commonest colour, yellowish-green, is caused by changes involving oxygen atoms at low pressure. Higher in the sky, and therefore visible at lower latitudes, the changes involve oxygen atoms at still lower pressure, and the light emitted is red. Rarer bluish, or red-edged green, displays are produced by pairs of oxygen or nitrogen atoms which have been excited, or have lost one or more of their electrons.

Earth and Fire

We are by the sea again, but now restrict our attention to the beach, which is part sand, part shingle, punctuated with rocks. Along this stretch of the coast, the colours are not striking. The rocks are brown and the shingle seems, at first glance, a mottled, mealy grey. A closer look resolves the shingle into lackluster pebbles of various pale browns and greys, mixed perhaps with some white ones, and a few which are dull black or purple. At the shoreline, however, the scene comes to life. Reflection from the wet surface gives highlights and the colours themselves become deeper and richer. The sand turns from matt fawn to gleaming ochre, and the pebbles look smooth as polished marble, and appear in as wide a variety of colours.

Few rocks are as dazzling white as Parian marble or the chalk Cliffs of Dover. But many are coloured only because they contain traces of some contaminant in minerals, such as quartz, limestone or gypsum, which if pure, would be colourless. By far the most common of these impurities is iron. Usually, each iron atom has shed three of its outer electrons on to neighbouring groups, but by absorbing some visible light, it can temporarily reannex one from an oxygen atom of any silicate, carbonate or sulphate group which may be close by. This transfer of electrons from oxygen to iron accounts for all the ochres, rusts, browns and reds in our rocks, sand and buildings. The colour is very sensitive to the structure and water content of the mineral, as illustrated by the change in colours when clay is fired. The blue-grey streaks in some clays and cream limestones are also caused by iron atoms, but by those from which only two electrons are lost. Prolonged exposure to air, or heating to form bricks, make the iron lose a third electron and change to its more familiar ochre form.

Since pebbles, and sand, are merely moveable and hence worn fragments of rock, why do they look so much paler? A grain of sand, being so small, has a very large surface compared to its volume, and so it scatters a high proportion of the white light which falls on it. The ochre colours of any iron it may contain are therefore much diluted, and the sand looks paler than the rocks from which it was formed. The finer the sand, the whiter it looks (and the same effect may be obtained by crushing demerara sugar or coloured glass). The paleness of pebbles arises in the same way: their surfaces are scratched and pitted from movements against other stones and so act as effective scatterers of light, regardless of its direction or wavelength. Hence their pale, dull look.

Rocks, pebbles, and sand all show darker, richer colours when they are wet, though the effect is less noticeable for rock, particularly if it has a fairly smooth surface. When light passes from one transparent material into another, that proportion which is scattered depends on the relative ease with which light travels through them. If light travels at almost the same speed in the two substances, there is less scattering than if the speed of light changes appreciably at the boundary. Since light is slowed down more on passing from air to stone than from water to stone, sand and worn pebbles scatter light more effectively if they are dry. When light travels from water to sand or pebbles, less of it is scattered and more enters the stone. Here light of some wavelengths is absorbed and that of others transmitted or reflected back to the observer, so the light which reaches us is less diluted and the colours darker and richer. The greater the scattering power of the dry material, the more marked is the effect of the water. New, shiny plastic, which reflects (rather than scatters) most of the light falling on it, is almost unchanged in appearance when it is immersed in water.

The wide range of pebble colours revealed by the sea is not entirely because of the presence of iron. Other metals also contribute, but the colours they generate arise from a change in orientation of electrons within a particular atom rather than through a temporary electron transfer from oxygen atom to the iron. As such changes are of low theoretical probability, colour is generated only when appreciable concentrations of the metal are present. The pink or purple or rose or amethyst quartz is caused by manganese, while minerals, such as malachite, which contain copper are often green or blue. In some minerals, the metal iron is surrounded by atoms of sulphur rather than of oxygen. Transfer of electrons from sulphur atoms to the metal is fairly easy, and is accompanied by intense absorption of light of a wide range of wavelengths. Such minerals are black.

Many of the colours of gems and semi-precious stones, as of more mundane rocks, are caused by the contamination, by traces of metal, of basically colourless, oxygen-containing materials. Ruby and emerald both owe their colour to chromium. The dramatic difference between the two is owed merely to the fact that the enveloping oxygen structure in ruby, but not in emerald, is under considerable internal stress. Sapphire is structurally similar to ruby, but contains iron and titanium instead of chromium. The colour of deep-green jade, like that of emerald, is caused by chromium in an unstressed oxygen environment. Paler green jade is coloured by iron atoms which have each lost two electrons, unlike the ochre colours which often arise when three electrons are removed from the iron. Turquoise, as can be guessed from its similarity to copper sulphate crystals and to weathered copper domes, owes its colour to copper.

Metal ions are not, however, the only components of rock which give rise to colour. Some minerals contain the bulky disulphide group clouds whose electron clouds are so diffuse that they overlap with those adjacent groups. The shared clouds which are formed are midway between "clasp" and "treacle" in type. They absorb visible light and give rise to a variety of colours: royal blue in Lapis Lazuli, black in Marcasite, metallic golden yellow in Iron Pyrites (Fool's Gold). Graphite, although a form of non-metal carbon, looks almost as shiny as a metal. The atoms form layers, and on either side of each layer is a continuous sheet of electron cloud, like a multi-decker treacle sandwich. And it is these layers of electron cloud which give graphite its metallic luster (see Figure 33).

Crystals of rubies, sapphires and other gems can now be grown artificially, and it is found that the colours are often improved by heat treatment. The colours of natural gems, too, can be permanently changed in this way. Zircon (zirconium silicate) for example, can be changed from brown to red, yellow, green, blue or colourless. Presumably the change in temperature either alters the detailed arrangement of the oxygen atoms around the zirconium ion or changes the number of electrons associated with it. But these improved colours may fade on prolonged exposure to sunlight, and so heat-treated gems are seldom displayed in jewelers' windows.

The colour of the semi-precious gem alexandrite is very sensitive to the light which falls on it. The mineral itself absorbs blue and yellow light. In daylight, it transmits much green light, together with some red, and so looks a fresh, yellowish green. Since artificial light contains a lower proportion of

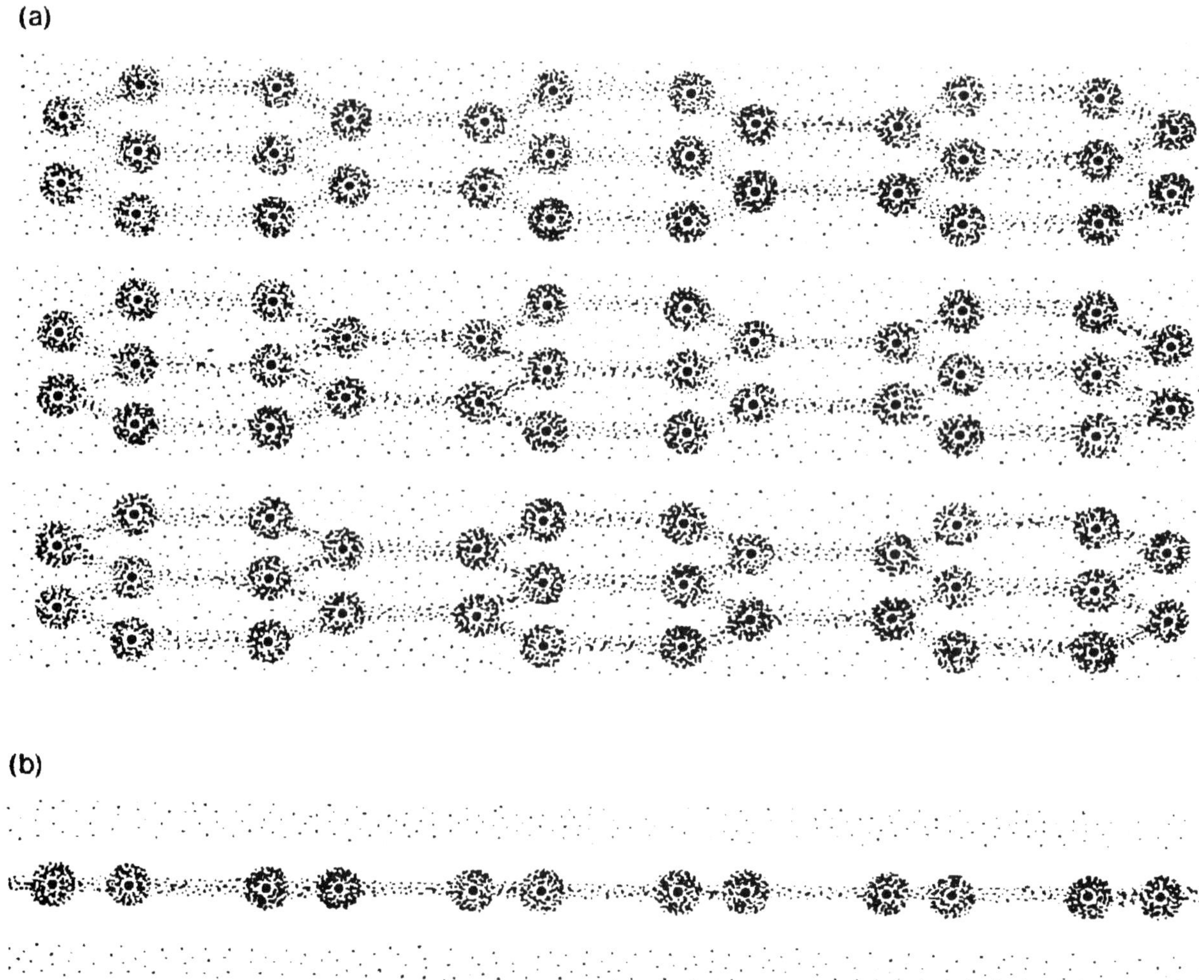

Figure 33. Shiny graphite. *The structure of graphite, illustrating (a) three layers of carbon atoms, and (b) end-on view of a single layer, showing electron cloud above and below the sheet of atoms.*

high-energy and middle-energy light than does daylight, so does the light transmitted by the alexandrite. In tungsten lighting, the gem transmits roughly equal amounts of green and red, so it looks yellow. By candlelight, which is of still lower energy, the alexandrite looks red.

But colour, as we have seen, is not always caused by absorption of light. The coloured sparkle of diamonds is like that of a particularly impressive dewdrop or chandelier. When white light passes from air into a diamond, the colours are spread out more effectively than they are when they enter glass, and a much higher proportion of the light is reflected internally from the back of a diamond than from the rear surface of a drop of water or a glass prism. On reflection, the spread of colours is amplified. Diamonds are cut so that the light is reflected at the inner surfaces of a number of facets. The various colours emerge from the front of the gem at markedly different angles. When the wearer, or the observer, moves slightly the light which enters the eye is first of one almost pure colour, then of another. Modern imitations may disperse and reflect light equally impressively. Their sparkle rivals that of a real diamond, though they lack its extreme hardness.

Some of the most beautiful colours of the mineral world are caused by optical interference. Precious opal, like soap solution, absorbs little visible light. It is made up almost entirely of silica and water. But part of the structure consists of regularly stacked spheres, and reflections from neighboring groups of these may interfere. Depending on the angle of viewing, light of one or more wavelengths is cancelled out. The opal acts as a diffraction grating. Legend maintains that the exact colour of an opal is sensitive to the well-being of the wearer, and it is indeed possible that the spacing between spheres varies with changes in temperature and in the humidity of the skin. The mineral labradorite shows similar iridescence, usually in the colour range from royal blue to kingfisher, green and gold. These peacock colours are superimposed on a background of dull grey, which is caused by thin sheets of oxides of iron or titanium embedded in a colourless felspar mineral. The iridescence arises through the interference of light reflected from different layers of oxide, the exact colour depending on the spacing and orientation of the layers and on the viewing angle. The less exotic iridescence observed by Goethe on "the surface of stagnant water, especially if impregnated with iron," interference also arises from layers of iron oxide.

We have seen that many solids change colour when they are heated. The change may be permanent. Clays and earth pigments, such as raw sienna, lose water on heating and acquire a much redder hue. Their structure is permanently changed, and their original ochre colour does not return if they are wetted. Some effects of heating can, however, be reversed. We may remember from our school days how blue copper sulphate crystals lose water and crumble to a white powder when heated, the blue colour being restored when water is added. This colour change, too, arises from the change in the environment of the metal, and hence in the exact arrangement of its individual electron cloud. This colour change has been used as a 'dampness' indicator for drying agents and 'weather pictures.' The pale pink colour, indicative of dampness, arises from cobalt surrounded octahedrally (by four particles of water and two chloride groups), whereas the brighter blue, dry-weather colour is produced when the cobalt is in the center of four tetrahedrally disposed chloride groups (see Figure 34). The blue is more intense than the pink because changes within a tetrahedron are more probable than those within an octahedron. Environment changes also cause purple crystals of chrome alum to turn green as they dissolve in water, and the "Cambridge" blue of a copper-sulphate solution to darken to "Oxford" blue if ammonia is added.

Some reversible colour changes can be produced merely by raising the temperature. Another survival from school chemistry is "zinc oxide; yellow when hot, white when cold." The hot form has sufficient energy to be able to undergo small changes in structure on the absorption of visible light.

Very hot solids (and liquids) glow. They have so much energy that they emit not only infra-red radiation but also low-energy visual radiation and become "red-hot." If their temperature is raised still further, they may become "white-hot," giving out energy over the whole visible range.

Many substances, when heated in the presence of air, combine with oxygen and change colour. A bright copper coin merely acquires a black coating of copper oxide, but for many substances, 'oxidation' is accompanied by burning. The light emitted by the flames often shows beautiful colours which depend on the substance which is being burned and on the rate of supply of both fuel and air to the different regions of the flame. We are so familiar with domestic flames from matches, candles, cooking gas and fires that it may seem surprising that many of the changes which take place within them are extremely complicated and by no means fully understood.

If we look at a steady candle flame, we can see three main regions: a transparent blue base, a grayish semi-transparent central cone and an opaque, bright-yellow outer cone. When the candle is lit, the wax liquefies, rises up the wick and vaporizes. Oxygen diffuses into the gaseous wax and combines with it, eventually producing carbon dioxide and steam while giving out considerable heat. At the high temperature produced, the wax breaks down into very small, highly excited groups of atoms (such as "dicarbon" and "carbon-plus-hydrogen") which, at the base of the flame, rid themselves of some of their energy by emitting blue light. Higher

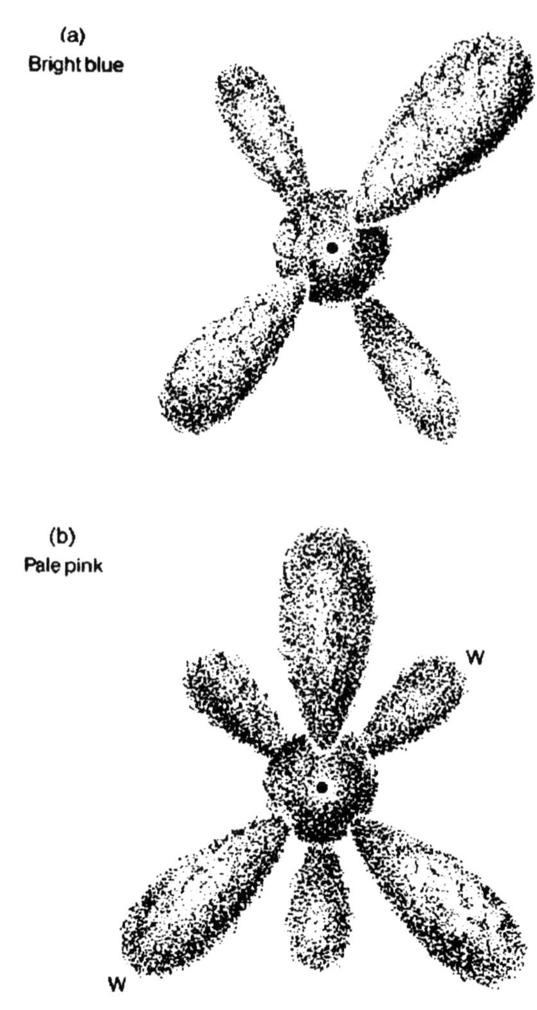

Figure 34. Fine blue, damp pink. *Clouds of electrons around a central cobalt nucleus in combination with chloride groups (a) when dry, and (b) after absorption of a little water, W.*

up the carbon atoms may join together and form relatively large conglomerates, or soot particles, which become "yellow-hot" and glow, forming the bright, opaque outer cone of the flame.

Flames produced when other substances burn may naturally contain other small, excited groups of atoms which will emit light of other wavelengths. Coke, for example, burns with a clear blue flame, produced by excited oxides of carbon. The flames of domestic cookers and heaters differ from those of candles or fires because air does not just seep into the hot gaseous fuel but is premixed into the unignited gas. In coal gas, the colour of the flame varies markedly with proportion of air in the mixture. A low ratio of air to fuel produces a yellow flame similar to that of a candle, while a high proportion of air to gas gives a hotter, clearer blue flame with a turquoise central cone, containing oxygen-plus-hydrogen groups. Natural gas is chemically more akin to candle wax, and when mixed generously with air, burns with a blue flame composed of an inner cone similar to that at the base of a candle flame—a paler, greener middle cone and a more purple outer cone.

Flames, like solids, can be strongly coloured by the presence of very small amounts of impurities. A crystal of table salt will colour the flame of a gas stove bright yellow. Pale mauve flames sometimes flicker over a particularly hot bonfire, and if any fine copper wire finds its way into a fire, it colours the flames emerald green. These colours are owed to individual atoms which have gained so much energy from the fire that one or more of their outer electrons has been promoted to regions even further from the center of the atom. The colour of the light emitted when the atoms revert to the state of lowest energy is characteristic of that particular type of atom. The yellow flame to table salt is exactly the same as that produced by washing soda, caustic soda or sodium bicarbonate and is caused by the presence of sodium.

Flame colours have long been used to identify chemical elements: a deep green flame is characteristic of copper, and pale mauve which is often seen over a wood fire, is caused by potassium, which is absorbed by plants from the soil. Nowadays, the intensity of flame colour can be used to measure both the amount of the element which is present and the temperature of the flame. Atomic flame colours are exploited more frivolously by manufacturers of fireworks, who have access also to less familiar substances. The heads of 'Bengal matches,' for example, contain either lithium, which produces a rich crimson flame, or barium, which gives a limegreen one. Relatively few elements, however, produce coloured flames, which accounts for the rather restricted palette available to the pyrotechnist.

Vegetable Colors

Since only a small fraction of dry land is covered with bare rock, sand or snow, or with buildings, minerals make a limited contribution to the colour of the Earth's surface. Seen from the air, most of the land, as any air traveller can testify, is covered with vegetation: forest, grassland, crops or scrub. During the growing season, leaves account for almost all the surface area of most types of plant. The landscape looks mainly green while the leaves are young, though the colours may change through yellow and red to brown as the year proceeds. But it is not solely the leaves which impart their colours to the landscape. A bare forest shows a range of subtle browns and the heather-clad hills of Scotland are smoky purple. Cultivation has brought us orchards of fruit blossom and fields of spring bulbs. European farmland is studded with patches of dusky-blue lucerne and acid-yellow rape. Few British wild flowers, other than heather, monopolize enough expanse to determine the colour of a distant landscape, but several provide more restricted patches of showy colour. Newly cut roadsides can be pink with willowherb or scarlet with poppies, and the floor of a woodland can look almost solidly coloured, white or blue, with anemones or bluebells.

Focusing more closely on to individual plants, we can see the immense variety in the colour of the flowers and also, perhaps surprisingly, of the leaves.

Cabbages may be greenish cream, bottle green, smoky turquoise, purplish blue, rich claret, or glossy black as an aubergine. The emergent shoots of daffodils are pale sulphur yellow, while bursting leaf-buds of peony shine like old mahogany.

Much of the beauty of vegetation in a landscape arises from its movement. If we walk through a beech wood towards the sun, we see light which has passed through some leaves and bounced off others, some of them shaded by their neighbours. So the light entering our eyes will vary greatly in colour and in brightness, changing with the breeze; and the forest will look quite different if we turn away from the sun. We can see a similar play of light and shade, yellow-green and blue-green, from the stripes on a freshly mown lawn. The mower bends alternate bands towards and away from the viewer. Those bent away from him reflect more light when observed against the sun and so look a lighter and yellower green. And when wind ripples a cornfield, the colour is as of shimmering velvet, and for the same reason.

Almost all plant colours are produced by substances which are themselves coloured. Colours which arise by interference or scattering are rare. Vegetable colours, like other coloured materials, absorb light of some, but not all, energies in the visible range. Green leaves, for example, contain chlorophyll, a substance which absorbs all colours except green. Its structure is complex, and somewhat like a badly made lace mat, ordered in the middle, but ragged around the edges (see Figure 35). At its centre is a single magnesium atom, stripped of its two outer electrons. Around it is a square of four nitrogen atoms enclosed in a flat, openwork arrangement of twenty carbon atoms. Outside this regular structure are a number of short, branched "arms" consisting of different small groups of atoms, and one "tail," a chain of about twenty carbon atoms. In this assembly, the most loosely bound electrons are those which lie above or below the "lace mat" or above and below its "tail." These rather mobile electrons can absorb rather small amounts of energy, in the visible and ultra-violet regions of the spectrum, but they readily revert to the more stable state by transferring their extra energy to some neighbouring substance.

It is this power of chlorophyll to act as an energy carrier that enables life to exist on earth. Green plants absorb energy from sunlight and use it to drive the process of photosynthesis in which complex energy-rich sugars are built up from the much simpler water and carbon dioxide which the plant takes in from the soil and from the air. Not only does photosynthesis trap energy from sunlight and store it in food, but as a by-product, it produces oxygen, which almost all living things need if they are to make use of energy stored in food. So to chlorophyll we owe not only our food but also the means by which we use it.

Also present in almost all green plants are members of a large group of yellow, orange and red substances which are closely related to the "tail" in chlorophyll. This electron-rich chain forms the backbone of the assembly (see Figure 36). Attached to each end is a ring of six atoms, and protruding from it are a number of small side-groups. As in chlorophyll, there are electrons on either side of the chain, and these can absorb energy in the visual region, giving rise to the colour of carrots (whence the group name of 'carotenoids'), tomatoes, sweet corn and marigolds. Carotenoids are also present in the leaves of most plants. Brown seaweeds owe their colour to absorption by both chlorophyll and carotenoids, but in flowering plants the green of chlorophyll usually swamps the colours of other substances. The yellow pigments show clearly in autumn, when the chlorophyll decays and loses its colour.

Another large group of vegetable colours, the flavonoids, produces the tints of autumn leaves, the purple shades of many new shoots and the varied hues of a large number of flowers. The parent substance, flavone, has a basic skeleton of three rings. Above and below its main skeleton, it too has clouds of loosely bound electrons which enable it to absorb visible light (see Figure 37). Variety of colour is provided by small branches of different groups of atoms around the rings by sugars and other substances combined with the flavonoids. Many of the colours vary with acidity. One group is red in acidic solutions, mauve in neutral media, and blue in alkalis. Substances of this type act as natural indications

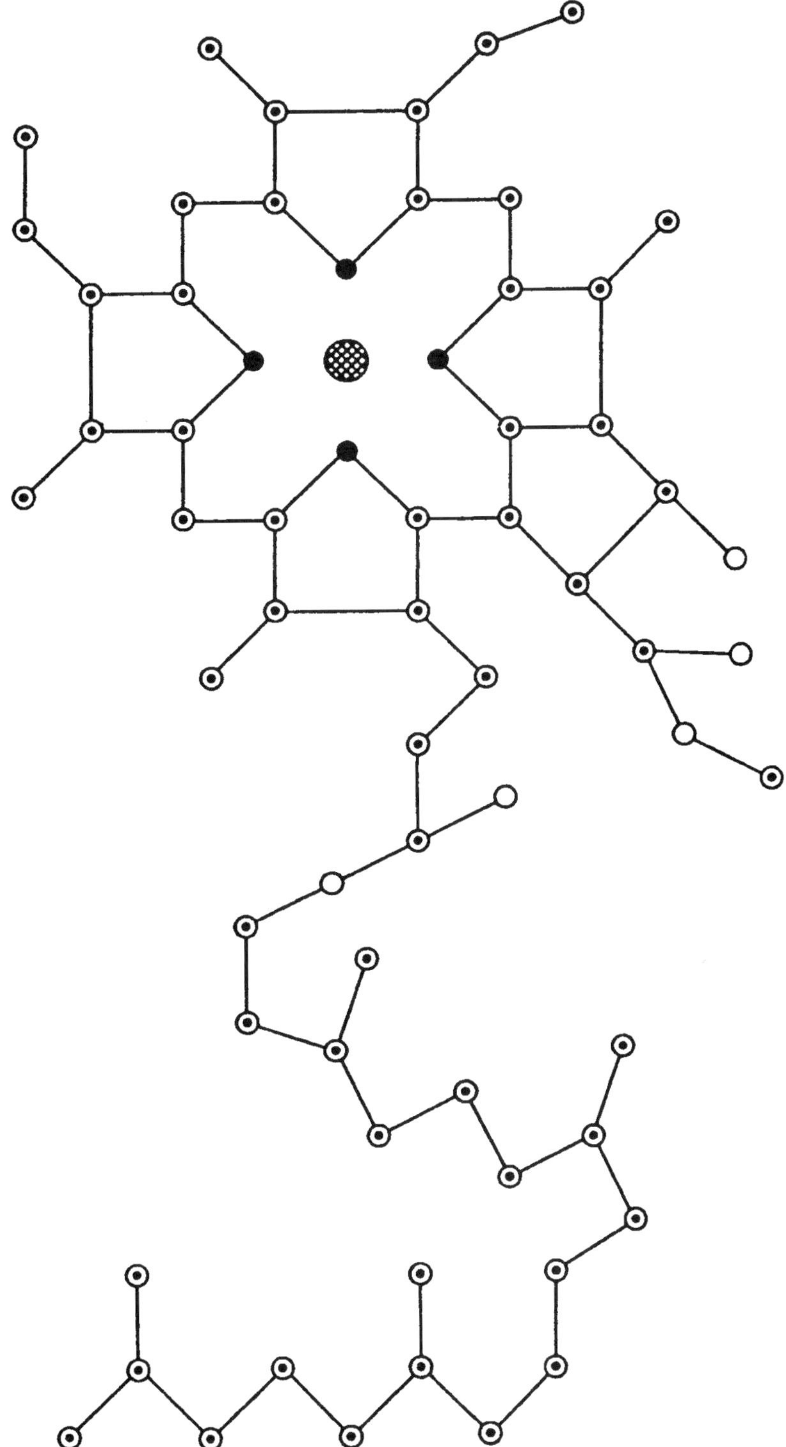

Figure 35. Leaf green *'Lace-mat and tail' skeleton structure of chlorophyll—α using the same symbols as in Figure 12. The central metal, represented by ●, is magnesium.*

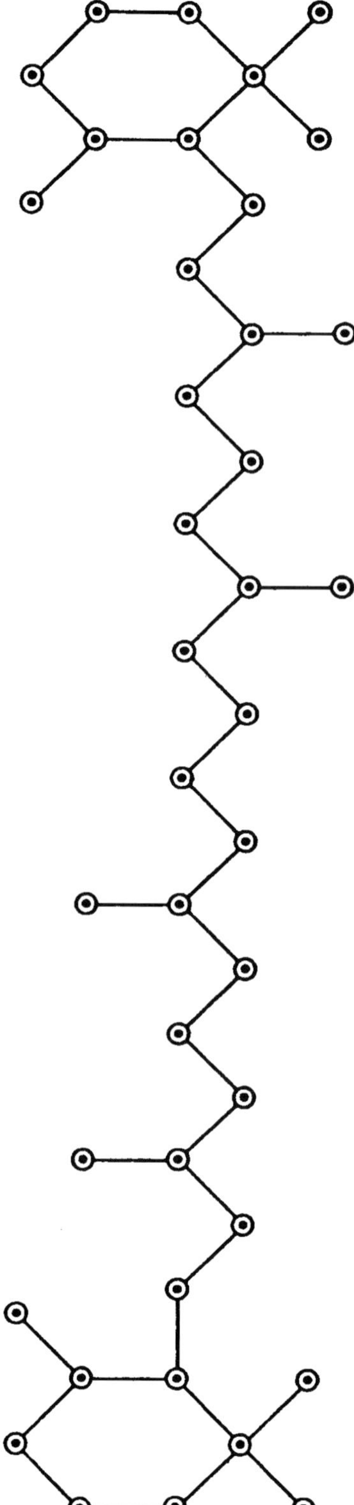

Figure 36. Carrot orange. *Skeleton structure of ß-carotene, showing carbon nuclei ⊙.*

of acidity. They are present in cornflowers, in which the pink variety has more acidic sap than the common blue form, in milkwort, which is pink on acidic, peaty soil and blue on chalk downs, and in milkwort and some types of forget-me-not, in which the acidity of the flower increases with its age. Another group of flavonoids is colourless in acidic media but turns yellow when alkaline. The two classes are named after their alkaline colours, the red-to-blue ones being called *anthocyanins* and the colourless-to-yellow ones *anthoxanthins*. Members of the two classes often occur in the same plant, and as each component will probably change colour at a different acidity, the final colour will show a complex dependence on acidity. The juice of pickled red cabbage, for example, is red only if it is acidic. If ammonia or washing soda is added, the acid is neutralized, and so the anthocyanins turn blue and the anthoxanthins turn yellow thus the juice changes through various shades of purple, blue and turquoise to green (see Figure 38).

The formation of flavonoids may be affected both by external conditions and by the health of the plant. The red anthocyanins which are responsible for many of the flaming colours of autumn leaves are formed most effectively in bright light at low temperatures, and so autumn tints are brightest when the days are clear and crisp. Some plants also produce red anthoxanthins if they suffer injury or mineral deficiencies. On the other hand, the natural red or pink colour of some flowers, such as stocks and sweet peas, can be destroyed by a virus which prevents the formation of anthocyanins.

Since many flower petals contain several carotenoids as well as anthocyanins and anthoxanthins, it is easy to understand the enormous variety of colours exhibited by flowering plants. One can sympathize with the view, implied by many a Victorian hymn writer, that God painted the flowers for the delight of man. However, since most flowering plants which are pollinated by birds and insects (rather than by wind) have showy flowers, it seems likely that these colours also confer some advantages on the plant. The way in which plant colours have evolved has been the subject of much discussion, but it seems clear that coloured petals do in-

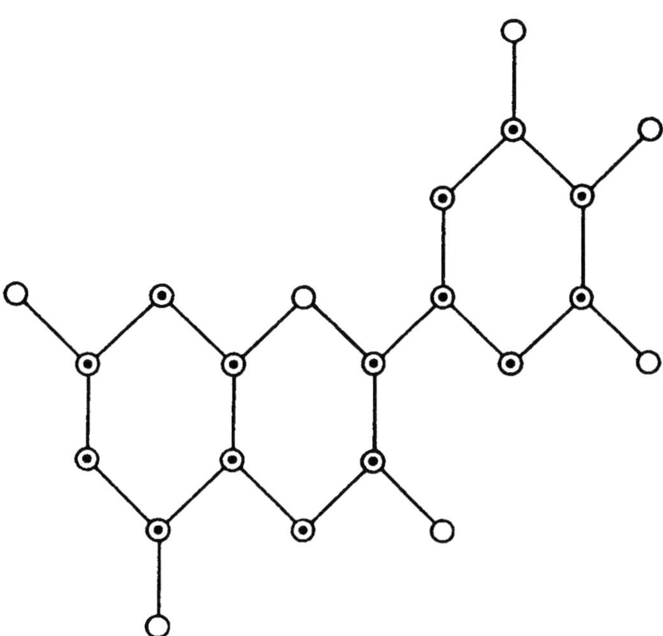

Figure 37. Delphinium blue. *Skeleton structure of the anthocyanin delphinidin, showing nuclei of carbon ⊙ and oxygen ○.*

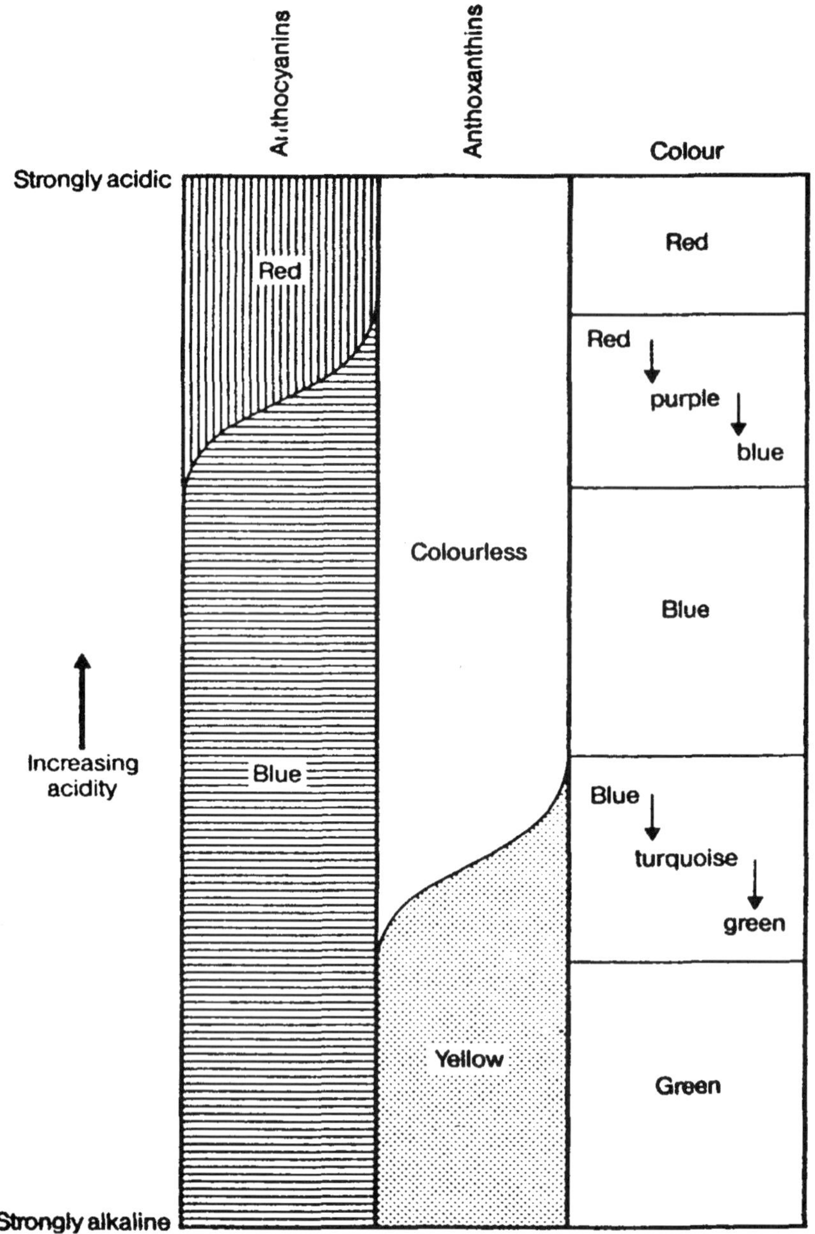

Figure 38. The colourful juice of pickled red cabbage. *If ammonia is gradually added to the juice, the colour changes down the sequence on the right.*

deed attract pollinators and that guidelines may lure them towards the nectar (and hence the pollen). Some members of the orchid family have flowers which closely resemble, in both shape and colour, the female of a species of insect. They are pollinated by the male of that species, who lands on the flower and attempts to copulate with it. The effectiveness of these devices depends, of course, on the ability of the pollinators to distinguish between different colours, but we shall defer discussion of colour vision, in animals and in man, until after we have looked at some of the colours of animals themselves.

Project Proposal

Color Contrast in Photography

Dark and Light, Hue, Warm and Cool, Complementary, Simultaneous, Saturation, Color Balance and Extension

Project Proposal

The idea is to create all seven contrasts with color photographs. You will be asked to either locate or set up color contrast situations that represent the seven basic contrasts, which we have studied, and then visually document them by using a camera. If you use a digital camera instead of film, be sure that you *do not* edit the color. If you are using film, you should not use filters, or any other means to enhance the color. The best method for learning is to either find or set up objects with their *original colors only*.

This project is designed to increase the student's understanding, recognition, and function of both dark and light and color contrast systems. Rather than the physical maneuvering of pigments, this project concentrates on developing a visual sensibility about the character of contrast, and removes the need to be concerned about pigment rendering techniques.

Project Specifications

- Make two photographs of each of the seven contrasts, for a total of 14 photos. Be sure that each composition is very different, one from the other. This way, you will discover new and various ways to see color contrast.
- Remember that creativity is at the heart of the designer/artist. Students should avoid repeating the same image.
- Photo compositions should be on glossy paper, whether digital or film processes for optimal clarity and saturation.
- Be sure that you take all pictures in either the *vertical* format or *horizontal,* but not both. Failure to

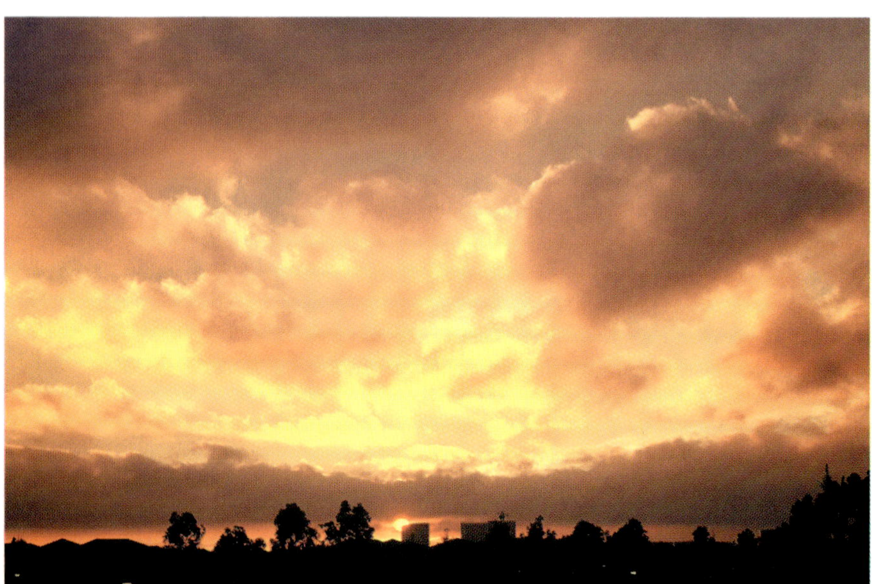

Southern California Sunset demonstrates the character of extreme contrasts.
Photo by Alan Burner.

do this will result in not being able to fit all photos on the board adequately.

- Spray mount the 14 compositions onto a 20" × 30" black illustration board. Be sure to label each composition by it's particular contrast. Labels should be neatly cut, all the same width and length. Do not hand letter. Labels should be well crafted and not distract from the photograph.
- There is enough space for 15 compositions. Since there are 14 photographs, use the 15th for a title card. Four by six inches with your name and other relevant information as your instructor requires.
- For color balance and extension, make one composition to represent *color balance* and one to demonstrate *extension contrast*.

Student Samples of Various Contrast

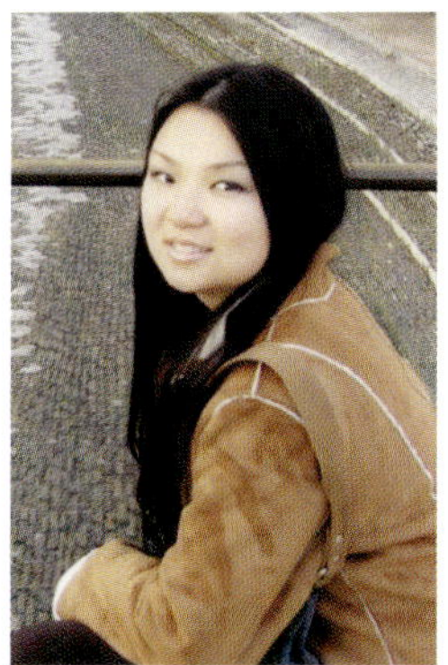

Jane Fonda Lo

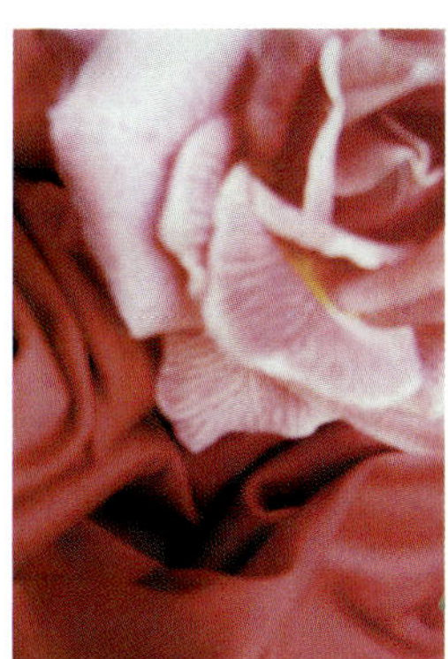

Saturation

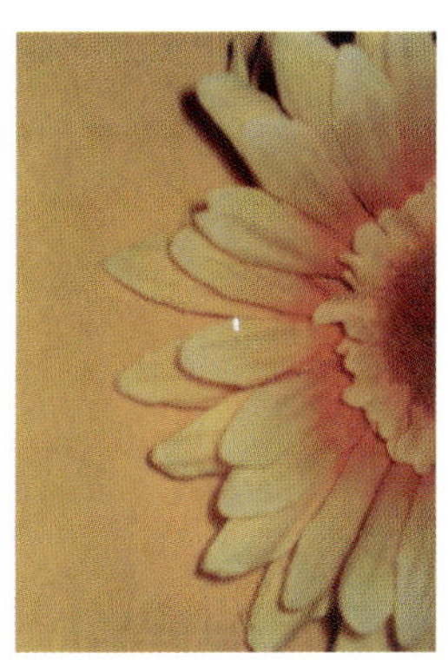

Saturation

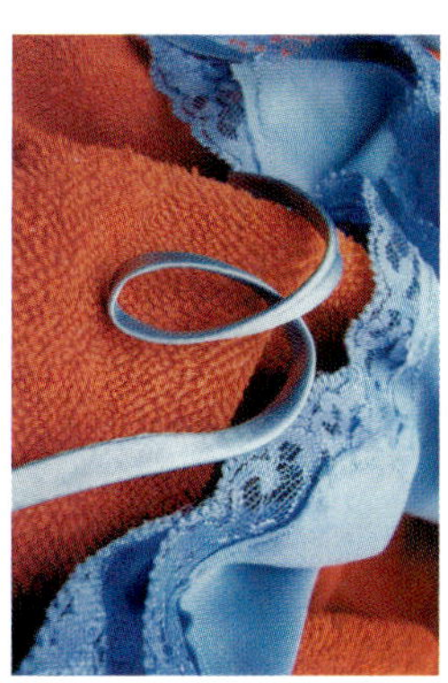

Complementary

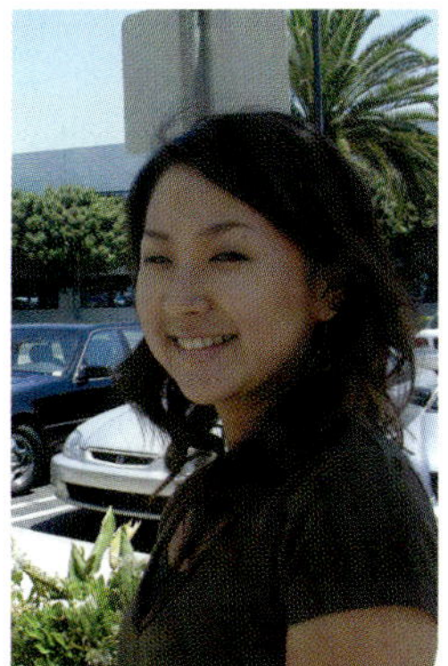

Ai Fujikawa

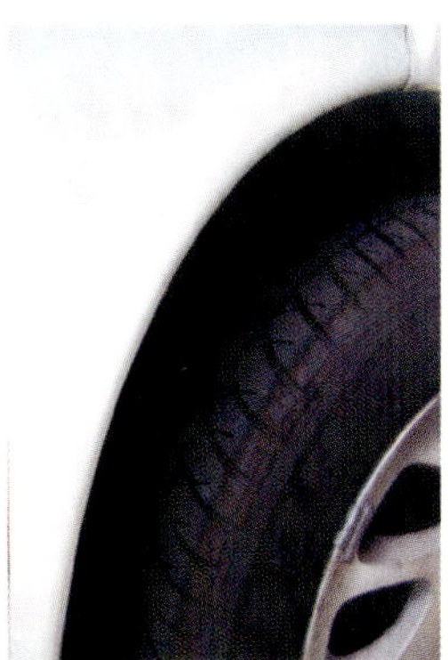

Dark and Light

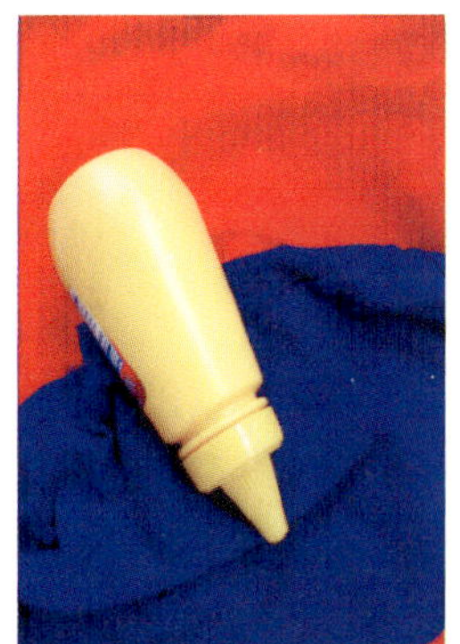

Hue

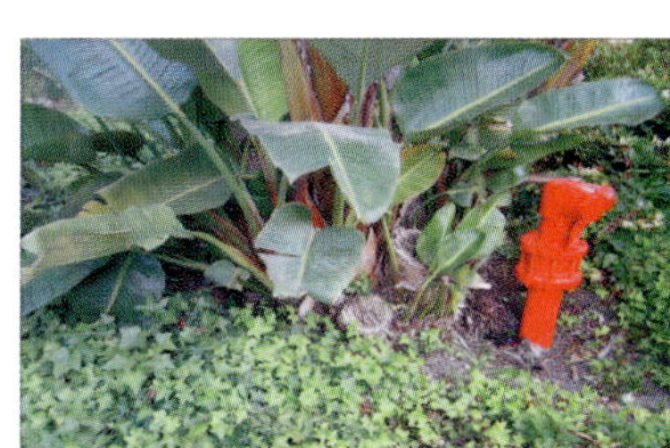

Contrast Extension

Tints and Shades
Value Systems

Mass, Volume, Illusion of Form in Dimensional Space, and Focal Points

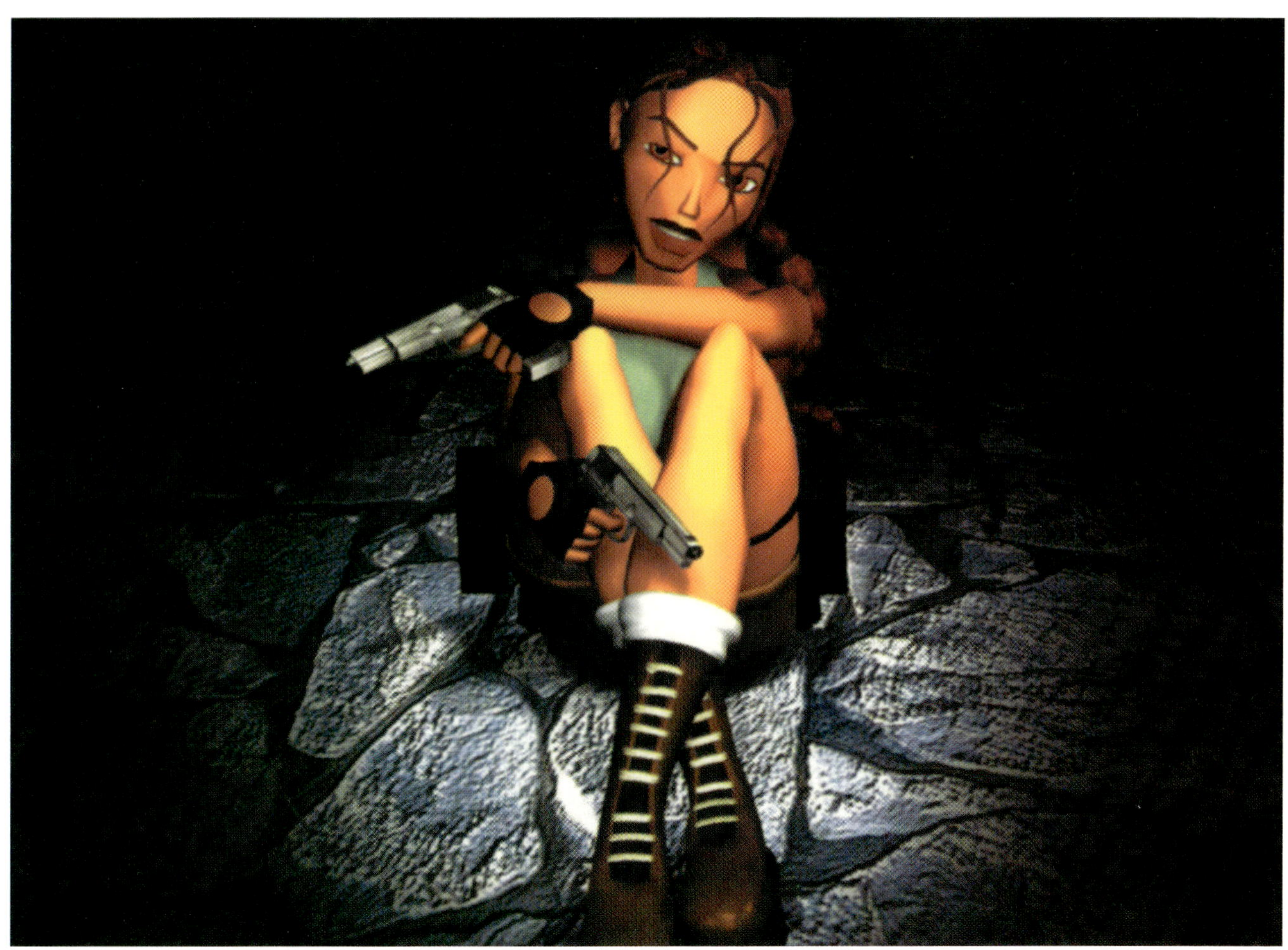

Lara Croft: Tomb Raider Series, PlayStation.
Used by permission of Eidos, Inc.

Chapter Four

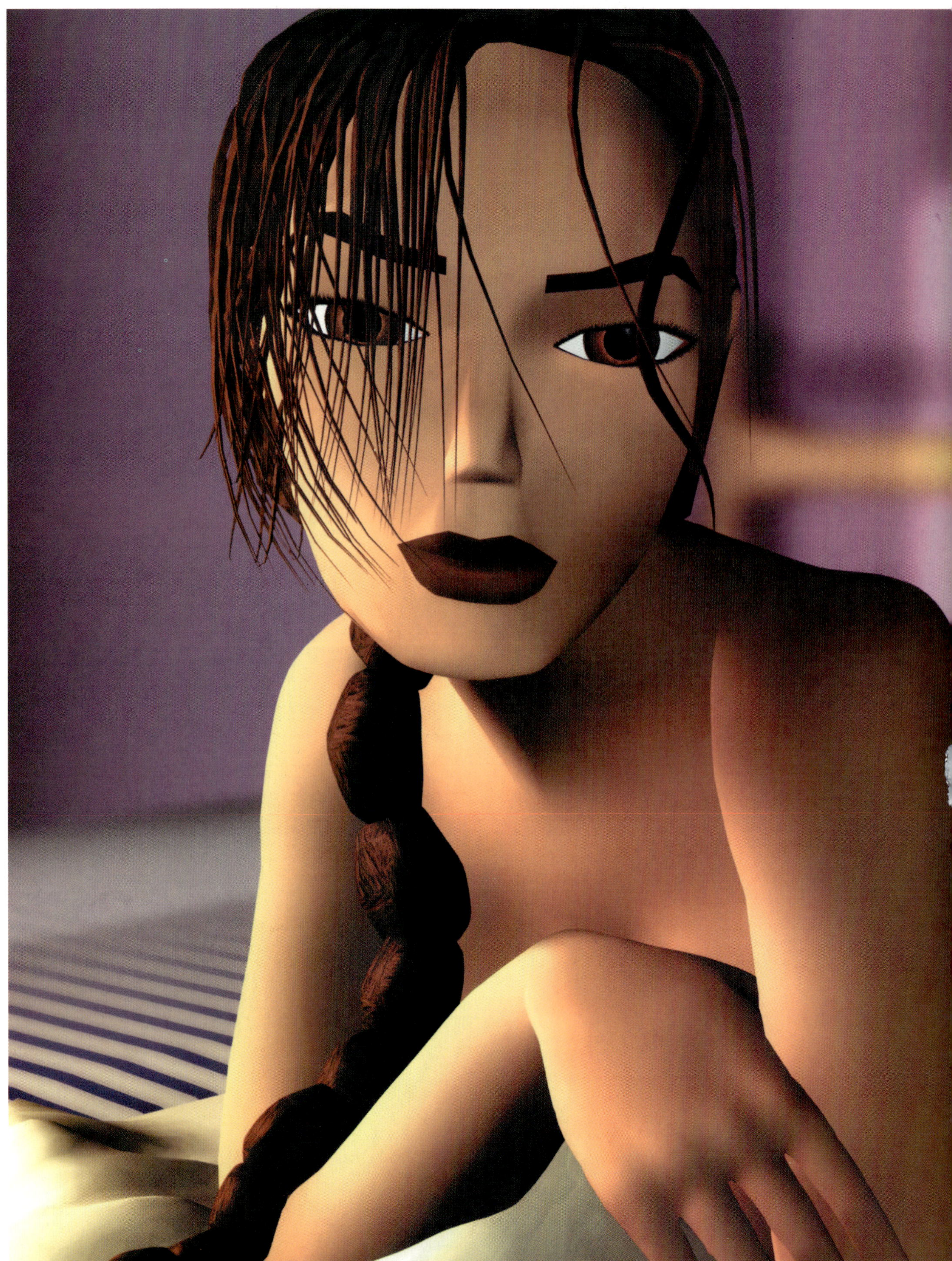

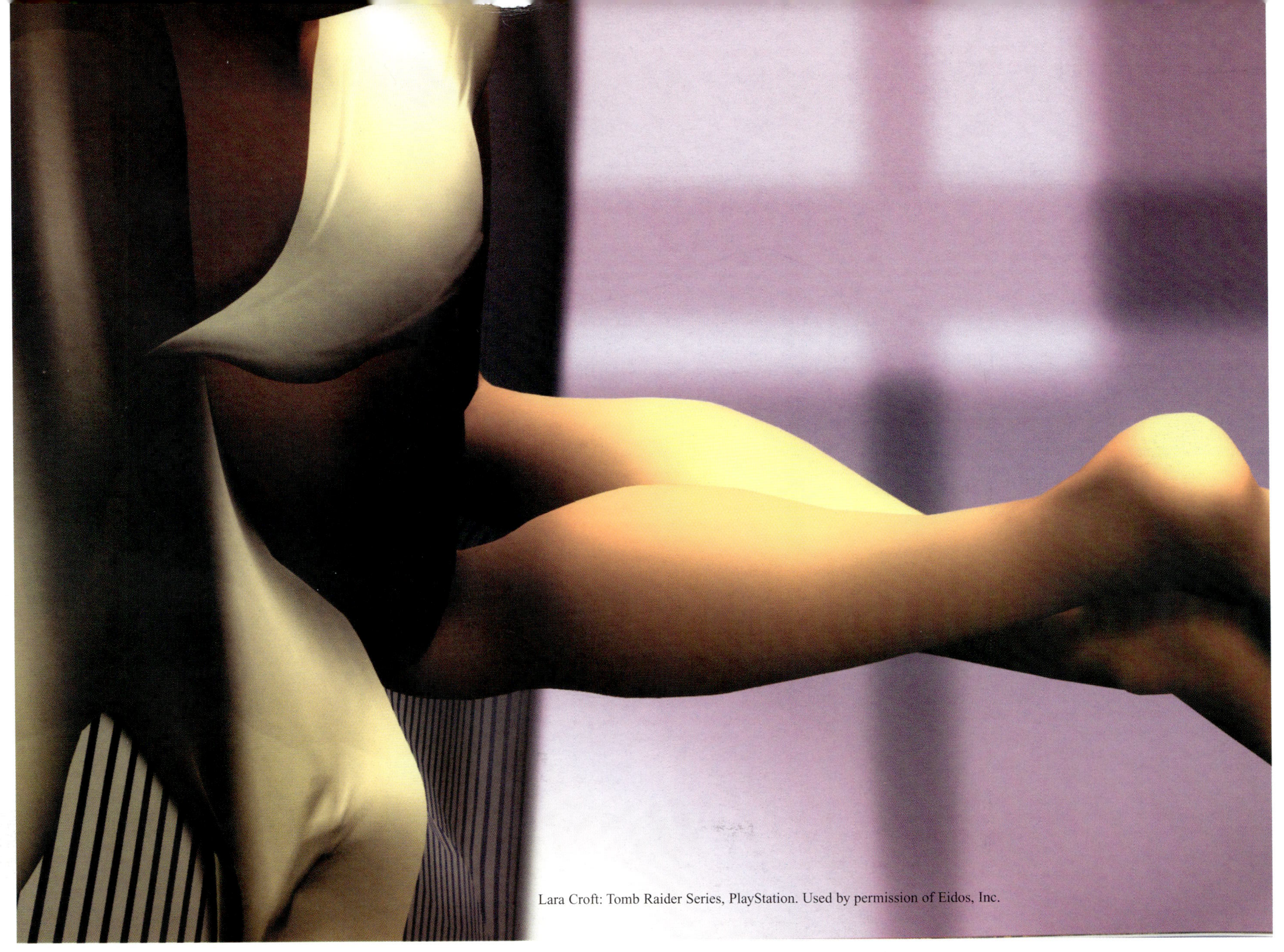

Lara Croft: Tomb Raider Series, PlayStation. Used by permission of Eidos, Inc.

Earlier in the text, we discussed values within chromatic and achromatic applications. In reality, *tints and shades* are another way of talking about value gradations—dark to light, chromatic values and black to white gradations. *Tints* refers to the addition of white and *shades* refers to the addition of black to a given hue.

Attributes of the Value System:

- Manipulation of tints and shades consistently throughout a given composition controls the overall tonal quality of the artwork.
- Tints and shades create atmospheric perspective, controlling the degree of the illusion of depth of space.
- Tints and shades produce the illusion of form, or three dimensions in space, as well as limits dimensional capabilities. Tints and shades represent mass and volume.
- Tints and shades create extreme value gradations, which produce high contrasting areas, or forms of high contrast. These results produce greater dimension and more obvious focal points.
- Illusion of surface texture.

In this chapter, we want to make investigations into tints and shades through specific examples in order to fully understand their exact functions. Without value gradations, all would be flat and without the illusion of reality. We will observe styles and time periods to see how tints and shades function as well as their overall importance in art.

Let's take a look at tints and shades (values) through a historical context.

Previous page illustrates magic of *tints and shades* by creating the illusion of 3-D form in space, in the reclining image of animation's Lara Croft.

The Classical World

Even the Romans understood the impact of tints and shades. As we take a look at some of the frescos in the luxurious capital of Italy, within the lavish homes in the city of Pompeii, we can see evidence of the artist's struggle to understand how gradations of values functioned to indicate space and form.

In the house of Marcus Lucretius Fronto, this frescoed wall is rendered with the figures of Mars and Venus on the left. In the central area of the panel, Eros can be seen with groups of servant girls, observing a scene nearby. We can almost detect the struggle of Roman artists, who were striving to develop the idea of creating three-dimensional figures in space. Even though there is still a reasonable degree of flat space felt in the wall fresco, there are obvious attempts to create mass (form), by value variations seen in the drapery and fabrics worn by the participants in the picture. Even though artists had not at this point refined the process of value gradations, it is evident that they were well into understanding the subject. Furthermore, this elegant pigmented wall exhibits competent hue contrasts, creating a marginal depth of space in the composition.

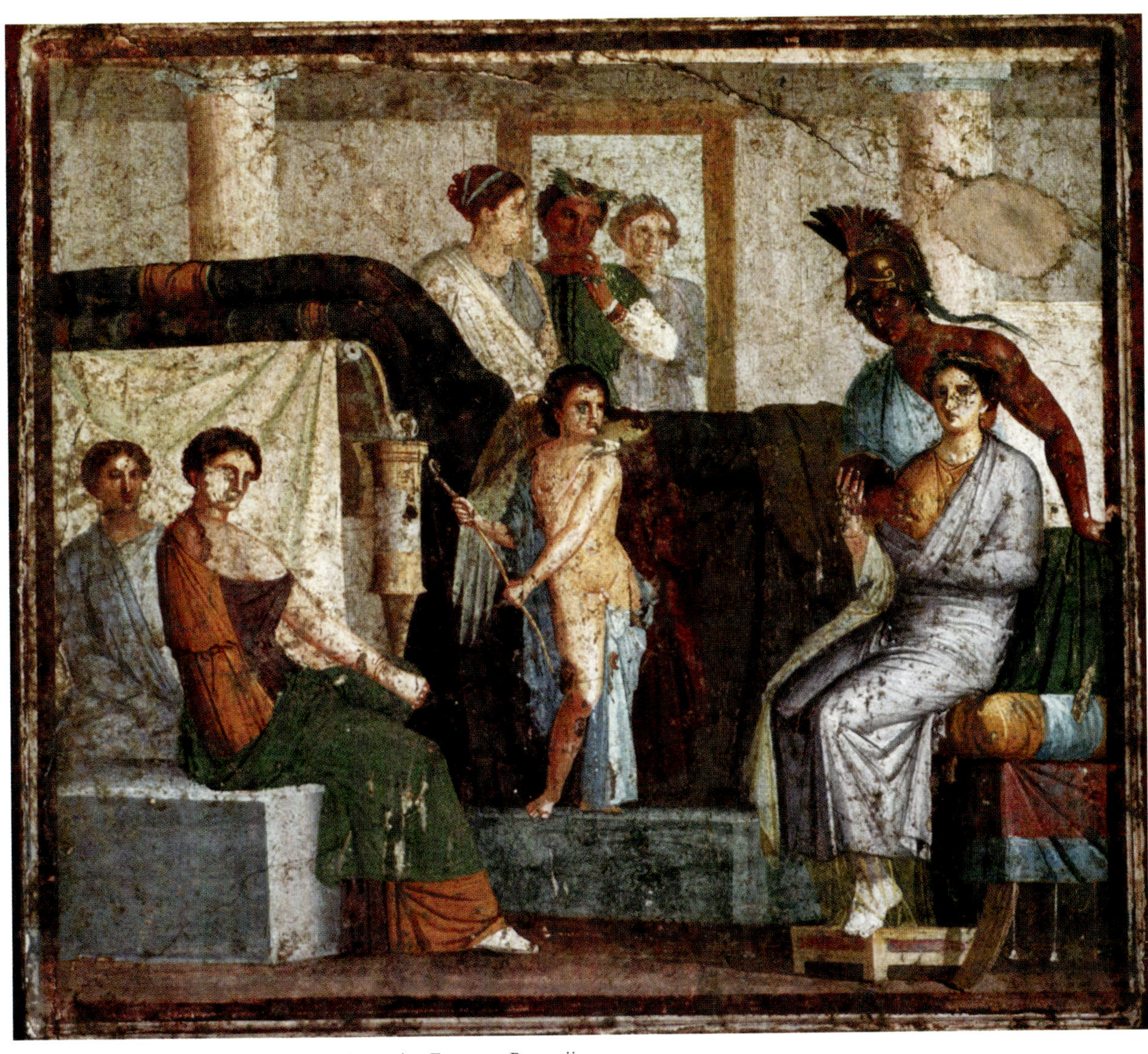

Fresco Painting in the House of Marcus Lucretius Fronto at Pompeii.

The Middle Ages

In 11th century Gothic cathedral windows we also see evidence of value variations within the individual glass constructions. The introduction of value gradations into stained glass was a major accomplishment early in the development of colors in glass. However, it wasn't until after the French Revolution that tints and shades were developed to their full potential. The variation of actual hues was not easily accomplished, but craftspeople did figure out how to introduce dark pigments into the colors of glass. The chapel window image found in St.

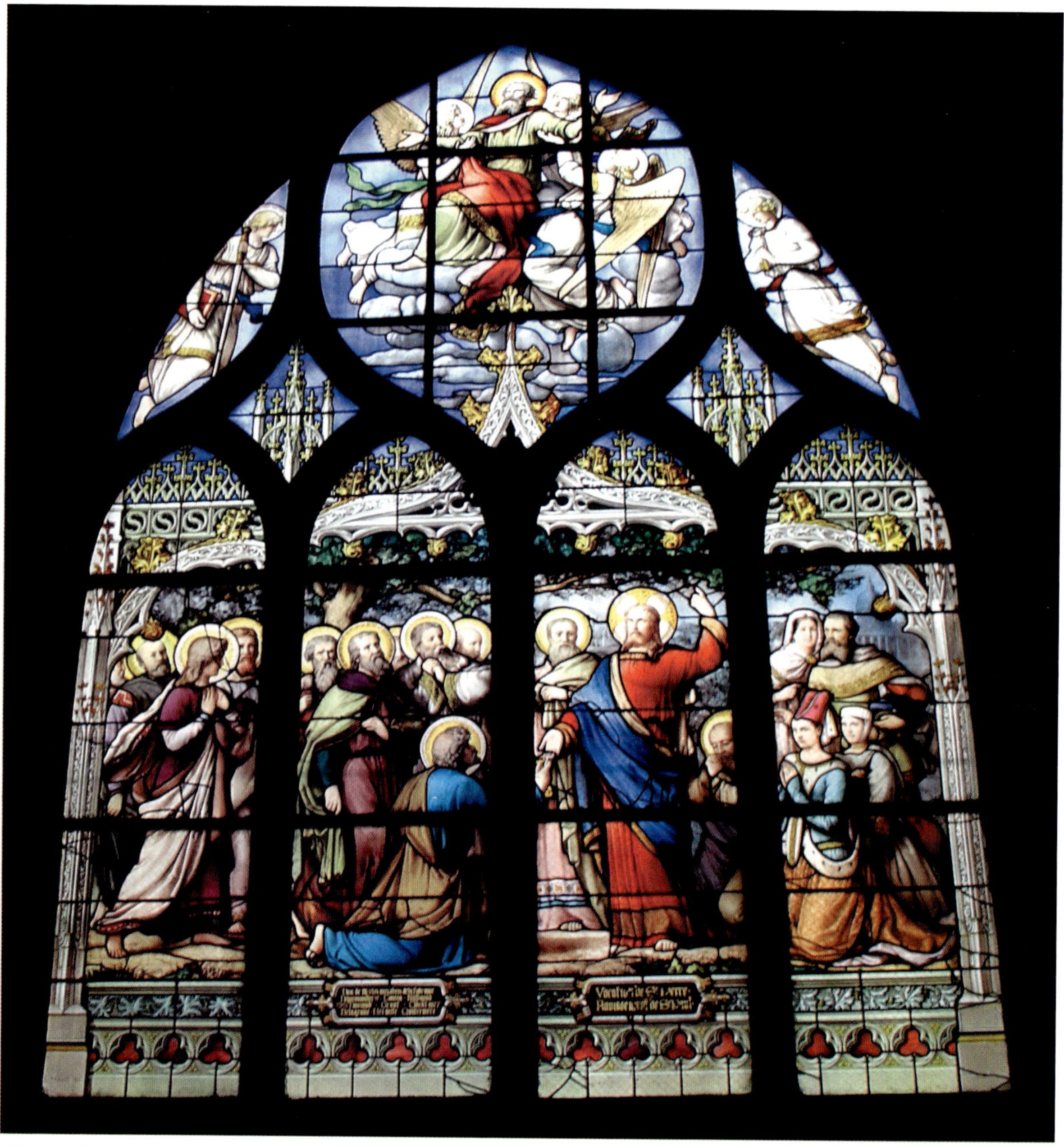

Chapel Window of the St. Severin Cathedral, Paris.
Photo by Alan Burner.

Severin Cathedral (opposite page) is an example of the important effect of tints and shades. The tints and shades of the drapery are skillfully controlled, creating the dimensional quality in the window. The values seen in the faces of Jesus and His Disciples is essential to establish the expression necessary to convey the emotion of the situation.

An even more definitive use of values is demonstrated in this archival chapel in *Notre Dame de Paris*. Here, we can see that tints and shades are very important in creating greater detail in the faces of the six figures. The delicate handling of tints and shades lends a believable texture to the skin and enhances the three-dimensional form itself.

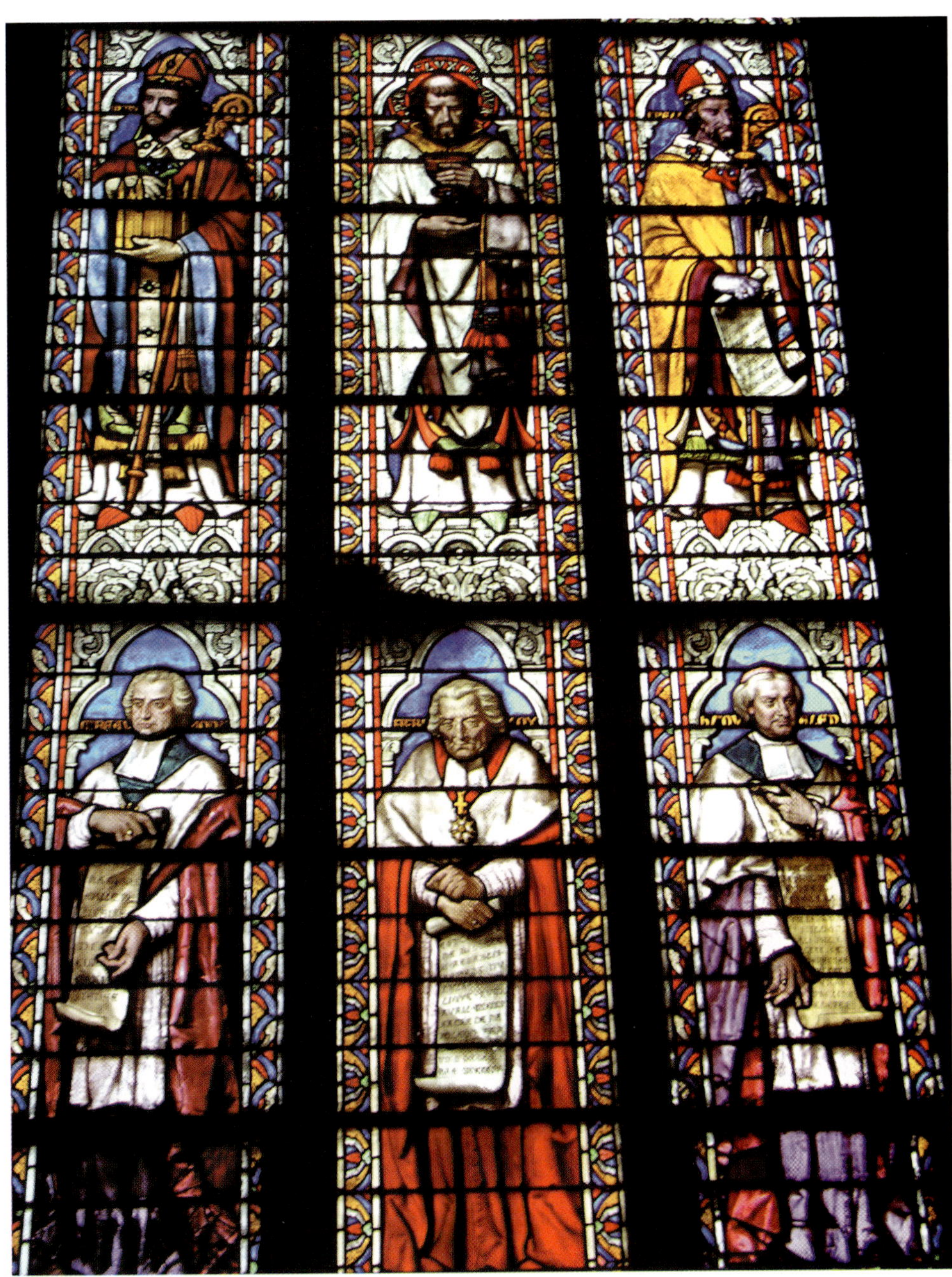

Partial Window in Archival room at Notre Dame de Paris.
Photo by Alan Burner.

The Renaissance Age

Early in Michelangelo's career, he knew that he was to be a sculptor. The problem was, the Pope needed walls embellished with Biblical references. This was a much higher priority for the church, since its message would be available in full grandiose visual format to both believers and non-believers. Basically, Michelangelo was told that he would need to conform to the wishes of the Pope if he was to survive as an artist in Italy. This was disconcerting to him, since he adored the medium of sculpting. In due course, Michelangelo painted for the Vatican by day, and sculpted for himself by night.

This bears mentioning because of his love for three-dimensional form. So much was his desire toward sculpting, that we see it conveyed, or converted into painted frescos. Many believe that he actually sculpted vicariously through his frescos, and thus his incredibly accomplished results seen on the Sistine Chapel ceiling. Never before had figures leaped off a flat surface in this manner. His ability to control *tints and shades* is astonishing to say the least. Michelangelo's control over value gradations was ever so tightly controlled, as if he was methodically chipping away at a sculpture. He meticulously developed his tints and shades.

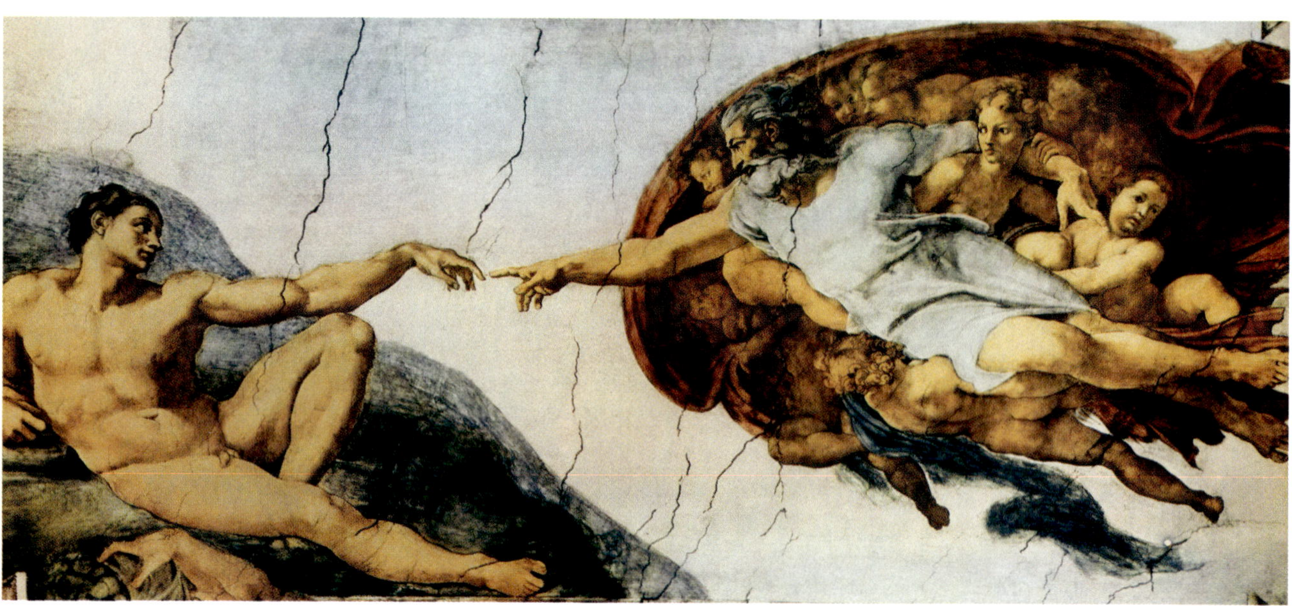

Creation of Adam (Sistine Chapel) by Michelangelo Buonarroti.

Modern and Contemporary

Shijo's imagery representing *Aiko's Dream* is predominately about chromatic tints and shades. These strange abstracts seem to set-up a certain flatness in the composition, while the tints and shades seen in the figures indicate a nominal degree of three-dimensional mass. This manipulation of tints and shades creates the *implication* of 3-D form, but not the *illusion*. Implication only infers a certain degree of form in space, but illusion produces the deception of being tangible. The intense yellow ground could be interpreted as the middle ground or background, and the same respectively for the violet triangular shaped area. The use of tints and shades tend to confuse the eye, and therefore create flat fractured planes of color, which seem to overwhelm the potential for constructing the illusion of mass. Basically, tints and shades produce a certain mass, as well as the deception that there is measurable depth of space in the foreground, middle-ground and background. The flat planes, however, minimize those effects by their complexity of placement. The composition effectively creates the *dream state*, in that it is somewhat unclear and confusing—nothing is absolute or makes complete sense. The tints and shades help to invent the mysterious nature of these abstract figures, as they transform from abstract simplistic forms to a more representational version.

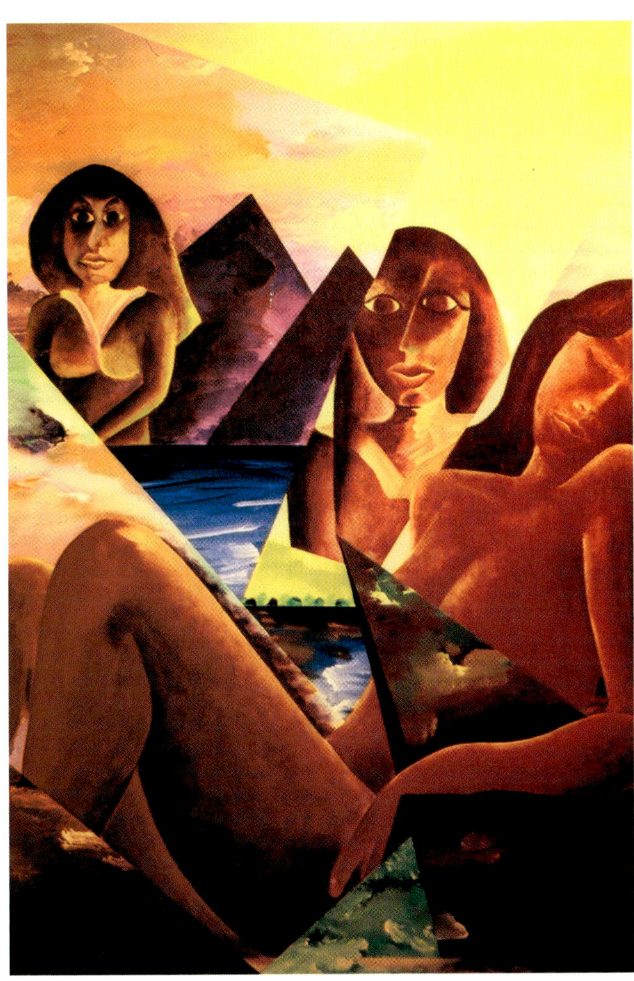

Dream of Aiko by Shijo

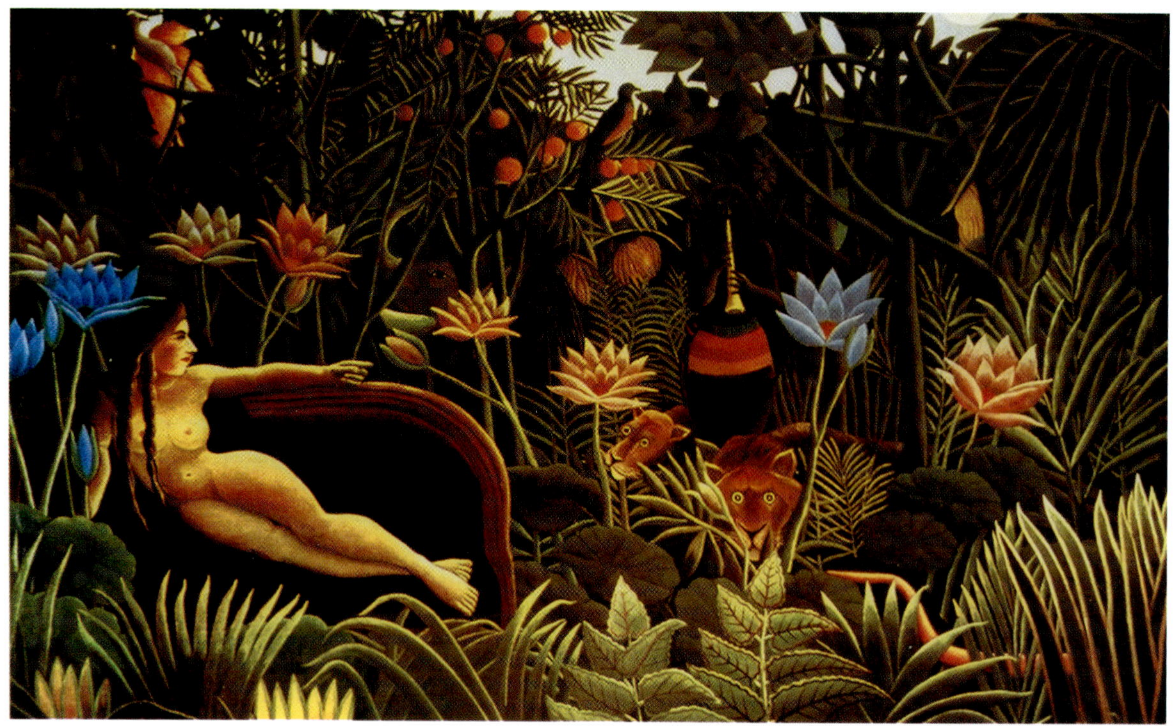

The Dream by Henri Rousseau.

Rousseau's dream imagery is abstract and simple. Like Shijo's work, the images do demonstrate a certain degree of three-dimensional mass, yet in a limited way. The tints and shades are extremely consistent in their dark to light gradations across the flora and fauna in the composition. The background is constructed of uniform dark value variations, while the foreground illustrates a commensurable uniformity of lighter value gradations. The uniformity of gradient values in the foreground, background and plant life, tend to greatly flatten the composition. We know there is the perception of spatial depth, but the painting lacks the actual feeling or illusion of that space. However, the contrast of a horizontal band of very light tints and shades in the extreme foreground, assists in creating limited illusional space.

The Animated World

Within the arena of *animation,* value gradations of tints and shades are imperative for creating certain types of contrast, which in turn create focal points, dimensional mass, volume and depth of space. The importance of tints and shades in animation, for example, can be illustrated by making a comparison between earlier animation and current applications in respect to their chromatic values.

Betty Boop, one of the early animated figures especially popular in the 1950s, was basically shapes defined by contour line, and then filled-in with color, which is void of any value variation (see Betty Boop image on the left). In the earliest years of animation, value gradations in the figure (since they were all black and white) were mostly nonexistent. It was totally up to the viewer to imagine that they were seeing a three-dimensional form. Later on, a flat cartoon personality was typically rendered onto a clear sheet of acetate material. Next, that sheet was then inserted over a background scene, which had a full complement of value gradations.

With the help of shaded backgrounds, it became easier for the viewer to imagine this flat figure to be a three-dimensional form. During the early years, when television was a fairly new commodity, the viewer's imagination was the key component for animated forms, in a generation of so many new inventions.

In the 21st century, we find that hand-painted cels are rapidly becoming a thing of the past, as we have advanced to the point where we now employ more advanced technology. Digital processes have enhanced animation capabilities, and of course made the process much quicker and more effective.

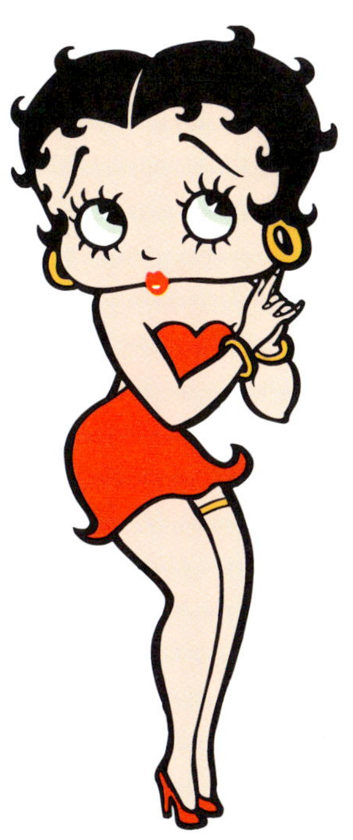

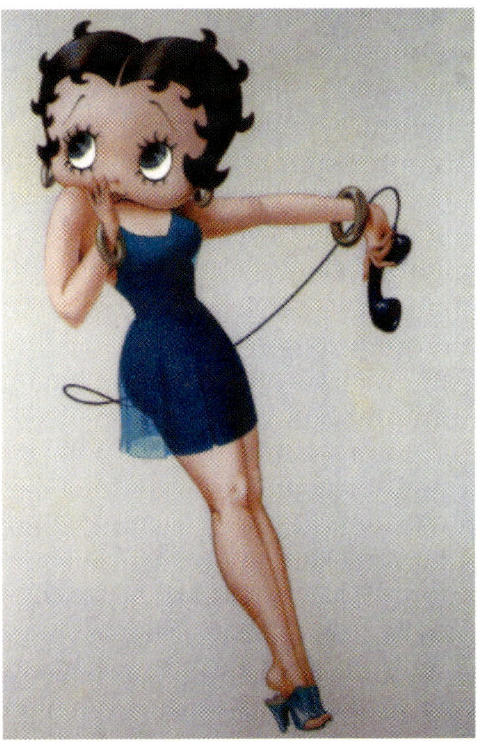

Betty Boop's image (right figure) now has been created with the advantage of added chromatic values. The tints and shades have created an extraordinarily more believable image dimensionally. In much of animation today, with some exceptions such as the Pokemon series, the heavy line is no longer necessary, since tints and shades have produced a more believable, three-dimensional form. The contour line form today may only exist as a stylistic emphasis, but not necessary otherwise.

Betty Boop. Classic Betty on Left. Right figure depicts Betty with added tints and shades.

Lara Croft (page 179), a popular contemporary animated figure, exhibits value variations which generate a very high contrasting composition, and makes no misgivings about the *emphasis* of the situation. She is alone, and a certain amount of fear grips the composition as she waits for the next event. The focus is on Lara Croft, but more specifically the weapons, and draws attention as to why she is there in that place. She is further accented by giving her form greater mass by the rapid transitions from light to dark values of the tints and shades.

The *fully reclined figure* of Lara Croft on pages 180 and 181 demonstrates tints and shades in the *chiaroscuro* value system, that is to say, the average gradation of dark to light, and back again. These value transitions here show us the importance of contrasts set-up by tints and shades. The light to dark areas create the three-dimensional effects of the body. Her upright legs illustrate the most extreme value changes, and also creates the maximum three-dimensional illusion. Compare the difference between her face, which is somewhat less dimensional than her legs. Dark and more subtle transitions of values occur in her face, while lighter and more severe gradations can be seen in her vertically extended legs. Her shoulders and arms reflect a moderate value range. Darker transitions in one area and lighter transitions in another help to create a greater sense of foreshortened space, moving the figure into its appropriate positions from the foreground to the background. Notice the slow transitions of shaded violets behind her right shoulder and arm. The contrast set up is significant between the right arm—with its rapid gradations of orange tints—and the background. The light tints of violet behind her elevated legs provide high contrast with the very intense light orange values of the legs.

Also apparent is the illusion of three-dimensional mass in space, as well as a certain perception of her skin texture. The slow and gradual yet wide range of warm orange contrasted against violet tints and shades create the quiet and relaxed mood of the character.

The Keys

Focusing our attention on the three comparisons of High Key #1, Intermediate Key #2 and Low Key #3, we want to bring to the reader's attention the issue of *High Key* through *Low Key* color.

High Key: Often, additions of white to a given color, or very light, intense color.

Intermediate Key: Would refer to the most saturated state of the color, between *high key* and *low key*.*

Low Key: Additions of black, or darker shades. It is the dulled down state of a given color.

The overwhelming brightness or intensity of Shenmue's portrait (facing page) generates a very spiritual and powerful image of an otherwise humble and unassuming young girl. This composition demonstrates the effects of *high key* color. Her face radiates and is surrounded by white light, as she appears to come from her own world, or universe. Her classical Japanese style of grace and elegance is emphasized, and the sophistication and dignity of the culture is sensed in part by this *high key* composition.

The composition of Lara Croft's gun battle (see top of page 192) *tonally* suggests a more *intermediate key* composition. There are dark areas which reflect a high contrast with the lighter values of the figure itself. There is a tension felt because of the extremes of higher keyed color in the figure and the low key colors in the background. The picture is neither high or low key compositionally, but somewhere in between.

In the composition at the bottom of page 192, the entirety of the space consists of particularly *low keyed color*. Rather than the extreme contrast of Lara's stressful gun battle, or the gentle contrasts of the Shenmue's portrait, we instead see a mysterious and suspenseful gaze, with very little contrast. This *low key* composition generates the element of suspense and secrecy, which is produced by the dulled colors, and in this case, the low contrast. Generally, a higher keyed color will have the effect of greater energy, whereas this low-keyed tone displays a cautious tension.

*Normally, we refer only to *high key* and *low key* color, which would then qualify examples #1 and #2 as high key. However, for greater clarity and preciseness, we have introduced *intermediate key*.

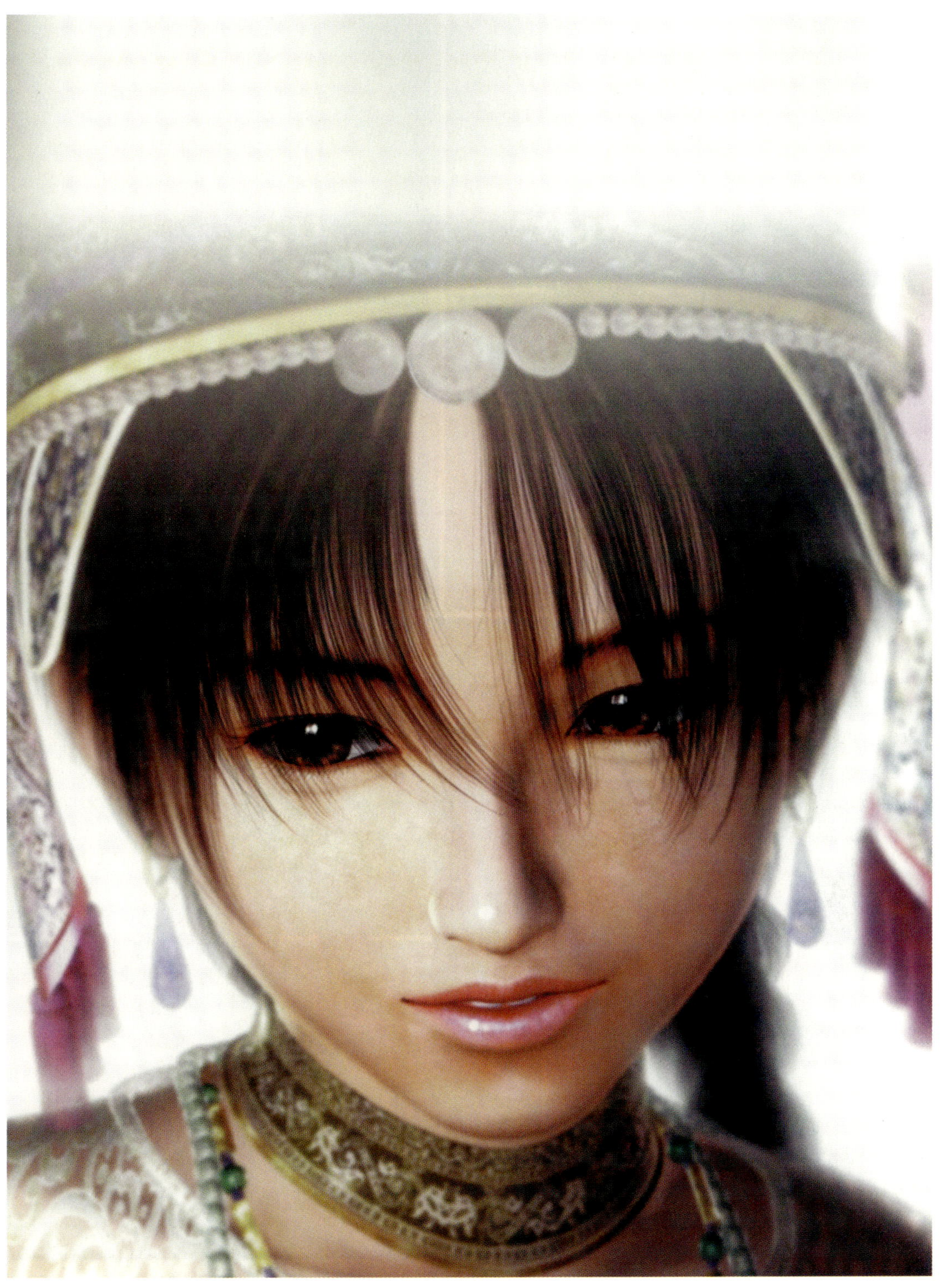

Shenmue, Dreamcast—Sega (high key #1).

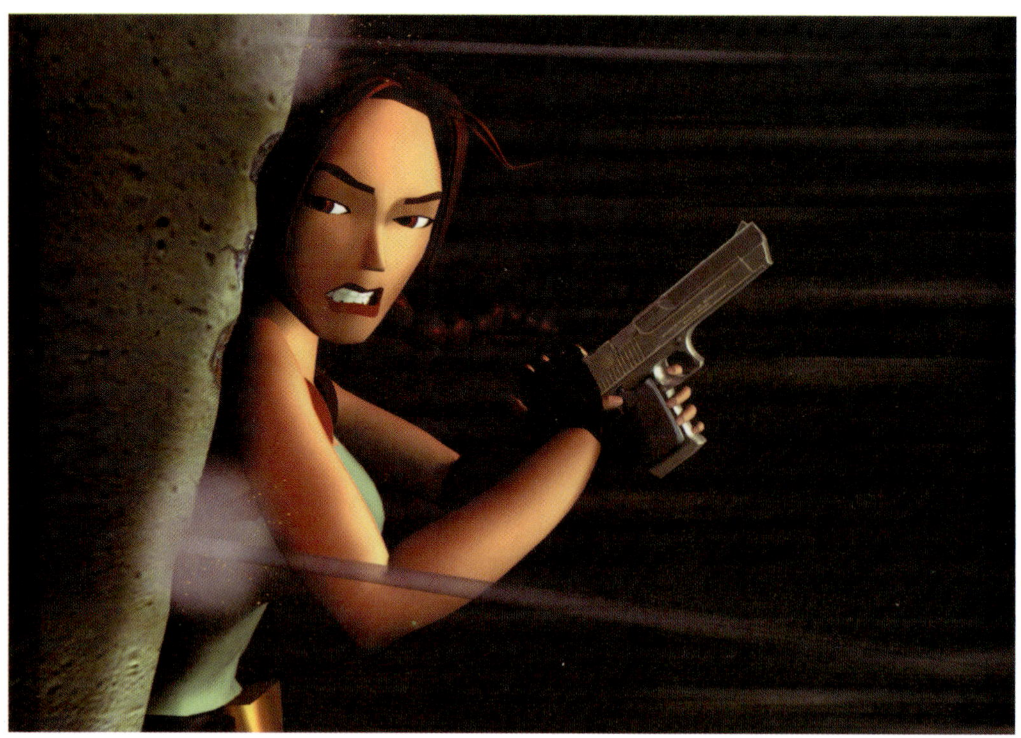

Lara Croft, Tomb Raider Series—PlayStation (intermediate key #2).
Used by permission of Eidos Inc.

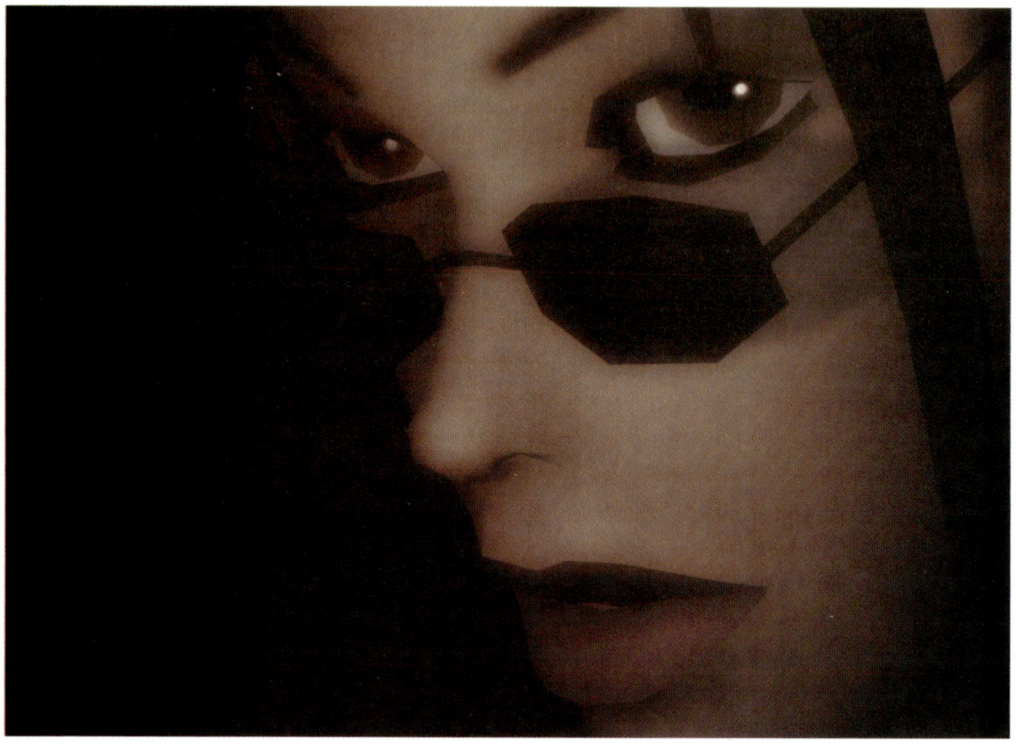

Lara Croft, Tomb Raider Series—PlayStation (low key #3).
Used by permission of Eidos Inc.

Early American Realism

Turn of the century American Realism artist Paul Cadmus records the famous event of Pocahontas saving Captain John Smith. Just as he is about to be slain for his illegitimate relationship with the young and seductive Pocahontas, she rushes in to protect him from death. He is spared because of her love for him, and as the story continues, all turns out well for them in this dynamic love story.

The dynamics of the Pocahontas love story are also visually reproduced in large part by the tints and shades effects, or value gradations. This drawing is exemplary of the *chiaroscuro* value system, with borderline *tenebristic* effects (see the *three types of value variations* following this discussion), which illustrates the illusion of three-dimensional figures in space. The *chiaroscuro* system builds up a gradient of dark to light achromatic values across the composition which develops physically powerful figures. It is the strong gradations of values in the borderline *tenebristic* effects which help to create the severity of the situation, as the drama grows and the theatrical positions of the figures act out their roles. The value gradations actually produce a rather harsh transition, which again accentuates extreme spectacle, with its dramatic diagonal figures in the composition. Pocahontas is the key figure, since the powerful diagonal line created by her form interrupts the vertical stance of the two warriors and the horizontal band of kneeling figures. The diagonal line of her body is continued by the standing warrior's shoulder and left raised arm.

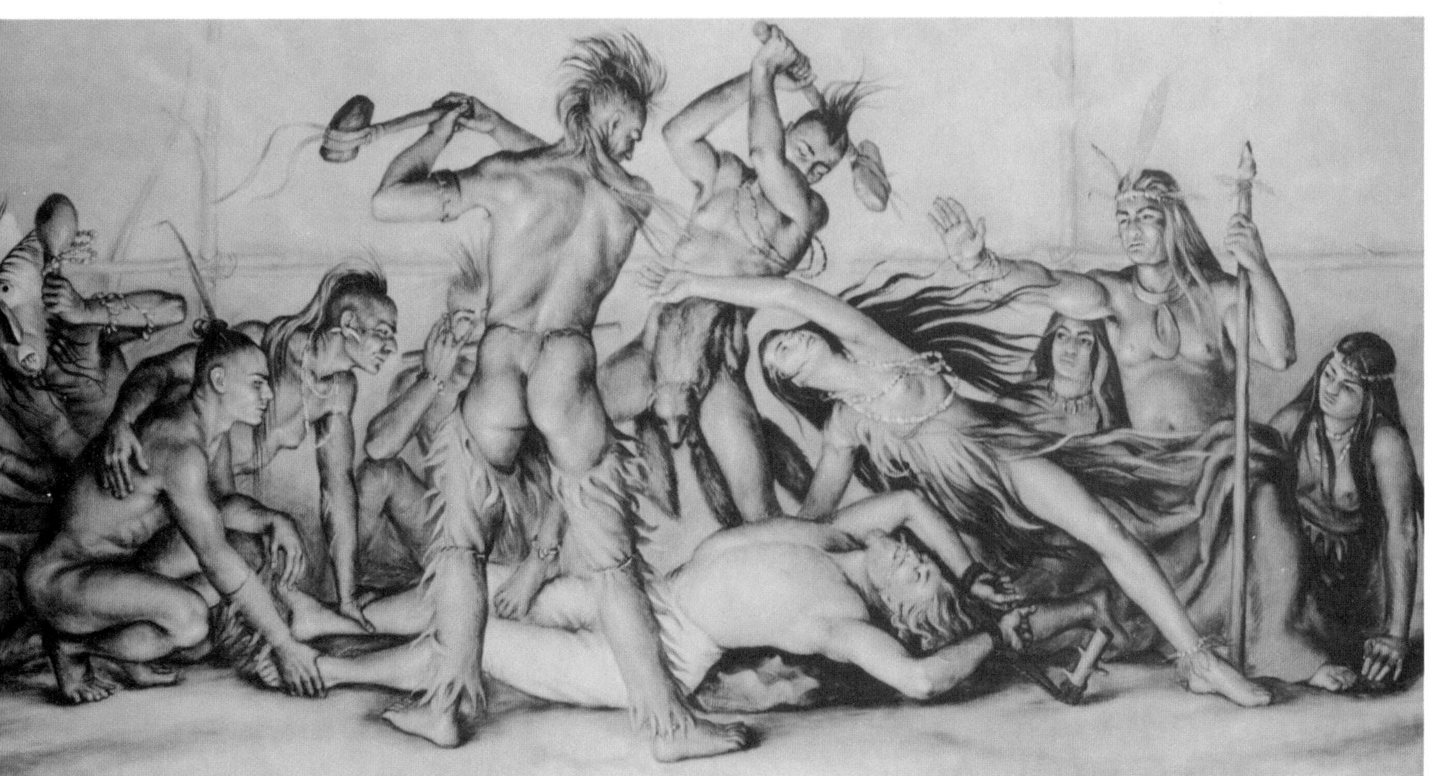

Pocahontas Saving the Life of Captain John Smith by Paul Cadmus.

Three Types of Value Variations, or Tints and Shades:

Sfumato

Sfumato is Italian for "vanished in smoke" literally, and it was Leonardo who actually created the term and effect himself. This type of value system can be observed in the Western world's icon—the *Mona Lisa*. Attributes of sfumato are those which create the most subtle and delicate gradations of value. Lisa's face is comprised of subtle nuances of value gradations, as a result of tints and shades. In fact, the entire composition is subtle and quiet with sfumato effects. Some say that it was not finished because of the lack of detail in the background, and compared to the face of Lisa, it certainly does lack the detail that we are accustomed to seeing. Yet the background has that smoky sfumato effect and the lack of detail helps us focus on the portrait of the lady herself.

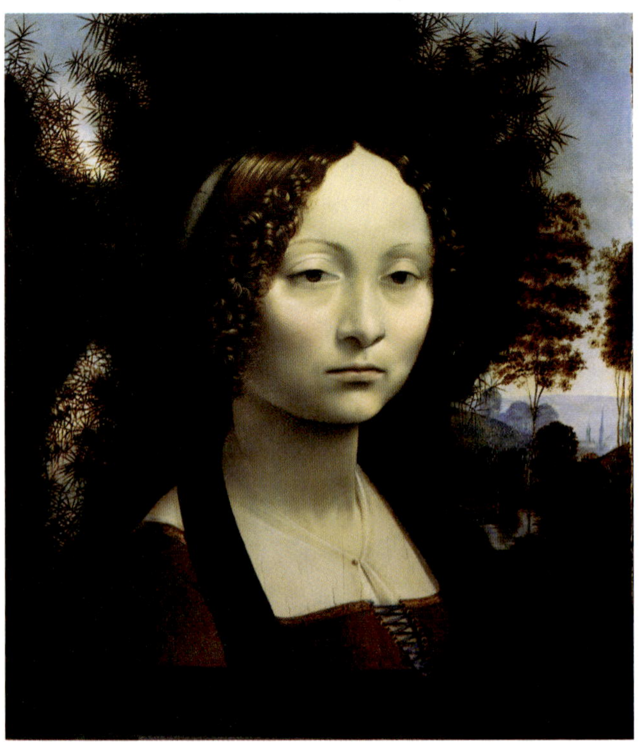

Portrait of Ginevra de' Benci by Leonardo da Vinci.

c. 1474.

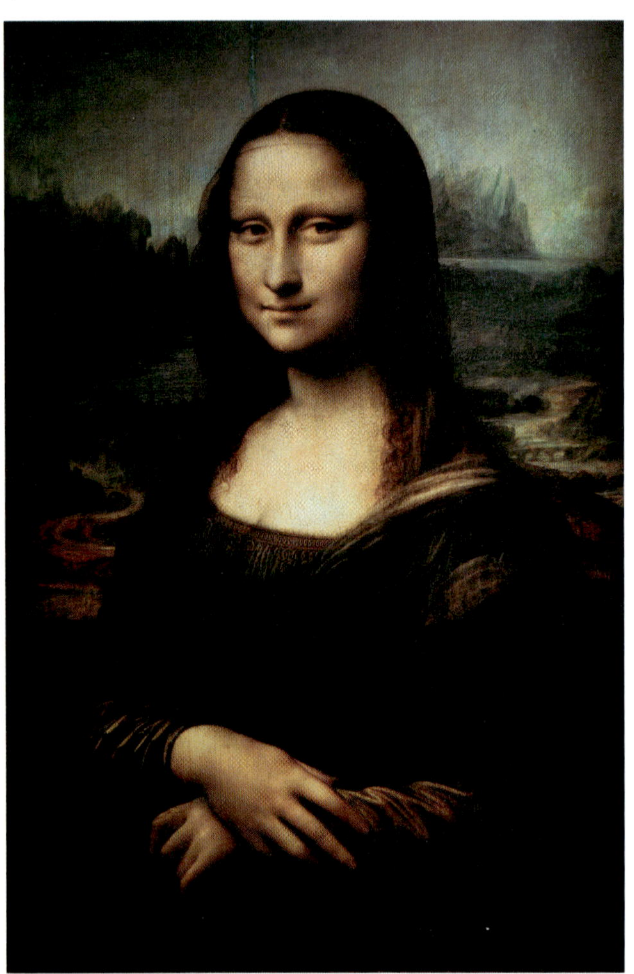

Mona Lisa by Leonardo Da Vinci.

A similar background can be seen in Leonardo's Florentine lady, the *Portrait of Ginevra de' Benci,* yet it is lighter. The background is not unlike Leonardo's *Mona Lisa,* in that it continues that *smoky* unfinished appearance so typical in his portraiture. Notice the emphasis of Ginevra's facial features. The gentle sfumato values drift almost unnoticed across her face, contrasted to the chiaroscuro effect of her soft but tightly curled hair.

The dynamic of the composition is in the dark values of the background foliage contrasted against the intensity of her face. It is the darkness that forces the viewer to focus more carefully at the portrait and to consider the person, or personality, of Ginevra. The lack of detail, or the smokiness of the background is in direct opposition to the very specific features of her face. In a more simplistic sense, we could say that the Ginevra portrait is comprised entirely of extreme tints and shades.

Chiaroscuro

This is actually a pattern of slow gradations of value, which shift from light to dark and back again throughout a given composition. It is the primary system used in tints and shades to produce believable illusion of three-dimensional objects in space. *Chiaroscuro* is neither extremely dark compositionally, nor is it exceptionally dark in its gradations. It is rather between sfumato and tenebrism tonally.

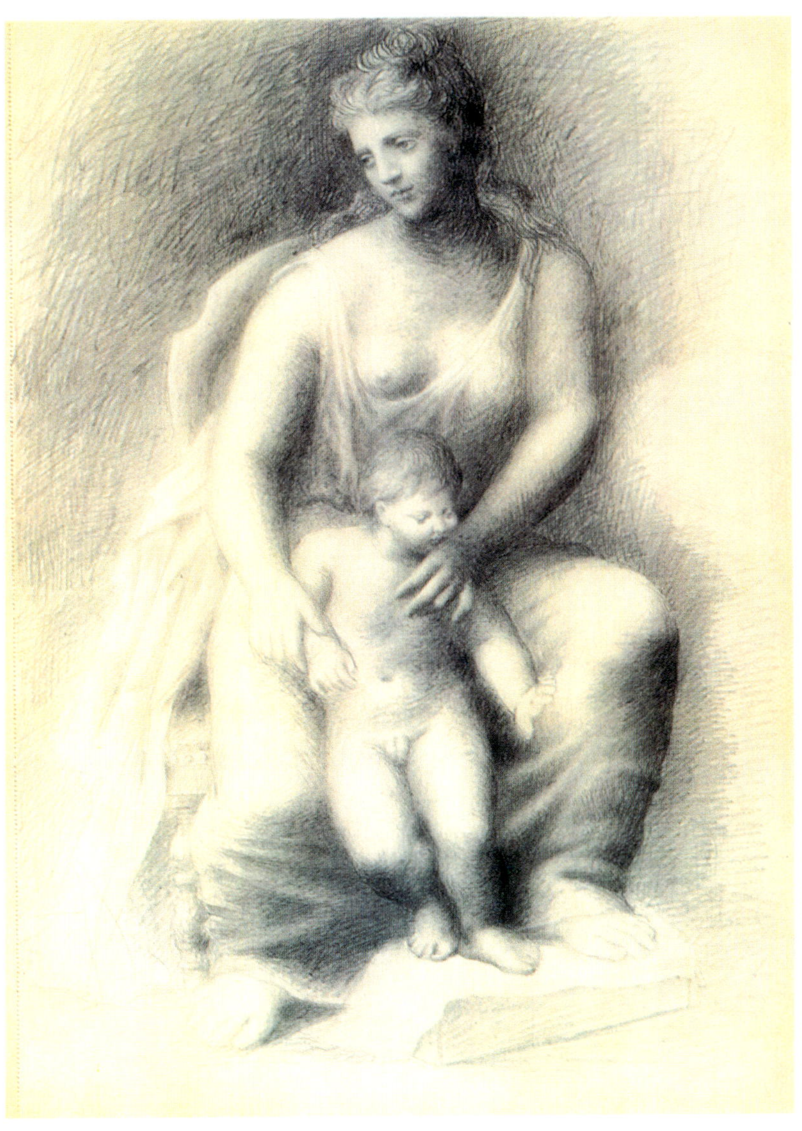

Renaissance Maternity. Dinard, Summer, 1922 by Pablo Picasso.
© Artists Rights Society (ARS).

Tenebrism

Tenebrism can best be described as extreme value changes. Often tenebrism is so extreme in its gradation, that it seems to shift suddenly from dark to light with little or seemingly no transitional area of gray values between. Tenebrism produces the most harsh tints and shades of the three value systems and is decidedly the most theatrical.

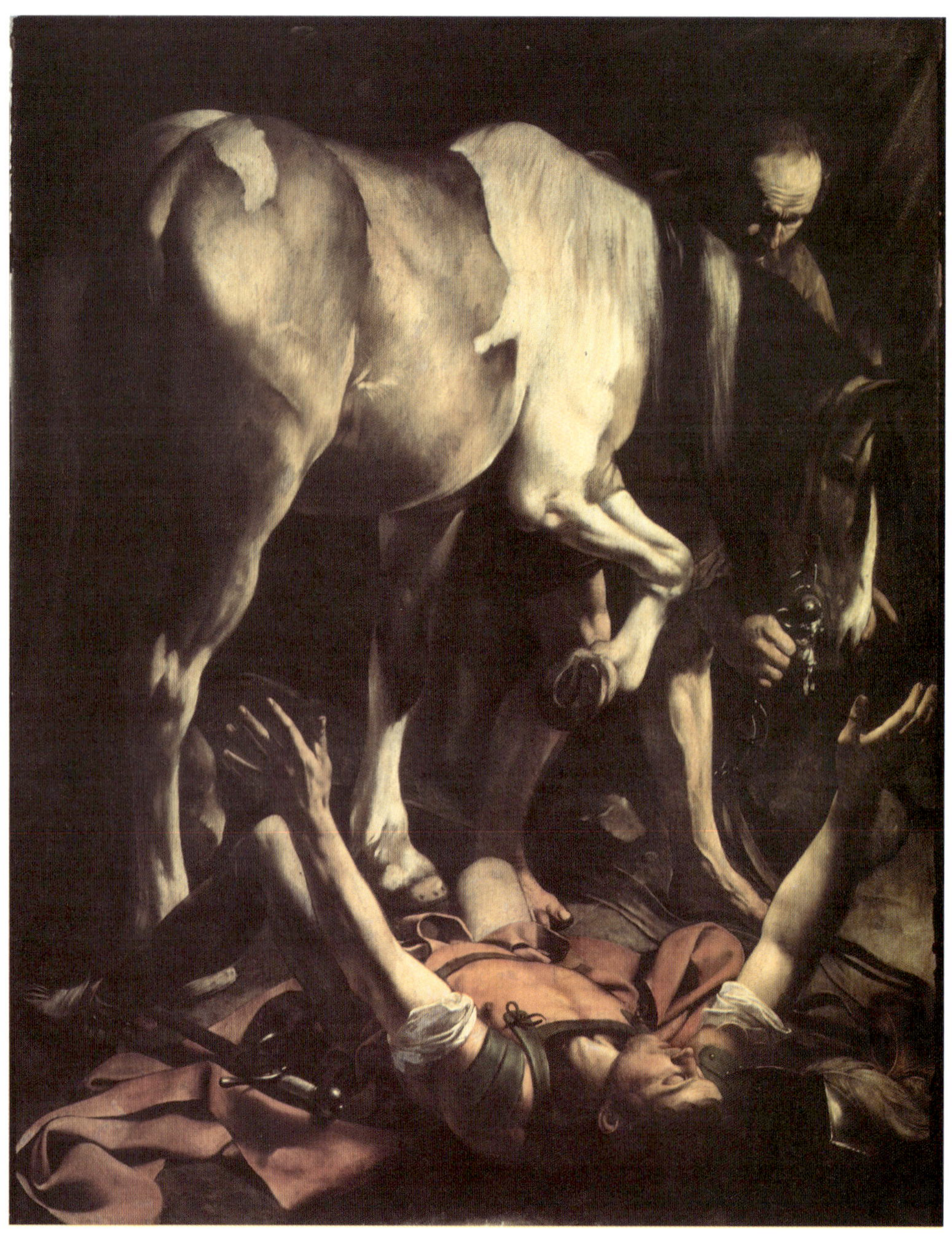

The Conversion of Saint Paul, by Michelangelo Merisi da Caravaggio.

In *The Conversion of Saint Paul,* as is often the case in Caravaggio's work, we see the effects of tenebrism in full force. This actual account of this event is found in the New Testament Book of Acts. To eliminate any confusion, it is necessary to point out that Paul's name before his conversion was Saul of Tarsus. Saul was a Roman officer who regularly persecuted Christians, not long after the crucifixion of Jesus Christ. Christians were brought to Jerusalem on a frequent basis, as sanctioned by the emperor, and were persecuted and/or put to death for their faith.

One early morning, Saul sets off on a regular mission to search for Christians. Suddenly, a burst of intense light illuminates everyone in the search party, and Saul himself falls off of his horse resultant of the intensity from the light. As Saul lays on the ground blinded by the light, the Lord begins to speak to him by saying, "Saul, Saul, why are you persecuting Me?" Saul inquires as to whom he is speaking, and after a short conversation, he is led back into the city, where he stays with a certain disciple for a period of three days. After three days have passed, Saul's blind eyes unexpectedly are opened again. Saul's physical sight is not the only thing that was restored. His *spiritual eyes* are also opened. Saul converts to Christianity, and now *Saul of Tarsus* has become *Paul the Apostle*, who grew to be one of the foundation saints of the church.

Caravaggio builds extreme light and dark transitional areas of tenebristic values, focusing on the fallen figure of Saul. Even though light is flooding the surface of the horse's left side, Saul is still the focus. All through the composition, tenebrism reigns with the extreme dark to light conversions, with a minimum of transitional gray tones. The mass or three-dimensional form of Saul's arms are very tenebristic values. We are looking at an undetermined amount of deep space, mass, and focal emphasis, all a result of values in tenebrism.

Finally, a beautiful execution of tinted and shaded pigments can be observed in the ceiling of one of many rooms within the Palace of Versailles (See photo on the next page). The immediate observation is the high contrast between light and dark. The figure in the corner of the ceiling is in high contrast with the dark, low key background. When standing in the room itself, it is almost impossible to discern whether or not it is the illusion of a three-dimensional figure, or an actual sculpture. The execution of value gradations in this painted ceiling is astounding, as the extreme high contrast of dark and light causes the form to "pop" away from the rest of the painted surface.

The Versailles ceiling demonstrates two of the three value systems. The smoky background of the ceiling seems very reminiscent of the *sfumato* effects, of Leonardo da Vinci's *Mona Lisa* or in *Ginevra de' Benci.* Also, the effects of *chiaroscuro* are responsible for the development of the illusion of three-dimensional mass in the foreground figure.

The maximum effect of contrasts of value are well planned by the architect and the artist. The highly recessed or vaulted ceiling omits much of the glare, which enters the room via the large palace windows (lower left corner). The optimal function of sfumato and high contrast is therefore allowed to accomplish its major function, which is to accentuate the figure and its mass.

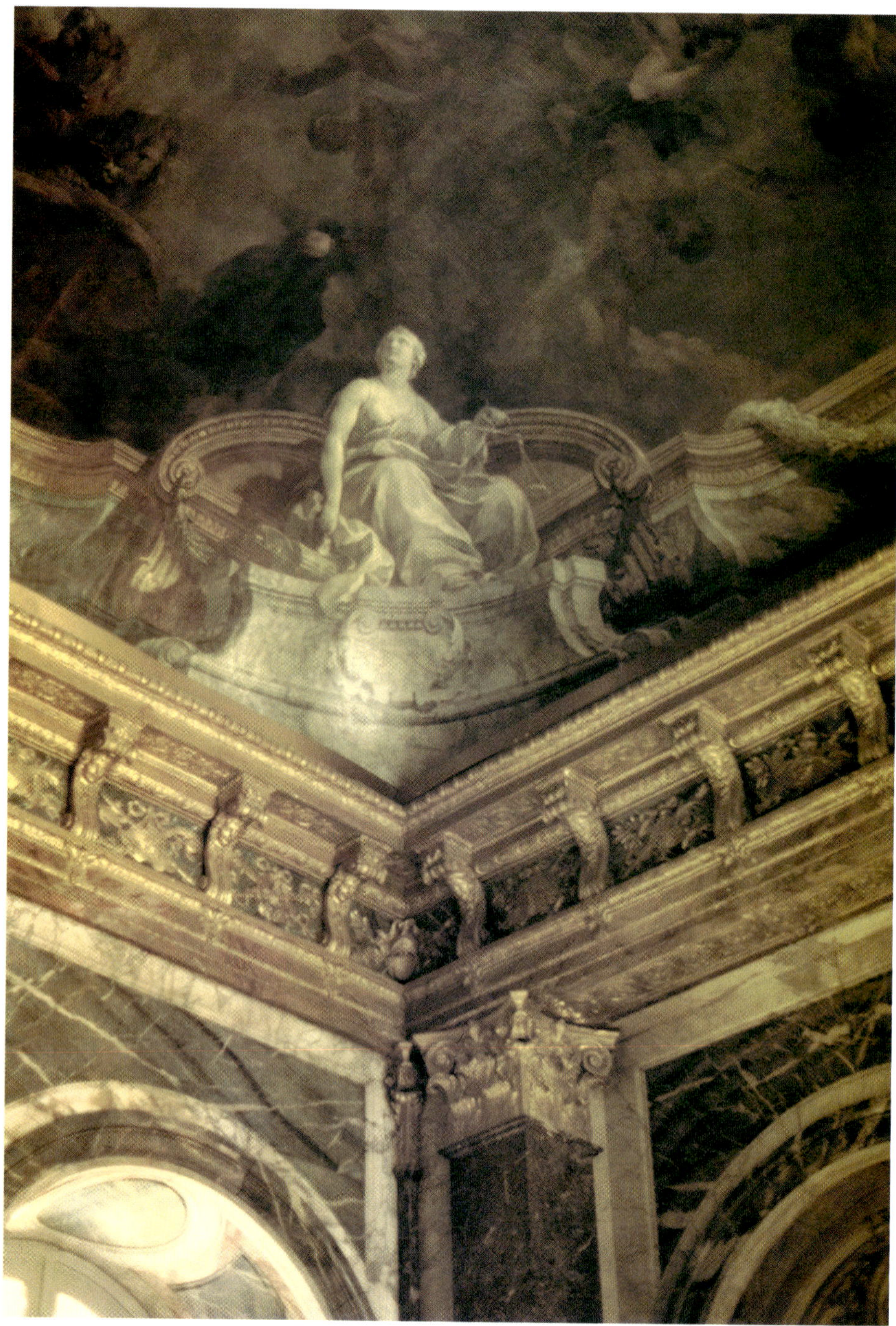

Interior Room; Ceiling Corner, Palace of Versailles, France.
Photo by Alan Burner.
Value systems can create startling 3-D illusion. At the Palace of Versailles, a figurative form is revealed in the corner ceiling, which makes us feel an illusional separation from the wall. High contrast between the background colors and the foreground figure aid in the effects manifested by the figure's value system. This is also referred to as a *figure/ground relationship.*

Reading Complement

Sensations of Colour

by Hazel Rossotti

The homogeneal Light and Rays which appear red, or rather make Objects appear so, I call Rubrifick or Red-making; those which make Objects appear yellow, green, blue, and violet, I call Yellow-making, Green-making, Blue-making, and Violet-making, and so of the rest. And if at any time I speak of Light and Rays as coloured or endued with Colours, I would be understood to speak not philosophically and properly, but grossly, and accordingly to such Conceptions as vulgar People in seeing all these Experiments would be apt to frame. For the Rays to speak properly are not coloured. In them there is nothing else than a certain Power and Disposition to stir up a Sensation of this or that Colour. For as Sound in a Bell or musical String, or other sounding Body, is nothing but a trembling Motion, and in the Air nothing but that Motion propagated from the Object, and in Sensorium 'tis a Sense of that Motion under the Form of Sound; so Colours in the Object are nothing but a Disposition to reflect this or that sort of Rays more copiously than the rest; in the Rays they are nothing but their Dispositions to propagate this or that Motion into the Sensorium, and in the Sensorium they are Sensations of those Motions under the Forms of Colours.

—Newton, *Opticks*

Since all Perception in the Brain is made
(Tho' where and how was never yet display'd)
And since so great a distance lies between
The Eye-ball, and the Seat of Sense within,
While in the Eye th'arrested Object stays
Tell, what th'Idea to the Brain Conveys?

—Blackmore, *Creation*

Do not the Rays of Light falling upon the bottom of the Eye excite Vibrations in the *Tunica Retina*? Which Vibrations, being propagated along the solid Fibres of the optick Nerves into the Brain, cause the Sense of seeing.

—Newton, Opticks

Two optic nerves, they say, she ties,
Like spectacles, across the eyes;
By which the spirits bring her word,
Whene'er the balls are fix'd or stirred.

—Matthew Price, Alma

Someone is given a certain yellow-green (or blue-green) and told to mix a less yellowish (or bluish) one—or to pick it out from a number of colour samples. A less yellowish green, however, is not a bluish one (and vice versa), and there is also such a task as choosing, or mixing a green that is neither yellowish nor bluish. I say 'or mixing' because a green does not become both bluish[1] and yellowish because it is produced by a kind of mixture of yellow and blue.

—Wittgenstein, *Remarks on Colour*, trans.
By McAlister and Schattle

During the day, owing to the yellowish hue of the snow, shadows tending to violet had already been observable; these might now be pronounced to be decidedly blue, as the illumined parts exhibited a yellow deepening to orange.

But as the sun at last was about to set, and its rays, greatly mitigated by the thicker vapours, began to diffuse a most beautiful red colour over the whole scene around me, the shadow colour changed to a green, in lightness to be compared to a sea-green, in beauty to the green of the emerald. The appearance became more and more vivid: one might have imagined oneself in a fairy world, for every object had clothed itself in the two vivid and so beautifully harmonizing colours, till at last, as the sun went down, the magnificent spectacle was lost in a grey twilight, and by degrees in a clear moon-and-starlight night.

—Goethe, *Theory of Colours*

[1]Translator's Note: Wittgenstein wrote 'greenish' here but presumably meant "bluish"...

Colours appear what they are not, according to the ground which surrounds them.

—LEONARDO DA VINCI, *Trattato della pi*

In the silent painted park where I walked her and aired her a little, she sobbed and said I would soon, soon leave her as everybody had, and I sang her a wistful French ballad, and strung together some fugitive rhymes to amuse her:

The place was called *Enchanted Hunters.*
Query:
What Indian dyes, Diana, did they dell
endorse to make Picture Lake a very
blood bath of trees before the blue hotel?

She said: "Why blue when it is white, why blue for heaven's sake?" and started to cry again…

—NABOKOV, *Lolita*

Why blue: when I asked Nabokov "Why blue?" and whether it had anything to do with the butterflies commonly known as the "Blues," he replied: "What Rita does not understand is that a white surface, the chalk of that hotel, does look blue in a wash of light and shade on a vivid fall day, amid red foliage. H.H. is merely paying a tribute to French impressionist painters. He notes an optical miracle as E.B. White does somewhere when refereeing to the divine combination of 'red barn and blue snow.' It is the shock of colour, not an intellectual blueprint or the shadow of a hobby…I was really born a landscape painter."

—A. APPEL, *The Annotated Lolita*

Every hue throughout your work is altered by every touch that you add in other places.

—RUSKIN

When Anaxagoras says: Even the snow is black!
He is taken by the scientists very seriously
because he is enunciating a "principle," a "law"
that all things are mixed, and therefore the purest
white snow
has in it an element of blackness.

That they call science, and reality.
I call it mental conceit and mystification
and nonsense, for pure snow is white to us
white and white and only white
with a lovely bloom of whiteness upon white
in which the soul delights and the senses
have an experience of bliss.

And life is for delight, and for bliss
and dread, and the dark, rolling ominousness of
doom
then the bright dawning of delight again
from off the sheer white snow, or the poised
moon.

And in the shadow of the sun the snow is blue, so
blue-aloof
with a hint of the frozen bells of the scylla flower
but never the ghost of a glimpse of Anaxagoras'
funeral black.

—D.H. LAWRENCE, 'Anaxagoras'

I had entered an inn towards evening, and, as well-favoured girl, with a brilliantly fair complexion, black hair, and a scarlet bodice, came into the room, I looked attentively at her as she stood before me at some distance in half shadow. As she presently afterwards turned away, I saw on the white wall, which was now before me, a black face surrounded with a bright light, while the dress of the perfectly distinct figure appeared of a beautiful sea-green.

* * * *

As the opposite colour is produced by a constant law in experiments with coloured objects on portions of the retina, so the same effect takes place when the whole retina is impressed with a single colour. We may convince ourselves of this by means of coloured glass. If we look long through a blue pane of glass, everything will afterwards appear in sunshine to the naked eye, even if the sky is grey and the scene colourless. In like manner, in taking off green spectacles, we see all objects in a red light. Every decided colour does a certain violence to the eye, and forces the organ to opposition.

—GOETHE, *Theory of Colours*

A given visual phenomenon may not be perceived at all unless it is actively looked for.

—Burnham, Hanes and Bartleson, *Color*

The difference is as great between
the optics seeing, as the objects seen.
All Manners take a tincture from our won;
Or come discolour'd through our Passions shown.
Or Fancy's beam enlarges, multiplies
Contracts, inverts and gives ten thousand dyes.

—Pope, *Moral Essays*

For they sometimes appear by other Causes, as when by the power of Phantasy we see Colours in a Dream, or a Mad man sees things before him which are not there; or when we see Fire by striking the Eye, or see Colours like the Eye of a Peacock's Feather, by pressing our Eyes in either corner whilst we look the other way. Where these and such like Causes interpose not, the Colour always answers to the sort or sorts of the Rays whereof the Light consists, as I have constantly found in whatever Phenomena of Colours I have hitherto been able to examine. I shall in the following Propositions give instances of this in the Phenomena of chiefest note.

—Newton, *Opticks*

Light and the Eye

The colours we see depend, we say, on the composition of the light which enters the eye. And this, in turn, depends on the composition of the original light and on the way in which the light is modified by encounters *en route* from source to eye, encounters with other light waves, with the media through which it passes and with objects off which some or all of it may bounce. Since we were less than two weeks old, we could experience variations in the composition of the light as different sensations of colour. But how?

In this section, we shall discuss the changes which occur when the light encounters the back of the eye. We shall discuss mainly human colour vision, both normal and anomalous, but will also mention colour vision in other vertebrates and in insects. We shall see that there is still much unraveling to be done before we can understand what happens *after* the light is absorbed by the eye—the optic nerve and the brain combine to play some odd tricks. Some of the sensations we experience seem but tenuously related to the encounter between light and eye. So while it is quite easy to give the spccifications (of wavelength and intensity) for a ray of light, it is vastly more difficult to specify a sensation of colour. None the less, as we shall see, there have been numerous brave attempts to do so.

The eye is commonly likened to a camera. The light enters a dark chamber through an aperture which can be varied in diameter according to the intensity of the light, and it is focused by the lens to a light-sensitive backing. In both camera and eye, the light produces only small changes in the photosensitive material, but these are the starting points for a long series of changes which take place during the 'processing' and which eventually produce either a photograph or a sensation.

In a young, normal, human eye (see Figure 43), the outer layer (the "cornea"), the lens and the eye fluids are almost transparent. When the light reaches the retina, on the inner surface of the eye, it passes through layers of transparent nerve fibers, between capillary blood vessels and on to the photosensitive cells at the ends of the nerve fibers. These are backed with a layer of cells which contain black pigment and absorb stray light. The whole eye is enclosed in a tough outer skin which is an opaque continuation of the cornea.

The photosensitive cells are coloured—they contain pigments which absorb visible light, and it is this absorption which forms the basis of our sense of sight. In the human retina, there are two classes of photosensitive cells called *rods* and *cones* on account of their (very approximate) shape. The rods are effective only in dim light and enable us to sense differences in brightness, while the cones respond to light of normal intensity and allow us to distinguish between different colours. So the eye behaves as a

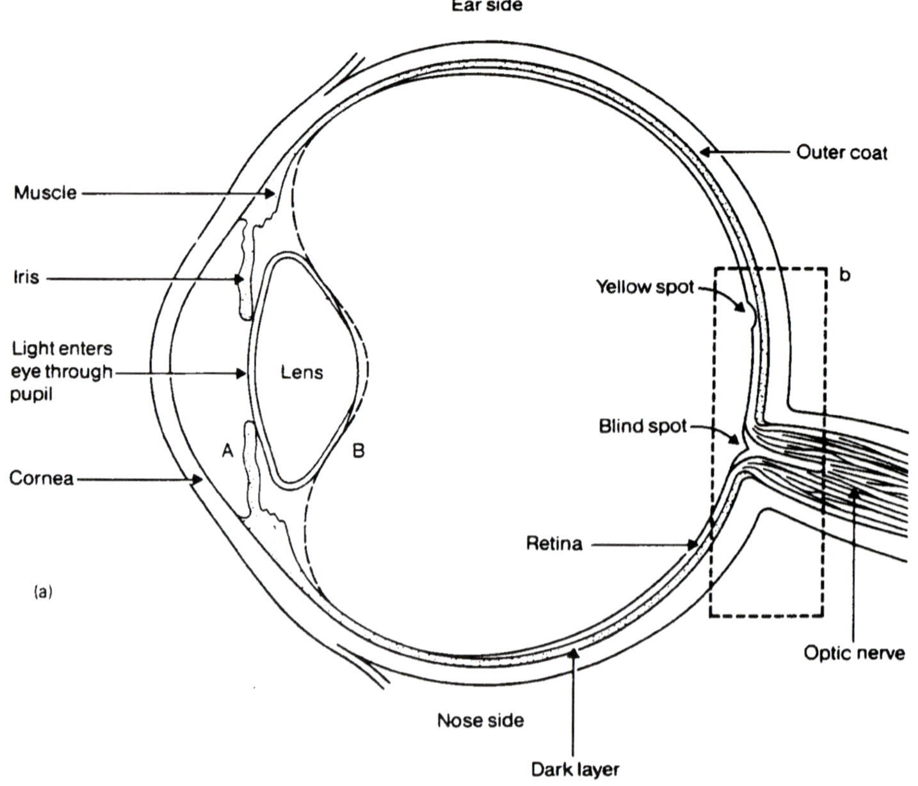
Ear side
Outer coat
Muscle
Iris
Yellow spot
b
Light enters
eye through
pupil
Lens
Blind spot
A
B
Cornea
Retina
(a)
Optic nerve
Nose side
Dark layer

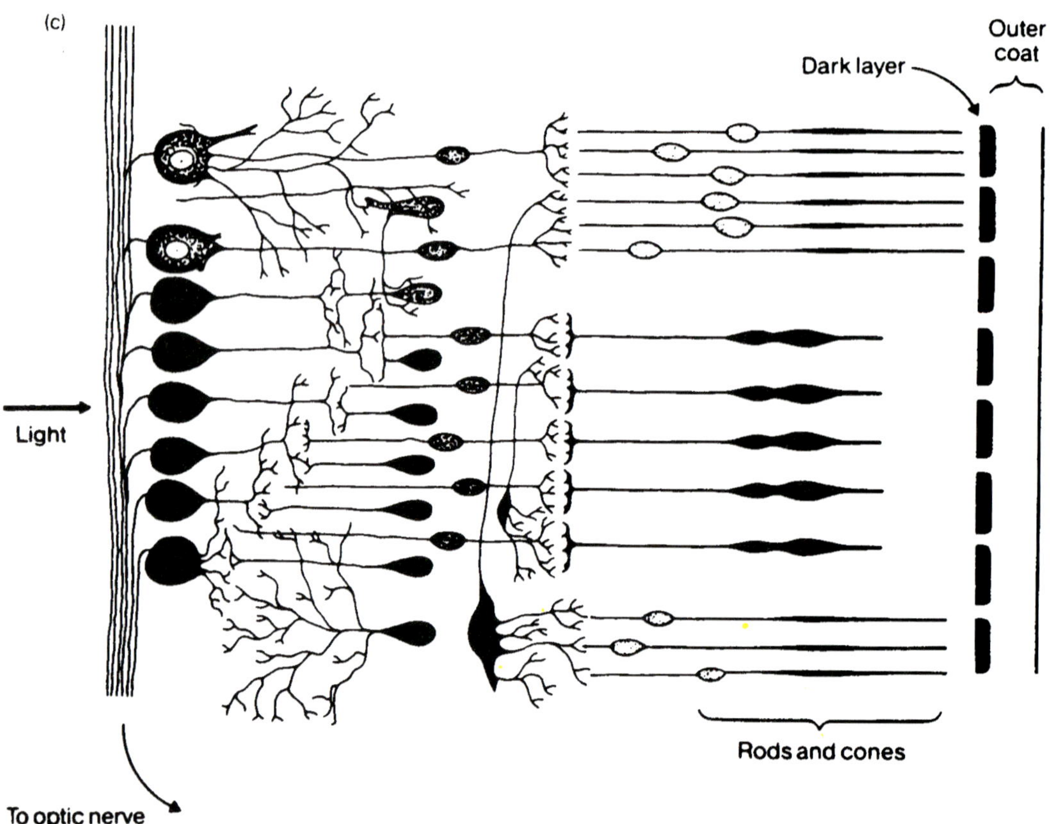
(c)
Outer
coat
Dark layer
Light
Rods and cones
To optic nerve

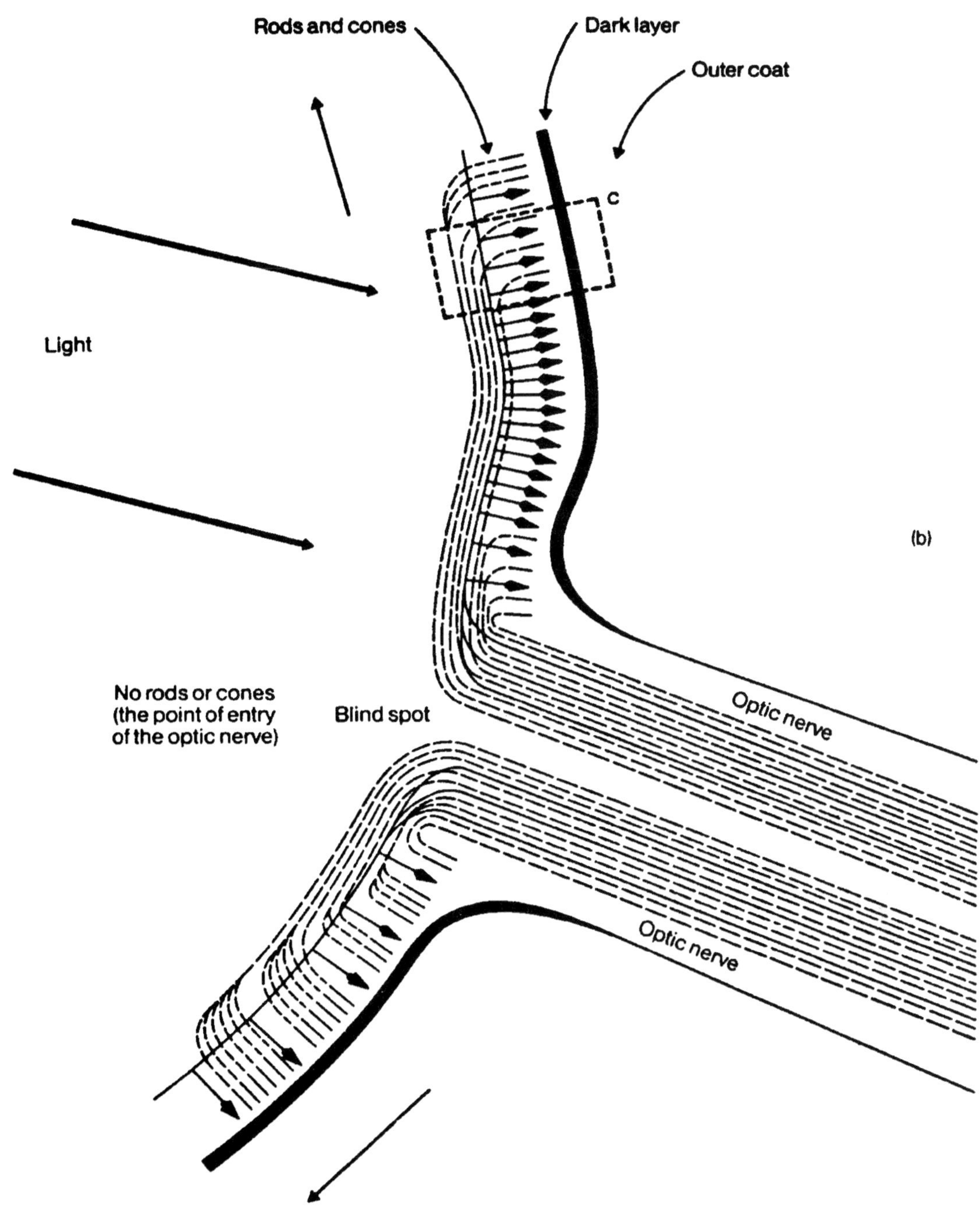

Figure 43. The human eye. *(a) Horizontal section through center. The cavities A and B contain fluid. (b) Enlargements of region shown in box in (a) above. (c) Enlargements of region shown in (b) above, showing section through retina. (Adapted, with permission, from Figures 2.17, 2.18, and 2.19 in R.W. Burnham, R.M. Hanes and C.J. Bartleson,* Color, *John Wiley, New York, 1963.)*

camera which contains two films, one for colour and one for black and white only, as well as a photochemical device which selects the film appropriate to the lighting conditions.

The rods and cones are not distributed evenly over the retina. Opposite the center of the lens is a small yellow-brown pit, the center of which (the 'fovea') contains only cones, 100,000 of them. There are no capillaries or nerve fibers between the lens and these foveal cells, but the pigmented edge of the pit absorbs some of the ultra-violet and blue light which might otherwise damage them. The rest of the retina is equipped with four million cones and 120 million rods. The concentration of the rods is greatest about 20° form the yellow spot, while that of the cones decreases with increasing distance from it. But there is one point on the retina, at the junction with the optic nerve, where there are no photosensitive cells of either sort. This is the "blind spot."

When light strikes a photosensitive cell, a photon may be absorbed, and if it is it will trigger off a series of changes which contribute to the sensation of vision. The probability of the photon being absorbed depends on whether the eye is adapted for bright or dark conditions, on the wavelength and intensity of the light and on the type of retinal cell on which it falls. We shall first see the way in which the rod cells respond, since these operate more simply than the cones.

It seems that all rods contain a single reddish-purple pigment called "visual purple" or *rhodopsin*, which consists of a protein combined with a substance called retinal, which like carotene, has a long backbone of carbon atoms, with small side-arms (see Figure 44). When we have been in the dark for a while, the carbon chain is bent and slightly twisted near one end, and able to fit into an indentation in the surface of the protein (see Figure 45). If dim light enters the eye, a photon may be absorbed by the carbon chain, which then straightens out, untwists and detaches itself from one of its moorings on the protein. This causes the shape of the protein indentation to change, and the other end of the chain to break loose. The pigment is bleached, and a signal may pass along the nerve fiber. This signal is identical for every proton absorbed, regardless of the

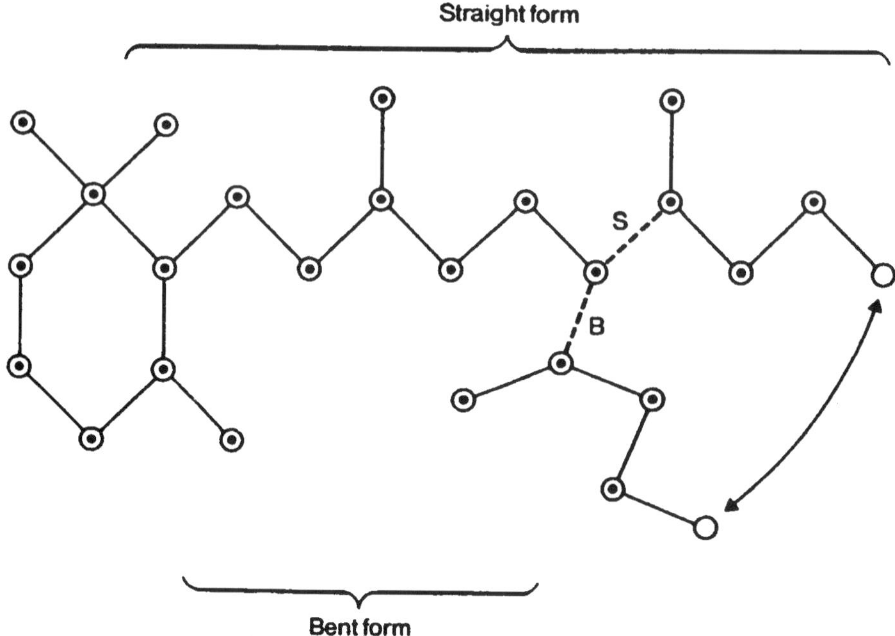

Figure 44. A light twist. *The skeleton of the light-sensitive substance retinal (cf. carotene, shown in Figure 36, page 87). The end of the tail can twist, to give a bent form joined to the backbone by the dotted line B, or a straight form, attached by line S.*

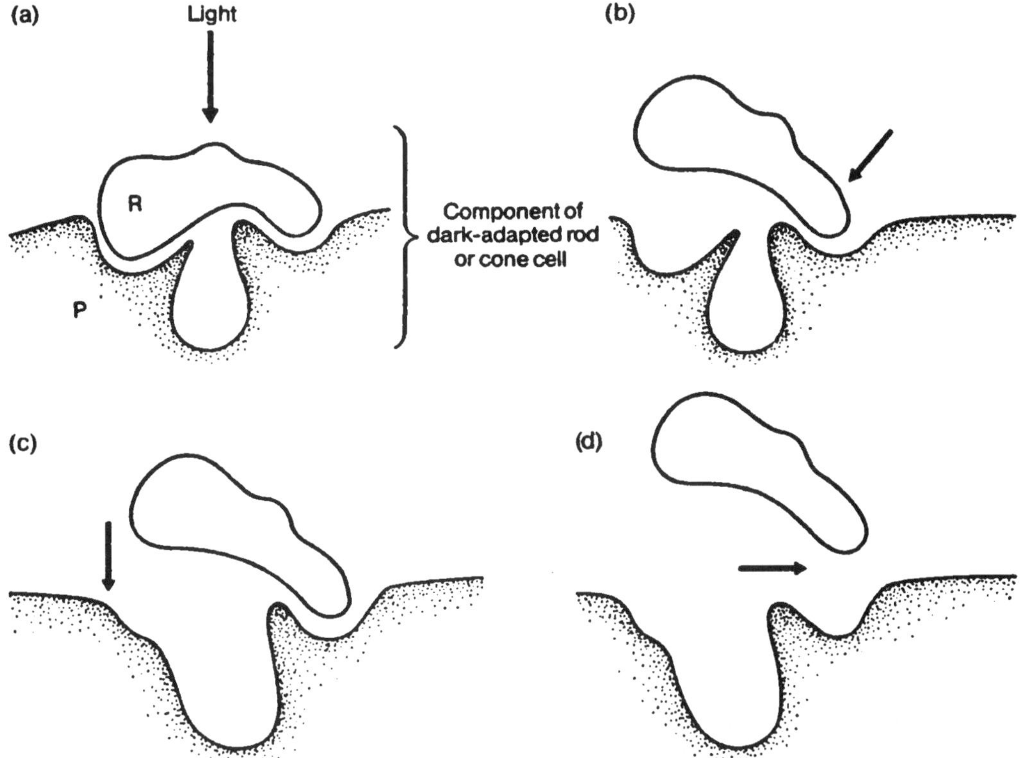

Figure 45. Changes in the retina. *Sketches to illustrate the mechanism of light sensitivity in the eye.*
(a) A dark-adapted retinal group R adopts the bent form and fits snugly on to the puckered surface of a protein, P.
(b) When the retinal absorbs a photon, its "tail" straightens and forces the "head" away from the protein base.
(c) The protein surface, no longer held in position by the retinal, relaxes, and changes shape.
(d) The "tail" of the retinal breaks away from the protein, initiating an electrical charge which is conveyed to the nerve.
(Adapted, with permission, from R. Hubbard and A. Kroft, Scientific American, *vol. 216, June 1967, p. 65.)*

wavelength of the light. The rod response is like that of a spring mousetrap which behaves exactly the same whether the rigger is released by a mouse or a rat (although the probability that it will be set off by one or other depends on the relative numbers of each around and their relative liking for the bait). The rod cells are not, in fact, equally sensitive to light of all wavelengths. Photons in the middle of the visual region are absorbed most efficiently (see Figure 46). When viewed by weak moonlight, the dark green leaves of a holly tree might seem a lighter grey than the bright red berries, because rods show their greatest sensitivity to green light.

If the illumination is increased, the rhodopsin remains bleached and the rod cell is inactive. But in dim light, the pigment, having lost its energy to the nerve, gradually reverts to its original, photosensitive state. The mousetrap resets itself spontaneously. Rods which have been inactivated by bright light readapt only slowly to the dark. The efficiency of our night vision increases markedly over twenty or thirty minutes and is not fully developed for about one hour.

Illumination which is bright enough to inactivate the rods is also bright enough to stimulate the cone cells and so to allow us to perceive colour. Cones respond to changes in the overall intensity of the light much more quickly than do rods and are fully adapted within seven minutes.

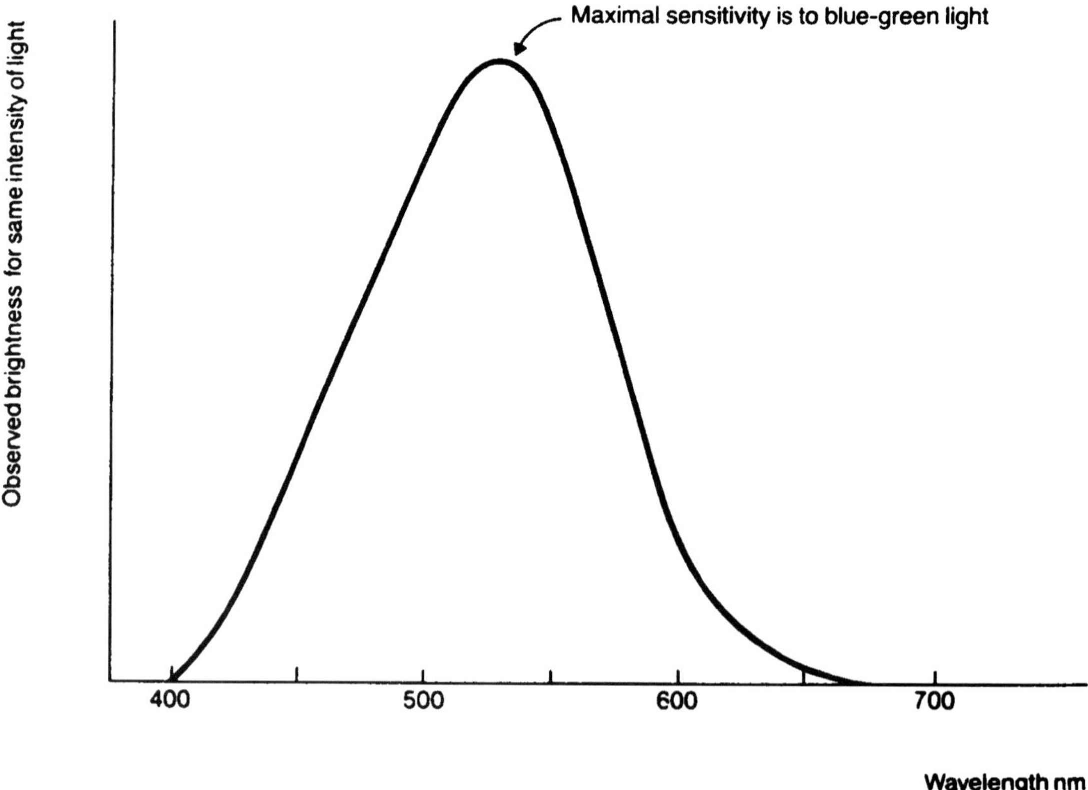

Figure 46. Brightness by night. *How the rod cells respond to light of the same intensity but of different wavelength.*

Each cone, like each rod, contains visual pigment, a molecule of which consists of a carotene-like carbon 'backbone' partially folded into a cavity in a protein molecule. Although the retinal backbone seems to be exactly the same as that in a rod pigment, the particular protein which forms part of rhodopsin has not been found in cones. In fact, there are three different types of cones, each containing a different sort of protein. So a cone will have one of three possible visual pigments. Each pigment absorbs light over much of the visual spectrum (see Figure 47a). The effect of the absorption of a photon is similar to that in rhodopsin, and does not vary with the wavelength of the light. For each photon absorbed, one carbon backbone straightens and one impulse passes to the nerve.

Each cone pigment, like rhodopsin, absorbs photons with varying efficiency according to their energy. Colour vision is possible because the three cone pigments differ *from each other* in their sensitivity to wavelength.

We can see from Figure 47b that one of the cone pigments (A) absorbs most efficiently in the orange part of the spectrum, while another (B) absorbs maximally in the green region. The third pigment (C), which absorbs less efficiently than the others, has its absorption peak in the blue, high-energy end of the spectrum. When we add together the separate contributions of the three pigments, we find (Figure 47a) that the total absorption also varies with wavelength, being most efficient in the yellow region. The percentage contribution of each pigment to the total absorption is shown in Figure 48, which perhaps provides us with the best key to the understanding of colour vision, because it shows us how the ratio of contributions varies with wavelength. Any light of "normal" intensity triggers off the three cone pigments in some ratio A:B:C which depends

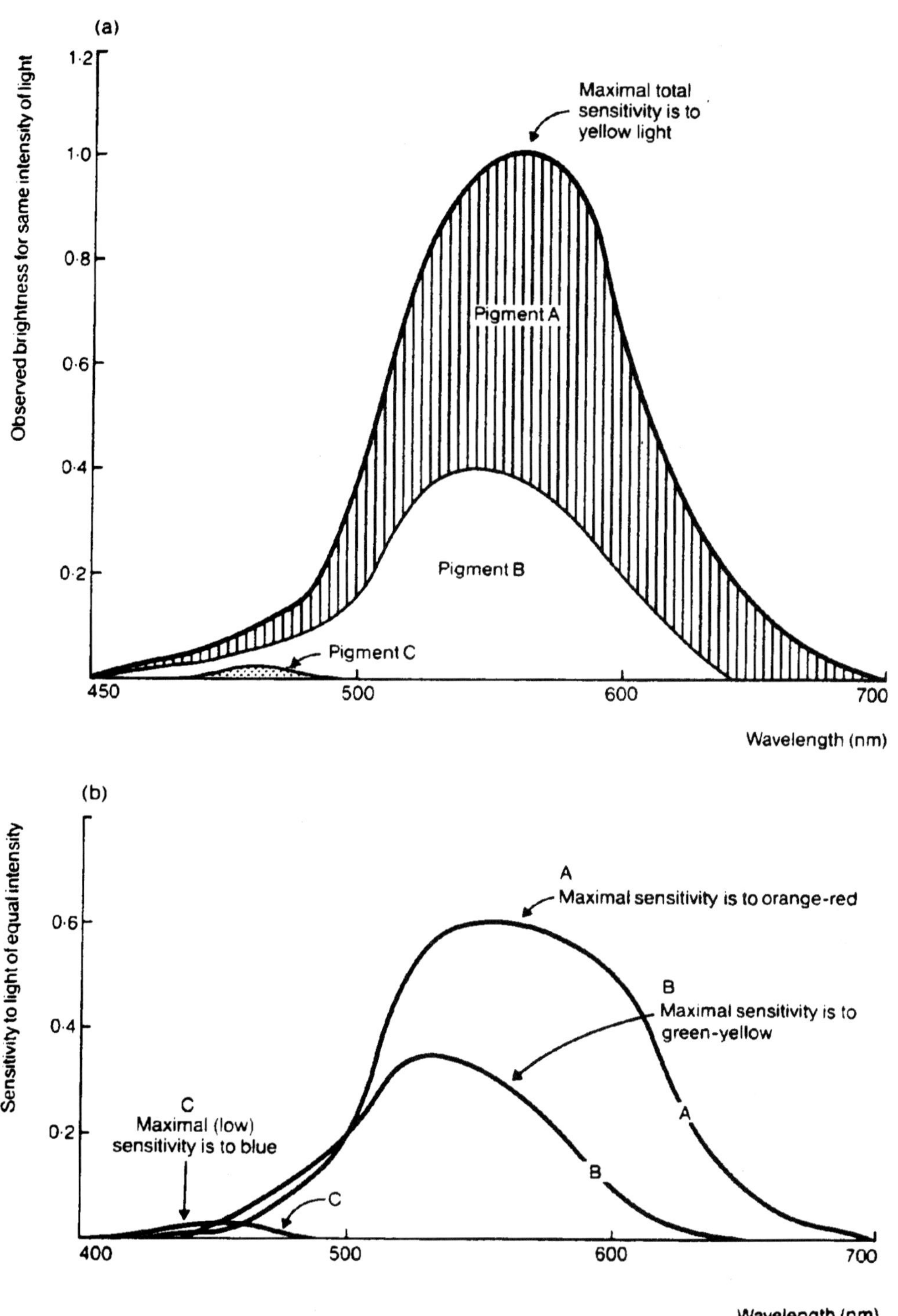

Figure 47. Brightness by day. *(a) The full line shows the combined response of the cone cells to light of the same intensity but of different wavelengths. The approximate contributions of the three systems of cone pigments are indicated by the differently shaded areas. (b) The approximate sensitivities of each of the separate systems.* The valves are those estimated at the cornea by Smith and Pakorny.

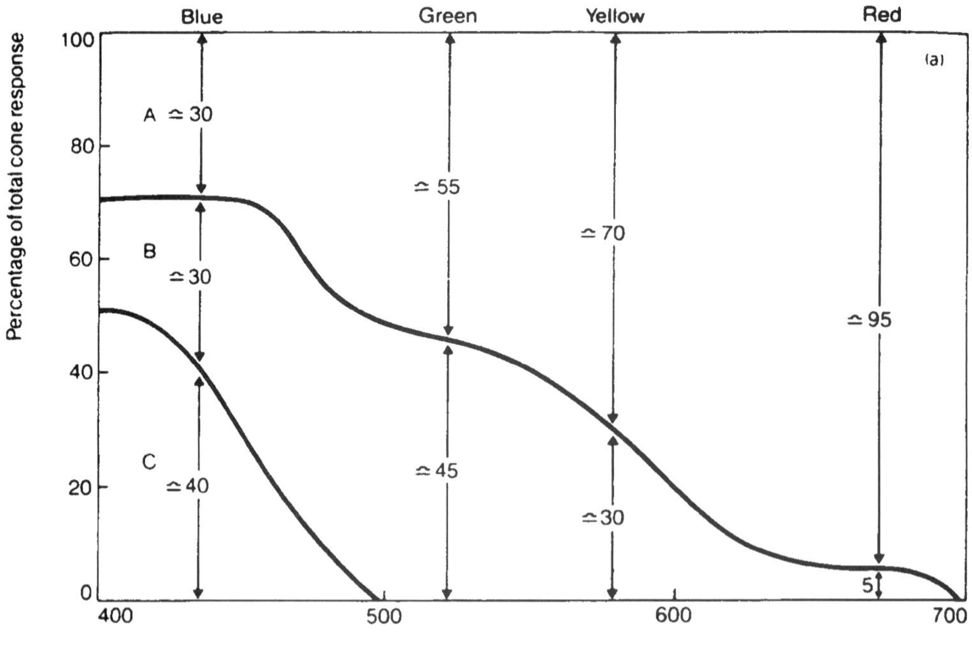
Blue
Green
Yellow
Red
(a)
Percentage of total cone response
100
80
60
40
20
0
A ≃ 30
B
≃ 30
C
≃ 40
≃ 55
≃ 45
≃ 70
≃ 30
≃ 95
5
400
500
600
700
Wavelength (nm)

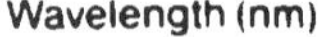

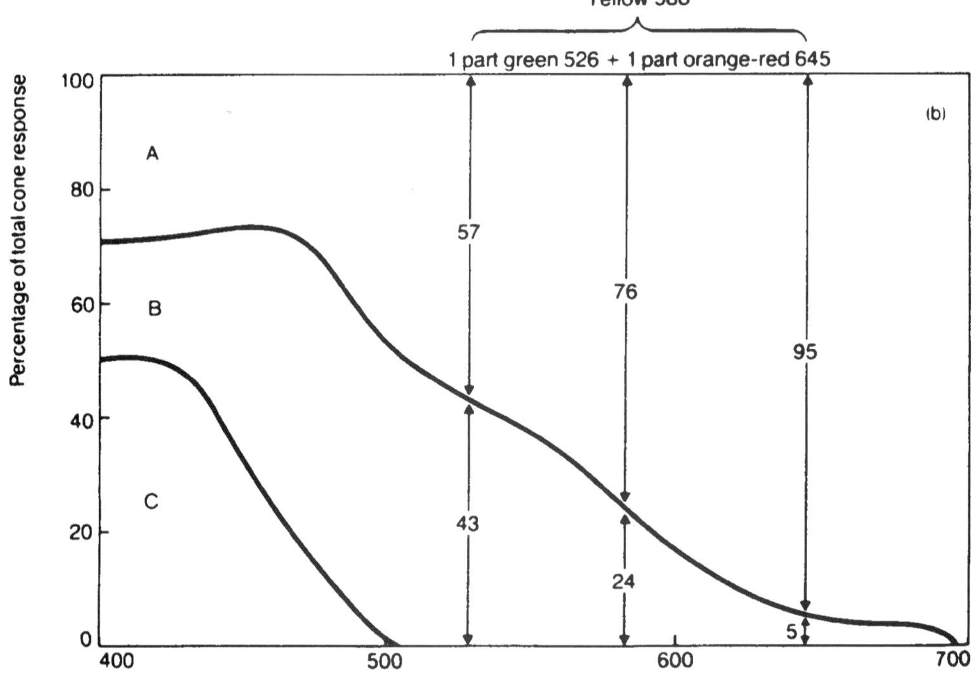
Yellow 588
1 part green 526 + 1 part orange-red 645
(b)
Percentage of total cone response
100
80
60
40
20
0
A
B
C
57
43
76
24
95
5
400
500
600
700
Wavelength (nm)

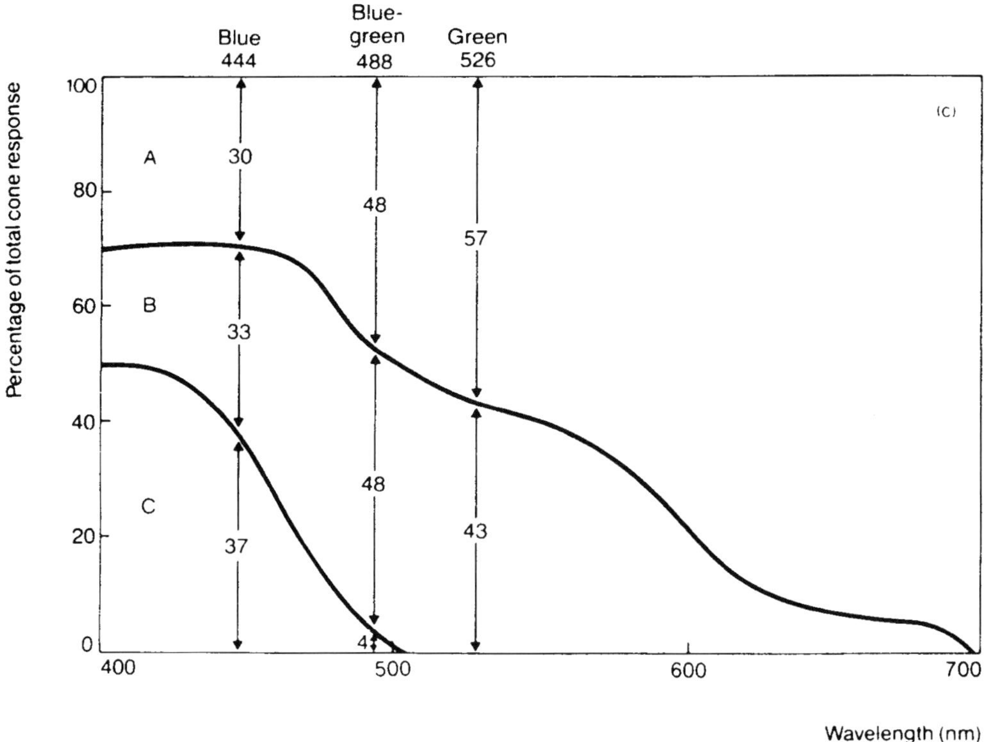

Figure 48. Cones and colour: *Approximate percentage of total cone response attributable to each of the three pigments.*
(a)The probable cone response rations A:B:C which provide the sensations of blue, green, yellow, and red.
(b)The sensation of yellow can also be obtained by combining the responses of cone pigments A and B to green light and to orange-red light.
(c)The blue-green sensation obtained from light of 488 nm can never be exactly matched by mixing blue and green light as the percentage of B-cone response is maximal in this region.

on the wavelength composition of the light: and it is this *ratio* which produces a particular sensation of colour. For example, a cone response in a ratio 33:42:25 gives a sensation of blue, while with one of 70:30:0 we perceive yellow (see Table 2).

Some response ratios can be produced both by the light of a single wavelength, and by a mixture of two lights, both of different wavelengths. We cannot distinguish by eye alone between a "pure" yellow light of one narrow wavelength range in the region of 580 nm and the mixture of green and orange-red lights which gives the same response ratio (see Table 3 and Figure 48b). Green light of 560 nm cannot, however, be matched by a mixture. sSnce this wavelength is the lowest at which pigment C makes no appreciable response, any mixture containing light of lower wavelength would stimulate some contribution from pigment C. Nor can blue-green light of 488 nm, where the response of B-cones is maximal (see Figure 48c).

There are also some "non-spectral" colours which can be made only by mixing. Mixtures of red and blue light give response ratios which do not correspond to that of any single wavelength light and which we perceive as shades of magenta (see Table 3). And if we mix blue, green and orange-red light of roughly equal intensities, we obtain white light of ratio about 63·5:34:2·5, which is almost indistinguishable from the white light obtained by mixing all visible wavelengths at equal intensity.

So the cones allow us to distinguish colours by day and the rods enable us to see shapes at night. But the rods sometimes also contribute to vision by day. An object at the very edge of our visual field (behind the lines joining one eye to opposite ear) seems monochrome because the light which reaches us from

Table 2. *Probable response of cone pigments to various wavelengths.*

Wavelengths (nm)	Approximate % of total absorption contributed by pigment			Colour
	A	B	C	
420	29	21·5	49·5	violet
460	33	42	25	blue
490	48	48·5	3·5	blue-green
530	57	43	0	green
580	70·5	29·5	0	yellow
600	80	20	0	orange
620	88·5	11·5	0	orange-red
660	95·5	4·5	0	red

Table 3. *Probable cone response ratios for some pure and mixed lights.*

Colour	A:B:C ratio	Wavelength of pure light of same ratio (nm)	Mixed light of same colour			
			%	nm	ratio	colour
Yellow	70:30:0	588	50	526	57:43:0	green
			50	645	95:5:0	orange-red
Blue	33:42:25	460			None	
Blue-green	48:48:4	488			None	
Green	63·5:36·5:0	560			None	
Red	95·5:4·5:0	660			None	
Magenta	64·5:23:12·5	None	50	460	33:42:25	blue
			50	660	95·5:4·5:0	red
White	63·5:34:2·5	None	34	480	43:49:8	blue
			33	540	59:41:0	green
			33	620	88·5:11·5:0	orange-red

it falls on the periphery of the retina where there are mainly rods and only few cones (see Figure 52). Slightly nearer the center of the retina, there are rather few cone cells, and the perceived colour is not quite the same as that produced when the same light falls on the cone-rich central region. It has been suggested that the sensation is attributable to the combined response of rhodopsin and of the three cone pigments.

The responses of rods and cones certainly both contribute to vision at the intermediate, twilight, intensities of illumination. When the light is bright enough for us to see some colour, but not bright enough to bleach the rods totally, the sensation is probably a result of the response of all four pigments. We have seen that rods absorb most efficiently in the green region of the spectrum (~ 500 nm), whereas the total cone response is most sensitive to yellow light (550 nm). As dusk falls, our eyes therefore become increasingly sensitive to light of shorter wavelengths. At twilight, our most sensitive response is to blue-green light (510 nm) and so, before all colours turn to greys, they become gradually more blue, an effect first reported in 1823 by the Czech physiologist Purkinje.

Night is not always devoid of colour. But although the full moon looks golden,* the moonlit world is colourless, as Walter de la Mare expresses it:

Slowly, silently, now the moon
Walks the night in her silver shoon
This way and that, she peers and sees
Silver fruit upon silver trees.

The intensity of sunlight reflected from the moon is just high enough to stimulate cone vision, at least in that part of the spectrum to which cones are most sensitive. But the intensity of the light which is reflected off other objects is so low that only rod vision occurs.

The stars, too, look silver, although spectroscopic analysis shows that they radiate light of composition which is often far from white, although too dim for our eyes to recognize it as coloured. The colours of the stars have, however, been photographed using very long exposures.

Both rods and cones have low sensitivity to light of long wavelength, and it is likely that the red light of a photographic darkroom, though strong enough to stimulate the cones, does not inhibit the rods. Sailors and airmen who need their eyes to become adapted for dark vision before going on night duty can grow acclimatized by wearing red goggles in a lighted room instead of having to stay in the dark. The US Armed Forces are issued with playing cards specially designed so that hearts and diamonds, normally represented in red on a white ground, may be distinguished by those wearing such goggles.

The low sensitivity of the retina to long wavelengths leads to the curious behavior of certain green celluloid eyeshades. Although seen through a single layer of celluloid, the world looks green, through a double layer, it looks red, and similar effects can be obtained with certain coloured liquids. When white light falls on the eyeshade, all the very low wavelength light is transmitted together with about one third of the green light, and rather little of other wavelengths. Since the retina is so much more sensitive to green light than to red, the resultant sensation is green, albeit a somewhat yellowish green. If this 3:1 mixture of red to green light passes through a second layer of celluloid, the red component is again transmitted almost undiminished, while the strength of the green is again reduced threefold. The 9:1 ratio of red to green in the emergent light is high enough to produce a red sensation, despite our low sensitivity to long wavelengths.

Anomalous Colour Vision

The normal human eye is by no means the only one capable of discriminating between light of different wavelengths. Many humans who have abnormal colour vision are none the less able to differentiate between light of different wavelengths, as are some species of animals.

There is considerable variation even in "normal" human vision. Some is individual, and some racial, as in the pigmentation of the lens and of the yellow spot. Changes may encroach with age, as when the cornea

*But the moon is not always golden. Occasionally an unusually high proportion of the blue component of the reflected light is scattered, or bent, away from the observer. A "harvest moon" or "hunter's moon" (or a rising sun) low in the sky looks redder than usual. During a lunar eclipse the colour of the moon may change, through orange to deep crimson. And "once in a blue moon," atmospheric particles from a volcanic eruption or forest fire may be of exactly the right size to scatter all light of low and medium energy, with the result that only the blue component reches the observer.

becomes opaque and perceived colours dull. Those successfully recovered from an operation for cataract often report a dramatic brightening of perceived colour. The lens pigment darkens with age, and so absorbs a higher proportion of short wavelength light. Many artists use blue less frequently as they get older, and Mark Twain compared some of Turner's later work to "a ginger cat having a fit in a bowl of tomatoes." Defective colour vision in humans is occasionally caused by injury, drugs or physical or mental illness. But of the eight percent of all men and .5 percent of all women who have abnormal colour vision, the great majority are born that way.

Albinos, who lack pigment in their skin and hair, also lack the black layer behind the retinal cells, which are therefore stimulated by stray light scattered inside the eye as well as by light from outside. Their vision therefore lacks clarity and the colours become diluted and less brilliant. The occasional person who is born without any cone cells will have very poor general sight. Relying on rod vision, he will shun bright light and be totally colour-blind. But most types of defective colour vision are the consequence of abnormalities in the cone cells.

Human colour vision has been widely investigated by means of experiments in which an observer is asked to match a given patch of light by mixing, in any proportion, a number of other lights. An observer with normal vision can match any colour, provided he has up to three others and can, if he wishes, mix one with the sample patch and then match this with a mixture of the other two lights. The need for three independent lights is a consequence of the presence of three cone pigments.

Some of the observers with abnormal vision can match any given colour by using only two lights, suggesting that they have only two photosensitive cone pigments. A very few people match by brightness alone, needing only one light. About six percent of the male population needs three, but produce matches which are quite unacceptable to those with normal vision. So it seems that defensive colour vision can arise either because one or even two cone pigments are absent, or because all or any of the cone pigments are different from the normal types.

The most familiar forms of defective colour vision arise from the absence of one of the three cone pigments. To about two percent of all men, green and red are both indistinguishable from grey. Others who can discriminate between red and green, confuse yellow, blue and grey. And yet another combination of two cone pigments allows normal discrimination of red, orange, yellow and green, although all light of shorter wavelengths appears blue-green.

We can see from Figure 48 how colour vision would be affected if we lacked one of the three cone pigments while the other two were unchanged. If either A or B was missing, colour discrimination would be possible at wavelengths below about 520 nm, where two pigments respond. At higher wavelengths, however, only one pigment is active, and only differences in brightness could be perceived. On the other hand, if C were missing, there would be response from two pigments over the whole visual range. Colour discrimination would be possible except in those regions where the vertical distance between the curves happened to be the same. Figure 49 indicates that cones containing only pigments A and B might give an ambiguous response over the wavelength range 420–520 nm (blue-green).

It is often emphasized that the colour vision of those who are classified as "colour-blind" is often only slightly more defective than that of the "normal" majority, who, as we have seen, cannot distinguish between, for example, "pure" yellow light and a mixture of red and green lights; or, indeed, between a large number of other pairs of "pure" and "mixed" light. Those with defective colour vision merely have more scope for ambiguity than do those with the normal, though far from perfect, ability to discriminate between light of different wavelengths. Since some jobs, however, involve the recognition or matching of colours, tests for anomalous colour vision have been devised. It is only from tests that many of those with defective colour vision learn that they have any abnormality. There are not a large number of situations, other than work, in which a tendency to muddle green and blue would be apparent, particularly as many of the normally sighted differ about whether a given hue in this range should be called blue, turquoise or green. The tests may be

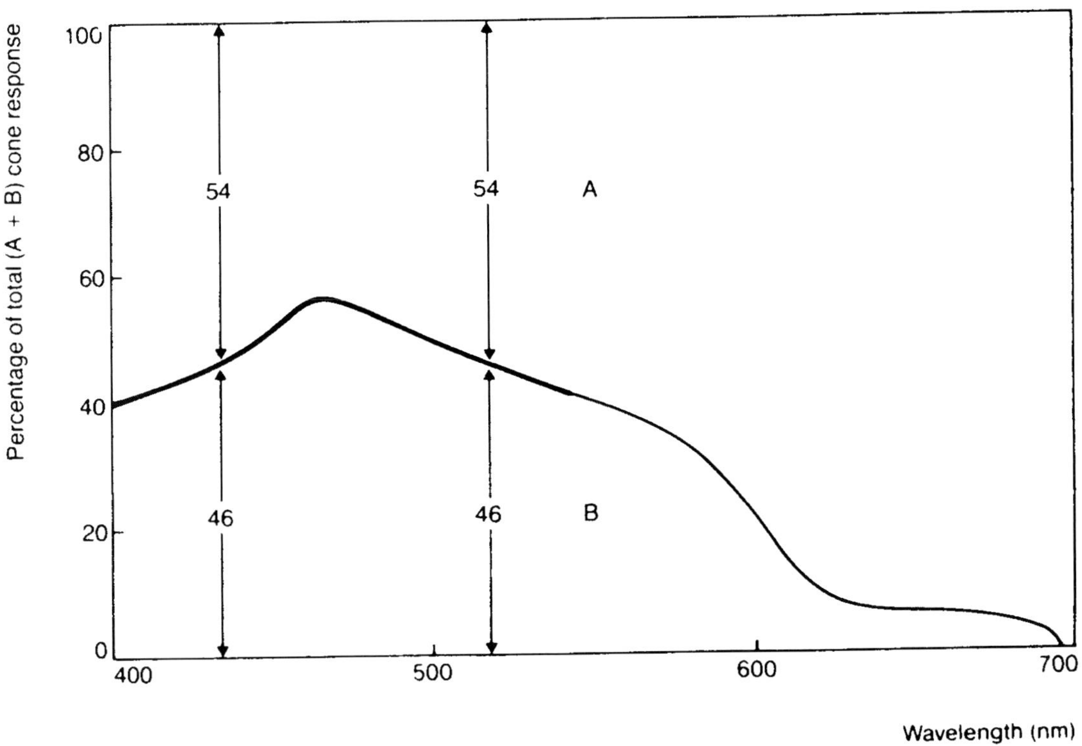

Figure 49. Blue-green ambiguity. *The likely effect of absence of pigment C on the total cone response, if the sensitiveness of pigments A and B were as represented in Figure 47 (page 115). For light of wavelengths above about 550 nm (thin curve), colour vision would be unaffected. But at lower wavelengths (thick line), the same response can be obtained from pure lights of two wavelengths (e.g. 430 nm and 573 nm) and of any mixture of them.*

strictly tied to the job and designed only to find out whether an applicant can match paint, cloth, printing ink, recognize signals or select the correct, colour-coded electrical resistor. Other more general tests may involve the naming of coloured lights and sorting large numbers of coloured samples into regular series involving a gradual change in hue. One common type of test uses cards covered with an irregular mottled display of spots in which are embedded others depicting numerals, letters, pathways or simple pictures. The figures differ from the background in colour, but not in lightness, and are designed so that each can be read only by those who can distinguish between the two colours of a pair. A set of such cards enables most types of defective colour vision to be detected. If the equipment is available, a person may be asked to match one light with a mixture of three, or two, others. Information about this ability to distinguish colours is given by the match which he selects, particularly if he is asked to match the same light a number of different times.

Most defective colour vision is hereditary. Red-green colour "blindness" is transmitted by a recessive gene, sex-linked to the male. So a male who has one gene carrying this defect will, in fact, be colour-blind, while a female will not be colour-blind unless she has two genes for colour-blindness, and such genetic "purity" is rare. But a woman with one such gene may transmit the defective gene to her children, although she herself will have normal vision. So her sons may be colour-blind and her daughters may, like their mothers, be carriers. Men, if they normal colour vision, cannot transmit the defect. A colour-blind son of a normal father must have inherited the defective gene from his mother.

It is not surprising that the incidence of a genetic defect of this type shows a regional variation. In some rather isolated communities, such as Fiji, it is very low (only 0.8 percent of the male population), whereas in Canada it is as high as 11.2 percent.

With nearly two centuries of hindsight, we can appreciate the observation reported by John Dalton, the chemist, that the geranium described by his friends as pink appeared, both to him and his brother, as sky blue by day and "red" by candlelight. He must have lacked the red-sensitive pigment, so that the mixture of red-blue light scattered from the flowers would be indistinguishable from the blue of the sky. In the candlelight, which contains little blue, the flowers, like any red object, would scatter little light that he could detect and so would look black. Anomalous colour vision of this type was long termed "Daltonism."

Colour Vision in Animals

It is, of course, much easier to study colour vision in man than in other animals. But we can try to find out if animals can distinguish between light of different wavelengths by attempting to train them to seek food from a container of a particular colour, regardless of the brightness of the colour or the position of the container. Experiments can also show whether or not a change in the wavelength of the light produces a different electrical response from the nerve of a light-sensitive cell, although the results of such measurements alone cannot tell us whether the animal experiences different colour sensations, as these depend on the connections between the nerve cells as well as on the sensitivity of the eye to wavelength.

The great majority of studies of colour vision have been on either vertebrates or insects. Although most vertebrates have simple eyes, very similar in structure to the human eye, they vary enormously in their ability to distinguish between colours. Mammals other than man often have poor or non-existent colour vision, although that of the macaque monkey is very similar to our own. Ground squirrels, who can distinguish between blue and green but are insensitive to red, are thought to have only two types of cone cell. The red squirrel and the guinea pig have only one type of retinal cell and so are totally colour-blind. Cats have very poor colour vision, but under good conditions, can distinguish blue-to-green colours from orange-to-red ones. It is thought that the proverbial red rag infuriates the bull by its movement rather than its colour, because no cones are present in the eyes of the cattle.

Many types of birds and fish are thought to have good colour vision, since colour plays an important part in some of their behavior. The Australian Bower Bird decorates its nest with various blue objects such as scraps of paper and china, juice from blue berries and feathers from smaller birds it has killed for the purpose. A male Robin will defend its territory against a shapeless bunch of red feathers, although not against a bunch of brown feathers or even against a stuffed juvenile (brown) robin. Owls, however, have only rod cells, and so are totally colour-blind. Three types of retinal cone cells have been found in hens and pigeons, whose colour vision is similar to our own. The eyes of many birds, including these two, contain coloured "filters" of oil droplets in the yellow-to-red range, but the effect of these on the colour vision of birds is not known. In the frog, colour vision appears to come with maturity—tadpoles seem to be colour-blind. Lizards, which are active only in daylight and have pure cone vision, seem able to distinguish between meal worms dyed different colours, while the nocturnal gecko, with pure rod vision, is colour-blind. Turtles, like birds, have coloured, oil-drop filters, but their colour vision seems to differ greatly from one species to another. Fish seem well able to distinguish colours. Sticklebacks and Siamese Fighting Fish react vigorously to red and blue in both courtship and defense of territory.

Though the compound eyes of insects have a totally different structure from the simple eyes of vertebrates, they contain visual pigments similar to our own. Many insects, such as bees, wasps, ants, dragonflies, butterflies, moths, beetles, cockroaches and houseflies, can distinguish colours, but usually in a

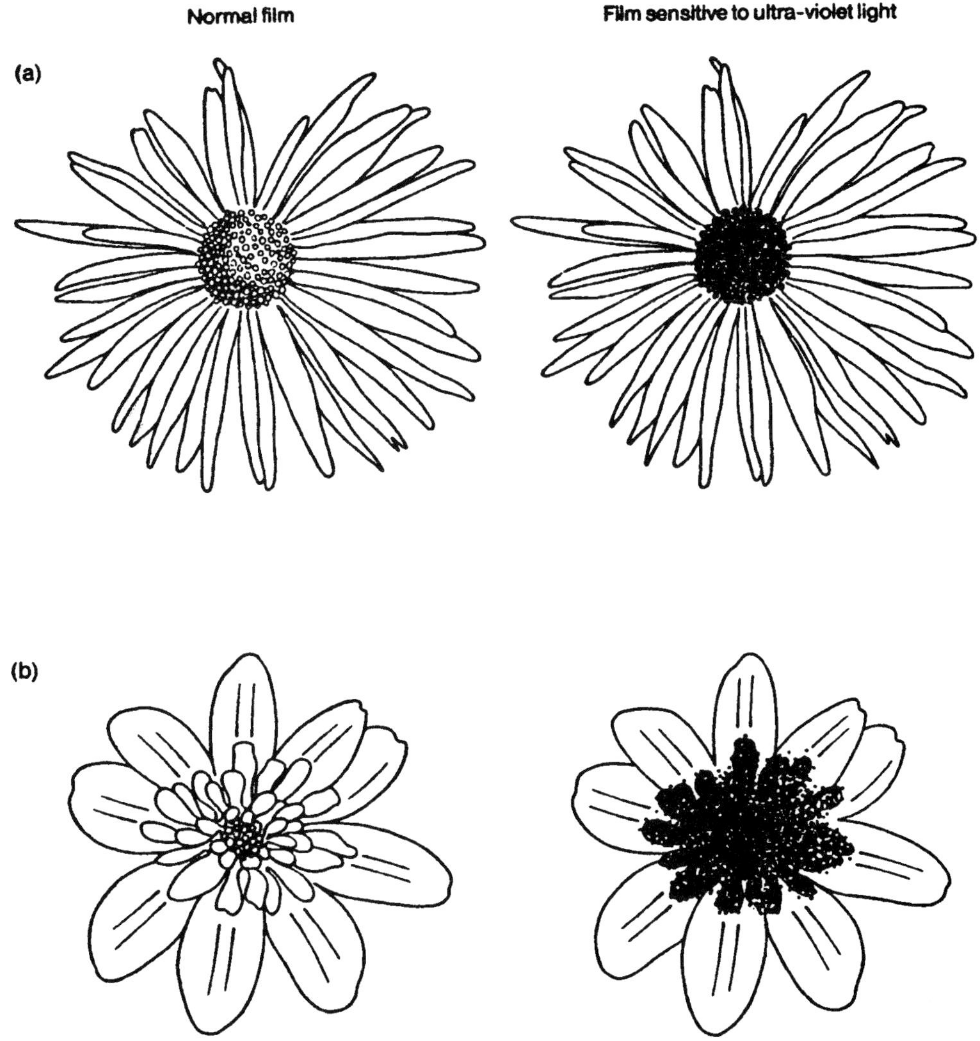

Figure 50. A bee's-eye view? *The photographs on the left were taken with normal film which responds mainly to visible light; those on the right were taken with film which records predominantly ultra-violet radiation. The outer petals of the flowers, which seem yellow to us, reflect "bee's purple" to the bee. The centers, which absorb ultra-violet and reflect only the yellow, would seem much darker, and could guide the bee to the nectar.*
(a) Leopard's bane.
(b) Lesser celandine.
(Reproduced with permission, from R. L. Gregory and E. H. Gombrich, Illusion in Nature and Art, *Duckworth, London, 1973.)*

range different from our own. And some have colour vision only in certain directions but are colour-blind in others. Some parts of their colour-sensitive insects respond to radiation of wavelength 390–300 nm in the ultra-violet range which is invisible to humans. But most insects are insensitive to red light. Exceptions are a few butterflies and the firefly, which can detect light of a wavelength as long as 690 nm; as indeed it would need to if, as believed, it uses the orange-red flashes of its species to find a mate. Ants, however, are blind to red. When a colony is illuminated by a spectrum from sunlight, they carry their larvae into the red region but avoid the near ultra-violet. In addition to colour vision, many insects, unlike humans, can distinguish between light which is of the same wavelength but polarized in different planes.

Much work has been done on the colour vision of bees, who can distinguish between lights in the three colour ranges: yellow (590–500 nm), blue-green (500–480 nm), ultra-violet (400–300 nm) (see Figure 50). For bees, the mixture of 440 and 360 nm and 650 nm, known as "bees' purple" by analogy with the mixture of the two extreme colours, red and violet, visible to humans. For bees, as for humans, there are pairs of complementary "colours" which together make up the whole range of the visible part of sunlight: ultra-violet and blue-green, yellow and violet, blue and "bees' purple." Since bees cannot see light of a wavelength longer than about 590 nm, they are blind to red and orange, and so it might seem surprising that they visit such red flowers as poppies. However, poppies reflect not only red light but also ultra-violet, and it is this which attracts the bees.

Photographs on film which is sensitive to ultra-violet light reveal complex patterns of guide-lines on petals of some flowers which to us look plain white or a single colour, but which are "variegated" in their power to reflect ultra-violet radiation. Similar "latent' patterns on butterfly wings are thought to play a part in recognition and in courtship. If bees are shown two blackboards bearing the directions "Bees may feed here" and "No bees allowed," the bees will always collect on the correct notice, provided that the permissive text is painted with a material which reflects ultra-violet light while the restrictive one is painted with Chinese white, which does not.

Although we have been able to establish that some animals can distinguish colours, only a few species have been studied in detail, and the part which colour plays in their lives is largely a matter of speculation.

The Eye and the Brain

Are the writers of the excerpts on pages 104-7 merely being fanciful? If not, how can we reconcile the phenomena they describe with our earlier interpretation of colour vision in terms of the absorption of photons by the three cone pigments? Our own experience confirms that there is more to colour than the composition of the light which meets the eye. Colours provoke emotional responses. They appear to vary when physics suggests they should not and, contrariwise, seem constant when it seems they should vary. We sometimes see colours in the absence of what we might think would be the appropriate light, and indeed, in the absence of any light at all. A great number of types of change can take place both in the retina and in the brain after a photon is absorbed.

Some of our psychological responses to colour may have a simple, geometrical origin. A red splodge often seems to advance from the page and to concentrate the viewer's attention towards its center, whereas a blue splodge seems to recede and to lead the eye outwards. The apparent movement of colours towards, and away from, the viewer probably occurs because the lens of the eye (unlike that of a camera) is made of a single material and so is subject to "chromatic aberration." Light of a different wavelength is bent, as by a prism or a raindrop, to a different extent. When the muscles which control the shape of the lens focus green light on the retina, the red light is focused a little behind it and the blue a little in front (see Figure 51). To see a red object clearly, the lens must be the same shape as we need to see a green object which is slightly nearer, and to see a blue object, it must be adjusted in the opposite way. So reds seem to advance and blues to recede.

The impressions that blues (and yellows) spread while reds contract may well be because of the way in which the cone pigments are distributed on the retina. We cannot see colours at the edge of our field of vision because only rods are present at the periphery of the retina, but as we bring an object nearer to the center of the visual field, we first recognize blue and yellow. Slightly nearer the center, we sense green, and still more centrally, we can see red (see Figure 52). It is not surprising that blue, which we can see at the wildest angle of colour vision, tends to spread, and that red, which is visible only fairly centrally, tends to contract.

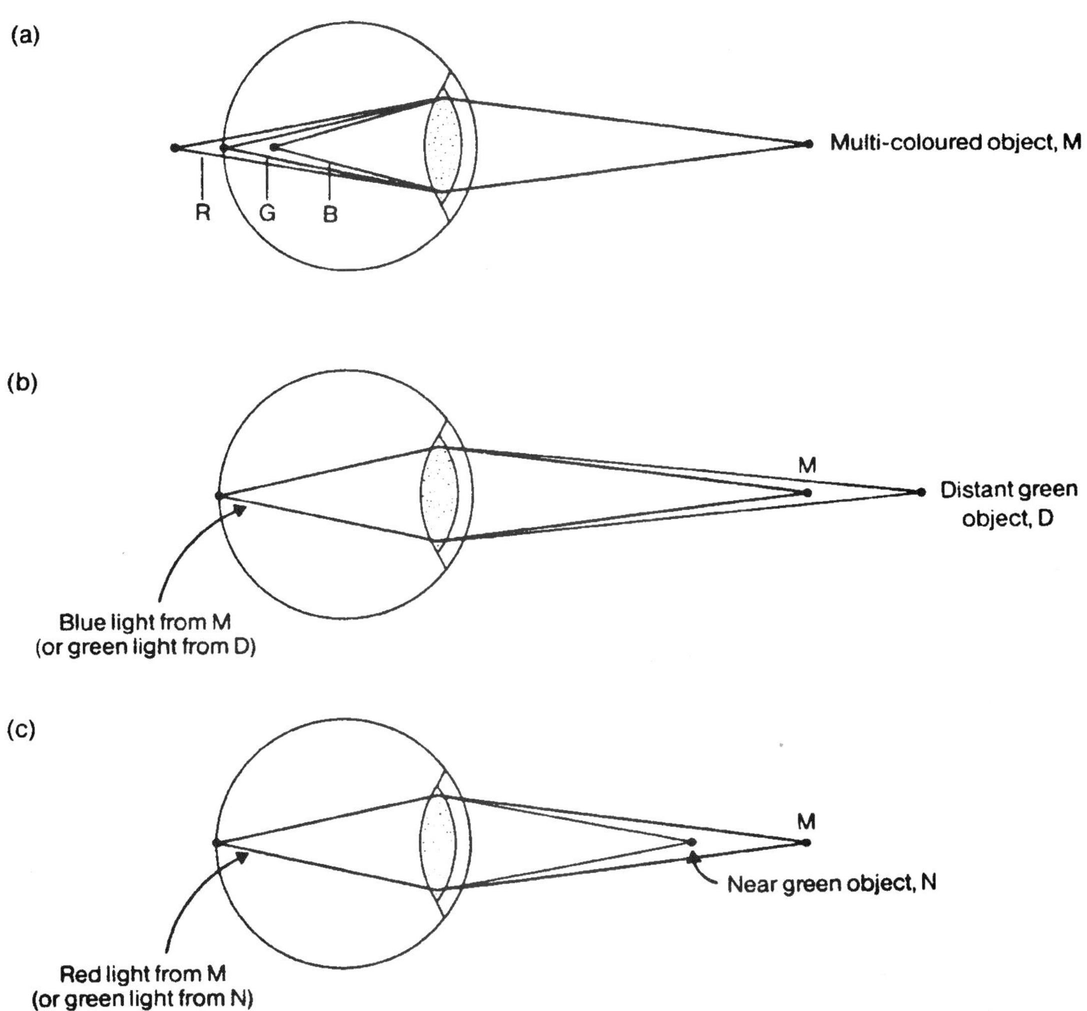

Figure 51. Colours which recede or advance. *(a) The eye receives light from a multi-coloured object, M, when the lens is adjusted to focus green light on the retina. Blue is focused slightly in front of it and red slightly behind it. (b) When the lens changes to focus the blue light from M on to the retina, the eye is adjusted for the clear viewing of green (or white) objects, D, which are slightly more distant than M. Blue therefore seems to recede. (c) Adjustment of the lens to focus red on the retina also allows clear vision of a green or white object, N, which is slightly nearer than the source of the red light. So red seems to advance towards the viewer.*

Colour sensations may depend on intensity as well as on wavelength, even when the cones alone are responding. As the light gets more intense, both orange and yellow-green approach yellow, while violet and blue-green both become more blue. Only in three cases, yellow, green and blue, does the colour seem to be independent of the intensity. These colours are termed "psychological primaries" because each can be said, whatever its intensity, to contain no element of any of the others.

We do not fully understand why, alone of all the colours, red, yellow, green and blue behave in this way, though the cause probably lies in the absorption curves of the cone pigments. Indeed, there are many large gaps in our knowledge of visual perception, and particularly of colour. But many of the effects mentioned in the chapter arise either from the highly complex set of nerve connections between the retina and the brain, or from the time lag in the recovery of a cone cell after it

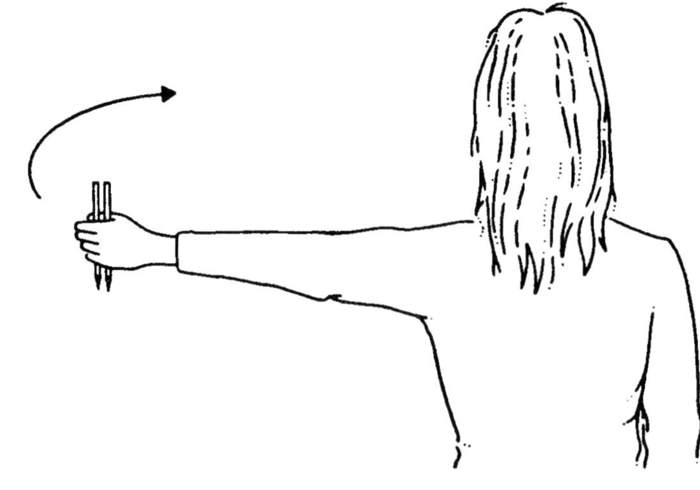

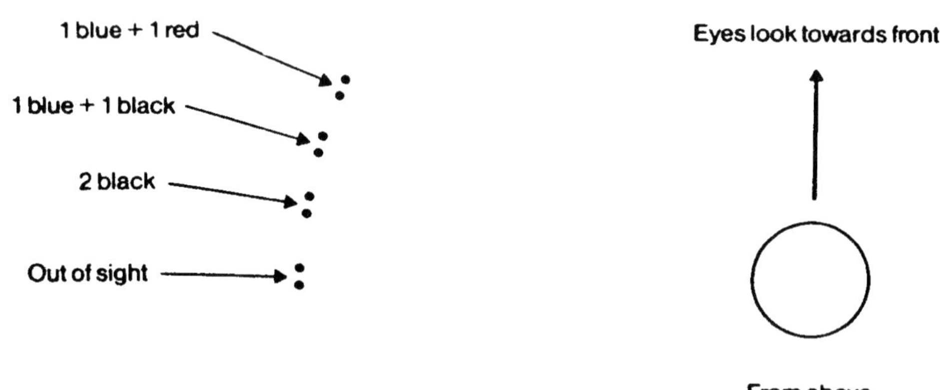

Figure 52. The corner of the eye. *The girl, facing forward, holds a blue pencil and a red pencil out beyond her ear, and gradually moves her arm so that they come into her field of vision. She first sees both pencils as black, then perceives the colour of the blue one, and finally recognizes the red.*

has absorbed a photo, or from a combination of both factors.

The rods and the cones are incorporated into very different "circuit diagrams." Impulses from individual rod cells do not travel directly to the brain, but first pass from a group of cells to a nerve center which transmits a signal to other centers, from which an impulse eventually reaches the brain. Since the signal may have come from any one of a hundred or so cells, rod vision is very sensitive, although its definition is not of the very highest. It is likely that impulses from adjacent nerve centers are combined to give information about the *differences* between their signals, which enables them to monitor contrast, and us to recognize shapes (see Figure 53).

Signals from the cones travel to the brain by various routes. Some cone cells near the center of the retina send combined responses straight to the brain, and this allows us to see extremely clearly, in colour, in light of normal intensity. Other cones seem to combine their signals so that the activity in one cell inhibits the response of neighboring ones. The cones seem to be able to monitor both brightness and colour (red/green and blue/yellow), and this could be achieved if the nerve connections were similar to

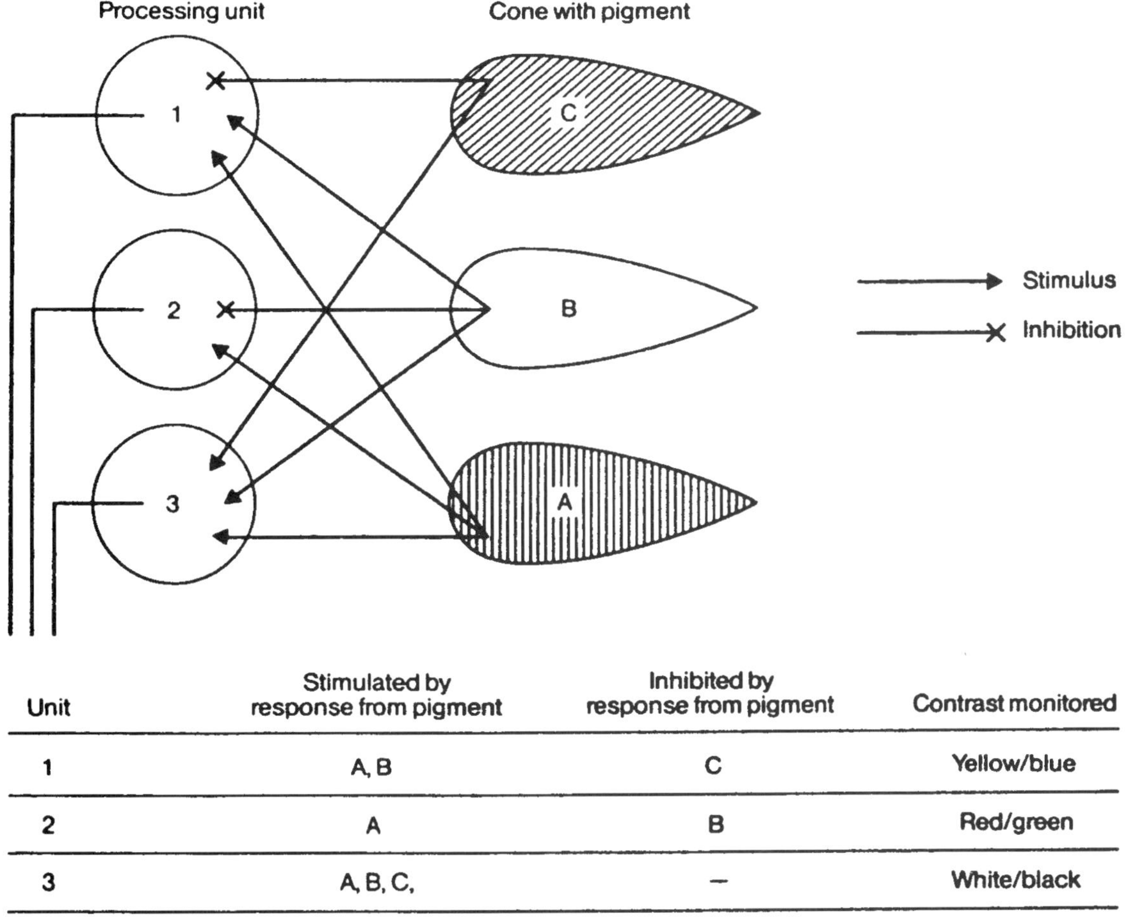

Unit	Stimulated by response from pigment	Inhibited by response from pigment	Contrast monitored
1	A, B	C	Yellow/blue
2	A	B	Red/green
3	A, B, C,	–	White/black

Figure 53. Connections for contrast. *A possible scheme of nerve connections which would allow cone cells to monitor contrast.*

those of the simplified scheme shown in Figure 53. A strong response from the cones must also be conveyed to the rod cells, in order to inhibit them when the light is bright.

It is thought that the first steps in the collation of cone responses occur in the retina itself, but that the brain performs most of the processing required to produce the sensation of colour. It is certainly the brain which combines the signals from each eye. Coloured stereoscopic pictures provide impressive application of binocular vision. A scene is photographed twice; once as viewed by the right eye of a stationary observer, and once as viewed by his left eye (see Figure 54). The right-hand one, printed in red, is superimposed on the left-hand one, printed in blue-green. This composite print is viewed through goggles with a blue-green filter over the right eye and a red filter over the left one. So the right eye sees black on blue-green, while the left eye sees black on red. After a second or so, the two signals fuse in the brain to provide a gleamingly three-dimensional impression in black on white.

Some people find that impressions from their two eyes do not fuse easily, if at all. The response of one eye sometimes entirely dominates that of the other, so that, when viewing a stereoscopic picture through coloured goggles, they would see a flat picture on a coloured background. A very few people, who have defective colour vision in one eye only, are in the unusual position of being able to compare the sensations produced by normal, and defective, colour vision, and to tell the normally sighted how the world

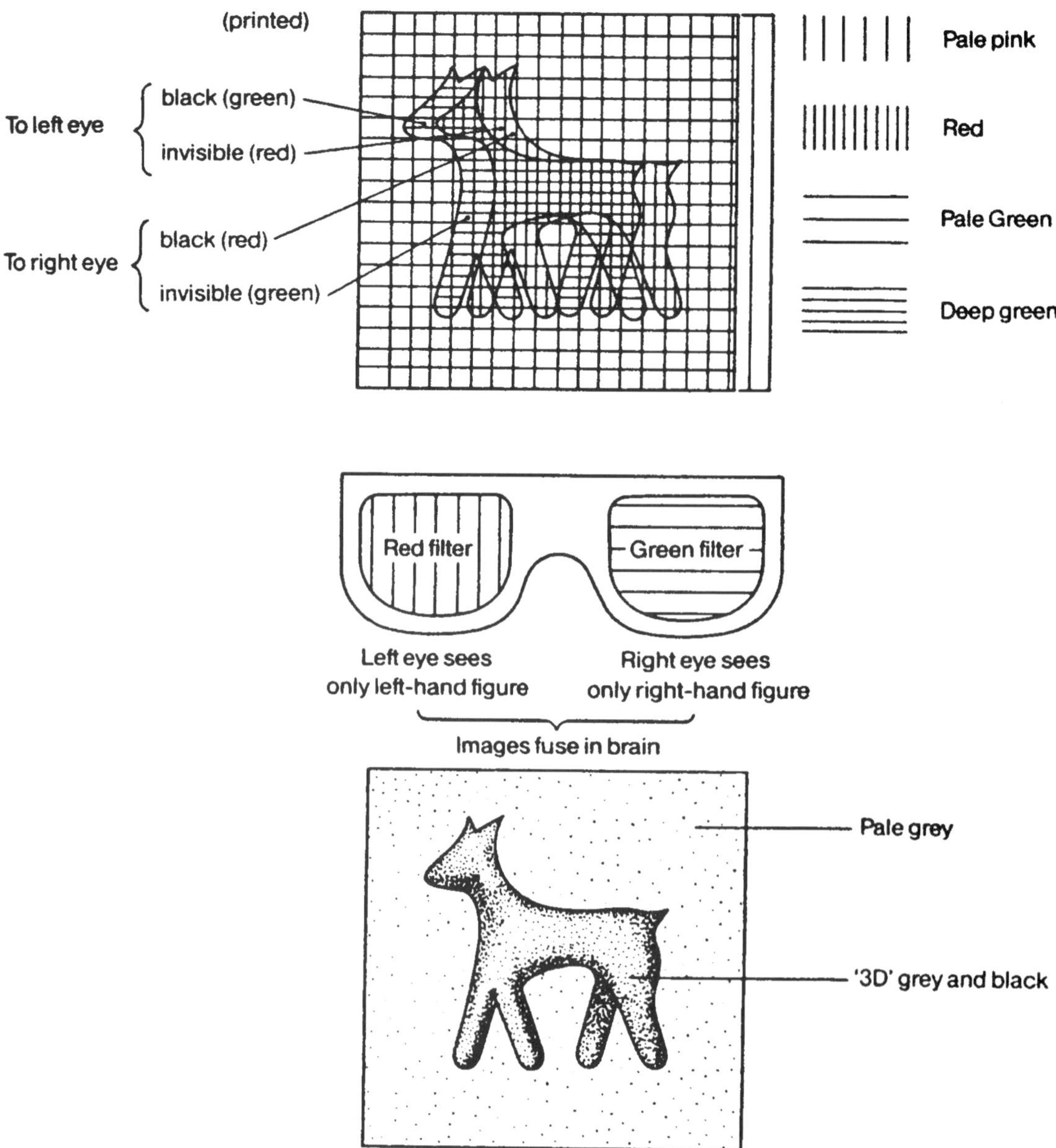

Figure 54. Stereo. *An illusion of depth is produced by the fusion of two images within the brain.*

looks to the 'colour-blind'. And if the defective eye is strongly dominant, their supposedly binocular colour vision will also be defective.

Some of the colour phenomena which have most captured the attention of writers and experimentalists alike are those in which the effect of light on one cone cell is modified either by the simultaneous response of neighboring cells, or by some previous response, in eye or brain. One such effect is the way in which the inhibition of one cell by another enhances colour contrast. If we stare at a bright red patch on a white card, it seems to develop a green line around the edge, whereas a yellow border appears around a violet patch. Sunlight on snow or whitewash looks yellowish, and the shadows bluish. But the light from the lit and shaded areas differs only in intensity. Its composition is the same. Even more impressive coloured shadows can be obtained in theater lighting.

In the same way, two patches of, say, blue and yellow, often look brighter, and more contrasting, when adjacent than when apart.

We know from studies of the electrical activity of individual brain cells that a cell which is receiving no stimulus is dormant, but it is not totally inactive. In the absence of any message from the optic nerve, it discharges steadily. When the retina is stimulated by a flash of light of a particular colour, the electrical activity of the cell may be greatly increased, or reduced to almost nothing, or totally unaffected (see Figure 55). Different cells respond differently to different wavelengths.

Some brain cells appear to respond to colour only if it occurs at the edge of an area. Such cells must play a crucial part in our perception of contrast, and hence of shape.

The boundary between two colours produces interesting effects. A patch of bright colour on a dark background appears, by contrast, brighter at the edges. A band of orange on deep green or brown appears almost to glow at the edges, like a strip-light, in much the same way as a series of wide stripes of increasingly paler grey seem, by contrast, to darken each of the boundaries. But at the precise junction between two colours of similar brightness, the colours may become slightly paler, and so the contrast decreases. The effect is most marked when the two colours are complementary. For example, when yellow and blue stimulate adjacent cones, the response is much the same as if both cones had been triggered off by white light. The yellow and blue mix, not outside the eye but on the retina, so each of the patches look paler at the junction between them than it does further into the main area of colour. This effect obviously becomes more important the smaller the patches of colour. As early as 1824, Chevreul warned tapestry makers to avoid placing complementary colours next to each other if they wanted to produce brightly coloured pictures. For the same reason, painters and stained-glass artists often outline areas of colour in black, or separate them by a white line. But optical mixing need not yield only white. A mosaic of red and green gives a vibrant yellow. Such effects have been much exploited in textile design and painting and are the basis of colour television.

Colours also become mixed on the retina if they follow each other more rapidly than about fifty stimuli per second. If the segments of a top are painted, the colours fuse when the top is spun (see Figure 56). Alternating slices of red and green become yellow, while blue and yellow become whitish, just as if lights were superimposed on a screen. A quite different effect, probably caused by different rates of recovery from fatigue to different wavelengths, is the stroboscopic colour we see when we spin certain patterned black and white discs (see Figure 57). The actual colours experienced depend on the observer, and vary with the speed and the direction of rotation, the particular pattern and the light source. The top shown here, designed by Sydney Harry, is at its most impressive when viewed by the light of a colour television set. Under fluorescent lighting it shows weaker colours, and under tungsten, or in daylight, none at all.

Colour sensations may change with time if one or more sets of cone cell become tired, as when an observer is shown a series of flashes of very intense red light (620 nm). The colour first seems red, then passes through orange and yellow to a green sensation, which holds for about thirty seconds before reverting gradually through yellow to orangish-yellow, where it then stays. It seems that the barrage of high-wavelength photons is too great to be monitored for long by cones containing pigment A. Once the response is triggered, the recovery time is too slow to maintain the appropriate response ratio A:B:C for 620 nm. So a higher proportion of photons is become fatigued, but since they absorb a lower fraction of the photons than do the A cones, they become slightly less tired. So after about two and a half minutes, the response settles down to give an orange-yellow sensation derived from a lower ratio of A to B responses than would be expected for 620 nm.

Fatigue also seems to account for the engaging apparitions known as "negative after-images." If we stare hard at a coloured pencil held against a white background for one or two minutes, and then remove the pencil, we can see a pencil-shaped patch of complementary colour which moves across the background as we move our eyes. A red pencil gives a turquoise patch and a green pencil a magenta patch. It seems that when we look at a red pencil, the cones respond, and become temporarily out of ac-

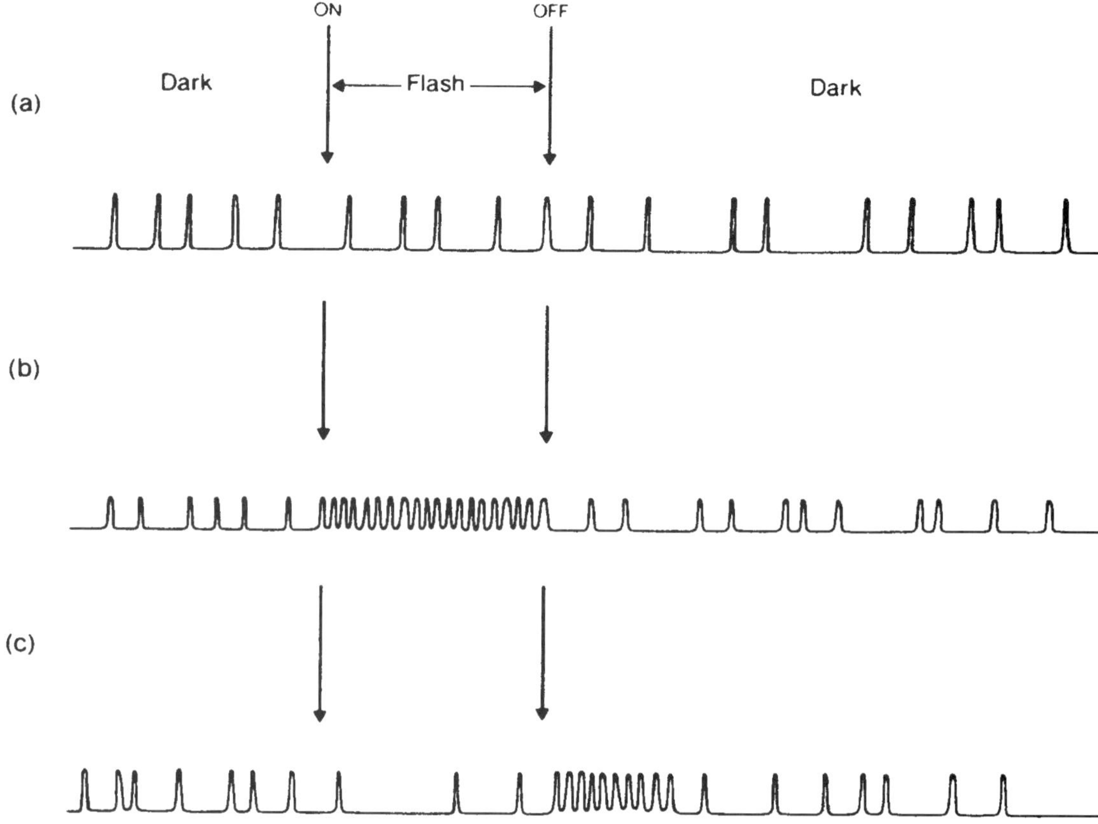

Figure 55. Brain waves. *Some types of electrical activity of individual brain cells subjected to a bright flash of light.*
(a) No response: the cell continues to "tick over," as in the dark.
(b) Activity increases during flash.
(c) Activity decreases during flash, but increases above normal level immediately afterwards.
Each cell may react differently to light of different wavelengths, and differently from its neighbors for light of the same wavelength.

tion in the A:B:C ratio appropriate to the wavelength. When white light falls on the retina, these fatigued cones do not respond, and the light from the background produces a "white" response in the unfatigued cones, but a "white-minus-red" (i.e. turquoise) response in the pencil-shaped region of the fatigued cones. After a minute or so, the cones become reactivated and the after-image fades. Doctors and nurses wear bluish-green clothes when they do surgical operations so that they are not distracted by the bluish-green after-images of blood.

But not all negative after-images are as simple as these, or as Goethe's "well-favored" tavern wench. In 1965, it was found that if the eyes are "primed" by looking alternately at green and black stripes in one direction (say vertical) and red and black stripes in another (say horizontal), then the negative after-images which are obtained when we look at black stripes on a white background are linked to the direction of the stripes. If we look at vertical stripes, we now see magenta, and if we turn the pattern through a right angle, so that the bars become horizontal, the colour changes to green. The connection between direction and colour can persist for hours, or even days, without impairing every day vision in any way.

The exact explanation of this effect has not yet been fully worked out, but it is believed to hold the

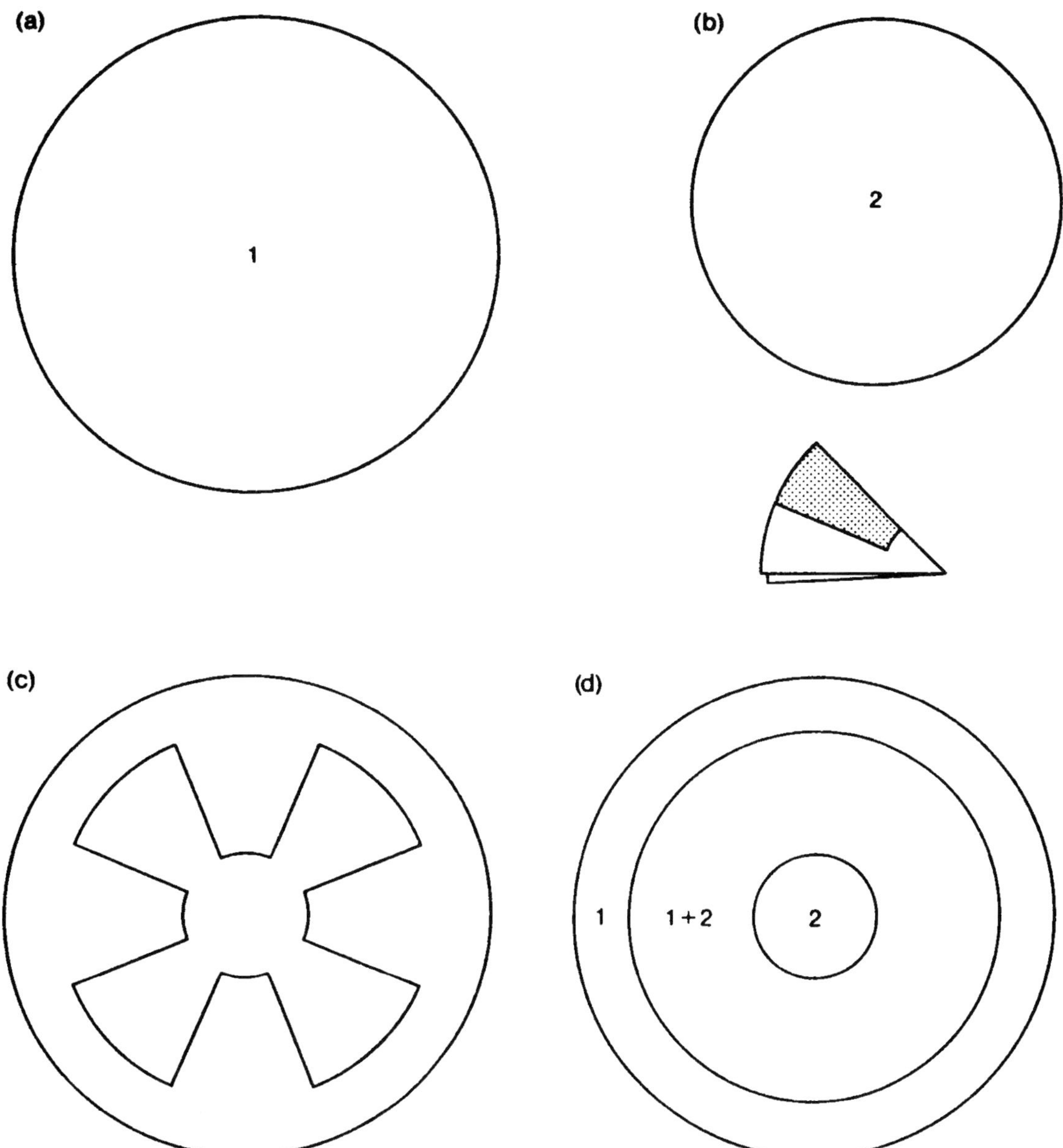

Figure 56. Coloured tops. *Do-it-yourself colour mixing.*
Circle of coloured paper (1) mounted on circle of stout cardboard.
Smaller circle of paper of different colour (2), folded as shown, with shaded region cut way.
Cut-out glued concentrically on coloured circle.
When the cardboard circle is mounted (securely) on a child's top, or on the circular sanding base of an electrical drill, colours 1 and 2 are mixed in equal proportions when the disc spins.
Best results are obtained with the brightest colours: a combination of fluorescent red and fluorescent green is particularly impressive.

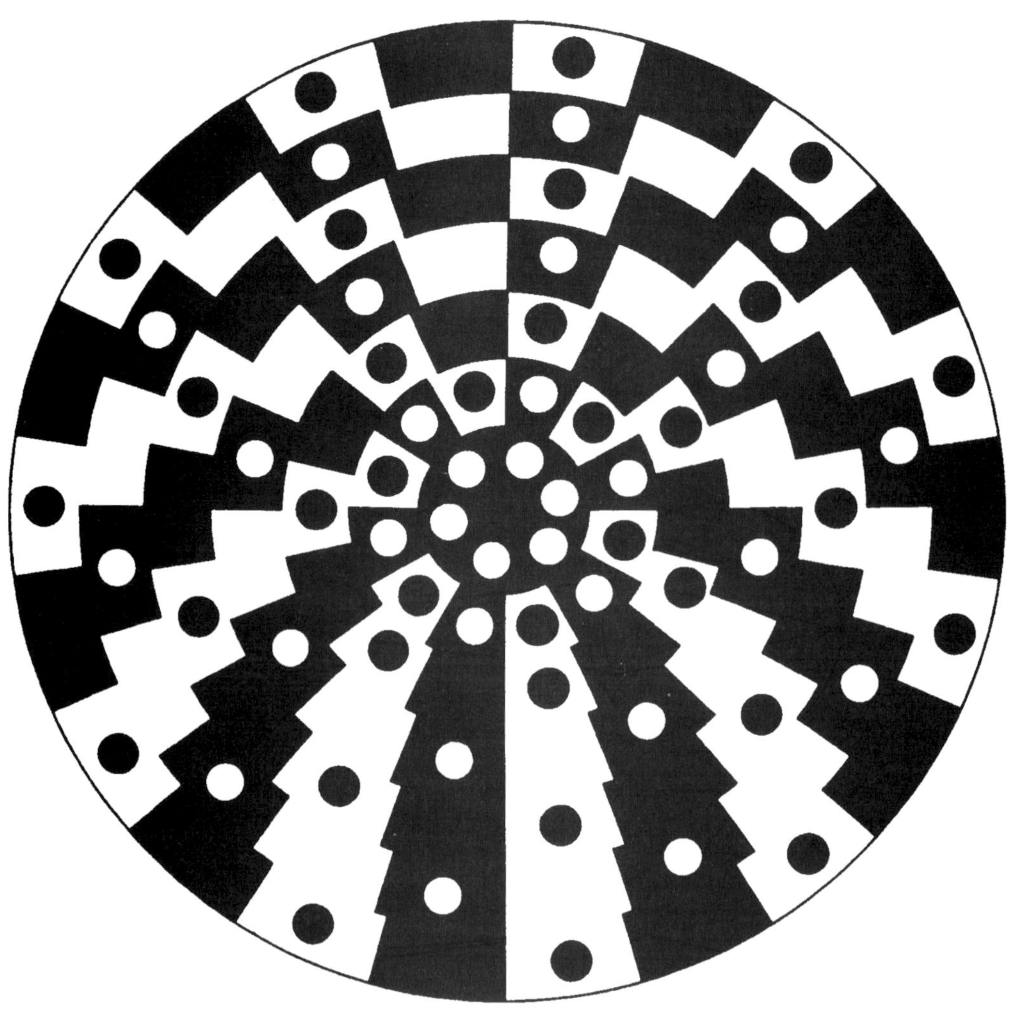

Figure 57. Sydney Harry's top. *The original is 14.3 centimeters in diameter, and mounted on heavy cardboard with a sharpened matchstick as axle. It is spun by hand.*

key to a greatly increased understanding of our perception of colour, and of the nature of simple learning and memory. One thing is certain. Much more is involved than the mere time which it takes a cone to recover from absorbing a photon.

Negative after-images of colour complementary to the object are normally obtained when the illumination is fairly even. Incandescent sources may produce a positive after-image, a fleeting company of the object. In a darkened room, we may continue to see a candle flame for a moment or two after it has been blown out. And if you have a short enough name, you may write your whole signature across the night sky with a lighted sparkler, for the colour lingers for an instant after the sparkler has moved on.

Perhaps the most impressive of all after-images is the "flight of colours" which we see after a very bright light has been shone into the eye, as when we have been examined by an oculist. Against a white ceiling floats a brilliant yellow patch with a magenta border, edged with turquoise around its changing amoeboid shape. The colours gradually change too, so that it becomes a negative after-image—blue, edged with yellow and red. The effect lasts for several minutes, changing shape and colour like a spreading oil patch.

Visual information can also be stored for much longer periods. We can remember some colours for years, and our memory can modify the colours we now see. If two shapes, representing a leaf and a donkey, are cut from the same piece of grey paper and placed on the same background, most observers claim that the leaf is a greener grey than the donkey.

A similar expectation may be one reason why we say that a donkey, lit by the setting sun, is brownish grey, although the light which reaches us from it is akin to that scattered by rust or copper in daylight. But the state of adaptation of the eye is also important. It is thought that the retina can adapt to wavelength composition of the illumination, if this differs appreciably from white light, in much the same way as it adapts to changes in intensity. Those who use cars with slightly tinted green glass will know that, seen through the windscreen or a closed window, the surroundings look "normal" and the glass untinted. The eye is adapted to a faintly green background. But if we then partly wind down a window, that part of the scene we see through the open window now looks distinctly pink, while the adjacent part, viewed through the glass, is tinged with green. After a minute or so, however, the contrast fades, and both parts of the scene look untinted.

More dramatic illustrations of the interplay of adaptation and contrast can often be seen in theater lighting. The stage is lit from two widely separated spotlights, one white and one red, so that their spots exactly coincide on the white background, which our eyes, once they have adapted to the pink light, see as white. A dancer appears, and blocks the beam from the white spot, and where her shadow falls on the background, the only light which reaches us is from the red spotlight. So we see a red shadow on a white background. Her partner then emerges from the opposite wings, and blocks the beam from the red light. So where he casts a shadow, only white light reaches the background. But we do not see his shadow as white on a pink background, because we already see the background as white. So, instead of perceiving it as pink-minus-red, we see it as white-minus-red—as turquoise. The shadows of the *pas de deux* appear, not as red and white on pink, but more impressively, as red and turquoise on white.

A similar effect has been exploited by Land, who showed that red and white light could be mixed in such a way as to give sensations over a wide range of colours. He made black and white positive transparencies, photographing each scene twice, once through a red filter, and once through a green one. He projected them both on to a screen, the first with a red light, and the second with a white one, and when the images were superimposed, obtained, in addition to red and black, a range of colours from turquoise, through green and yellow, to orange.

We do not yet know if the mechanism by which we adapt to the colour of the illumination takes place in the eye or in the brain. But there seems to be a series of brain cells, each of which picks up processed signals from a very narrow band of wavelengths. Between them, they span the visible spectrum, and it seems that each discernible colour (including the non-spectral purple) is associated with its own set of brain cells. Of these cells, a number will respond only in the presence of the background illumination. Thus some of the cells which respond to changes in the intensity of red light (but are insensitive to changes in the intensity of other colours) will respond to red *only* if it is mixed with light of other colours. Pure red light produces no activity in such cells. It may well be that observations of this type will eventually help us to understand why the perceived colours of objects depend so little on the light which falls on them.

But the extent to which the colour of an object seems to remain constant also depends on who is looking at what. The colour of a real donkey seems to change less with the illumination than does the colour of a donkey in a picture. The colours of a naturalistic painting vary less than do those of a bold pattern, which are themselves more constant than an abstract picture with ill-defined regions of colour. To a large extent, what we see depends on what we expect to see. Even to an artist, a donkey may, at a brief, casual glance, look donkey-coloured. But if the artist is thinking about incorporating the donkey into a painting, he will be more sensitive to the light reaching him from the donkey at that particular moment than to the average colour which the donkey would have if viewed by a layman in diffuse light.

Colour sensations may often be even more dramatically altered by, or even produced by, factors other than light. Some forms of hysteria and hallucinogenic drugs enhance appreciation of colour. Hallucinogens often provide experience of brightly coloured patterns which bear little relation to the real world, and those about to suffer attacks of epilepsy or migraine may see coloured rays and geometrical shapes before an attack. The blind, particularly if they are old, may have similar sensations, akin to seeing "golden rain" and coloured patterns. In childhood, a pressure on a closed eye was enough to produce patterns as exotic as Catherine Wheels or peacock tails. In adult life, a firmer touch, preferably on the upper part of the eye, is needed to produce an inferior but none the less impressive result. Electrical and mechanical stimulation of the optic nerve and the visual areas of the brain can make us see colours, as can some acute illnesses, and even a strong magnetic field. And so, of course, can memory and dreams. But although we can experience an immense variety of colour sensations produced in these different, non-visual, ways, we have as yet only a negligible understanding of any of the mechanisms involved.

Chapter Four Project Proposal

The Project—Tints and Shades: Mass and Deep Space

The Project:

On a sheet of 18" × 18" watercolor paper render 12 spheres of varying sizes. You should form *three yellow, three orange, three green* and *three white* spheres. Anytime that you paint or create a sphere on a surface, be sure that you make a cast shadow, so that the ball will appear to sit appropriately on the plane. Additionally, linear perspective should not be the main vehicle for creating the illusion of space—nor should overlapping—but rather chromatic value gradations. The spheres should have the illusion of three-dimensional mass by the manipulation of tints and shades. You must not only create round spheres, but produce the illusion of deep space, whether by dark contrasts or *chromatic value gradations*. There will be four groups of three spheres, which will illustrate either warm tints and cool shades or cool tints with warm shades.

The spheres need to have a light source, and should therefore be illuminated from one side or the other. The sphere then will demonstrate *highlights* to *base tones (see example on following pages),* creating effective transitions of light to dark chromatic values across the surface of the ball:

- A *warm illumination* creates a *warm tint and shade,* but a *cool cast shadow.*
- A *cool illumination* creates a *cool tint and shade*, but a *warm cast shadow.*
- Use the blending, stippled or broken color technique, or as demonstrated. Below are suggested formulas, which will aid in your decisions. They are not "written in stone," only possible methods of color choices for the painting of spheres. You are allowed to make appropriate changes, as long as you achieve a convincing composition of spheres in deep space.

Three Yellow Spheres:

- *Highlight* (warm tint) is white to very light tinted yellow.
- *Light tone* is light to medium yellow.
- *Half tone* is saturated yellow.
- *Base tone* or shade is yellow-orange. Shade with black.
- *Reflected light* is light orange-yellow.
- *Cast shadow* is cool-dark blue or violet tints and shades.

Three Orange Spheres

- *Highlight* (warm tint) is white to lightest tinted yellow-orange.
- *Light tone* is yellow-orange to saturated orange.
- *Half tone* is red-orange.
- *Base tone* is deep red-orange shaded with black.
- *Reflected light* is light red–orange.
- *Cast shadow* is cool-dark blue or dark violet.

Three Green Spheres

- *Highlight* (cool tint) is lightest tinted yellow-green.
- *Light tone* is light green to saturated green.
- *Half tone* is saturated green to shaded blue-green.
- *Base tone* is blue-green shaded with black.
- *Reflected light* is light blue-green.
- *Cast shadow* is deep shaded warm-red to red-orange.

Three White Spheres

- *Highlight* (warm tint) is white to lightest possible tinted yellow.
- *Light tone* is lightest yellow to lightest violet.
- *Half tone* is lightest yellow with violet shades. Mix them when partially *stiff*, so that you will not cancel the yellow.
- *Base tone* is violet.
- *Reflected light* is lightest violet tints.
- *Cast shadow* is cool deep violet

Reference:

Tints and Shades

When referring to *tints* we are moving from gray to *white*:

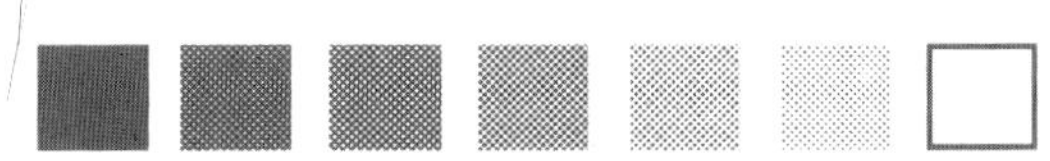

When referring to *shades* we are moving from *gray* to *black*:

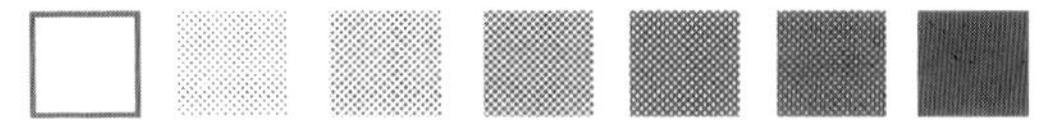

Project Objectives Summary:

- To formulate a proper understanding of how *tints* and *shades* function, particularly in terms of creating the illusion of three-dimensional *mass* and *depth of space.*
- To further clarify the effects of warm and cool temperatures and their effect of creating *believable shapes in space*, as well as, facilitating mood variations.
- To form a clearer understanding of how value gradations function in all chromatic functions.

Please see the following image for an example of student resolution to the project proposal.

The Value Sphere:

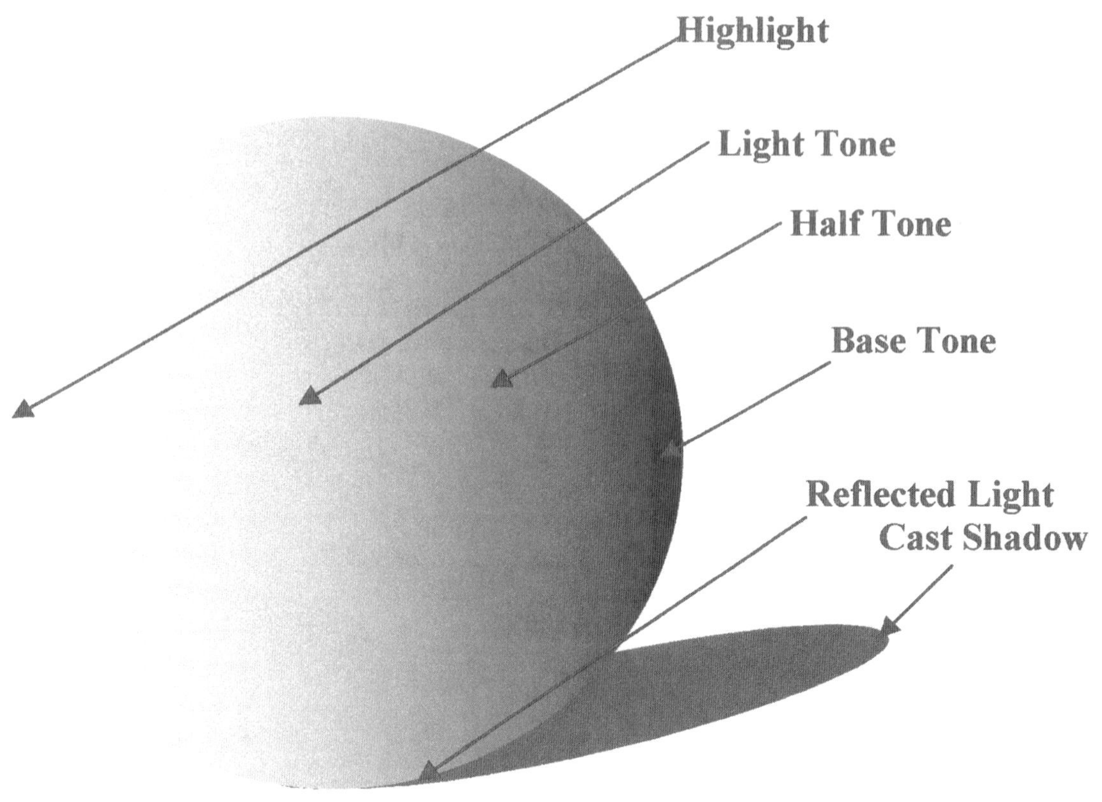

Student Examples:

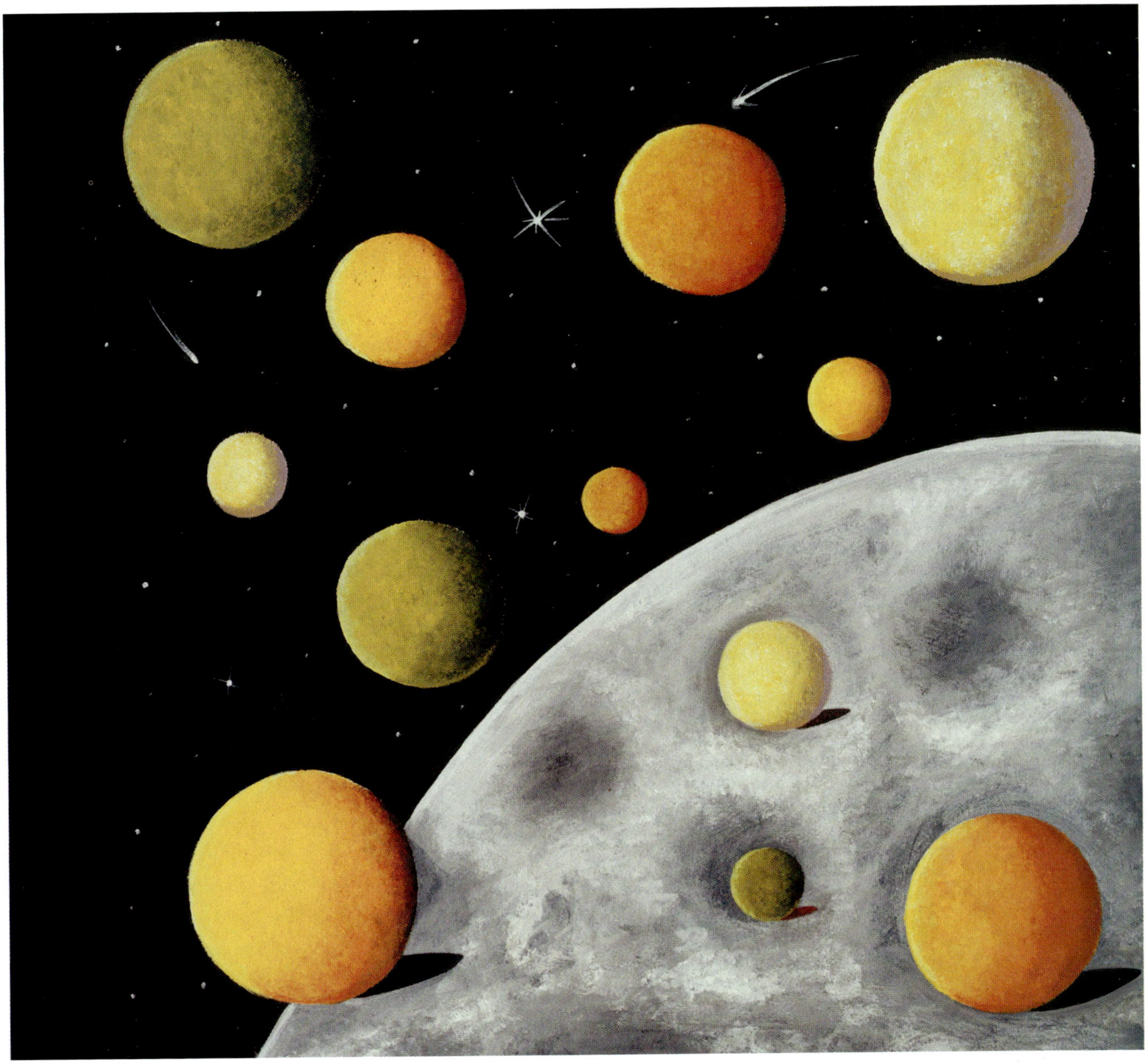

Twelve Spheres in Space by Sarah Chea

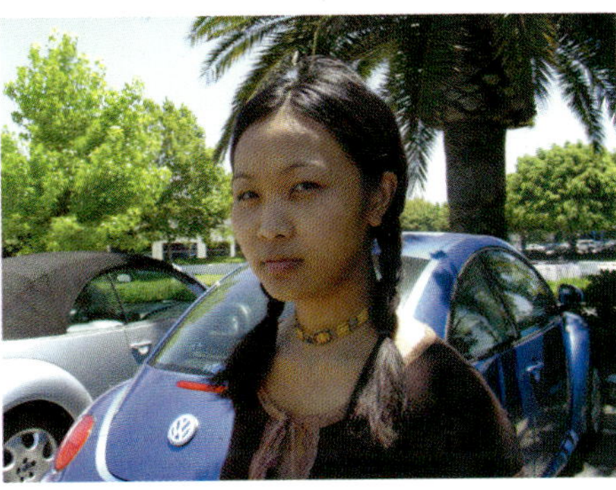

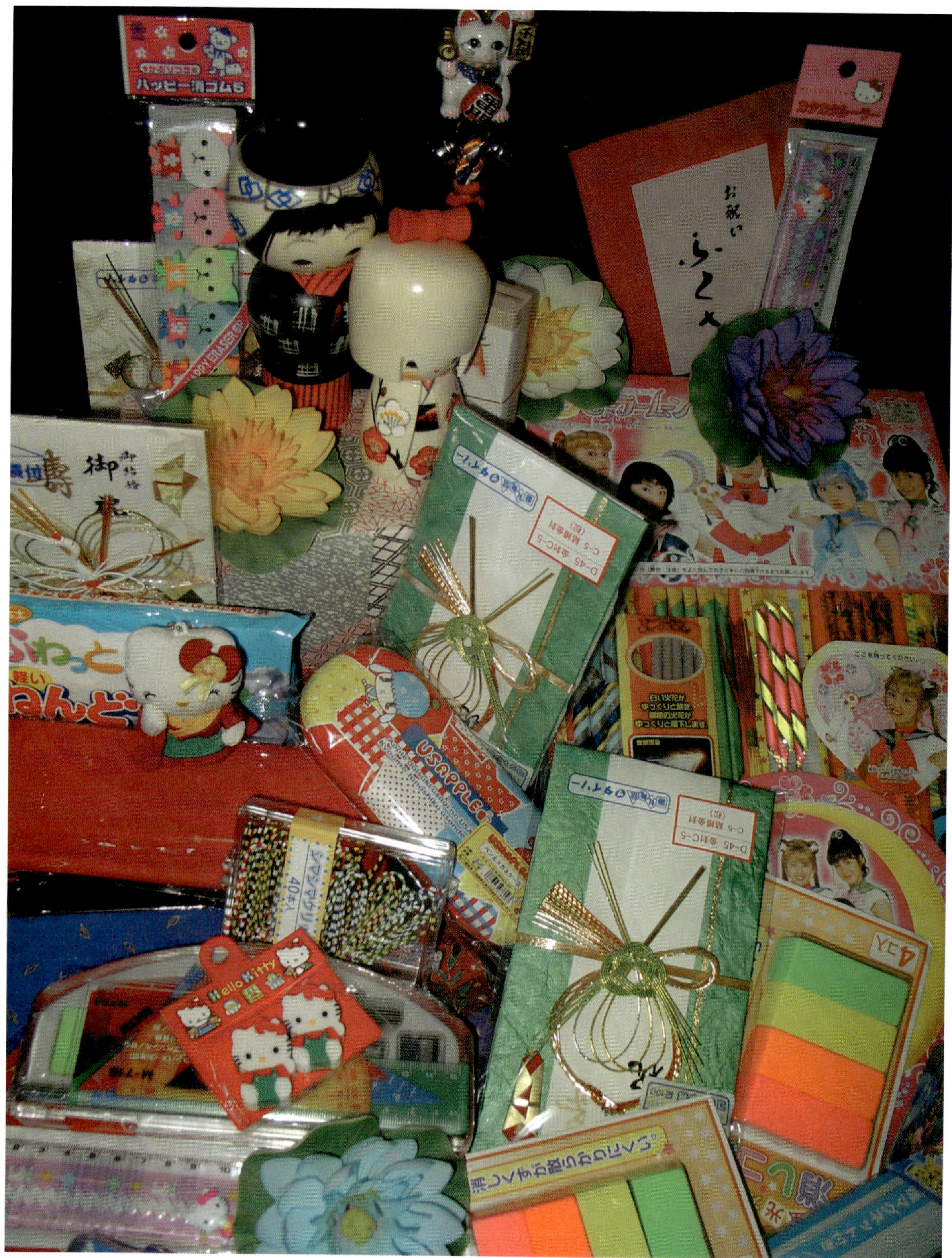

The Japanese Market. *In Japan, the packaged product's key emphasis concerns the bringing of color into focus. Reds and greens are always dominant in everyday merchandise. Color and color harmonies are paramount in Japan in terms of "making the sale." Rich saturated harmonies of color reach-out to the customer, and they are easily enchanted by the energetic pulse of hues. It is the "authority of color" to manipulate the senses.*

Color Harmony

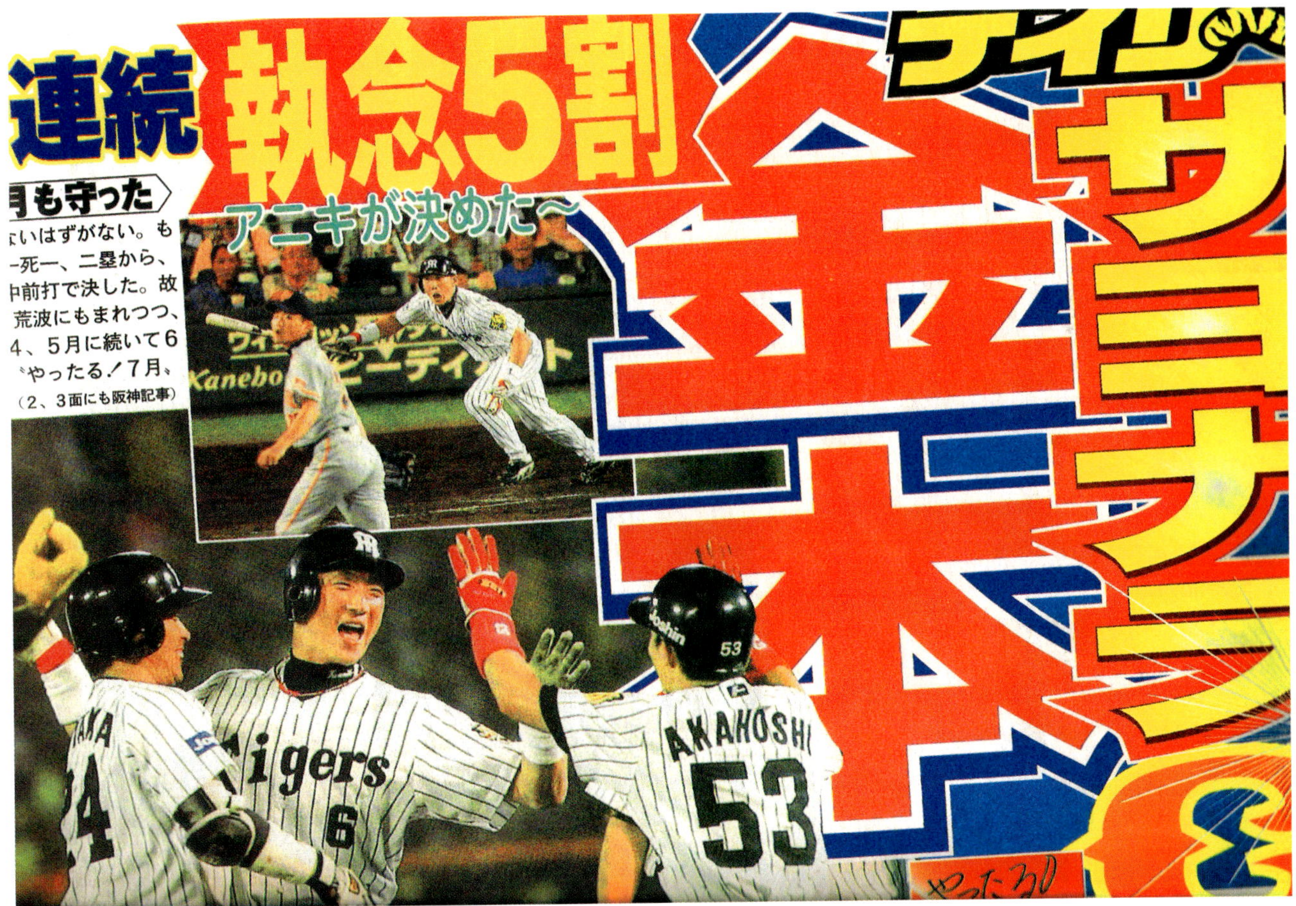

July 1, 2004 Sports Page Announces Tigers Victory: The Color Harmony of Commercial Contemporary Japan.
Photo by Alan Burner.

Chapter Five

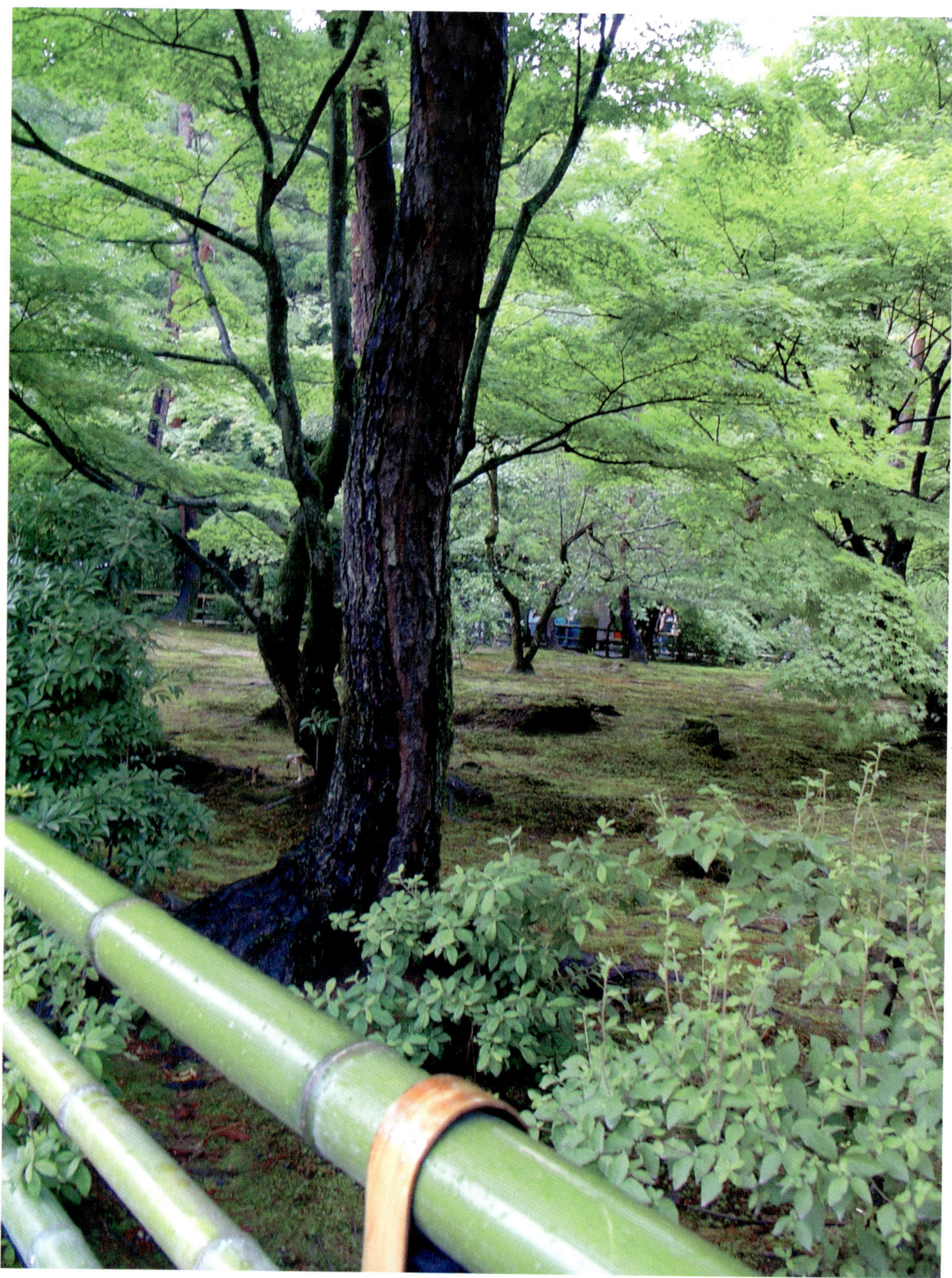

Tranquility of a Dyadic Color Harmony of Green Foliage and Dark Red Bark.
Photo by Alan Burner.

Introduction to Color Harmony

The harmony of color refers to the effect of color combinations on the human psyche and human spirit. Specifically, color harmony results when two or more colors are brought together to create particular moods and emotional responses by the viewer. In the first part of this chapter, we will study the conventional western approach to color harmony. Next, we'll focus on the Orient for our summary of color's composite parts. While color harmony serves similar functions from culture to culture, its composite hues vary considerably, as do the symbolic representation of those combinations. The second part of this chapter will entail the study of color as seen by the Japanese aristocracy in the Heian period one thousand years ago.

In all situations and professions that require color resolutions, there are general hue formulas or color marriages which function optimally. The term *harmonious* can be used to define colors that are different from each other, as the same color with various values, or for colors that are only minimally different from one another.

Johannes Itten, a well known color theorist in the earlier part of the 20th century, said that color harmony should not be considered "subjective", but rather should be moved into the "objective" arena. His comments were based mostly on the physiology of *afterimage* effects. An example of afterimage is gazing at a saturated *red square* for a few minutes and then closing the eyes, only to see a *complementary green square.* The same is true of an orange square, which produces a blue square and a yellow square to violet. The eye will always *demand the complement* of what is also known as *successive* contrast. In order to support objectivity in color harmony we need only to refer to the color circle. Our standard model illustrates that red is opposite of green, yellow to violet, and orange to blue. When we mix those complements, they have the effect of canceling each other to produce the achromatic value of gray. Imagine Wilhelm Ostwald's theory, for example; whose hypothesis of the color circle would actually put yellow opposite of blue, rather than violet. The result would not be gray, or the cancellation of color, but the two would instead create *green.*

Johannes Itten said that color harmony must be objective, while Wilhelm Ostwald believed that it should be subjective. We know that Ostwald felt that his theory about harmonies was justified, because certain groups of colors were "pleasing." These days we understand, however, that aesthetics are not the criteria alone, but there is more to it, in that it does not formulate well, in its all too simplistic approach (please see Ostwald's theory for greater clarity). On the other hand, color harmony cannot be entirely and unequivocally objective in all aspects. There has to be some room designated for subjectivity, even though it is certainly more objective by conventional standards. There are certain rules about color that cannot be denied, such as the *physiological* effects of successive contrast and simultaneous contrast, which has its place in the objective quadrant of color harmony. However, there are exceptions to the rules in some cases, since there are those who will always see color quite differently. We can say to any one person that their personal choice of color arrangements do not fit the conventional model of harmonic chroma, yet their choices will not always allow us to be overly dogmatic as long as people are individuals.

This brings us to *subjective* color. Certainly we can decide on any number of color harmonies or arrangements of our own choosing. That is not in and of itself the problem. There are certain formulas (harmonies), which presented in proper arrangement, produce specific and desired emotional results. Staying away from those factual conventions is sometimes risky when attempting to produce a very definite mood.

Subjective color is this: adherence to the rules or boundaries of color harmony conventions to a degree, with the freedom to chose those color harmonies which suit your needs. It is subjective in that you are free to make certain decisions about saturations, intensities, values, tints, shades, contrasts, color proportions, etc. There are many color harmony variations—too many for us to effectively be able to cover in this text. Instead, we'll cover six traditional examples referred to as dyad, triad, tetrad, hexad, analogous and monochromatic color harmonies.

Monochromatic Color Harmony

Monochromatic harmony refers to a composition of one color with gradations of that color's values. So, if we select blue, the composition will consist only of gradations of blue values. The blue can only be changed by tints and shades, or the addition of white or black respectively. In this case, the composition's temperature will be cool, demonstrating the application of light, medium and dark blues.

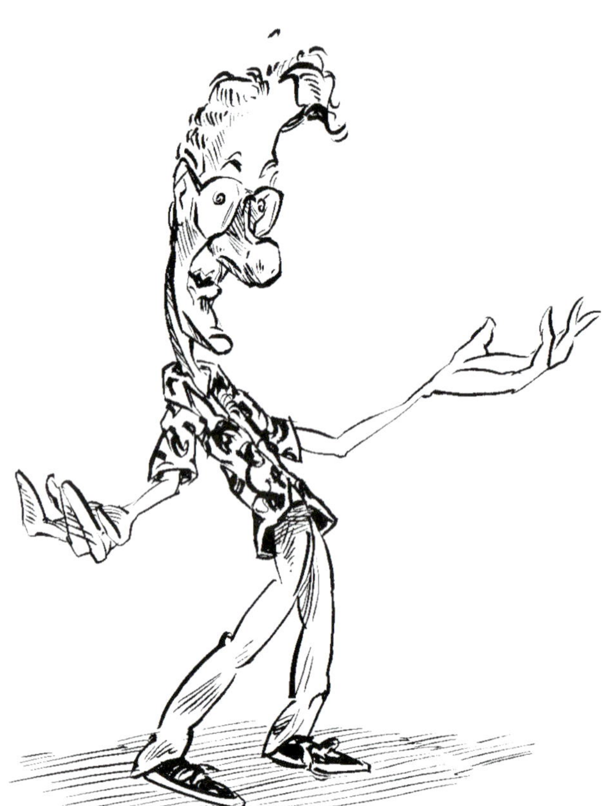

Monochromatic Figure
©Richard Ewing

Two Nudes by Picasso is an excellent example of one color with varying values. The entire composition is comprised of light, medium and dark values of orange. The monochromatic use of color creates a very sculptural and stone-like appearance to the figures themselves. The lack of color variation focuses the eye on the sculptural quality of these two figures.

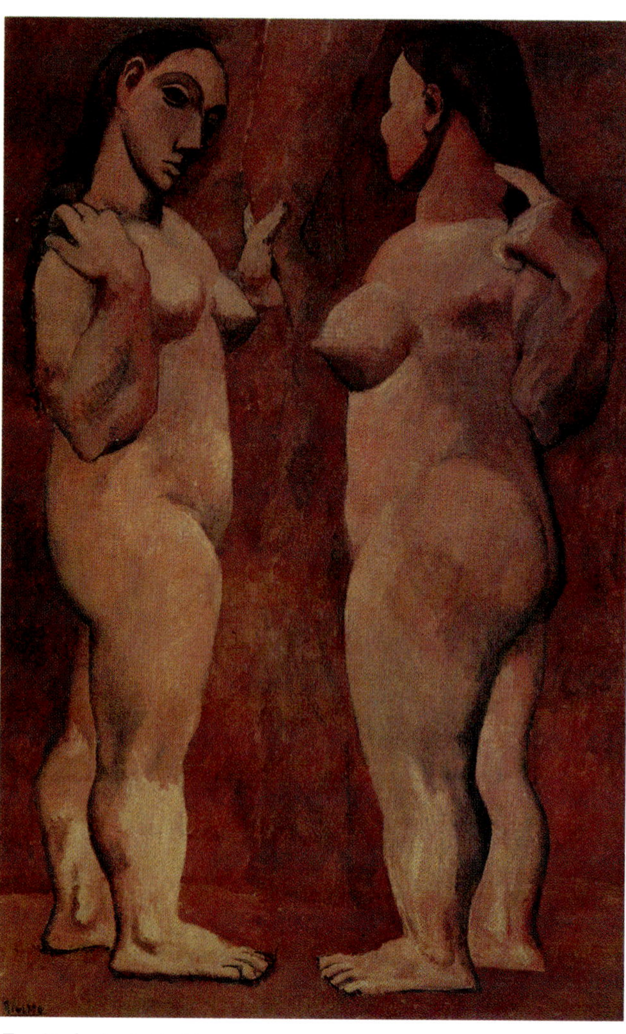

Two Nudes by Pablo Picasso.
©2003 Estate of Pablo Picasso/Artists Rights Society (ARS), New York..

Dyad Color Harmony

Dyad color harmonies consist of red and green, orange and blue and yellow and violet combinations. They are known as complementary colors. The complements are always comprised of one primary and one secondary color, or one warm and one cool color, respectively. Using the twelve-hue color circle, they are always diametrically opposite.

Typically, dyadic values will be opposite, as seen in Helen Frankenthaler's composition. The yellow values are a very light translucent tint, whereas the violet areas on the right side and top portion of the composition are commensurately shaded and opaque. This is the nature of the dyadic harmony, that is to say, an extreme tint as well as an opposite extreme shade. Dyads can exist at any point on the color circle, as long as they are symmetric to the center of the color circle. Intermediate colors apply in the same manner. Dyad harmonies are perhaps the simplest of the color harmonies.

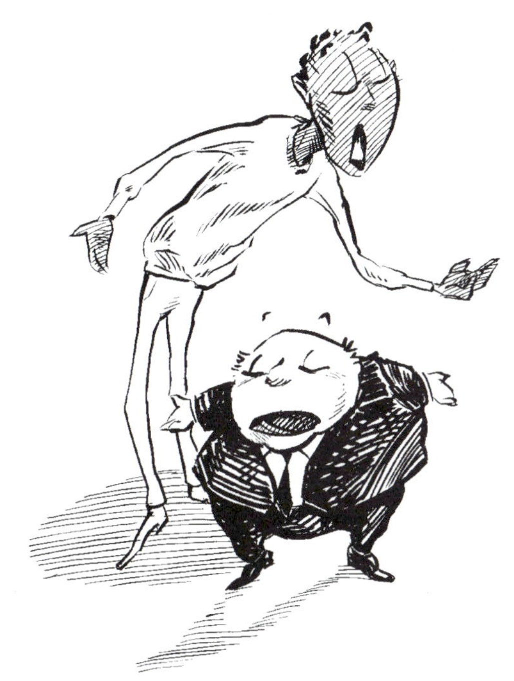

©Richard Ewing

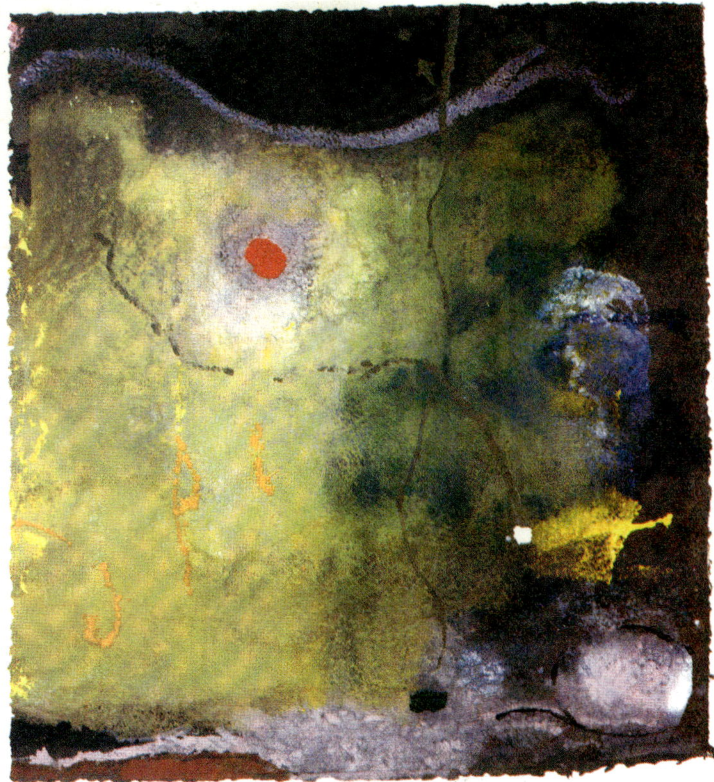

The Other Side of the Moon by Helen Frankenthaler.
Source: Knoedler & Company.

Triad Color Harmony

Yellow, red and blue are the strongest of the color harmonies, and are known as the *primary triads.* Some are triads of intensified color, or tinted triads, while others are significantly shaded reds, yellows and blues.

A secondary triad would be orange, green and violet, and is seen clearly in Diebenkorn's painting *Berkeley No. 52.* There are more gradients of orange throughout the picture plane, yet the existence of violet and green are significant enough to create a true secondary triad. It is necessary to remind the reader at this point that triadic positions are at the points of an equilateral triangle within the color circle.

Intermediate triads are:

- Yellow-orange, red-violet and blue-green.
- Yellow-green, red-orange and blue-violet.

Split Complements also create a triadic color harmony, but the triangle is not equilateral.

Instead, the configuration of a split complementary from yellow, for example, would be yellow, blue-violet and red-violet. The violet itself is no longer part of the harmony, because one-half of it is moved to the left, and one-half to the right. The remaining colors are as follows:

- Violet: Yellow-orange and yellow-green
- Orange: Blue-green and blue-violet
- Green: Red-violet and red-orange
- Blue: Yellow-orange and red-orange
- Red: Blue-green and yellow-green

Jan Gossart, a 16th century renaissance painter (see *Danae* on opposite page), illustrates a skillful use of split complements, seen by the yellow-orange background buildings, the red-orange columns and the blue cloak on the isolated foreground figure.

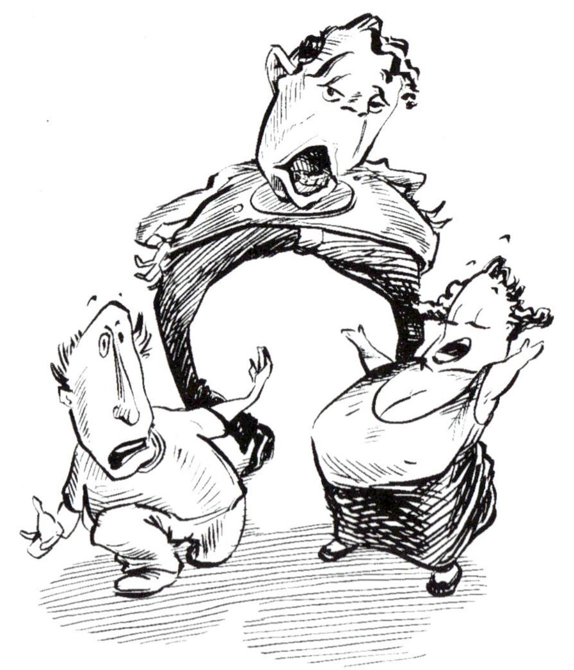

©Richard Ewing

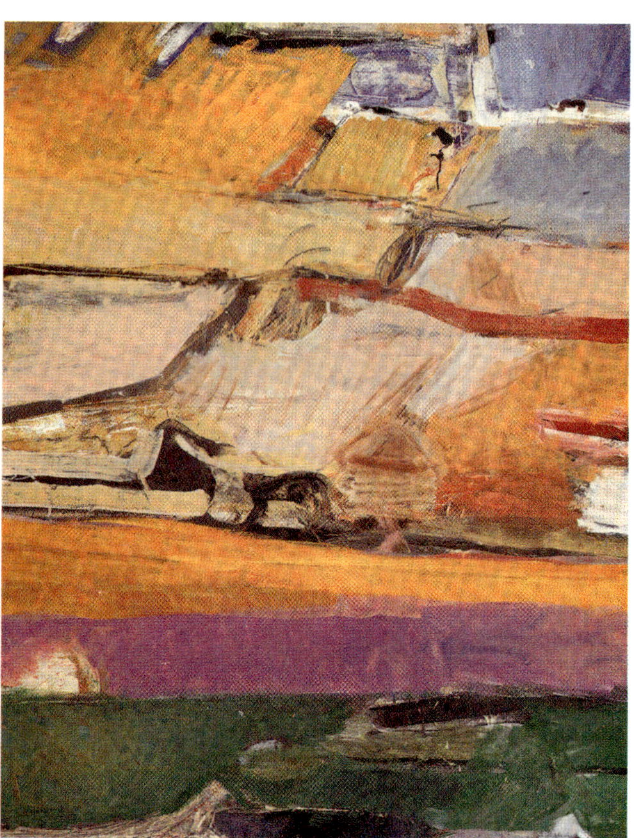

BERKELEY, NO. 52 by Richard Diebenkorn.
Gift of the Collectors Committee, Image © 2003 Board of Trustees, National Gallery of Art, Washington, 1955.

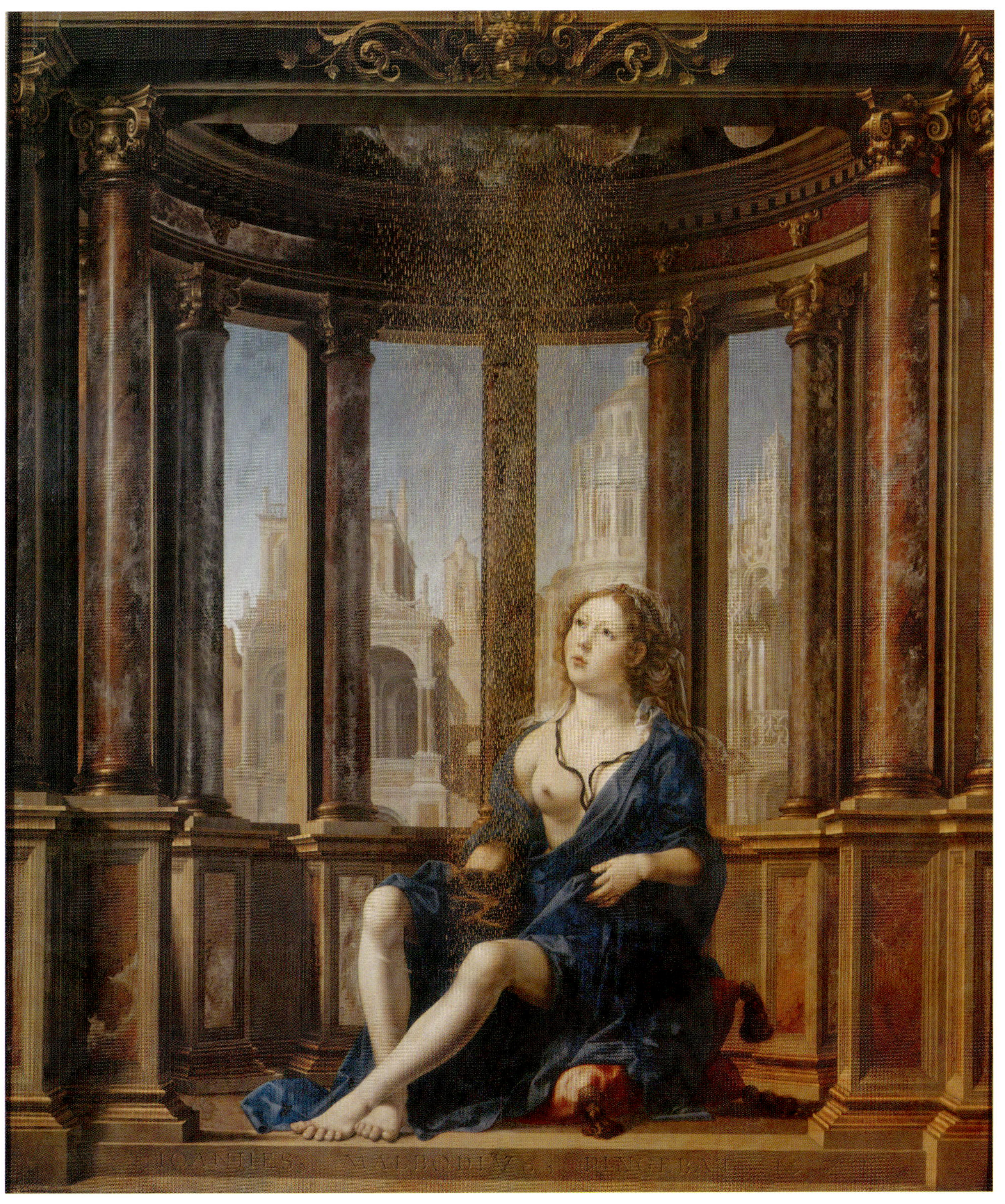

Danae by Jan Gossart.
 Alte Pinakothek, Munich, Germany.

Tetrad Color Harmony

The *tetrad* harmony incorporates the use of two pairs of complementary harmonies in a single composition. Those complements are derived by a perfect square inscribed within the color circle. Each of the connecting points of the square indicate the colors, which are to be used.

Three Harmonies of the tetrad square:

- Yellow, violet, red-orange and blue-green
- Yellow-orange, blue-violet, and red and green
- Orange, blue, red-violet and yellow-green

Another tetrad can be formed by the use of a rectangle inside of the color circle, instead of a square. These pairs are:

- Yellow-green, red-violet, yellow-orange and blue-violet
- Yellow, violet, orange and blue

The composition of Raphael's has deep green curtains in the upper right and left corners, and on the outer robe of the right side figure. On the central figure of Mary, she wears a blue-violet outer robe with red. The left side figure is adorned mostly with yellow-orange with a bit of red. The surrounding ground of blue-violet is also apparent.

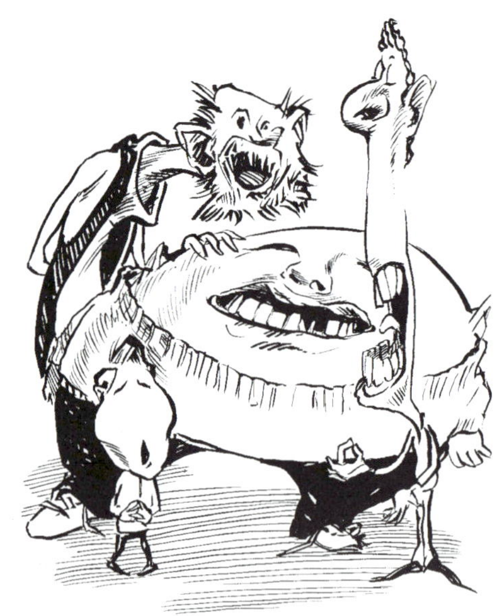

©Richard Ewing

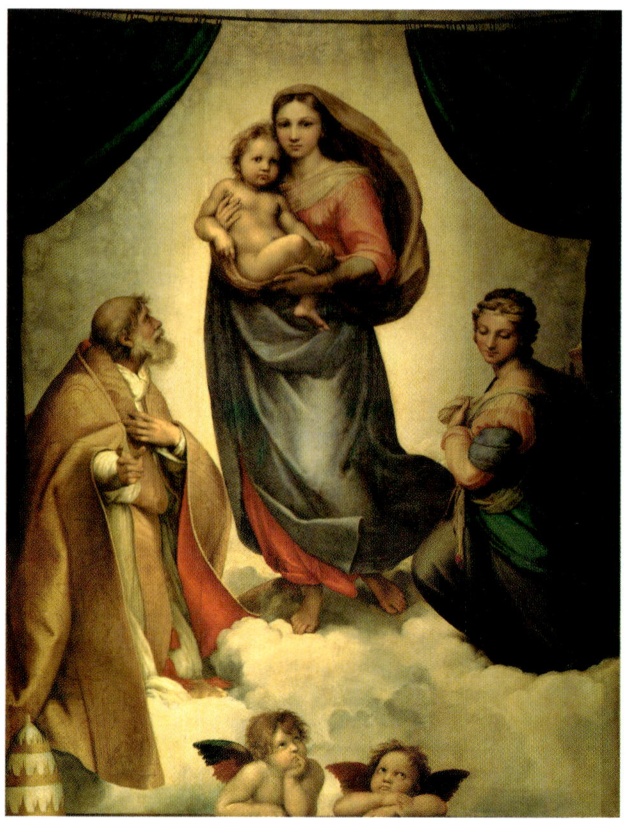

Sistine Madonna by Raphael.
Erich Lessing/Art Resource, NY.

Hexad Color Harmony

Hexad harmonies are derived from a hexagon inscribed within the color circle. The hexad harmony is more complex, in that it incorporates three complementary pairs in one harmony, or in any given composition. Hexads are different in that they only give us two possibilities of color harmonies:

- Yellow-orange, blue violet, red-orange, blue-green, red-violet, and yellow-green.
- Yellow, violet, orange, blue, red and green

Black and white can also join a square tetrad in order to produce a third possibility (hexad), even though it is not a full chromatic hexad (see *Sixteen Candles* 1992).

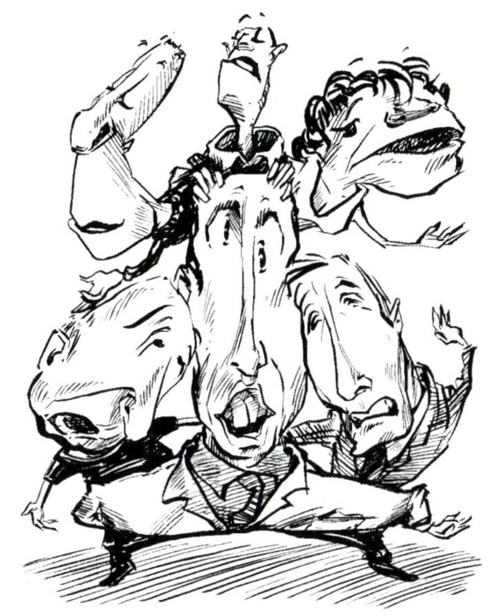

©Richard Ewing

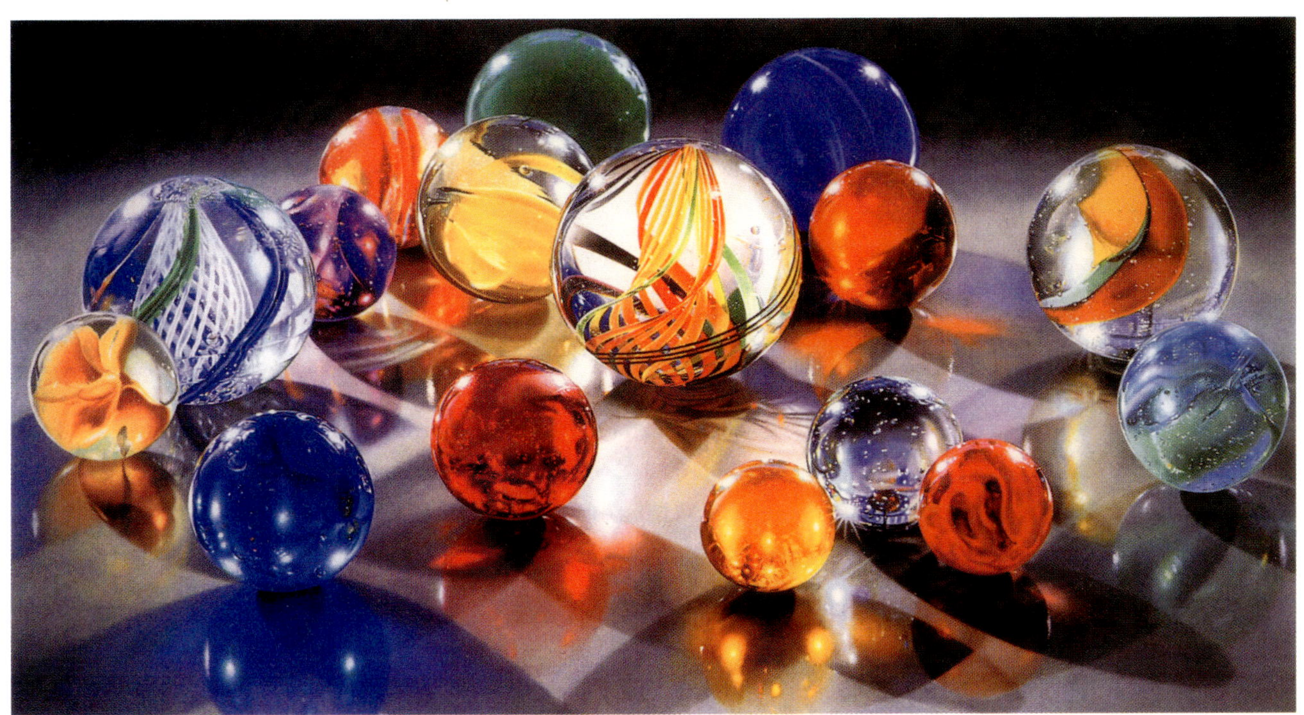

Sixteen Candles 1992 by Charles Bell.
Used by permission of the Louis K. Meisel Gallery, New York.

Analogous Color Harmony

Analogous color harmonies are a family of hues, which exist side-by-side on the color circle. As few as three, and as many as *five* colors are normally used to qualify as analogous. They must all be joining colors on the circle, side by side. Both warm or cool harmonies may create an effective temperature mood.

Warm analogous harmonies can be created (for example) by:

- Yellow, yellow-orange, orange, red-orange, red or
- Red-orange, red, red-violet and violet

Cool harmonies can be created (for example) by:

- Yellow-green, green, blue-green, blue and blue-violet
- Green, Blue-green, blue, blue-violet and violet

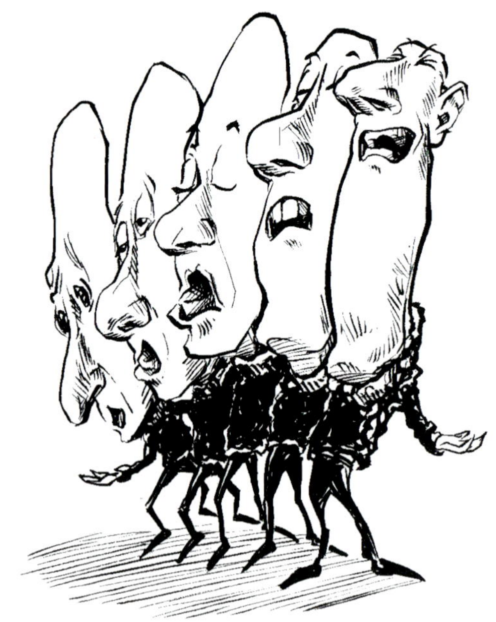

©Richard Ewing

The dividing line between warm and cool temperature is usually considered between yellow and yellow-green, and violet and red-violet. Yellow-green becomes a type of warm, even though it has established a coolness, and red-violet becomes a type of cool even though somewhat warm by nature. The yellow-green is a combination of one warm and one cool color, giving the yellow a certain cool quality. The red-violet is a combination of one warm and one cool, as well, producing a cool-ness to the red.

This highly abstracted painting is constructed of rigid orange verticals and calm horizontals of yellow, red-orange and red. De Stael builds his landscape by incorporating a warm analogous color pallet into the composition.

If we were to use temperature of color as a reference to this painting, we would then have to say that it perhaps reflects a warm summer day. On the other hand, if we were to use the color symbolically, we may be tempted to call it a cool autumn day.

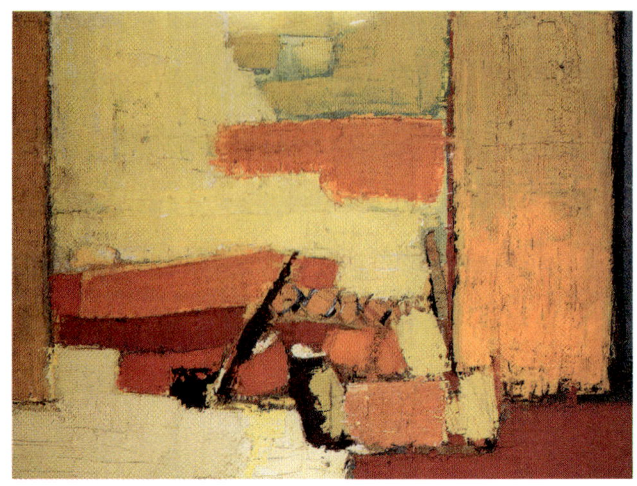

Countryside by Nicolas De Staël.
© 2003 Artists Rights Society (ARS), New York/ADAGP, Paris.

Below, *André Lhote* creates an analogous warm and cool harmony by using blue, blue-violet, violet, red-violet and red. Although there are both warm and cool hues, the overall effect is that of a somewhat warm composition. The redness of the figure, with the warm red-violet, seems to slightly dominate the temperature of the painting. The combination of warm and cool reflects a moderate temperature zone, to say the least.

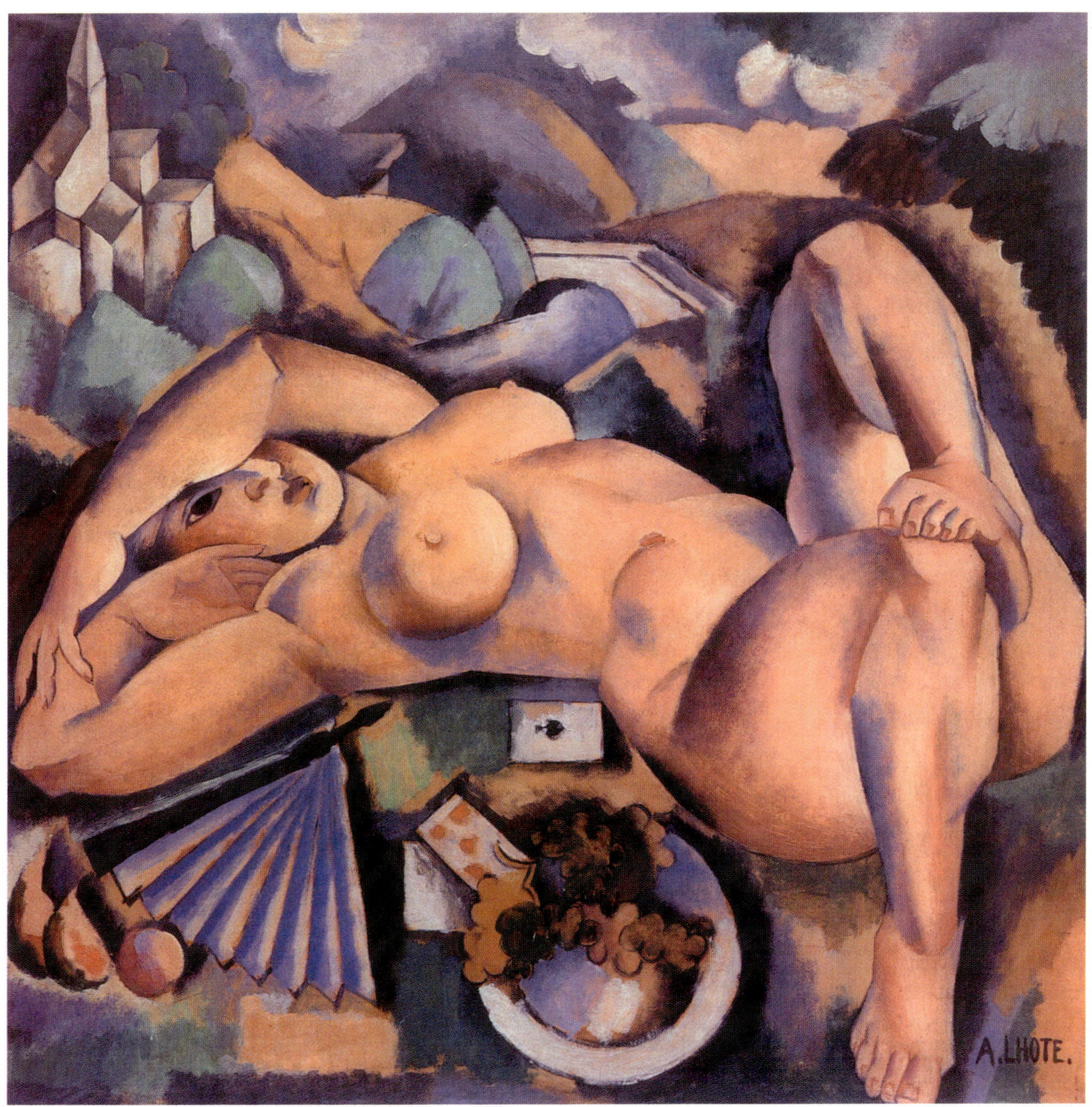

Bacchante by André Lhote.

Japan: A Land of Color Harmony

Since the earliest recorded history of the Japanese, color harmony has been an important aspect of the culture. In fact, color is at the core of its aesthetic sentiments, as we will see early in the Heian period and then in the newer and more contemporary Japan.

Color is especially at the center of concerns for architecture, ceremony, dress (fabric design), and the Japanese garden. We will take a brief look at the specific color harmonies that represent Japan and the sentiment of its people.

Two Color Harmonies for Two Different Japans

Red and green dyadic harmony is part of Japan's history, from early times. A typical scene that exemplifies the recognition of Japanese landscape is the saturated red architecture contrasted with the green foliage of nature. There already exists the symbolical harmony, or at least commonness of materials, between architecture and nature, in that the structures of wood have been constructed from the very source of its contrast, the product of the green leaf. The artificial structure of wood has been painted red, which is in complementary color to the natural green foliage.

In the frame below we see a 50/50 balance of red and green, where neither color overpowers the

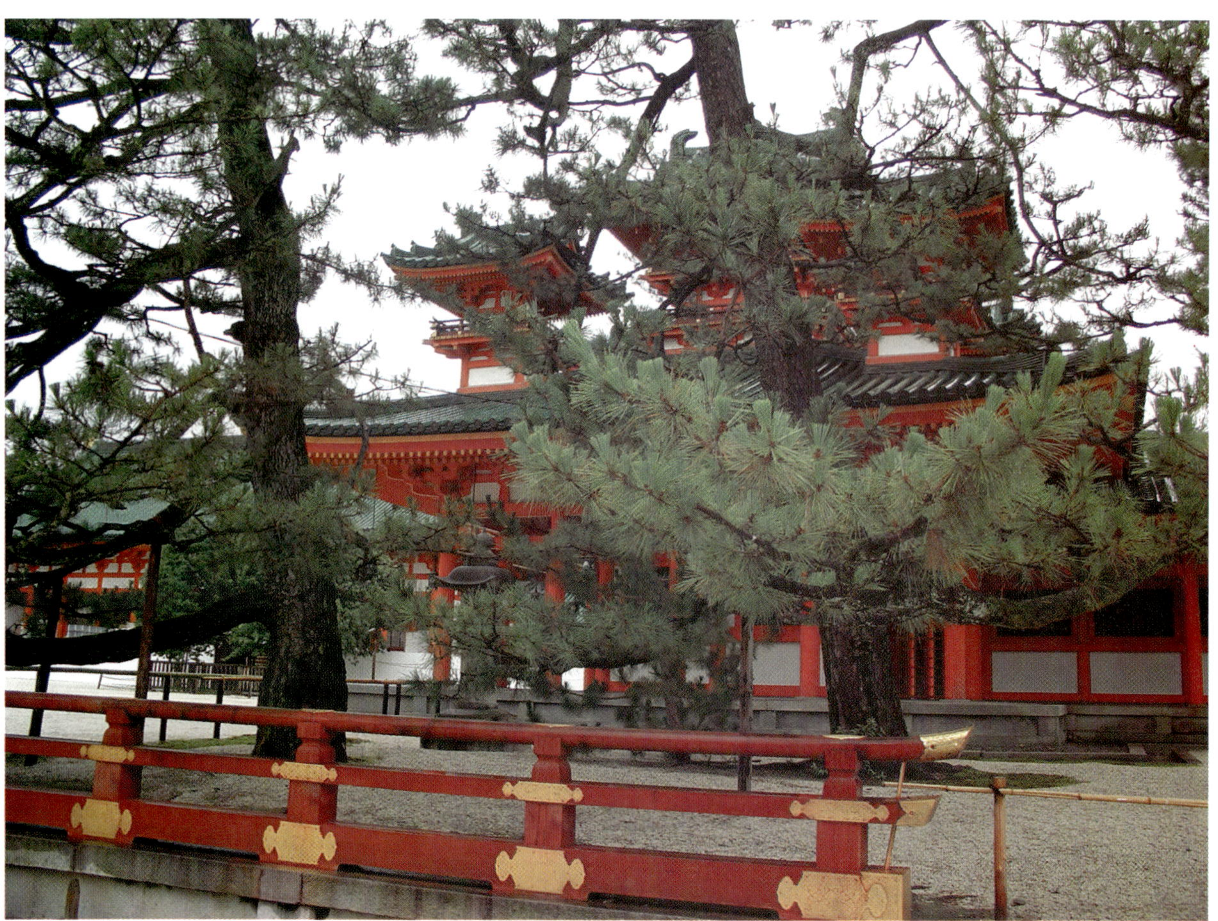

Heian Shrine, Kyoto, Japan.
Photo by Alan Burner.

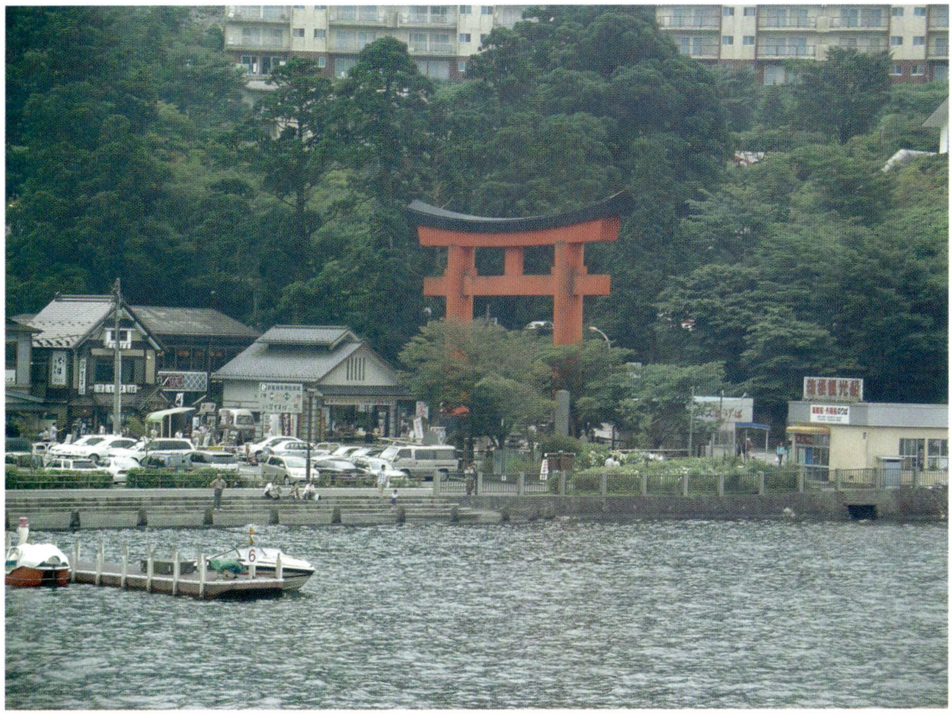

Tori Gate at Hakone, Japan.
Photo by Alan Burner.

other. It is this *dyadic color harmony* that prevails all over traditional Japan, and represents traditional Japanese color harmony. In a broader range of green landscape, it is the green which complements the red, and the red complements the green.

The red Tori gate in the distance is most definitely a focal point, and yet it does not dominate the entire town because of the enormous amount of green landscape. The green of the surrounding area gives greater saturation to the gate, and the red of the gate certainly produces a more saturated green. It is the saturated red, which denotes *importance* in architecture, and it is the contrast of these two colors that signifies that which is constructed, as opposed to that which is natural.

It is also the effect of red and green dyads that create harmony with the garden itself. In the *Component of a Garden Shrine* composition, the light indigo ground of stonework serves to separate the natural from that which is not. The grayness of rock surfaces gives equal credibility to both the red and the green of the composition.

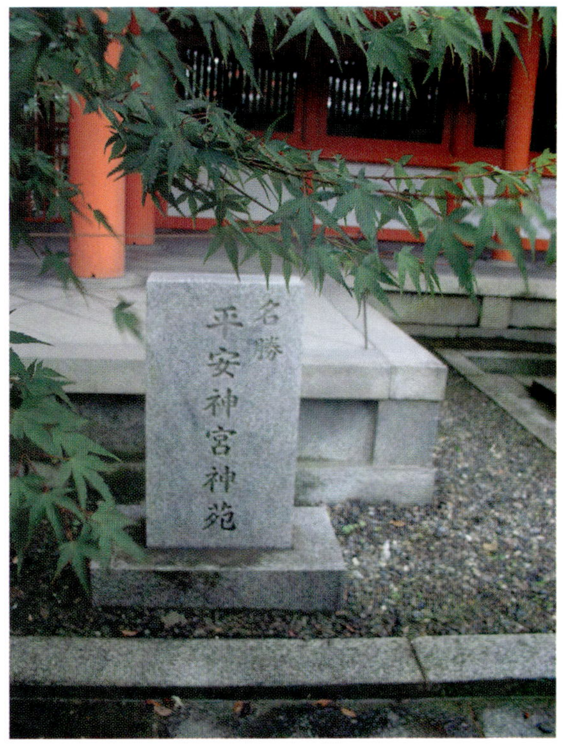

Component of a Garden Shrine.
Photo by Alan Burner.

Basically, the pond scene (below) is a *monochromatic* green color harmony, excepting the person in the center wearing red. We could almost call this contrast of extension, had the red patch been just a bit larger. Notice the variance of green values in the garden. All the values of green foliage are planned very carefully, for optimal effect.

The monochromatic greens in the garden's foliage had a very quieting effect on students and faculty members. The tranquility in such a calm color harmony, is quite amazing. Add a soft, steady rain to the mix, and you will find it difficult to leave. The careful planning and placement of green hues are the success of this color harmony.

Elegant moments of harmony
Perhaps Murasaki's pond.
A work of art in beauty's rest
Rain splashed surface
Dances on lily pads of green.
Washed tranquil from the world
My heart is at peace
I can love again.

Shijo, Kyoto, June 2004

It is often the case, whereby one finds it impossible to express adequately, the experience of a given moment in time. As artists and designers, we struggle to express those times with words, music, and color

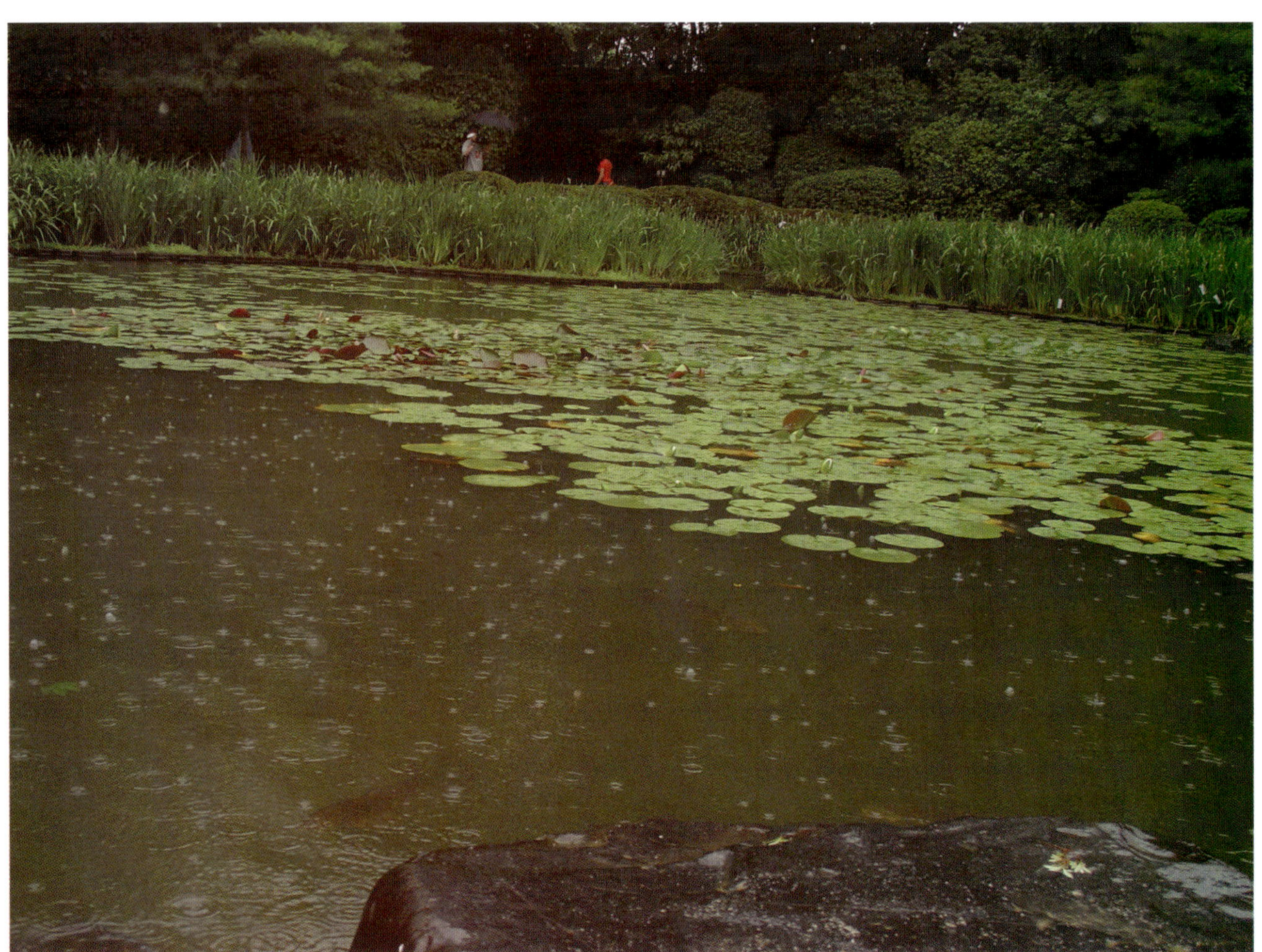

Heian Shrine Pond on a Rainy Day, Kyoto.
Photo by Alan Burner.

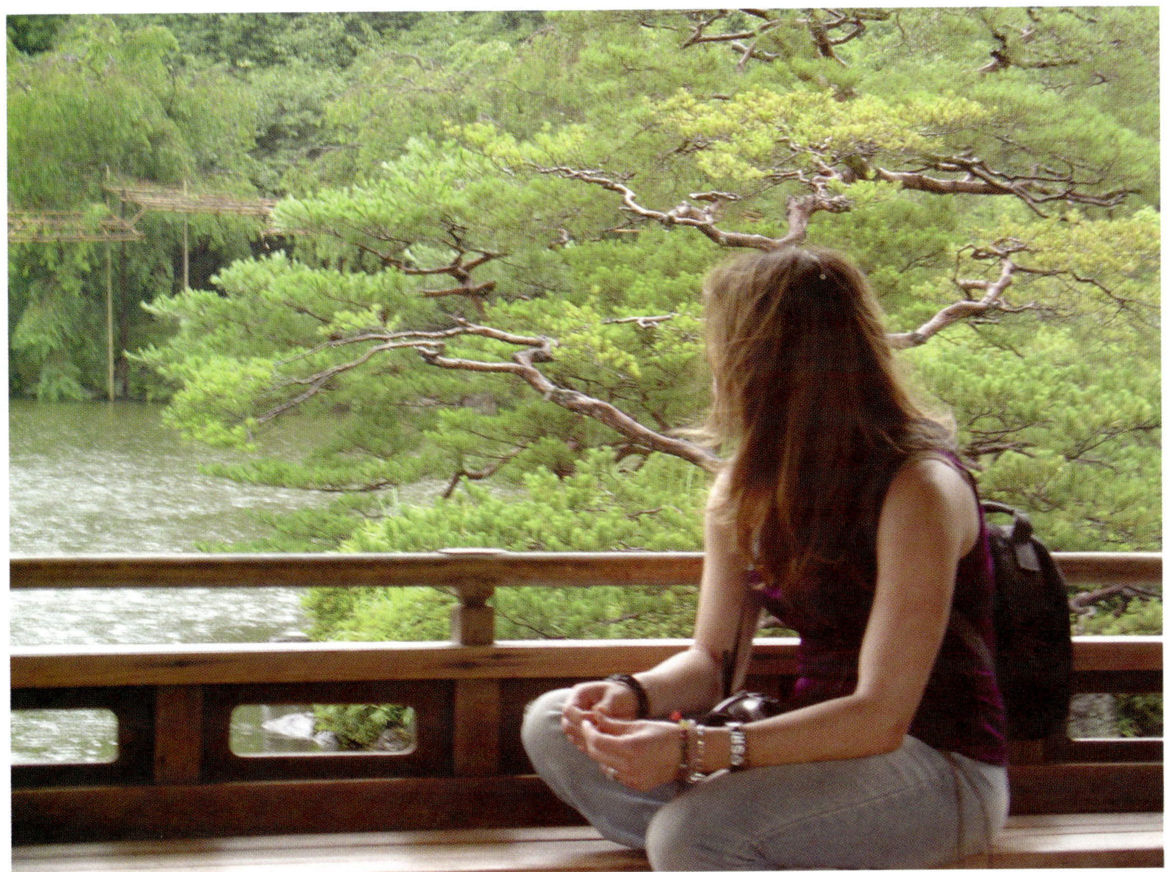

Remembering a Sacred Moment of Tranquility with Kristi. Heian Shrine Pond, Kyoto, Japan.
Photo by Alan Burner.

visuals, often to no avail. The more that we understand the issues with color attributes, in this case *harmony*, the more proficient we become in conveying our message. Let us not forget that it is the message or content of the color visuals that is responsible for translating the information to the viewer or customer. Color is mood!

We have briefly discussed the typical colors which represent the older order of Japan, as well as, the traditional colors of Japan. Now, lets take a look at the colors of *contemporary* or current day society in Japan today, specifically within its larger cities. There is, of course, the old and the new, which exist side by side currently within most larger cities, but we want to focus on Japan's largest city, in order to make a solid point.

Flashes of primary colors yellow, blue and red are everywhere in the city of Tokyo. These triadic color harmonies have become symbolic of the new modern age for Japan's largest cities, especially Tokyo. This is not really surprising, since the primary triad color harmony is the most powerful of all harmony combinations, and the idea is to capture the buyer's attention. At first sight, it would seem as though one sign would distract from the others, but it is the overall effect that draws crowds into the street. The Japanese are great team workers. By day, the streets are fairly calm and business is as usual. At night, signage had better be able to produce at least the same level of energy as the next, or one's business is liable to be engulfed in the night storm of primary harmonies.

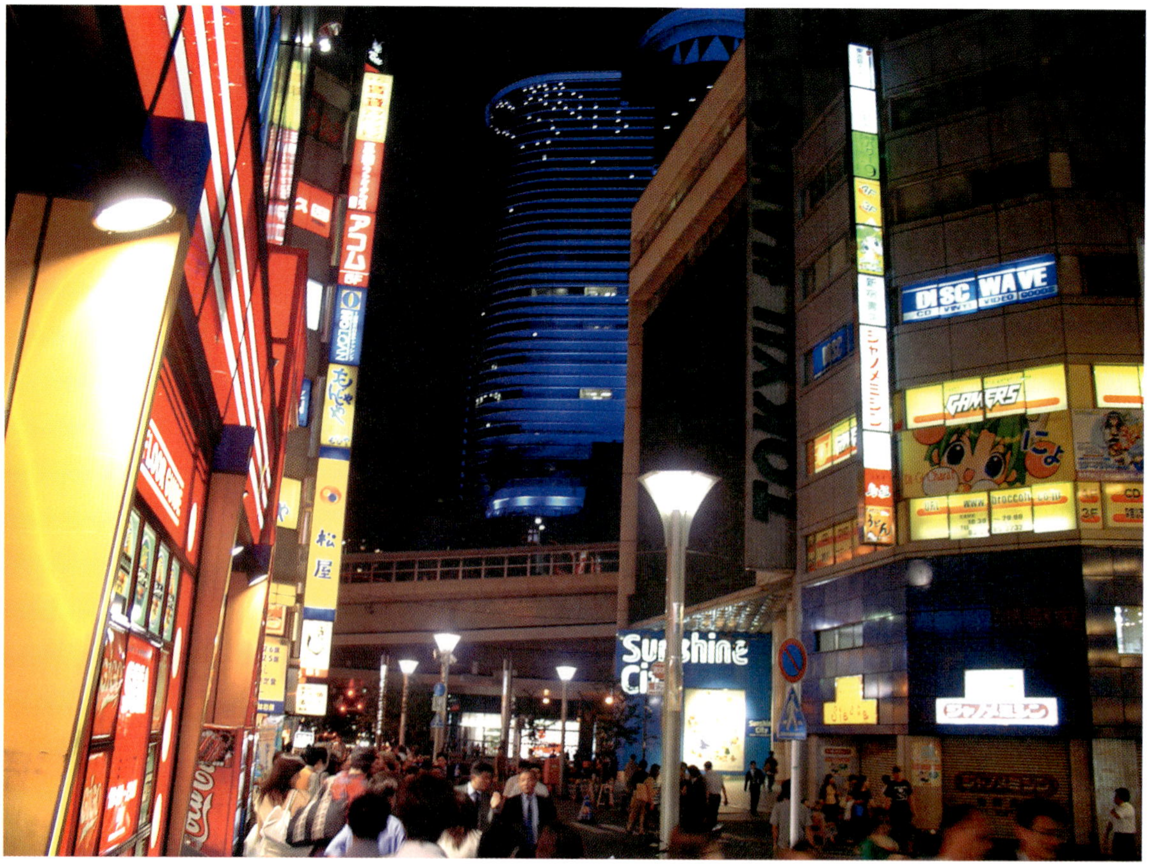

One of Many Tokyo Shopping Districts.
Photo by Alan Burner.

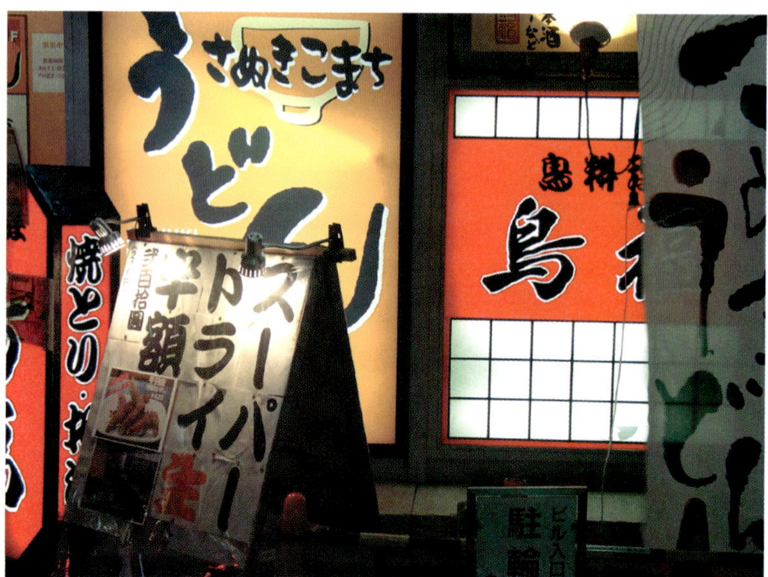

Small Udon Shop: Signage Must Compete Also. Tokyo.
Photo by Alan Burner.

Even the small stores must struggle to keep up with the energy and excitement of colors generated. By day all businesses are at equal standing, but by night when the crowds come out, the competition of color signage is intense.

A typical Tokyo shopping district (see surrounding images) is not simply amplified with visual primary harmonies, but color is audible as well. As one strolls the street, loud and commensurably energetic music seems to replicate the city's *visual clamor*. It is the symbolic stimulus blender, where all of the senses seem to overload into the proverbial buying frenzy. The trap has been set and is sprung. Basically, the energy of the city's yellow, red and blue harmony creates the energy, which requires further support in the form of music. The city is the new Japanese society, which is in direct contrast with the old traditional quiet complementary harmonies of red and green. This is but one example to illustrate the emotional and mood appeal of color harmony—one is tranquil, and one is energized.

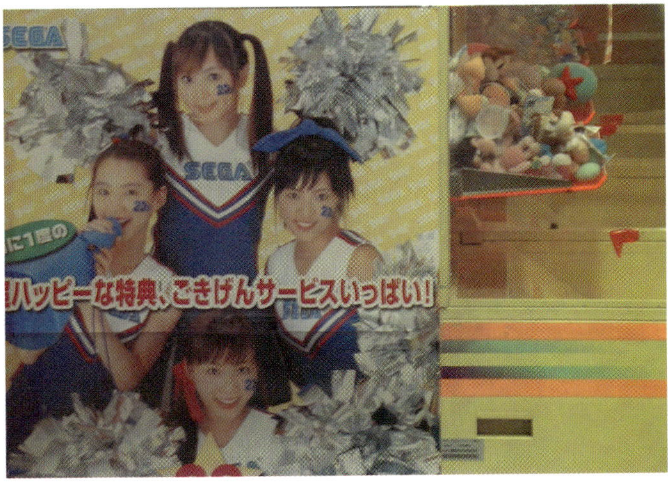

Primary Colors Prevail on Sega Poster, Tokyo.
Photo by Alan Burner.

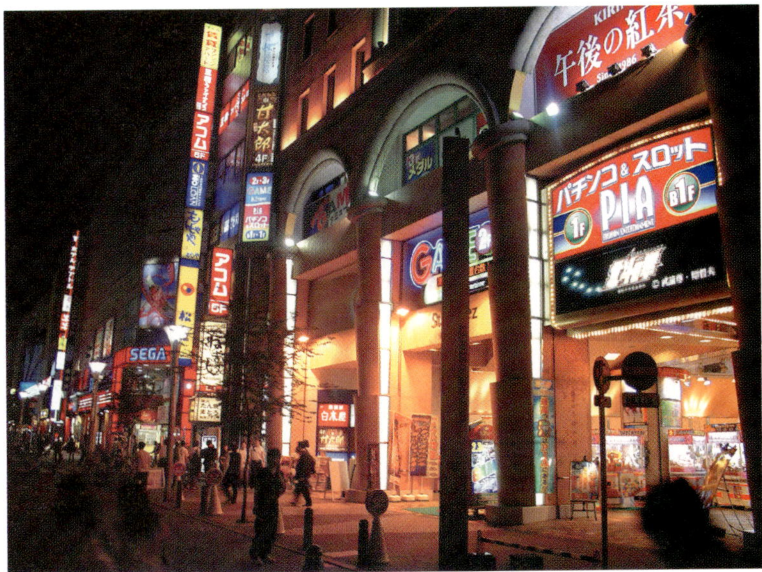

Primary Harmonies of a Game Palace Lure the Customer, Tokyo.
Photo by Alan Burner.

Introduction to Japanese Heian Period Color Harmony and Aesthetic Sentiment

Another important feature, and focus of this chapter on traditional Japanese color harmony, takes us back one thousand years ago to the Heian period in Japan; in particular, the aristocratic population of nobility up to the Emperor himself. This was a very important time for Japanese history and the development of Japanese aesthetic sentiment. Our basis for this period will center around Japan's most important literary achievement, the novel known as *Genji Monogatari,* or the *Tale of Genji.*

The author of this novel, the *Lady Murasaki Shikibu,* wrote this almost exactly a thousand years ago, the closest estimation is between 1004–1006. This novel is one of the worlds longest fictional texts, and is clearly Japan's most acclaimed novel throughout its history. The *Genji Monogatari* in Japan would be commensurate to *Shakespeare* in England, in terms of literary achievement and fame. All school children study the Tale of Genji in Japan. The novel is a fifty-four chapter love story, that takes place in eleventh century court life in Japan. It is Japanese aristocracy at its best—the emperor, empress, princesses, princes, ministers of the left and right, and ladies-in-waiting—all contribute to court life as aristocrats. They are concerned with a host of political factions, which helps to install them or their son's and daughters in a higher position within court life. The tale centers around Prince Genji, who experiences victory and defeat at court, the joys of life as an aristocrat and the grief of exile, all from his own doings.

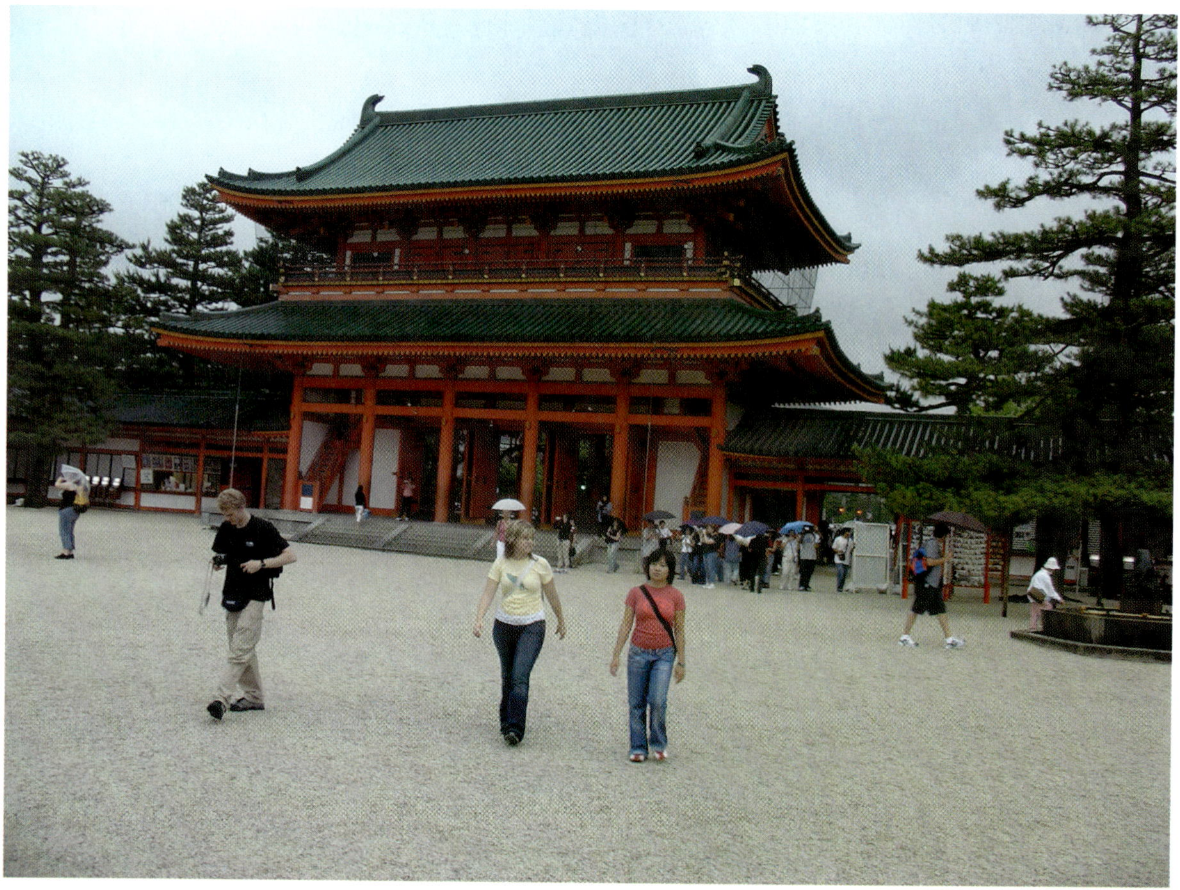

Heian Shrine with Author's Students, Kyoto, Japan, 2004.
Photo by Alan Burner.

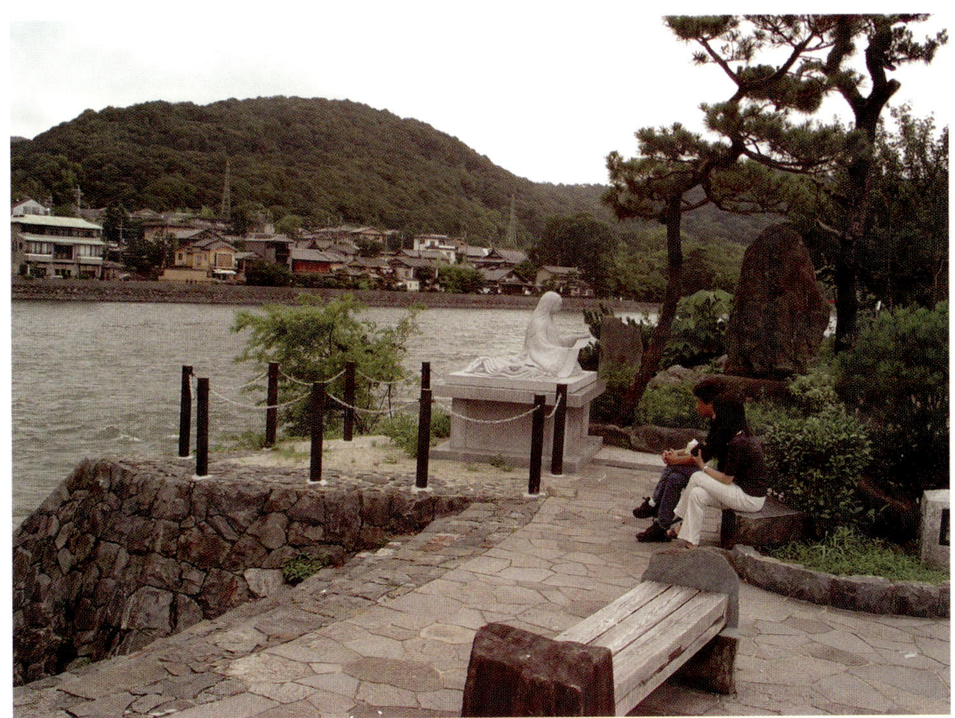

Gravesite of Murasaki Shikibu in Northern Kyoto.
Photo by Alan Burner.

The tale begins with color as an important issue. The author's name, *Murasaki* means *purple,* and part of her family name means *wisteria,* which is a lavender cascade of clustered blossoms, typically seen around Japanese gardens in the spring. The word lavender (light purple or violet) refers to *affinity*. You will see in the following essay, that affinity is a very important word. The fact that Murasaki Shikibu's name makes reference to these things gives important clues to look for within the essay itself.

Within the Japanese Heian garden itself, color was (as it still is) an important issue: the proximity of lighter greens to darker greens for contrasts; the positioning of moderate greens as opposed to intermediate areas of color, and so on. The appropriate colors of bark, such as the red bark of a pine tree, the light-red flower of a cherry tree, or the white of a lotus blossom, are equally important in their placement.

Within court life, there is also the all important aesthetic of appropriate dress. Fabric colors and motifs of the season must be appropriately layered to match the colors of a spring garden, for example, or autumn colors. For a lady to display poor taste in assembling the wrong color harmonies, would mean a certain loss of status at court. The knowledge of

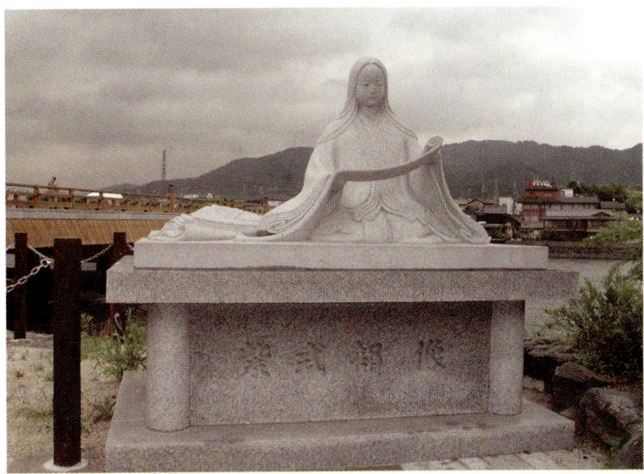

Close-up of Murasaki Shikibu's Gravesite in Northern Kyoto.
Photo by Alan Burner.

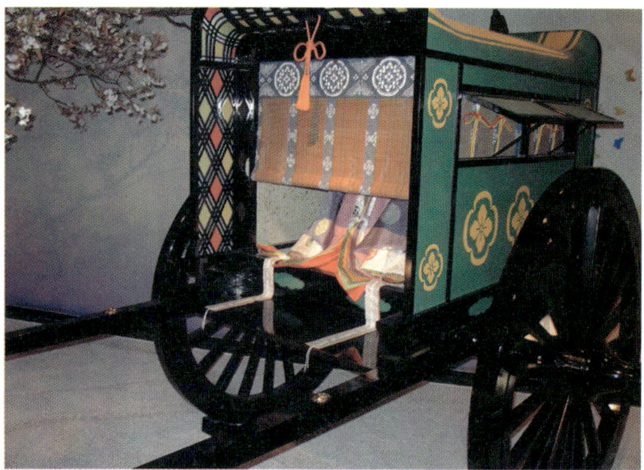

Court Carriage with Typical Layered Robes for Women, Genji Museum, Northern Kyoto.
Photo by Alan Burner.

proper color harmony uses at court was imperative for a lady.

Color was at the center of aesthetics, but there was much more to it. It was the court ladies who had command of artist sensibilities. Painting, poetry, music and writing were mostly the prowess of the aristocratic women. A woman's worth had much to do with her accomplishments in the arts. In fact, it is believed that in reality, it was *The Tale of Genji* that was largely responsible for the installation of Murasaki Shikibu at court.

Murasaki, both in the *Genji Monogatari* and the author, were gifted in the arts—painting, poetry, writing, and music. They had a special affinity for

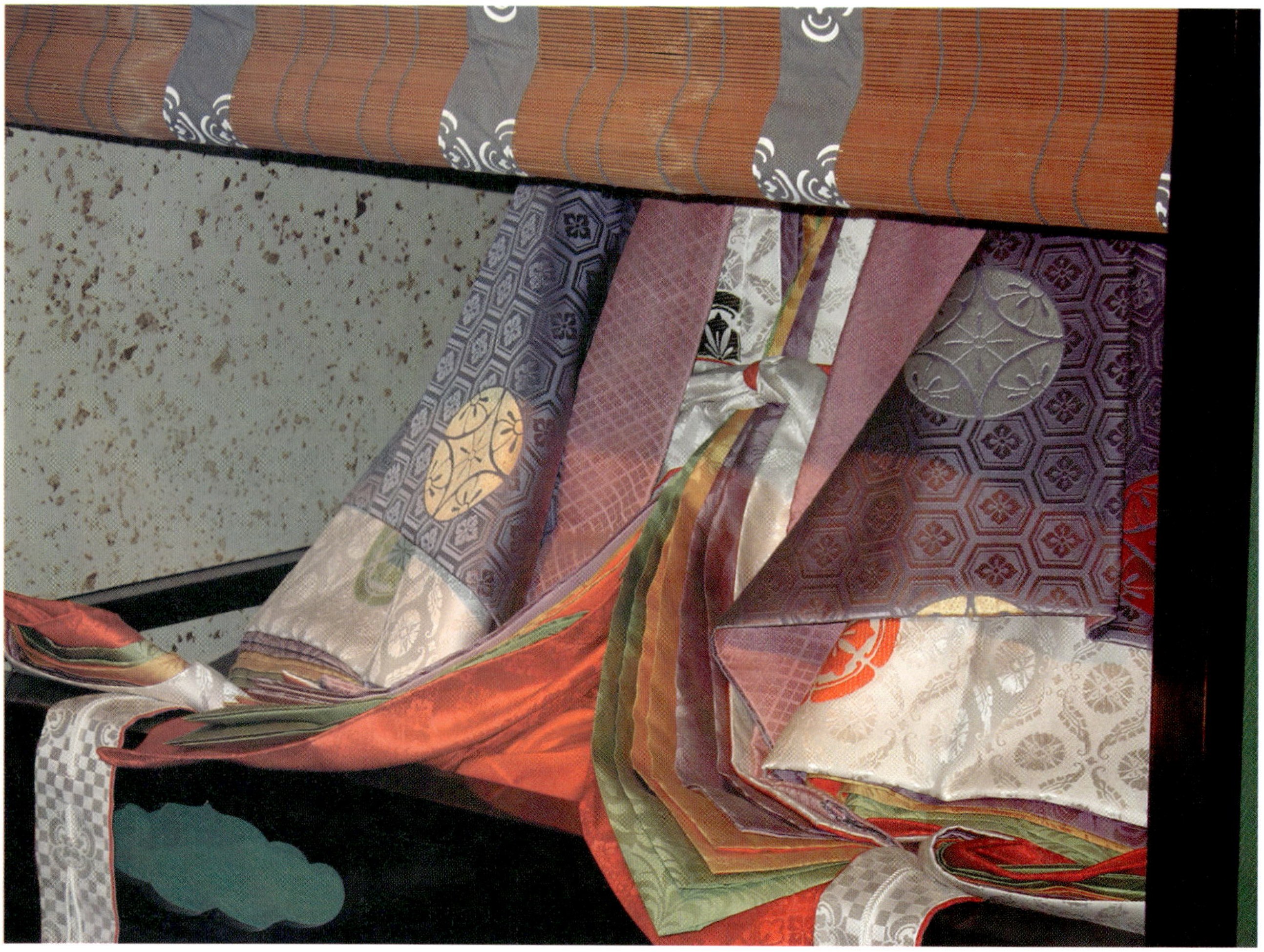

Typical Layering of Court Lady's Robes, Genji Museum, Northern Kyoto.
Photo by Alan Burner.

harmony, with many art forms, as well as color. Here, a mock of Prince Genji is seen "peeking" to catch a rare glimpse of Murasaki playing the koto.

Below, a very early morning at Atami, Japan, is caught with a calm, quieting monochromatic blue color harmony. Note that the tranquility factor differs from the Heian pond (page 244), with its green monochromatic color harmony, and Atami Bay's (below) blue harmonies create very sedate or tranquil environments. Both the Heian Shrine's pond green monochromatic color harmony and the Atami Bay Blue harmonies are the result of a very sedate environment. It is easy to see why blues and greens are felt as calm colors.

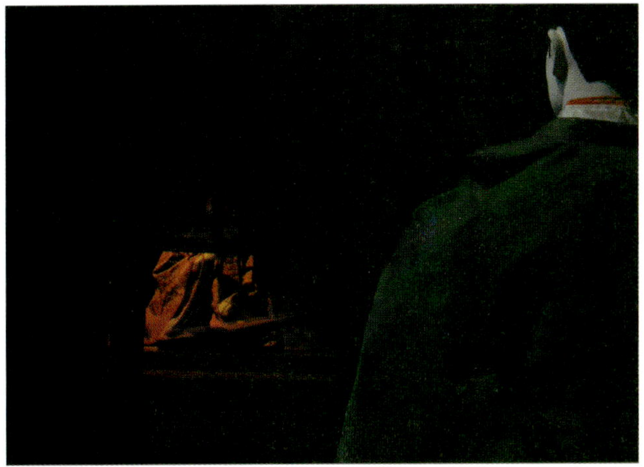

Genji Steals a Look at Murasaki's Musical Prowess, Genji Museum, Northern Kyoto.
Photo by Alan Burner.

Atami Bay, Atami-shi, Shizuoka.
Photo by Alan Burner.

A Case for Color Harmony: Japan 785 A.D. to 1186 A.D.

Color harmony is based on methodical color associations. Harmony continues to be the convention by which particular themes are established, as well as mood development and the creation of specific emotional content. These color accords are not exclusive to one culture, but are the vital link to expression for most social orders in the world today.

We find that by traveling through times past there have been standard color harmonies established, yet they have varied greatly from culture to culture though the stretch of time. Certainly we cannot expect all families of colors to have the same meaning for every group of peoples, yet no matter what group of people we belong to, we all understand the value of color harmonies. Whether by the creation of mood through color, or the ability to focus attention to one or more areas in a composition, or the symbolical overtones, we intuitively understand harmonic legitimacy. Familiar color associations can be seen around the world. As we look at certain ethnic groups, we consider the costume form of dress of peoples in Africa, Polynesia, China and Japan, or the Native American Indians across the United States, to name a few.

The organization of harmonious color schemes requires a certain sensibility. One culture in the distant past, particularly sensitive to this, was from the continent of Asia. As we travel back a thousand years in time, we visit the mother of aesthetic awareness—the Heian period in Japan. Here, emperors and empresses ruled over an aristocratic court of superior aestheticians, as princes and princesses procured the ultimate of all art forms. Whether dealing with aesthetics or politics the Japanese, in some way or another, made important color decisions on a day-to-day basis.

Japan, 785 to 1186 a.d.

Color played one of its most important historical roles within the ranks of Japanese aristocracy, during the turn of the first millennium. Nobility wove color harmony into the warp and woof of court life, from dress habits to garden aesthetics. One of the single most important aesthetic aspects, or art forms of the day, was the particular attention paid to how one was to dress each day. The obsession with court dress was practiced by all aristocrats, and was an important aesthetic statement about one's taste and sensibility, as well as one's position at court. This was particularly true of women in high court positions.

Interestingly enough, women had far fewer steps in their rank structure than did men. Yet what they lacked in color rank steps, was more than compensated for in the number of layers of clothing required for females. In fact, as we will see, the splendor of color in women's dress created a dazzling spectacle, which could only have been described by *comparing the scene to a painting.*[1]

Let's begin our harmony studies, by making critical observations about this unique culture, specifically its dress habits, as well as the total aristocratic court scene.

Dress Code and Rank System in Heian Court

In the Heian Court ranking system there were 30 grades of subject rank. With only a few exceptions, all of the highest three ranks, and most of the fourth and fifth ranked subjects, were actually permitted to attend the emperor at what was referred to as the Courtier's Hall. People from the fifth rank and up

[1]*Murasaki Shikibu, Her Diary and Poetic Memoirs*, Bowring, Richard. Princeton University Press, 1982 Page 49, sc. 7. Murasaki Shikibu refers to Lady Saisho as she sleeps; "She lay with her head pillowed on a writing box, her face all but hidden by a series of robes, dark red lined with green, purple lined with dark red, over which she had thrown a deep crimson gown of unusually glossy silk; she made an enticing scene. Almost convinced that she had stepped right out of a painting, I pulled back the sleeve that covered her face."

were considered the high ranking nobility, therefore; the sixth rank and down were considered low ranking, or minor positions.

The importance of dress in rank for the aristocrats was essential. The restrictions of color that were imposed at court allowed others to interpret the rank of another, even from a distance. This signaled what form the approaching relationship would take before actual human contact, and the color itself would make it possible to discern the difference between a courtier of the fifth rank, and that of a sixth ranking courtier.

Since it was those of the 5th rank and above who received most of the attention at court, it is appropriate to focus on these higher ranks, particularly on the top three ranks. The lower ranks were not as elaborately dressed as the higher aristocrats. It was the visual structure of color harmonies combined that would indicate rank, which was more profound and well defined in the higher orders. In order to concentrate and focus on the vast complexities of all the ranks of dress, both men and women would typically allow themselves the occasional distraction of *okashi*.[2] This is a particularly relevant and important expression in aristocratic court dress, as it relates to its affinity with nature. It is the quality and sensibility of *okashi* that draws our attention to the beauty and awe of court dress. It is that sudden awareness of beauty in court ceremony, with its various displays of color and motion, that forms the concept of the court's affinity with nature.

Dress Code and Types of Gowns for Women

Dress codes varied depending on the type of function which was being performed. Everyday dress was different than ceremonial dress, just as clothing worn in the spring time was in contrast to autumn, winter, or summer wear. Dress was traditionally changed before each of the four seasons began. This meant that specific colors represented each of the four seasons, and the robes of the aristocrats were changed accordingly. Consider the following example as Kenshi prepares her ladies-in-waiting for the Hojogi retreat:

> "That evening, the ladies-in-waiting assembled before her in all their finery. Princess Teishi wore a coat in fallen-leaf colors over aster robes. Kenshi was a white figure, her two or three robes matched by her complexion." [3]

The particular colors, textile types, and layers involved, could become quite complex depending on the occasion and office held by the person in question. Also, court dress, governmental dress, and attire of those residing at home varied as well. It is because of the infinite complex nature of aristocratic dress codes, that I have decided to concentrate on court dress of the higher ranks for women. It was

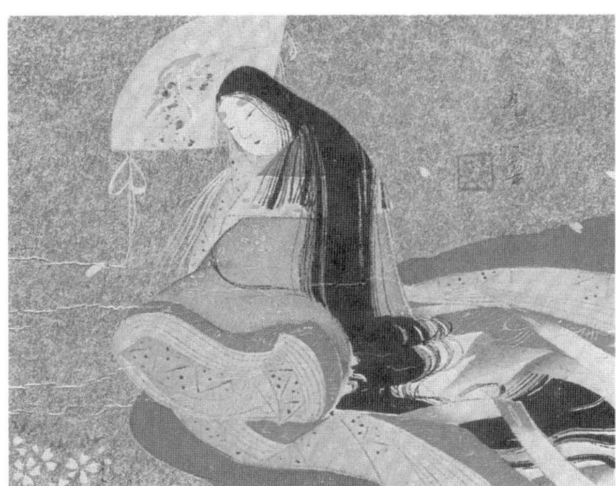

Typical Court Dress
[Also see Ladies in Waiting of Lady Tamakazura's Court (detail), last page of this chapter]
From the Genji Monogatari Emakimono

[2]OKASHI. Okashi is the term used to express the beauty of the moment. Okashi is based on surface beauty such as court ceremony, color, action, and fabrics. Okashi can be expressed seasonally as spring. Spring illustrates the suddenness of being awe struck over beauty, as the new blossoms discovered on a tree, or an immense rainbow after a rainstorm. Spring, for example, is very Okashi!

[3]*A Tale of Flowering Fortunes*, William H. and Helen Craig McCullough. Stanford University Press 1980, Stanford, CA Page 744, Vol II.

not unusual for a court lady to wear as many as fifteen layers of fabric types. Some of these variables will be covered later in the body of this text.

Fabric in Rank

Listed below are the fabrics that were restricted for wear according to rank and office. It is important to remember that certain types of fabric and color harmonies were to be worn according to rank. There were even restrictions about the appropriateness of color to fabric combinations. Certain color and textile harmonies were often considered either appropriate or inappropriate, depending on the event and time of year. These conventions applied to both women and men.

Lower Rank: Plain and unfigured fabric, and bombycine.

High Rank: Damasks, gossamers, brocades, and certain types of embroidery.

Highest Rank: Deep *red* damask, embroidered *green* silk, and complex embroidered scenes on silk.

Many of the textiles seemed to indicate a certain kind of affinity with the body, clothing, and nature itself. The human form, natural textiles, and the physical aspects of nature will also be discussed in this text. We will analyze this particular form of affinity by illustrating that court fashion was the harmonious link between the human body and nature.

Dress Definitions for Women

The following are a couple of examples and descriptions of formal court dress, as well as the types of fabrics (for men's dress see the supplementary notes).

Jacket (Karaginu): This was the outermost piece, and was usually the most elaborate. It was made from a variety of different silks, and depending on rank, it could be very elaborate. Sophisticated embroidery was common on this piece in the higher ranks. It was waist length.

Mantle (Uwagi): Refers to full length, but falls short of being the same length as the trousers. The mantle could be either printed fabric or plain. Mantles were made of different types of silk; bombycine or brocade.[4]

Robes (Itsutsuginu): Refers to sets of unlined robes which are combined together to create a specific color. Usually made of various silk gauze materials, gossamers, and damasks[4] The first few layers are normally gauze, with the remaining layers being less sheer, made of either gossamer or damask. Layers can be as few as three and as many as fifteen.

Gown (Uchiginu): Refers to trousers worn under the layers of lined robes. Most often, this piece was a crimson color, and made from beaten silk.

Train (Mo): The train was the longest piece. Usually made from silk, and/or brocade.

Rank Offices of Women

Before listing rank as it relates to women, it is important to point out that official rank was not awarded to women. Rank existed more in the form of "offices held" by women, which gave her commensurate privileges with a man's rank, but without the same authority. These were *palace* ladies-in-waiting, as opposed to ladies-in-waiting in *private* households.

[4]GAUZE. A very sheer fabric made from silk, usually worn closest to the body in layering techniques.
GOSSAMER. Sheer silks, but less sheer that gauze.
DAMASK. Another one of the silks. Because of it's weave, produces a very satiny effect. Used as lining with gossamer.
BOMBYCINE. Also a silk fabric. Bombycine is a rich fabric between damask and brocade.
BROCADE. Any silk that has been woven into patterned colors, other than the sheer silks.

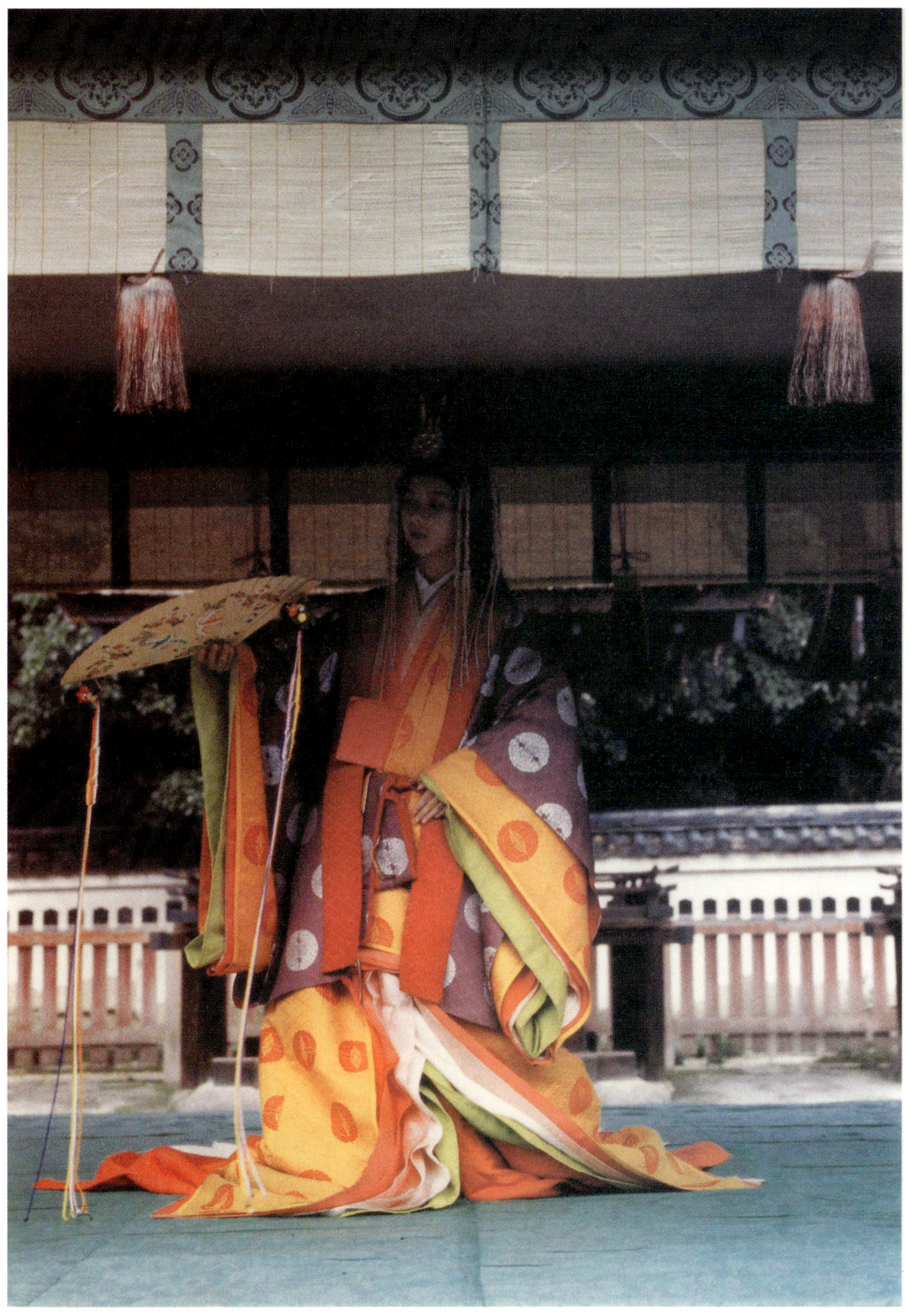

Head Priestess of Shimogamo Jinja. She Wears the Juni-hitoe, Twelve Layers of Silk Color Harmony, Weighing over Thirty Pounds. This is similar to Robes Worn in Tale of Genji.

Joro Class (upper grade): Small group of ladies who were authorized to wear the forbidden colors and fabrics. This group consisted of the *Mistress of the Wardrobe*, two *Principal Handmaids, assistant Handmaids* of the 3rd or 4th rank;—*daughters* and *granddaughters of the Ministers of State.*

Churo Class: (middle grade) This was the largest group, and consisted mostly of *Handmaids* and *Palace ladies*. (Myobu)

Gero Class (lower grade): These ladies helped to sew costumes and related work. Usually belonging to *daughters of Stewards* and *Shinto priests* of leading shrines. These ladies-in-waiting were selected for office according to their skills in calligraphy, poetry, artwork, music, taste in dress and manners. Usually, the lady who would demonstrate the highest degree of skill was the one who received the highest office at court.

Color Codes in Court Dress

One of the most complex problems in understanding court dress is that of the proper use of color. The applications can only be *generalized* here, since they varied considerably depending on rank and occasion, not to mention the exceptions granted for wearing certain colors. Below are the general color codes as they existed at Heian court:

Low Rank (6th rank and below): Pale reds, most blues, browns, and certain yellows.

High Rank (5th and above): Yellow-green, white, silver crimson, pale green, green over white lined with red, and yellow-green over red[5]

Highest Rank: *Forbidden Colors*[6]; red and purple combinations, purple, yellow-green figured material, and deep purple (strictly forbidden color)

Monks and Mourning Attire: Gray

The Story of Affinity within the Japanese Aristocracy

The primary objective of this survey is to determine if there was an effort on behalf of the Heian court aristocracy, to create the perfect affinity between themselves and actual nature. The main, or direct link in creating that affinity most certainly would have to exist within the realm of court dress. The establishment of three types of affinity links at court will be discussed as follows:

1. **Indirect link to indicate affinity** or intermediate links refer to implicating affinity through an alternate source, rather than a direct reference link. Indirect links include artwork, architecture, and interior furnishings. They are affinity indicators which are not as closely related to the person(s) in question.
2. **Surrogate link to indicate affinity** can be either a "stand-in" for the conventional link or method, or a substitute for the subject. Specifically, the exterior structured garden, or a person such as Ukifune can act as a surrogate link or form.
3. **Direct link to indicate affinity** can be seen in court dress (Fabric/clothing). Direct links are specific references to affinity. Directness must be involved with animate subject matter such as silk (silkworm), wisteria fiber (wisteria plant), and mulberry cloth (mulberry tree), are used as direct links, with the human form to create affinity with nature.

[5]Yellow-green over red could only be worn by the ladies-in-waiting of the Joro office (rank), and only pertains to jackets of figured silk, and to printed trains.

[6]Forbidden Colors. Forbidden colors could only be worn by those of the Imperial family, or the highest of court nobles. Forbidden colors varied somewhat with each new emperor.

The *direct link* is the most important of the three links, and is the chief connecting factor in aristocracy's affinity with nature. The various links will be discussed within the framework of four basic Japanese text sources:

1. **From *Genji Monogatari:*** the chapter "The Picture Contest." This chapter involved an art competition between the Lady Akikonomu and the daughter of To no Chujo. The contest was important politically, since the results would be the installation of Akikonomu (winner of contest) as consort to the Emperor.
2. **From *Genji Monogatari:*** the chapter "Butterflies." This chapter records another contest involving Akikonomu. The Lady Akikonomu's fall garden was challenged by the Lady Murasaki and her spring garden.
3. **From *The Pillow Book of Sei Shonagon:*** the chapter "The Lady of the Shigei Sha." Lady Shigei Sha sent a letter off to her sister, the Empress, informing her that she intended to visit her in the near future. The apartments of the Empress were decorated and cleaned to a greater degree than ever before, as well as preparation of the ladies-in-waiting who were also dressed more elaborately than normal.
4. **From *Genji Monogatari:*** the chapter "Ukifune." Ukifune is the illegitimate daughter of the eighth Prince, and half sister to Oigimi and Nakanokimi. She becomes the victim of two male courtier's desires, who's names are Kaoru and Niou, and is whisked away to a small mountain cottage. Politically she is weak, as she does not have strong court backing, and ends up living out the rest of her life secluded in the mountains. Ukifune was known for her beautiful hair and petite size.

Beginning with "The Picture Contest," we are told about an elaborate gathering of Heian court aristocrats in order to determine who was the most accomplished artist. This contest was very important, as it would determine the outcome of a *significant court appointment—t*he selection of consort to the Emperor.

Lady Fujitsubo, Emperor Suzaku's consort, decides that because of recent endless debates on aesthetics in court, and the large number of people involved, that she would split the art contest into two sides. On the left side would be the *Akikonomu faction*, favored by Prince Genji, and the *Kokiden faction* would be on the right, which was favored by To no Chujo. Each side had a number of ladies-in-waiting as participants, and each side was in serious competition for their respective ladies, Akikonomu and To no Chujo's daughter. The ceremony begins with the following scene:

> **"The day was appointed. The careful casualness of all the details would have done justice to far more leisurely preparations. The royal seat was put out in the ladies' withdrawing rooms, and the ladies were ranged to the north and south, and the courtier's seats faced them on the west. The paintings of the left were in boxes of *red sandalwood* on sappanwood stands with flaring legs. *Purple Chinese brocades* were spread under the stands, which were covered with delicate *lavender Chinese embroidery*. Six little girls sat behind them, their robes of *red* and their jackets of *white* lined with *red*, from under which peeped *red* and *lavender*. As for the right of Kokiden side, the boxes were of heavy *aloes* and the stands of lighter aloes. *Green Korean brocades* covered the stands, and the streamers and flaring legs were all in the latest style. The little page girls wore *green robes* and over them *white jackets* with *green linings*, and their singlets were of a *grayish green* lined with *yellow*. Most solemnly they lined up their treasures. The emperor's own women were in uniforms of the two sides."[7]**

[7] *The Tale of Genji*, Murasaki Shikibu, page 314.

It is significant to note that it was the ladies who sat near the paintings, not the men. In this description, the dress (fabric) of the ladies-in-waiting and the page girls began to resemble a oneness with the art work itself, not the men (it was the women who were the connoisseurs of art). If we examine the descriptions of the scene carefully, it becomes more difficult to separate the *inanimate art form from the animate.* It is also important to consider the following comparisons seen in the previous paragraph, in order to see this concept more clearly:

Paintings on the Left

1. Paintings in boxes of red sandalwood on sapponwood stands.
2. Purple Chinese brocades under stands.
3. Little girls wore red robes.
4. Jackets were white lined with red.
5. Red and lavender peeped from under the jackets.
6. Oborozukiyo dressed the same as the littlegirls

Paintings on the Right

1. Paintings in heavy aloes and boxes on lighter aloes stands.
2. Green Korean brocades covered the stands.
3. Little girls wore green robes.
4. Jackets were white with green lining.
5. Singlets were grayish green lined with yellow.
6. Kokiden dressed the same as the little girls.

The art of dress not only served as an aesthetic element as well as a messenger to signal that a competition was in progress, but also illustrated that the paintings had created a type of affinity with the fabrics worn by the ladies-in-waiting. The imagery and colors of the costumes as well as the paintings, would illustrate a considerable affinity, when considering the similarities of garden images and colors:

- The *red sandalwood* in contrast to the softer *tones of aloeswood*, yet the very fragrant quality of the aloeswood exits.
- Not only are the colors in contrasting complements, but the country from which the brocades originate are different. Also, the brocade is *under* the stands on the left, and *over* the stands on the right. As we continue down the list, *red robes* contrast and complement *green robes, red lining* to *green lining*, etc. Since the time of the year happens to be spring, it is significant to note the play of *color* symbolism in dress. An example of this is the *purple brocades* and the *green jackets*, symbolic of the *plum tree* with its *green leaves* contrasted with the *purple plums*. The *white blossoms* seen in the jacket contrasted with the *green leaves* in the lining, etc. This preview of comparisons serves to illustrate how an *indirect* link is involved with linking people to nature through art.

It is important to note here just exactly what types of paintings were presented. These paintings were known as *emakimono*, which essentially means "narrative paintings." The *emakimono* assumes the form of a hand scroll (presented in a wood box—see last page illustration). When rolled out from right to left a story appeared. First the narrative section preceded by painted scene, usually consisting of a minimum of six, but usually more, illustrations.

The Suma emakimono decided the fate of the contest in the end, and was brought out by Prince Genji. These paintings contained scenes of Genji's exile on the Suma coast, where he had experienced extreme hardships in his struggle with the forces of *raw nature*. Gradually, Genji became part of these natural surroundings, as the effects of raw nature continued to physically batter him down. His robes illustrated the same subdued colors as his natural surroundings as he was tormented by constant storms, and his robes were wet from the rain, as his body yielded to the winds of the Suma coast. With those images of the Suma coast in mind, the emotion of Genji's experience gripped those at court. They fought back the tears brought on by the visually powerful scrolls, as they felt the pain of their fellow aristocrat. Genji Monogatari records this:

> **"....but there was no describing the sure delicacy with which Genji had quietly set down the moods of those years. The assembly, Prince Hotaru and the rest fell silent, trying to hold back the tears. They had pitied him and thought of themselves as suffering with him; and now they saw how it had really been. They had before their eyes, the bleakness of those nameless strands and inlets. Here and there, not so much open description as poetic impressions, were captions in cursive Chinese and Japanese. There was no point now in turning to the painting offered by the right. The Suma scroll had blocked everything else from view. The triumph of the left was completed."[8]**

As the others looked on with To no Chujo, they were tremendously moved by the emotional content of the paintings. In fact, the *colors* and content of the artwork was so effective, that most of those present had to struggle just to keep back their tears, as their hearts and minds were at one with Genji. The question that remains is; how is it possible for a group of paintings to move people to such emotion?

In order to understand the emotional qualities of those paintings, it is necessary to establish the importance of the Emakimono, and it's linking ability. There were three basic functions of this art form:

1. **Entertainment:** The most beneficial aspect of these scrolls pertained to the ladies-in-waiting, who were basically women of leisure. What better way to pass the time than to produce a *color document*, or to enjoy a good story. With this abundance of time they were also able to perfect other art forms, such as writing, poetry, costume design (dress), music, and creation of the structured gardens.
2. **Competition:** Most importantly, and the particular purpose behind the picture contest, was the competition for court appointments. That very important political function was the reason for Akikonomu's installation as consort to the new Emperor; Genji had won the contest for her with his Suma scroll.
3. **Historical Documentation:** In Japan, these scrolls have provided valuable information, from one generation to the other. The "Emakimono" is the visual source of information for what we know about Japanese Heian/Kamakura court life.

Because of the entertainment, competition, and documentational factors, we can see some very good reasons why the court developed this unparalleled sensibility. The paintings, which had accompanying poems, most likely had the same effect on the court observers (Suma Scroll), as an emotionally moving film does in the 20th century.

It is important to re-emphasize the startling effect that the Suma scrolls may have had on the others. Their hearts and minds were at one with a man who had experienced a form of affinity with raw nature, as he began to blend with nature. Accustomed to living around the structured and protected environment of the court life, Genji had felt the untamed wrath of raw nature, suffering the repeated effects of the storm. The paintings reflected the colors of his agony.

Up to this point we have been dealing with the idea of an *indirect link, such as art.* However, before examining the concept of a *direct* link, it seems more in order to examine the notion of a type of *surrogate* link. Art, architecture, poetry, interior furnishings, can all be considered a "surrogate" link, depending on the subject. However, in this text the *strongest* link is more committed to the *structured garden* and *court dress.*

Certainly it can be said that in particular places and certain times of the year, the natural forces of nature can be very harsh in Japan. These forces are very

[8]*The Tale of Genji,* Murasaki Shikibu, pages 314–315.

frightening and destructive at times, as was the account of Genji's exile on the Suma coast. It seems as though the aristocrats at court experienced the Suma coast through an intercessor, or *surrogate link,* the painted colors of the emakimono compositions.

There were some possible reasons for the need of *surrogate* elements. Perhaps, because of the awesomeness of raw nature, they preferred to create their own environment, as they wanted to see it, rather than the way it actually appeared. Conceivably, being surrounded by such wealth and security for such a long period, they became too vulnerable to the insecurity offered by the real forces of nature. If that were true, a definite need for a substitute would have been created.

The *Lady Sei Shonagon's* aesthetic concepts, define very well why the surrogate system existed. Many times, the Lady Shonagon is the *direct* link. To see that clearly, we turn to the *Genji Monogatari* chapter "Butterflies."[9] In "Butterflies," the issue of the *garden as an affinity link* surfaces again. The subject of court dress becomes successor and superior over the structured garden, as the garden acts as a mediator between the aristocrats and real nature.

The Butterfly Conspiracy

In order to discuss this thoroughly, it is first necessary to go back to the earlier chapter "Maiden" in *Gengi Monogatari.* Akikonomu wrote to Murasaki in a poem about the beauty of her autumn garden, inferring that *autumn* was the superior month to display a garden. Months later, in the chapter "Butterflies," as Murasaki's *spring* garden began to flourish she decided that it was time to respond to Akikonomu about the superiority of spring. She not only responded to Akikonomu with a poem, but dressed up some of her little girls to represent butterflies and birds. Once they were fully costumed, they proceeded to Akikonomu's residence to deliver floral offerings from Murasaki, while Yogiri delivered the poem: "She chose eight of her prettiest little girls to deliver them, dressing four of them as birds and four as butterflies. The birds brought cherry blossoms in silver vases, the butterflies "yamabuki" in gold vases. In wonderfully rich and full bloom, they completed a perfect picture."[10]

There was a type of indirect reference in that scene, since the butterflies and birds were presented as a *perfect picture painting*. Yet at the same time, the *direct link* of affinity became more obvious in the *costumes of the children, as they fluttered around the garden.*

Affinity with nature was not only created within the confines of the garden, as we discussed about the *surrogate* link, but also in the *direct* link of dress. We not only observe the garden as an altered form of nature, but it can also be observed as a *motif* in the dress fabrics, art, and architecture. Imagine that we can see courtiers, ladies-in-waiting, and the children dressed with similar motifs all in the garden together. The furnishings as well as the apartment walls are finished in fine animal and floral motifs, which also correspond to those on the robes. As they move out into the garden, these motifs begin to merge with the actual forms of nature themselves. The *colors* match the *season*, as well as the infusion of *color* harmonies seen throughout the structures, gardens, paintings and fabrics. The picture becomes one of total affinity as the aristocrats—including the mock butterflies and birds (little girls)—move about within the natural elements that they represent.

All of the aristocrats were dressed with floral patterns and various motifs of nature. As they move among masses of blossoming plants and trees, they move in and out of similarly decorated interiors. Suddenly, the scene merges visually into a beautiful oneness—an infusion of affinity has been created. Consider the following account:

> **"The music for the dance of the Kalavinka bird rang forth to the singing of warblers, to which the waterfowl on the lake added their clucks and chirps, and it was with very great regret that the audience saw the dance come to an end. The**

[9]*The Tale of Genji,* Murasaki Shikibu, pages 418–429.
[10]*The Tale of Genji,* Murasaki Shikibu, page 422.

butterflies seemed to fly higher than the birds as they disappeared behind a low fence over which poured a cascade of yamabuki."[11]

Even the ending was perfect, as the butterflies and birds flew at different levels, both higher than the yamabuki fence. Suddenly they seemed to merge all together with the yamabuki, then in a moment they disappeared.

Akikonomu was greatly moved as she answered Murasaki's presentation:

"I weep in my longing to follow your butterflies. You put up fences of yamabuki between us."[12]

It was as if the Lady Akikonomu had felt a longing to experience this affinity with nature for a moment, as if to enter a dream state of oneness with those around her and nature. She had observed a visual blending of that scene, if only she could have been a part of it, to experience the *union of the elements.*

The affinity element is illustrated once more when Prince Hotaru appeared suddenly at the competition, only to have learned that Tamakazura (Genji's adopted daughter) was already receiving letters from many of the courtiers. Since he was also interested in her, he proceeded to attach a spray of wisteria in his cap, swaying around like a willowing plant. He then said; "If there were not something rather special to keep me here, I think I would be trying to escape. It is too much, oh, really too much." He then refused to drink any more, as he had consumed too much already. He continued by saying, "Lavender holds me and puts me in the mind of things. I mean, let them say what they will, to throw myself in."[13]

He divided the spray of wisteria at that point, and gave one of them to Prince Genji.

In Heian Japan, the meaning of the color *lavender* was *affinity*, and so the wisteria sprays were indicative of the Prince's interest in Tamakazura. Having given her father half of the wisteria flowers, he said:

"Please hold yourself in abeyance beneath these flowers, to judge if the plunge would have the proper effect."[14]

As we can see, affinity links were not always as dramatic and overwhelming as was the garden contest. Instead, it was subtle—the wisteria flower became a symbol of union between two people. Similarly, the color of lavender had reminded them of the union of two.

Seasonal dress was a powerful unifying element. When certain guests on Akikonomu's side arrived, they were issued formal attire with the *appropriate spring colors and motifs.* In order for people in court to successfully merge with nature a strict code was necessary. The codes for proper *colors*, fabrics, and prints were adhered to as each season changed from one to the other. The attempt to become part of nature in the fine art of dress sensibility was constantly sought after by court aristocracy.

The following record from the *Tale of Flowing Fortunes,* illustrates that spectacle of seasonal changes of color. At the *Golden Hall* (see following pages) dedication in the year 1022, a description of Kenshi's ladies by Michinaga, went like this:

"Viewed from a distance as a brilliant sun rose in the sky, the very blinds screening the ladies in attendance on the various personages seemed extraordinary, to say nothing of the scene as a whole—the bombycines in *fallen leaf (yellowish-brown lined with yellow), maidenflower (yellow lined with green), bellflower (blue lined with green), and lespedeza colors (reddish purple lined with green),* and the *violet* curtains, shading to *purple* at the

[11] *The Tale of Genji,* Murasaki Shikibu, page 423.
[12] *The Tale of Genji,* Murasaki Shikibu, page 423.
[13] *The Tale of Genji,* Murasaki Shikibu, page 421.
[14] *The Tale of Genji,* Murasaki Shikibu.

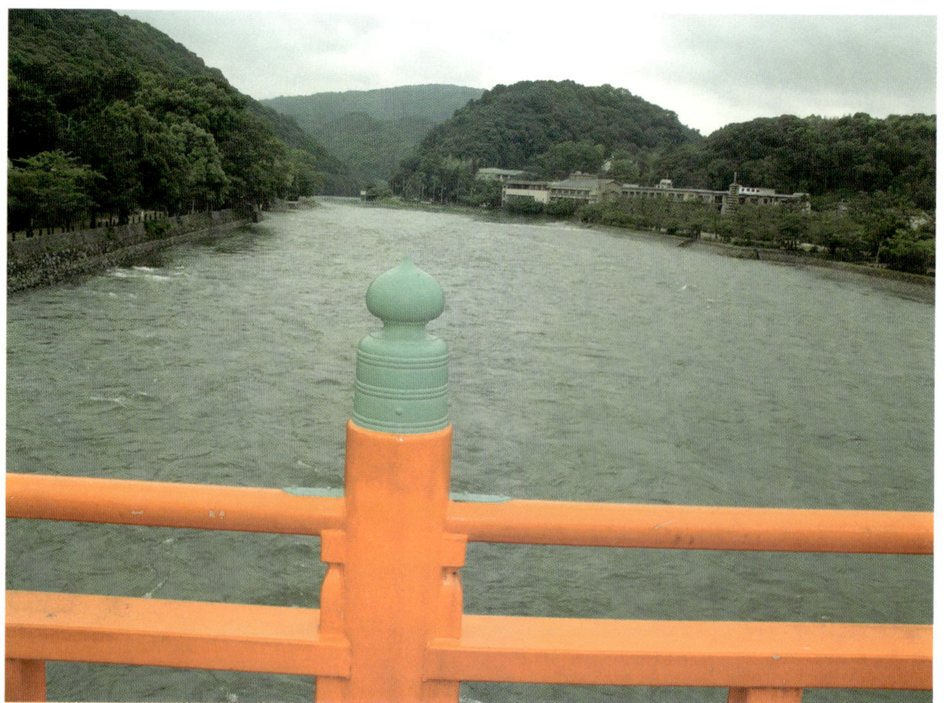

The hills of northern Kyoto, the area where Murasaki Shikibu wrote the *Tale of Genji*.
Photo by Alan Burner.

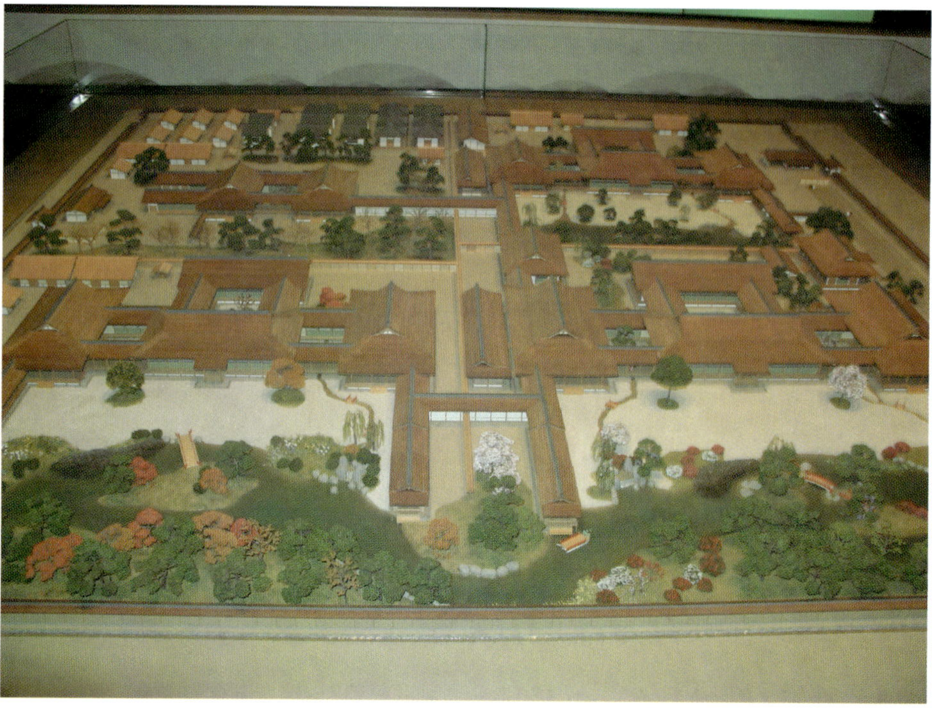

Model of the Heian Court Residences and Palace Area.
Photo by Alan Burner.

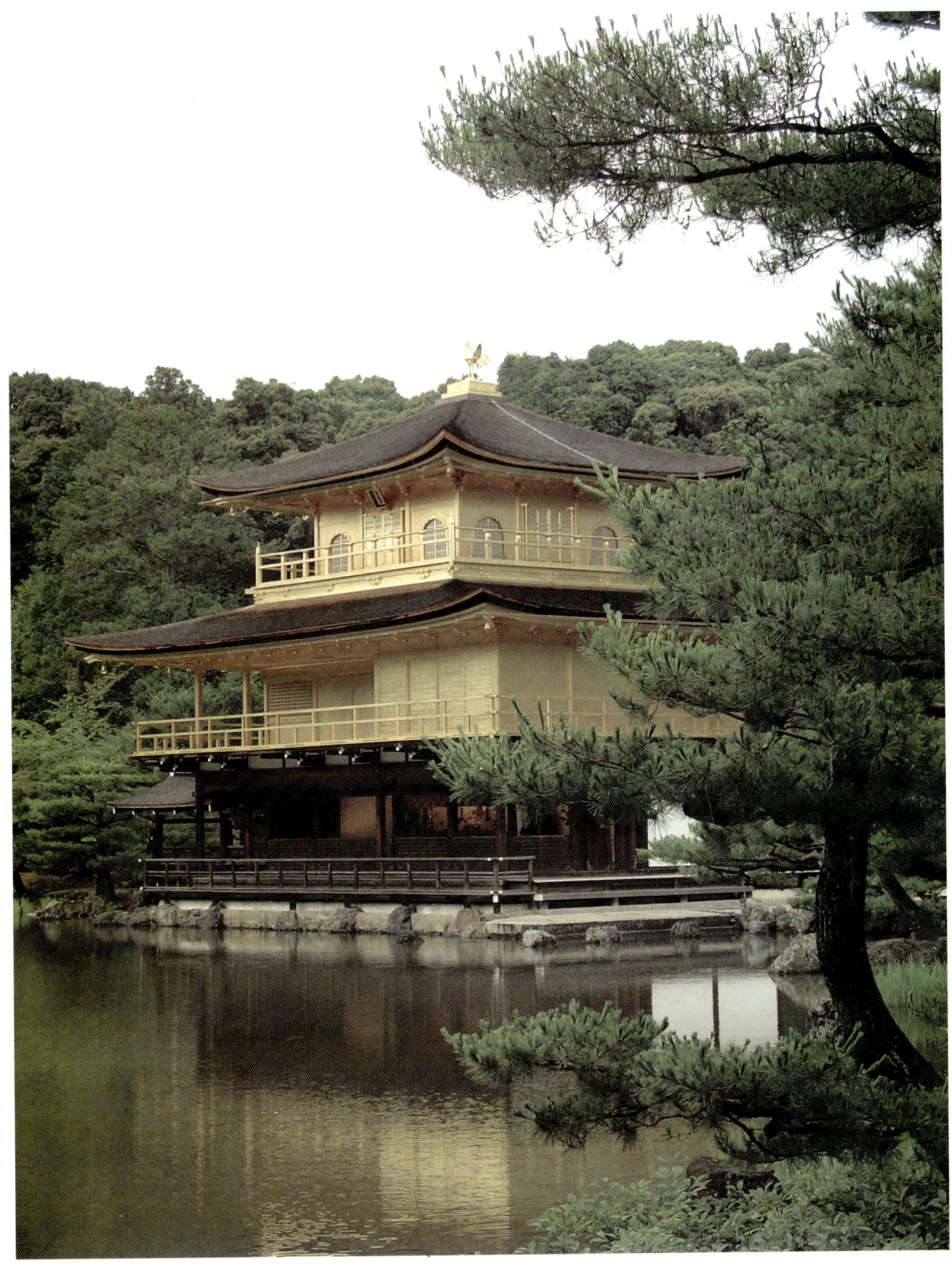

The Golden Hall, Dedicated in 1022 A.D., Kyoto, Japan.
Photo by Alan Burner.

bottom, with their ornamental cords, cluster-dyed streamers, and elegant paintings appliquéd in *gold* and *silver* dust. Indescribably splendid sleeve openings and skirt edges spilled out from behind the blinds, so dazzling to the spectators that they could scarcely distinguish one from the other. *Red plum* and *wild-pink* peeled silk *(shiny material)* inner robes shone with brilliant luster, and there were bombycines and gossamers in *bellflower, maidenflower, lespedeza, fallen leaf,* and *rue* colors *(white with green lining),* ornamental cords, formal jackets, trains—but I could not possibly describe everything. All the triple-layered *red* trousers were made of damask."[15]

These ladies were described much like one would talk about a beautiful sunrise. In fact, the beginning of the record began with a certain hint of affinity, as the "brilliant sun" was brought into the picture. The morning sun began filtering down through the delicate screens, into the room and onto the robes of the various ladies-in-waiting. Continuing with that aesthetic awareness, the *colors of the robes* were described in terms of their relationship to nature. (Bombycines in *colors of fallen leaf, maidenflower, bellflower,* and *lespedeza.*) Finally, a certain oneness was complete as "they could scarcely distinguish one from the other." The ladies in full court costume with their *colors of floral designs,* against the *colors of the natural setting,* had become visually unified.

Looking further into the concept of a direct link to affinity in court dress, the focus will remain mostly on women's dress for the following reasons:

- Women were the primary object of art—often more so than the artwork itself—as we see in the "Picture Contest."
- Women's clothing was more complex and elaborate than men's dress, and more layers were worn at one time.
- The affinity connection with women was much stronger, especially since skin tone was important for them. It should be noted here that women were more akin to the arts than were men. Women were totally involved with all of the arts and were well noted for their prowess in the arts.
- "The Picture Contest," and "Butterflies" chapters were primarily about women.
- Usually, it was the women who were in control of putting those functions together, and therefore they were responsible for the aesthetic success of the particular event.

In order to further understand the development of affinity and to cultivate its connections, it is logical to continue by discussing *court dress* as it relates to the *interior of a structure.* After which we will move to an outdoor scene in the highly organized garden. The first worthy example is an interior scene, as recorded by Sei Shonagon titled, *When the Lady of the Shigei Sha Entered the Crown Prince's Palace*:[16]

One day, the Lady Shigei Sha entered the Palace where ceremonies were being carried out with great splendor. She suddenly began thinking about the fact that she had never seen her sister the Empress. The following month, she wrote the Empress a letter advising of her intensions to visit. When the time had come, the Empress began decorating the Palace apartments, more elegantly than she had ever before attempted. All of her ladies took great care in order to prepare themselves in the same manner. It is interesting to note here that "court procedure" dictates that the life of a court lady was mostly lived out within the interior world only. It was a rare occasion for her to exist to the outside world other than for travel. For this reason, it was even more important for the ladies and their interiors to function as one.

---

[15]*A Tale of Flowering Fortunes,* McCullough, page 548.

[16]*The Pillow Book of Sei Shonagon,* Ivan Morris. Trans ed. (New York; Penquin Books), page 128, #20.

Our concept of these interior spaces is based on old woodblock prints, narrative scrolls, and various written documentations. Based on these sources, we will briefly discuss those interiors as they may have looked in the apartments of the Empress.

The interior spaces were very sparsely furnished, and for good reason. Moveable screens, sliding screen doors, curtains, and certain other walls were decorated with scenes of nature's landscapes and floral motifs. As often mentioned, the costumes were elaborately designed with motifs similar to their outside gardens. It would not be uncommon to see their robes of springtime consisting of embroidered garden motifs similar to their gardenscapes. Colors of their robes and jackets were in complementary color arrangements, and often commensurable to the existing colors in the garden itself. Therefore, when the ladies either entered an interior space or exited into the garden, the beginning connection with nature was born. The cycle of movement in and out of gardens and structures completed the picture of affinity.

The typical costume for a lady-in-waiting consisted of the following:

- One formal ***Jacket*** worn as the outermost covering. Usually designed with embroidery in a nature landscape motif. (Higher ranks)
- One ***Mantle*** underneath the jacket. Usually an animal, (cranes, etc.) or floral type of motif on a fairly dense silk, normally printed motifs as opposed to embroidered work. (Also depends on rank)
- One ***Train*** made of silk, 5 to 6 feet in length. Normally brocaded, depending on rank. Worn from the waist down about 12″ past the end of the hair. (Depending if hair is full dress code length.)
- ***Robes*** were the layers worn underneath, and range from three to fifteen layers, combined to create *seasonal colors*. Sheer silks only were used.
- ***Trousers*** were worn underneath robes. Partially exposed, made from beaten silk. Always crimson in color.

Note: For complete details on dress, see introduction and supplementary notes.

In the transition towards affinity, Sei Shonagon records more concerning preparations for the Lady Shigei Sha:

> **"In the morning, I attended the Empress while her hair was being dressed. A four-foot curtain of state had been placed across the main hall, facing the back of the room. Her Majesty was seated in the front part of the room, while a group of ladies-in-waiting were gathered behind the curtain of state. Hardly any furniture had been put out, only a straw mat with a cushion for her majesty and a round brazier."**[17]

It seems somewhat curious that there were so few pieces of furniture in the rooms, but then the reason for the sparse apartment interior becomes obvious. When we visualize the scene, imagine all of the ladies-in-waiting behind the curtain of state. Within the interiors, to one degree or another, there would be *harmonized colors* in patterns, nature landscapes, floral motifs on the costumes, etc. Also, objects in the room reflected similar decorations such as curtains, screens, and other prominent areas, as well as in the traditional *tokonoma* (recessed wall area). Certainly, when we consider the possibilities of all aesthetic elements in the various rooms, there would have been no need for much else, without creating clutter and confusion.

Another noteworthy point about the furniture within the interiors, was the feeling of impermanence that also prevails in nature. Seasonal change was not only involved with dress, but almost equally important was the seasonal change of interior space.

[17] *The Pillow Book of Sei Shonagon.* Ivan Morris, page 129.

Obviously, anything of permanence would have made it much more difficult to change the seasonal motif.

If the interiors did not coordinate with dress and with the season represented by the gardens, the ability to achieve true visual oneness would have been impossible. Seasons change, as do interior spaces and fabric types at court commensurately. The ladies of the interior had become living art forms, and were responsible for the aesthetic furnishings. The visuals must have been astounding as suddenly, the apartment interiors were transformed into a type of protected indoor garden.

Continuing in the development of affinity with nature, Sei Shaonagon elaborates on the virtues of the Empress's complexion:

> **"Unusual though the combination was, Her Majesty looked beautiful. The color of her clothes went perfectly with her complexion and, as I gazed at her, I was impatient to have a proper look at the Shigei Sha to see whether she was equally pretty."[18]**

It is precisely in that statement that the final link is formed. Favored among all women in court were the ladies with the lightest skin. Skin *coloration* and *tone* had to be perfect, or at least what they determined to be the most revered for standards of beauty.

In establishing a link to their natural surroundings, whether indirect, surrogate, or direct; the affinity source had to begin from the inside out, from the human form to the exterior jacket. The visual transition of affinity from human animate form to inanimate motifs had to be accomplished slowly, and more importantly, with subtlety.

Beginning with the inner most form (the human body) and then slowly making a visual transition from the inside robe to the outside jacket, the perfect complexion was first accompanied by the most sheer of inner robes. In many cases, the lightest color was worn closest to the skin, and usually white was the choice when dealing with seasonal dress. The visual transition from the surface of the skin to the first fabric was to be subtly varied in tone, and it was the most crucial step in creating affinity with outward surroundings as well as creating the perfect art form, the court lady. After the first of the sheer layers were put on, another type of sheer robe was applied, but with somewhat darker and more colorful layers. Many of the first layers were a very sheer silk known as gauze, and several layers were worn in the beginning transition. After the first layers, a sheer, but less transparent silk robe of gossamer was put on. A somewhat thicker and even less transparent damask (silk), was finally added to complete the inner robe layering.

As suggested before, the most significant event in the creation of affinity with nature occurred in the layering process. It is safe to conclude that the proper selection of robes required the utmost skill in dress sensibility in order to complete the perfect dress scenario. The plan was to create gradations of silks one over the other, building expressive layers of fabrics until the final jacket crowned the assembly. These surface relationships created the framework to indicate the affinity experienced by the aristocrats.

---

[18]*The Pillow Book of Sei Shonagon.* Ivan Morris, pages 129–130.

Color Blending

Hue combinations in these surface relationships created specific *seasonal colors,* appropriate for the particular season represented. This particular method of robe layering was commonly referred to as *color blending,* which produced court favorites such as *yellow-green* (a *green gauze* robe over a *yellow gauze*). The fabrics had to be sheer enough for the layering to be accomplished. One *color* is shown through the other, yet part of each robe had to demonstrate its *saturated color,* as well as its translucent nature. So, part of the robe was to be seen as a *saturated green,* and the other which was a combination of the two colors, would appear with its intensity changed to *yellow-green.*

Gossamer and damask were used over the gauze in the layering process, but the combination of the two colors in these fabrics, did not create the suggestion of affinity in the same way as gauze. These two fabrics were considerably less sheer, or more opaque, and for that reason could not be blended in the same sensitive manner as gauze material. Normally, robes made with gossamer and damask were lined, gossamer lined with damask, or in some cases, damask lined with gossamer. The skill of overlapping materials was referred to by a specific name; *"Sweet Flag"* and *'"China Tree,"* and both were considered *summer colors.*[19]

Sweet flag robes consisted of a green robe with red lining. These were a court favorite to wear against the yellow-green gauze. *China Tree* robes were *pale purple* with a *green lining.* Again, the *blending of colors* was a very skilled art. Too much subtlety between layers, joined with *colorful outer garments,* would have down played the effect of the inner robes. Conversely, robes of too much *intensity* could downplay the mantle, train, and especially the jacket, all of which would have prevented any unifying of fabric with the person wearing the costume. The perfect progression of color layers, was necessary in order to achieve perfect *color blending* with the exterior garments.

That brings us to the *mantle, train,* and the *jacket.* These garments were the *connectors* between the animate form (aristocrat) and the inanimate exterior layers, thus the creation of affinity. Exterior costume articles were made from heavier fabrics, embroidered heavy silk jackets, printed mantles, and heavy brocades or printed trains. An example of specific subject matter represented on the fabric was recorded by Murasaki Shikibu, when writing about Governor Michinokuni's wife:

> **"When they finished serving, the women went out and sat down by the blinds. Everything sparkled in the light of the candles, and some women in particular stood out. Lady Oshikibu—wife of the Governor of Michinokuni and His Excellency's envoy, you know—had a beautiful train and jacket, both embroidered with the Komatsubara scene at Mt. Oshio. Tayu no Myobu had left her jacket as it was, but her train had a striking wave pattern printed on it in silver, not overly conspicuous but most pleasing to the eye. Ben no Naishi had a train printed with a very unusual design, as a crane standing in a silver seascape; as a symbol of longevity it was a suitable complement to the pine branches on the embroidery, a real touch of genius. Lady Shosho's embroidery, decorated with silver foil, was not quite up to the same standard as the others and everyone found fault with it.[20]**

The types of fabrics and their organization, subject matter (motifs), and use of color all perform the task of creating a single unity or *harmony* with the sparkling lights of the candles. We can well imagine the effect of the candle light reflected on the textured silver jackets and trains. Most of the specific

[19]*A Tale of Flowering Fortunes,* McCullough, page 226.

[20]*Murasaki Shikib; Her Diary and Poetic Memoirs.* Richard Bowring; Trans, ed. Princeton University Press. (Princeton, New Jersey 1982), page 67.

hues remain unspecified, yet we have an idea as to what they were, simply by remembering conventional summer color harmonies.

The scene was well planned. Instead of utilizing a floral motif or the *color blending* techniques to create the harmony, it was more about the unifying element of light. *Color* was still associated with strongly in the event, since we understand that light is the source of color. Imagine for a moment the captured light during the evening, as it mingled within the colored fabrics with silver landscapes, then suddenly reflected off into the interior of the room, visually illuminating the jackets, and everything around them. The robes, mantles, trains, and jackets have all been *harmoniously connected* now, and within the costume a certain statement about the transitional processes of affinity has been made. We can well imagine the delicate inner-working of light transferring from one element to the other.

The Completed Scenario of Affinity

Now that we have completed the costume, the stage can be set in order to complete the scenario of affinity. To accomplish this, an imaginary situation has to be created, by combining the accounts of the "Lady of the Shigei Sha," "The Picture Contest," and "Butterflies" into a single event. We can easily visualize the interior apartments where the Empress, Shigei Sha, Sei Shonagon, and various ladies-in-waiting are installed. Imagine that they are all wearing formal court dress with their favorite embroidered jackets. The interior structure has been lavishly and carefully decorated, as the screens, doors, and curtains, are all in the same motifs as those who are in attendance. The blending of visual aesthetics between the animate forms of the ladies in costume and the inanimate forms of the interior apartments is complete.

Arriving now at the Picture Contest, we see they are all present as contestants. All of the most talented ladies-in-waiting are arriving to take their places for the competition, and once more we see that the stage is set as the *indirect* link to the paintings. The paintings actually become somewhat obscured by the intensity of the costumes, and if it were not for the emotional intensity of the Suma scroll, certainly they would be. However, the *brilliance of color* in court dress has caused a certain blending, or oneness between the artwork, and the fabric. Court dress performs a certain amount of its own blending along with the emotional qualities of the Suma scrolls, in that they are both intense. One visual indication is by the *dress*, the other is emotionally indicated by the painted *scrolls*. Even with all of this evidence, one more link is still necessary to make this affinity complete.

The strongest link appears to take place in the *Genji Monogatari* chapter "Butterflies." Children are dressed as *butterflies* and *birds* and are scattered among the 'yamabuki' flower. Ladies-in-waiting, courtiers, various attendants, and of course the Emperor and Empress, are also involved within the garden environment. All are in formal court dress, and all are dressed with related garden and nature motifs, as the organization of court dress blends with and complements the highly structured garden. Not only are the people *linked* to raw nature, but now the costume fabric produced by the silk of the silk worm, has moved back into its place of origin, the garden. This *surrogate* link is also used as a connector between the direct link, and the raw aspects of nature outside of the court confines. With the visual linking process completed, we see the perfect affinity; a picture of nature with court aristocracy.

One final brief observation about this surrogate connection is best illustrated by the *Lady Ukifune.* Murasaki Shikibu writes about her in the last five chapters in the Tale of Genji. One of the outstanding features Ukifune was so well known for was her hair. When discussing the *surrogate* form of the garden, it was presented in terms of linking the *motifs* of court dress to raw nature. Commensurate with that; Ukifune's hair would have been a *surrogate* form, linking her body to the costume and its *motifs*.

This takes us back to the transitional stage of linking the "white skin" of the lady to the exterior jacket. There could have been, at times, difficulty in blending the skin tones with the first robe, depending on the colors that were chosen. However, the dark hair—which is a product of the body—could have been used to link the body to the fabric by virtue of its high contrasting nature. It would serve as an alternate source as mentioned above, but also as an *additional* linking device. Whether used as an *alternative* source in connecting the body to the costume, or as an additional supplement to help the robes connect. The hair was very important as part of the actual costume. The ideal hair length at court, was approximately three inches longer than the height of the lady. Looking at the narrative scrolls, especially those of the Genji Monogatari, the hair flows down through, and *mingles with the jacket, mantle, and train,* dispersing in and out of the *color folds,* creating a strong bond between the elaborate fabric, and the lady herself.

While the robes are successful in marking that subtle, but all important transition, the hair adds the perfect touch. The raven black hair contrasts sharply, yet at the same time blends, with the beauty of the court costume. The hair is not only a visual connection, but also creates a physical oneness with court dress.

There is a certain difficulty about presenting a completely clear picture of court dress. We are not able to appreciate, or fully comprehend it, in that we are limited by the amount of visual documentation, and of course, the inability to go back in time to observe the actual spectacle. More important, we realize that even if we were able to be in attendance, it would have been impossible to adequately describe such an exquisite event.

One of the masters of court aesthetics, Sei Shonagon, said this when she wrote several times about the frustrated attempts to provide an adequate description:

> *"It would be foolish to attempt a description of the courtier's costumes, which were so splendid that they made everyone think of a grove of cherry trees in full bloom."*[21]

If you have ever been to Japan in the spring, you know exactly what a powerful statement that was. Cherry trees in full bloom are a short-lived spectacle, rivaled only by summer fireworks. As summer approaches, the blossoms fall from the trees, creating a blizzard of color movement.

Summary of Affinity with Nature Linking Process

- Light skin
- First inner *robes* of the most sheer of gauze
- Additional *robes* of gossamer and damask: sheer silks
- A *mantle* of heavier silk. Printed/unprinted.
- A *train,* usually printed or brocade: natural motif
- The *Jacket,* usually embroidered with natural motifs. (Higher Ranks)
- *Interior* apartments with related motifs and colors
- The *paintings* of an art contest. Link of aristocracy to nature
- The structured *garden.* Murasaki's garden: nature motifs, human form in perfect visual harmony with garden/fabrics. Ultimately links to *raw nature*

Dress Definitions for Men

- *Over-Robe (Ue no kinu):* This was the outermost robe. Similar applications apply with men as with women concerning type of fabrics and designs.
- *Over-Trousers, Over-Shirt (Ue no hakama):* These are worn together with over-robes as formal court costume.
- *Under-Robe (Shitagasane):* This was a formal undershirt.
- *Trouser-Skirt (Oguchi):* This was a wide, red trouser-skirt. Large openings in the legs.
- *Trouser-Skirt/Divided Skirt (Hakama):* Worn by both men and women.
- *Silk Trousers (Sashinuki):* These were worn loosely, and were laced.

[21] *A Tale of Flowering Fortunes,* McCullough, page 466.

- *Head-Dress:* This was given by the Emperor to nobility. The head-dress signified the fifth rank and above.
- *Baton:* The baton was ceremonial, and was given only to the highest ranking gentlemen at court.

Fabric in Rank

Listed below are the fabrics that were restricted for wear according to rank and office. It is important to remember that certain types of fabric and color combinations could be worn according to rank—even the colors used on particular fabrics had restrictions. Applies to men and women:

Lower Rank:	Plain and unfigured fabric, and bombycine.
High Rank:	Damasks, gossamers, brocades, and certain types of embroidery.
Highest Rank:	Deep red damask, embroidered green silk, complex embroidered scenes on silk.

Many of the textiles of that time period, seemed to indicate a certain affinity with the body, clothing, and nature. The human form, natural textiles, and the physical aspects of nature have been discussed. We have analyzed this affinity illustrating that dress was the harmonious link between the aristocrats (human body) and nature.

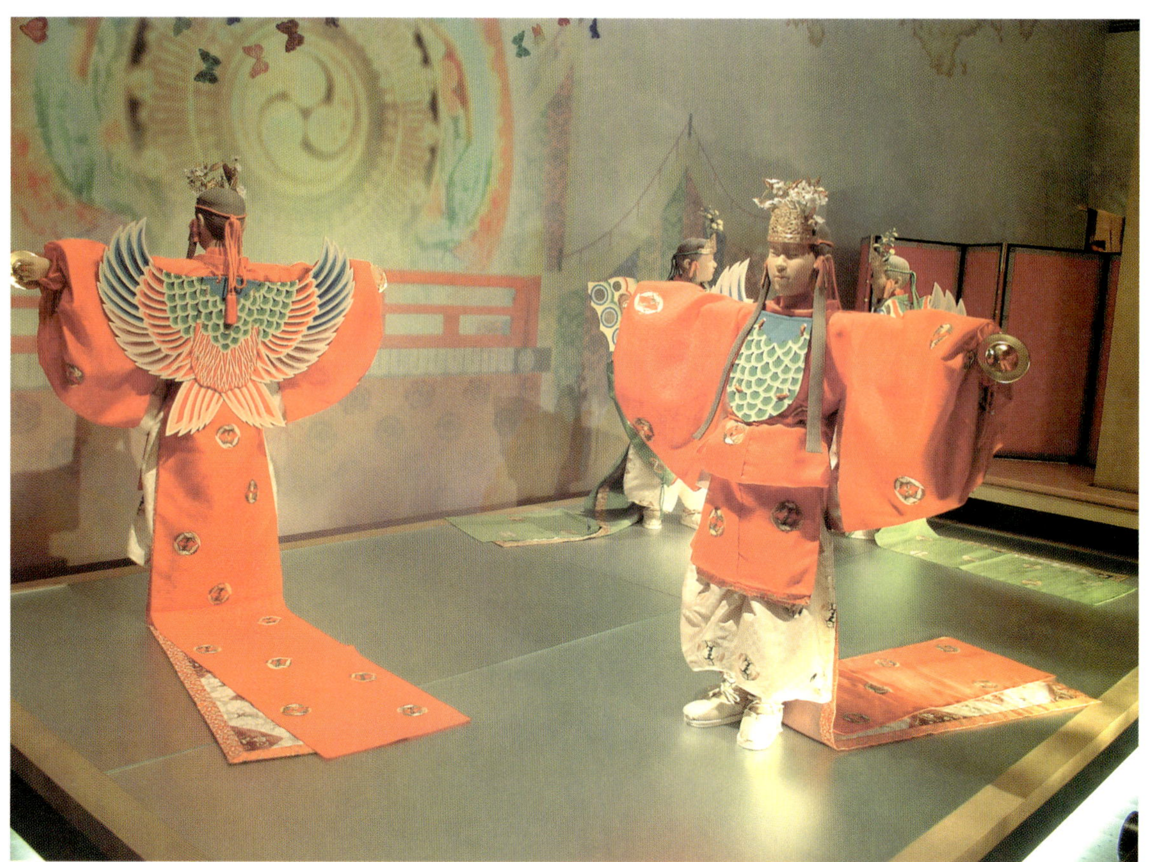

Heian Court Dress for Men, Genji Museum, Northern Kyoto. Photo by Alan Burner.

Rank Offices of Men

Only the highest offices of rank have been discussed in this text because of their complex nature. Brief descriptions of the top five ranks are presented below:

Chancellor	Often this rank was left vacant unless a man could be found of outstanding character. In short, he was the role model for the emperor. He was the highest and grandest of all the Ministers of State. Known as Daijo Daijin.
Minster of the Left	Next and most powerful of the ministers. Known as Sadaijin.
Minster of the Right	Substitutes for Sajijin, and at times even has more power than him, depending on his ties with certain political and family factions. Known as Udajin.
The Palace Minster	Has considerably less power than the top three positions. This post is normally occupied by a much younger person, perhaps in his early thirties. Known as Naidaijin.
Major Councelors	Mostly of the Fujiwara family, but occasionally a Minamoto family member, usually in their fifties or sixties. An elite group who was second to the Ministers of State. Known as Dainagon.
Middle Councelors	Had to be of suitable birth, and have served in lower positions. Normally a post for a young man in his twenties. Known as Chunagon.

Summary of Heian Court Harmony

Color harmony is responsible for the arrangement of color relationships, by which we are able to develop specific themes. As we know from the previous reading, aristocrats created elaborate themes from specific color harmonies. These accords were created to match the mood of the particular season or event being celebrated. The following is a summary example of seasonal color harmonies:

Late Summer (early autumn) Color Harmony:

One typical color harmony of late summer, or more accurately early autumn, is seen in the following reading section; "Dress Code and Types of Gowns for Women"

> **"That evening, the ladies-in-waiting assembled before her in all their finery. Princess Teishi wore a coat in *fallen-leaf* colors over aster robes. Kenshi was a white figure, her two or three robes Matched by her complexion"**

The aster was a combination of various light purples with green lining, purple with a brown or dark orange lining, or brown (dark orange) with a yellow-green lining. Early autumn colors were evident by the correlation to the season. Some leaves of various brown/orange colors were falling, while other leaves of green, and yellow-green remained on the tree. The fabric worn by the aristocrats was in perfect color harmony with the surrounding seasonal elements. Even careful attention was given to the colors of the inner linings, so that they would carefully harmonize with the skin color. Everything had to be in perfect harmony—color, imagery, and celebration.

Early Spring Color Harmony:

One of the most elaborate events cited in this particular study was "The Picture Contest," from the previous reading section; "The Story of Affinity Within the Japanese Aristocracy" (refer to that section for the story).

Consider once again, the color harmonies of "The Picture Contest";

1. Boxes of *red sandalwood* on sapponwood stands.
2. *Purple Chinese brocades* under stands.
3. Little girls wore *red robes.*
4. Jackets of *white lined with red.*
5. *Red and lavender* peeped from under the jackets.
6. Lady Oborozukiyo dressed the same as the little girls.

1. *Heavy aloes* and boxes on lighter aloes stands.
2. *Green Korean brocades* covered stands.
3. Little girls wore *green robes.*
4. Jackets of *white lined with green.*
5. *Grayish-green* lined with *yellow.*
6. Lady Kokiden dressed the same as the little girls.

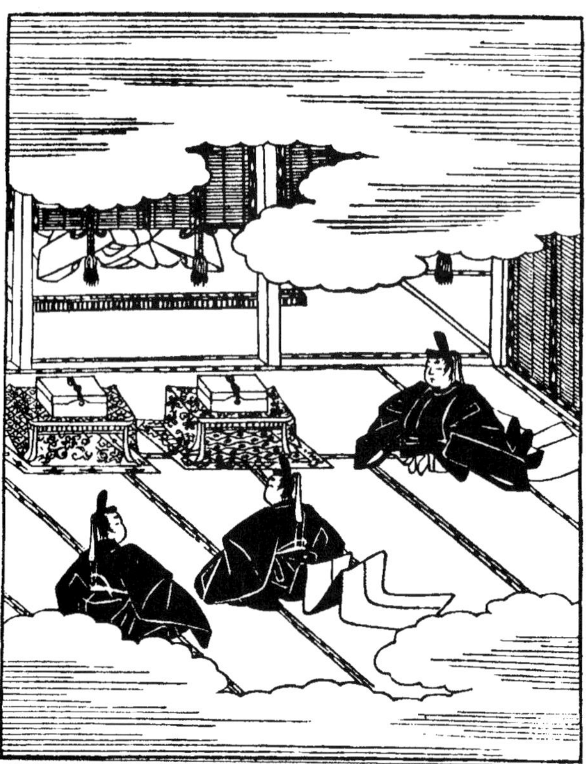

Prince Genji, Prince Hotaru and To no Chujo take their positions at the Picture Contest.

Springtime colors were represented in both teams such as the greens and yellow-greens, which could also be seen on the foliage of the plants. Yellow, lavender, purple, red, and white were all colors of various blossoms throughout the gardens. The colors that the aristocrats wore matched the colors of spring, as well as the motifs that could be seen embroidered on the fabrics.

In "The Picture Contest," we even see harmonies between the contestants. One side had purple brocades, while the other had green, thus setting up a secondary color harmony. One side wore red robes with jackets of white lined with red, the other wore green robes with jackets of white lined with green—the perfect complementary harmony. Finally, one side wore red and lavender gossamers, and the other grayish-green and yellow—again, springtime color seen in the two complementary harmonies of one team contrasted with the other. One can only imagine the awesome sight, as the ladies-in-waiting and their little girls performed in such harmonic splendor.

The text continues to tell the story of how Prince Genji judged the contest, influenced by his previous exile on the Suma coast, an island of isolation and fierce storms. The trials and tribulations were almost more than he could bear, especially having been accustomed to being a prince in the highest aristocracy of the land. Finally back at court, Genji judged the painting contest and he immediately observed that the paintings on the left were superior. The left had painted the Suma Scroll, but the colors were so moving that the prince as well as everyone else had to fight back the tears. The colors of the emakimono were so perfect that the exact mood of the severity of the exile could be felt—the paintings were the perfect visual documentation of his pain on Suma.

In "The Picture Contest," we see just how important the effects of color harmonies are. The use of color to create contrast between the two teams in the competition was evident. The extreme mood and emotional aspects observed on the human psyche was profoundly seen in "The Picture Contest."

Project Proposal

Color Harmony

Monochromatic, Dyad, Triad, Tetrad, Hexad and Analogous Harmony

Project Proposal

This project incorporates all six color harmonies into one composition (see student examples that follow). Make seven harmony divisions, side by side, representing all harmonies. Beginning with the left side of the composition, the first harmony vertical bar should be monochromatic. The next succeeding harmonies from left to right will be dyad, triad, tetrad, hexad and analogous. Select the appropriate motif that will fill the composition from side to side, and then transfer the image onto watercolor paper.

First, photocopy your motif. Then fill the entire reverse side of the copy with a heavy application of graphite. Next, center and lightly tape the image onto the watercolor paper (graphite side is face down). Now, begin to trace contour lines of the image with a pencil, until all contour lines have been traced over. When you are certain that you have traced all lines, carefully remove the photocopy to reveal the transferred image. You are now ready to begin painting your harmony color bars.

Remember, everything that you have learned in the previous chapters should be applied to this project, as well. Saturation, intensity, values, contrast, tints and shades and now, color harmony, should all be considerations for incorporation into the composition.

Project Specifications

- Working composition should be centered carefully on the watercolor paper. 140 lb. paper works well for most projects.
- Carefully measure and then tape-off the assigned size of the composition. Artist or drafting tape works well for easy removal.
- Clean, hard-edged lines should be part of your consideration, in most cases.
- Presentation is always paramount. The precision techniques of a crisp, clean composition can often make a big difference, so be sure that the neatness factor is always part of your routine.
- Painted compositions should have a white, gray or black border.
- Electronic applications, or printed compositions should be matted for presentation.

Project Objectives

1. The student should demonstrate knowledge of the properties of past chapters; Saturation, intensity, value, contrast, tints and shades.
2. The student should be able to recognize the seven variations of color harmonies.
3. The student should be able to incorporate the use of color harmonies, in order to manipulate emotional and mood responses.
4. The student will learn the appropriate use of color harmony functions and ramifications. (If your instructor requires a computer application for this project, then select the required image and scan it to the computer).

Student Examples of Six Individual Color Harmonies

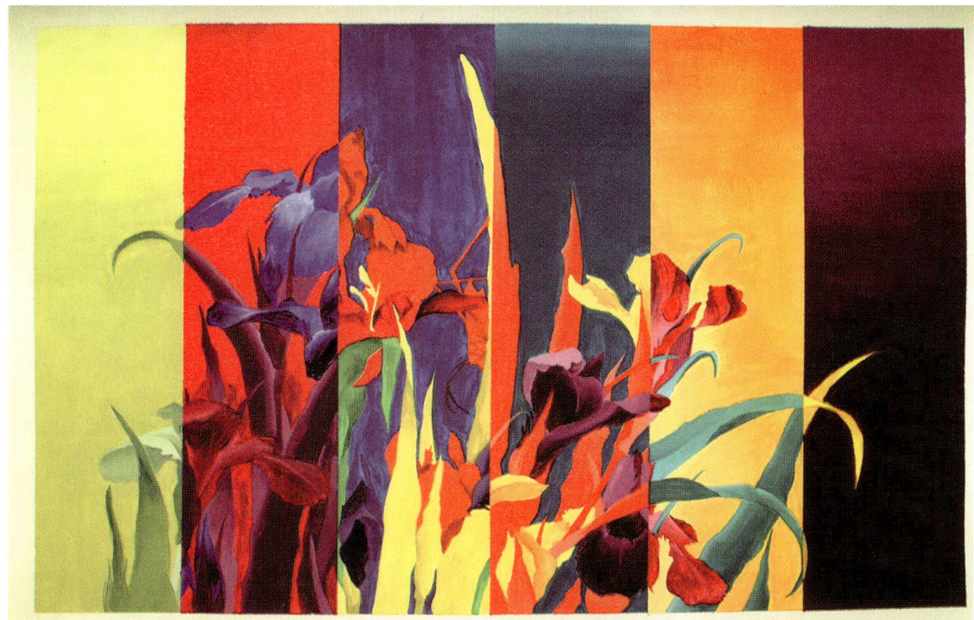

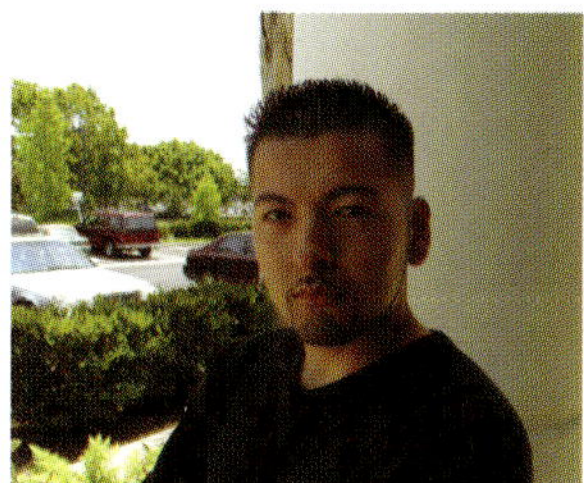

Leonardo Gonzalez:
Japanese Irises

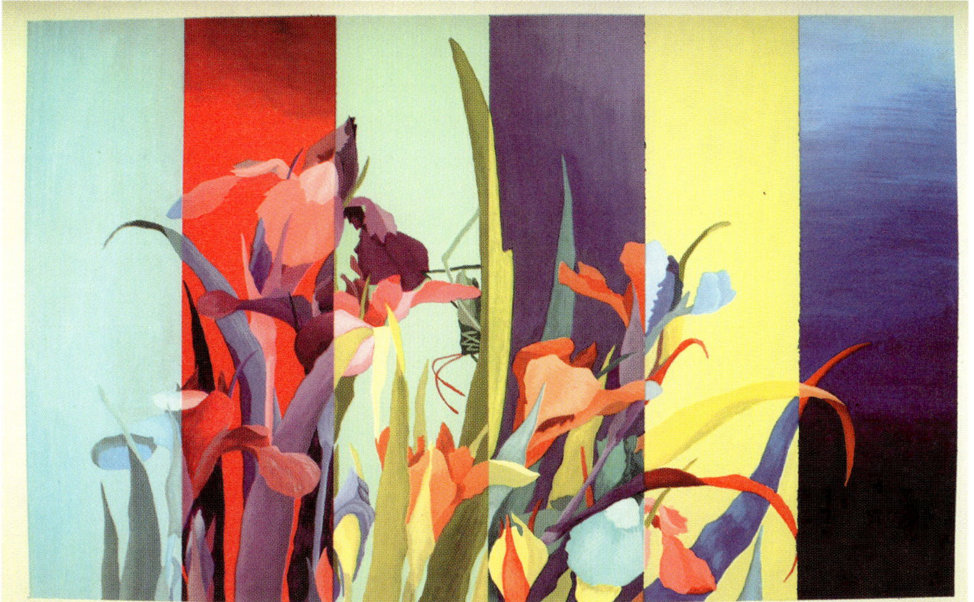

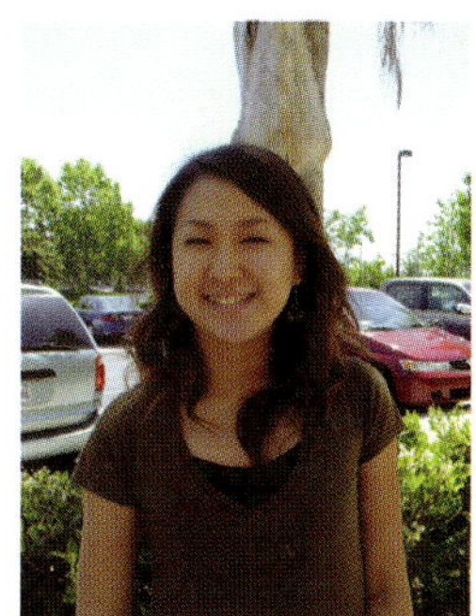

Ai Fujikawa:
Japanese Irises

This example illustrates six color harmonies, from left to right: Monochromatic, analogous, triad, tetrad, hexad and dyad. Notice that the harmonies create a certain ambiance or emotional quality in each student's painting. In some cases, different harmony sections generate a different mood, as well.

Written Project Proposal

Color Harmony

Monochromatic, Dyadic, Triadic, Tetrad, Hexad, and Analogous Harmony

This written assignment will serve as a tool to assess your observation skills and sharpen the student's ability to recognize and effectively use color harmonies. Please answer the following questions regarding Japanese Color Harmony Sentiment, as thoroughly as possible:

- Name the specific color harmony/harmonies in the *Picture Contest.*
- Who won the contest and why?
- What do you think the actual colors were of the *paintings (emakimono)* themselves, and why? In particular, what would be the colors of the Suma Scrolls and why?
- Are there specific color harmonies in the *Tale of Flowering Fortunes?*
- What was the objective of the *Butterfly Conspiracy?*
- What do you think the colors of the *Butterfly Conspiracy* are, and do they represent color harmonies?
- Give two examples and discuss their function, of color blending at court: one example for *spring* and one example for *autumn*.
- What is the connection between color harmony and affinity?
- Discuss emotional factors in any two situations in the essay. How do the events and color harmonies represented promote a particular mood?
- Why is color harmony at the heart of Japanese aristocracy in the essay?

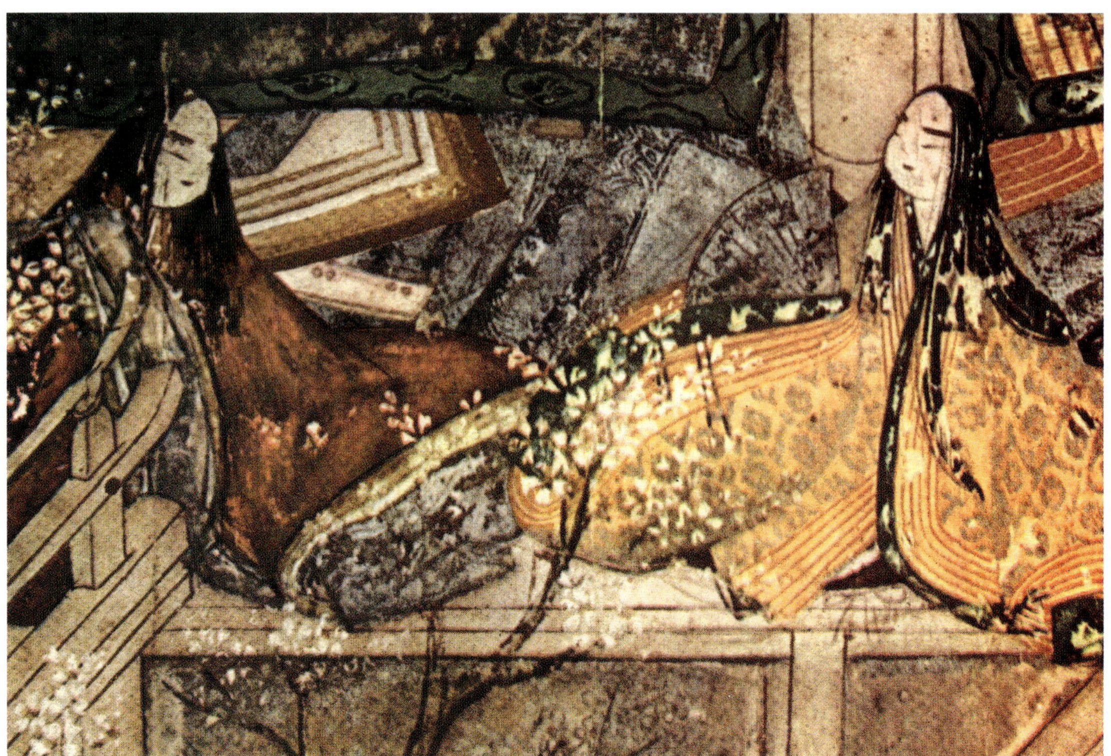

Tale of Genji, Lady Tamakazura's Court

Color Expression

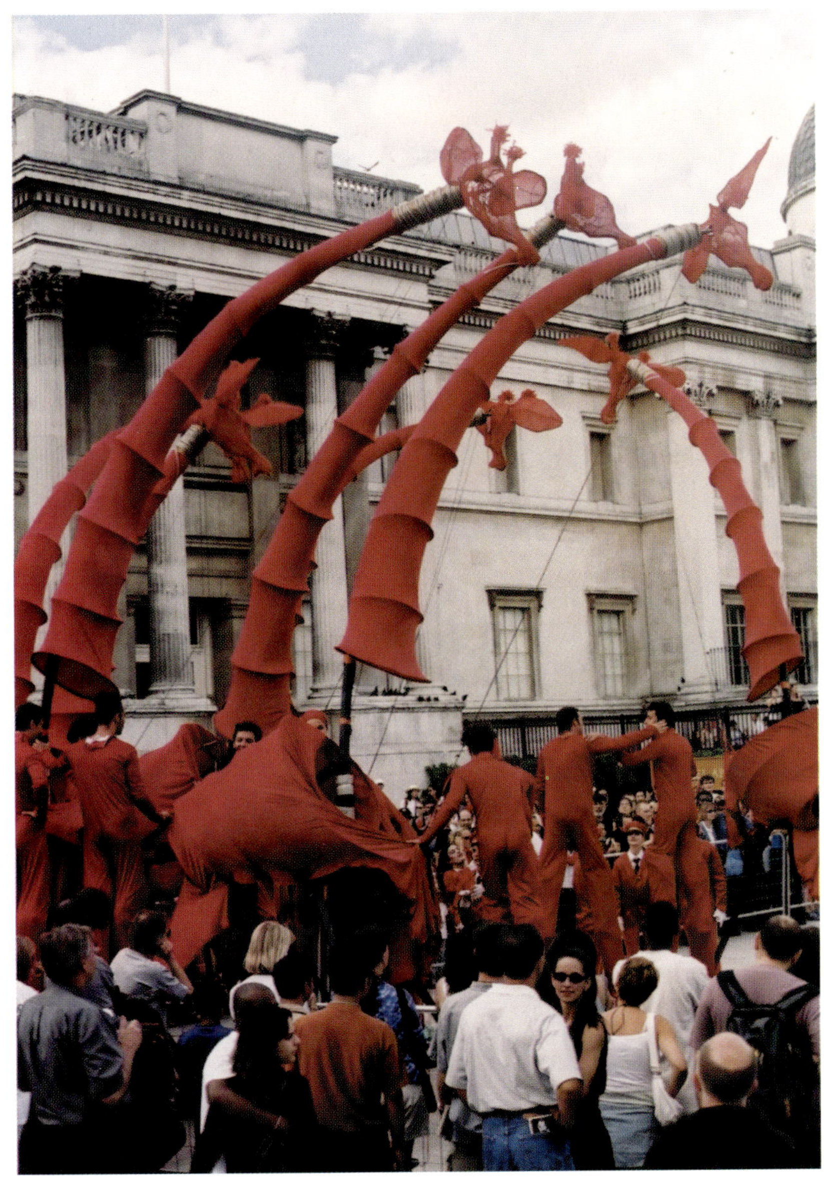

Performance of Red Giraffes—Trafalgar Square, London
Photo by Alan Burner.

Chapter Six

Introduction to Color Expression

Color expression translates into emotion, which is then revealed as *mood*. Expression is about using color itself, in order to bring about a certain mood in a given composition or situation. A very important aspect to understand about color is that each color has certain features, such as *character* or *personality*. It becomes necessary to learn how color functions, in order to effectively manipulate the viewer's emotional response.

Expression has been at the heart of the art world historically in most art forms, from poetry to architecture. As we move through this chapter, we want to look briefly at some examples of *color expression* concerns found in: architecture, interior design, sculpture, painting, poetry, prose, culture, nature, abstract and non-objective, performance art and stage lighting.

Color Expression in Architecture

The great cathedrals of the world, as we have studied earlier, are expressive of the glory of God and His kingdom. The greatness of this mighty architectural form is an expression in and of itself, in order to manipulate the senses. To cause the awesome feeling of heaven's vastness and its glory, and to evoke further contemplation about its rewards. The massive sculptural exterior (see following page), as well as the color-illuminated volume of the interior, with its majestic colored windows, serve to put the worshipper in the appropriate standing of humility with God himself. It is the smallness of one's existence, as opposed to the overwhelming greatness of the creator.

The following color expression categories serve to illustrate the various forms by which color is involved with when creating effective emotional or mood appeals:

Typical Applications *That Apply to Color Expression:*

Tonal Variations	Symbolic	Emotion/Mood
Light (pale)	Important (noble)	Celebration (happy)
Bright (tints) [Intensity]	Winter	Hate
Vivid (purity)[Saturation]	Spring	Love
Deep (shades) [Value]	Summer	Peace/Tranquility
Dark	Autumn	Chaos
Dull	Cold/Cool	Depressing
Grayish [Light to grayish category will demonstrate variances of 10% to 100% densities]:		
Transparent	Hot/Warm	Sensuous
Dense (Opacity)	Sophistication	Passionate
	Cultural	Quiet

This chart is a sample of color expression categories or elements, which can be used either separately or in a formulaic manor to create effective emotional (mood) appeals.

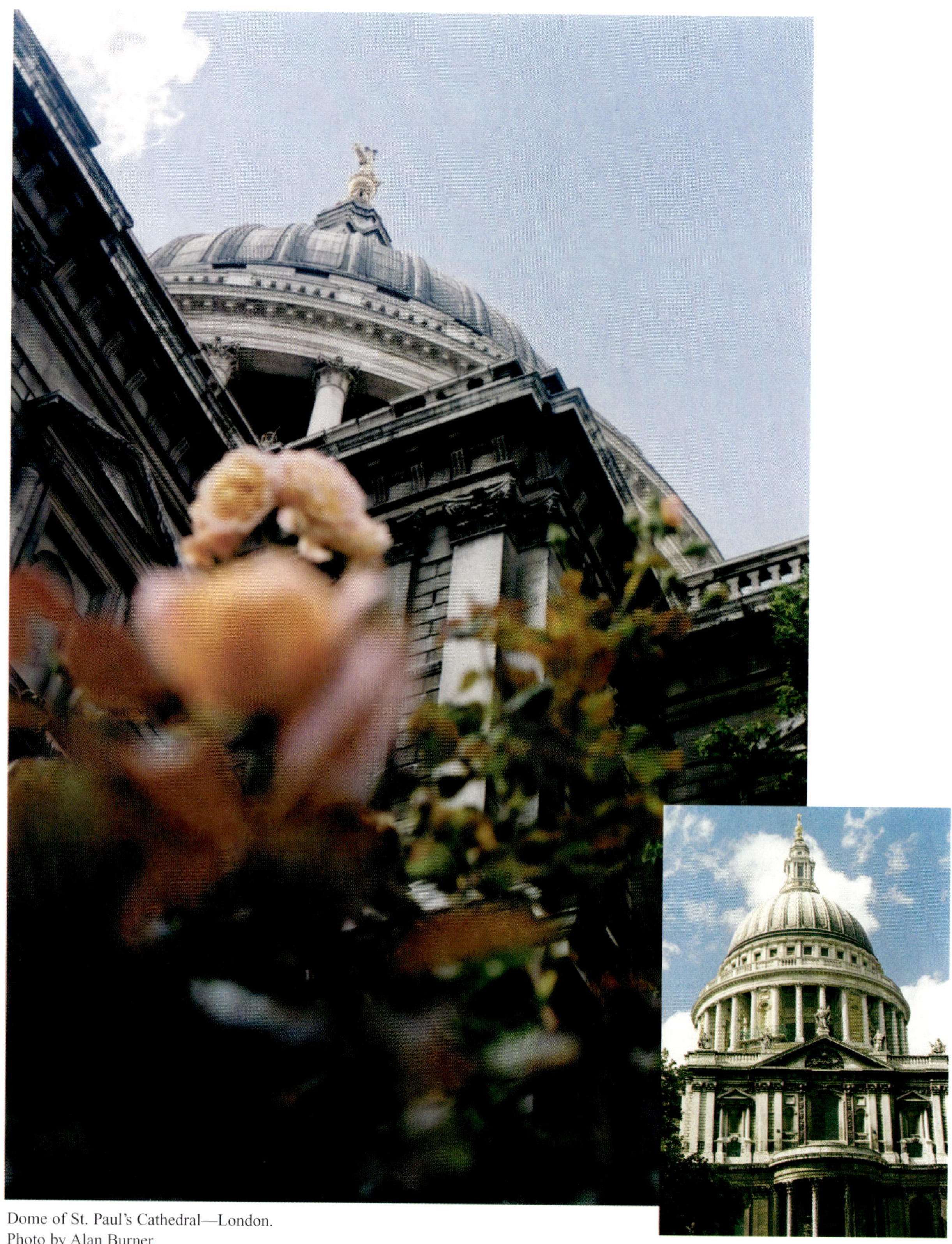

Dome of St. Paul's Cathedral—London.
Photo by Alan Burner.

Dome of St. Paul's Cathedral, London.
Photo by Alan Burner.

Interior Design

Color expression makes its way into every situation, and is vastly important to interior designers as well. Interiors can bring the level of emotion to many different stages, depending on the clients desire. Whether coming home from an intense day of work, or creating a social event such as a dinner party, one's interior space can be vital to the emotional state. Few color expression functions are as important as creating the appropriate interior ambiance for a home or office.

Color harmony in the office space can create the ultimate productive environment for each worker. Color affects mood, and that translates into how efficient the workload is processed each day. At home, a relaxing and warm environment is often the choice of many, and color choices in the living space make for a more restful evening and a better day ahead.

The example of our Feng Shui dining room is a simple but effective concept. There is a total harmony of wood objects of various hues of orange, which creates a warm inviting ambiance with its more subtle complementary contrast against the cool blues of the outside water.

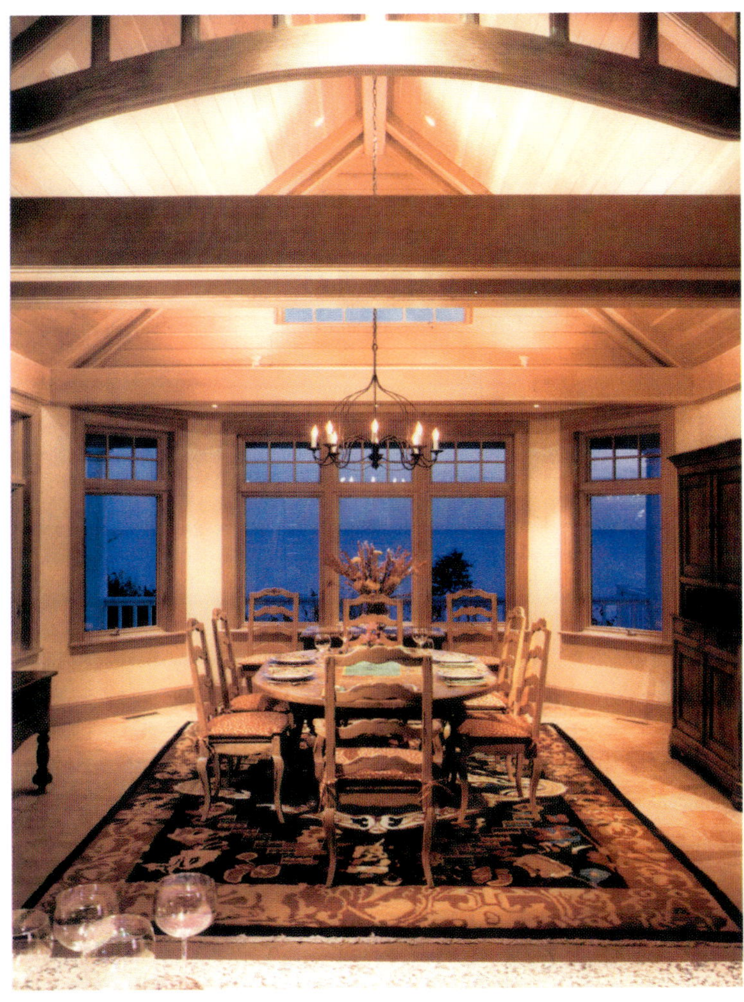

Feng Shui Dining Room Overlooks a Tranquil Body of Water.
© Sheila Emery Watson Guptill Publications.

Color Expression in Sculpture

Behind the choir in Notre Dame de Paris are high-relief, carved wooden panels (below) of sculptural forms. In this case the sculptures, or high-reliefs, do require color. The vertical position of the figures and architectural forms create a very rigid construction. Additionally, the horizontal line created by disciples and cross-members of the remaining structural design generates a stable feeling, yet lacks in drama or dynamic. Color is essential here in order to evoke a feeling of respect, warmth and life everlasting. Here, after the crucifixion, death and resurrection of Jesus Christ, Thomas examines the wounds, as the two are observed by the remaining disciples through the windows.

The saturated *red* areas in the background create a symbolic and very passionate response, about the suffering and shed blood of Christ, both before and during the raising of His body on the cross. The *violet* robes are that of a king's royal colors, contrasted with the intensity of yellow (gold) contrasting flower petals.

The deep shades of yellow, which dominate the mood of the relief create a very somber scene. Saturated, or even intense yellow would have created an atmosphere of celebration, and in and of itself, would have been an appropriate mood. However, the events which led up to the resurrection (crucifixion) were horrible and extremely painful. It would have been therefore, inappropriate to have any type of *dominating* vivid color, in relationship to the scene. Instead, the joy of the disciples about Christ's resurrection, is somewhat subdued by the painful events which preceded this particular occasion, depicted here on the backside of the choir chamber. The somberness

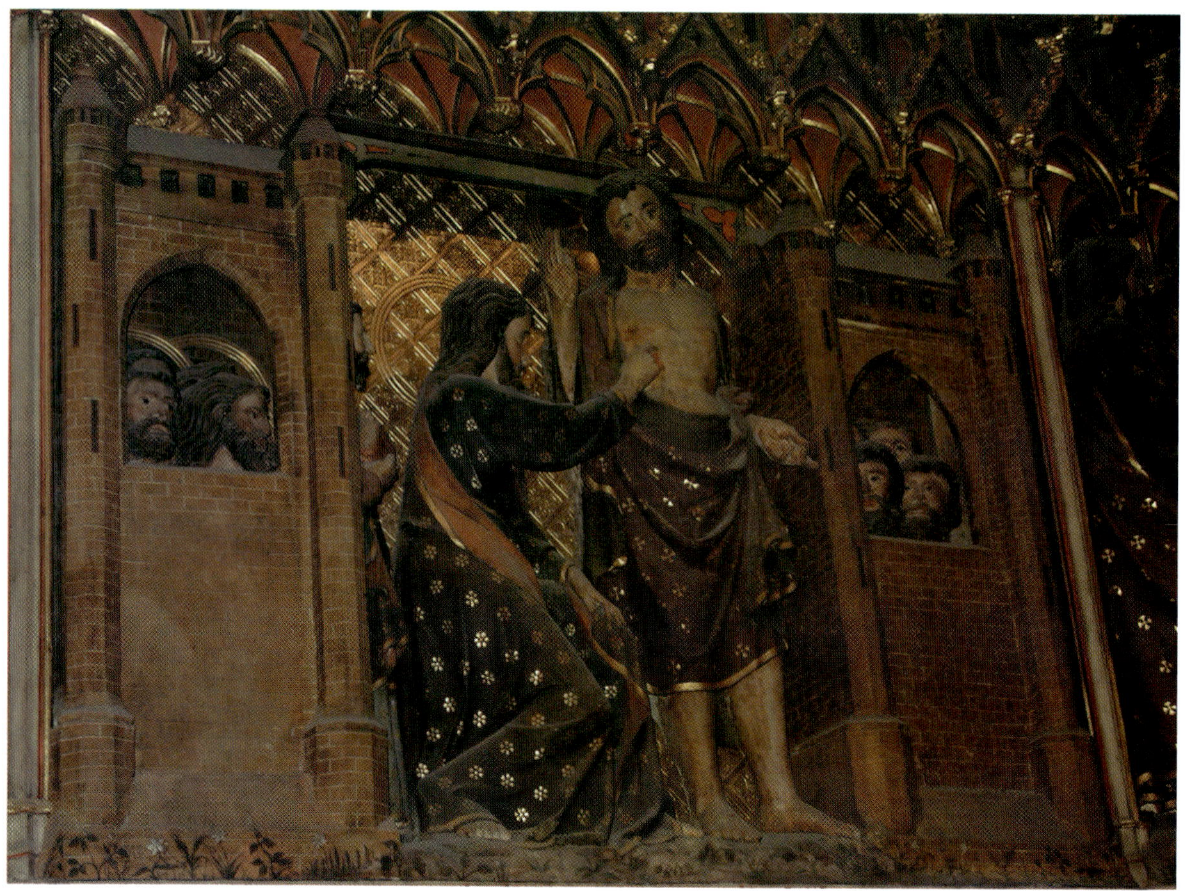

Interior of Notre dame de Paris, Thomas, Disciple of Jesus Checks the Wounds of the Risen Christ
Photo by Alan Burner.

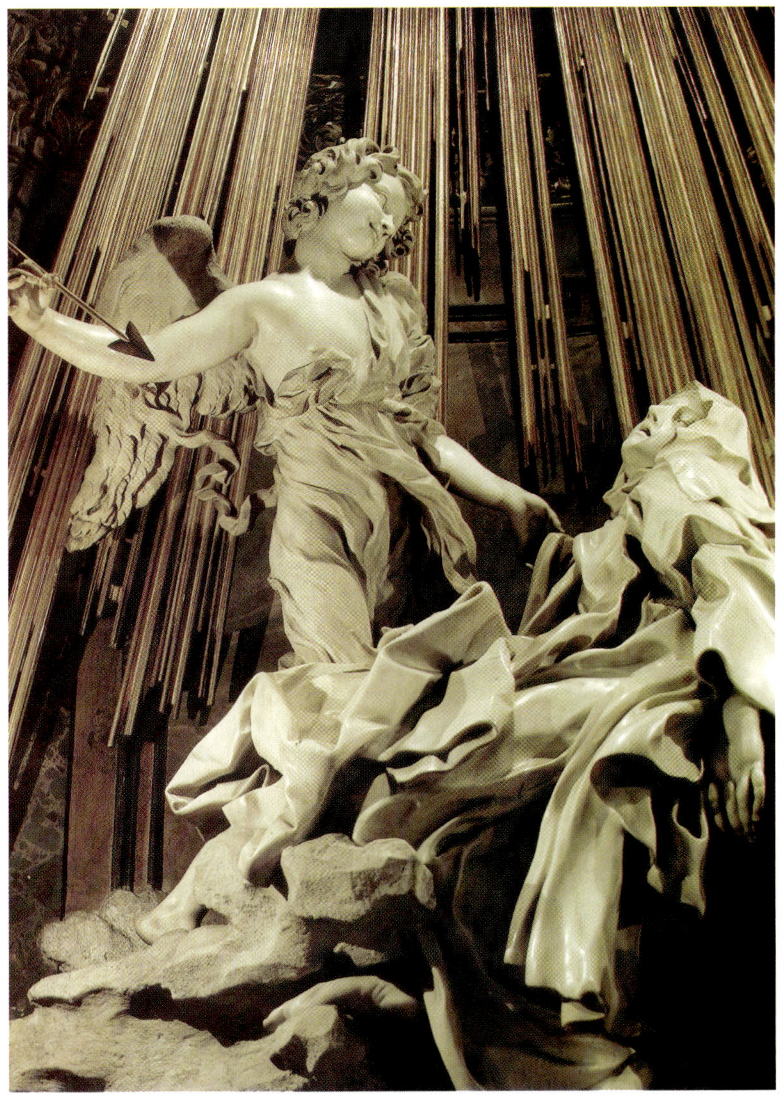

The Ecstasy of St. Teresa by Gian Lorenzo Bernini.
Santa Maria della Vittoria, Coronado Chapel, Rome.

of shaded or dark yellows, against the more saturated red and intensified smaller areas of gold (yellow) seem to create the most appropriate of moods here. The following sculpture by Bernini, however, presents a different attitude about the need for color expression:

Bernini's sculpture *The Ecstasy of St. Teresa* (see above) illustrates just how expressive three dimensional sculpture can be. The scene, depicting her heavenly dream, dominates the area within the Coronado Chapel in Rome. Her facial *gesture* elaborates on the intensity of her dream, and the diagonal figure helps to further emphasize and support the main components of extreme *expressional* form. It is independent of color, or the need for it, in this case. The passion and pleasure observed through diagonals of *physical expression* in the sculpture is sufficient in and of itself. However, it is quite the opposite with color expression. Color expression or emotion does not need representational form, facial appearance, or any other element or feature to demonstrate mood, or to be able to complete its *expressive component.*

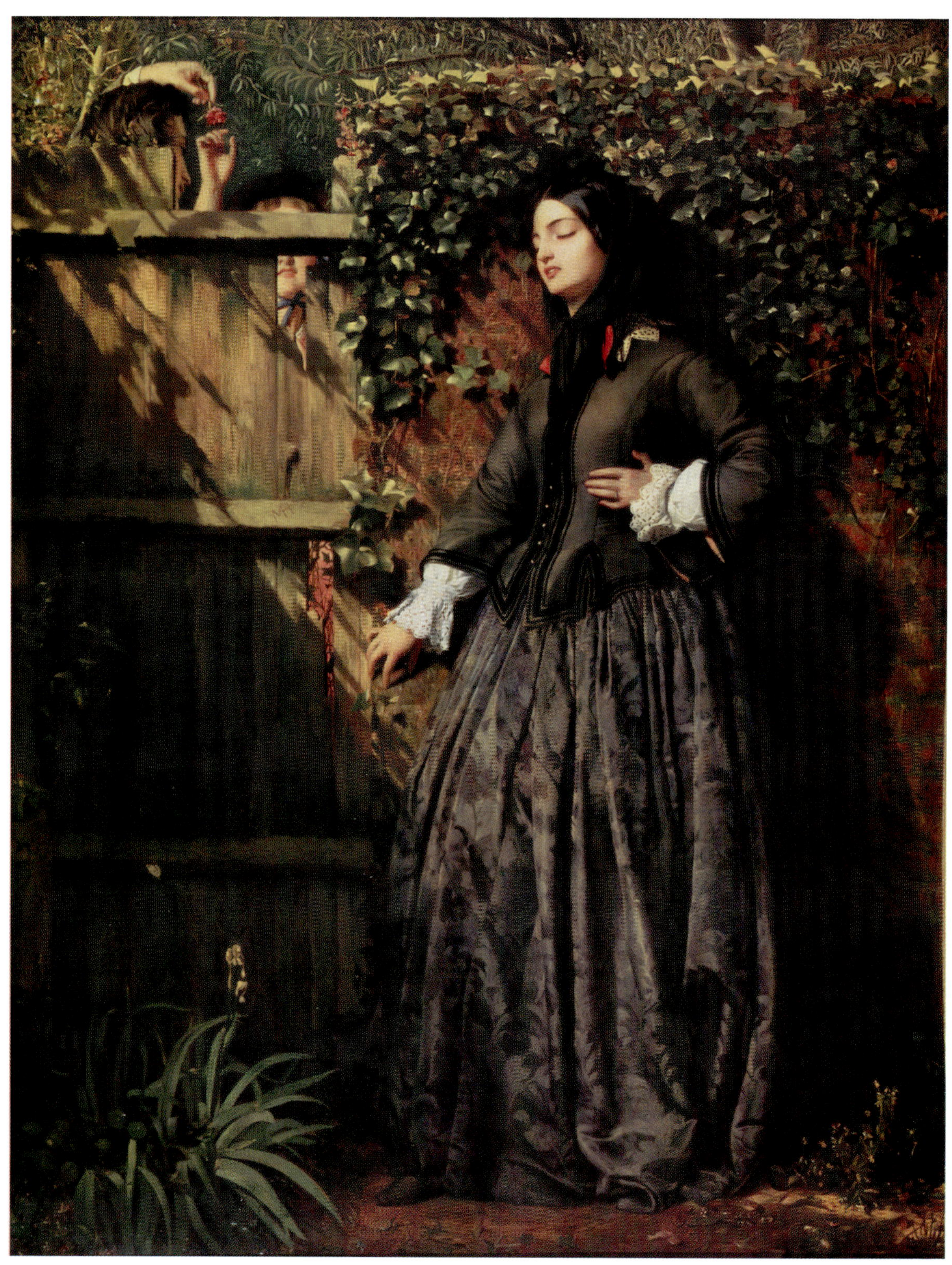

Broken Vows by Philip Hermogenes Calderon.
Tate Gallery, London / Art Resource, NY.

Color Expression in Painting

In Calderon's *Broken Vows* (see facing page), we see that the facial expression in this painting is paramount to the entire composition. The face of the foreground figure illustrates a range of emotions. Her moods are apparent, as she has gone from the intense feeling of the probability that her suspicions have been correct, to the transformation of painful disappointment. The *expression form* focuses directly on her face, as the directional light illuminates the most important aspect of this painting. Typically we rely on this type of painting to give us the obvious information about the mood of any given painting. The examples of architecture, sculpture and painting are particularly obvious when creating an expression, which translates into the emotional factors of a composition. However, we do want to take a look at the less obvious, and most suggestive and authoritative elements of expression, which is color itself.

In the beginning of this book, we discussed Van Gogh, but it bears repeating in this chapter, since he was one of history's most magnificent purveyors of *color expression*.

Arles, the town of Van Gogh's favorite memories, was painted repeatedly, as if he was reliving his most memorable and pleasant days vicariously through his paintings (see *Street in Saintes-Maries* below). This is color expression in its finest moment, where color is not dependant on form or shape. Even though we understand that there are structures and foliage, we also know that the painting does not depend on the realistic nature of imagery for expression. It is rather, the saturated and intensified nature of colors, that set the mood in this painting. His color expressions are energized fields of vibrant warm and cool hues, which give the viewer a perspective on his emotional state as well as how fond he is of the area.

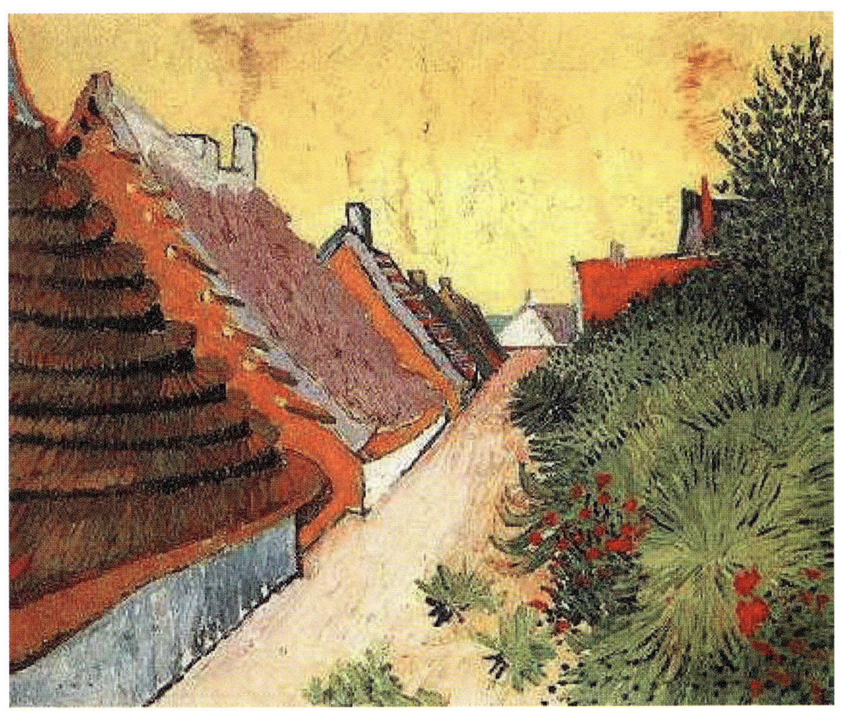

Vincent Van Gogh, *Street in Saintes-Maries,* Arles, June 1888.
Private collection. Christie's Auction, New York, 19. 5. 1981.

Color Expression in Poetry

In order to understand the subtle nuances of color expression on the psychological plane, we may approach it more successfully first through descriptive writing. The next sequence of examples are found in two of Shakespeare's works. The first example is from the Sonnets.

<u>Sonnet 23</u>
As an unperfect actor on the stage,
Who with his fear is put besides his part,
Or some fierce thing replete with too much rage,
Who's strength's abundance weakens his own heart;
So I , for fear of trust, forget to say
The perfect ceremony of love's rite,
And in mine own love's strength seem to decay,
O'ercharged with burthen of mine own love's might:
O let my looks be then the eloquence
And dumb presagers of my *speaking breast*,
Who plead for love, and look for recompense,
More than that tongue that more hath more expressed.
O learn to read what *silent love* hath writ:
To hear with eyes belongs to love's fine wit.

In his poetic sentiments on love, Shakespeare often uses complex forms of repetition to paint his picture. Within these multifaceted structures, we see the subtlety of color. How does this work? Lets take a closer look at *Sonnet 23* for additional insight and inspiration about expression.

There are key words to consider, such as *speaking breast, silent love*, and *to hear with eyes*. We can relate *the speaking breast,* to "speaking from the heart", as a verbal expression, that is felt deep in the soul, and then communicated to the lover. *Silent love* and to *hear with (the) eyes* work together then, in what we refer to today as "the *look* of *love", and* it is *"love's fine wit",* that can only notice that expression. True love, in fact, does not often have an oral *expression,* but it must be *"read"* in the *expression form* of *silent love.* The method that we use to relate to this, is found specifically in the phrase *...to hear with eyes*. Really, it is completely unnecessary to understand color as it relates to form, when we deal with the component of *color expression* itself.

To hear with (the) eyes goes much further than that, however, when we think of the words carefully. When we look at a color composition, what is the emotion that we feel? To feel the *sensation* of mood by a physical visual color, is somewhat like *hearing with eyes*, in a sense, in that both components are perceived in a spiritual, or inward sense. Whether we feel love or color's mood, they are both (in this case) felt emotionally.

Can you hear with your eyes, when you look at the *Girl With A Pearl Earring* (below)?

Vermeer's painting has been one his of crowning achievements. There is something mysterious and magnetic about this young girl's gaze.

Use this painting as an example, to analyze and develop your sensibilities about recognizing the attributes of color expression. See whether or not you can write a full analysis about three aspects. First, try to identify the actual *emotional* appeal and *mood* qualities of the "Girl With a Peal Earring". The painting is somewhat mysterious and alluring, as she seems to suddenly turn around and confront the

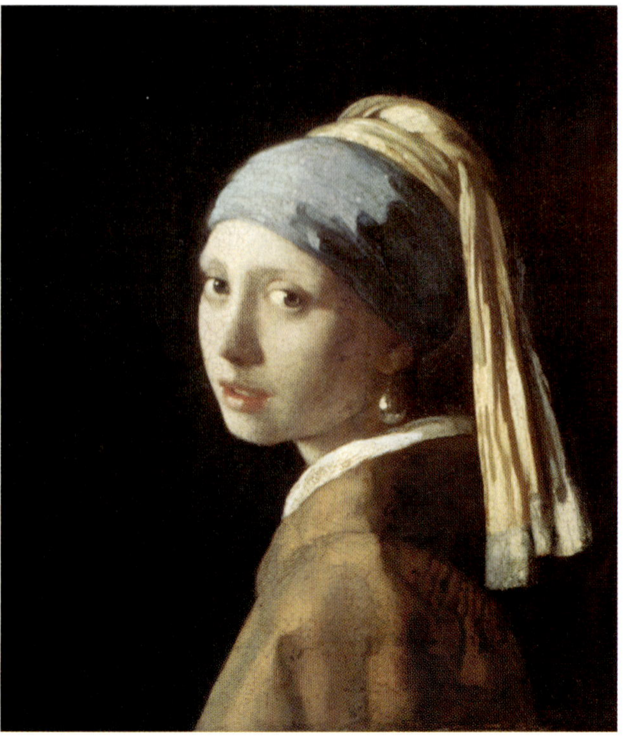

Girl with a Pearl Earring by Jan Vermeer.

viewer. Secondly, discuss this portrait in terms of how much that *mood* manifestation relies on her facial expression. I propose that she possesses both an element of innocence and sensuality. Thirdly, how does color develop the mood, or help to express the mood, of the painting? Which is the more powerful aspect, facial expression or color expression?

Based on the emotional (feeling-sensation) and mood (frame-of-mind/disposition) aspects—which are *mysterious, alluring, innocent* and *sensual*—try to develop a subjective analysis about color expression, using this painting as an example.

Color does not depend on form or recognizable shapes. Color is completely independent upon any other element of art or design. Color is expressive in and of itself, and needs no additional supportive element. Some say that color depends on form, but in reality it can even escape those boundaries, as we will see more clearly in Chapter Seven. It is color expression, which can single-handedly create emotional content, and the moods associated with it. Franz Marc's *The Fate of the Animals* (below), speaks volumes about the effects of impending war on innocence. Color speaks loud and clear as it dominates the composition, creating a mood of terror. It is only after color has affected its emotional debut that line direction and abstracted animal forms begin to aid color in its total outcome. Franz Marc was part of a popular art movement in the early part of the 20th century aptly known as *German Expressionism.*

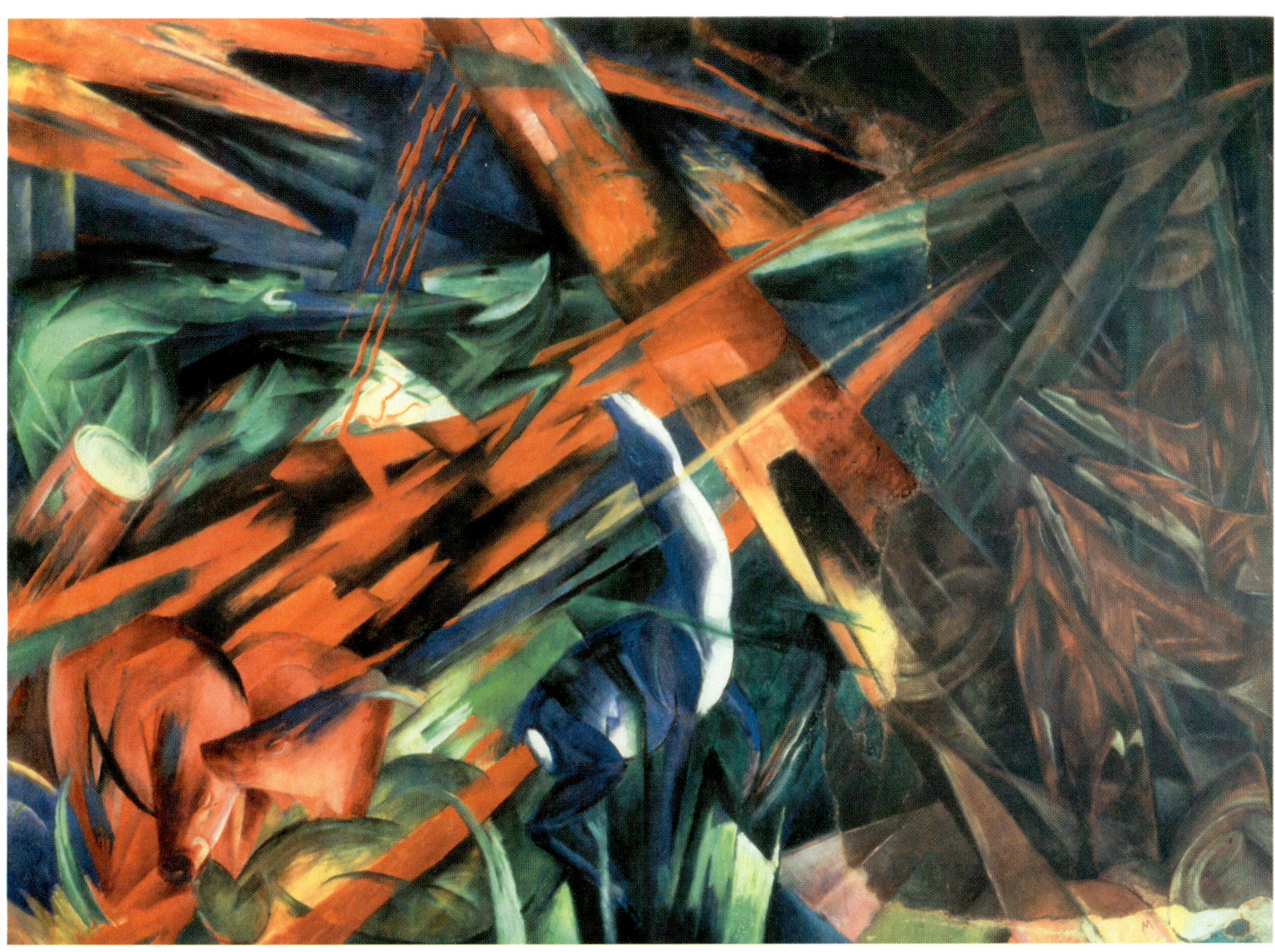

The Fate of the Animals by Franz Marc.

The color of expression in *Red and Green Complements of Aiko* (right) creates a very passionate response to her approach with the flowers. There is a subtle sensuality that reverberates throughout the photo, resulting from the diagonal of saturated red flowers. There is also a visual poetic sensibility between Aiko and the flowers. The redness of her hair, red lips and flowers all set up a visual mood connection.

The Red Studio only deals with color expression. The outlined shapes and occasional color differentials, have very little affect on the overall emotional appeal of this composition. It is clear to most that this is about color only. The expression of red in the Matisse painting is the force that actually creates mood. We immediately think "this is about red", but do we want to know why, or how it effects us physiologically?

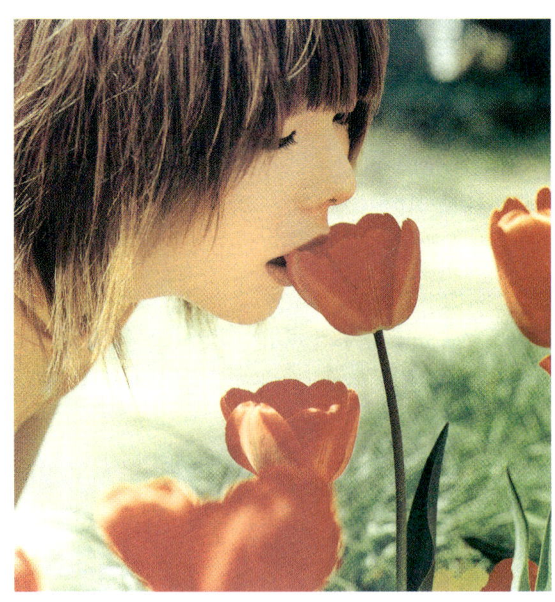

Red and Green Complements of Aiko.

We should be able to develop enough sensibility to color, as if to be able to *hear with (the) eyes*. The emotional expression of color is felt by the "ears of

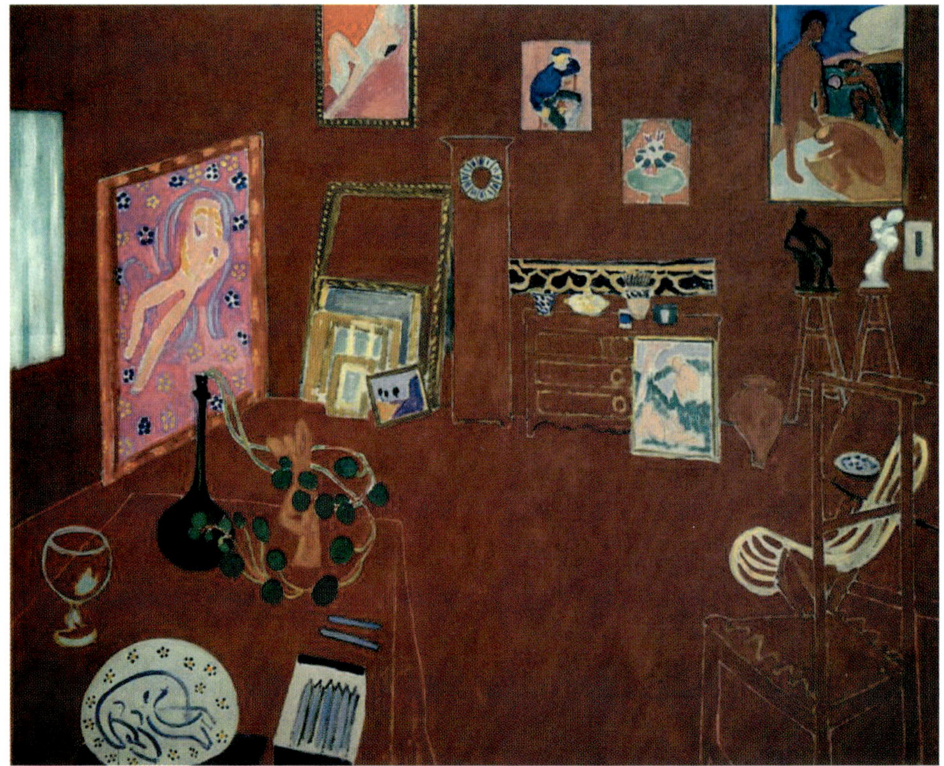

Henri Matisse: *The Red Studio.*
The Museum of Modern Art, New York.

the spirit", that is the essence of mood associations to color, such as the uplifting feeling of a celebratory yellow, or the seductive ambiance created by a saturated or deeper red, for example. Color is felt. Red is not just symbolic, but is felt or heard by the inner-spirit of humankind.

Romeo and Juliet, by William Shakespeare

Try reading through Shakespeare's sonnet again, and allow yourself to *feel* the colors of the poem.

How does the sonnet feel and what *mood* does it set for you? Does the reading of *love's fine wit* generate an image in your mind, or a pattern of colors? Perhaps colors will be red and green complements, or a range of blues and blue greens with violets hues?

When you read through the sonnet again, try to feel what the colors of the poem are.

Color Connection in Prose

A story of integrity and passion, Romeo falls in love with Juliet, and their feuding families hamper their efforts to marry. The Montague family (Romeo's) and the Capulets (Juliet's), are enemies constantly at war with each other. It is a story filled with the highest degree of passion, a prototype for the quintessential love story, filled with high emotion and conflict.

Romeo is only interested in love, he is the lover who immediately becomes infatuated with a beautiful woman. When Juliet appears on the scene, it is Rosaline who has been holding Romeo's attention, but in spite of his romantic advances, Rosaline remains indifferent toward him. Suddenly, he is in love again, but this time the woman of his desire holds him in a love grip, such as he has never before experienced. She is intoxicating to the degree that he completely forgets about Rosaline.

To this point in Romeo's life, his concept of love is quite superficial, and certainly his ideas of love are skewed to say the least. He has been obsessed with the idea of love, rather than the reality of it. When Juliet comes into his life, he seems to learn what love actually is, as evidenced by his stunning and passionate love poems.

Romeo's personality is impulsive, passionate, energetic and immoderate. He is extreme.

Juliet, on the other hand, is clear-headed, determined, strong, loyal, and somewhat naïve.

She is from the aristocracy, which does not give her the broad freedom Romeo enjoys. So it is that one night, he sneaks into the courtyard of the Capulet family, his own family's sworn enemy, and ultimately up to Juliet's room to consummate their marriage, which had been kept a secret.

Juliet's parents finally reveal their intention for her to marry their choice, whose name is Paris. Juliet is unable to reveal that she is secretly married to Romeo, and so she conspires with her nurse to drink a potion, which would make her appear to be dead. When she is finally put in the family crypt, the potion would wear off, after which time, Romeo would come to her aid, and they would be able to live happily ever after without their family's reproach.

The night arrives when she takes the temporary poison, after which a messenger would fetch Romeo to let him know the plot. The problem is, that the messenger is detained, and Romeo never hears of the plot, only that she is dead. He hurries off to her tomb, reaching it only to find (as he believes) that she is dead. Torn with grief and despair, and unable to face life without her, he commits suicide and falls at her side dead. Just then, Juliet's potion wears off and she discovers his dead body next to her. Juliet, unable to continue her life without him, puts a dagger to her chest, and falls dead on Romeo's body:

> "Yea noise? Then I'll be brief. Oh happy dagger.
> This is thy sheath-there rust and let me die"
> (Juliet, Act 5, Scene 3)

Emotional Transference to Color Expression in Romeo and Juliet

Here, two people so desperately in love, a passion and joy so rarely experienced, turns to agony and tragedy. This is a story of love expression, so how could we translate the expression of emotion, or mood content into abstract color expression?

The tragedy of *Romeo and Juliet* is *prose* expression, which easily converts into color expression. The life of Romeo and his persona is quite different from that of Juliet, and yet their goals are the same. There is, in fact, a spectrum of expression as the story unfolds. The intensity by which Romeo is able to love seems unparalleled in Shakespeare's plays. Romeo's epithet is that of being skilled at love, or being a lover. This is all brought into focus when Juliet appears, and he becomes so star-struck, he all but forgets Rosaline. Juliet loves Romeo with equal energy, yet she is more level-headed in most of her approaches; whereas Romeo is mostly spontaneous.

Try to imagine in your mind's eye, that Juliet's character and reactions to Romeo are strong, level-headed and loyal, and her love is without compromise. Her nature, as the entire play reads, seems to imply hues of deep blues, indigos and rich violets, as they pulse through the composition. Romeo's temperament on the other hand, creates an environment of highly intense and charged colors. Orange, the color of energy and the yellow of joy and celebration, juxtapose and dance across the composition to contrast with their complements.

Later in the story, it is elucidated by various hues of red to dark red, which begin to permeate the picture plane. Finally, the tragedy creates the darkest of violets, reds and even orange hues. The story becomes the spectrum of expression, or color.

Color Expression in Culture

Color expression is often the dominant element in festivals of the great countries around the world. Very dynamic color expressions can be found in Japanese festivals, celebrated throughout the year. The festival celebration is usually centered around a float belonging to a particular shrine.

Color expression is evident in the *Kamikawa-bandori*, as it is in every Japanese festival. Once again, as we studied in Chapter Five, the typical colors of contemporary Japan (Red, yellow and blue) are revealed, but this time in a traditional setting. The extreme intensity of the moment is important; the *saturated color* emphasizes and expresses the energy of the people, music and chants during the progression to the shrine. Color and its ability to ex-

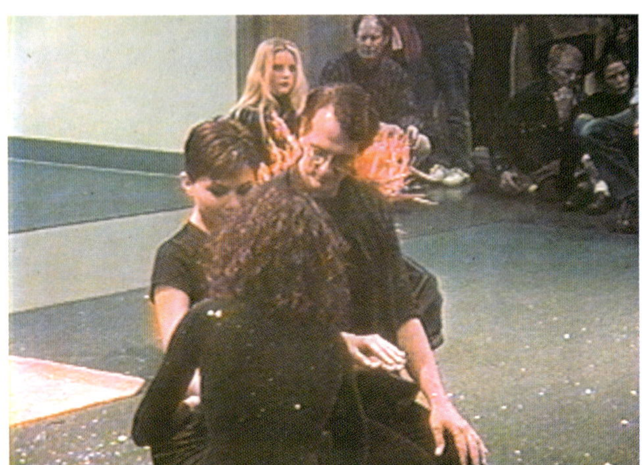

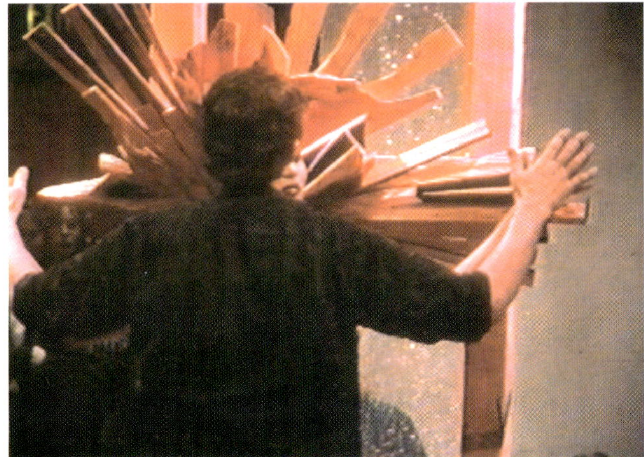

Alan Burner and Joanna Abelo rehearse a contemporary version of Romeo and Juliet. *Video Still.*

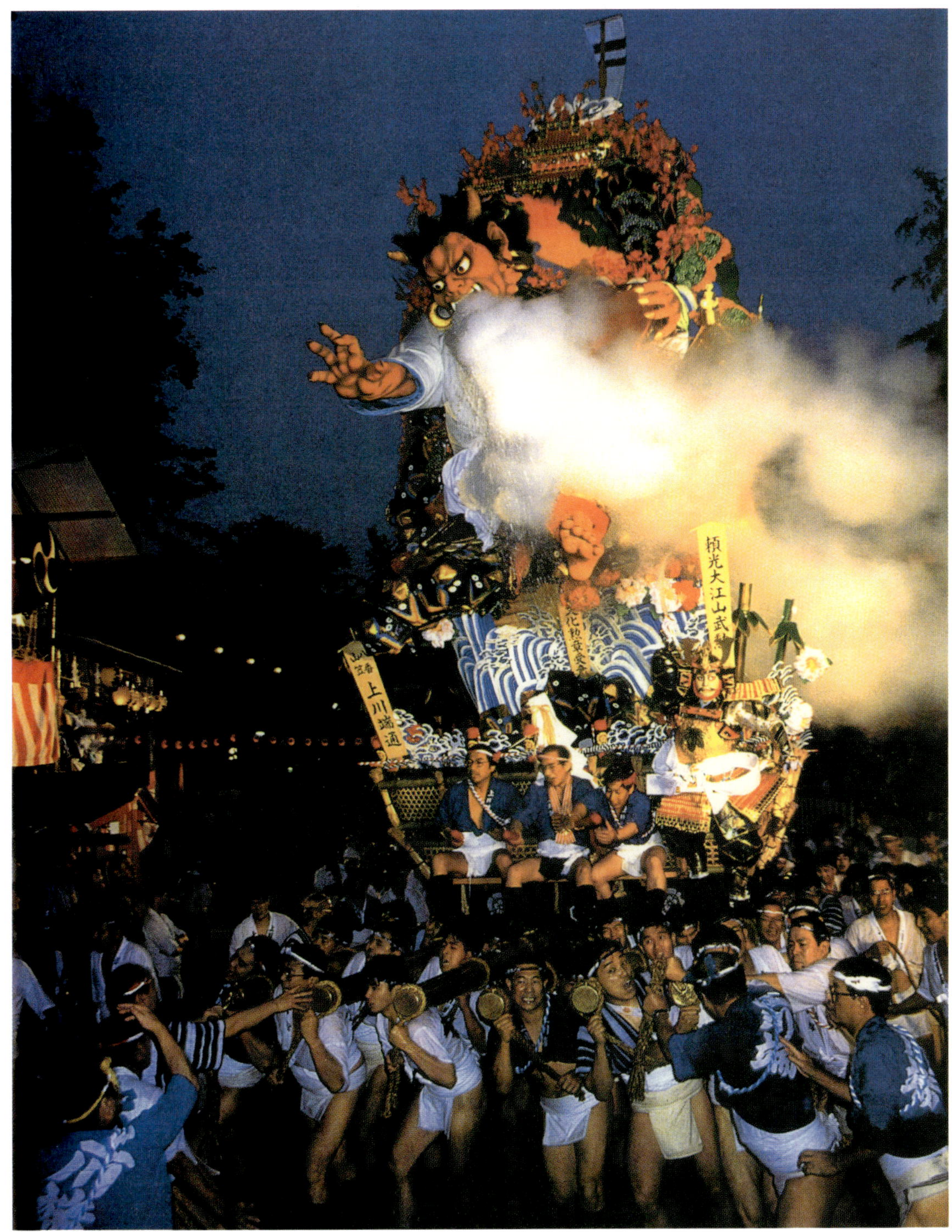

Kamikawabandori Float During the Hakata Gion Yamagasa Festival

press the sentiment of the people during festivals is paramount to its success.

In Japan, the expression of red is powerful and always dominates at festivals. Red is one of, if not the most, influential colors there are. The character of red has the most variations of emotional and mood components of any color, and it has the most appeal. People are drawn to the power of red for all generations, with its full repertoire of expression.

Color Expression in Nature

The *Valley Curtain* (below) signifies just how important the role of color expression can be. The reasonably saturated orange curtain, creates a powerful and ominous state of being, as it contrasts against the complementary blue sky. The saturated contrast of orange against the dull greens and tinted blues of the ground surfaces create an abrupt and threatening wall as one drives down the road toward it. The sheer scale of the saturated orange wall allows one to imagine how cautious and apprehensive one could actually feel, driving towards this gigantic curtain. The *expression of orange* is energized and almost overwhelming to the point of trepidation.

Finally, we take a look at Christo and Jeanne-Claude's blue umbrellas in Japan (opposite page), and the yellow umbrellas in California (opposite page). It is significant to note that the umbrellas in Japan are more densely packed together, whereas the California landscape is peppered with umbrellas far and wide. It is much like the two societies, in that Japan's people and architecture are more closely crowded together, whereas in California comparatively, there is more space per populous. One of the most interesting aspects of the work is the color ramifications. Anyone who has spent time in Japan can tell you that water is not a scarcity. Since the annual rainfall in Japan is about 60 inches, we could naturally conclude then that the umbrellas would represent the perceived notion of an abundance of *blue water*. In contrast, California is very dry, with very little rainfall or water, accompanied by frequent sunny days. The yellow umbrellas seem to mirror the yellow, yellow-orange grasses that typically coat the hills in Southern California, as well as it's source

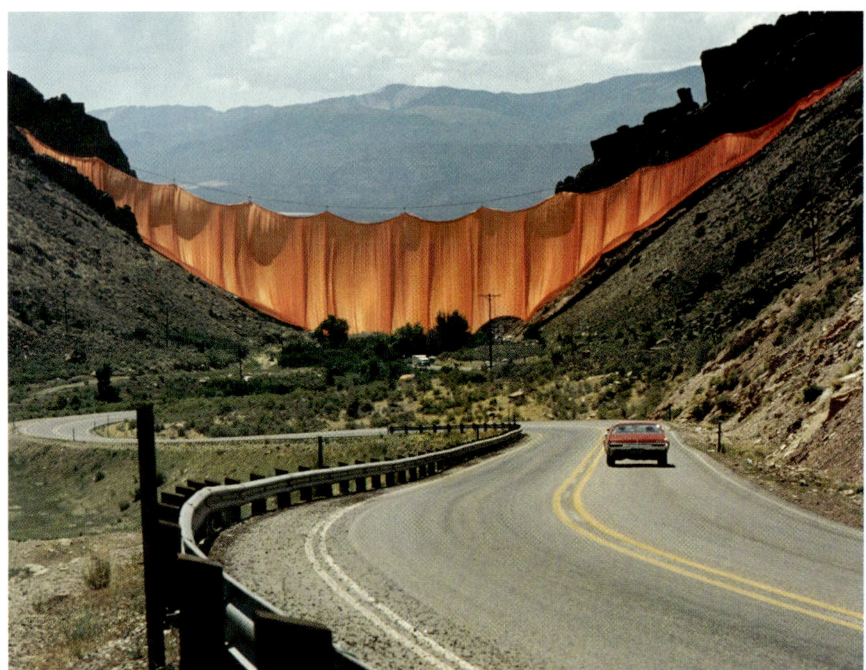

Valley Curtain, Rifle, Colorado, 1970–72
Christo & Jeanne-Claude
Photo: Harry Shunk Courtesy of Wolfgang Volz
©1972 Christo.

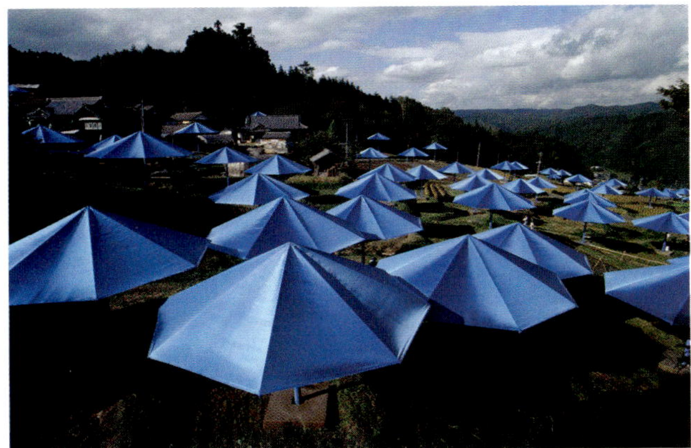

The Umbrellas, Japan - USA, 1984-91
Christo & Jeanne-Claude
Photo: Wolfgang Volz
©1991 Christo

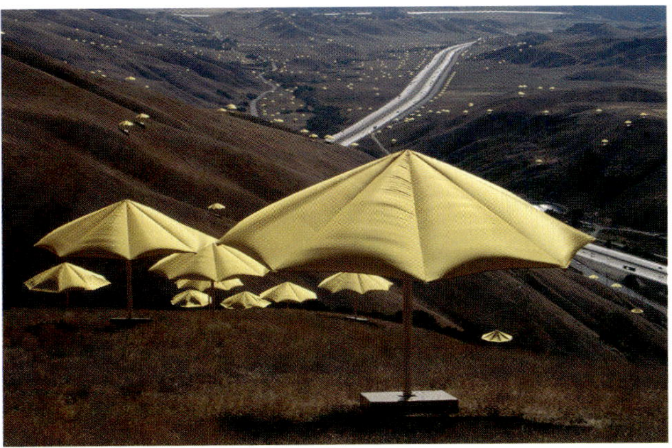

The Umbrellas, Japan - USA, 1984-91
Christo & Jeanne-Claude
Photo: Wolfgang Volz
©1991 Christo

of dryness—the sun. This expression of color is very symbolical in the natural disposition of these two lands. The prevailing and saturated cool blues clustered through the Japanese fields, lies tranquil with the saturated green rice paddies. The blue carries the eye through the fields quickly, while the warm saturated yellow umbrellas lead the eye more slowly and harmoniously through the hills of California, pulling the eye back further and further into the distant background. It is almost as if the blue umbrellas are emphasizing and creating a greater serenity, producing a very calm and harmonious functional color. The warm yellow umbrellas stimulates, or raises the temperature of the already warm and sparely populated environment in this part of California. Both blue and yellow fulfill the functional *expression of color*, by revealing the character of the land surface, by which the colors temporarily exist.

Color Expression in the Abstract and Non-objective

Hans Hofmann, an American Expressionist, was a key player in the development of what we now know as *abstract expressionism.* His canvasses abound with color expression, with surface texture, shape and color. The artwork incorporates the use of saturated color with powerful and masculine shapes. Hofmann's work epitomizes the authority of color to create extreme *mood* in the viewer. His works are primarily about the physiological color effects, rather than the object. Hans Hofmann's *Yellow Table on Green* (above) does not require perspective accuracy, any more than it does with other traditional values in painting. It is simply about emotional responses.

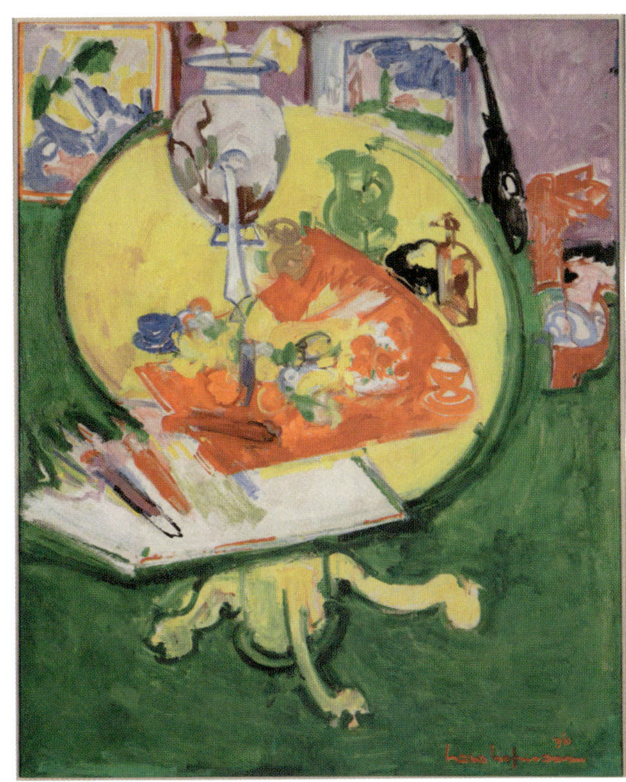

Hans Hofmann, *Untitled (YellowTable on Green),* 1936
George Braziller, Inc.

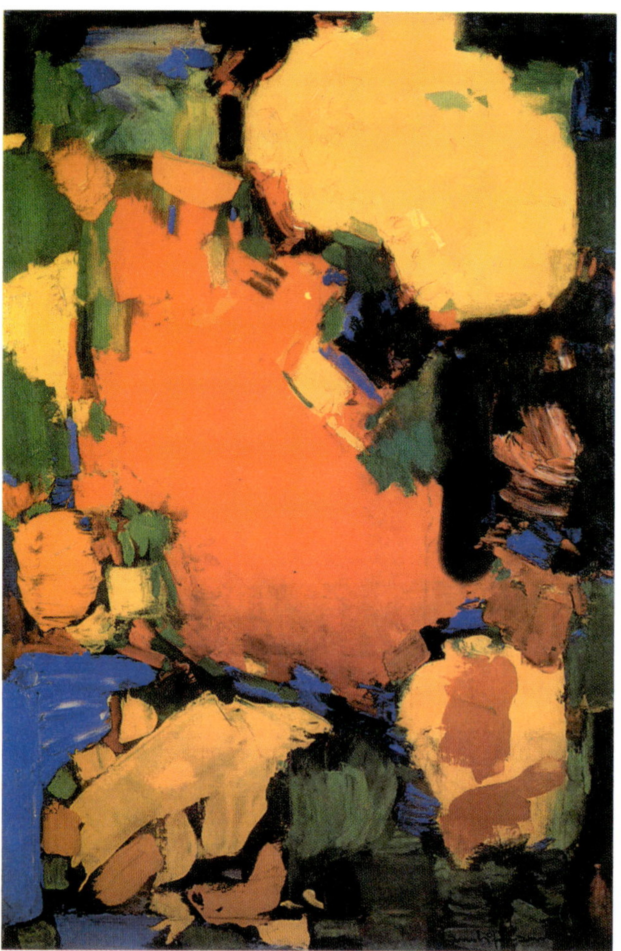

Hans Hofmann, *Voices of Spring,* 1959.
Collection of Mr. and Mrs. Gilbert H. Kinney.

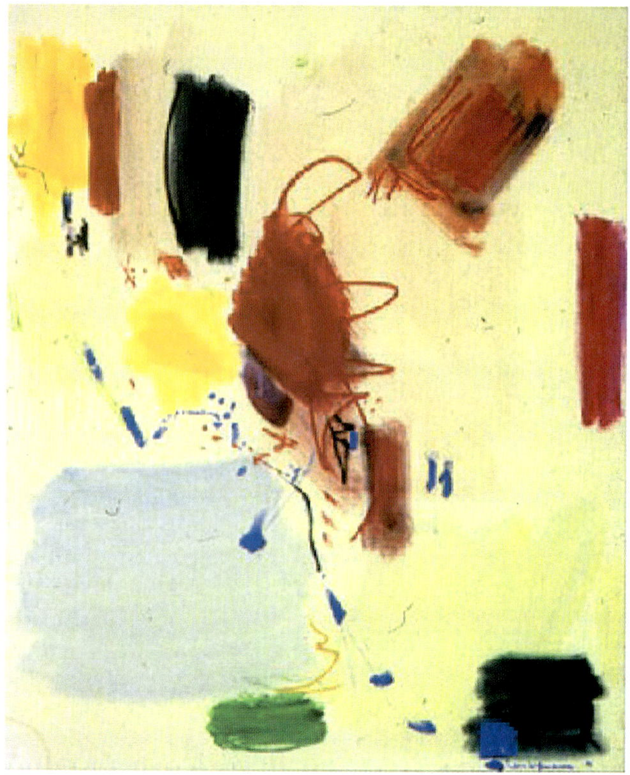

Hans Hofmann, *The Voice of the Wind,* 1961 .
Private collection, Pasadena, Calif., courtesy Riva Yares Gallery, Scottsdale, Ariz., and Santa Fe, N. Mex.

Voices of Spring (above) has much to do with learning to *hear with your eyes.* We use phrases such as "one picture is worth a thousand words", meaning that often times it is difficult to explain a situation or object. Rather than struggling to figure out how to use the right words, the visual product often speaks loud and clear for itself. The painting itself is a type of controlled chaos, in that there are patches of color that seem energetically applied, and exhibits a well planned structure of carefully thought-out hues. It is, as it is with much of Hofmann's work, a medley of color shapes, and color is seen once again as independent of shape or form. This painting supports the philosophy about color, that is to say, "why can't we simply give color the respect it deserves. Do we need to validate color with form and shape? Look at *Voices of Spring*, isn't color grand! Look just how beautiful the primary and secondary colors are, so filled with emotion."

The Voice of the Wind (above) requires the viewer to completely participate. As one looks at the composition, the first thing that is noticed is the appearance of random color. The placement initially may seem once again chaotic, and yet on closer inspection you will see an ordered placement of color shapes. It does in fact, produce the "sound of the wind", as we understand the nature of wind, demonstrated here. There are leaves, which seem to be

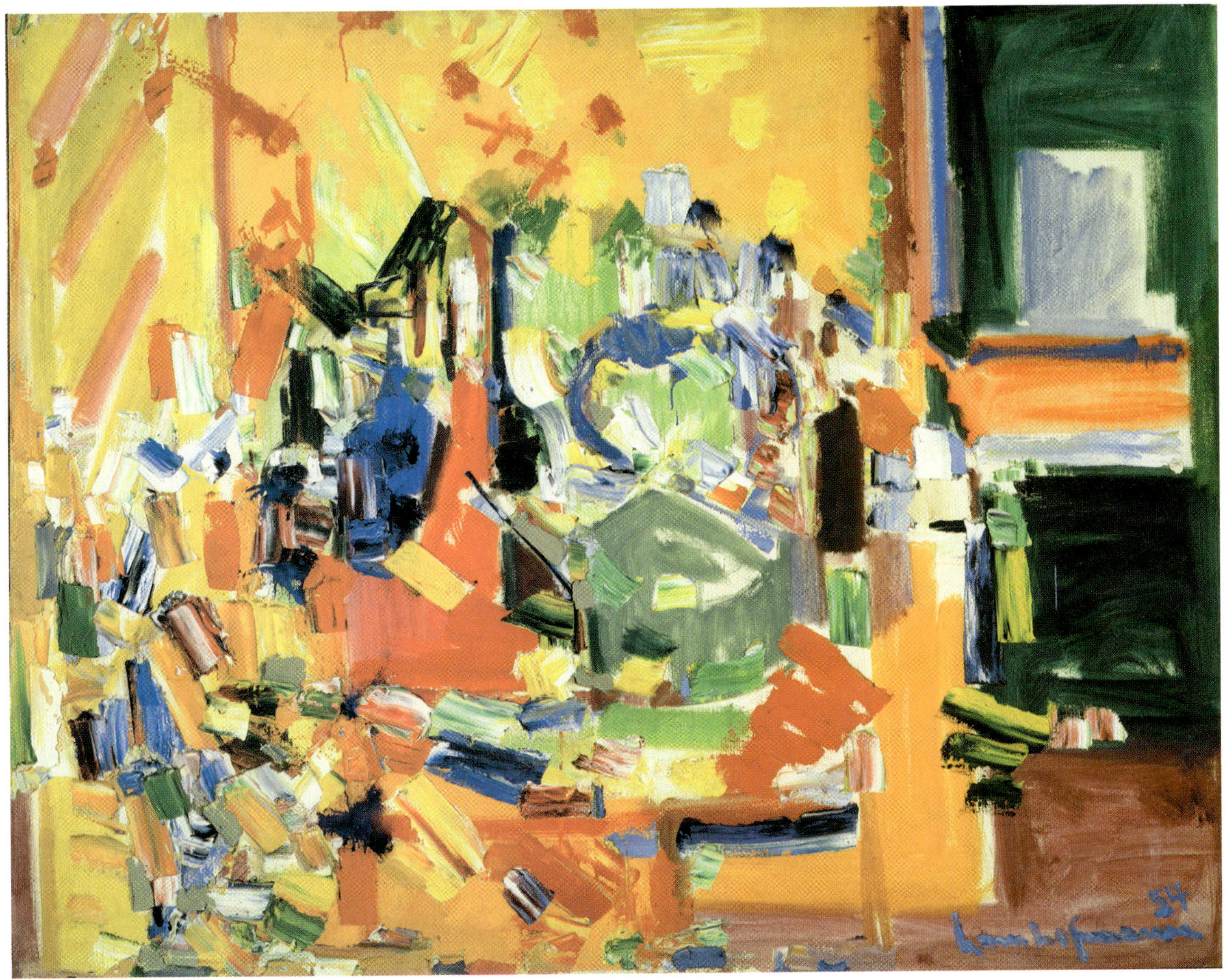

Hans Hofmann, *Orchestral Dominance in Yellow,* 1954.
Whitney Museum of American Art, New York. Partial and promised gift of Betty Ann Besch Solinger in honor of David M. Solinger 95.262.

blowing upward and the *voice of the wind* is turbulent, as a sudden autumn gust. Colors move in cadence to the centralized saturated red strokes of paint, which move diagonally to control the flow of other subservient hues. It is the expression of wind in color.

Orchestral Dominance in Yellow (above) is indeed orchestrated. Almost as if to be a musical composition, the yellow and yellow-orange are fragmented, dancing patches of vibrant color throughout the composition. These colors seem to have a real sense that they have been composed and played out by the artist/conductor. This canvas can be played many ways, but a specific effort has been made to evoke a particular mood on the viewer. This is *color expression* manipulating the senses. Colors in Hofmann's paintings are built very carefully as structured color compositions, which are filled with drama, as well as emotional content. Color functions simultaneously as both chaos and control, and as spontaneity and order.

Green, Red, Blue by Mark Rothko.

One of the great artists of expressive color was Mark Rothko (above). In his earlier years, Rothko's work consisted of vast color fields of non-objective vibrant color. As he aged, his color pallet evolved from saturated to darker color, dark grays, and finally to black. Before his death in 1970, his paintings were no longer vivid color fields, but they had transformed into emotional fields drained of color, as he neared his death. Rothko painted extensively about color's expressive character. Exploring human emotions through the spectrum, his paintings are passionate and seductive, and evoke a pure mood through each and every color investigation. In the truest sense, Rothko's color is not relegated, or subservient to form. Instead, color commands the attention and dictates the mood of the viewer. When standing before one of Rothko's large canvases, one feels the true sensation of that color, as if to feel emotionally the temperament of that color, and react to it accordingly.

In Shijo's *Libera Me Domine* (opposite page), we must first acknowledge the style. We will refer to the work as contemporary Gothic painted constructions. The painting incorporates fragments of Renaissance concerns, as well as expressionist surface treatments. The more free-spirited application of red and yellow hues in the background is seen here as a more expressionist approach. The remainder of the painting, with its gilded framework, statuary and the pulpit alludes to Gothic, Greek and Romanesque attitudes. The deep red hues are contrasted with the intensities of yellow and yellow-oranges, which complete a very somber and perhaps fearful mood, as the day of judgment materializes. The gray façade acts as a buffer, or neutralizing zone transitioning into blue. Taken from the Requiem Mass, the occasional Latin phrases, and the blue tints and shades of the statuary add some degree of stability, calmness and hope about the outcome. Observe the difference between the achromatic version and the chromatic. It is easy to see just how important color (color expression) is to establish the severity of the message, regardless of the form. It is of utmost importance to under-

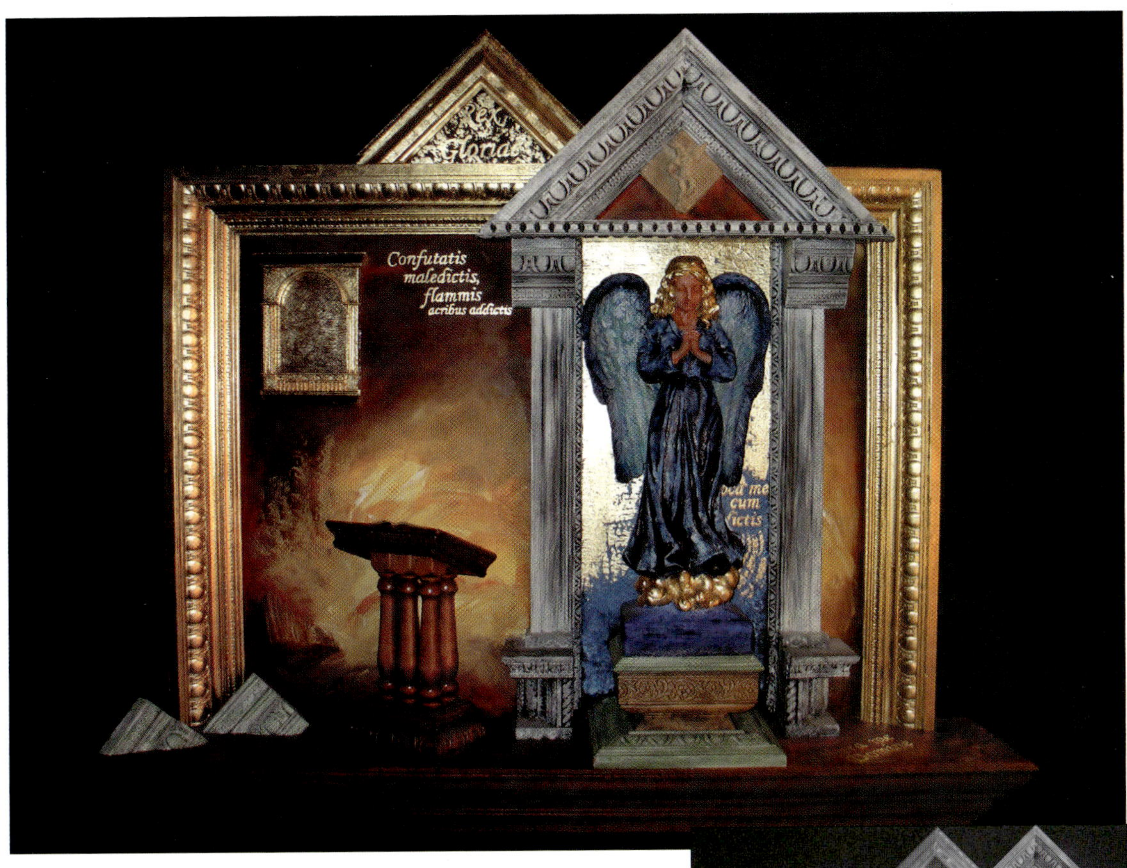

Shijo, Libera Me Domine
Photo by Alan Burner.

stand that color is the absolute authority to create this very serious emotional statement.

Color Expression in Performance/Stage Lighting

The lights are turned down, the candles lit and set in place, and Aiko waits for Akihiko's return (next page). The setting is somewhat obvious as to her intent, as she waits for her husband. The hues range from intense yellow to deep red-oranges, and then to deepest red-orange in the background. There is warmth generated not only from the candles, but every color in the frame is warm and inviting. The intense yellow of the candles create enough light to enhance the figure of Aiko, which in this very dim and soft red-orange light, becomes very sensuous and alluring. Any other harmony combinations of color expression would simply not work. Imagine her on stage as the lighting technicians change the colors of the stage to

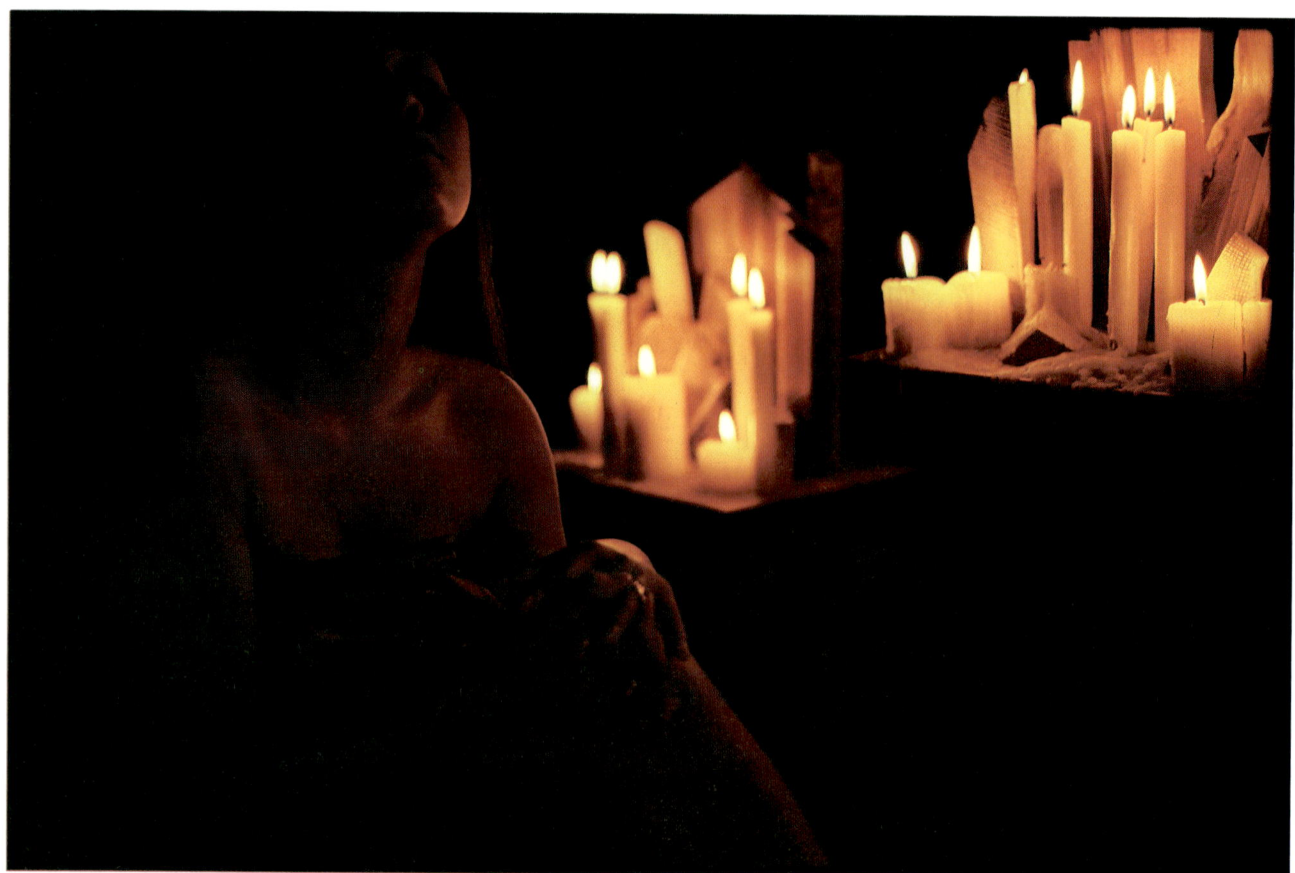

Shijo, *Aiko Prepares for Akihiko's Return* [Video Still].
Photo by Alan Burner.

blues and blue-greens, or perhaps cool violets to warm violet. The mood would not have the same appeal, the emotional ambiance would be more cold and calculating, or perhaps just too calm.

Setting the appropriate mood is paramount in stage lighting design. A well orchestrated performance is solidly based in *color,* usually enhanced by special lighting techniques, which take the audience through specific emotional expeditions. Lighting technicians have prior knowledge of the script's contents, and spend a considerable amount of time planning and incorporating the exact color sequences into the duration of the performance. This is a vital function that serves to manipulate specific mood responses. The all important aspects of performances, opera, musicals, etc., depend on color to *enhance* and in most cases *create* the mood. A *cool stage* (green, blue, violet) will create calm and even tranquil *moods,* whereas a warm stage (yellow, orange, red) generates a charged and energized presence.

The Dreamscape (next page) presents us with a different color expression. The figure is calm as is a tranquil horizon. *The Dreamscape* is another example of the effects of stage lighting. The levitated figure creates an immediate calm, though somewhat rigid, first by virtue of the *horizontal relaxed* line of her body, but more importantly, by the high intensity red-orange of her body. The composition is somewhat mysterious with its warm hues, and it keeps the

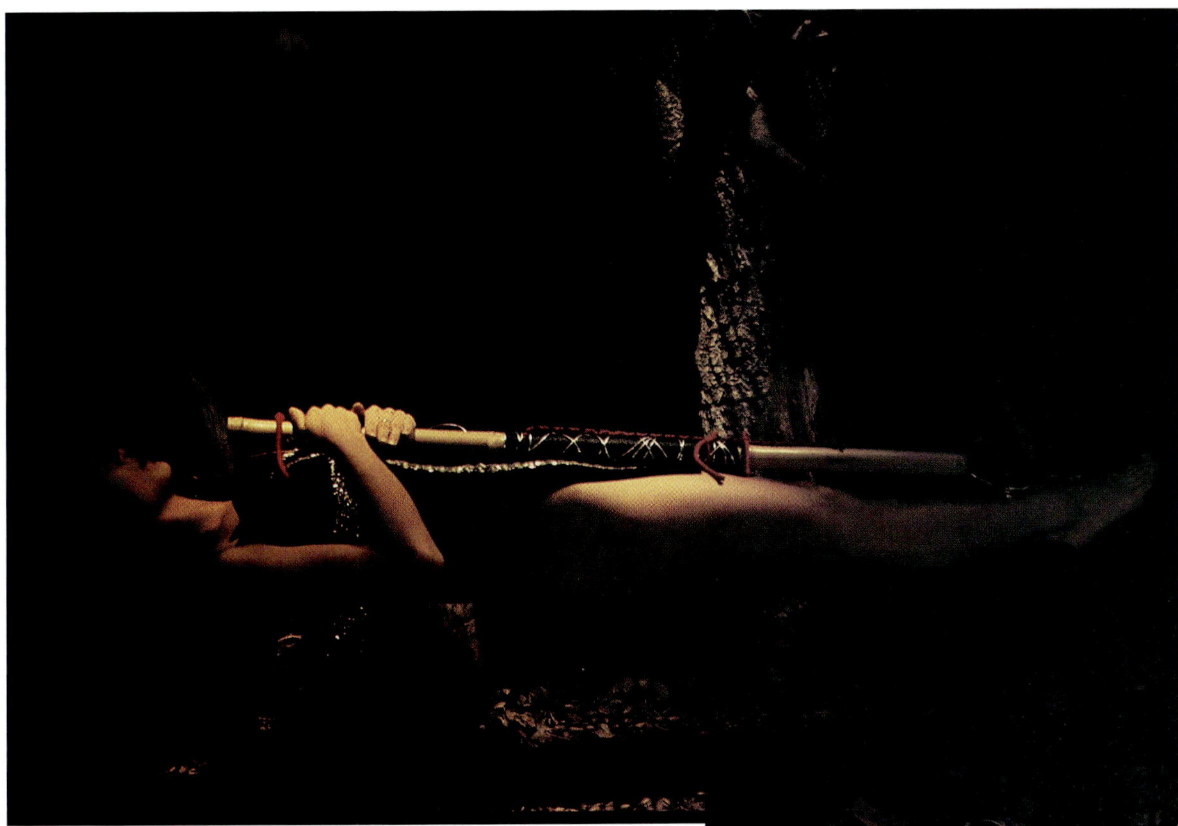

Shijo, *Preparation for the Ceremony; The Dreamscape* (video still)
Photo by Alan Burner.

viewer too curious to be able to relax, or create a total calm ambiance.

Color expression in this frame, has similarities, and yet very different mood effects are perceived from *The Dreamscape*. Her form is relaxed, as is the figure in the above frame, and yet there is a striking difference. Her *vertical stability* creates a certain strength architecturally, that the above does not possess. The most noticeable difference is color. Violet, green and orange are the dominant colors in this set, and it is without question that violet is the most prevalent of the hues present. The strength and stability of the standing vertical figure, is reinforced by the *strongest* and least intense color in the spectrum, which is of course violet. The color expression in this set forges a very dynamic feeling, even with a vertical and static form in place.

Shijo, *Amy Relaxes Between Film Sequences on Stage.*
Photo by Alan Burner.

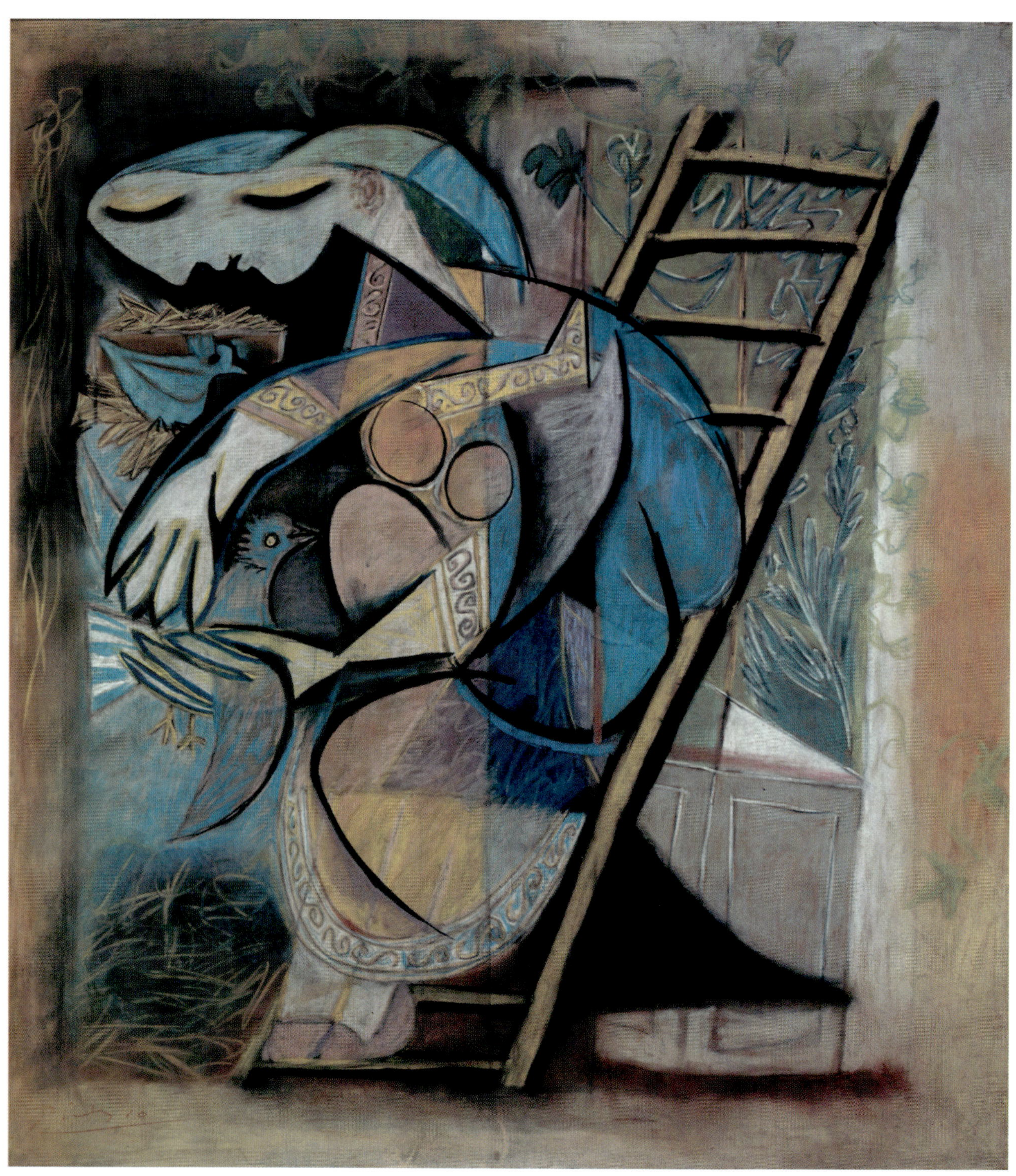

Woman with Pigeons by Pablo Picasso.

Advanced Color Expression

Pablo Picasso, one of the 20th century's most successful artists, will be the focus for the remainder of the color expression discussion. Actually, he was one of the wealthiest and most successful artists in recorded history.

Picasso was what we refer to as a "form" artist, as opposed to a "colorist." That is to say, even though he incorporated color into much of his work, it was his prowess with shape and form that we know him by the most. Abstract form, simple form, large and small forms, juxtaposed forms fragmented in space, all were about his style. Some of these forms involved color, some did not. At times he would use a full color pallet, other times only a wash of color would complement the forms in the composition. The use of color as expression depended on his own life experiences. His work was about the man himself, which basically narrows down to his various relationships with women.

Still, Picasso knew the importance of color expression quite well. After all, he was usually the source of upset with the women in his life (below). Look at *Sad Olga* to see his use of somber washes of color throughout the composition, which corresponds to the expression on her face. *Olga Apprehensive* is endowed with considerably more color hues, and the colors are more specifically located in the painting. The red-orange tones seem to create some degree of tension, and thereby supporting the idea that there is a fair degree of apprehension about Olga's face. *Olga Hurt*, on the other hand seems to have lost any emotional ability to hold up her facial expression. That is to say, the color has drained from the composition, only to leave deep shaded red to orange tones. The limited monochromatic nature of this portrait seems to express more fully a deeper sadness and hurt.

These color enhanced portraits continued to change, as the representational aspects become continuously more abstracted, and the shapes distorted.

Picasso no doubt knew he could be more expressive of his emotions about toward his subject

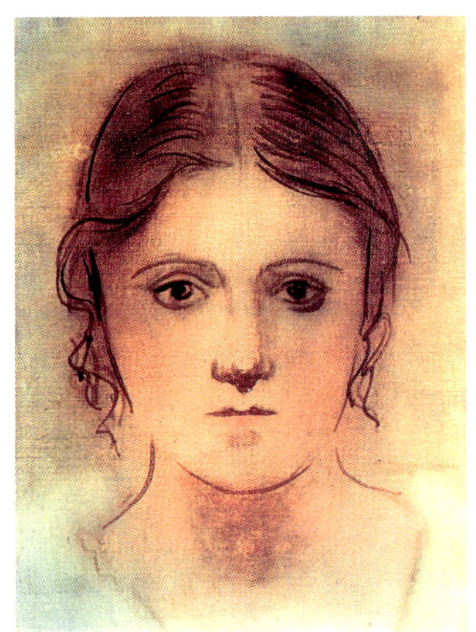

Pablo Picasso, *Sad Olga,* Paris

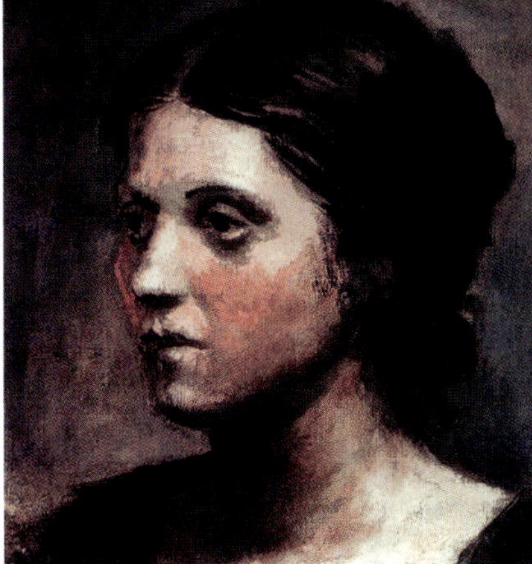

Pablo Picasso, *Olga Apprehensive,* Paris

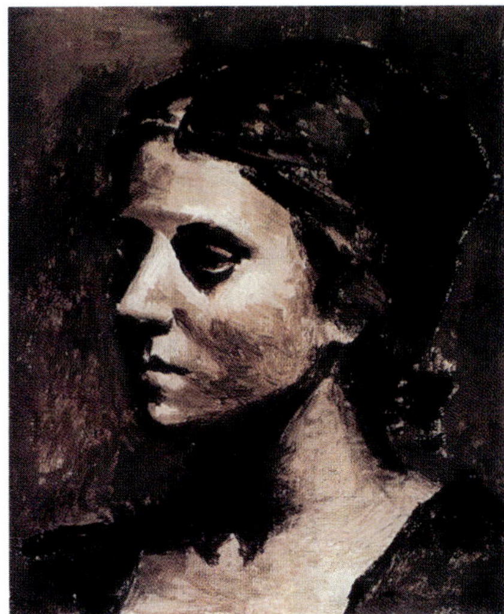

Pablo Picasso, *Olga Hurt,* Paris, Autumn

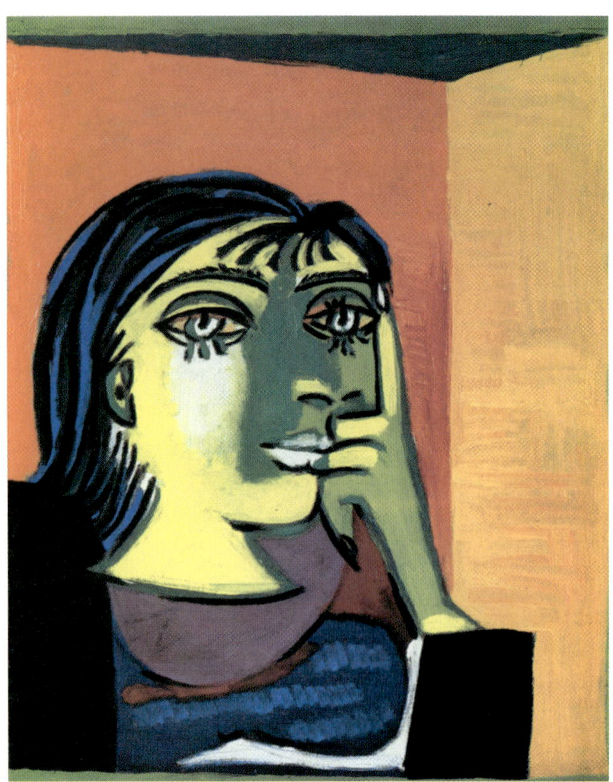

Portrait of Dora Maar, 1937 by Pablo Picasso.

matter, if nothing more than to fragment, destroy and then reinvent their form.

Picasso's extramarital affairs took their toll on his wives and he became increasingly more distraught about his relationships. His compositions of fragmented planes and shapes—simple contour line drawings without color—began to express the condition of his emotional state.

It is most certainly color expression which portrays the mood of this portrait of Dora Maar (above). Everything else about the composition is subservient to color, and it is this hexad harmony of primary and secondary saturated complements that tell us of his strong emotional attachment to Dora. In this case, it is the destruction of typical or conventional color, which is replaced by unconventional color to translate the emotion.

Picasso exclaimed many times, in slightly different sentences, "Every act of creation is first of all an act of destruction" or "To paint is to destroy." Picasso knew full well about the *act of destruction,* he was after all the grand purveyor of this sentiment and action. He not only destroyed the lives of his lovers and wives, but that of his own children as well. Picasso's infidelity was the reason for the pain and suffering of his family, lovers, and himself. Everyone in his life, especially those close to him, gave repeatedly of their energies, until they had nothing left to give. Picasso would then move on to the next victim, stolen energies unrequited. His own granddaughter writes concerning his accomplishments as a human being, rather than his success as an artist:

"Isolated inside Notre-Dame-de-Vie, he died in the same way as he had lived: alone, which is how he had wanted to be. He had made this cruel statement: When I die, it will be a shipwreck. When a large ship goes down many people in the vicinity are swept into the whirlpool."

It's true, many people were swept into the whirlpool. Pablito, my inseparable brother, committed suicide two days after our grandfather was buried at Vauvenargues. My father, the frail giant, died two years later feeling desperately orphaned. Marie-Therese Walter, the inconsolable muse, hanged herself from the ceiling of her garage in Juan-les-Pins. Jacqueline, the companion of his last days, also committed suicide with a bullet in her temple. Later, Dora Maar died in poverty surrounded by the Picasso paintings she had refused to sell, so she could preserve for herself the presence of the man whom she idolized.

*I was meant to be one of the victims as well. If I'm still around, I owe it to a lust for life and struggle, which I inherited from a grandfather I dreamed about. And who wasn't there"**

Picasso left a path of destruction everywhere he tread. As he continued painting, he destroyed images, planes and peoples lives, all for the sake of his art. He continued to destroy, rearranging his expression

*From Picasso, *My Grandfather by Marinqa Picasso,* Riverhead Books, 2001.

of life with his women. He reinvents the form over and over, in order to fit his own expressive needs.

In May of 1937, Picasso turned his attention to one his greatest works ever produced. This time it was not about his own personal destructions, as much as it was about the destruction of a town called *Guernica* (following page). On April 26, 1937, German Nazi warplanes began their surprise attack on the town of Guernica. The headlines read "*Mille bombes incendiaries lancees par les avions de Hitler et de Mussolini reduisent en cendres la ville de Guernica*" (A Thousand Firebombs dropped by Hitler and Mussolini's Planes Reduce the Town of Guernica To Ashes).

The entire city of Guernica was destroyed in a matter of a few hours. Many reports said that the town glowed an eerie deep red-orange—not unlike dying embers in a camp-fire—the evening after the destruction of Guernica. It was total carnage and chaos upon an innocent, unsuspecting civilian town. The German war machine had prevailed without a struggle.

Picasso labored with many sketches, working and reworking his plan to show the world the calamity in his native Spain. The painting itself is somewhat of an enigma, and so we will explore briefly the two interpretations that are most obvious. One could declare what is reasonably obvious, in that the painting is about the destruction Guernica. All of the figurative forms have been through the extreme agony of a bomb attack because of the Nazi forces, and so the destruction of buildings, a couple of animals, and human forms indicate that the painting is purely about the physical destruction of the town. There are four women, one male, a baby, a horse and a bull, which dominate the figurative element. The people and horse are all in death's grip, as the agony prevails. The bull, it is said by many, is the Nazi General Franco of Spain, surveying his path of destruction. There is however another interpretation, or at least opinion of the content in the mural.

Another approach to the mural is seen in light of Picasso's real life, consider the many spiritual destructions symbolized on this canvass. The figures represent women who have been emotionally and spiritually shattered. The horse also represents women, in either interpretation, which is generally agreed upon. In the bullfight, the horse saps the strength from the bull, which is Picasso himself. Picasso then surveys his own path of destruction. The faces in the composition all seem to turn in the direction of the bull, and he looks back on the destruction to survey the consequences of his life.

The following essay documents much of the development of Guernica, through a discourse about "Weeping Women," which are seen in his sketches and paintings in preparation for Guernica.

Picasso's

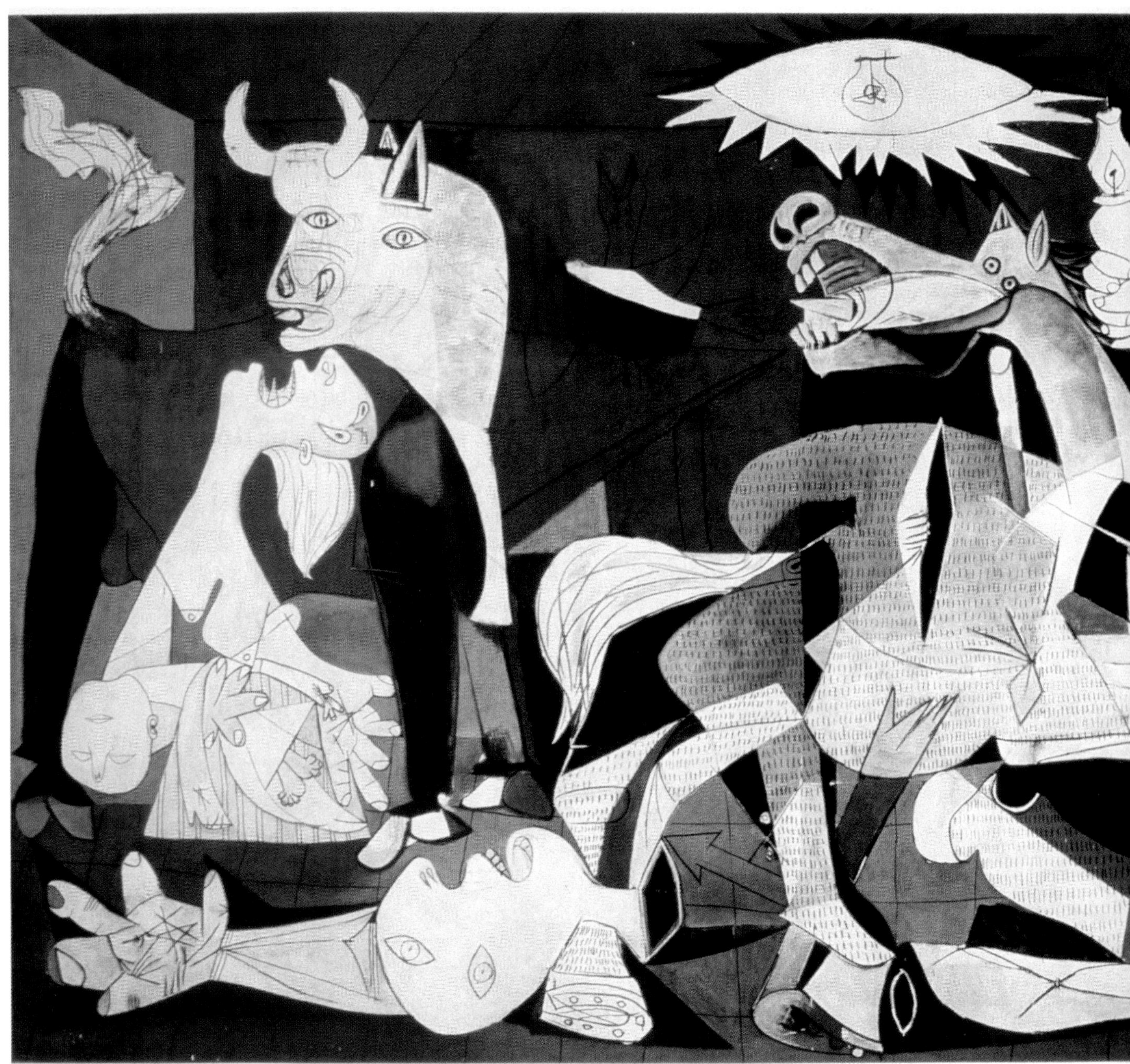

Guernica by Pablo Picasso May/June 1937.

Guernica

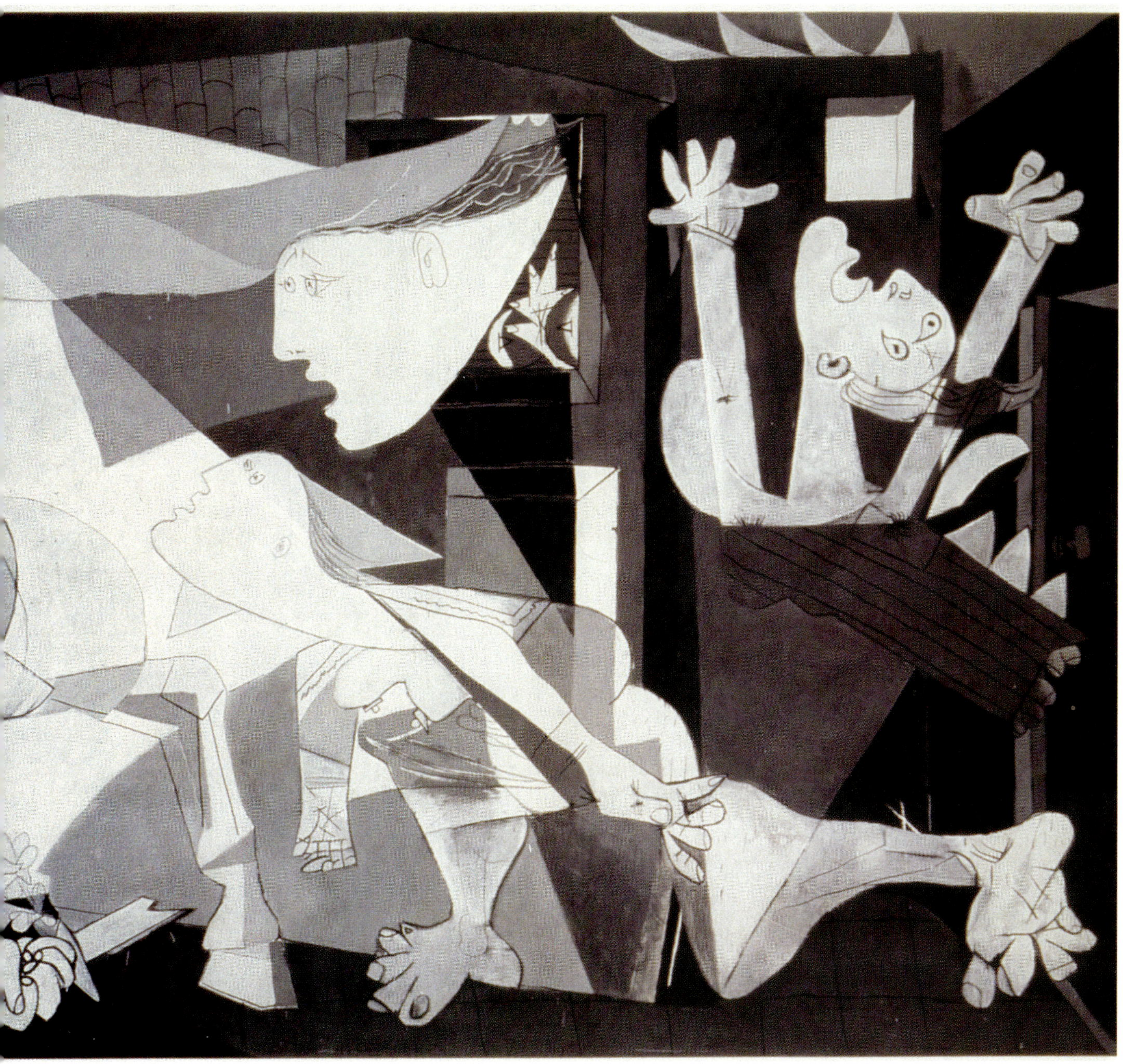

READING COMPLEMENT

Picasso and the Weeping Women: The Years of Marie-Terese Walter and Dora Maar

by Judi Freeman
Los Angeles County Museum of Art

". . .Picasso sends us our death notice. . ."

"To take up a pen, line up words as if they could add anything to Picasso's *Guernica*, is the most useless of undertakings. In the black-and-white rectangle of ancient tragedy, Picasso sends us our death notice: everything we love is going to die, and that is why right now it is important to die, and that is why right now it is important that everything we love be summed up into something unforgettably beautiful, like the shedding of so many tears of farewell."

—MICHEL LEIRIS, 1937

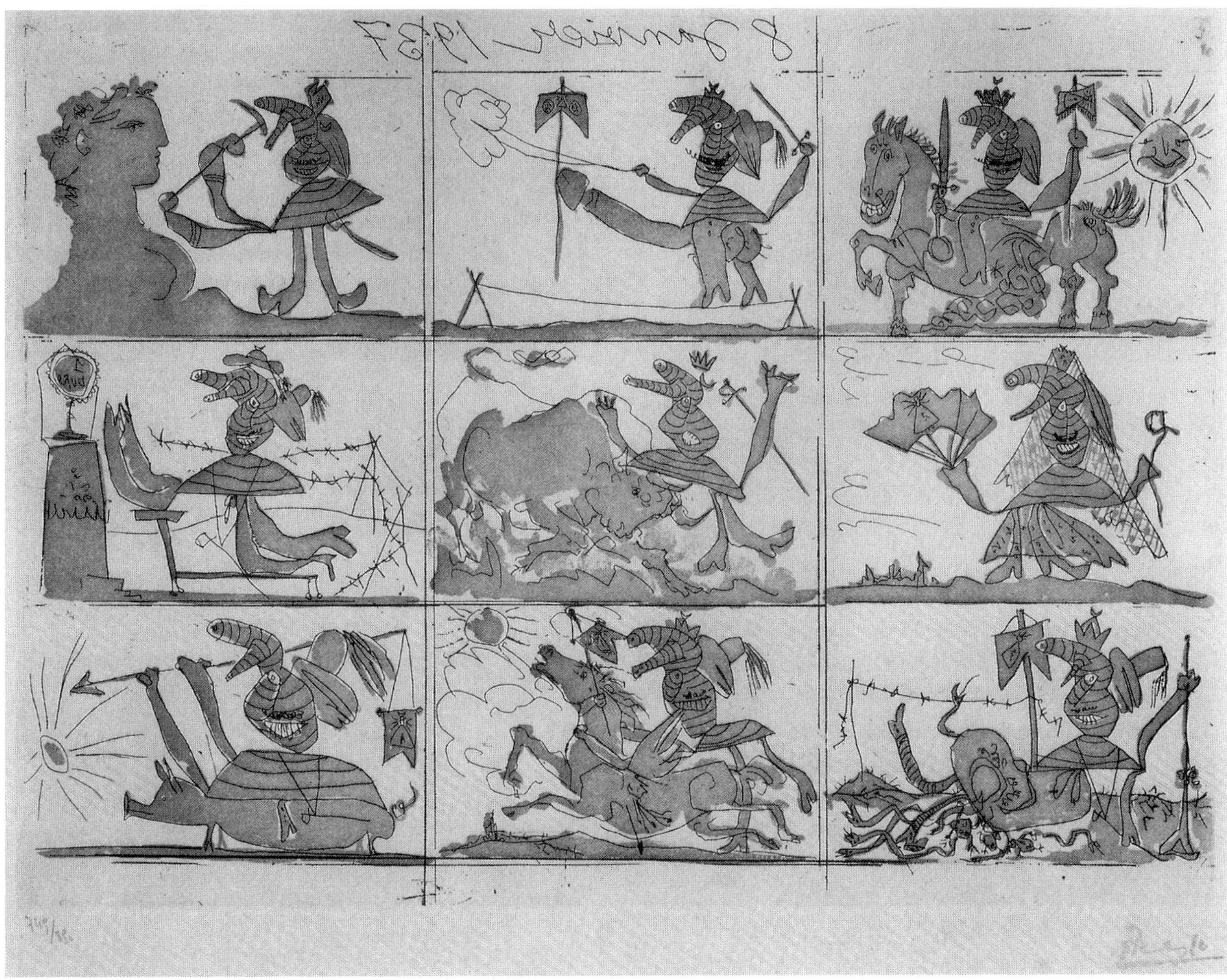

Figure 1

Dream and Lie of Fanco (scenes 1–9) 8 January 1937 (with aquatint added 25 May 1937) Etching and aquatint on paper 12 3/8 × 16 5/8 in. (31.4 × 42.1 cm) © 2003 Estate of Pablo Picasso/Artists Rights Society (ARS), New York.

On 8 January 1937 Picasso began etching his *Dream and Lie of Franco.* Each of the two prints was divided, comic-strip-style, into three rows of three scenes. Picasso worked on them from left to right, but as printed they read from right to left. He completed all but four of the eighteen scenes by the end of the next day. In the first scene (Figure 1, upper right) Franco appears as a composite scarecrow/jellyfish with enormous tentacles and an elephantine head. He is astride a disemboweled horse. Next he has dismounted and exposes his hairy scrotum and an enormous penis. In the third frame he raises a pickax to a female bust. In the fourth, he stands in the foreground, clad in a traditional Spanish mantilla and comb and holding a fan, with a city on the distant horizon. A bull, symbolizing Spain generally and the Spanish Popular Front's resistance specifically, attacks him in the fifth scene. Kneeling at a makeshift altar surrounded by barbed wire, Franco prays in the sixth frame. In the seventh he gives birth

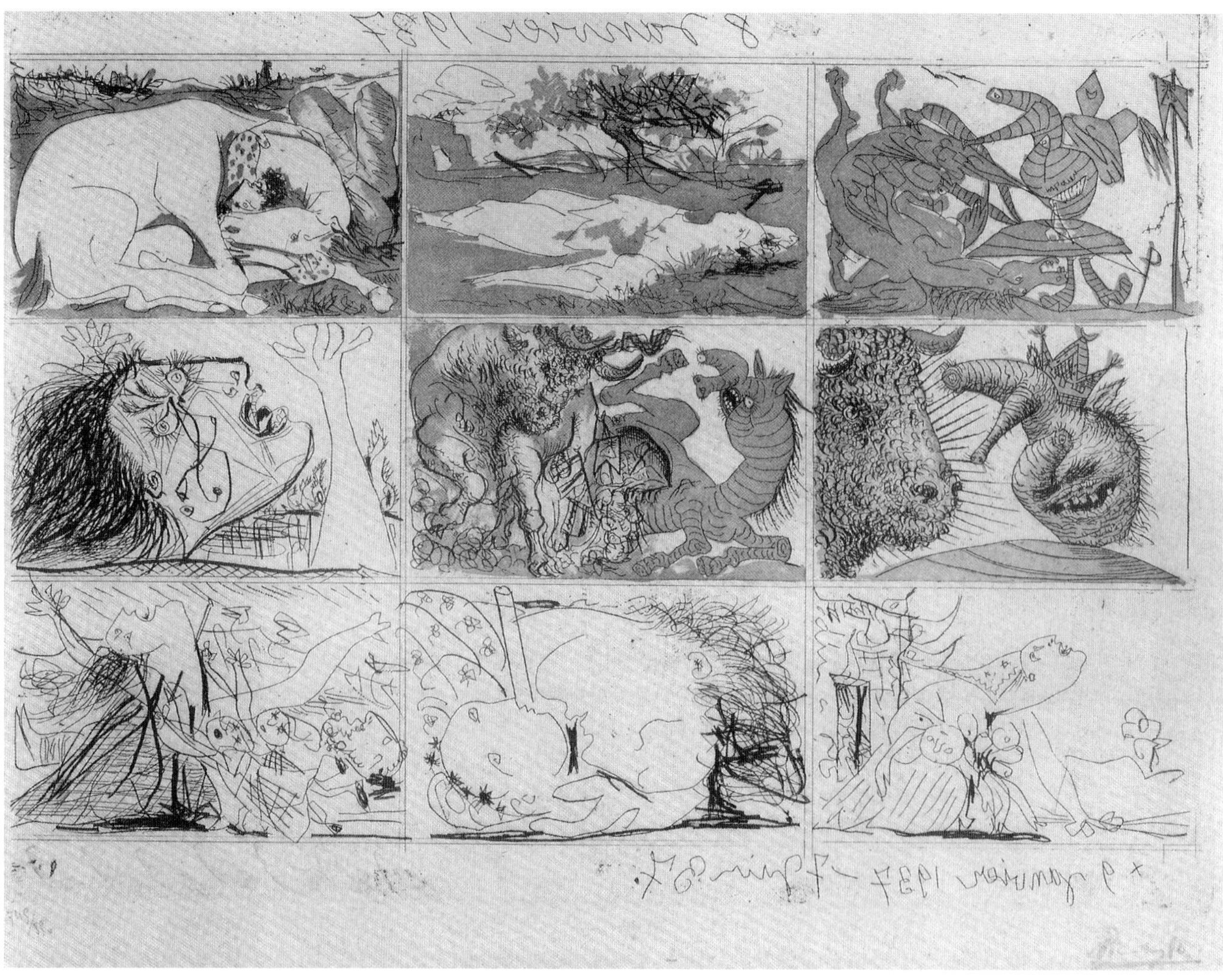

Figure 2

Dream and Lie of Franco (scenes 10–18) 8 January 1937 (with aquatint added 25 May 1937 and final four panels added 7 June 1937) Etching and aquatint on paper 12 3/8 × 16 5/8 in. (31.4 × 42.1 cm) © 2003 Estate of Pablo Picasso/Artists Rights Society (ARS), New York.

to an array of snakes and disembodied heads. He strangles and lances his horse in the next scene, so that by the ninth he no longer rides astride an animal but has been metamorphosed into half-monster, half-pig. In the tenth scene, beginning the second plate (Figure 2), Franco devours his dead horse's innards. The remnants of battle appear in the next two frames: a wounded woman lies on the ground amid burning buildings in scene eleven, while a dead warrior and horse dominate scene twelve.

Scene thirteen is a bust-length portrait. Franco, no longer the clean-shaven monster of panels one through ten, now is scruffy and hairy, an even more grotesque specter. He resembles a flayed animal or a caricature of Ubu Roi, the protagonist of Alfred Jarry's eponymous play, and is not dissimilar to Dora Maar's 1936 close-up photograph that she titled *Portrait of Ubu* (Figure 3). Both Picasso and Maar were fascinated by the story of Ubu Roi, and he makes several appearances in Picasso's oeuvre

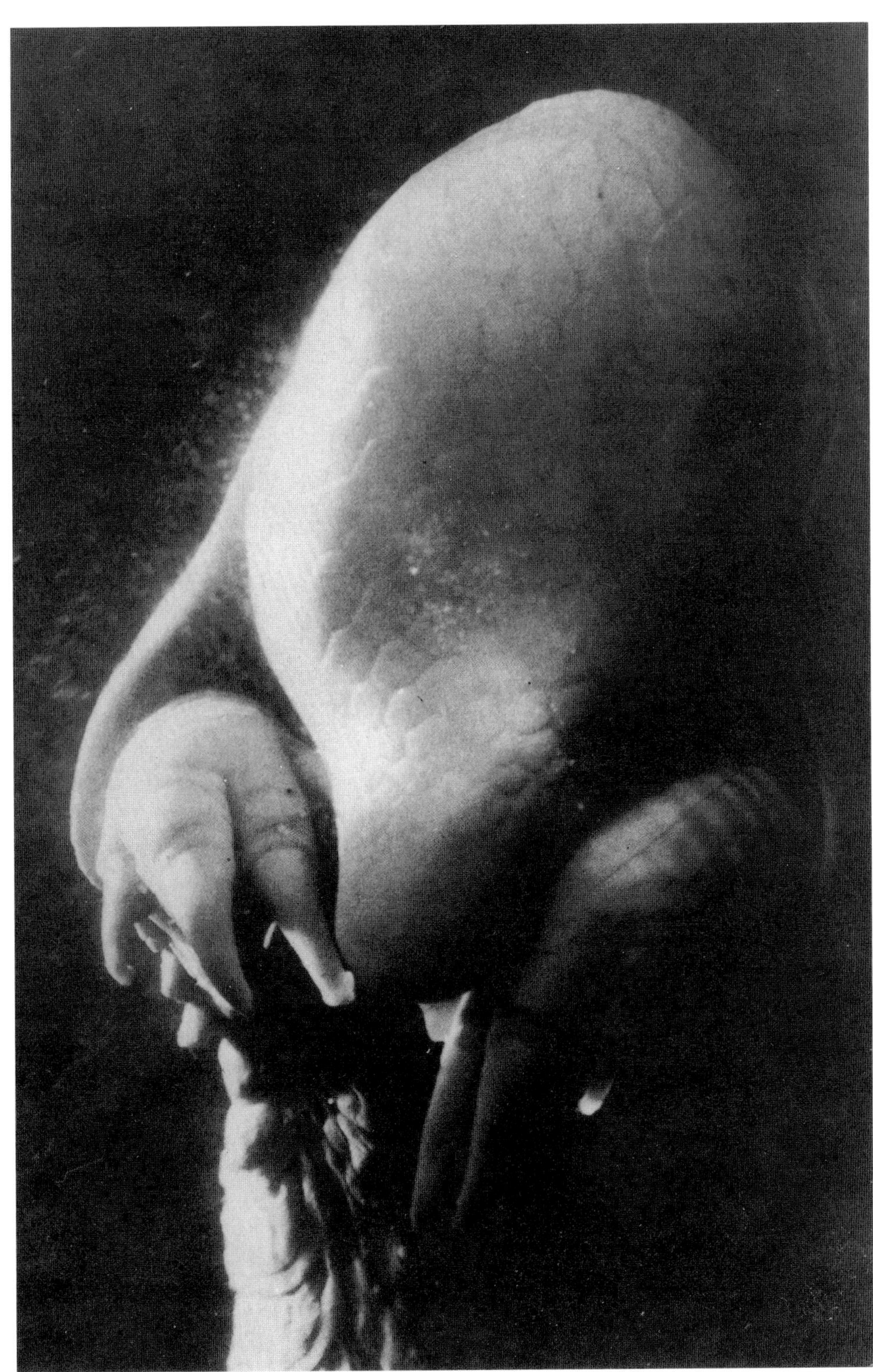

Figure 3

Portrait of Ubu by Dora Maar © Copyright 1936 Dora Maar. Reprinted with permission of the National Gallery of Australia.

(see Figure 70, for example). Here Franco comes face-to-face with the head of a bull. In the next frame Franco's head (not mostly shaven) is appended to the body of a disemboweled horse, he is confronted by the angry bull. This scene contains the densest and most violent activity on the second plate. Picasso completed the final four frames five months later, on 7 June. Dramatically different from the previous fourteen, these last scenes contain victims of Franco's wartime atrocities. Frame fifteen (Figure 4) depicts a weeping woman, hands reaching upward and hair disheveled, with burning phallic forms in the distance. A wailing mother holds her dead child as she flees from a burning house in frame sixteen. Frame seventeen is a closeup of a fallen couple—the dead warrior from scene twelve and the female bust from scene three—caught in an embrace. Scene eighteen is an elaborated version of sixteen. Here two terrified children cling to their distraught mother as she stands before her fallen husband.

The prose poem by Picasso accompanying the two prints in the published folio vividly evokes images that underscore the horrors of the attacks of Franco and his forces: "swords of ill-omened octopuses dishrag of hairs from tonsures standing in the middle of the frying pan," writes Picasso at the beginning of his text. His images become increasingly grotesque: "beauty products from the garbage truck—rape of the ladies-in-waiting in tears and in large tears—on shoulders the coffin stuffed with sausages and mouths…lantern of lice where the dog lies knot of rats hiding place of the palace of old rags—the flags that fry in the frying pan writhe in the black of the sauce of the ink spilled in the drops of blood that shoot him." Sounds reach a crescendo:

> *cries of children cries of women cries of birds cries of flowers cries of wood and of stones cries of bricks cries of furniture of beds of chairs of curtains of pans of cats and of papers cries of odors that scratch themselves cries of smoke pecking at the neck of the cries that boil in the cauldron and of the rain of birds that floods the sea.*

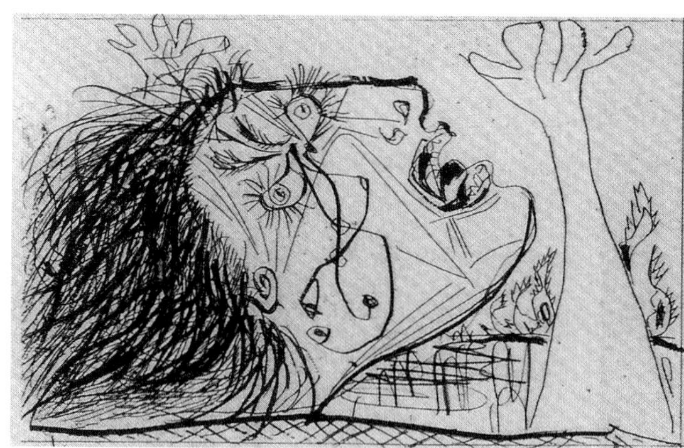

Figure 4

Detail: scene 15 of *Dream and Lie of Fanco* © 2003 Estate of Pablo Picasso/Artists Rights Society (ARS), New York.

Clearly Picasso's preoccupation with *gritos*—cries, screams, howls, shrieks—increased between January and June. He obsessively wrote in his notebook nearly every day beginning 25 January and continuing through the month of February. The texts are laced with powerful sensory allusions: the odors of flowers or perfume, the textures of liquids, the colors of things, the inflections of music. A verbal permutation introduces his entry of 20 February: "raging toothache in the eyes of the sun pique—pique raging sun-ache of the teeth in the eyes—eyes in the teeth pique of raging sun-ache pique eyes in the teeth of toothache—of the sun pique of raging eyes flower."

Just as this entry explores different combinations of the same elements, so too does his study of female heads (Figure 5). He captures these misshapen faces in various configurations. Within each head floats a pair of eyes, almond-shaped slivers punctured by circles filled with dots. Many of the heads have snouts in place of noses, chunky, bulging projections of flesh. All have nostrils reduced to short strokes. Most have mouths; some of these mouths consist of elongated ovals, while others are gaping orifices. Some are filled with teeth, usually square but occasionally rounded. From between several sets of teeth, knifelike tongues protrude.

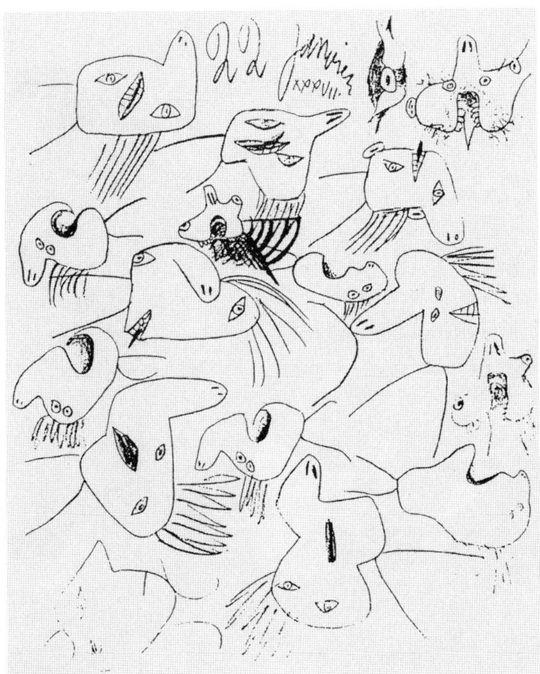

Figure 5

Study of Women's Heads 22 January 1937 Pencil on blue paper 10 5/8 × 8 1/4 in. (27 × 21 cm) © 2003 Estate of Pablo Picasso/Artists Rights Society (ARS), New York.

These women are clearly related to the weeping women. None has tears, but all have other features that will be quoted in the weeping women images. All allude to women contorted by violence and horrific pain. On the very same day, 22 January, Picasso drew an extremely graphic rape scene on a similar scale (Figure 6). The intensity of emotion contained in the weeping women could easily be excerpted from a violent scene of this nature. The rapist has a gnarled, monstrous, animal-like head, identical to the one on the upper right of the sheet of women's heads. The victim's face is that of an animal in agony. Her mouth is a large oval, a dark hole from which presumably a piercing scream of astonishing intensity emanates, with circumferential teeth pointing toward the center.

Tears and cries of pain, as features of the face, were not exploited by Picasso alone. His preoccupations were shared by his contemporaries as well as by previous generations of Spanish artists. A tradition of weeping women exists in Spanish religious sculpture, particularly in statues of the Virgin Mary. The *mater dolorosa* was a favored theme with sixteenth and seventeenth-century Spanish painters.

Among contemporary artists there is an unmistakable stylistic echo of Picasso's verses for *Dream and Lie of Franco* (and his subsequent notebook jottings) in the 1937 poetry of Joan Miró:

> *The flaming tree of the peacock's tail that bites the snouts of bats smiling before the charred corpse of my grandmother who was buried by a dance of transparent glass nightingales with rocket wings who dance the* sardana *around the phosphorescent carcass while pecking with the gold of their pincers the metal seeds of silver cypresses rushing down in waterfalls from the grandmother's big toe.*

Miró wrote this on 2 October 1937, using phrases reminiscent in both style and substance of

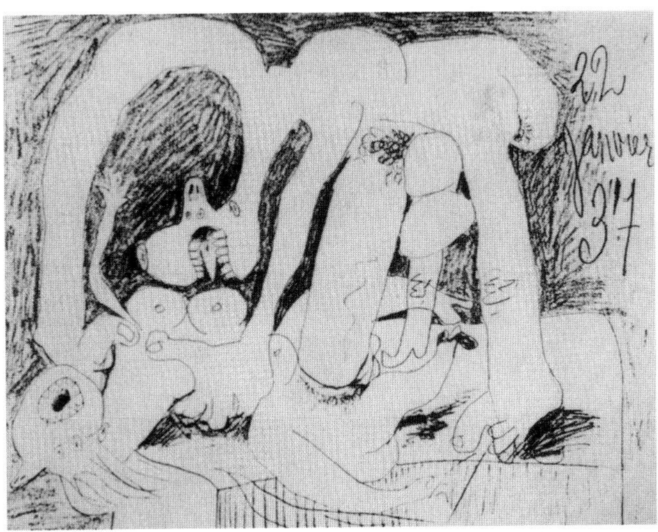

Figure 6

Rape 22 January 1937 Pencil on paper 8 1/2 × 10 7/8 in. (21.5 × 27.5 cm) © 2003 Estate of Pablo Picasso/Artists Rights Society (ARS), New York.

Picasso's "raging toothache in the eyes of the sun pique." Miró drew a sheet of heads (Figure 7) that sit atop bodies comparable to those in Picasso's *Rape*; they open their mouths to scream, they crane their necks to see, they gape in amazement. Such abbreviated, organically inspired forms appear also in the work of fellow Spaniard Julio González; his *Head* of 1935 (Figure 8) is an iron arc interrupted by short strands of hair at the very top, a gaping mouth with shardlike teeth at the bottom, and a looming eye with long lashes at the center. This reductive sculpture contains a pathos akin to any of Picasso's studies on the sheet of women's heads.

The *Rape* and *Study of Women's Heads* mark an unusually intense involvement with violent imagery during January 1937. Picasso's predilection for the

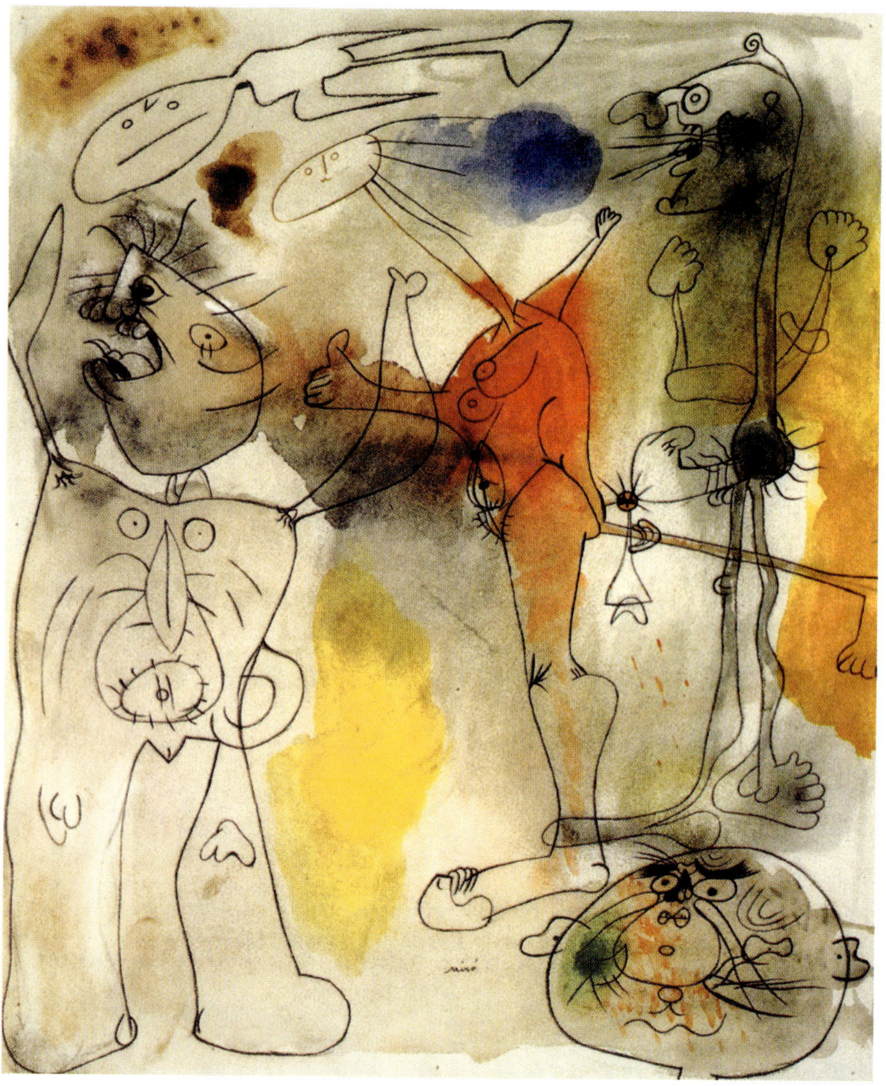

Figure 7

Joan Miró *Persons Haunted by a Bird* 1938 Gouache, crayon, watercolor and charcoal on paper 16 1/8 × 13 in. (41 × 33 cm) © 2003 Successió Miró/Artists Rights Society (ARS), New York/ADAGP, Paris.

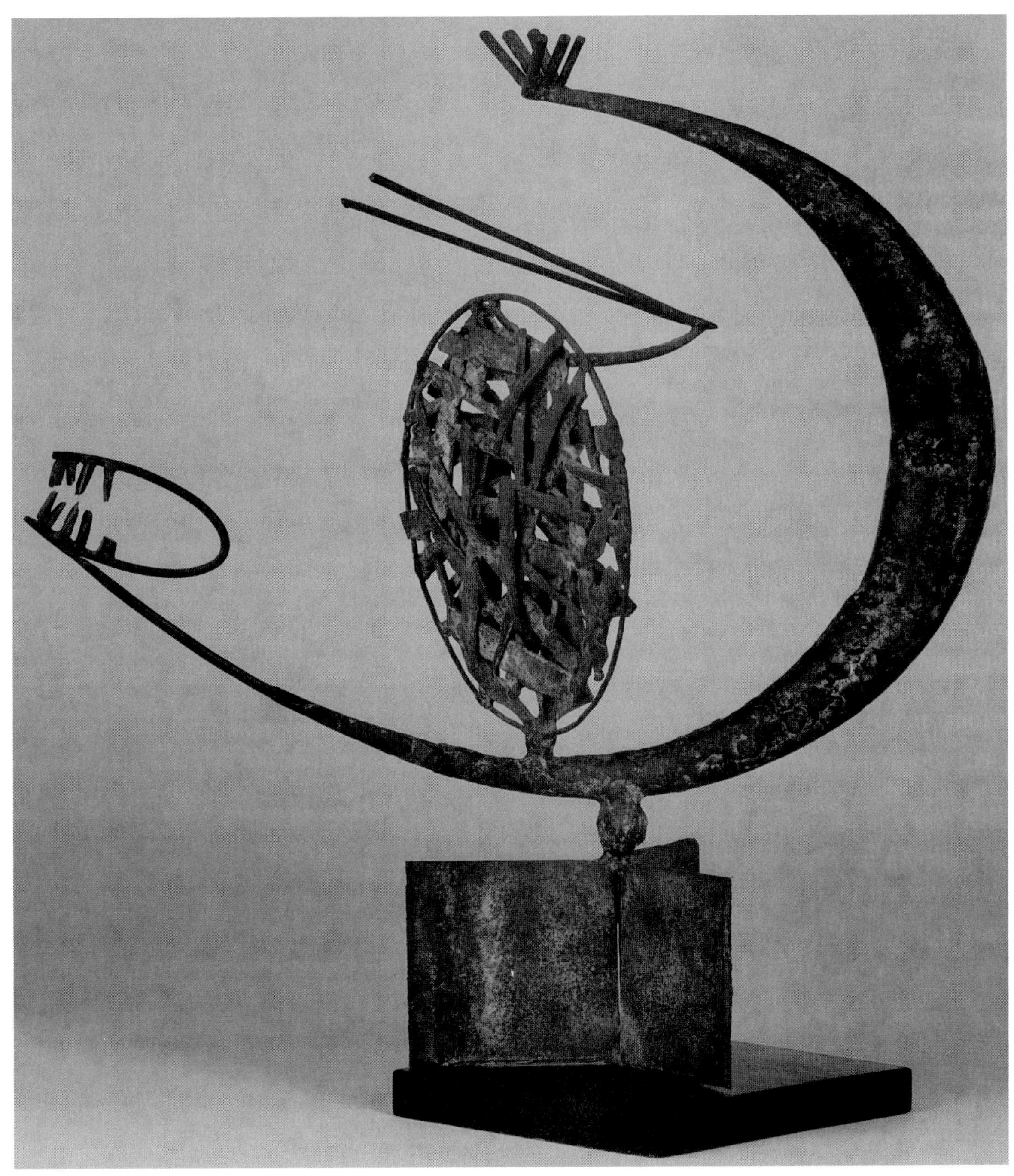

Figure 8

Julio González *Head ("The Snail")* c. 1935 Wrought iron 17 1/2 × 7 11/16 × 15 1/4 in. (45.1 × 19.5 × 38.7 cm) Digital Image © The Museum of Modern Art/Licensed by SCALA/Art Resource, NY.

subjects of these drawings was a fitting preparation for the invitation that he received in January, from representative of the Spanish republican government, to design a large mural for the Spanish pavilion at the International Exposition in Paris that summer. His sympathies for the Spanish republican cause were clear in the equally violent *Dream and Lie of Franco.* Early in February he returned to the scarecrow-like figures from *Dream.* Now devoid of Franco's menacing features, these were transformed into bathers (Figure 9). In his effort to find an allegorical theme to explore for the Spanish pavilion, Picasso incorporated characteristics of these bathers into a series of works he embarked on in April depicting the artist and his model in the studio. On 18 and 19 April he drew at least fourteen sketches, trying to work out the compositional elements. The most revelatory was the sixth in the group (Figure 10), in which two reclining nudes are contorted and elongated, their heads wrapped within their arms. This drawing—with its highly detailed and exaggerated studies of individual body parts—holds the greatest suggestion of tension and violence of any in the series. Along the left side of the sheet Picasso lavished great detail on certain key body parts: an eyeball; a pointed tongue protruding between jagged teeth and a pair of lips; twisted fingers seen from the side, front, and back; a nose with pronounced nostrils; an erect nipple and its aureole.

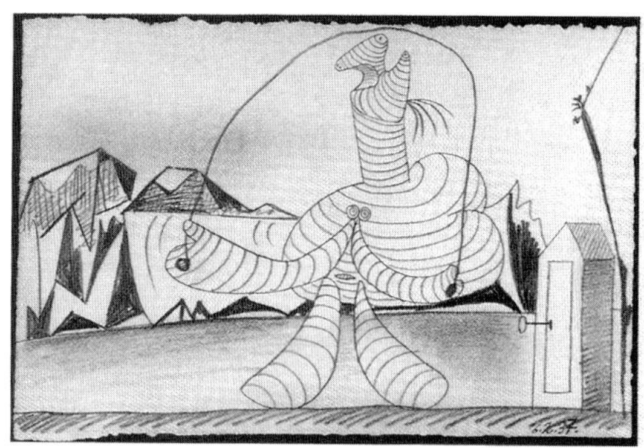

Figure 9

Bather by a Cabana Skipping Rope 6 February 1937 Pencil on Paper 6 7/8 × 10 1/4 in. (17.5 × 26 cm) © 2003 Estate of Pablo Picasso/Artists Rights Society (ARS), New York.

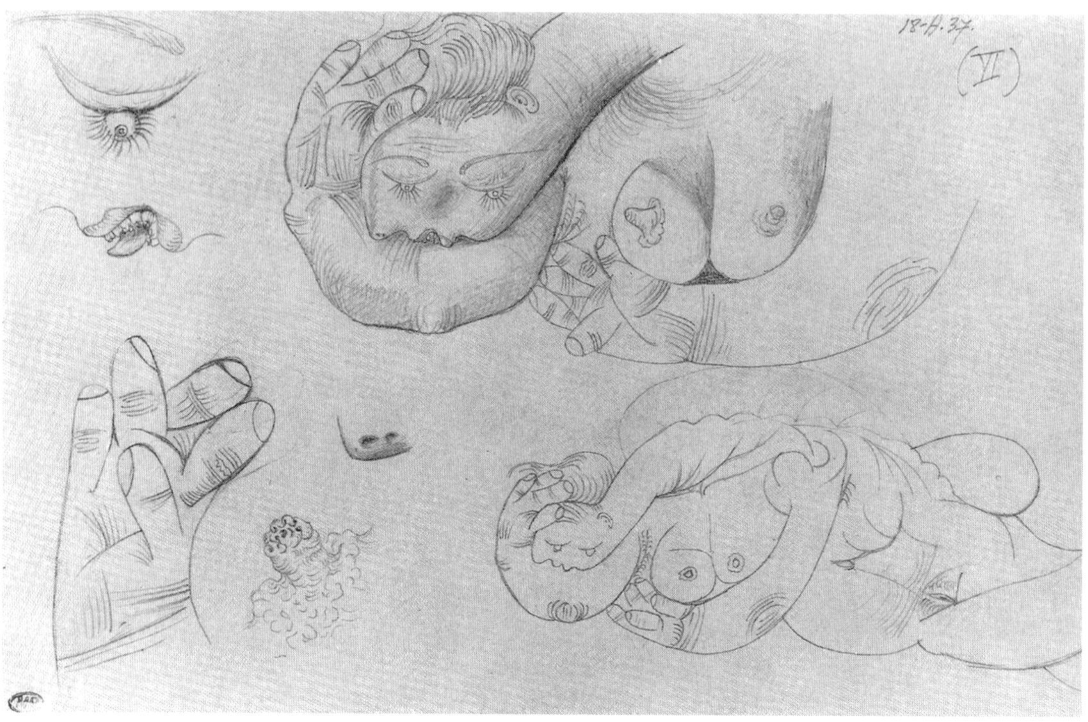

Figure 10

The Studio VI 18 April 1937 Pencil on paper 7 1/8 × 11 in. (18 × 28 cm) © 2003 Estate of Pablo Picasso/Artists Rights Society (ARS), New York.

By 1 May Picasso had abandoned his initial theme—artist and model—in favor of an allegorical encounter between bull and horse. Later he coyly observed, "My work is not symbolic…only the Guernica mural is symbolic. But in the case of the mural, that is allegoric. That's the reason I've used the horse, the bull, and so on. The mural is for the definite expression and solution of a problem and that is why I used symbolism." His six initial sketches, all created that Saturday, 1 May, are experiments in different arrangements of the two animals. The third sketch (Figure 11) features several humans as well, including a woman holding a lamp and a standing, distraught form at the center right of the sheet. This figure, head tilted back and toothy mouth slightly open, is the first indication that Picasso was interested in depicting states of intense emotion in his mural.

Three sketches of horses made the next day confirm his intention. One of them (Figure 12) shows an animal in agony, its tongue a sharp wedge thrust upward. The head is tilted back, the mouth is thrown open, and the massive teeth sit like stubs on the gums. In another of the sketches the teeth are neatly aligned. In this one and the third they seem about to fall out as they sit precariously on the edge of the muzzle.

One week later, on 8 May, Picasso's thoughts about the composition took a dramatic turn. New to his concept for the mural was a mother carrying the body of her wounded or dead child (Figure 13). This figure was almost certainly inspired by the news coverage of the violent events in Guernica (in the northern, Basque region of Spain) that had appeared in Paris newspapers during the previous week. On Monday, 26 April, German planes from the Condor Legion acting in support of Franco's forces bombed central Guernica repeatedly. Toward the close of market day the town was overrun by fire and for the most part leveled.

Paris learned the news the following day; *L'Humanité's* headline read: "Mille bombes incendiaries lancées par les avions de Hitler et de Mussolini réduisent en cendres la ville de Guernica" (A thousand firebombs dropped by Hitler's and Mussolini's planes

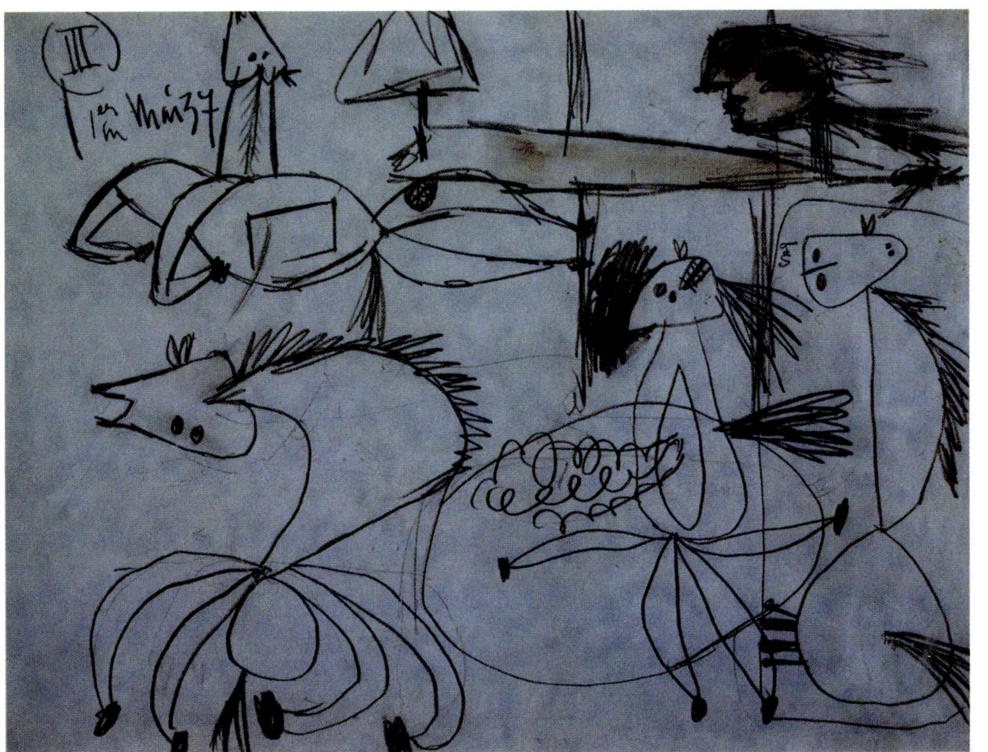

Figure 11

Guernica: Study for Composition 1 May 1937 (III) Pencil on paper 10 5/8 × 8 1/4 in. (27 × 21 cm) © 2003 Estate of Pablo Picasso/Artists Rights Society (ARS), New York.

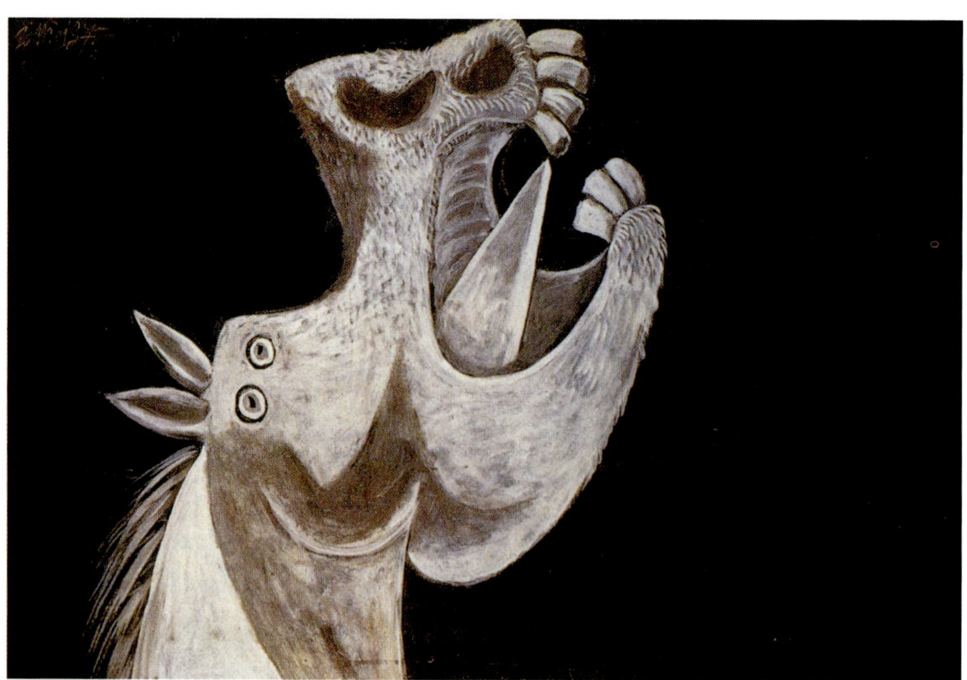

Figure 12

Head of a Horse 2 May 1937 (I) Oil on canvas 25 5/8 × 36 1/4 in. (65 × 92 cm) © 2003 Estate of Pablo Picasso/Artists Rights Society (ARS), New York.

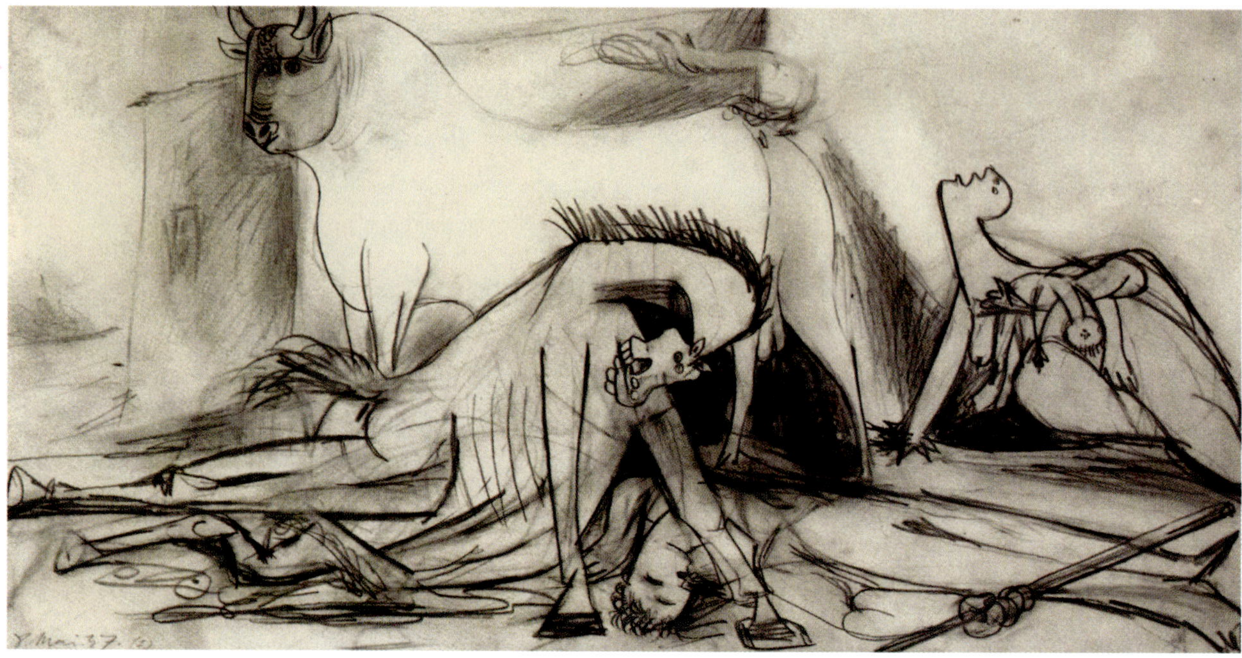

Figure 13

Guernica: Study for Composition 8 May 1937 (I) Pencil on paper 9 1/2 × 17 7/8 in. (24 × 45.5 cm) © 2003 Estate of Pablo Picasso/Artists Rights Society (ARS), New York.

reduce the town of Guernica to ashes). While other newspapers initially covered and then abandoned the story, *L'Humanité* vigorously pursued it. On 29 April it published a vivid account of the carnage (translated from the preceding day's London *Times*) by a British correspondent in Bilbao who had been to Guernica the day after the bombing:

> *At 2 a.m. today when I visited the town the whole of it was a horrible sight, flaming from end to end. The reflection of the flames could be seen in the clouds of smoke above the mountains from ten miles away. Throughout the night houses were falling until the streets became long heaps of red impenetrable debris. Many of the civilian survivors took the long trek from Guernica to Bilbao in antique solid-wheeled Basque farmcarts drawn by oxen. Carts piled high with such household possessions as could be saved from the conflagration clogged the roads all night. Other survivors were evacuated in Government lorries, but many were forced to remain round the burning town lying on mattresses or looking for lost relatives and children, while units of the fire brigades and the Basque motorized police...continued rescue work till dawn.*

The president of the Basque region, José Antonio Aguirre, issued a statement reprinted in many papers:

> *Before God and before history that will judge us I swear that for three-and-one-half hours German planes bombed with inconceivable destruction the undefended civil population of Guernica, reducing the celebrated city to cinders. They pursued with machine-gun fire the women and children who were frantically fleeing.*

The accounts of these horrific events ignited the passions of Popular Front activists in France. The traditional May Day celebration in Paris brought out more than a million demonstrators, who marched from the Place de la République to the Bastille to express their outrage and appeal for aid to the victims.

May Day was Picasso's first day of concerted work on the Guernica mural. He initially expressed his reaction to the events in Spain by using his preferred symbolic combatants: the bull and the horse. By 8 May accounts of the individual human tragedies in Guernica had clearly permeated his thinking. The inclusion of the mother and child (and their consistent appearance henceforth in his scheme for the picture) demonstrates this. In Figure 13 the mother has an extended trunk for a neck that protrudes from one long mass of flesh encircling the body of a limp child. Her cast-back head, shown in profile, is composed of an open, toothless mouth, a slight protrusion for a nose, and two dotted ovals for eyes. Picasso drew her head in a single rapid stroke, then added lines to alter the neck slightly. This quick, self-assured gesture indicates his certainty about the face, the pose, and the emotional tone.

The motif is further elaborated in a second drawing done that day (Figure 14); a shawl, draped around the mother's head and shoulders, serves to cover the child. The child's blood stains the mother's breast and hand. She looks upward. Her face conveys the intensity of the horror. Her teeth, lips, and tongue are defined in exquisite detail; her nose is now further developed, thanks to comma-shaped nostrils; her eyes now have eyebrows. Her mouth is slightly open; she is speaking, screaming, wailing.

The next day's drawing, an ink close-up of the mother and child, provides further information (Figure 15). As Picasso lavishes greater attention on the mother, the child becomes increasingly doll-like, with abbreviated, caricatured features. The mother's mouth is open wider; her eyelids appear for the first time and define her expression; her brows are bushier and pinched together. She appears shocked but not helpless, angered but not enraged, whereas her predecessor seems dazed and distraught. Picasso was of course aware of the ways in which his most minor graphic decisions would alter the viewer's perception of his subject's emotions. Placed on a ladder (Figure 16), the mother looks like a recumbent dinosaur

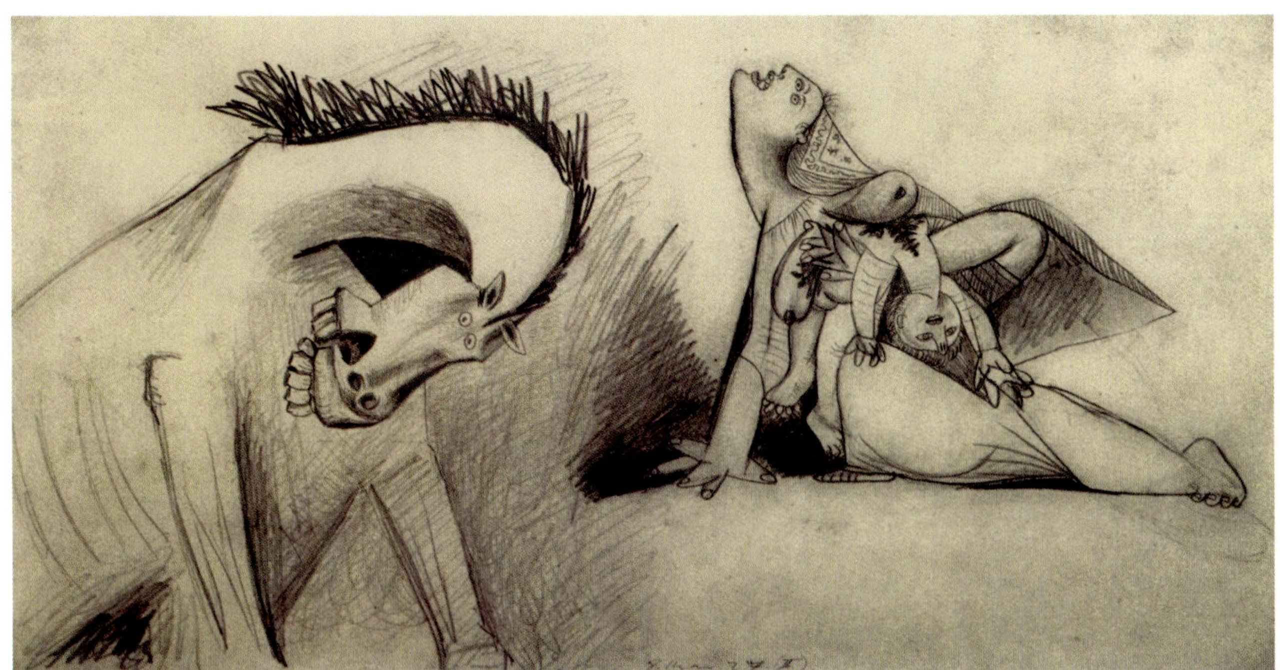

Figure 14

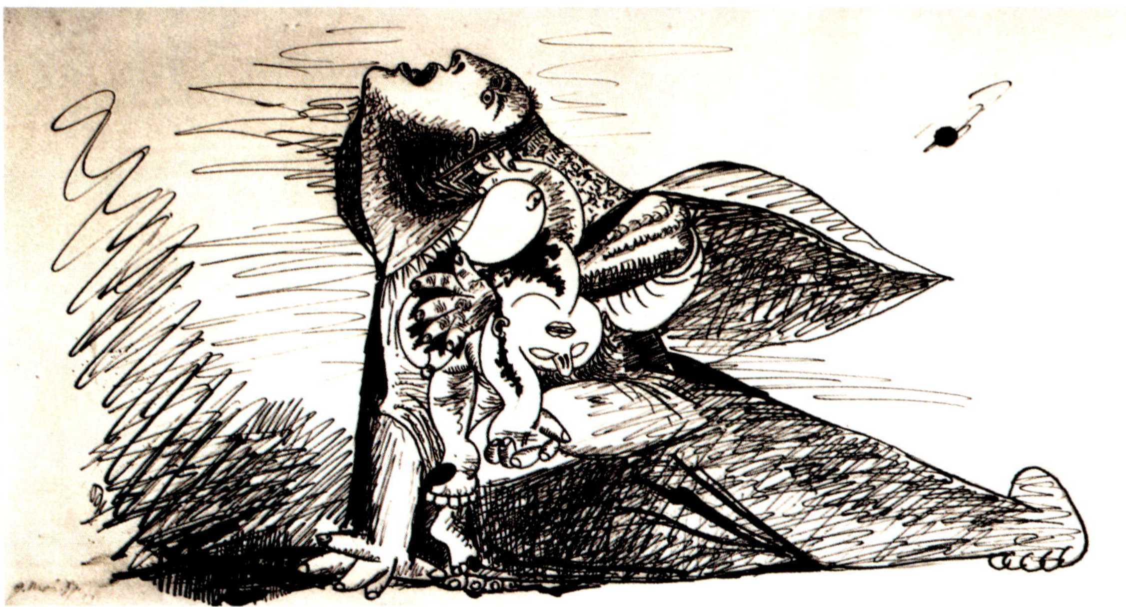

Figure 15

Mother with Dead Child 9 May 1937 (I) Ink on paper 9 1/2 × 17 7/8 in. (24 × 45.5 cm) © 2003 Estate of Pablo Picasso/Artists Rights Society (ARS), New York.

turned upright. Her head is thrown back 180 degrees. Several strokes of ink define the tears falling from her eyes. Her tongue, now rounded, dangles in her open mouth, while her teeth are studs on her lips. Her hair forms a clipped cap of strands that, like the tongue, creates an angular protrusion. All of these elements contribute, along with the extremely contorted poses of the two figures, to a sense of their physical and mental agony.

Later that day, 9 May, Picasso drew a study (Figure 17) for the mural's overall composition into which he integrated the mother with dead child. She kneels at the lower right, the child in her arms, her head is tilted backward. Her profile is minimally detailed, much like the mother in Figure 13. Two other women appear in this scene. The first is an embellished version of the woman holding the lamp in Figure 11. Now she holds a candle and stares with amazement. Her lips are parted, but she appears speechless. Her wide-open eyes and arched brows communicate her horror. The second appears at the far left, framed by a doorway. Her jagged profile and elongated neck-body resemble those of the mother with dead child at the right. The concept for all three women originated in Picasso's earlier sketches for the mother with dead child, which in turn had their origins in his many drawings of women's heads. There is a clear lineage, then, back to January 1937 (and even earlier) for these ideogrammatic women-signs.

Most of the following day, 10 May, was devoted to studies of the bull and horse, with the exception of one sketch, *Mother with Dead Child on Ladder* (v) (Figure 18). This drawing is the first colored version of the theme, and its hues are vibrant. The mother is wide-eyed and aghast. Her mouth is a dark, gaping orifice. Her nose is less rounded and more angular than in Figure 16, and her mass of hair is framed by thickly applied green crayon. Surrounded by saturated, intense color, she embodies a heightened, macabre violence.

On 11 May Picasso began drawing the mural itself. He translated the minute sketches of the previous weeks onto a canvas of enormous scale—more than 11 feet high by 25 feet wide. He must have changed some elements in the process of applying them to the canvas because the differences between his most recent compositional study (Figure 17) and the first version of the actual work (Figure 19) (photographed by Maar in his Grands

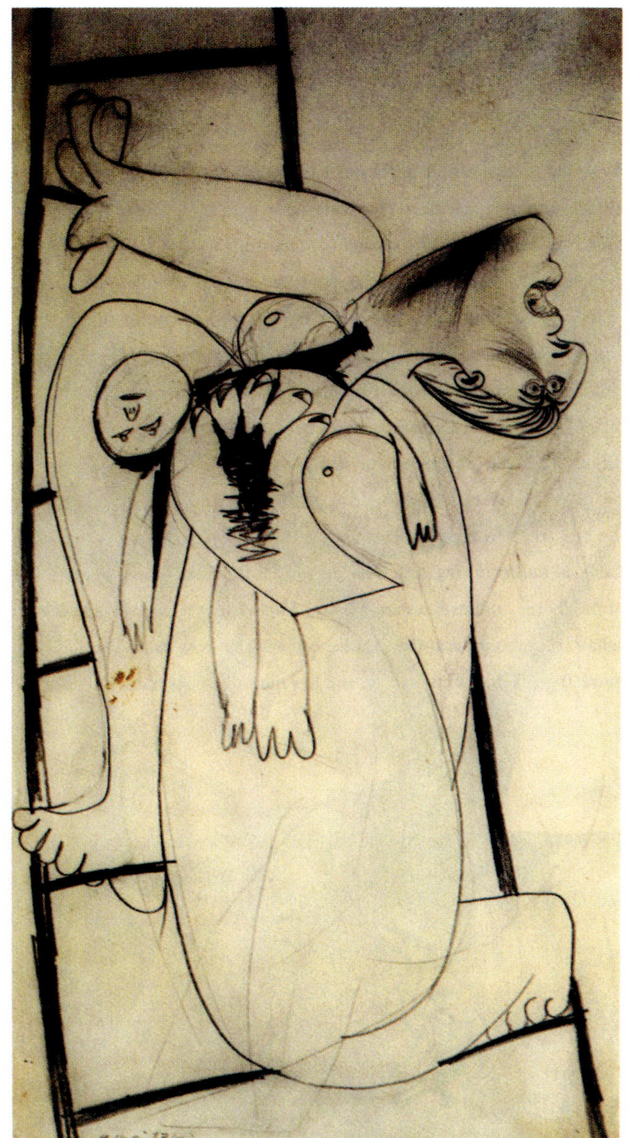

Figure 16

Mother with Dead Child on Ladder 9 May 1937 (III) Pencil on paper 17 7/8 × 9 1/2 in. (45.5 × 24 cm)

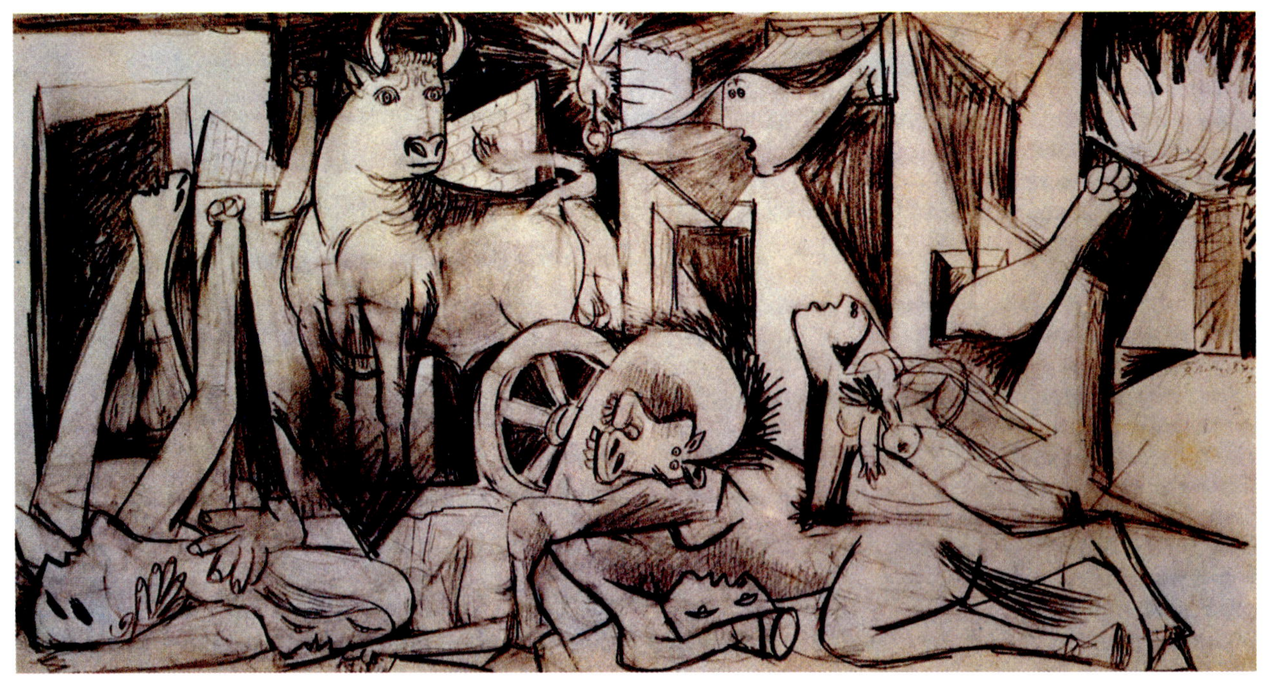

Figure 17

Guernica: Study for Composition 9 May 1937 (II) Pencil on paper 17 7/8 × 9 5/8 in. (45.5 × 24.5 cm) © 2003 Estate of Pablo Picasso/Artists Rights Society (ARS), New York.

Augustins studio) were dramatic. The stage set defined by Picasso in his 9 May study—with a flaming building on the right and a doorway on the left—is now somewhat reduced in size. The doorway at the far left has disappeared. The bust-length wailing woman previously situated there has been replaced by a mother with dead child, resembling the pair that appeared in the first 8 May study. Another wailing woman, this one without a child, appears with raised arms at the far right of the canvas. The many lines running through her suggest that Picasso debated about how he would configure her. Three other women appear. One lies dead along the bottom right edge of the canvas. Another appears to kneel at center right, holding the dead woman. Her face resembles the mother in Figure 17, but she looks plaintive rather than distraught or agitated. Above her is the woman holding the candle, who plays such an essential role in the final mural. The latter two are witnesses rather than emotional participants in the scene.

Over the next six days, a period of intense work, Picasso filled in sections of the canvas. He began to define its dark and light areas. He added a large round sun above the wounded horse and filled the fist (which first appeared in a 19 April drawing on the theme of the artist and his model) with a sheaf of wheat. This fist would disappear when he revised the mural several days later. He slightly refined the horse's position and shifted the placement of its teeth. These were minimal changes, but within the next several days Picasso completely redrew the horse's head, inverting it. Save the addition of hands to the woman at the lower right, who now appears to be running or fleeing, Picasso left the women essentially unchanged.

On 20 May he turned his attention to the animals in the scene, completing four studies of the

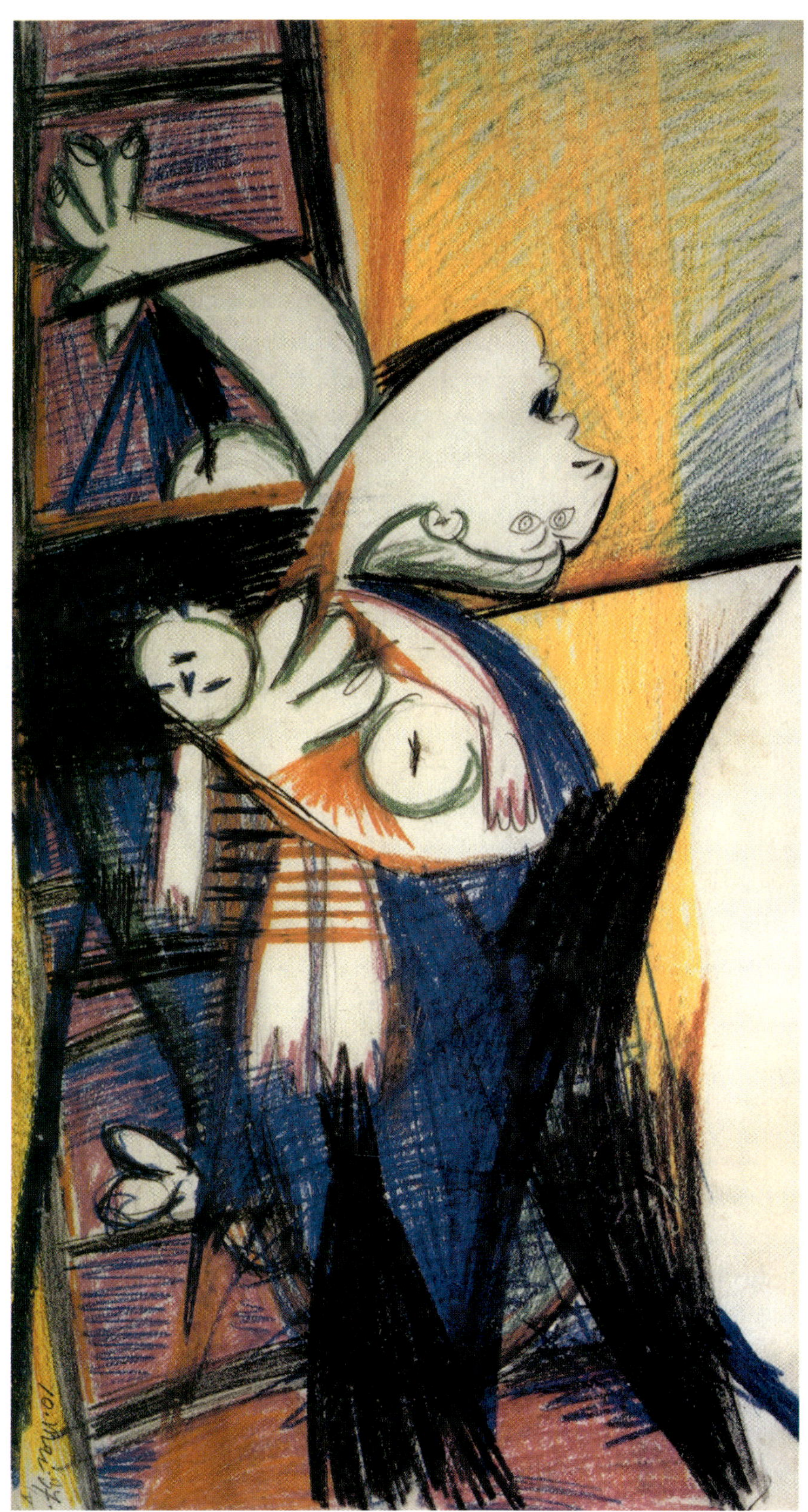

Figure 18

Mother with Dead Child on Ladder 10 May 1937 (v) Pencil and crayon on paper 17 7/8 × 9 5/8 in. (45.5 × 24.5 cm) © 2003 Estate of Pablo Picasso/Artists Rights Society (ARS), New York.

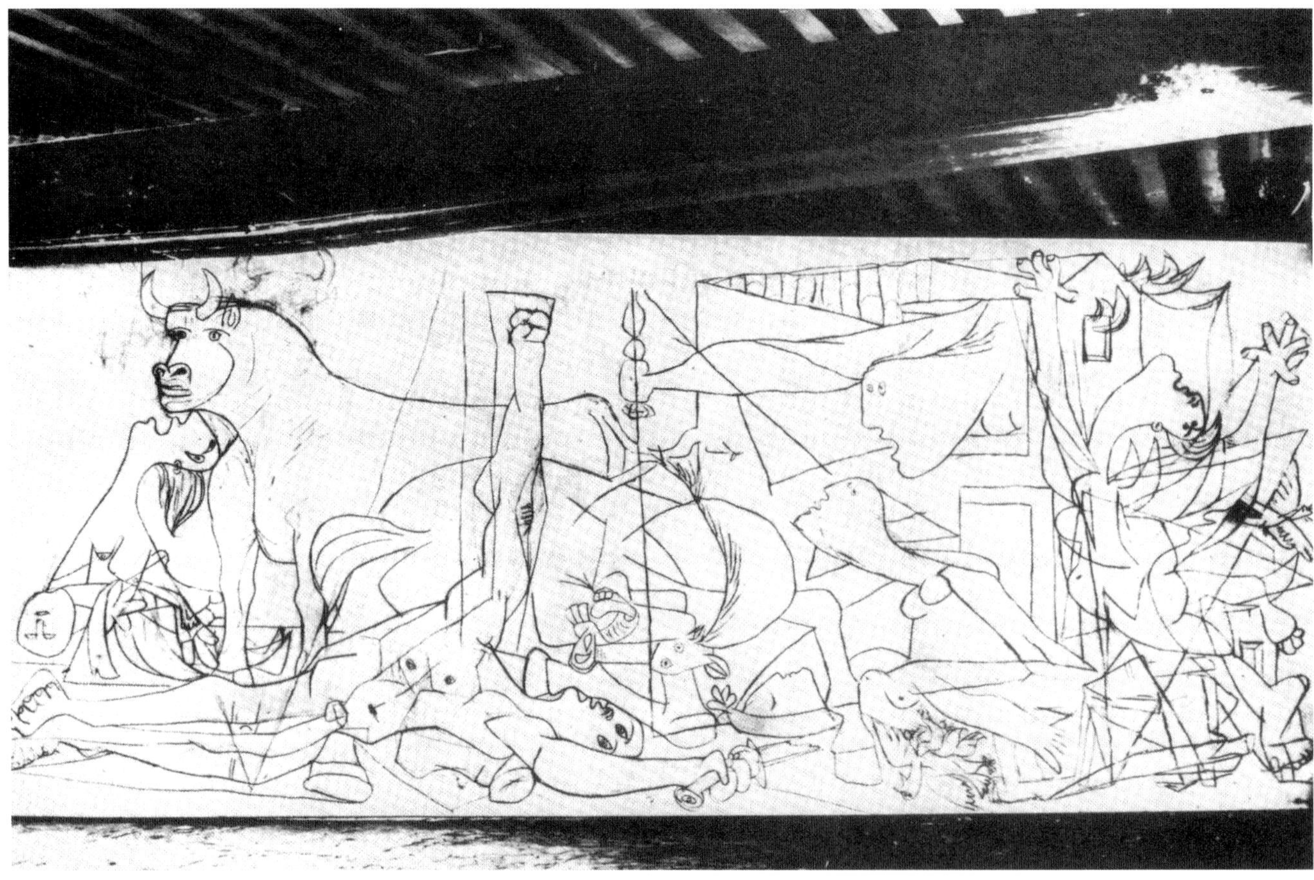

Figure 19

Dora Maar *Guernica*, state I Photographed on 11 May 1937 from Judi Freeman, “Picasso Sends Us Our Death Notice,” *Picasso and the Weeping Women: The Years of Marie Thérèse & Dora Maar,* 1994, PP. 24–61. Copyright (c) Rizzoli International Publications Inc. Reprinted by permission.

heads of the horse and the bull. In one (Figure 20) he drew numerous eyes: eyes like butterflies, insects, birds, goblets, flames. At this moment it is clear that he was considering which of these to use as the eyes of the bull, but later that day he incorporated two of them into his sketch of a woman (Figure 21). This is very probably a study for the figure at the far left of the mural as it was then conceived: the mother holding the dead child. Her eyes are connected teardrop shapes. One contains a butterflylike form. Her brows are two intersecting wedges, considerably more minimal than those used in previous figures. The lack of physiognomical detail in this area makes it difficult to read her expression and attitude.

Picasso provides considerably more articulation in the mouth area. Her lips are shaped and modeled, her teeth are drawn in three dimensions, and her tongue is a spike. The form Picasso gives to the mouth is highly erotic. Its lips are labia, its tongue a sharpened clitoris. None of Picasso's *Guernica*-related women up to this point had mouths on which so much attention had been lavished. Her nostrils are bulbous, shaded commas, and her single ear is an enlarged version of the simplified eyes found in his January studies. Her hair is now a series of thin, dangling lines.

Whatever Picasso was attempting in this drawing, he did not immediately incorporate it into his

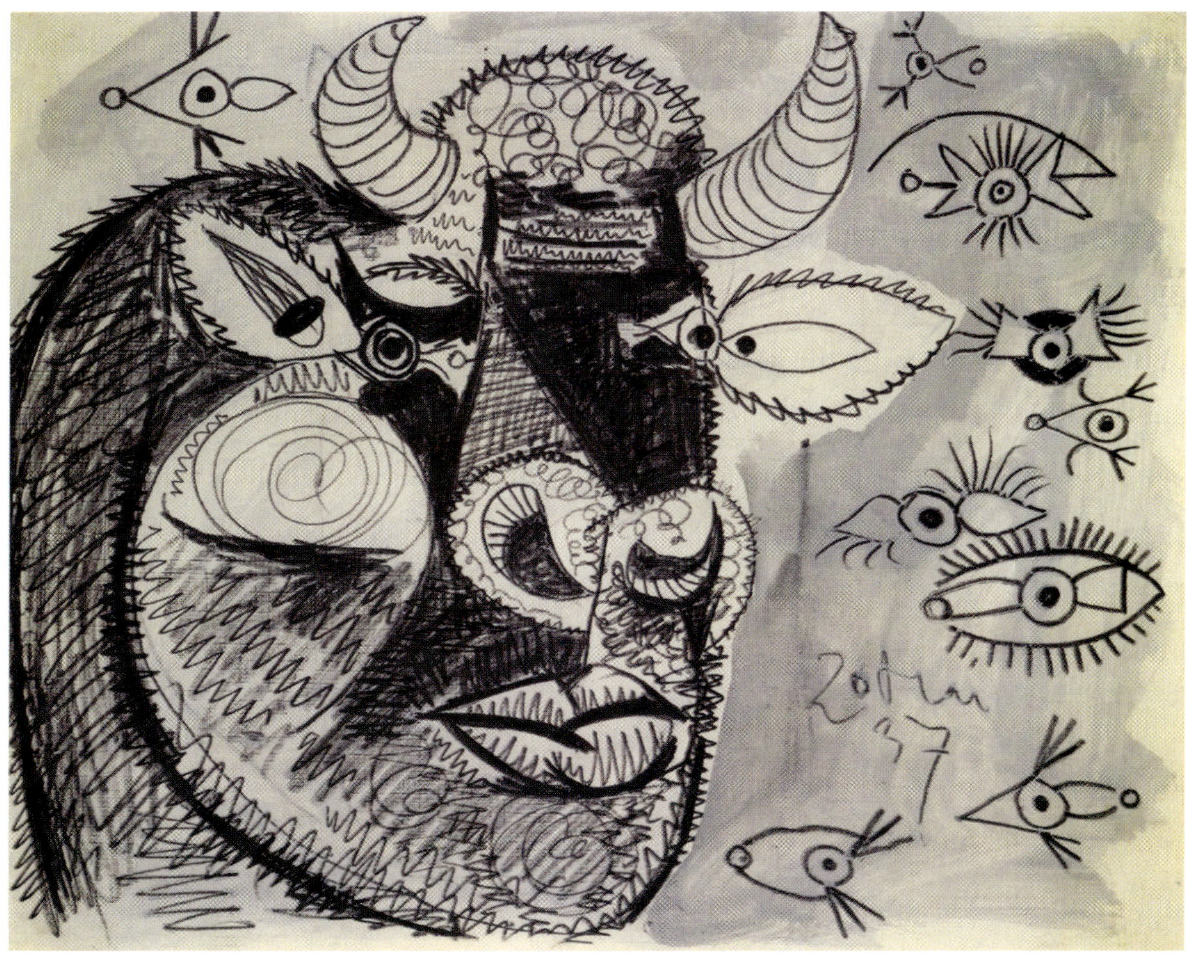

Figure 20

Head of a Bull with Studies of Eyes 20 May 1937 Pencil and gouache on paper 11 3/8 × 9 in. (29 × 23 cm) © 2003 Estate of Pablo Picasso/Artists Rights Society (ARS), New York.

mural, as demonstrated by the photograph Maar took no later than 24 May (Figure 22). Much of Picasso's energy thus far had been devoted to the arrangement of the bull and the horse. The bull, with its human eyes based on the 20 May study, is turned around and now faces the woman with dead child. Picasso's completion of the dark and light areas of the canvas emphasizes the blade of the horse's tongue and the teeth standing, as they seem to, on their roots. The horse's mouth is much more menacing than the woman's in Figure 21— there is clearly a different threshold for anger and violence among animals than humans. Picasso focused considerably more attention on the female figures during this phase of *Guernica*'s evolution. The hands of the figure at the far right have been completely repositioned; one remains up, the other is now down. The neck has become highly contorted. The bulbous commas of her eye are filled with enlarged pupils. Picasso also clothed the fleeing woman at the lower

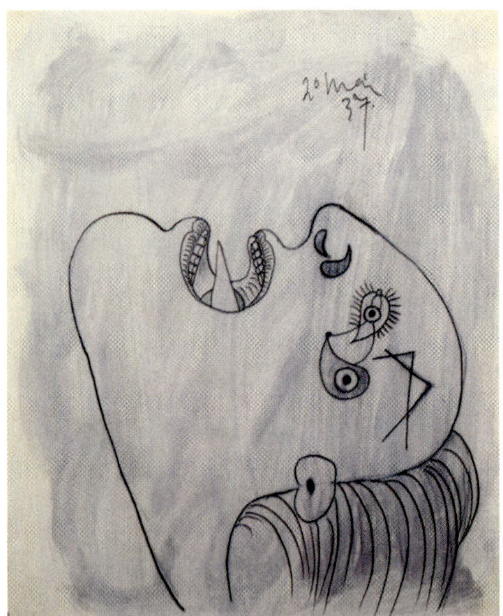

Figure 21

Head of a Woman 20 May 1937 Pencil and gouache on paper 11 3/8 × 9 in. (29 × 23 cm) © 2003 Estate of Pablo Picasso/Artists Rights Society (ARS), New York.

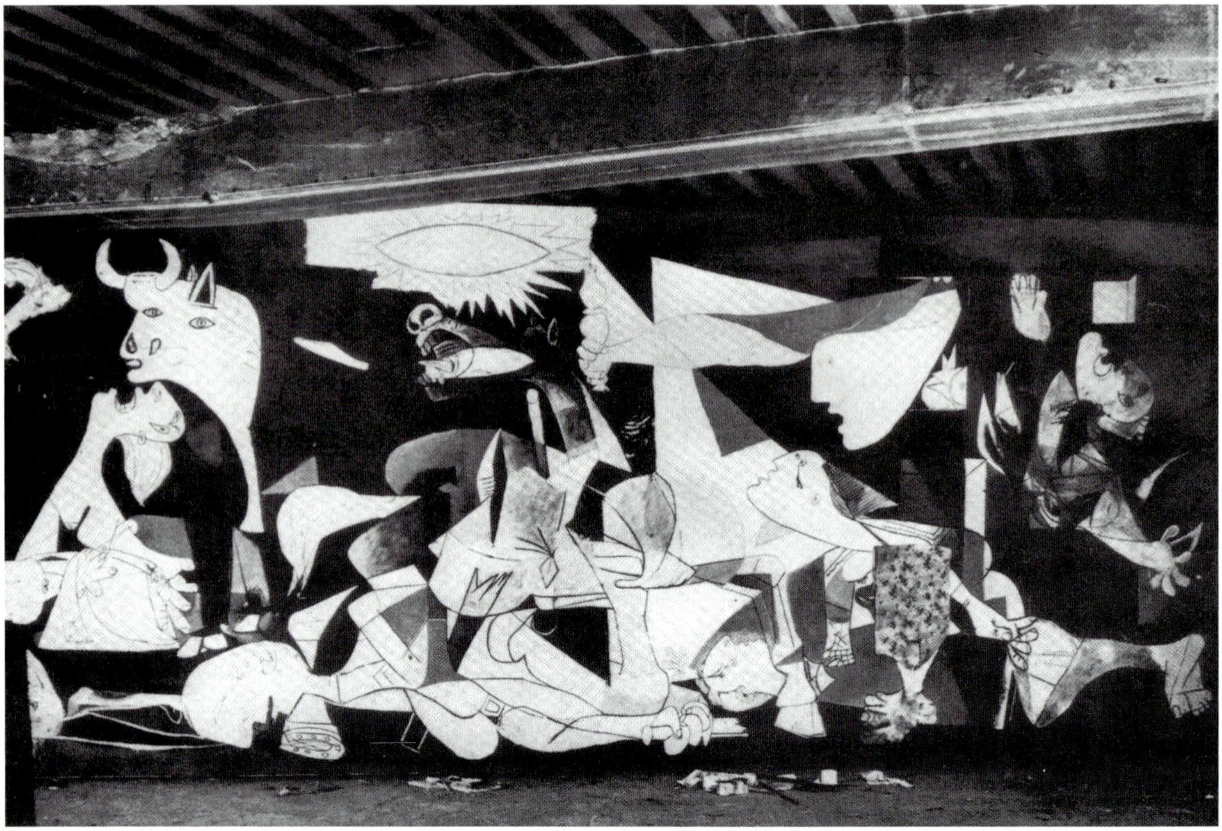

Figure 22

Dora Maar *Guernica*, state IV Photographed between 20 and 24 May 1937 from Judi Freeman, "Picasso Sends Us Our Death Notice," *Picasso and the Weeping Women: The Years of Marie Thérèse & Dora Maar,* 1994, PP. 24–61. Copyright (c) Rizzoli International Publications Inc. Reprinted by permission.

right by applying collage elements to mimic a kerchief and a floral dress. In subsequent revisions of the mural these additions were removed.

Two heads of 24 May (Figures 23–24) suggest that Picasso was continuing to explore alternatives, although these visages never appeared in the final mural. These are the first weeping heads among the preparatory drawings and paintings created for *Guernica*. Their tears are like splayed multipronged rakes. In the first (Figure 23), tears drop from each

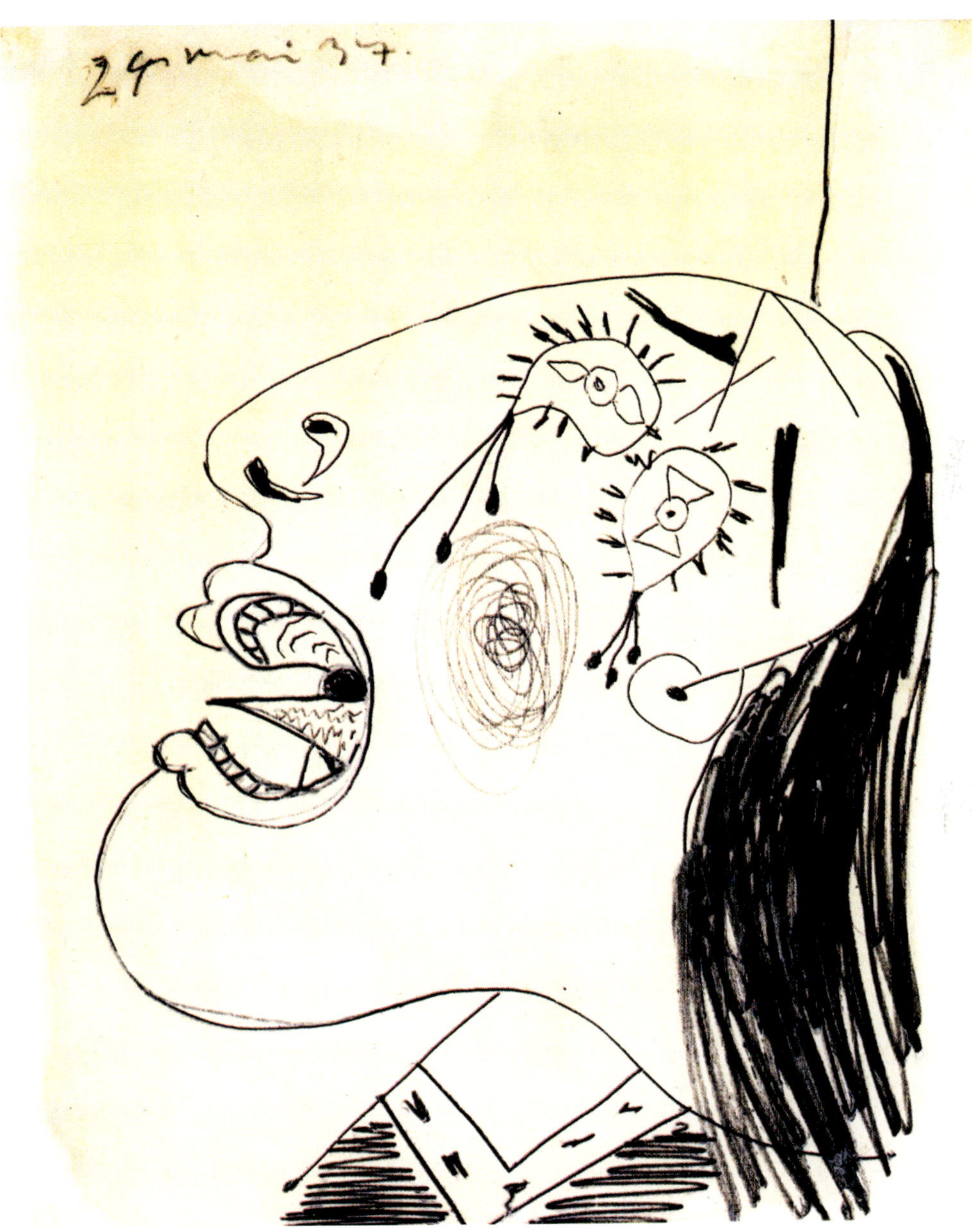

Figure 23

Weeping Woman (I) 24 May 1937 Pencil and gouache on paper 11 3/8 × 9 in. (29 × 23 cm) © 2003 Estate of Pablo Picasso/Artists Rights Society (ARS), New York.

eye. Her eye sockets resemble cells with cilia; one contains a bow tie, the other a wrapped bonbon. She has dark eyebrows and a furrowed forehead. Picasso drew the contour of her face in two rapid strokes. The texture of the mouth receives considerable description; the tongue is scaled and the palate is ridged. The teeth are neatly aligned and rounded.

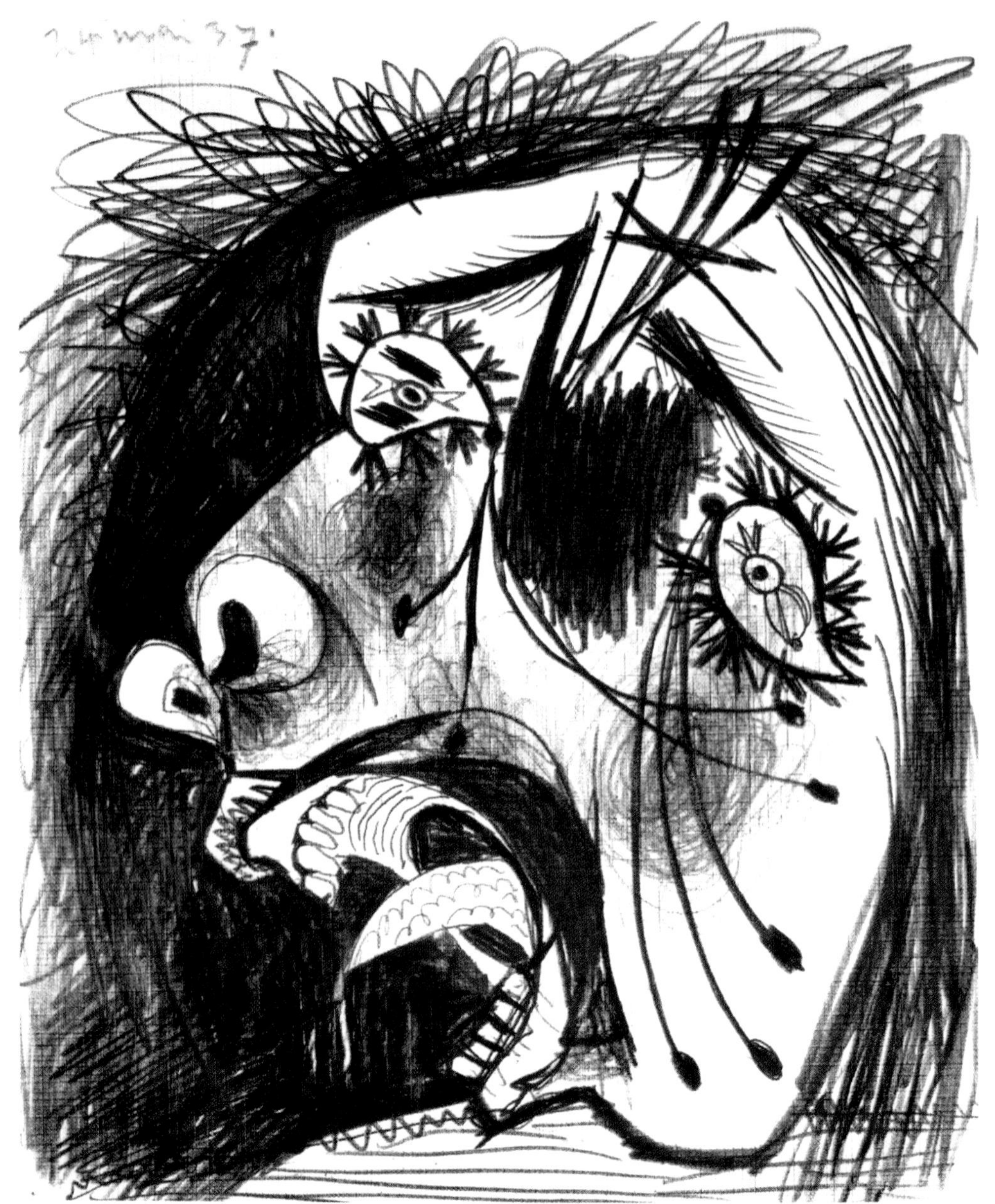

Figure 24

Weeping Woman (II) 24 May 1937 Pencil and gouache on paper 11 3/8 × 9 in. (29 × 23 cm) © 2003 Estate of Pablo Picasso/Artists Rights Society (ARS), New York.

She wears makeup, or so the circular lines on her cheek suggest.

Within a single day Picasso's approach toward representing the weeping women took a new direction. In the second version of 24 May (Figure 24) the irregularly shaped face is more a mask than an observed head. It is surrounded by a mass of dark, unruly hair. Set beneath thick eyebrows, her teardrop-shaped eyes fall to either side of her face and appear to contain elaborately wrapped candies. Her tears trace random paths across her cheeks, in contrast to their more controlled formation in Figure 23. Her lashes are clusters of spiky leaves. Her bulbous enlarged nostrils are joined to form a snout. Picasso experimented with rapidly scribbled patches of line on her cheeks, between her eyes, and around her mouth, whose fleshy lips form a gaping hole containing jagged teeth and a knifelike tongue.

A third weeping woman (Figure 25), drawn 27 May, is also disheveled, the result of lines rapidly scribbled on virtually all her features. Such hasty gestures indicate the certainty with which Picasso

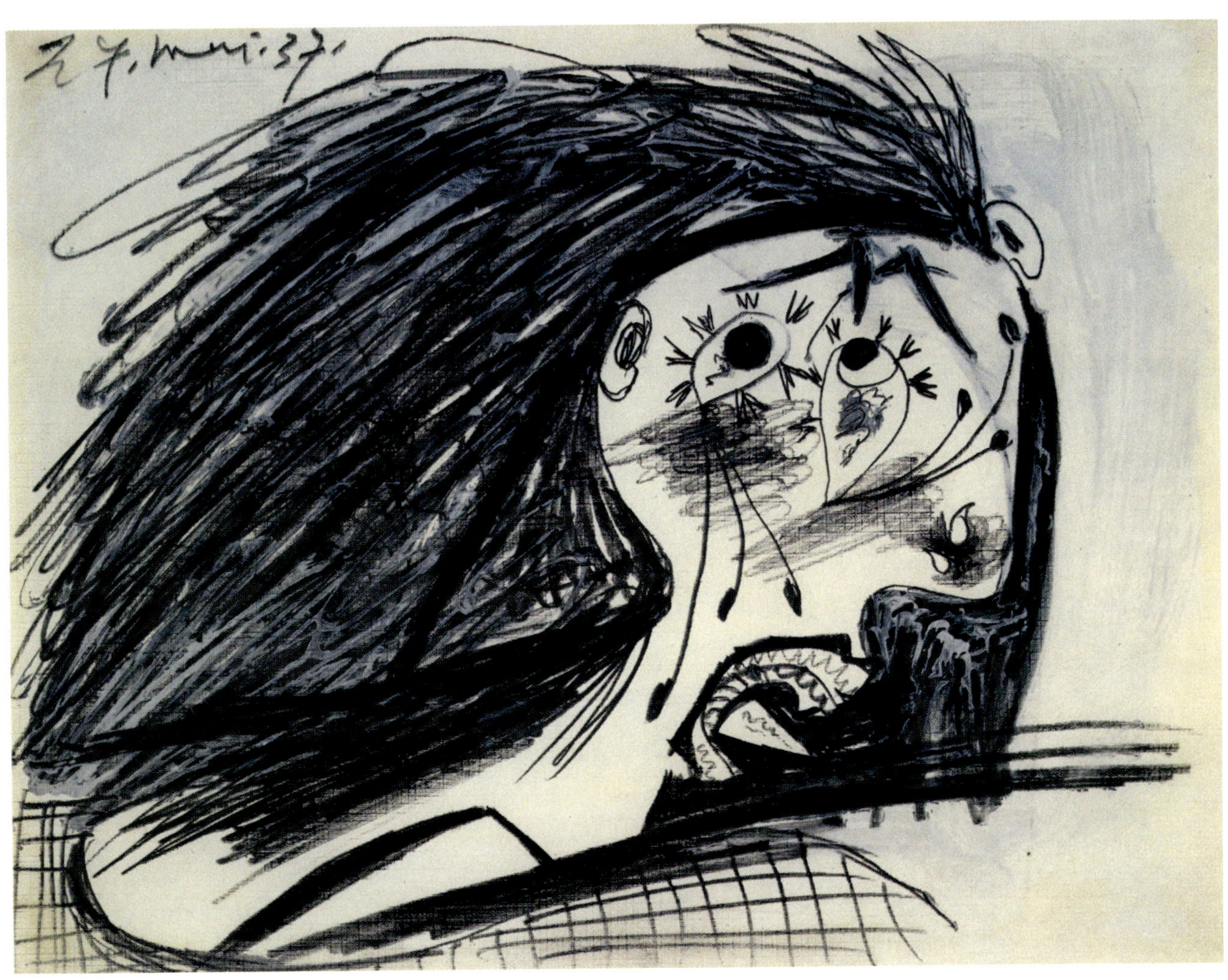

Figure 25

Weeping Woman (III) 27 May 1937 Pencil and gouache on paper 9 × 11 5/8 in. (23 × 29.5 cm) © 2003 Estate of Pablo Picasso/Artists Rights Society (ARS), New York.

executed these figures; he labored over the elements he had yet to finalize and rapidly sketched those with which he was less obsessed. Her eyes now come together on one side of her face, and her eyebrows are two prominent angles retraced several times. Her right ear is presented as two overlapping ovals on the side of her head, while another ear is visible at the top. A quickly executed series of teeth and the texture of her lips are the result of several looping strokes. Her tears both fall and rise, defying gravity, and her hair, as in the previous drawing, is a mass of scribbles. Evidently Picasso was considering the question of clothing. These three women wear, respectively, a dotted V-neck collar, a striped crew-neck shirt, and a checkered blouse.

The women's heads of 20 and 24 May (Figures 21, 23) and those of 24 and 27 May (Figures 24–25) indicate two degrees of emotional distress Picasso considered in developing the figure of the falling woman at the right of *Guernica.* He appears to have been willing to explore extreme states in his studies, but in the evolving mural he adopted relatively toned-down expressions for his figures. When his work on the mural was recorded on the 27th (Figure 26), the visage of the falling woman, like the face of the mother with dead child at the left side of the can-

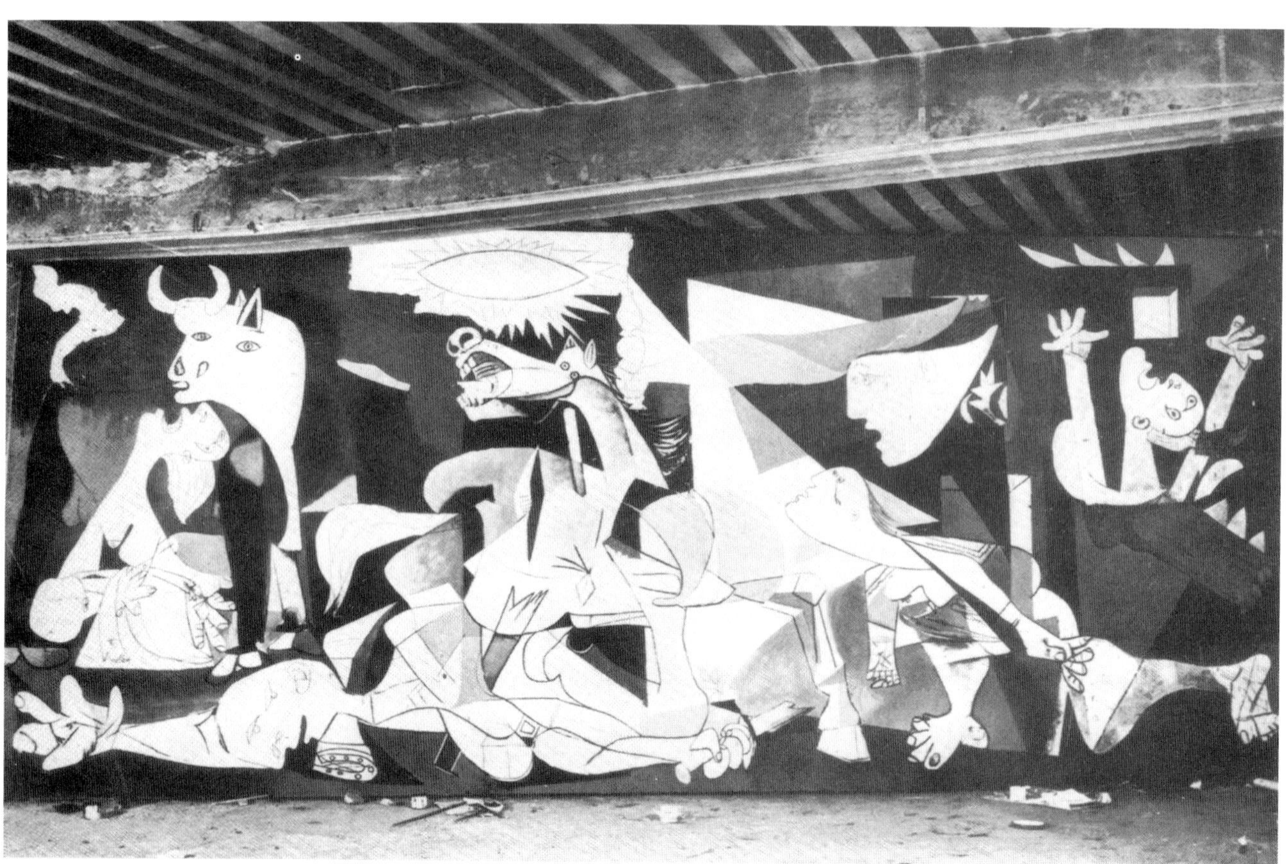

Figure 26

Dora Maar *Guernica*, state v Photographed around 27 May 1937 from Judi Freeman, "Picasso Sends Us Our Death Notice," *Picasso and the Weeping Women: The Years of Marie Thérèse & Dora Maar*, 1994, PP. 24–61.

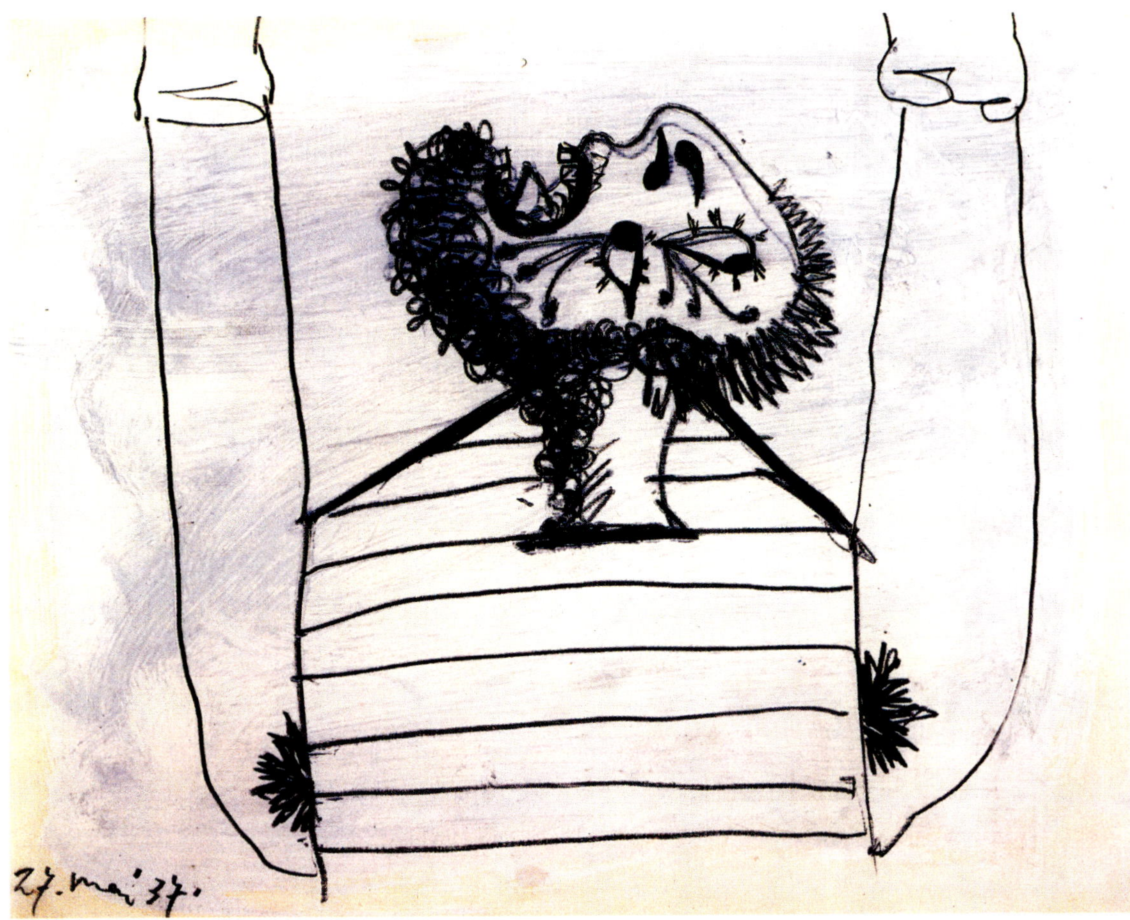

Figure 27

Falling Man 27 May 1937 Pencil and gouache on paper 9 × 11 5/8 in. (23 × 29.5 cm) © 2003 Estate of Pablo Picasso/Artists Rights Society (ARS), New York.

vas, most closely resembled the 20 May drawing. Picasso once again altered the position of her arms, now resolutely having them point upward, with open hands desperately reaching for something to hold on to. Although he had considered replacing her with a weeping man and rapidly sketched one that day (Figure 27), he evidently rejected changing the figure's gender and retained the concept of two women framing the composition.

The following morning, 28 May, Picasso resumed sketching the mother and dead child. For the first time the mother weeps. In his first study of the day (Figure 28) he endowed her with the teeth of the rearing horse of 2 May (Figure 12). Her teardrop-shaped eyes are weighted by their pupils, with pronged eyelashes attached to each. She has no ears, and her nostrils are darts, a motif appearing here for the first time in the studies for *Guernica.* Her general configuration is essentially unchanged from the one already painted on the mural. What Picasso endeavored to resolve was her facial expression.

His approach in the second drawing of the day (Figure 29) was far more experimental. Here, Picasso applied actual tangled hair to the mother's head. She now looks upward, her head tilted back at the same 90-degree angle that Picasso had used in

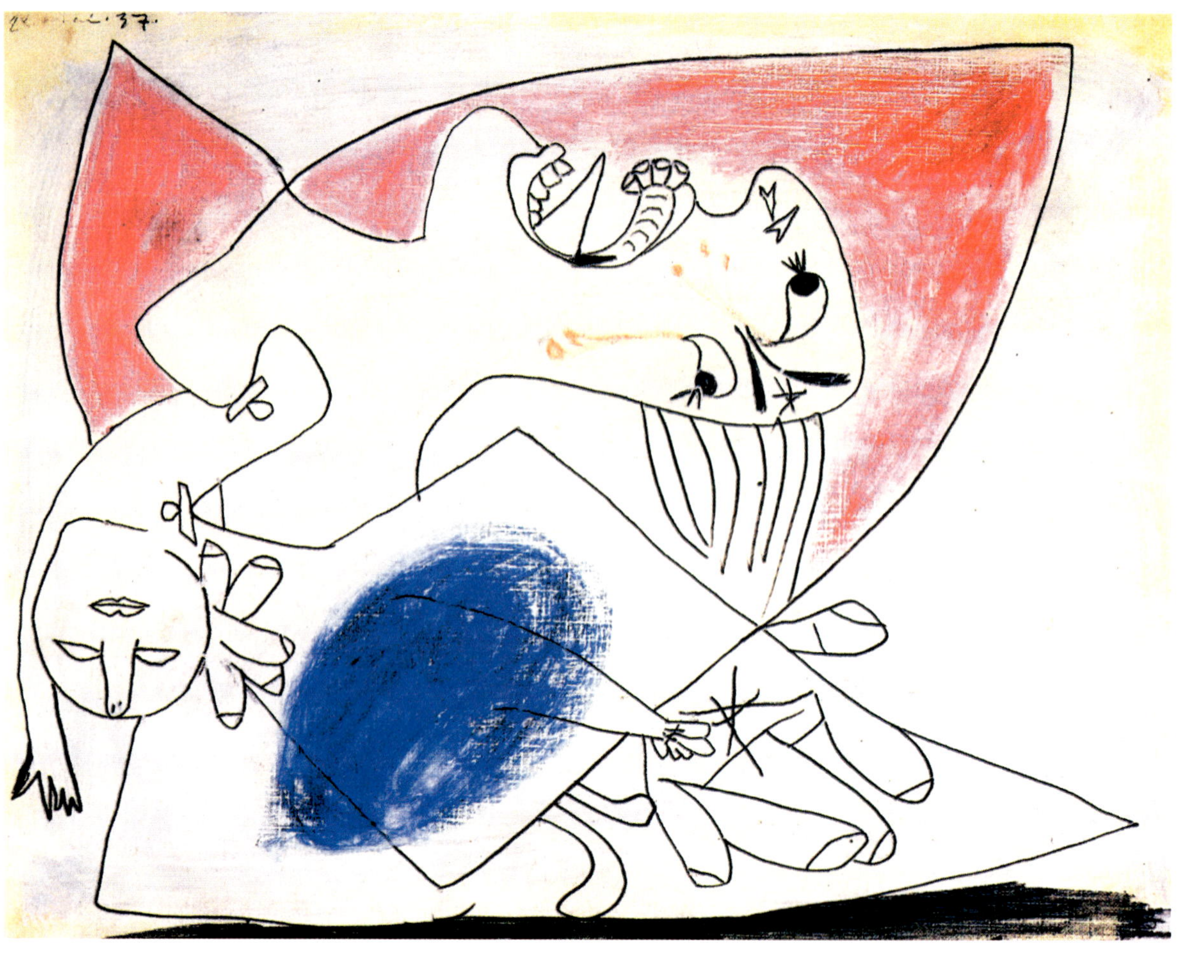

Figure 28

Mother with Dead Child (II) 28 May 1937 Pencil, crayon, and gouache on paper 9 × 11 3/4 in. (23 × 30 cm) © 2003 Estate of Pablo Picasso/Artists Rights Society (ARS), New York.

the falling woman. This drawing is a marked rethinking of the entire left side of the composition, from the architecture (Picasso now considered placing a burning building there) to the woman's pose (it mirrors that of the fleeing woman at the canvas's lower right). The mother is now in a state of frenzy—and for good reason. A lance runs prominently through the child's body, yet the child, arm upraised and mouth open, appears to be still alive, though barely. The scene is one of utter terror. The mother simultaneously flees, shields, and reaches for help. Her tongue and teeth jut out of her wide-open mouth; her eyes roll back in her head, while tears stream from them.

That Picasso elected not to incorporate such a violent image into the mural is significant. Once more he chose the more restrained approach, with suggestive but not blatant figures. He resolved to let the figures' faces convey the emotion of the scene, believing that these images, read in the aggregate, would effectively express his anti-Franco, pro-republic message. He now devoted his energies to refining the motif. His color study of a weeping woman from the same day (Figure 30) is a compro-

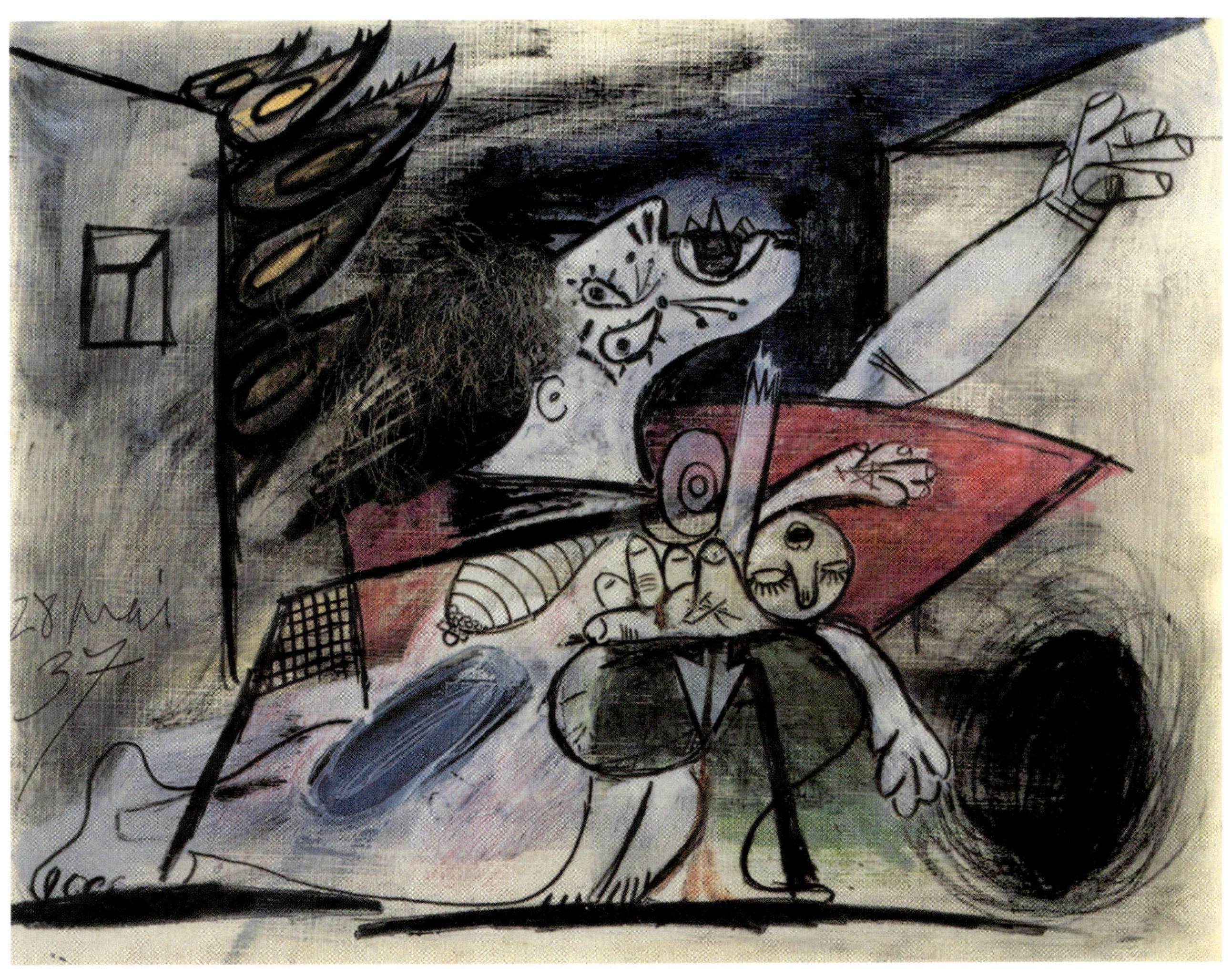

Figure 29

Mother with Dead Child (III) 28 May 1937 Pencil, crayon, gouache, and hair on paper 9 × 11 3/8 in. (23 × 29 cm) © 2003 Estate of Pablo Picasso/Artists Rights Society (ARS), New York.

mise between the more restrained versions (Figures 21, 23, and 28) and the more radical solutions (Figures 24, 25, and 29) of the previous week. The scribbled hair last seen the day before (Figure 25) and the sprouting lashes first appearing on 24 May (Figure 24) adorn a head of simplified contour. There is an ear at the top of the face and another where the head meets the neck. Tears flow in long arcs downward along the cheeks; the comma-shaped nostrils seem to be tears of another sort. Picasso labored over the mouth, carefully drawing each tooth, describing the upper and lower palates, and shaping the lips. These weathered lips and rotten teeth are suggestive of the peasant population of Guernica. They underscore the likely metaphorical relationship between Guernica's inhabitants and the weeping women Picasso had planned for the mural. The application of orange to the tears strangely animates the face, in a macabre reference to the "made-up" ladies of Paris—initially seen in the artist-and-model studies—that Picasso had eliminated from his monochromatic mural.

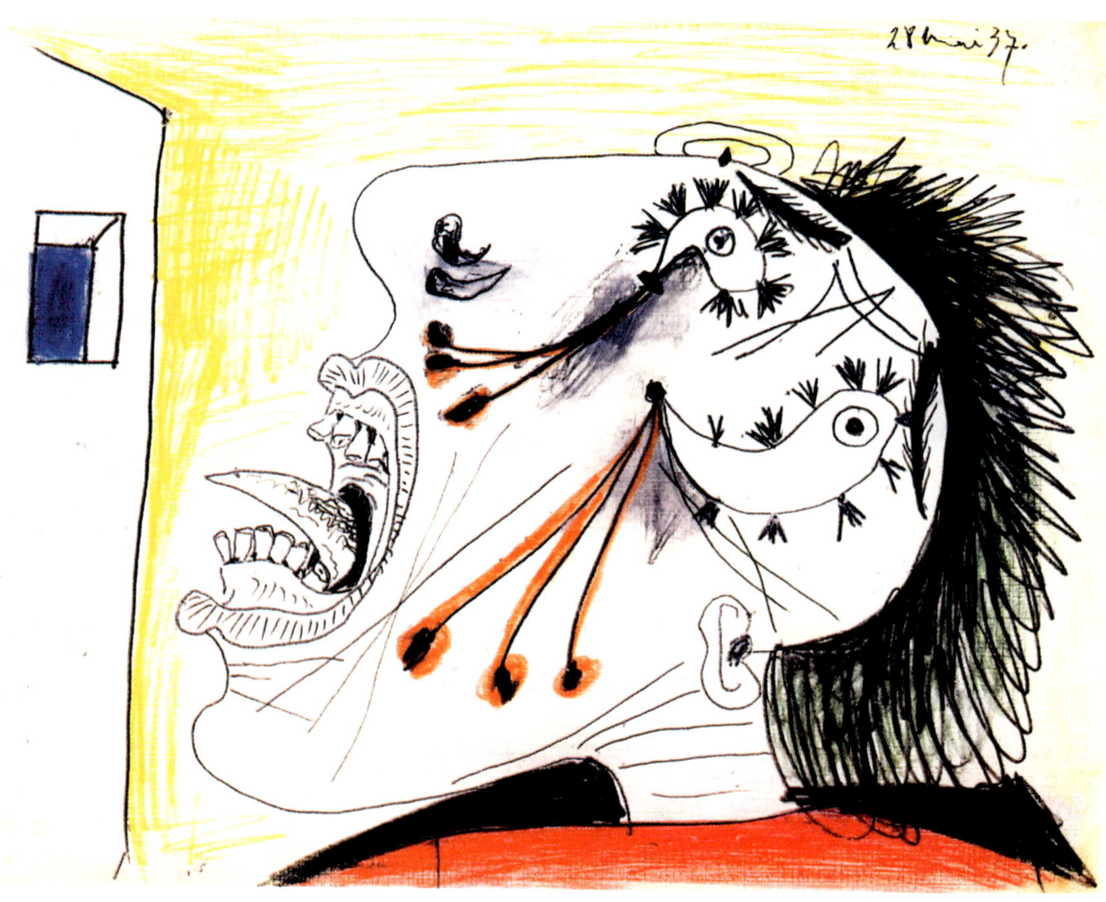

Figure 30

Weeping Woman 28 May 1937 Pencil, crayon, and gouache on paper 9 × 11 5/8 in. (23 × 29.5 cm) © 2003 Estate of Pablo Picasso/Artists Rights Society (ARS), New York.

Picasso did not work during the last weekend of May. Most likely he spent part of his time visiting Walter and their daughter Maya at Ambroise Vollard's house in Tremblay-sur-Mauldre. A single sheet drawn the following Monday, 31 May (Figure 31), contains several images. A weeping head is superimposed on a burning building and a large hand. The head is crossed by a swath of yellow flame, or smoke, emanating from the building. The juxtaposition suggests that this study, like the 28 May sketches, is related to the falling woman. The reappearance of the burning building demonstrates that a suggestion of the devastation that prompted the women's weeping was essential to Picasso's underlying concept. The eyes have become thickly outlined mollusks encircled in blue; the lashes still sprout in clusters, but the eyebrows look like stalks of wheat. The nostrils are darts again, now encircled. We see every tooth and its root. The woman has several strands of tentaclelike hair at the nape of her neck in addition to thin hairs elsewhere. Her tears consist of thin, orange rivulets; the drops at the ends are echoed by thick, vertical streaks of blue and green. The increased intricacy of this drawing indicates that Picasso was now fully immersed in the question of how best to express grief and despair. He

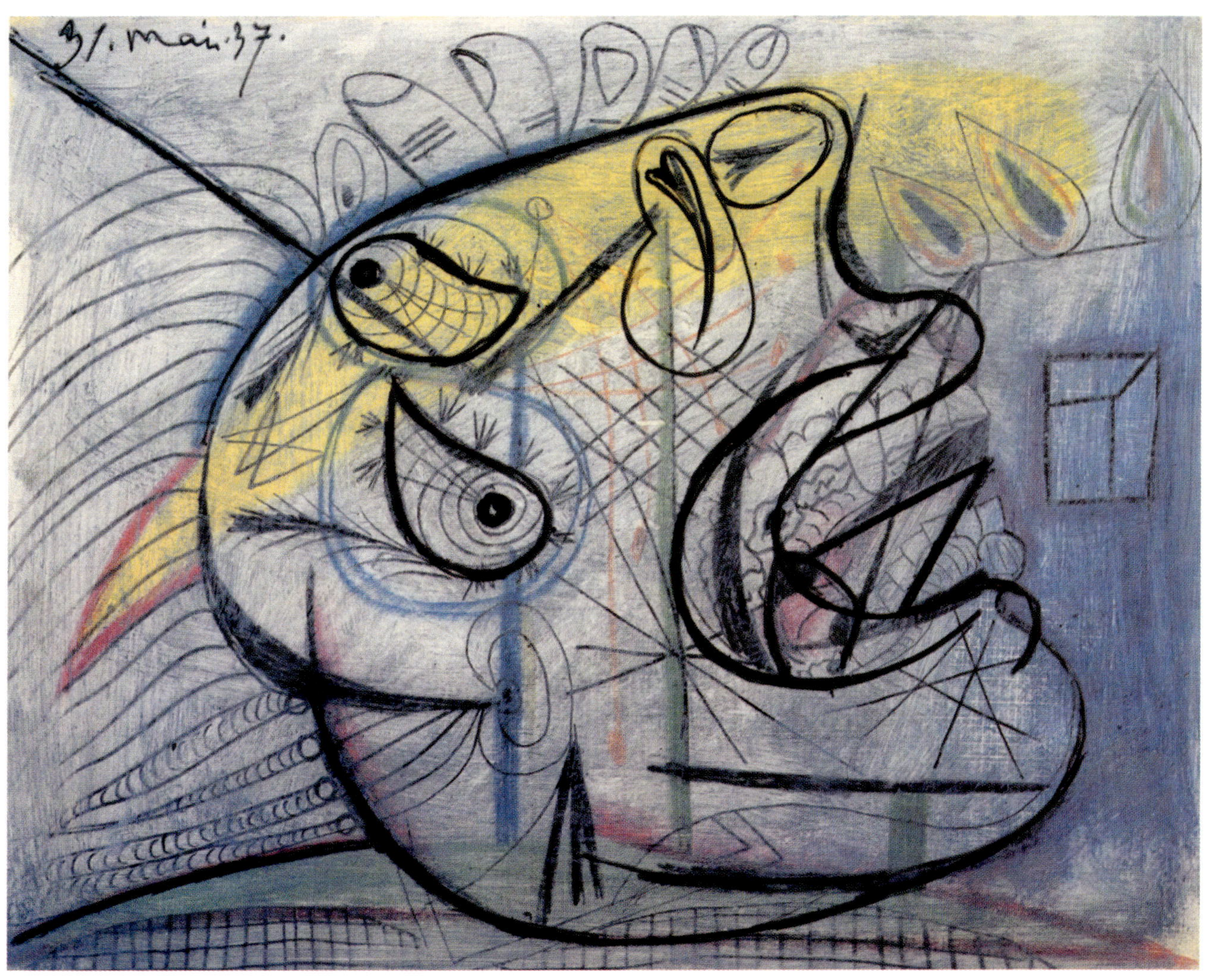

Figure 31

Weeping Woman (IV) 31 May 1937 Pencil, crayon, and gouache on paper 9 × 11 5/8 in. (23 × 29.5 cm) © 2003 Estate of Pablo Picasso/Artists Rights Society (ARS), New York.

was actively articulating each feature in a manner previously unexplored, and his addition of color now cast the entire head in an eerie glow.

Despite these explorations, however, the painted portions of the mural itself had not changed significantly by the time it was photographed around 1 June. He added several collage elements of wallpaper, but the figures remained unchanged. It is likely that Picasso visited the pavilion sometime during the first week of June, and that he assessed the location and environmental situation of the mural. José Lluis Sert, one of the pavilion's architects, probably visited Picasso in his Grands Augustins studio at this time to ascertain his progress. There was considerable concern among the pavilion's organizers that the mural would not be ready in time for the opening.

Though Picasso would remove the pieces of wallpaper from the canvas in the next several days, the painting was very close to its final form. Nevertheless, he continued to make sketches related to the weeping woman and the dead warrior. Three extraordinary weeping heads date from 3 June. One (Figure 32) is a slightly modified version of Figure 31. Extraneous detail is eliminated and individual features are sharpened. The eyes are still mollusks, but their lashes are minimal; the eyebrows are clearly defined stalks of wheat. Tears now stream only from tear ducts, marked by stars. The nostrils are darts transformed into elongated hearts with halos. The mouth is less crowded, though there are far too many teeth lined up along the lower palate and six large teeth along the upper. The tongue is an unadorned triangle; the lips are modeled with six short curving lines. The ear is now crescent-shaped, and its auditory function is conveyed by the diverging lines emanating from it. The hair consists solely of tentacles. Patches of color enliven the forms but do not add substantive detail.

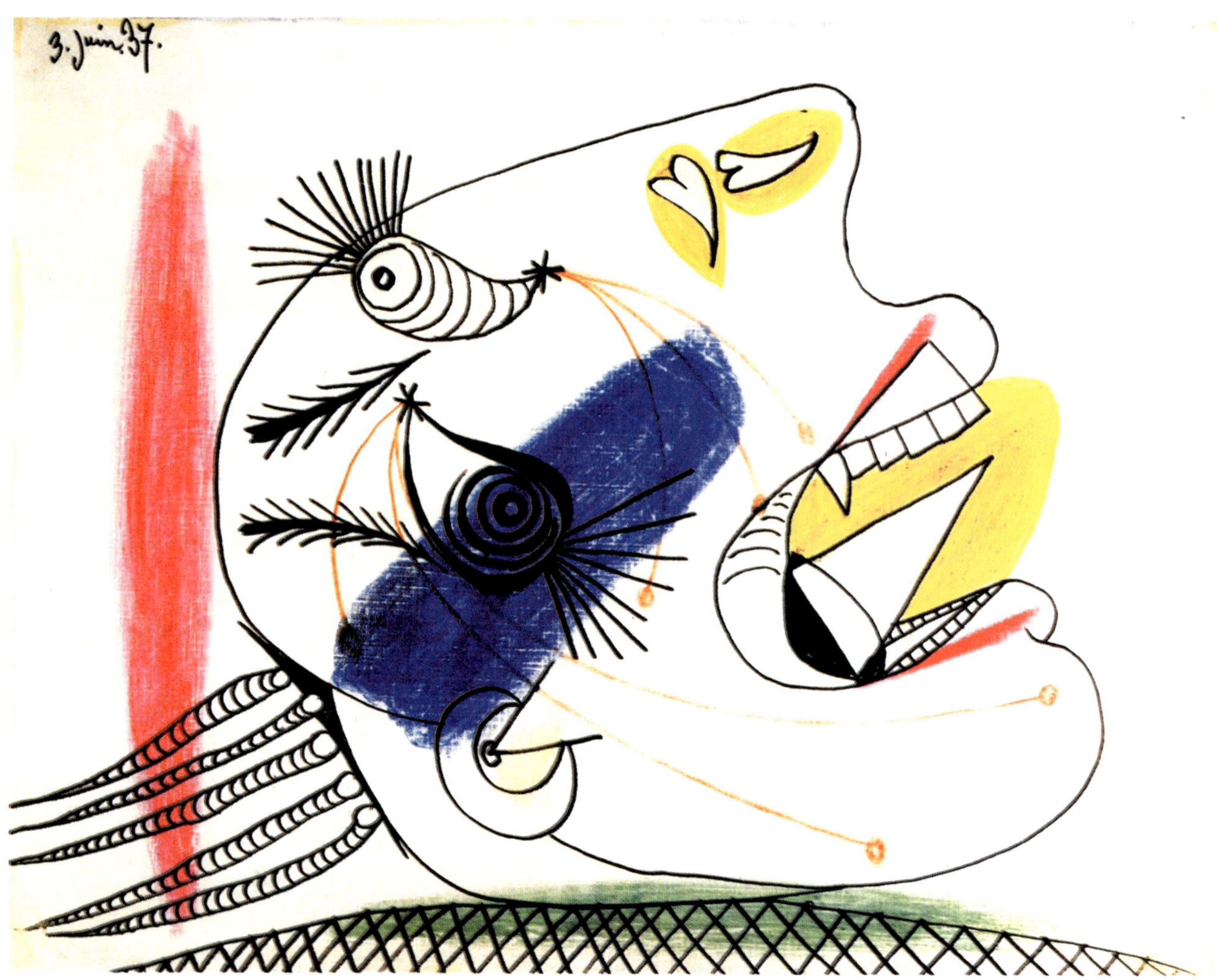

Figure 32

Weeping Woman (V) 3 June 1937 Pencil, crayon, and gouache on paper 9 × 11 5/8 in. (23 × 29.5 cm)

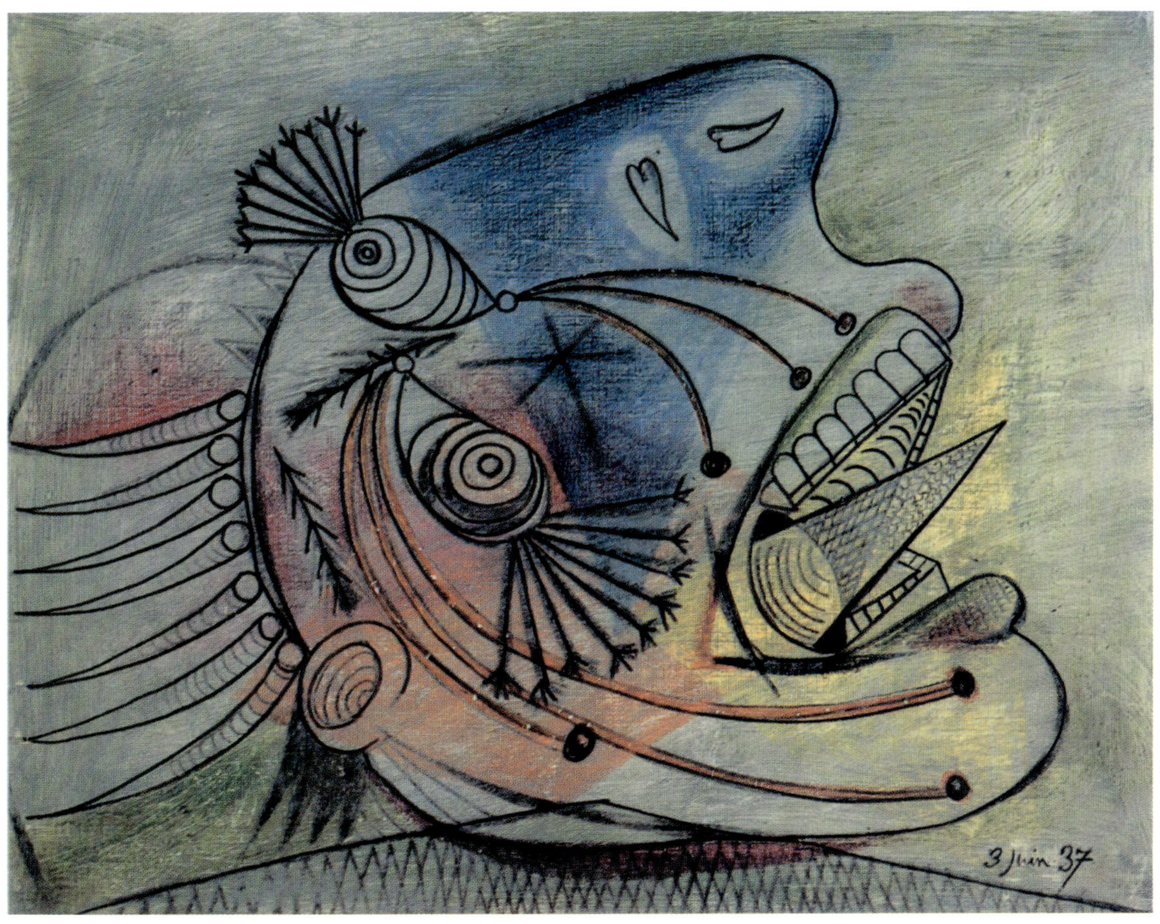

Figure 33

Weeping Woman (VI) 3 June 1937 Pencil, crayon, and gouache on paper 9 1/4 × 11 1/2 in. (23.5 × 29.2 cm) © 2003 Estate of Pablo Picasso/Artists Rights Society (ARS), New York.

In Picasso's second pass at the theme that day (Figure 33) planes of blue, red, and yellow intersect on the face, and the head, topped by small, triangular flames, is set in front of a field of green. This woman has long, thick lashes, and her tears amplify the contours of her face. Her ear is hollow, like the mouth of a horn. Her teeth are neatly aligned, and her tongue is now richly textured. Picasso in fact reversed the placement of the textures on the upper surface of the tongue so that what is most visible on the tip of an actual tongue is, on the tongue of this woman, furthest from the tip. Picasso's attention to such minute anatomical detail indicates how very thorough was his experimentation with these figures. The third drawing of the day (Figure 34) is the most chaotic. The tentacular hairs are falling over. The tears run in serpentine patterns along her ill-defined cheek. The precise contour of this head is difficult to discern where it disappears along the hairline. Her mollusk eyes now contain several concentric circles, and lashes extend from them like dangling wires. The teeth have multiplied, and the wedge of the tongue has been softened. Her ear has become a frame with sound waves visualized inside it.

Beginning with the 31 May drawing (Figure 31), his renderings of the weeping women depart from previous versions. They are more readable as mon-

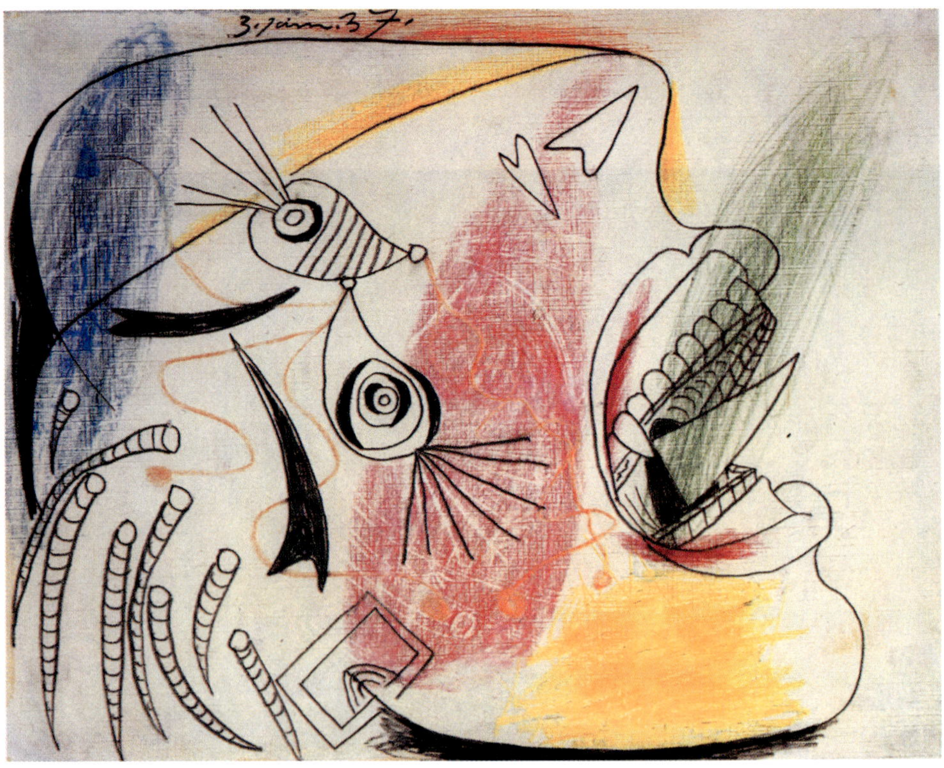

Figure 34

Weeping Woman (VII) 3 June 1937 Pencil, crayon, and gouache on paper 9 × 11 5/8 in. (23 × 29.5 cm) © 2003 Estate of Pablo Picasso/Artists Rights Society (ARS), New York.

strous masks than as expressive faces. Picasso did not use any of them in *Guernica.* The very fact that he was preoccupied with them—indeed with nothing but them—in the closing days of completing the mural suggests that he was considering last-minute options to alter aspects of the painting. With the aid of sketches made during the week of 31 May he continued to make changes to the fallen warrior and to other small areas, but essentially he was concluding his work. Maar's final photograph prior to the completion of the canvas was taken around 4 June, and the painting was delivered to the pavilion a week or so later.

"In the panel on which I am working, which I shall call *Guernica,*" wrote Picasso, "and in all my recent works of art, I clearly express my abhorrence of the military caste which has sunk Spain in an ocean of pain and death." This ocean of pain and death consumed him. He continued to consider alterations throughout the day that the canvas departed his studio. Although the mural arrived at the pavilion in mid-June, the architects thought Picasso would continue to work on it until the inauguration on 12 July, which he apparently did not. Picasso told Sert: "I don't know when I will finish it. Maybe never. You had better come and take it whenever you need it."

"It was necessary for the pictorial expression to be horrible, for the outlines to weep, for the discolored color to be one of sadness, for the whole to be a penetrating clamor—tenacious, strident, and eternal," observed Jaime Sabartés, Picasso's secretary and confidant. Picasso's absorption in each individual feature of the women's faces and his repeated reworking of those features was the key to his effort to attain this clamor. Films made of Picasso's *Guernica* contain footage where the camera creeps along the surface of the canvas, slowly taking in every minute detail and nuance. This was Picasso's desired effect, and his studies attest to his methodical search for the most suitable motif for each figure. Picasso unleashed his *Guernica* (Figure 35) for the world to share in the town's—and the artist's—tragedy. With the painting's departure from his studio Picasso abandoned for a time the themes of the mother with dead child and the fallen warrior. The one motif he could not relinquish was that of the weeping woman. Her visage haunted him. He drew her frequently, almost obsessively, for the next several months. She was the metaphor for his own private agonies.

Chapter Six Project Proposal

Dynamics of Color Emotion

Interestingly enough, we are going to execute color judgments about an achromatic mural. Picasso poured out his emotions onto the canvas, and so we shall attempt to do the same, yet with *color expression,* rather than his gray scale painting approach.

At this point in your color investigations, we have learned about the importance of color expression to measure emotional responses. We are going to face a new challenge in this project by recreating *Guernica* in full color. Please remember, this project is cumulative, in terms of the elements of color. The student will incorporate the use color seen in previous chapter, such as saturation, intensity, tints and shades (values), contrast, and harmony. These color properties should be demonstrated in the mural itself.

We want to find out if we can enhance the mood of *Guernica,* by using particular color harmonies. The painting is quite effective about illustrating the emotional factors of war. Picasso was tremendously successful at shape and form expression, but we want to find out if we can manipulate color to fit the mood of this composition.

Remember to incorporate ***mood of carnage*** when selecting your color harmonies.

The Project

This project can be done as an individual, group or a class. The proposal here will incorporate teams of four people per *Guernica* mural.

1. Make teams of four students each.
2. Divide the *Guernica* composition into four equal parts (as shown on the following *Guernica* example), which each student should then select as the section that they will render. Each student's quadrant will be a 12" section of the *Guernica* composition.
3. Before painting the team mural, make a watercolor paper test tile replicating a smaller section of your quadrant, which best represents your opinion of carnage. Perhaps a 10" square portion of that quadrant will be sufficient in order to show your other team members what you have in mind.
4. After presenting your "test tile" to the group, and everyone is satisfied with the results, it will be time to begin the actual painting. Suggested size is 21 1/2 × 48 (Your instructor may want to give you a different size). Be sure that you don't use a board that is more than 3/8" thick, or it will be too heavy. Plywood, particle board, etc., are suggested and can be cut to size at your lumber center.
5. Lightly sand the edges and give your board a coat of white, or gesso to neutralize the surface.
6. Project the image (slide with slide projector for example) onto the board surface, and then trace the entire image of *Guernica* onto the board.
7. Now, you are ready to render the color onto the shapes of *Guernica*.
8. At this point, you need to consult with your other team members, as to what exactly your intensions are. You will need to determine color choices, texture, tints and shades, as well as, contrast, saturation, intensity and value issues.
9. Although each quadrant is side-by-side, make sure that there is no line between that would indicate four different people worked on the project. It should have a variance of color harmonies throughout, but the shapes and forms must be juxtaposed where each quadrant begins and ends.
10. Remember to paint around the outside edges of the board, so that the wood, or natural material is not revealed.
11. Carnage, terror, apocalypse, and pandemonium are appropriate moods to create. Put yourself emotionally into the city during the attack, and then imagine that you are walking through the aftermath on that evening. Imagine the dull glow of huge embers, the heat, and the smell of

death, as you make your color choices and then begin to render color on the surface. The proper music selection will also help you to feel the mood as you work. Remember, the wrong selection of audio sounds can reduce the effects as well, so make careful selections.

12. Above all, remember to communicate and collaborate effectively, with respect for the other opinion, and be willing to make compromises if necessary.

Project Objectives

- Be able to create the appropriate *emotional response* to the word *carnage,* incorporating the most effective selection of color harmonies, which will enhance the mood of *Guernica*.
- To demonstrate the independence of color. Signifying that color can be liberated from the constraints of conventional shapes and form, and be able to reassign color to a less objective form, thus allowing color to function in the absolute freedom of expression.
- To determine whether or not the expression of color is appropriate in all cases, even in a predetermined achromatic composition.
- Be able to *validate* color choices and harmonies, which purposes are to elucidate and evoke specific emotional responses.
- To demonstrate successful work in a teamwork environment, exercising critical thinking and project solution skills.
- To demonstrate knowledge of all previous chapter contents, which incorporates the use of color elements such as: saturation, intensity, value, contrast, tints and shades, harmony, and emotional (mood) ramifications. The composition should demonstrate knowledge of high and low key color, balance, and hard-edged line, not to mention excellent presentation (craftmanship).

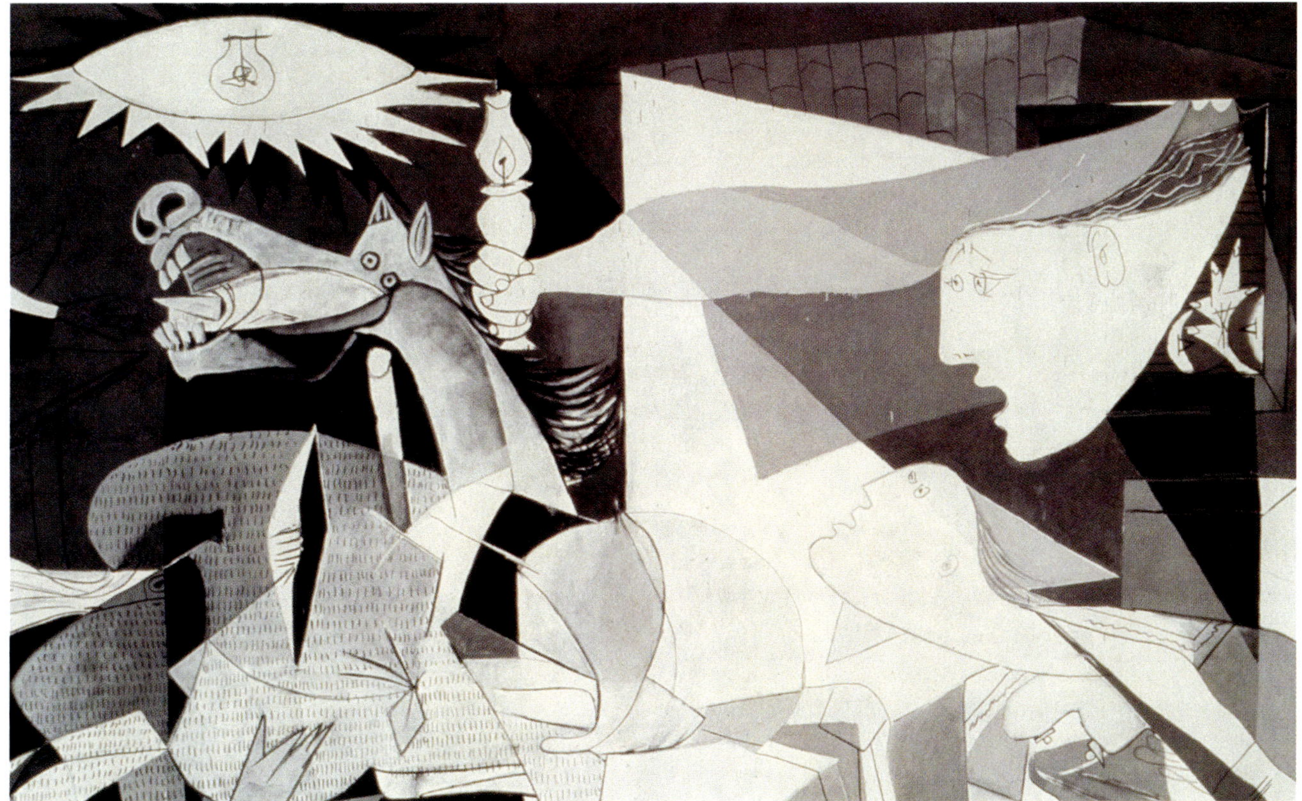

Guernica (detail) by Pablo Picasso May/June 1937.

Student Project Example—Guernica

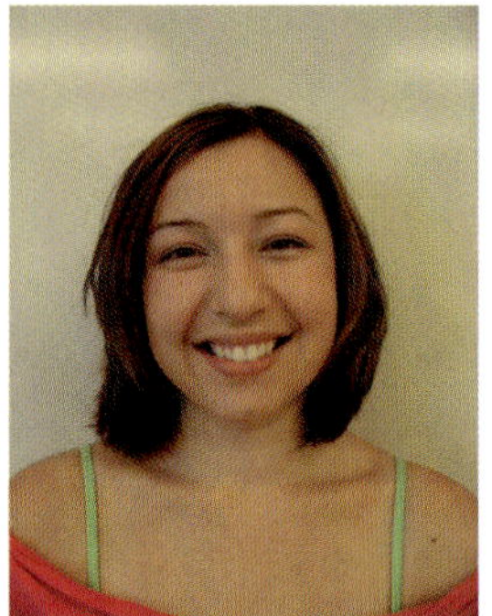

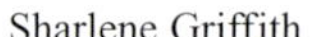

Sharlene Griffith

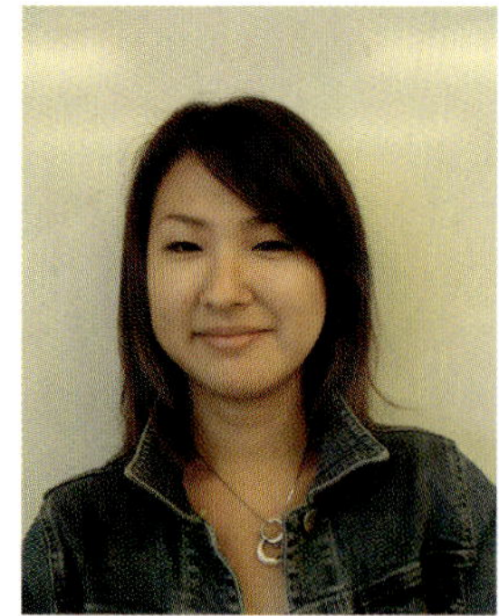

Ai Fujikawa

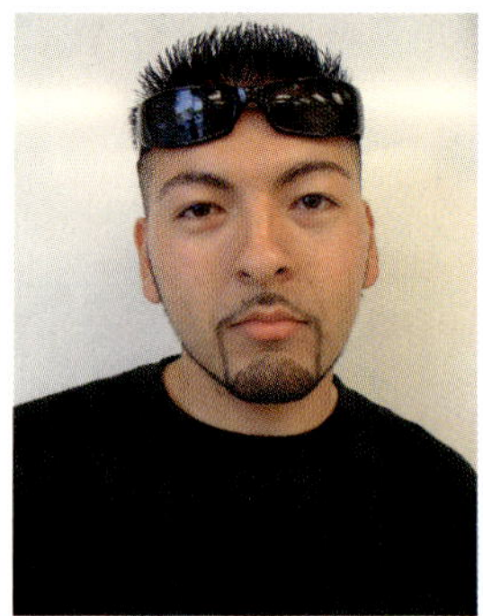

Leonardo Gonzales

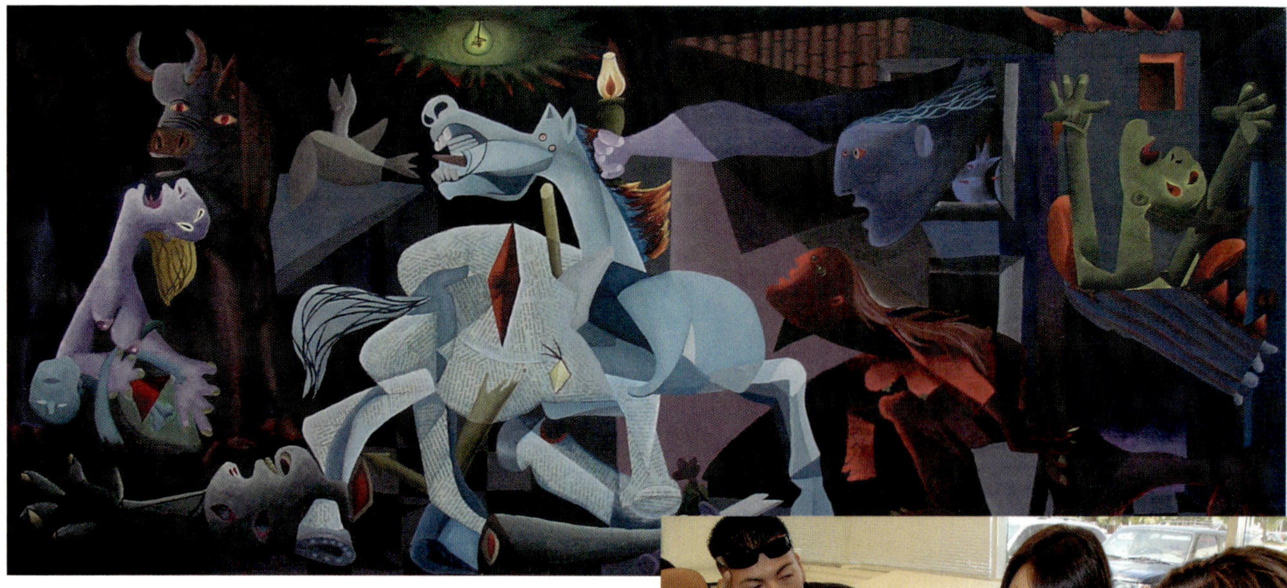

Students are now in final completion stages, but carefully go over the details before their critique. Students must be able to defend the quality of the work, as well as validate and defend their choices of color harmonies during the presentation. Students will be asked to discuss the calamity of Guernica, what it means to them and to identify color-to-mood components. Students should make sure that they have covered the many aspects of color they've learned, such as: value gradations, intensity, saturation, warm and cool, contrasts, tints and shades, color harmony, and the emotional aspects of color.

THE SPIRITUAL DIMENSION OF COLOR

One Step Beyond the Expression of Color: Transitions of the Intangible to the Physical

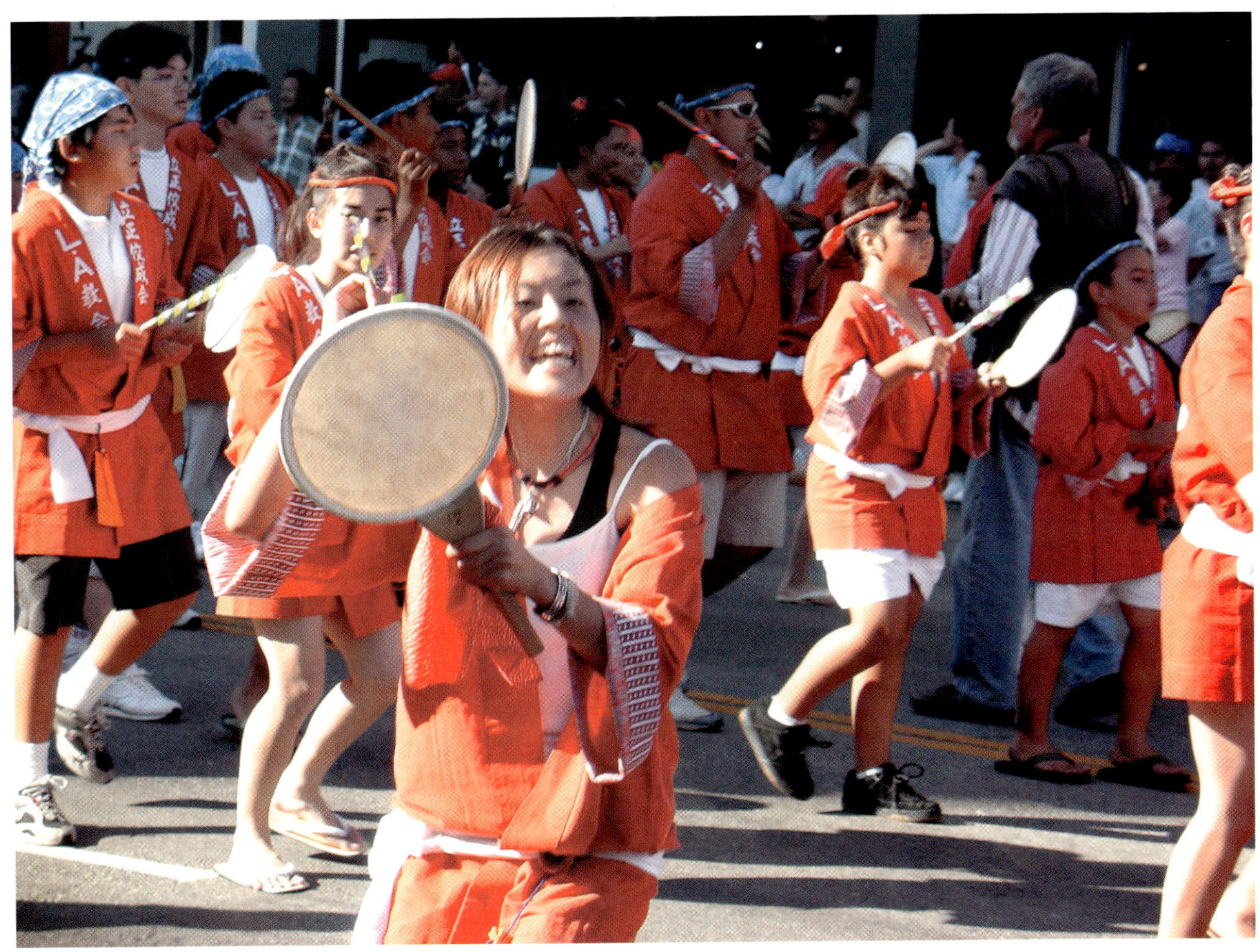

Nisei Week Celebration in Little Tokyo, Los Angeles 2004
Photo by Alan Burner.

CHAPTER SEVEN

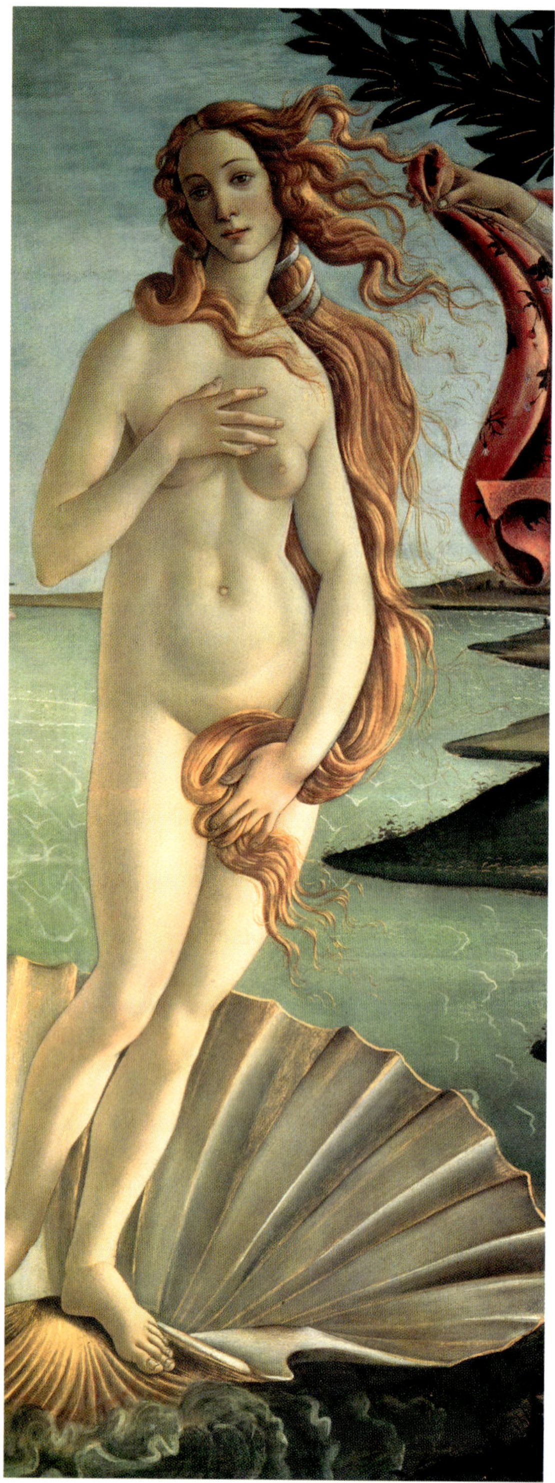

The Birth of Venus—detail of Venus by Sandro Botticelli (1444–1510).
Scala/Art Resource, NY.
Uffizi, Florence, Italy.

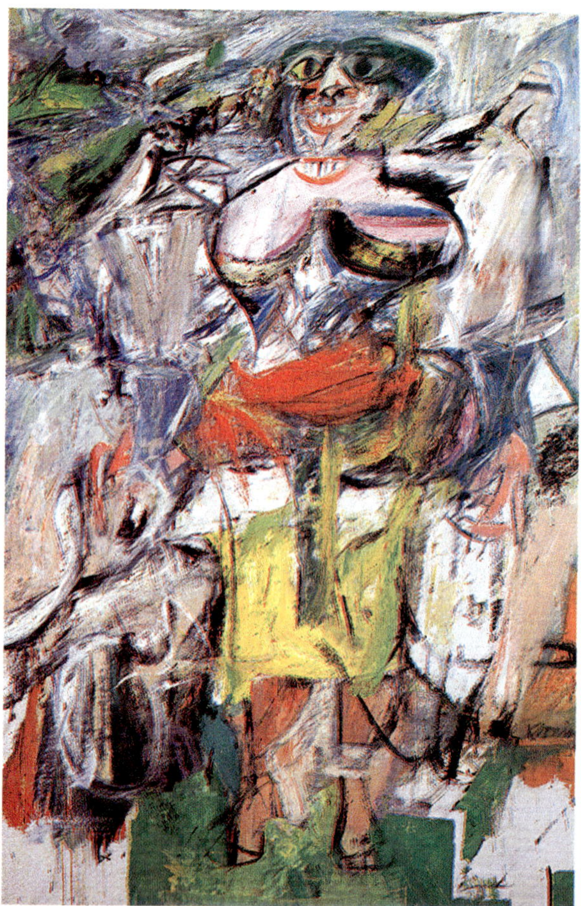

Woman and Bicycle by Willem de Kooning.

Introduction to the Spiritual Dimension of Color

Color's spiritual dimension first requires clarification as to what the word *spiritual* specifically refers to. The term spiritual is often misunderstood regarding the impact of color on the spirit. The subject is complex by nature because we are dealing with the unseen or intangible. This subject is a step beyond the *expression of color*, in that it can function separately from the material world and has no particular required shape or form. It is at times somewhat ethereal, while at other times it is nothing more than sensation waiting for a physical manifestation. Wassily Kandinsky, one of the art world's great intellects of the 20th century, referred to the Greeks and Romans and their preoccupation of expressing external realities. Kandinsky was inferring that the Greeks and Romans were not dealing with the spiritual as we define it, but only the superficial layer of human life. Kandinsky refers to this distinction as "The Spiritual in Art".

There actually is a connection between how the Greeks envisioned themselves and the spiritual; it has a lot to do with the human body and the gods of the Greek culture. However, when we discuss the term spiritual, we are referring more to a total inner being and a person's responses in all aspects. The spiritual dimension should not be confused with the "religious" aspect of the inner person, since that is but one category. Rather we are looking at the inner being in its entirety, and not so much the individual characteristics and responses to a particular aspect of spiritual functions.

It was the Greeks who brought us *idealism,* which attempted to represent or recreate the human figure within a framework of perfection. They were obsessed with the concept that humankind could be "super-perfect," as they sculpted the figure to appear much better than humanly possible. The Romans then adopted the Greeks sensibility about physical perfection in their artwork as well.

After the Greeks, the Roman empire began to copy the styles of sculpture and architecture. Soon enough, the Roman empire fell, which ushered in the *Middle Ages*, whereby Greek and Roman influences vanished. A thousand years later, during the Renaissance (rebirth of the classical Greek/Roman arts), people such as Michelangelo, Raphael, Botticelli (see previous page) and Leonardo Da Vinci began faithful studies of the old classical forms. The Renaissance painters were careful to study Greek classicism, since they wanted to paint exactly as the outward world appeared. This period mostly addressed the exterior, or appearance of the outward shell of a person, and their environment. In the 20th century everything changed. Artists such as Willem de Kooning (see facing page) dealt very deeply with the inner person. Through the physical medium of paint Kooning demonstrated that there were some serious psychological ramifications to his attitudes concerning women. He had done just the opposite of the Greek and Romans by actually destroying, or tearing the figure apart, perhaps attempting to show the "imperfection" rather than the "idealism" in humankind.

And last, but not least, we remember that it was the Greeks (Chapter One) who hypothesized early in history about the atom. The paintings on the following page illustrate a transition of the *spiritually perceived* energies within the atom into physical color. These paintings are a concept of these normally unseen forces.

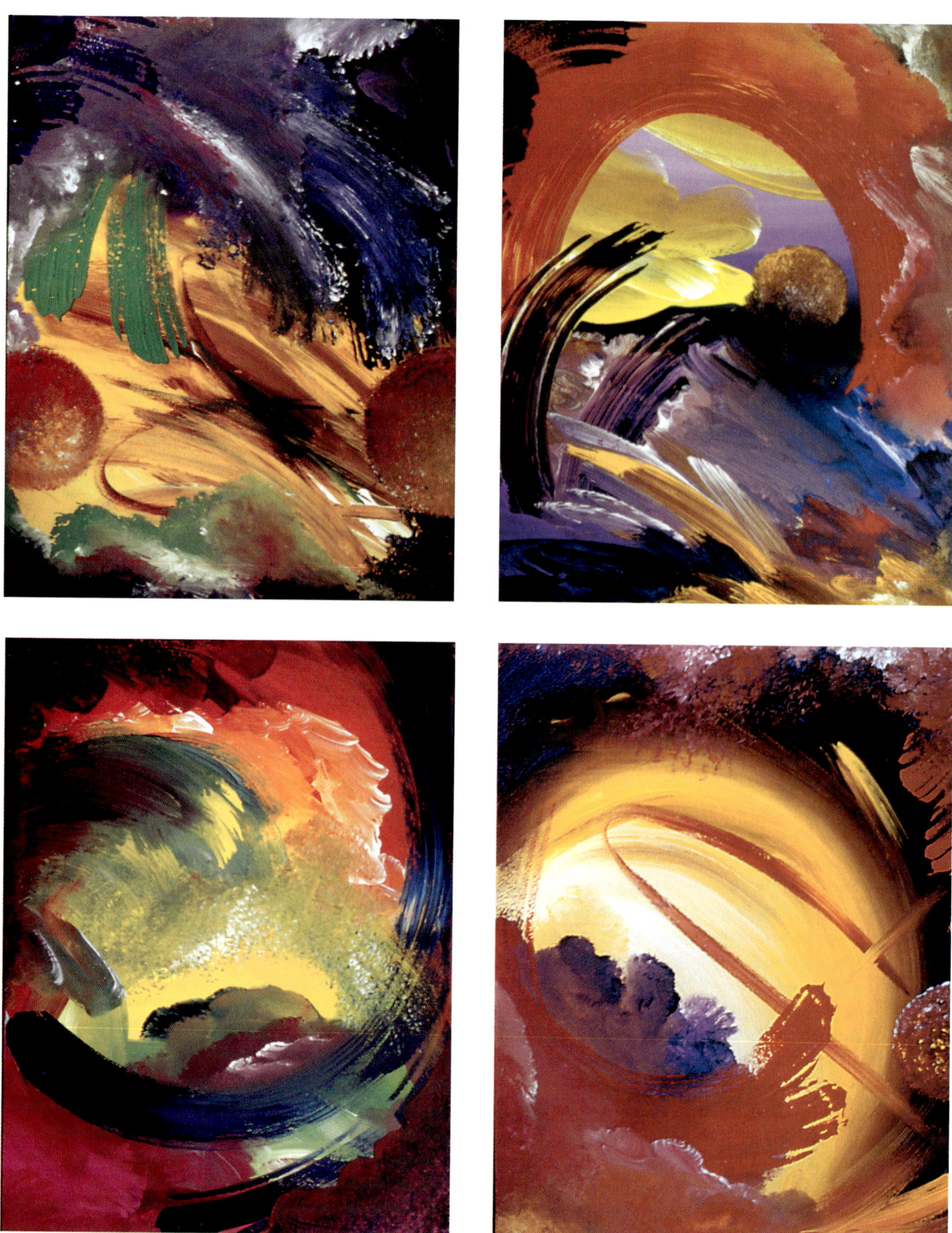

Shijo, *Ode to the Greeks: Visions of Quarks.*
Abstract color responses to the forces within the atom, whereby energy sources can be felt inwardly and interpreted by outward physical reactions. Even the contents of an atom can be felt and produce certain mood color responses.

Spiritual Persuasions

Kandinsky, an artist/intellectual from the Bauhaus, said "the relationships in art are not necessarily ones of outward form, but are founded on inner sympathy of meaning." It was Kandinsky who laid a solid foundation that color could and should not be limited to recognized forms. The artist Mondrian had stated earlier that color must be "liberated" from the confines of standard forms. Representation should therefore be more about the ***inner spirit***, rather than an outer representation. Take for example the portrait. One can either execute the outer appearance of the person, or the inner spiritual essence. Obviously, the physical result will be quite different. While the *outer image* or portrait will be obvious to the viewer, one may not recognize the demonstration of a pure *spiritual color* rendition of the inner, or spiritual, essence of the person. This concept begins to be seen by the tempestuous nature of Picasso's relationship with Dora Maar.

When we presume to render or print a person's portrait, we are actually attempting to capture the essence of the person, as well as the physical likeness. There are numerous issues when attempting to capture the essence of who that person is, because we are limited by the exterior physical reality. When we paint the likeness of the outer representation of the person, we are basically saying "What you see is what you get", because there is no other information about the subject available.

In the first *Portrait of Dora Maar* (below), we really are not seeing exactly "who" Dora Maar is, or how Picasso feels about her entirely, because we only see his outward representational expression of her. Although there is a certain mood captured in the drawing, we are still very limited as to what conclusions we can assume about her. In the painting of *Dora Maar Seated 1937* (following page), we can see quite a difference. Her image has been abstracted down to the simplest gestures. The primary colors of red, blue and yellow highlight her facial

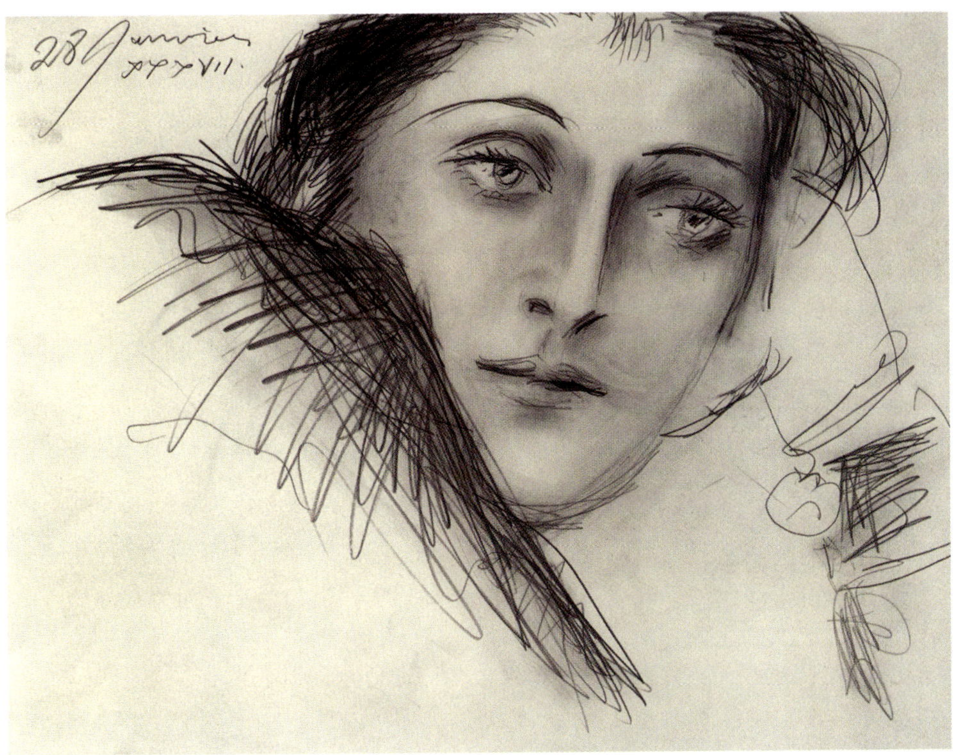

Portrait of Dora Maar by Pablo Picasso.

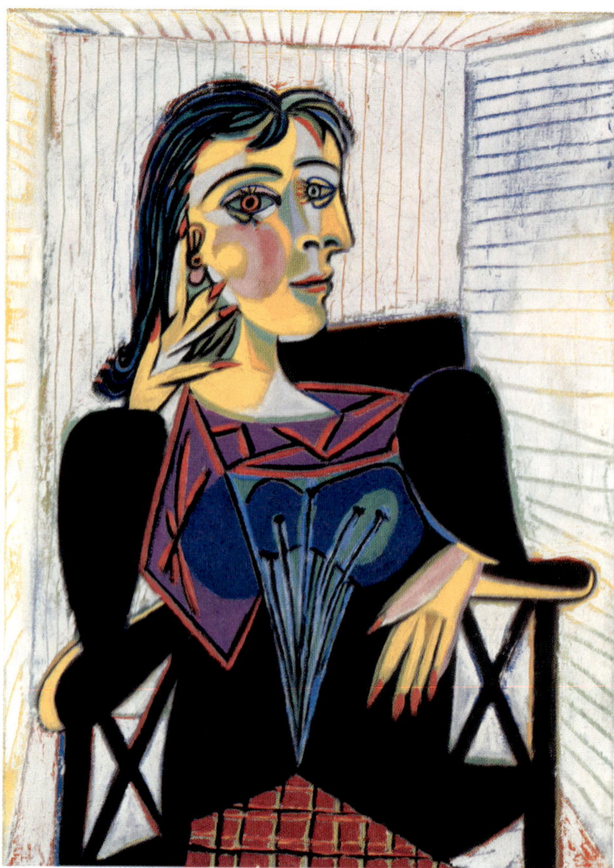

Dora Maar Seated, 1937, by Pablo Picasso.
Réunion des Musées Nationaux/Art Resource, NY

tones, as well as the composition itself. There is an ambiance of casual tranquility and bliss about her portrait, which tends to indicate that his relationship with her *at this point* was not as turbulent as it was often reported to be. The portrait seems to have a more spiritual direction, as it would indicate *his emotional response* to who she is, or *her inner actual self,* and has little or nothing to do with outer physical representation.

Looking ahead to a different artist, we turn to the French painter Paul Gauguin, who indicates that he is very much in tune with the spiritual aspects of color.

Gauguin creates a certain separation between the actual reality of Christ crucified on the cross (facing page), and his own whimsical vision of himself crucified, as the painting seems to become more of a visual autobiography. The actual Biblical report, tells us that Mary the mother of Jesus, Mary the wife of Cleophas, and Mary Magdalene sat at the feet of Christ. Instead, Gauguin paints three peasant women who take the place of the three Marys. The painting has much to do with color expression, and more importantly, alludes to spiritual qualities of color. Here, the dominant yellow in the composition is in serious contrast to the dark thundering sky reported at the time of Jesus Christ's death. The yellow is very harsh, and does not seem to reflect its usual upbeat and celebratory nature. The mood of the crucified Christ is in serious conflict with the usual character of yellow and psychologically alters one's perception of both the event and the color. Gauguin typically simplifies his forms toward the spiritual arena of color, albeit not to the point of pure spiritual expression.

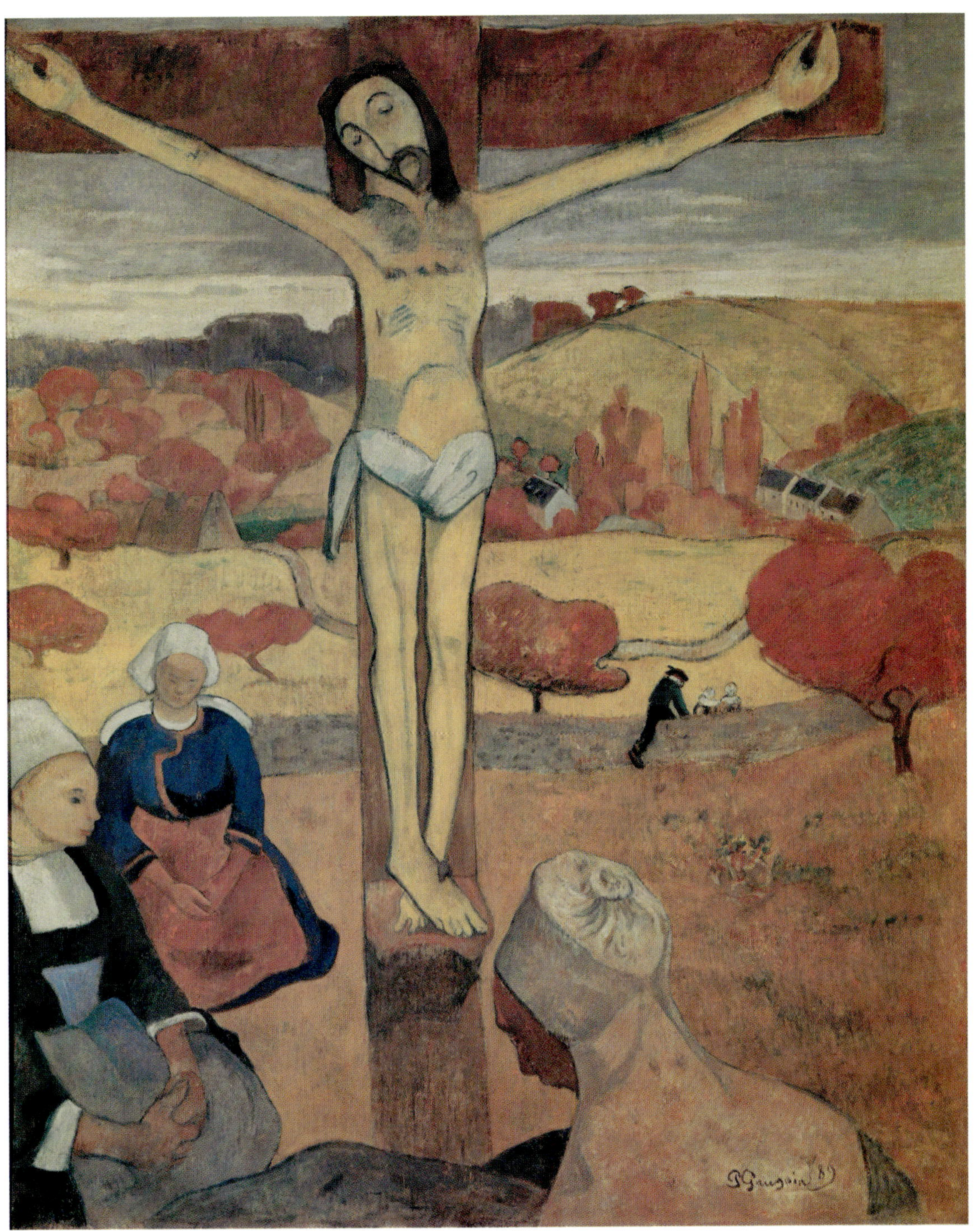

The Yellow Christ, 1889, by Gauguin.
Erich Lessing/Art Resource, NY.
Owned by Albright-Knox Art Gallery, Buffalo, New York.

Turning to Salvador Dali's *The Metamorphosis of Narcissus* (below), with its very symbolic imagery, reminds us of the dream world, which we all have experienced during our lifetime.

Dali's work helps to open the window into the spiritual world in order to better understand the more ethereal world of dreams. Dreams are part of the spiritual world, as opposed to the tangible exis-

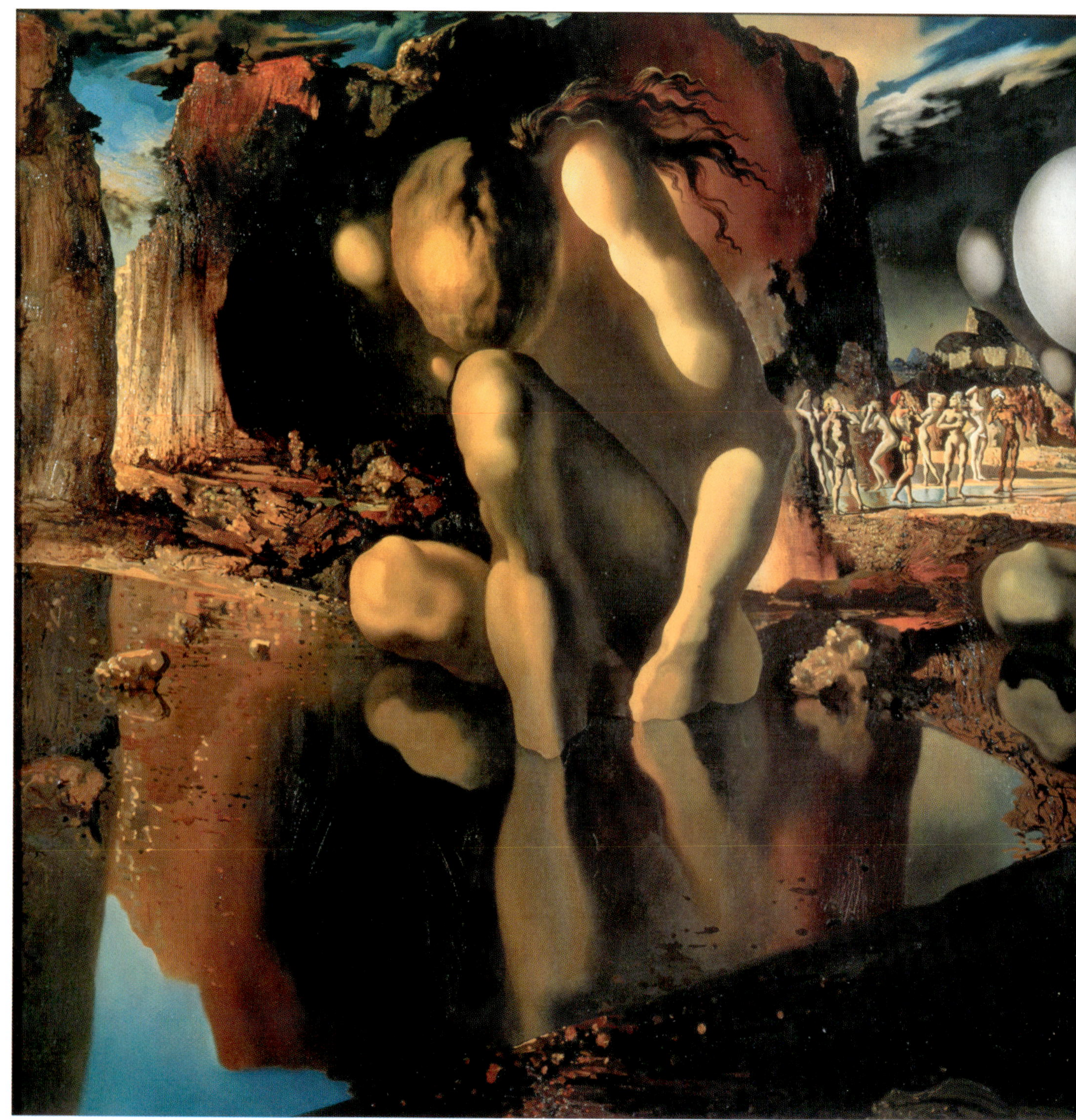

tence of the physical world. Often times, the spiritual expression of color relates to the dream world, where colors are sometimes unlimited in form and shape, and are often difficult to define, or perhaps vague as to their existence. In the physical world forms and shapes are well defined, and in fact color is usually relegated to the parameters of those areas, such as a red apple or a yellow lemon. These forms have assigned colors because the color belongs to that object. The lemon is validated by its color, whereas conversely the color of yellow does not need an object to validate its own existence. In this case, the lemon confines color to its own form, and yellow cannot extend beyond those required boundaries. In the spiritual, or non-tangible existence such as a dream, color cannot be limited to those conditions. Yellow can exist without limitations. The spiritual part of the human being, whether awake or in a dream state, can imagine or see color without limitations, as color travels beyond any form or peripheral vision.

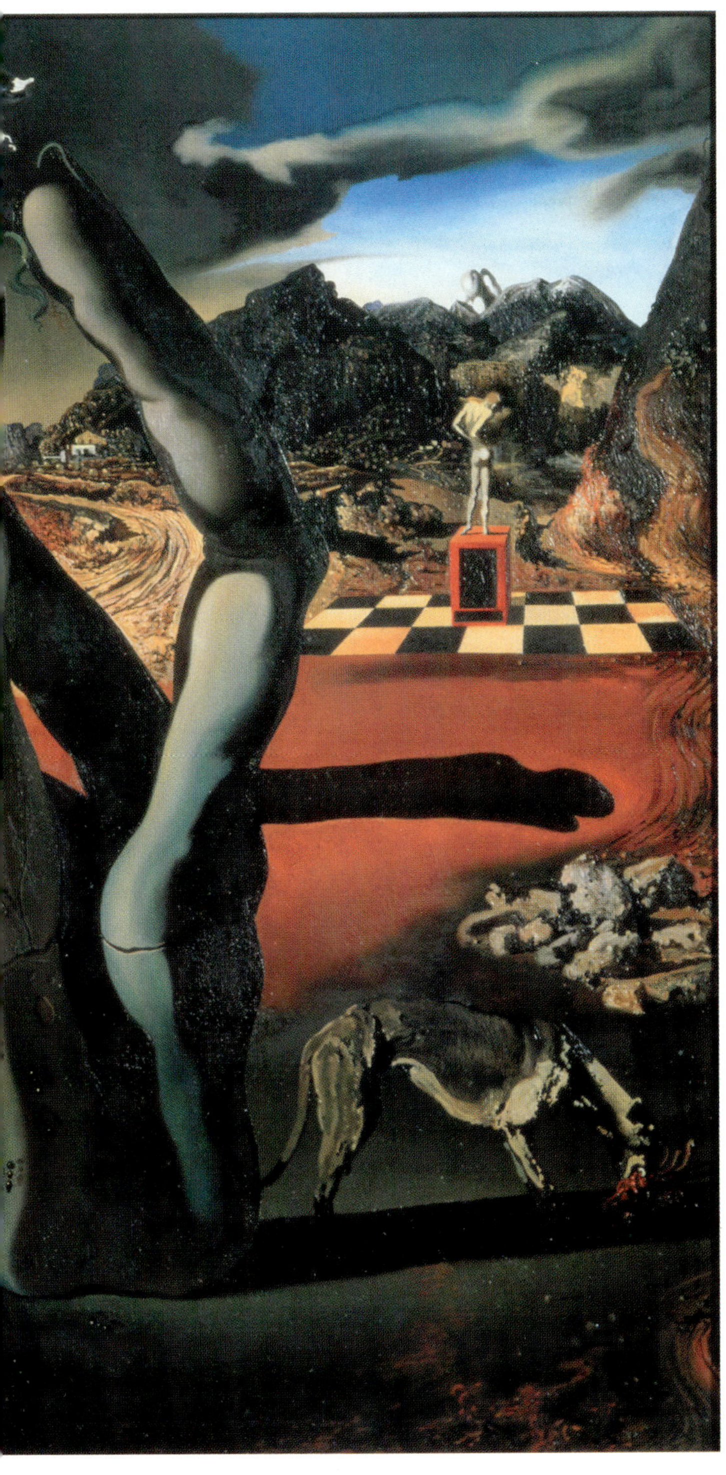

Another aspect by which we can observe the function of the *spiritual expression* of color, is to look at various words. *Love,* for example, can be a very emotional aspect of human experiences, and extends deep into the spiritual or non-tangible world. Love seems limitless until we attempt to express it physically. There are a number of complexities interpreting love into an accurate *measurable* expression in the tangible physical form. We know that there are limited physical expressions that indicate love, but to what *degree* becomes quite another issue.

The use of color in the *spiritual context* is much the same. The limitations are nonexistent until we attempt to bring it into the physical world. We understand then that dreams, for example, are limitless since they are attached to the spiritual world, more than they are to the physical.

When Salvador Dali attempted to paint one of his dreams, his limitations became obvious as to the struggle of spiritual transference into a physical space. The etherealness of a dream cannot be adequately manipulated onto a pigmented canvass. We know that this was at the heart of Kandinsky's manifest as well.

The Metamorphosis of Narcissus (1937) by Salvador Dali.
Tate Gallery, London/Art Resource, NY.
Tate Gallery, London, Great Britain.

Let's take a look at the evolution of the spiritual expression of color through the work of Wassily Kandinsky.

Sketch for Achtyrka (below) is a good beginning point to see how Kandinsky's work actually evolved to the spiritual level. The artwork itself has several factors to consider. Form and shape are obviously important to this piece, but color holds its own against the elements. In this first case scenario, we can see that color, form and shape are equally dependent. At this point we cannot make a case for one being more dominant or important than the other. We can see, however, that he is wandering away from the restrictions of form to a degree. The brush stokes of broken color are beginning to soften the boundaries of color.

Kandinsky's *Winter Landscape I* (facing page), begins to show that the forms are becoming more simple and abstract shapes, and the composition seems to be more about color than imagery. Color expression clearly dominates the picture plane, and we begin to see the evolution of color dominance in Kandinsky's work. The subject matter is much less significant compared to the mood created by the icy blues and harsh yellows. Here, Kandinsky works with the ultimate idea that color can be independent of formal representation, and that it alone holds at least equal weight with any other element.

Kandinsky's imagery in *The Garden I* (facing page), is becoming more spiritual in expression than the previous two paintings, in that the imagery is more difficult to discern. The *color* is now becoming the most important expression of the composition with its saturated ambiance. Instead of seeing imagery first, the most immediate attribute of this painting is *color.* Color is being freed of its bondage, and allowed to express itself with almost total independence from any shape or form. This rich and vibrant

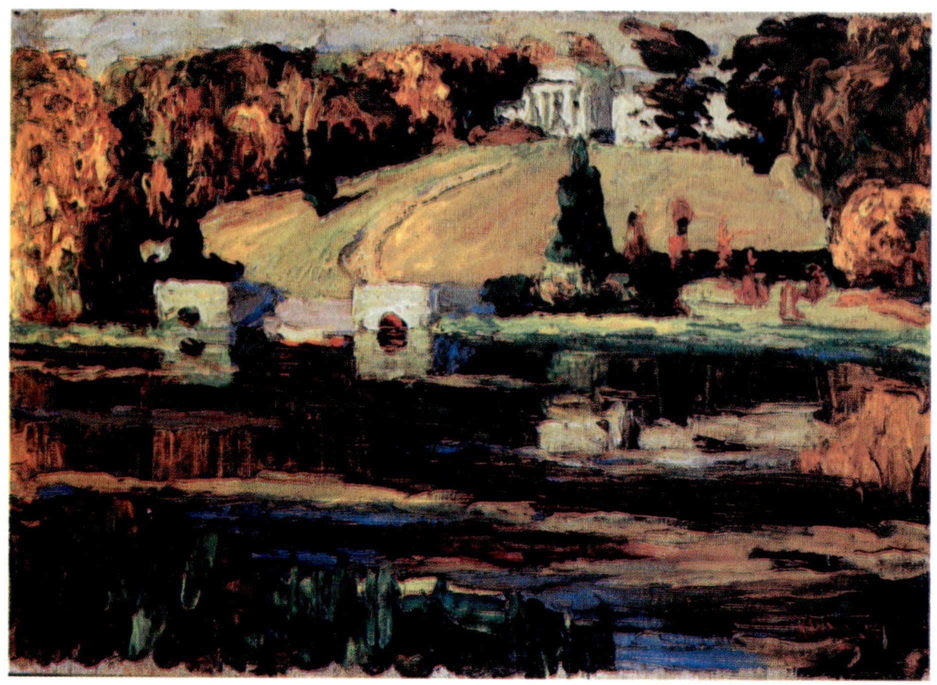

Sketch for Achtyrka, Autumn, 1901, by Wassily Kandinsky.
Städtische Galerie, Munich.

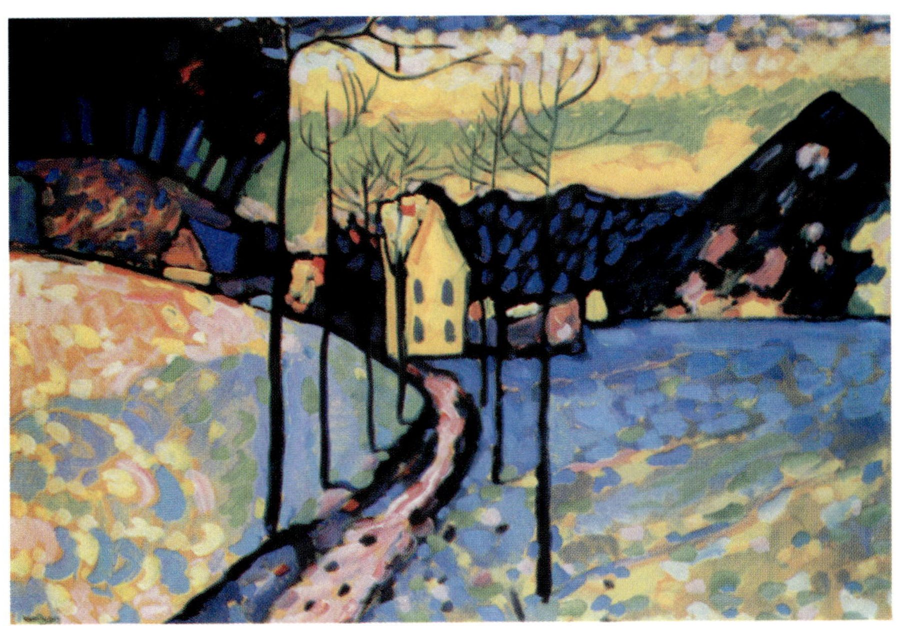

Winter Landscape I, 1909, by Wassily Kandinsky.
Erich Lessing/Art Resource, NY.
Hermitage, St. Petersburg, Russia.

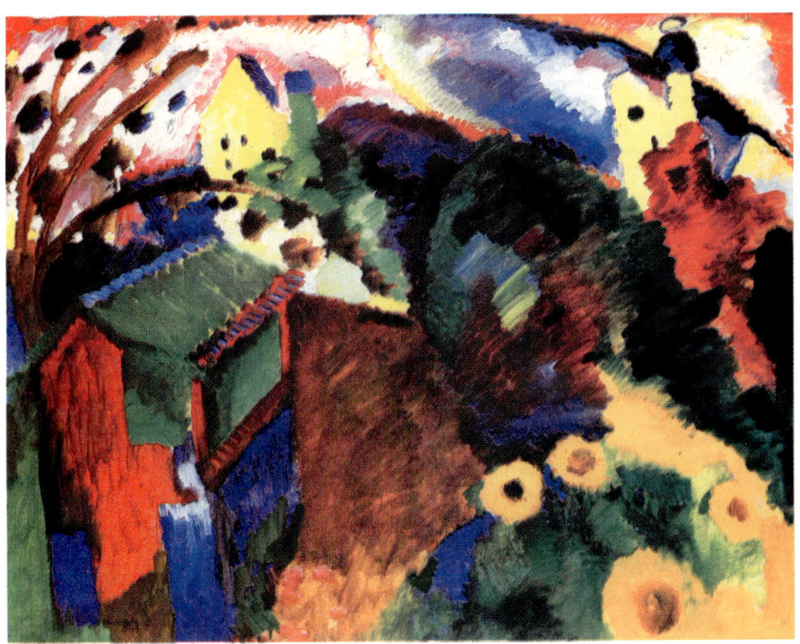

The Garden I, 1910, by Wassily Kandinsky.
©2004 Artists Rights Society (ARS), New York/ADAGP, Paris.

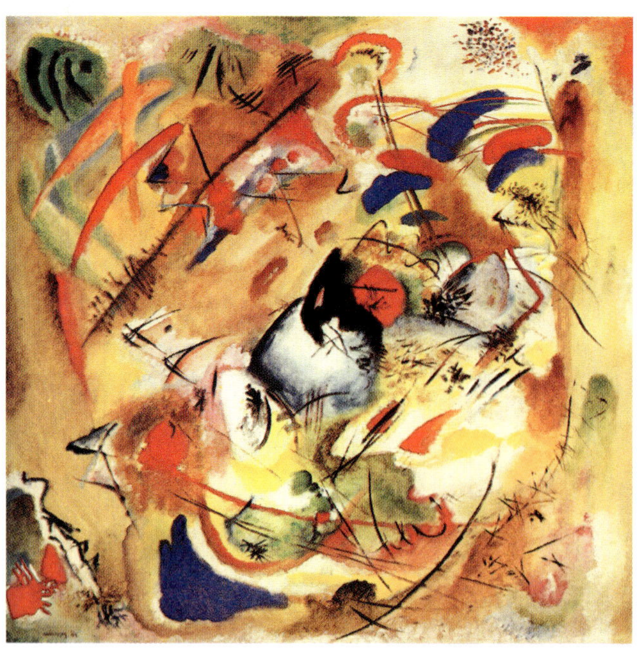

Dream Improvisation, 1913, by Wassily Kandinsky.

color composition pulls the viewer's eyes into the composition, and holds one's attention solidly. It is an extravaganza of color harmony.

Finally, Kandinsky creates the supreme spiritual expression in *Dream Improvisation.* The object has been destroyed, in order to reveal the pure spiritual expression of color. In many ways the painting is much like a dream sequence, in that it has an etherealness of color, where specific images blur in a cosmos background. More than that, a dream produces real emotion, mood that you actually wake up with and are physically affected by. The intangible dream can produce physical results based on content and color associations.

In *Dream Improvisation*, yellow profoundly effects the mood aspects of the composition, in that it is full of raw energy. Any possibility of a recognizable form has been eliminated, and color forms abound as the dominate expression of the spirit. Color in the physical world, must of course be linked to form, and at some point, color will have limitations as to its size and shape. In this case yellow is limited to the actual boundaries of the canvas. However, within the spiritual realm the perception of yellow does not have a form requirement; its area of coverage or size is therefore only limited as it exists in the mind's eye.

Kandinsky exclaimed that "The canvas is my enemy," giving reference to the difficulties of imparting spiritual creativity, or rendering of the *spiritual into the physical world.* Our emotions and concepts are of a spiritual, non-tangible nature, whereas the canvas is a physical limitation. The emotional issues and content of the story lay locked in the soul until paint is applied to the canvas surface. The tangible product — the canvas — becomes a tool to express what is being felt by the artist; yet, it is an imperfect vehicle.

In the chronology of change, from the physical to the spiritual emphasis, we have briefly examined Pablo Picasso, Paul Gauguin and Wassily Kandinsky. Picasso worked passionately to systematically and rationally destroy the image as we know it, by dividing and reconstructing from his inner

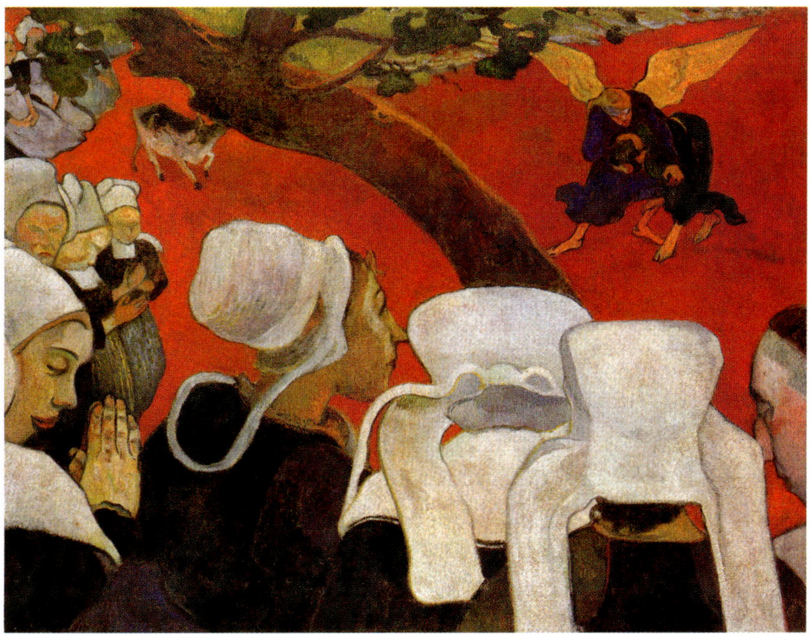

Vision After the Sermon or Jacob Wrestling the Angel, 1888, by Paul Gauguin.

self, responding to his emotional state. Picasso said that he painted what he knew, not what he necessarily could see. He applied what he observed in the physical world, but with a more emotional or spiritual connection.

The French artist, Paul Gauguin was, however, one of the most faithful painters dealing with the spiritual connection of color, and this concept is more fully realized as we continue to examine his work.

In *Vision After the Sermon,* Gauguin examines the emotional aspects of the *passion* with which Jacob wrestles the angel (background), more than his concern for any realistic form or perspective space. In reality, the composition is very flat, as the red background seems to advance into the viewer's space. Dealing with the spiritual responses was not about green grass, or dark shaded orange soil, but saturated red, which represents the spiritual struggle. The agony and passion by which Jacob wrestles the angel through the night, is felt by the emotion brought forth in the saturated red hues. Again, he was not at all concerned with physical representation of the world that he saw, but the spiritual reality of the inner person that he knew.

At this point, we would like to examine more of Kandinsky's philosophy about color and the pure spiritual, where only the forms of color and directional line exist. The subject matter or content may often times only be known by the lyrical emphasis of poetic or musical motions within the canvas, or merely by the title of the work. His compositions must be felt, experienced and carefully considered as only the colors of spiritual responses can record.

The subject of the spiritual in art merits further investigation in order to fully understand all of its ramifications. Let's take a look at how music factors into the visual art of color.

Color and Music Relationships

There is a relationship between visual color and music that is undeniable. In fact, Kandinsky elaborates extensively on the relationship of the spiritual between color and music. His canvases often reflect a type of symphony in color, titling some of his most important works as though they were musical "compositions."

Although there are differences in some comparisons generally, the use of terms and their connection to color are often strikingly similar. It is important to make a connection both in spiritual terms and vocabulary. Please observe some of the similarities between vocabularies of music and color theory:

Music Theory	Color Theory
* **Pitch:** Do, Re, Mi, Fa, So, La, Ti (This is a musical alphabet of seven) (Colors of light equal seven)	**Spectrum:** Red, Orange, Yellow, Green, Blue, Indigo and Violet.
* **Modes:** Seven Scales (Organization of a sequence of pitches into an articulate arrangement)	**Spectrum:** Red, Orange, Yellow, Green, Blue, Indigo and Violet.
* **Chromatic Scales:** (consecutive pitches) [All 12 notes in octave arrangement upward and downward]	**Color Circle:** Made up of primary, secondary and intermediate color (12 hues total)
* **Octave: Interval Between Two Tones** (12 semitones altogether)	" " " "
* **Key Signature:** Sharps and flats that appear at the beginning of a staff, which indicates the key of a musical work (sharp and flat notes).	**High Key and Low Key Colors:** Designates the tonal intensity or dullness (composition's character of lightness or darkness).
* **Chords:** Major triad and minor triad (Simultaneous sounds of three or more notes.	**Color Cords:** are harmonies of color created by primary and secondary color triads, as well as, dyads, tetrads, hexads, analogous, etc.
* **Harmony:** Is a arrangement of simultaneous tones.	**Harmony:** Methodical color relationships that are made up of specific color chords, which create a basic structure for a composition.
* **Four Part Harmony:** Basically, functional harmony is comprised of triads. When the root of a triad is doubled, it becomes a four-part harmony.	**Tetrad Color Harmony:** Four colors which are indicated by intersecting lines of either a square or rectangle drawn inside of the color circle.

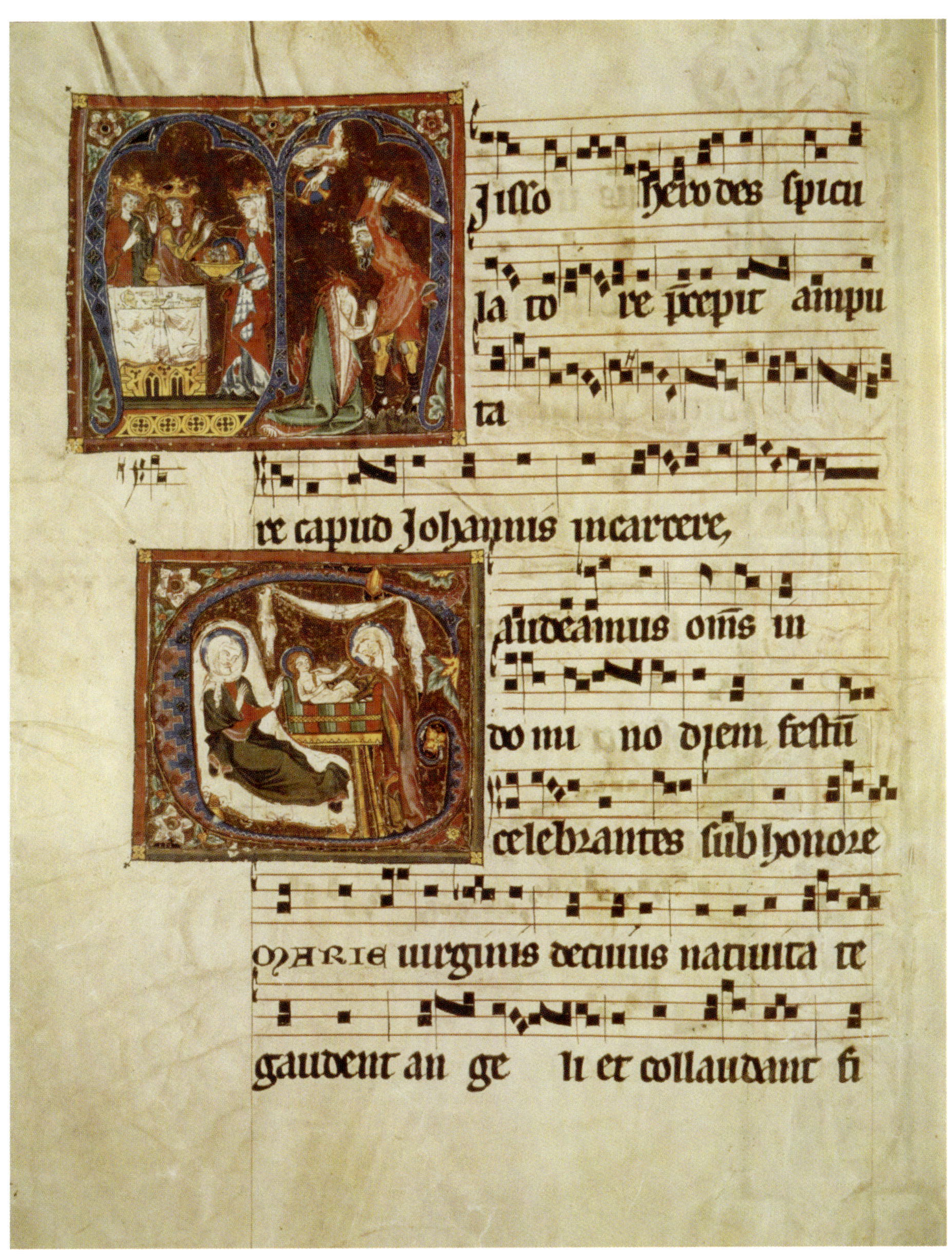

The Gradual from St. Katharinenthal, c.1312.
Zurich, Schweizerisches Landesmuseum, and Cantonal Museum of Thurgau, Frauenfeld, Ms. LM 26117, folio 190 verso.

The previous page is a page from one of the earliest and best examples of illuminated Gothic choir books. *The Gradual from St. Katharinenthal* (previous page) is basically a book of choir responses, sung alternately by two groups during church services. The words and the musical notes on the page have their origins from the spiritual inspiration of the inner person. The page then represents the spiritual, as *physical* responses in the form of musical notes and text. These are then sung as chants by the monastic population in the great gothic cathedrals of Europe. The page, then, is the physical evidence of the non-tangible spiritual existence.

There are some very similar functions between color and music. Some are not quite the same, yet there still remains a certain relationship between the two definitions. *Music* is the audible component, and *color* is often the visual interpretation of a musical piece. It is very common for a color painter to listen to his or her preferred musical selection before and during the act of painting, solely for the emotional and mood factors that help to establish the tone of the work, yet to be rendered.

It was Kandinsky who named many of his paintings after musical compositions. His attitude was that a painting may be created by the methodical orchestration of abstract and non-objective color applications. *To create a successful spiritual response of color onto a tangible surface (painting), is to conduct an orchestra of instruments, all with their specific tonal variations, into one cohesive work of art, or musical composition.*

In fact, it is clear that many of his compositions were nothing more than a visual *operetta* of color. *Operettas* often consist of music, dancing and the spoken dialogue, which are more simplified versions of an *opera*. The opera then, is a complex and more formalized performance of music and singing.

Kandinsky's *Composition X* has the appearance of a well-conducted symphony of color and form. This canvas of hard-edged, rigid color shapes is free-spirited and lively, as it moves upward on the picture plane. This painting is *orchestrated color*, from the inner spirit of the emotional and inspirational realm, into the physical visual world. It is nothing more than the evidence of mood and feeling from within the artist.

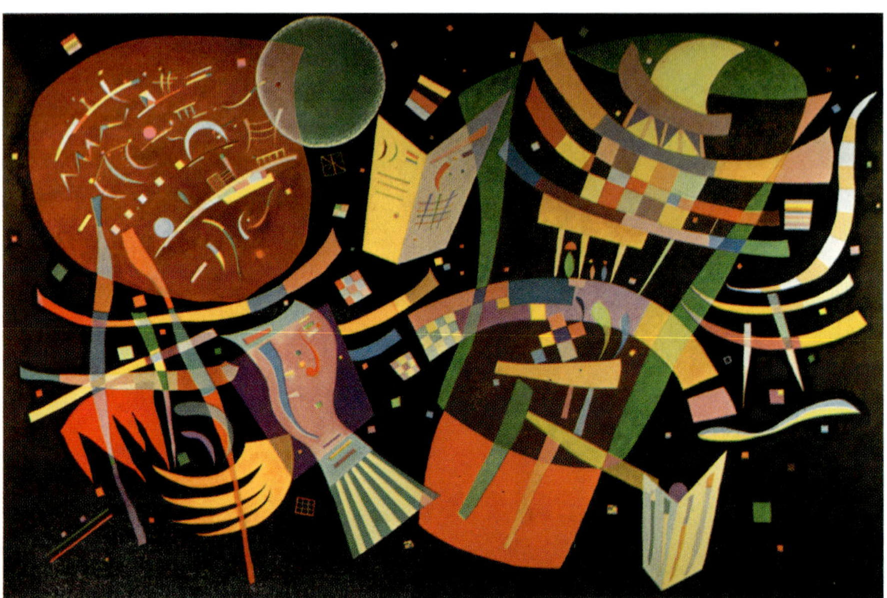

Composition X, 1939, by Wassily Kandinsky.

When contrasting *Composition X* with the previously discussed *Dream Improvisation* (opera version by comparison), we realize that the word "improvisation" in the world of music is basically the same as in other life disciplines. It is the performance of a harmonious piece, without prior reading of the music. It is spontaneity in a controlled manner. *Dream Improvisation* is more of an *operetta* by appearance, with a more color energized yellow presence. Softer edges of dispersed color flow in several directions, and the composition's character seems to be more spontaneous by its first impression. Both compositions employ a totally different harmonic gesture and mood composite, and yet are similar in gesture. They are just as two musical compositions would be dissimilar, even though conducted by the same composer.

What is the Sound of Color?

Having discussed all of this, we then need to realize that *color* possesses certain *sound* implications. The sound of color can be perceived in many ways. Think of musical instruments that you are familiar with and assign the most accurate color to it. When we try to imagine a *bass note* representing *yellow*, we immediately understand that it cannot be possible. It is not the character of a bass sound to be light and cheerful. A flat, as opposed to a sharp note in like manner, must be considered as to its color interpretation, or assignment as well. A flute or a harp would not be violet, since a true violet is very strong and exhibits little or no intensity. Violet is a very heavy, or weighty color, and carries a certain somberness or even oppressive mood. A more appropriate color then, would be perhaps *yellows, lighter greens and light blues*. *Violet* might then belong more appropriately to certain percussion instruments, such as tenor or bass drums.

When pairing music with color, the very first thought about the transference of color into sound can be witnessed in Kandinsky's *Red Oval,* and the dynamic of Japanese Taiko drums. Look at the similarities between the *vigorous expression* of Mari Nakano and the *color energies* seen in the *Red Oval.* Taiko is explosive, energetic, and creates bone-chilling moods, just as does color itself. The *reds, oranges* and *yellows* are, of course the energetic sounds of Japanese Taiko drums. The very animated, multi-directional, color explosion seems to replicate the extreme dynamic of a Taiko performance.

Taiko and color are always in league with one another. Red and black costumes replicate the contrasts found in the extreme tonal qualities of Taiko. At times

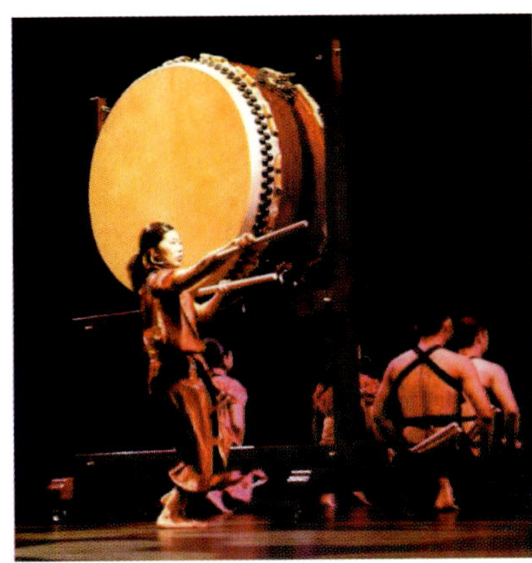

Mari Nakano, Production Still of Taiko Drummer, Home 2
TAIKOPROJECT © 1998–2005.

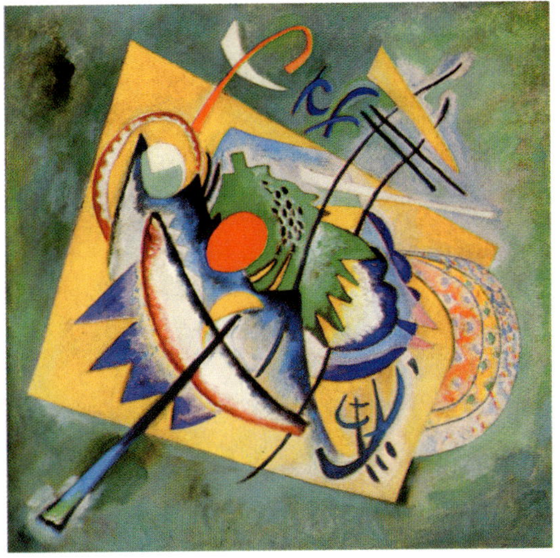

Red Oval, 1920, by Wassily Kandinsky.
©2004 Artists Rights Society (ARS), New York/ADAGP, Paris.

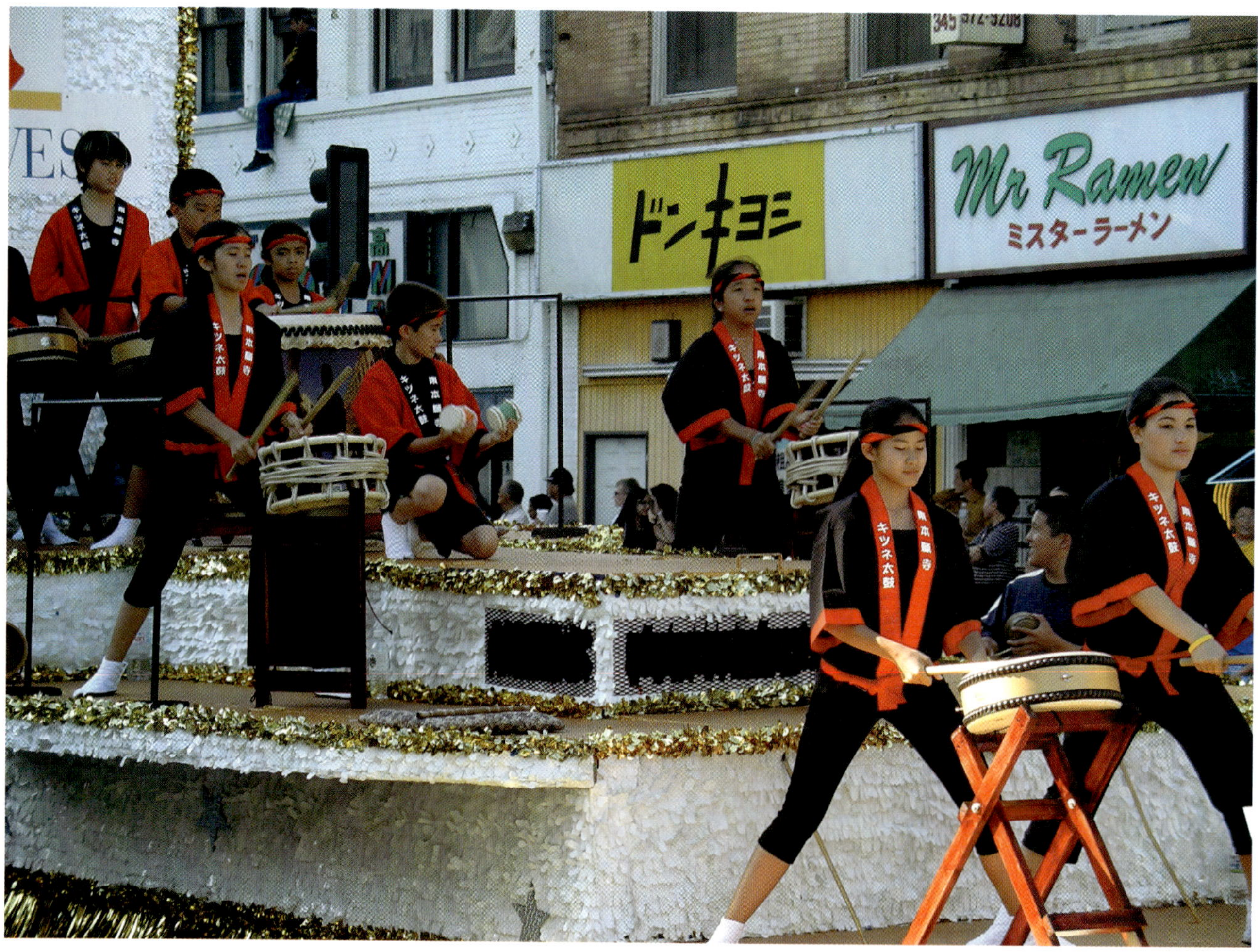

Taiko Performers in Nisei Week Parade, Los Angeles 2004.
Photo by Alan Burner.

the sound of color was black, heavy and slow. Other times along the parade route, the sound of red was more aggressive, fast and even angry.

Notice that the colors of the performance stage of Taiko is well thought out. In two of the examples, a fairly saturated red is incorporated with the Taiko performance. We remember that the power, thunder and intensity of energy is very indicative of the nature of red. The spirit of Japan is embodied within the sound of the drum and the energy of the performers, as well as the color red. Historically, Taiko has been associated with Shinto and Buddhism, as well as war time drums to intimidate the enemy or as a method to drive off evil spirits. Today, the thundering rhythm of the drums create spiritual awe, in their stern and forceful command. It is conceivable that if Kandinsky had been at the Taiko performance, he may have perhaps been inspired to have painted the *Red Oval* (previous page). Looking at the photograph of the Taiko, we cannot see the movement first hand, so obviously one is limited by the comparison between the painting and the Taiko images. The spiritual connection of interpretational possibilities is certainly there. If the reader has attended a Taiko performance, then it is clear as to the focus of this comparison.

Encountering a professional Taiko performance is one of the most spiritually moving experiences one can have. It is the intangible sound that perme-

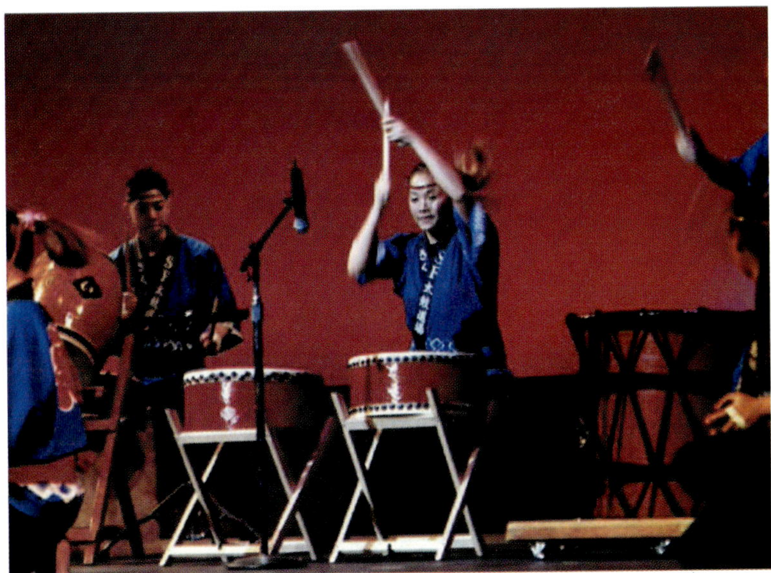

Taiko Dojo, Taiko Drummer, San Francisco.
Photos property of San Francisco Taiko Dojo. Copyright © 2005.

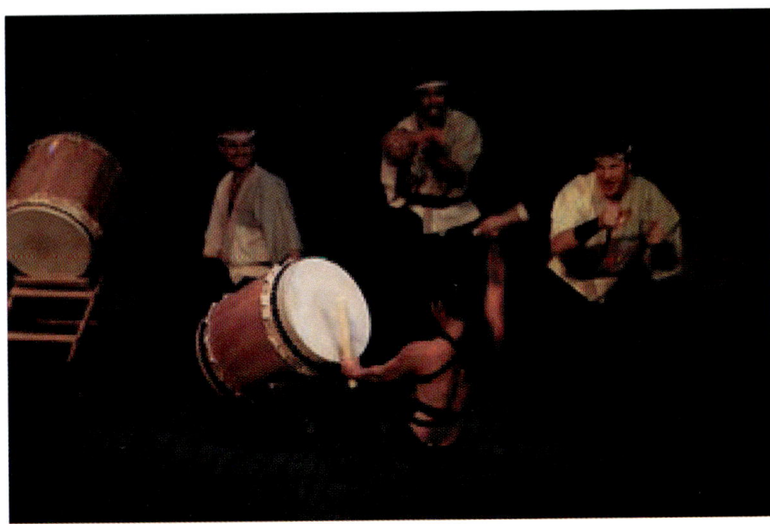

Stanford Taiko, Hanabi.
Used by permission of Stanford Taiko and Stanford Music Department.
Whether you prefer digital or pigmented applications, practice interpreting the spirit of the above two compositions into pure color emotion.

ates the soul, reaches deep down spiritually, and inspires physical creativity. It is probably one of the most dynamic expressions of the spiritual part of humanity. It remains the challenge of the visual artist today, to be able to inspire and create that kind of emotional response through color.

Verdi's Requiem Mass

Another example of the spiritual effect is through the amazing work of Verdi's Requiem Mass. Few examples serve better to affect a visual emotional color response through music. The words to the Requiem *Lacrymosa* are;

> Mournful shall be that day,
> When there shall arise from ashes
> Guilty man to be judged.
> Therefore spare them Lord,
> Good Lord Jesus,
> Grant them rest.

The lament is repeated as the tempo continues to control the mood, with its quiet and mournful timbre. The title of the piece and the first word Lachrymose (mournful) creates a somber tone of weeping and misery. Yet, there is hope for the redemption of the dead reflected in the construction of mood in this very spiritual music.

The Requiem begins very softly, and slowly builds into the sounds of hope, only to drop into mournful depression once again. The spiritual ambiance of the Requiem seems to alternate between the despair of losing someone to death, and the hope of their eternal salvation and rest. As one listens to the music, one understands the somber and weighty spirit of the music. Interpretations of the Requiem into color expressions could be seen through deep reds and deep warm violets, or perhaps darker blues. The spiritual rendition of color is relegated to very specific colors and values, in order to maintain the mood integrity of the musical composition.

Continuing with the color assessment, it would be possible to intermittently see the deeper

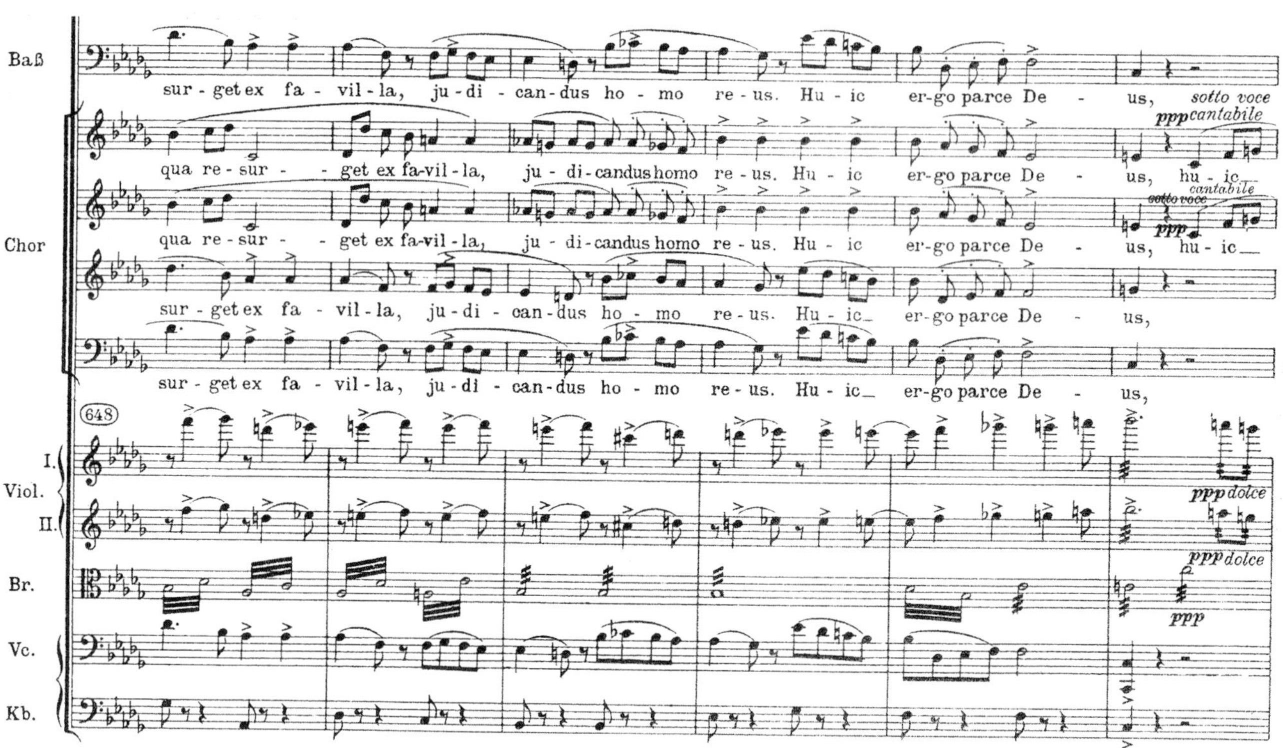

Section of the Musical Composition from Giuseppe Verdi's Requiem

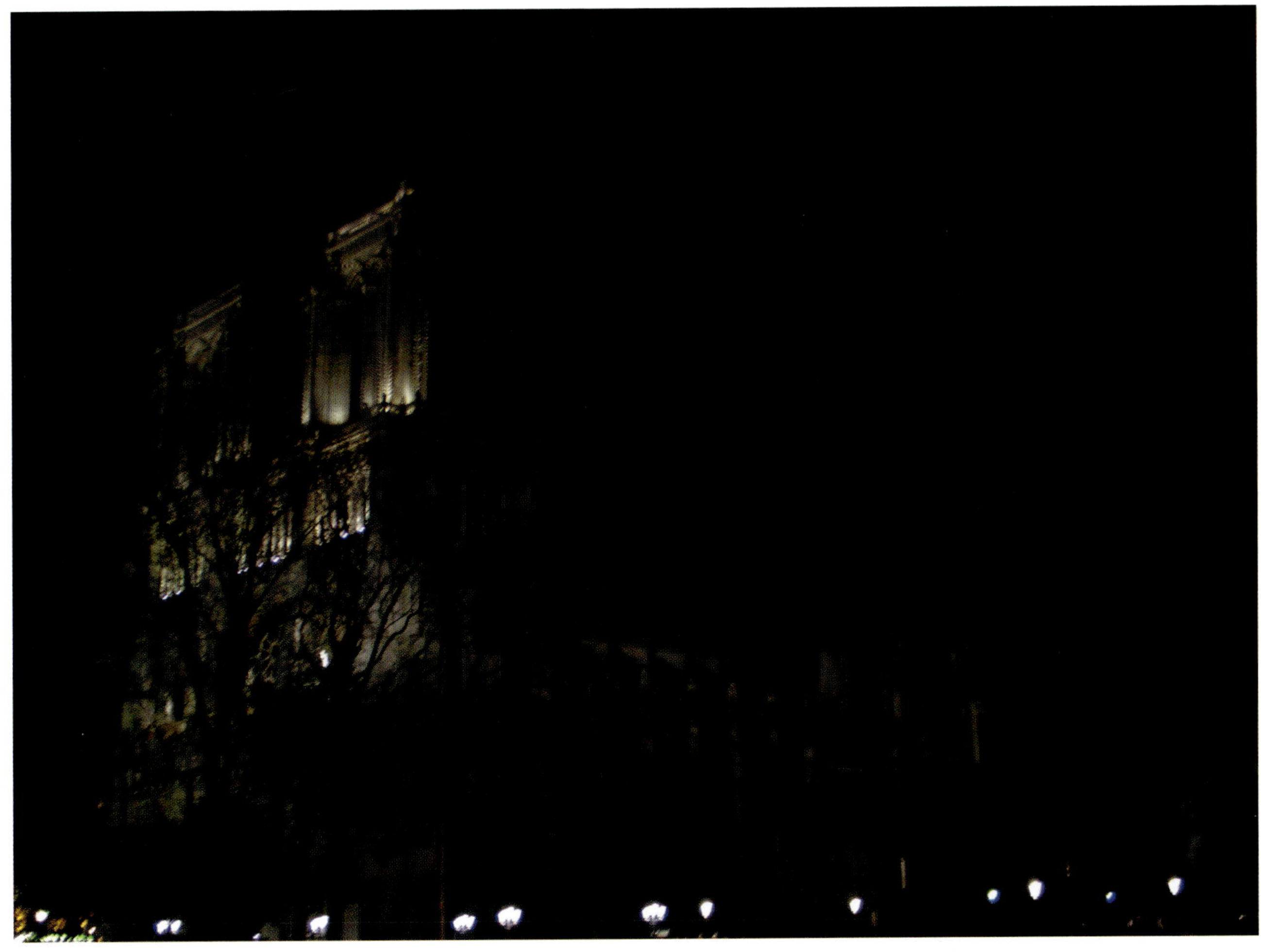

Cathedral Notre dame de Paris at Night.
Photo by Alan Burner.
The mood component at the cathedral is very different, especially when the Requiem is performed in the evening.

reds and warm violets transform into more saturated or intense colors of red, orange or perhaps yellow. These would provide the enhancement of the composition's element of hope in the midst of despair.

In the case of the *Requiem composition,* it is most often experienced in a church or cathedral setting. The emotional variances of *sound* and *color* influence the mood of the worshipper, which in turn creates an atmosphere of awe, respect and dignity. Kandinsky's canvas' and his application of colors are very much like a musical composition, a concert, a poet's journal, or the performance of dancers with their expression of body gesture.

Color in Performance: Dance

Dance and music have a very ethereal connection to their nature, among other attributes. We have learned that the spiritual properties of one's self are often manifested through the physical world, such as hand and body gestures. The human form is capable of revealing a multitude of spiritual issues, whether extreme *body language* or subtle gesture.

A most compelling issue is that of the complex nature of the human being. The body itself is a completely separate entity from the real-self, the body being *thoroughly physical* and the inner self, *wholly spiritual*. The two are often at odds with each other. The corporeal deals with the "right now", or tends to be more *animal* in terms of its basic needs, while the spiritual, conversely, involves itself more with the "timeless," whose attributes are to be *insightful* and sensitive. It is the music that inspires and moves the spiritual forces from within, and the body then interprets by giving the intangible sound a physical form or representation. *It is important to remember that it is the same with revealing the nature of color. We are inspired from within and create from without.*

Dancers on stage are attempting to convey a story, which until now has been locked-up tight in their souls. A performer chooses just how much of

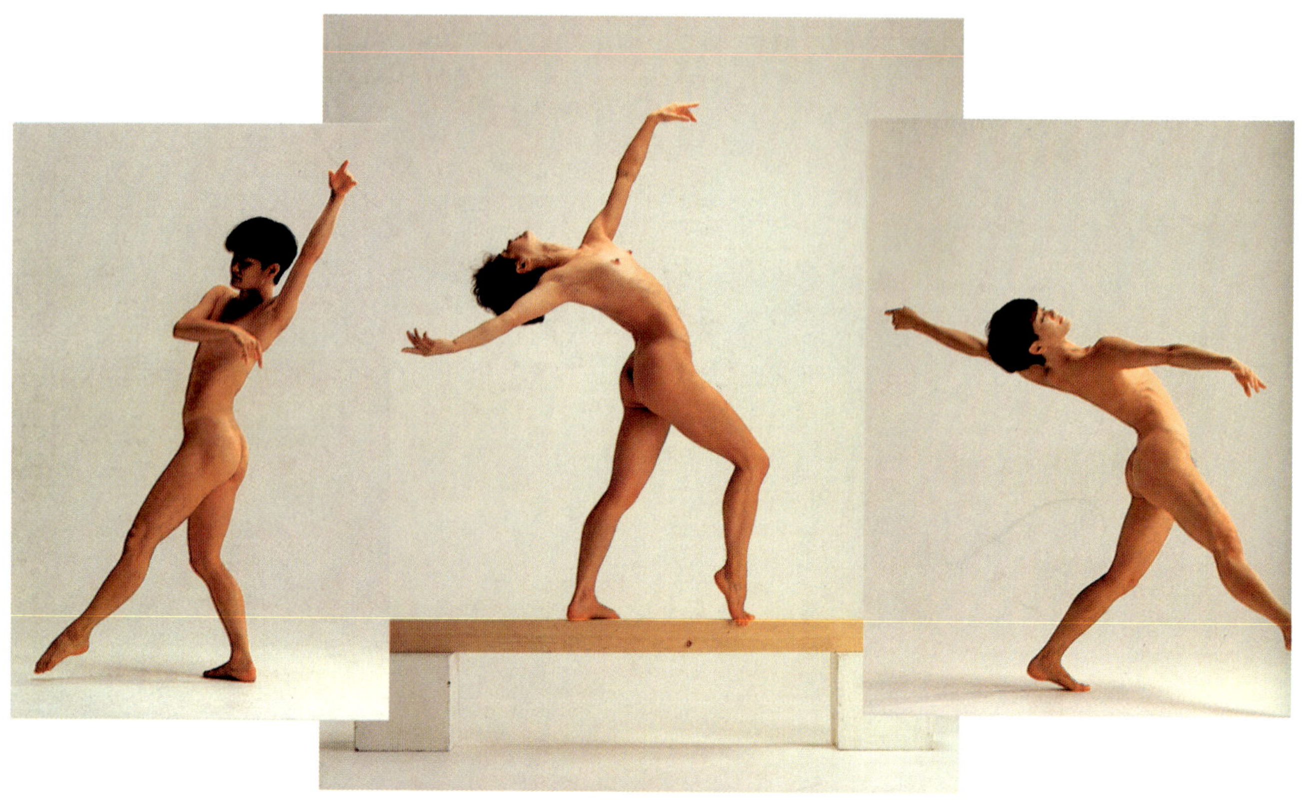

Pure form body gesture in dance demonstrates physical responses to mood influences or inspiration upon the spiritual or inner person. In the same respect, color is influenced directly from the spiritual link of the individual.

Visual Suggestion of Physical to Spiritual Transference

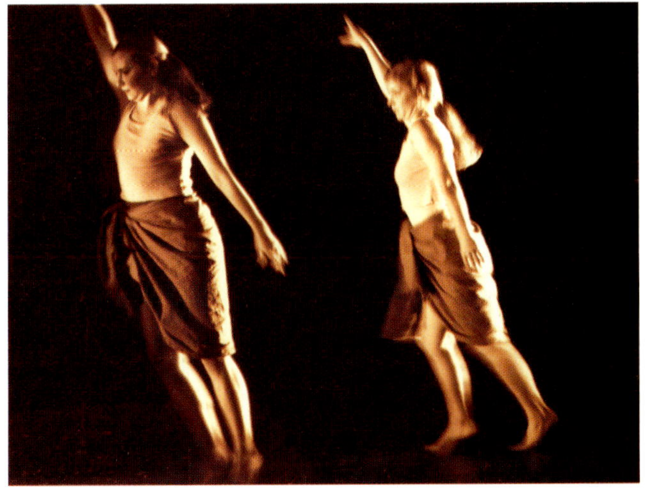

Using slow film, this sequence is a limited way of illustrating a type of transformation from the physical to the spiritual. The dance begins as pure physical representation in this frame. This visual form begins to transform into a less recognizable shapes (next frame) as it takes on a more spiritual sensibility, or perhaps a type of transforming manifestation.

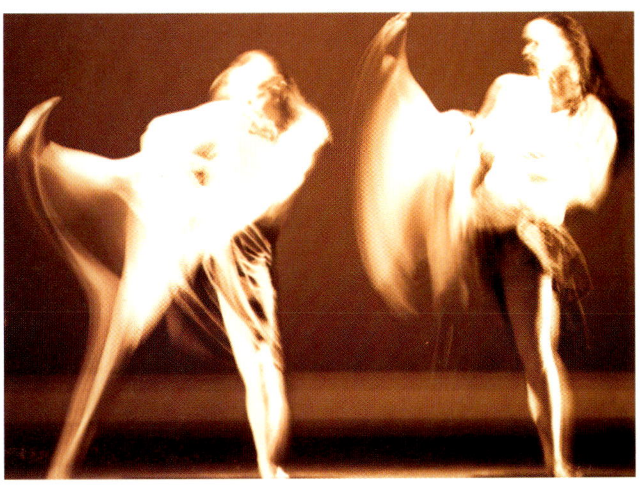

As the dance intensifies, the film is unable to capture the exact image, and instead we begin to see the movement of the figure, more than the body itself. It is the realistic image being transformed to the abstract form. This is especially noticeable on the left side figure, as the movement of the foot extending from the floor to eye level creates the image of movement. It is this area in which we are most interested. It is the essence of the dance.

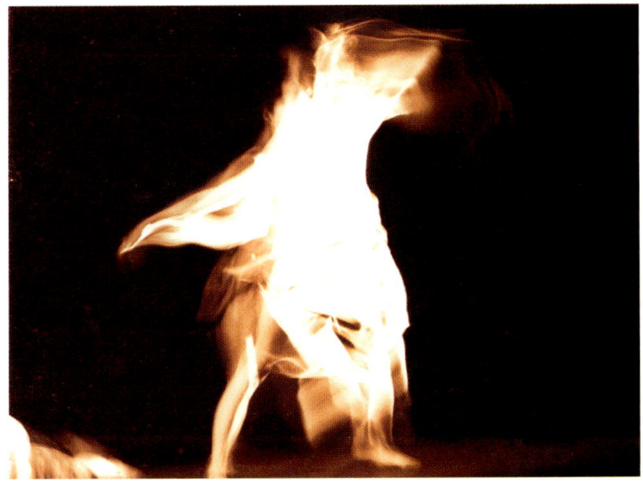

Finally, the dance reaches its high point. As the figures seem to unite, the image becomes more ethereal, leaving us with the essence of the figure. This ghost-like image has taken the form of pure energy, which seems to be overcoming the representational or physical form. The physical form, in a sense, has been destroyed and we are left with a type of visual manifestation of the spiritual (if that were actually possible).

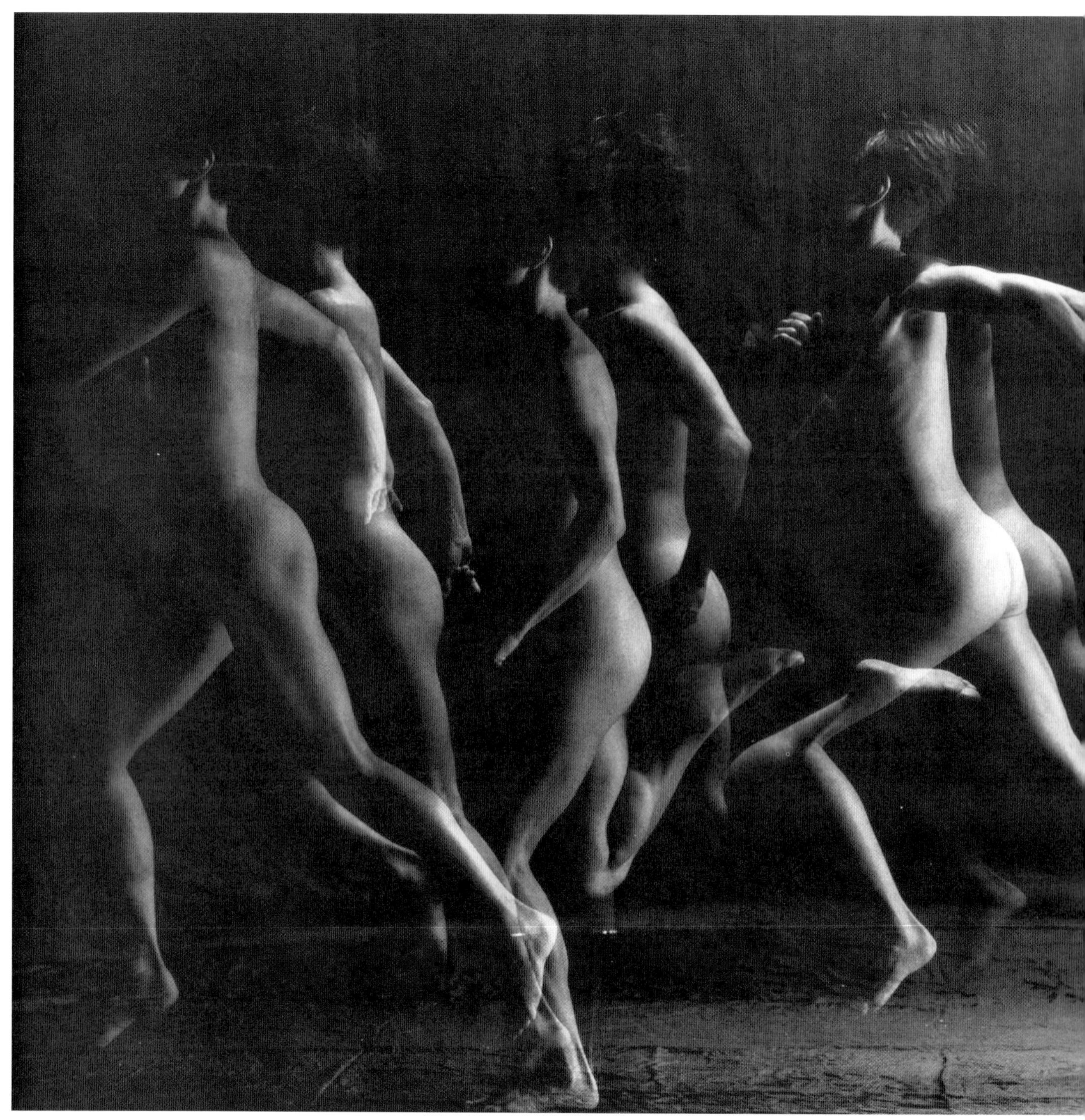

Body gesture is the pure form response to the spiritual or inner being of a person. Commensurately, the application of color is often the same, and is one of the purest expressions of mood.
Continuous physical responses to inner spiritual inspiration. There is a spiritual *energy* which is revealed by body movement. Color is *energy*, as well. Try to translate this composition into what you think may be the appropriate colors, which match the mood.

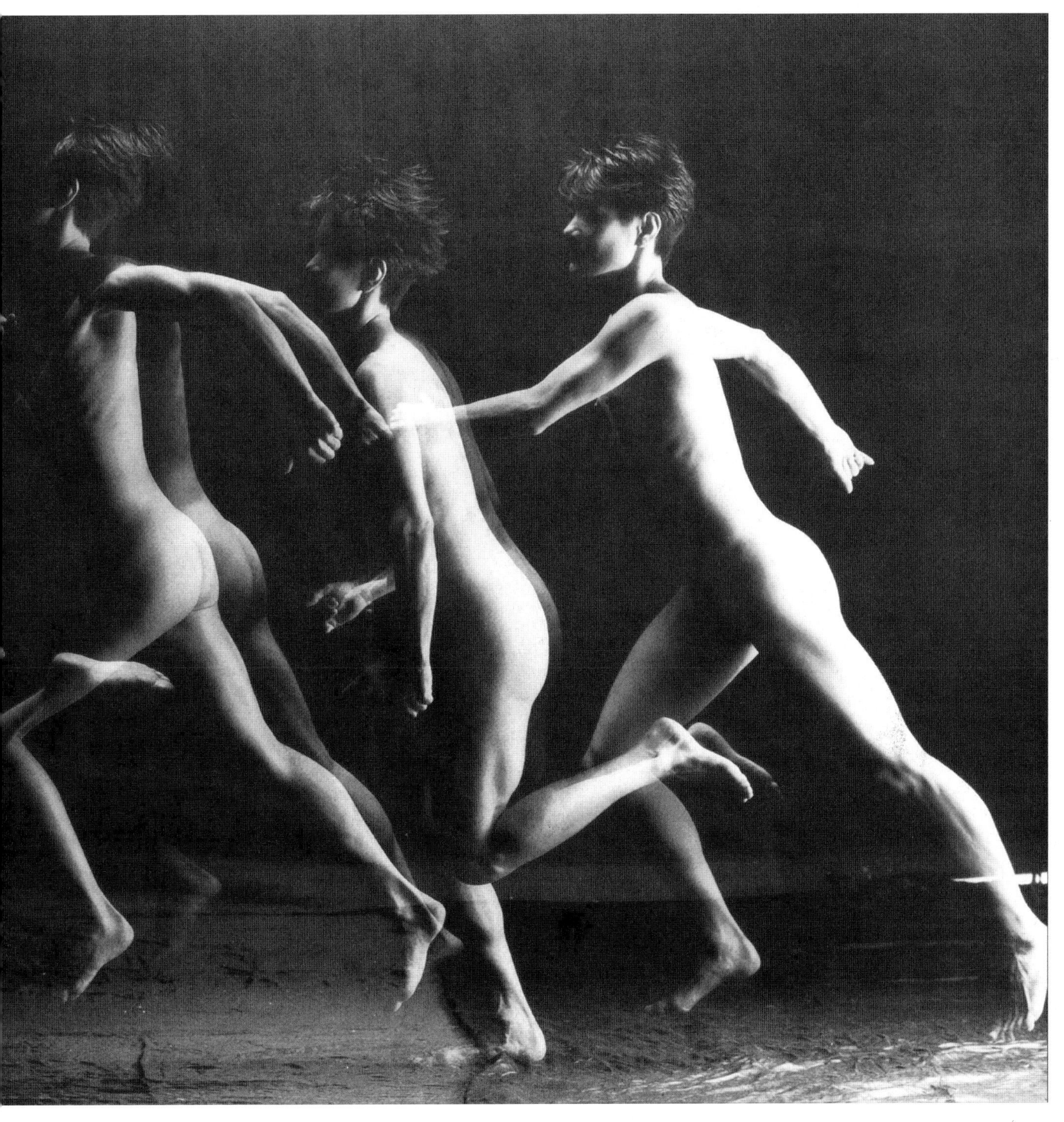

that story to reveal, while parts of it remains sealed behind the heart's door, just as the artist/designer creates the mood of the story with color.

Judging by this last picture, it is easier now to understand the concept of the spiritual. It also helps to identify the process of color abstraction, as abstraction leads the way towards the nonobjective. This figure illustrates such a strong presence, or suggestion of the ethereal by its captured energy. In this case, if the physical world can help lead our eye to the spiritual connection of color, then we have mostly accomplished our task of understanding what Kandinsky refers in his essay on "The Spiritual in Art."

Color in Performance: Performance Art

Continuing with the concept that there is a psychological connection of color to a physical act or response, we turn to a more contemporary version of art, which became popular in the second half of the 20th century, known as performance art. Often conceptual in nature, performance becomes a content-laden, one-time event. It often becomes an intangible idea presented by certain physical nuances.

The video still *Miko no Inori* (The Shaman Girl's Prayer, page 367)—is a performance art installation performed at the Osaka-Kansai International Airport, just south of Osaka, Japan. Mori's physical image has been dramatically altered to become more cyborg than human. Her silver and white costume, as well as white hair, convey a message of aloofness, as her icy light blue eyes set her apart from society's norm.

During the performance, she chants a prayer repeatedly, while rotating a crystal sphere. The sphere is then passed from hand-to-hand, as well as lowered from her face to her pelvis and back again. Each time she raises it to her face, she tenderly and passionately stares deep into its contents. Throughout the performance one of the most mysterious elements is the manner in which she looks into the ball, causing the viewer to speculate its meaning. For this particular performance Mori selects the new Osaka International Airport, which is a harsh, cold, futuristic and very busy environment. It is a place where tens of thousands of people travel through each day, each with a particular agenda and life experience. As she performs in the busy airport, travelers walk slowly by pretending not to see, others stop and watch, while still others walk by gazing slowly. Mariko has become partly a *tempting young girl*, and partly a *well-behaved involuntary doll.*

The spiritual connection in this art form rests in the artist's symbolic gestures, fabrics, and facial features, which are continually evolving. Her message can never be fully comprehended without Mariko's interpretation, as it can often be with other art forms such as music and dance. There is an element that we understand from each type of performance, dance, musical composition, painting and so on, simply because the artist has been effective in his or her physical interpretation of the original spiritual concept.

The Color Assessment in this example invokes a dyad (complementary) harmony of warm *passionate oranges*, and *icy defiant blues.* Orange because of *her* adoring responses to the sphere and the *viewer's* reaction to the "tempting young girl." Blue because of the icy cold aloofness and hard-edged appearance of the altered state of Mariko, as well as the tranquil nature of the performance itself.

Interestingly enough, the work of Mariko Mori and Wassily Kandinsky accomplish similar spiritual objectives, and yet the approaches have become very different as Mori *cherishes* the image, while Kandinsky tries desperately to *destroy* it.

If we were to substitute the word *color* instead of *image* in Mariko's declaration, we would have a fairly good assessment for the process of the emotional and spiritual ramifications of color. Read it through again, and see just how well her statement about images also works for color itself. Color creates and manipulates emotional responses . . . emotional and spiritual mood components are validated . . . *through color.*

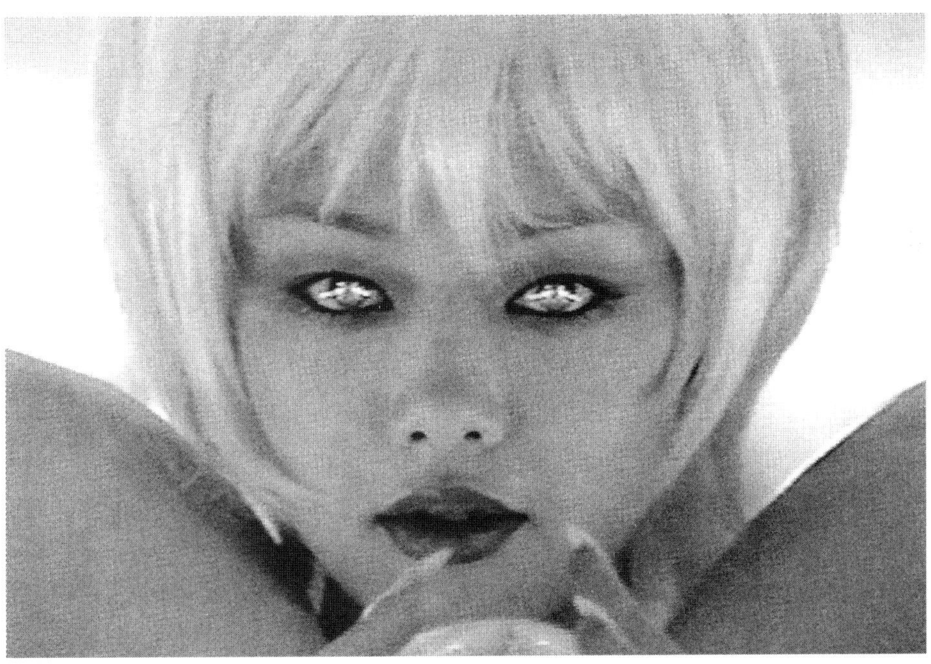

Mariko Mori, *Miko no Inori*

"I've always tried to say that things are two sided.
One side of the system is critical; the other is.....Celebration.
Everything is validated...through *images*.
People believe in this power—they are used to *images* being manipulated, and being manipulated themselves, by *images*."

Mariko Mori, 1995

Color in Poetry

Let's briefly consider color and poetic forms. Since we are using various art forms in order to express the nature of the spiritual use of color, *poetry* can be no less important. In Jozan's poem, there are two distinct words by which to focus—the *rain* and the *petals.*

Secondary words would be *red* and *white.* The life of a monk was to forsake the world as we know it and follow a simple and uncomplicated way of living. Possessions were objects which weigh down the heart, or spirit, anchoring one to the world. Typically, the Japanese monks of old would take refuge in the forests, rejecting carnal ways. Contact with other people was, in some cases, rare. What normally drew attention to the average person became a monumental event in the life of Jozan. His life was so focused on the simple that a blossom petal falling prematurely from the force of the rain was an event.

The rain's hastening of falling flower petals disturbed the poet because he loved spring and the seasonal flowers. His concern became very spiritual, as he transformed into a butterfly, chasing after each petal. Whether he was concerned about saving the petal, or experiencing every last moment of the petal's glory, his desires about them were very real and emotional. Energetic orange hues and saturated violets seem to fill the imagination's composition. The mood of the environment is urgent, as the butterfly expends enormous amounts of energy to retrieve the petals. Turbulent fluttering, the energy of orange, and deep subdued concerns of violet emotion fill the night skies as Jozan is filled with anxiety about the whole event.

Night Rain—Worrying About the Flowers

I sigh on this rainy late spring night:
the reds and whites that filled the forest are falling to the dust!
Late at night, my soul in a dream becomes a butterfly
chasing after each falling petal as it flutters to earth.

Ishikawa Jozan
(1583-1672)

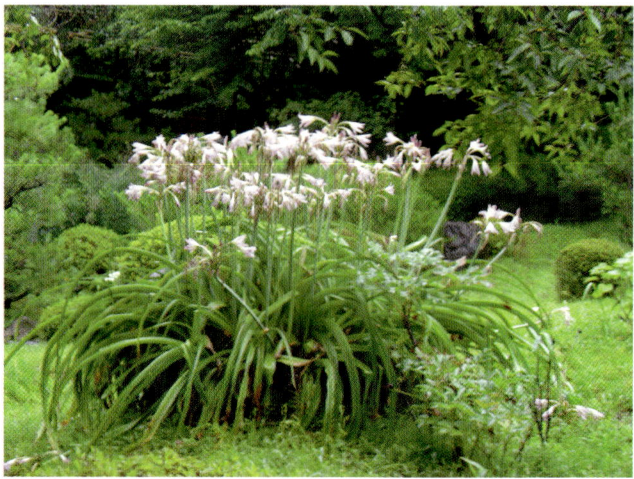

Blossoms of Heian Shrine Garden.
Photo by Alan Burner.

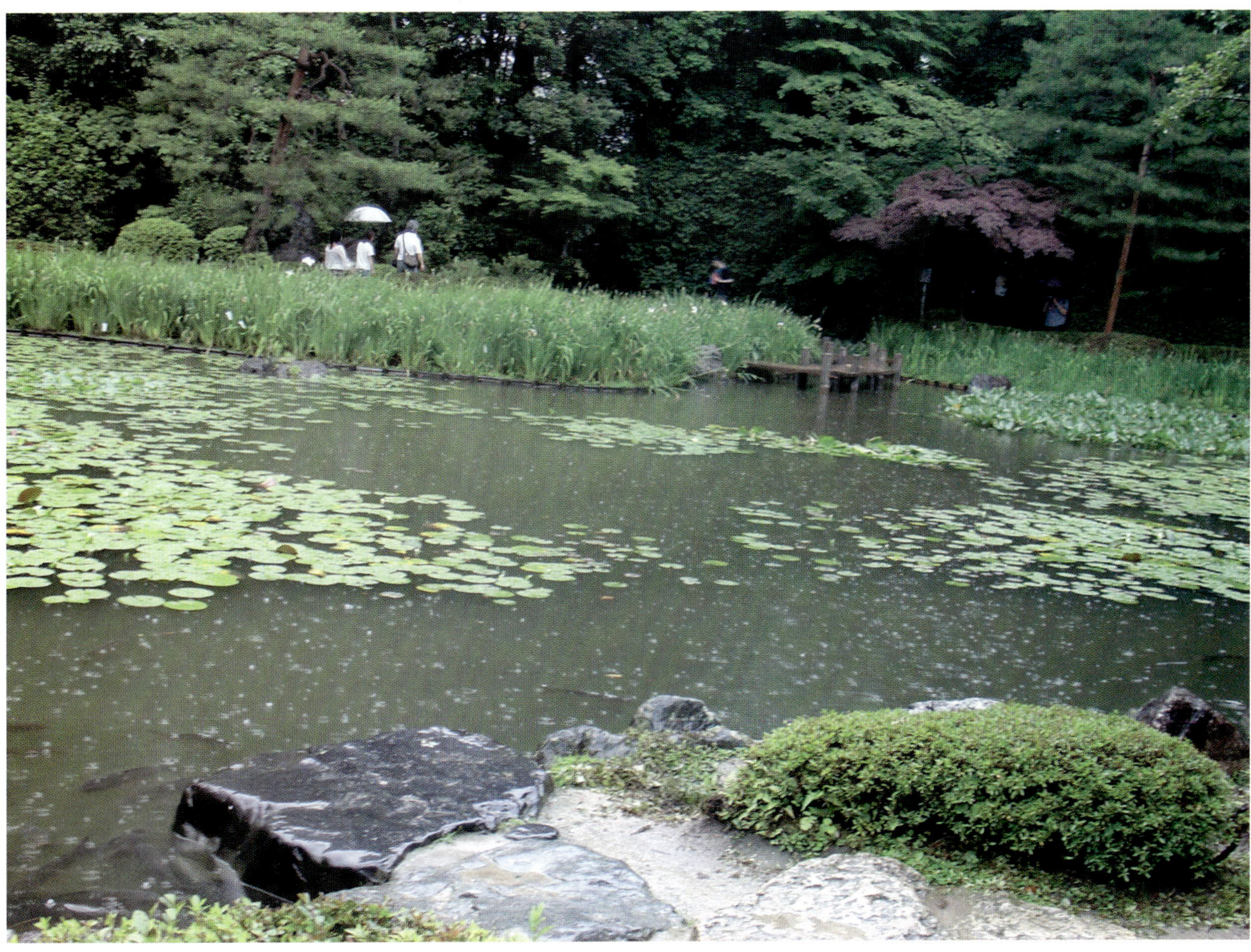

Heian Shrine at Kyoto, Japan, Morning Rain on the Pond.
Photo by Alan Burner.
Certainly Jozan would have appreciated the tranquility at the Heian Shrine pond in Kyoto. Rather than a heavy rain knocking petals to the earth, which distressed him in his earlier poem, a gentle rain splashes across the serine still waters of the pond. The perfect tranquility in this scene has a very spiritual ambiance, as the greens and blues generate very specific mood nuances. The rain is the *sound* of monochromatic green.

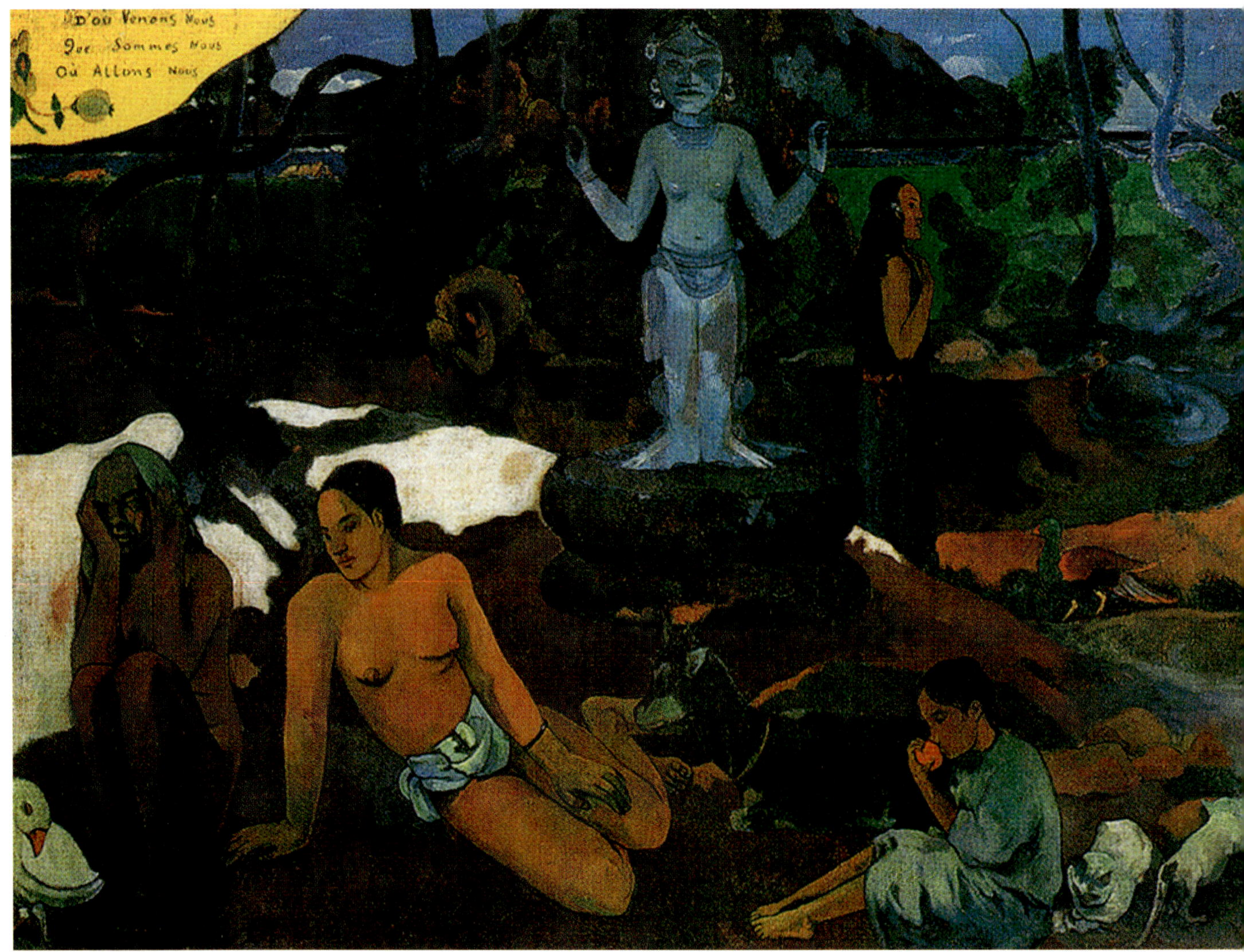

Where Do We Come From? What Are We? Where Are We Going? by Paul Gauguin.
1897. Oil on canvas, 139.1 × 374.6 cm (54 3/4 × 147 1/2 in.). © 2004 Museum of Fine Arts, Boston, Tompkins Collection; 36.270. Photograph © 2004 Museum of Fine Arts, Boston.

Kandinsky wrote that Gauguin's paintings were in reality "tragic or passionate poems."

Where Do We Come From? What Are We? Where Are We Going? (p. 370–371) is evident of Gauguin's *color poetry*, as the a specific story is told here. This very emotional composition, laced with blues, greens and oranges, presents a somber poetic rhythm of spiritual responses. Gauguin's paintings, of course, present the idea that color is of primary concern, not perspective and figurative accuracy. This seems very obvious to us now, since we have a clearer understanding that there is a very spiritual component in the use of color.

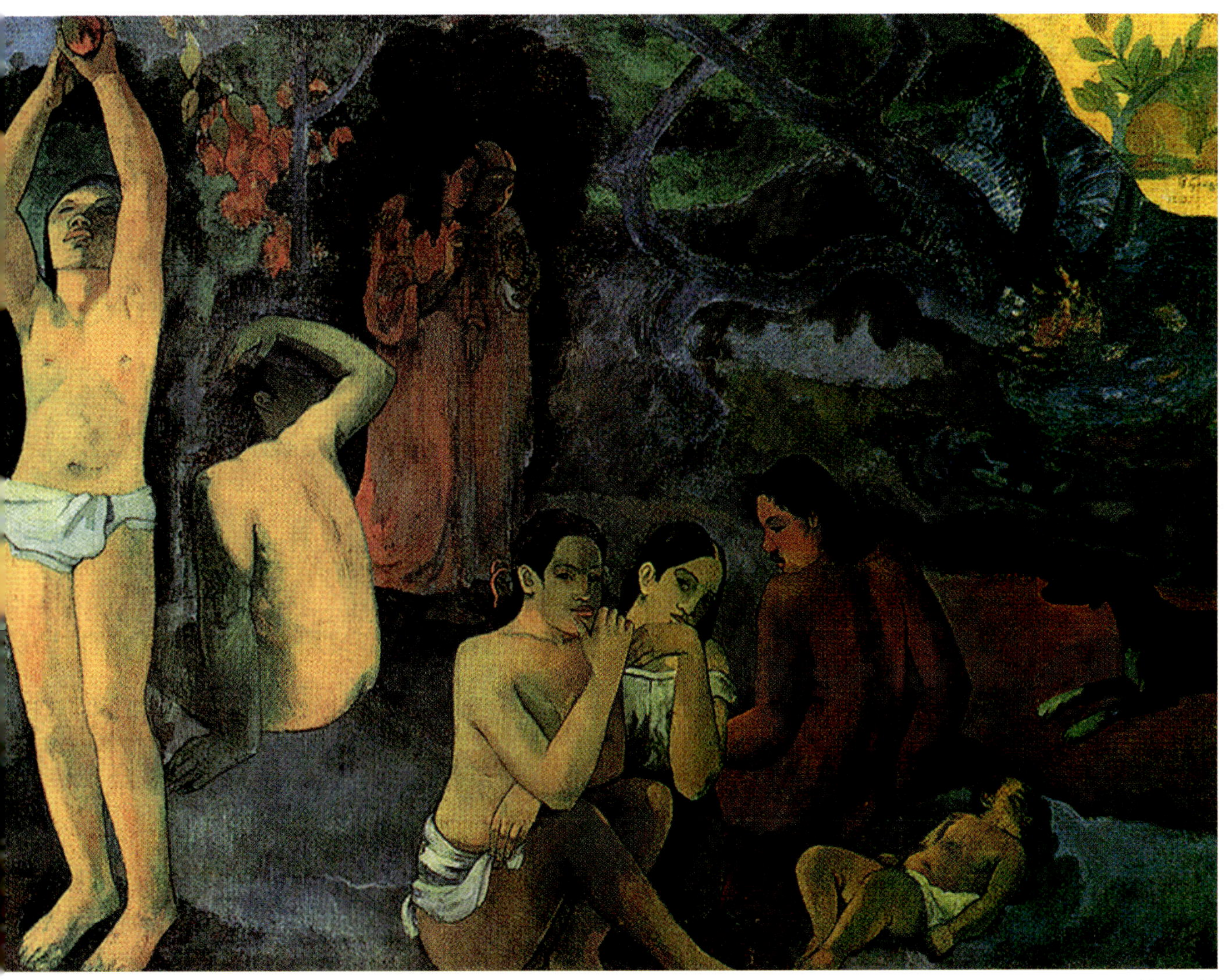

Gauguin's painting is as *spiritually* full of feeling (poetic) as it is *visually* lyrical (poetry). The work reads much like a *musical* composition, with its visual and spiritual accomplices. It is a painting from the heart, mind and soul of the artist himself, choreographed with warm and cool imagery, which seems to flow through the entire painting.

Moods of Color

Color is both fantasy and reality,
It is the master of desire and the evidence of the spirit.
An element supreme, free from influence
And in all respects an extension of the soul.
It dominates with harsh persuasion and gentle maneuvers.
People unknowingly expect this behavior,
And want to be persuaded.

Shijo, 2000

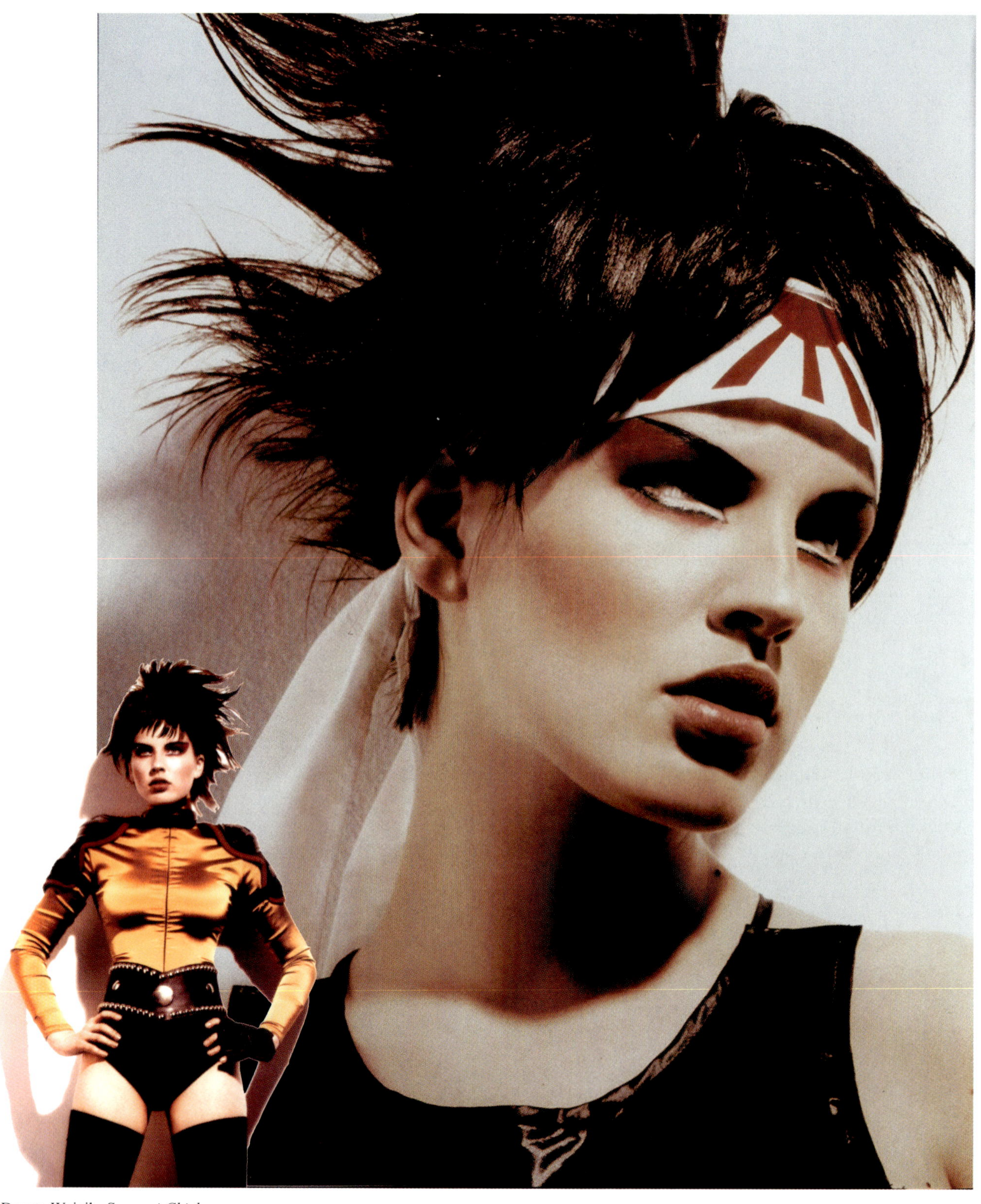

Dorota Wojeik, *Samurai Chick.*

Project Proposal: The Spiritual Dimension of Color

Project Proposal: The Spiritual Dimension of Color

Much of Kandinsky's art career, especially after the Bauhaus, was spent in pursuit of the psychological effects of color. Kandinsky, a master colorist, believed that color was a spiritual matter and like Mondrian thought that color should be liberated from the conventions of the form. Since human emotion is a spiritual function, it cannot be confined to any particular representation or physical shape. As we have discovered, the single most important characteristic of color is the expression of emotional states, or the mood element by which it generates. Kandinsky illustrated that human passions such as love and hate were shapeless. Additionally, just as music does not have physical form, we have seen that it can construct various types of emotional responses into the physical world through dance and various dramatic expressions. We therefore have also learned that all human emotions can be interpreted through the color vehicle into a tangible form.

Kandinsky proclaimed that the canvas was his "enemy," as he struggled to translate true spiritual emotion, by means of physical color pigments. He captured the energy created by the music, using it to render the paint onto the canvas in abstracted or non-objective forms. This was the liberation of the spectrum from its usual confines of traditional form.

Project Proposal with Subtractive Color: RYB

This can be accomplished in many ways. What we will be attempting to do is create an abstract or non-objective painting from a realistic or representational photograph, using acrylic or water color mediums. Your instructor may want to select a particular image for you to interpret, or you may be instructed to interpret the Dorota Wojcik portrait, as the student examples reflect.

- Working from a photograph, or image assigned to you, recreate that representational image, translating it into a spiritual expression of non-objective color (see *note*).
- If you assigned the Dorota Wojeik image on the facing page, try to interpret the energy, expression and mood of the image.
- This often works well when selecting the appropriate music to match the image. Audio inspiration, in addition to visual inspiration, is always better. Remember that your selections are totally subjective, as long as you can *validate* your solution.
- See the following student examples:

Note: *This project can be done with a photograph, poem or musical composition, or all three. Rather than a photograph, one could simply interpret a musical composition (intangible) into a physical representation (tangible) of the mood, which the music creates. The same can be said of a poem as well. Using all three in symphony is a bit more complex, but enhances the student's mood sensitivity, as well as critical thinking skills.*

Student Examples

The following is a composite of student responses to a photograph (referred to as the *original*) seen on the facing page of the Project Proposal titled: Dorota Wojcik, *Samari Chick.*

Students were asked to respond to the nuances of the portrait: What is her portrayed personality? What emotions and moods are projected? Is it energetic, calm, angry, etc.?

They were also asked to select the appropriate music, which they felt would relate to the image, as well as their painting itself. All works were executed with acrylic paints.

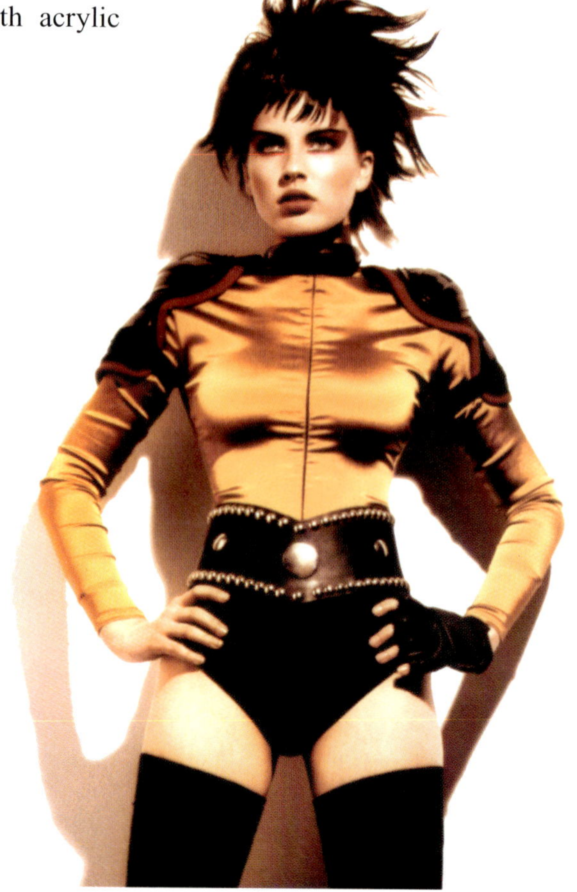

Dorota Wojeik, *Samurai Chick.*
© Michael Thompson, 2001.

Student Example #1

This student's composition interpreted the photograph in a very "Kandinsky-esque" rendering. Although it is reasonably successful, try to break away from doing the same thing that Kandinsky did, and use your creative imagination. After all, these compositions should be straight from *your* inner response, not an exterior copy of familiar technique.

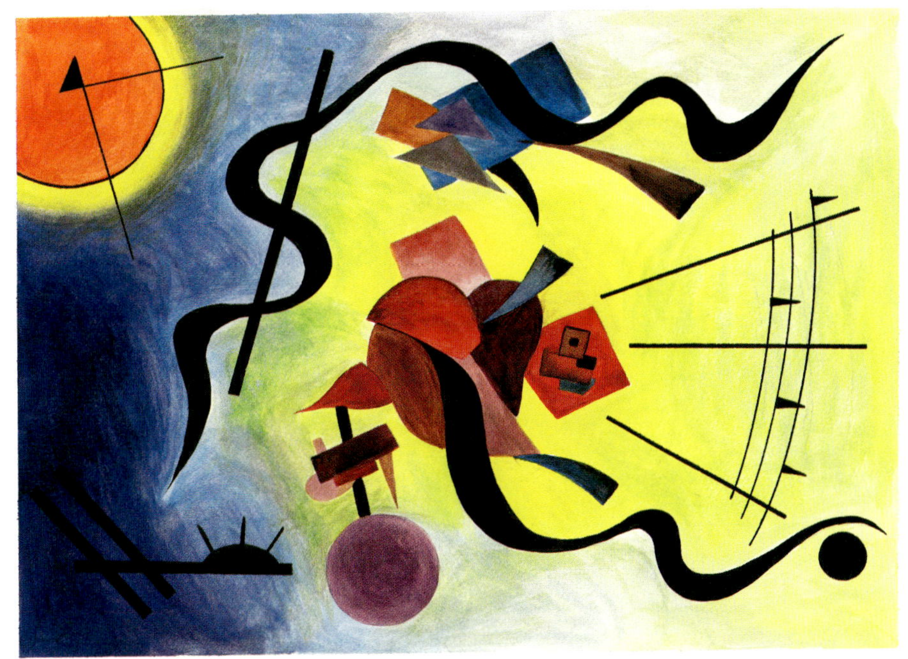

Student Example #2

This student example was accomplished with the air-brush technique. In this composition there are figures that materialize in the composition, which are abstracted, rather than non-objectified. With this technique, the lines are not as harsh and rigid as the previous example.

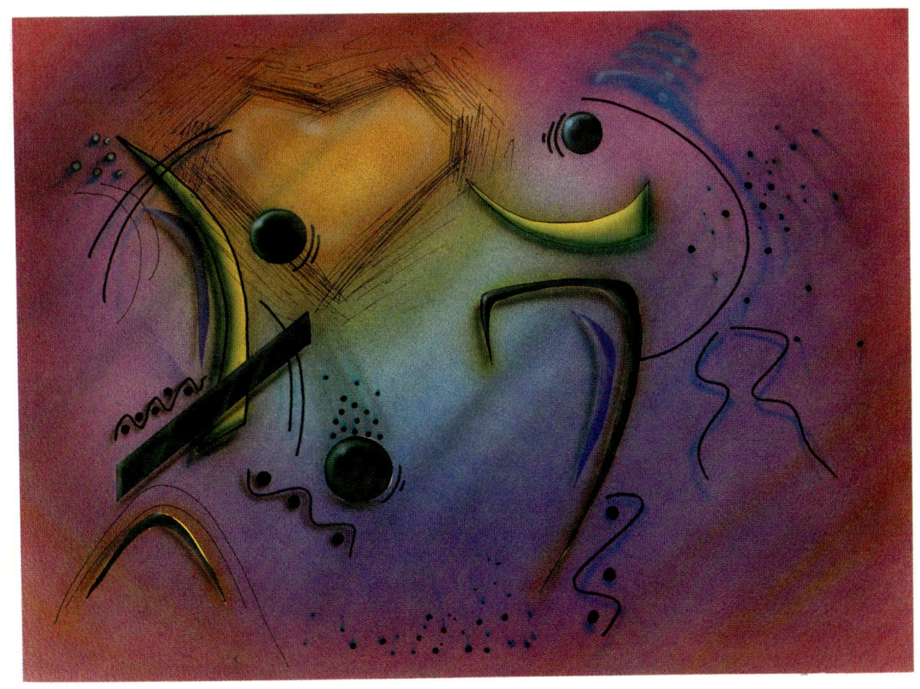

Student Example #3

This example is more minimalist than the previous. The figures have been de-objectified so that only the essence, or spiritualness can be revealed. The combination of line to background mood seems to be accomplishing the passionate and energetic quality of the original photo.

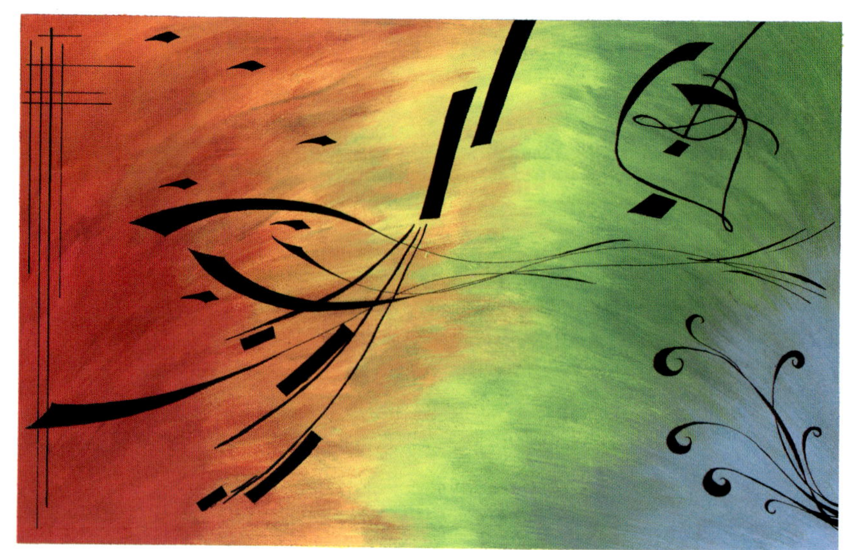

Student Example #4

Student example four has incorporated hard-edged solid stationary shapes, and contrasted them against the high tempo brush-strokes. The contrast of saturated blue and then red of shapes conflict with more intensified lighter background hues.

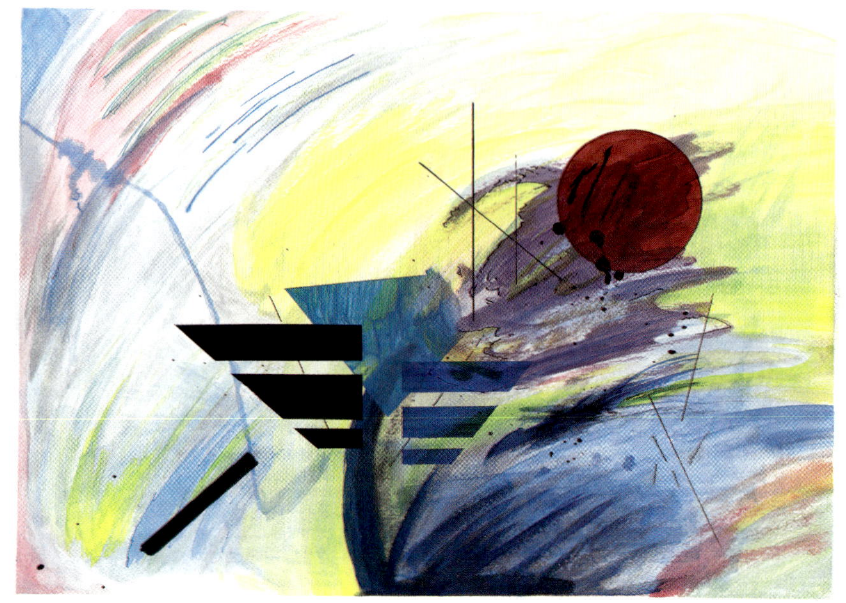

Student Example #5

This student's work has an odd tranquility about it, even though there is a contrast in terms of directional line. There seems to have been a type of explosion from the center of the composition. There is movement and dynamic, which addresses the energy in the original photograph, but the dominance of light blue controls just how much energy can be interpreted here. This composition is exemplary of the student's general nature, which is calm and one who loves inner peace. She has succeeded in transforming her spiritual character onto a tangible surface, as well as interpreting the energy of the photograph.

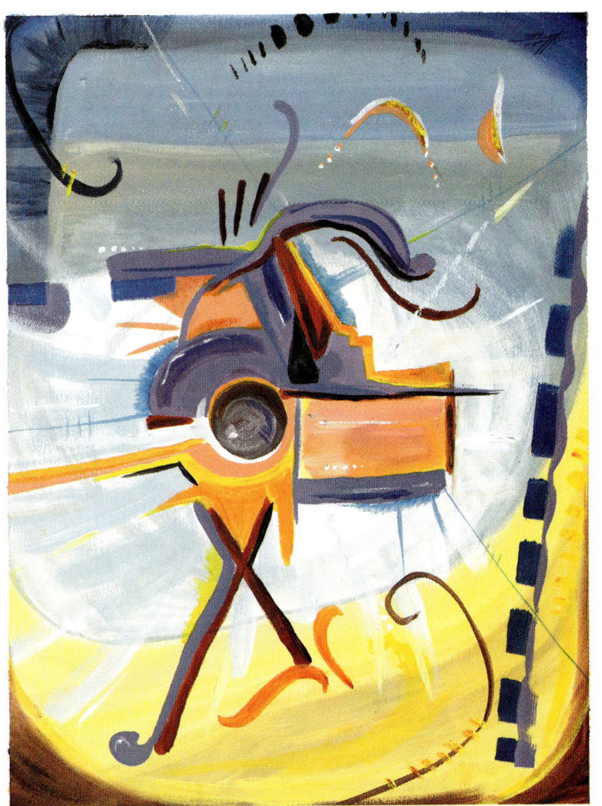

Kristy Beckett, *Dancers.*

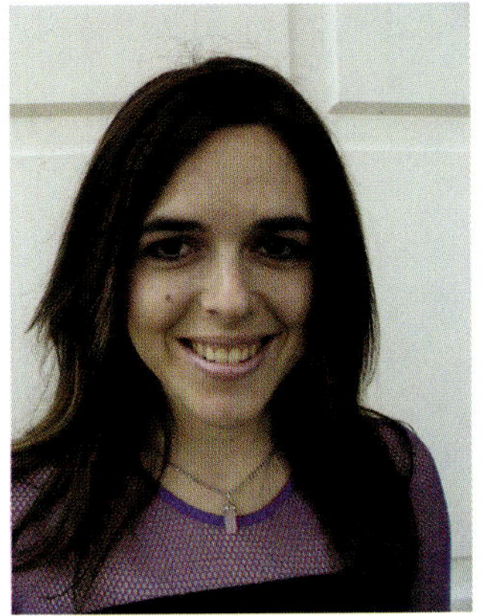

Kristy Beckett

Chapter Summary of the Spiritual Component to Color

Salvador Dali's painting will serve for our closing discourse on the spiritual aspects of color. Exactly how do we perceive the spiritual connection to color? What comes first, the inner inspiration or the outer? Is the dream inspired or created at the inner spiritual point, or is it the outer influences in life that inspire the content of a dream? One thing that does seem apparent is that normally dreams are influenced by forces in the physical world.

Salvador Dali tells us about his dream via the painting, which was originally inspired by a hanging pomegranate with a bee flying around it. The dream was then caused by external stimuli, the dream was built around the pomegranate alone, and then abridged by the artist in the form of a physical painting. What began in the physical world grew into the spiritual world and then recorded back into the physical existence again.

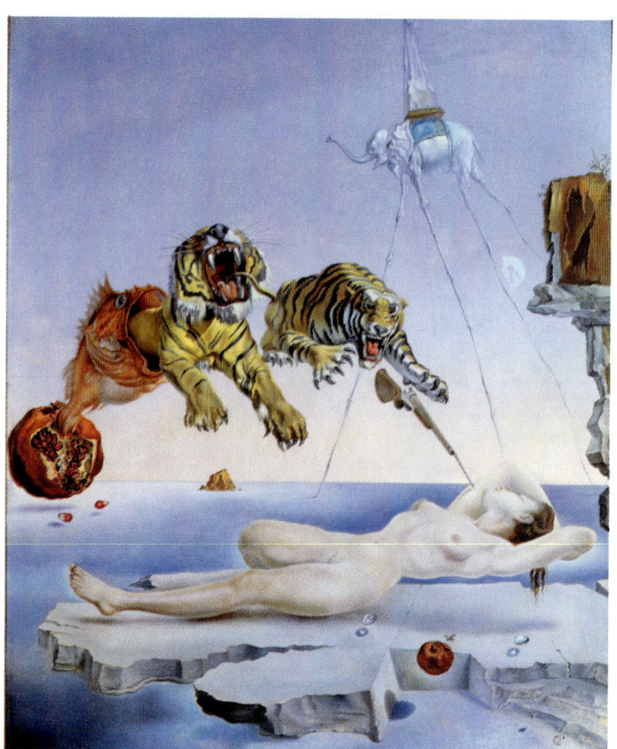

Dream Caused by the Flight of a Bee Around a Pomegranate, A Second Before Waking Up, 1944, by Salvador Dali.
Nimatallah/Art Resource, NY.
Fundacion Coleccion Thyssen-Bornemisza, Madrid, Spain.

The Pomegranate Dream—The Painting

Gala, Dali's companion, lay suspended over a concrete or rock slab. The whole event should be rather terrifying, and yet it seems somewhat calm by nature. Out of the pomegranate springs a harsh figured fish, which in turn spews a tiger from its mouth, after which yet another tiger leaps from the previous mouth. Just before the tigers are able to sink their claws into her, the sting of the rifle's bayonet (bee sting) awakens her.

The composition is that of extreme contrasts. Gala hovers so peacefully over the slab, and yet the tigers are frenziedly attacking. There is an emotional suggestion of terror by way of the contrasting figures, and yet it is very calm and peaceful. The slab, Gala herself, the horizon, and tigers are all horizontally located, which further enhances the tranquil environment. The quiet mood of blues and violets further confuse the intended urgency of the imagery in the composition, and the painting then becomes as a true spiritual representation in the physical world, albeit the limitations of size and realistic images.

The aspects of the *spiritual dimension of color* cannot be understated. No matter what the student's career objectives are, a thorough knowledge of how color's character effects the inner dimension is necessary. We have seen where the spiritual dimension is influenced by the physical world (i.e. dreams), or where the spiritual inspires the physical responses. Fine artists, graphic designers, interior designers, animators and web designers to name a few, must be able to fully comprehend and develop flawless color skills. One of the most important keys to a successful career as designers and artists is to be color proficient in all aspects.

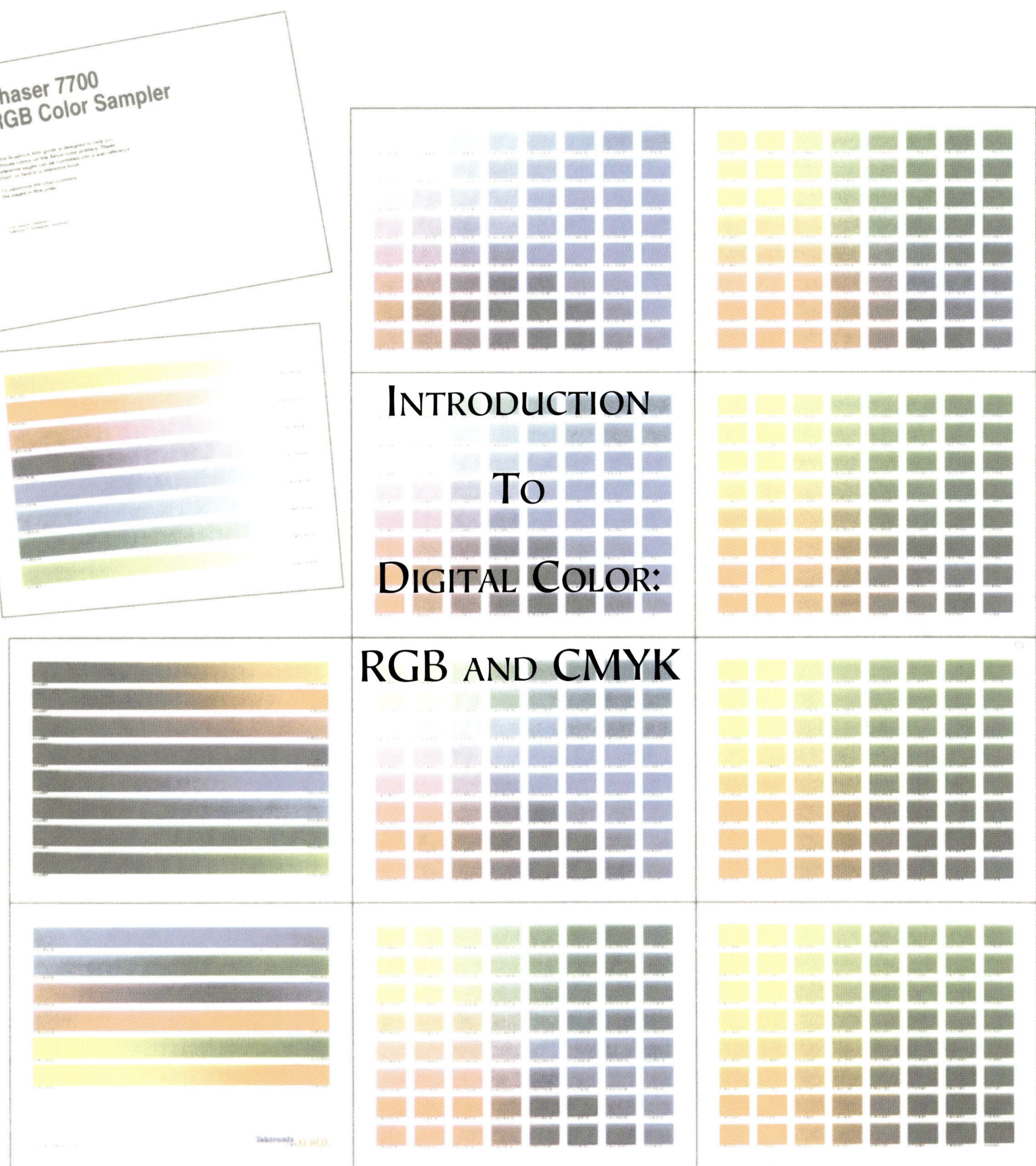

Introduction To Digital Color: RGB and CMYK

Digital Color: RGB and CMYK

We will now briefly introduce digital color, which typically applies to specific color applications such as Photoshop, Illustrator, Quark and InDesign. The subject matter then, requires extensive training in a computer lab situation with it's own related and specific materials and text. The purpose of this introduction is to simply acquaint the student with the function of the RGB and CMYK process.

You will remember that we discussed the nature of subtractive and additive color in the beginning of this text. It is important at this point, as many students will begin to work with digital color more often, to identify more carefully just how additive and subtractive color relates specifically to the digital processes.

We are no longer dealing with pigments in the sense of oil, acrylic, watercolor, or other fine art mediums, but rather the process of color reproduction and color correction. In this case the ultimate goal is to reproduce a perfect color corrected composition, via printed inks.

While we know that the primary subtractive *pigments* mixed equal black (RYB), we also know from earlier discussion, that the combination of all colors of *light* equal white. The RGB, or primary colors of light are additive, and consist of red, green and blue. (Remembering back to the beginning of the text, we discovered that there were bundles of quarks located in protons and neutrons. Each bundle of three quarks contain one red, one green and one blue quark, which combined produced white light.) The CMYK, or the primary colors of pigments (inks) are subtractive, and they are known as cyan, magenta and yellow. Since cyan, magenta and yellow inks do not mix to an accurate black, there is no other choice but to add black proper. The "K" in CMYK refers to "key", which basically separates it from blue ("B"). An example of the CMYK subtractive process is to look at specific color combinations. It is important to note that the CMY to RGB are different in some ways than we have previously studied concerning the color circle. Here is the difference: cyan's complement is red, magenta's complement is green, and yellow's complement is blue. So therefore, the *additive RGB* has a *subtractive complement* of CMYK.

Computer monitor colors are generated by white light, but the printed inks of the same images are subtractive color. What this means is that the imagery that you print from the monitor onto the paper, is going to yield much different results. A designer can never hope to have the same luminous results on paper as is seen on the screen. Color processing and editing will always be essential to a process, whereby RGB is converted to CMYK. The quality and type of paper that is used will often exaggerate the lack of appropriate colors as well.

In terms of the complementary colors, that is of the RGB and CYMK, we find that the we have to think about them differently. As white light shines onto the surface of yellow ink, for example, it is the yellow ink that absorbs, or subtracts all of the blue light, and produces a mixture of red and green light, which we see as yellow. Cyan absorbs red light and reflects green and blue, and magenta then absorbs green light, which then reflects red and blue. The student may recognize that the mixing of lights are explained very differently than we discussed in the first and second chapters. Before we were mixing physical pigments and applying them to a paper or canvas surface. The process was different, since the application of wet pigment does not change significantly from wet to dry state (depending on the paper), whereas RGB additive colors are quite different when printed in subtractive CMYK inks.

Remembering back to Chapter Four, we learned about rods and cones at the back of the eye, and their special function. We know that *rods* are sensitive to intensity, or brightness, whereas *cones* are exclusive to color ranges, such as the RGB light. Rods and cones function differently according to, for example, what type of day it may be. On a very foggy day rods would be the dominant functioning element of the two, since rods deal with brightness, more than cone's role of color. Imagery on digital equipment is going to assign different tasks to *rods to cones*, as it does viewing an acrylic painting, or the printed CMYK composition.

Please see CMYK and RGB Color Sampler Charts immediately following the Project Proposal.

Project Proposal with Digital Color: RGB to CMYK

As with the previous project, create a composition translating mood and emotion into a non-objective color response. This time you are creating the color composition with the RGB, or additive colors of light, typically seen on your computer monitor, for example in Photoshop, Illustrator, Quark or InDesign. Your RGB composition will then be translated into the CMYK for producing subtractive color prints.

- Produce three compositions which replicate a perceived mood within a given picture, such as the previous project proposal. Your instructor will give you the appropriate image to interpret. (Some find that this project is more challenging in terms of inspiration).
- As you will be experiencing color difference between the screen product that you produce and the printed copy, it will be important to do adequate color corrections in order for the mood, or spiritual, component to function. Many students find this even more of a challenge, since the computer program alienates the designer somewhat from the inner person. Try not to allow technology to interfere in the process of interpreting the project.
- Be sure to use high quality gloss paper.
- Leave a white border around the compositions.

Note: *Since CMYK color spaces are normally smaller than RGB, be sure to store your finished images in RGB for as long as possible, since you will be discarding valuable color information as soon as you make the conversion to CMYK.*

Student Examples:

The following three compositions are various responses to the same original photograph, but each composition belongs to a different musical arrangement. These examples are a student's non-objective response to the energy and spirit of the portrait of *Samurai Chick.*

Try to determine the emphasis of line and shape as they relate to color emotion. What mood do you feel and why? Is it color, line, or both that supports your evaluation? What exactly is happening between the relationship of line and color. How do they function together, or is one independent from the other in the function of the composition?

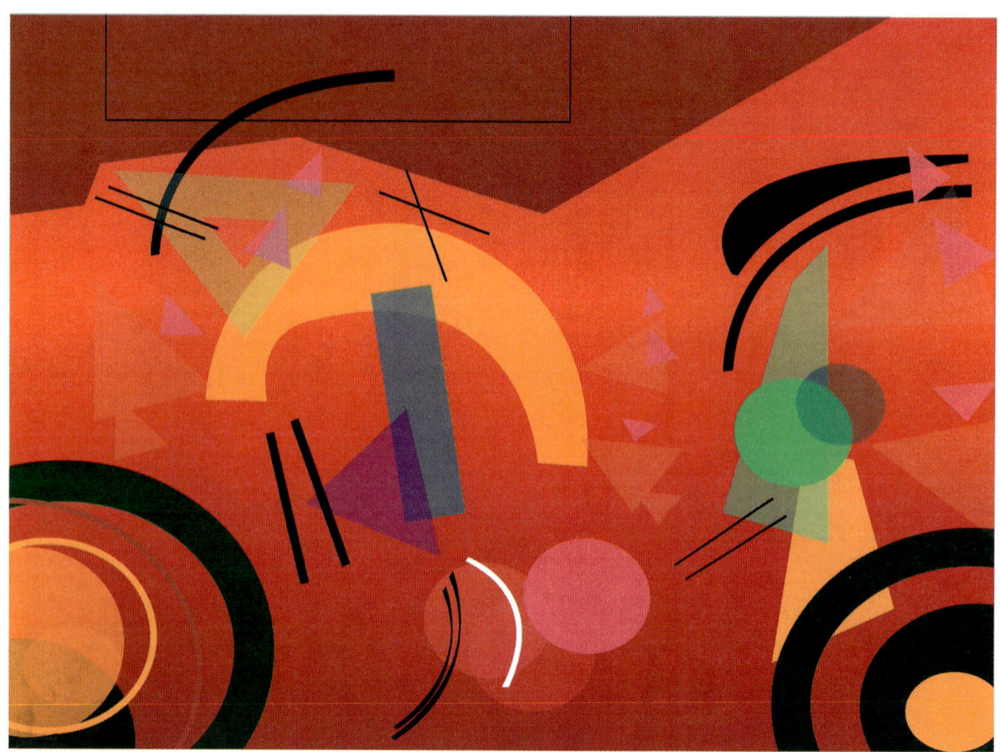

Student Composition #1

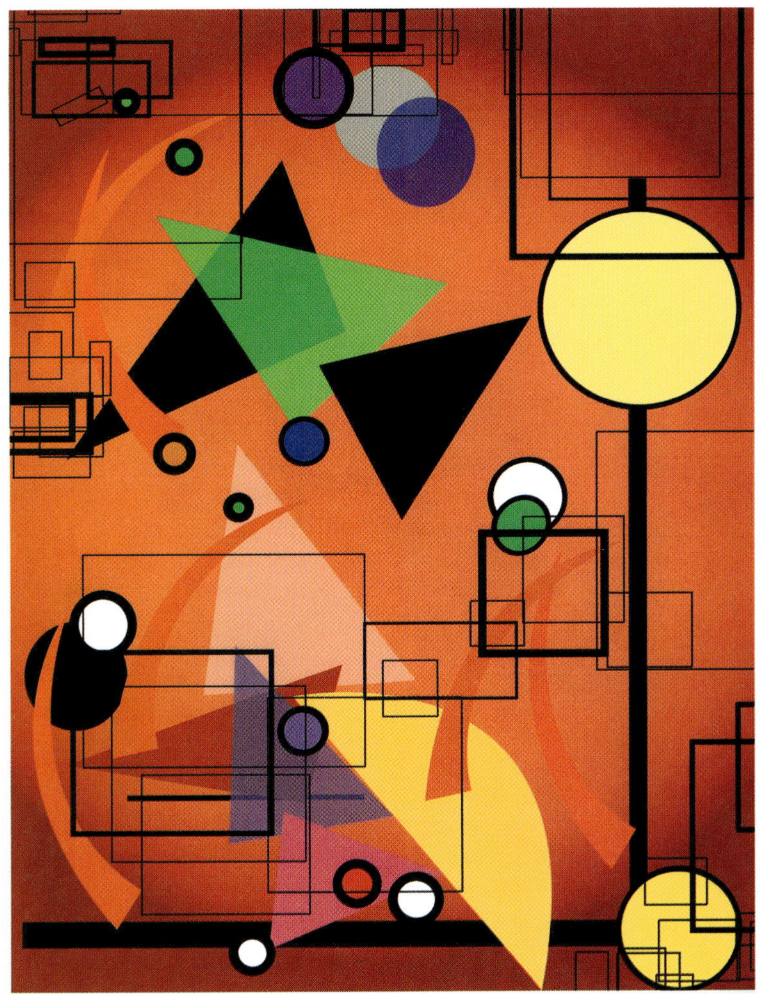

Student Composition #2

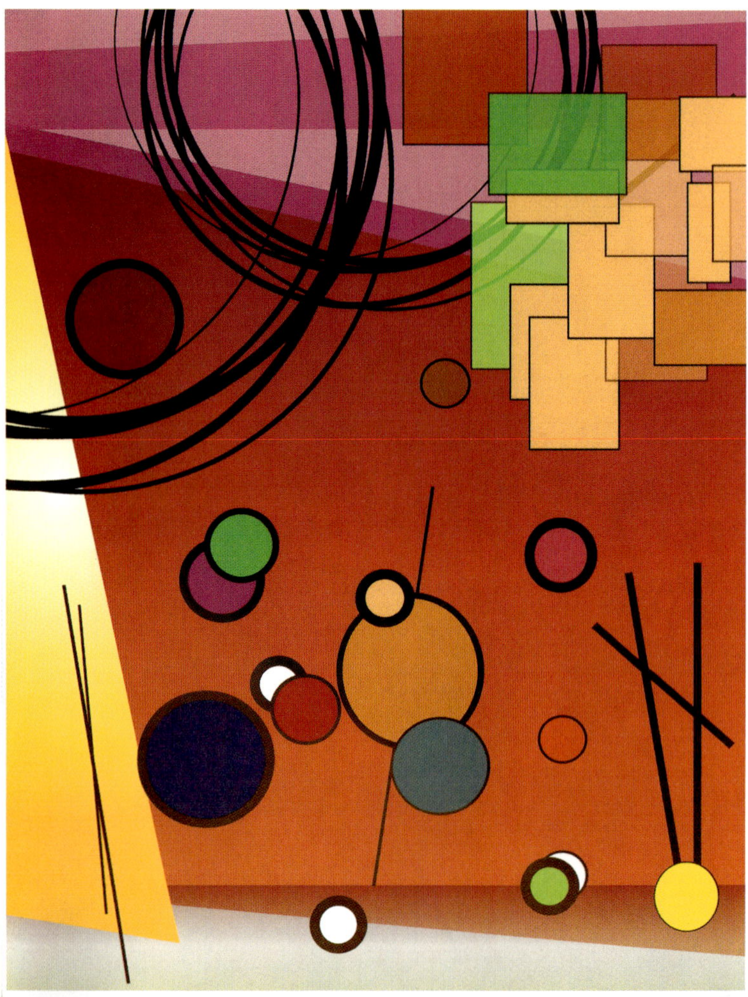

Student Composition #3

CMYK/RGB Color Sampler Charts

The following graphic arts guide is a recreation of one that was originally produced to assist the user in the selection of colors on Xerox color printers. It is also useful to the student of this text in order to determine accuracy and appropriate selections of color and color harmonies, as well as a guide for tints and shades, values, etc. Additionally, it serves to assist in the further understanding of the color charts and project proposals in chapters one and two, in terms of saturations and intensities, and is a good reference guide as to the properties of each hue. The CMYK (first set of charts) and RGB (second set of charts) Color Samplers indicate under each color patch the constituents of cyan, magenta, yellow and black of that particular hue.

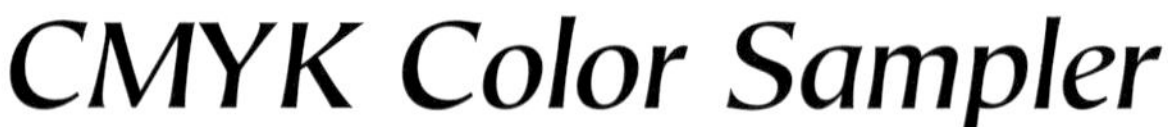
CMYK Color Sampler

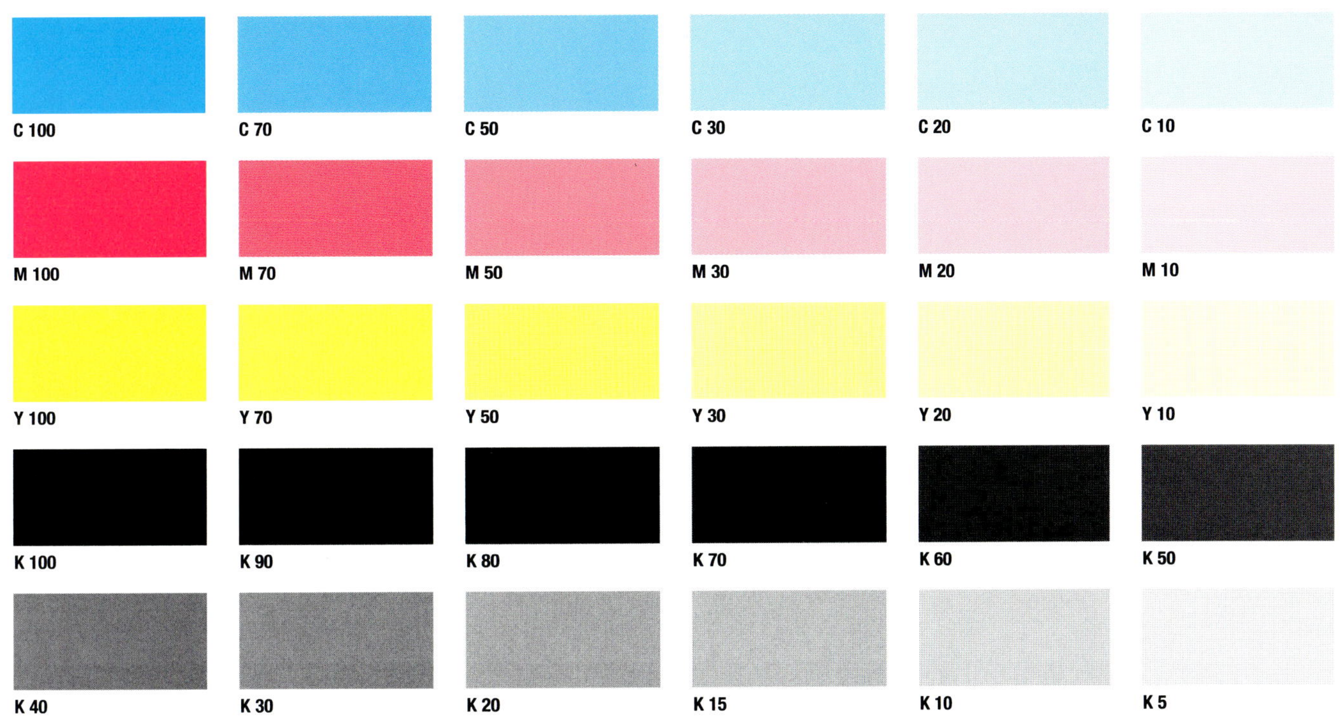

C 100 C 100 M 100

C 100 C 100 Y 100

M 100 C 100 M 100

M 100 M 100 Y 100

Y 100 C 100 Y 100

Y 100 M 100 Y 100

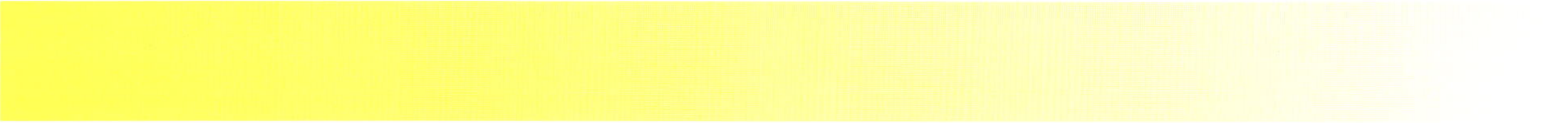

Y 100

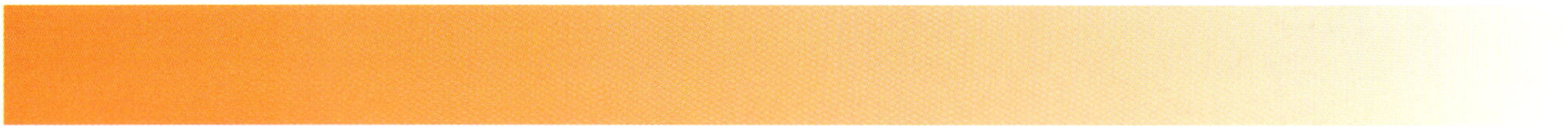

M 50 Y 100

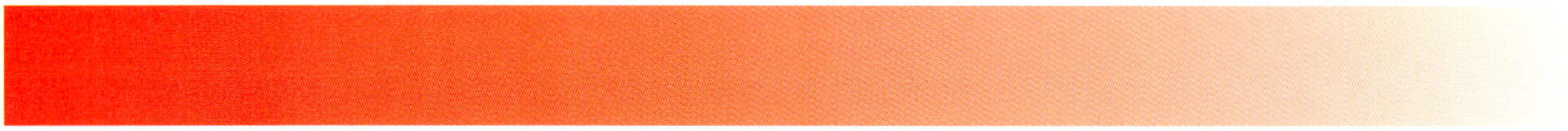

M 100 Y 100

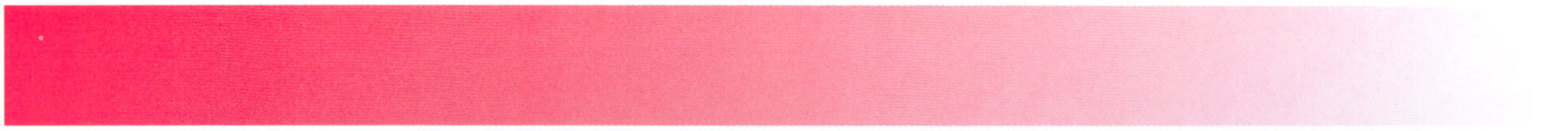

M 100

C 50 M 100

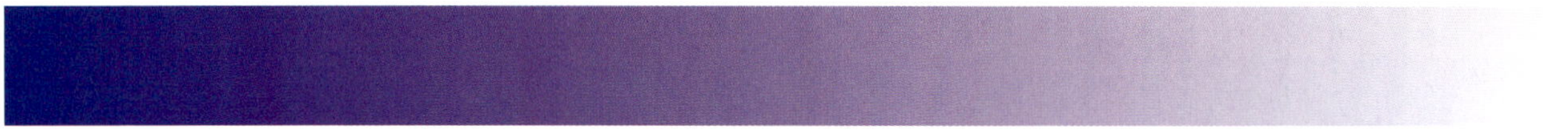

C 100 M 100

C 100 M 100	C 70 M 100	C 50 M 100	C 30 M 100	C 20 M 100	C 10 M 100
C 100 M 70	C 70 M 70	C 50 M 70	C 30 M 70	C 20 M 70	C 10 M 70
C 100 M 50	C 70 M 50	C 50 M 50	C 30 M 50	C 20 M 50	C 10 M 50
C 100 M 30	C 70 M 30	C 50 M 30	C 30 M 30	C 20 M 30	C 10 M 30
C 100 M 20	C 70 M 20	C 50 M 20	C 30 M 20	C 20 M 20	C 10 M 20
C 100 M 10	C 70 M 10	C 50 M 10	C 30 M 10	C 20 M 10	C 10 M 10

C 100 Y 100	C 70 Y 100	C 50 Y 100	C 30 Y 100	C 20 Y 100	C 10 Y 100
C 100 Y 70	C 70 Y 70	C 50 Y 70	C 30 Y 70	C 20 Y 70	C 10 Y 70
C 100 Y 50	C 70 Y 50	C 50 Y 50	C 30 Y 50	C 20 Y 50	C 10 Y 50
C 100 Y 30	C 70 Y 30	C 50 Y 30	C 30 Y 30	C 20 Y 30	C 10 Y 30
C 100 Y 20	C 70 Y 20	C 50 Y 20	C 30 Y 20	C 20 Y 20	C 10 Y 20
C 100 Y 10	C 70 Y 10	C 50 Y 10	C 30 Y 10	C 20 Y 10	C 10 Y 10

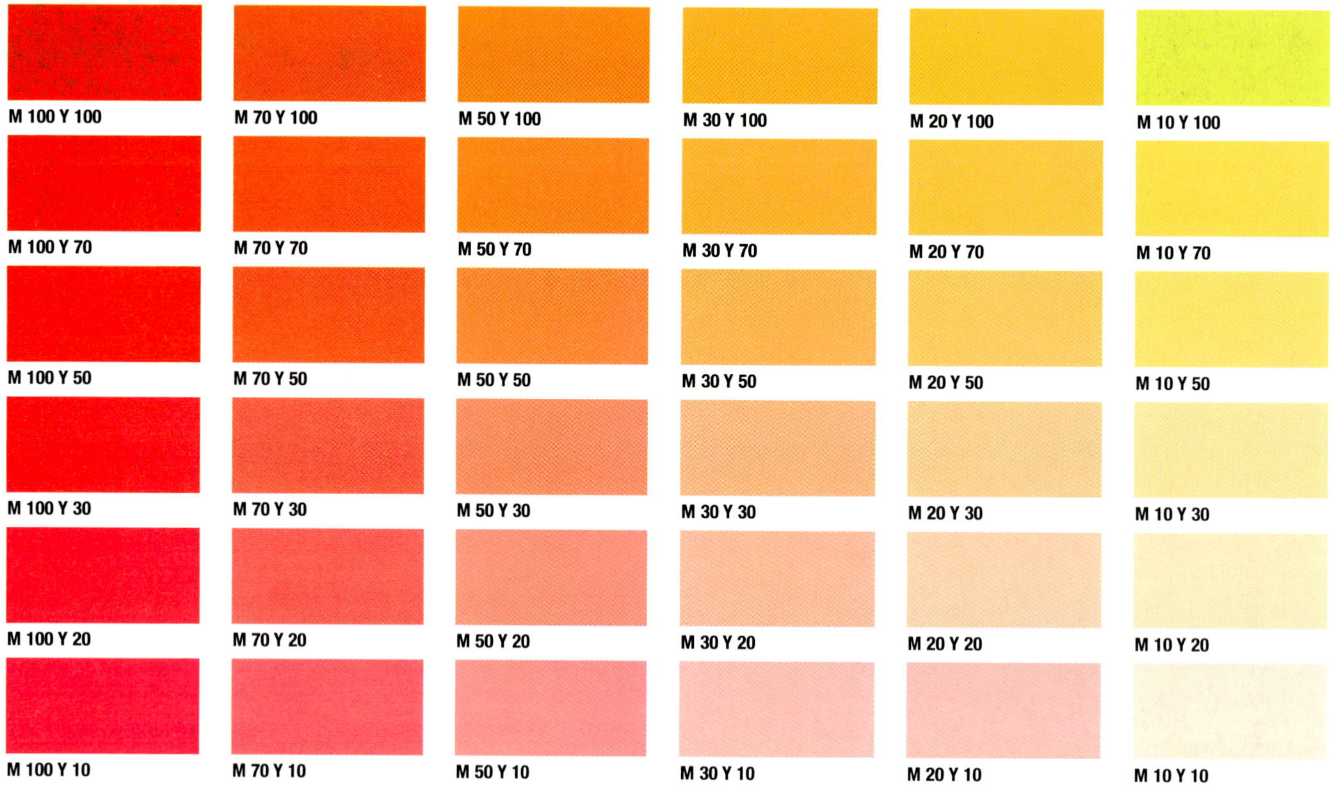

M 100 Y 100 M 70 Y 100 M 50 Y 100 M 30 Y 100 M 20 Y 100 M 10 Y 100

M 100 Y 70 M 70 Y 70 M 50 Y 70 M 30 Y 70 M 20 Y 70 M 10 Y 70

M 100 Y 50 M 70 Y 50 M 50 Y 50 M 30 Y 50 M 20 Y 50 M 10 Y 50

M 100 Y 30 M 70 Y 30 M 50 Y 30 M 30 Y 30 M 20 Y 30 M 10 Y 30

M 100 Y 20 M 70 Y 20 M 50 Y 20 M 30 Y 20 M 20 Y 20 M 10 Y 20

M 100 Y 10 M 70 Y 10 M 50 Y 10 M 30 Y 10 M 20 Y 10 M 10 Y 10

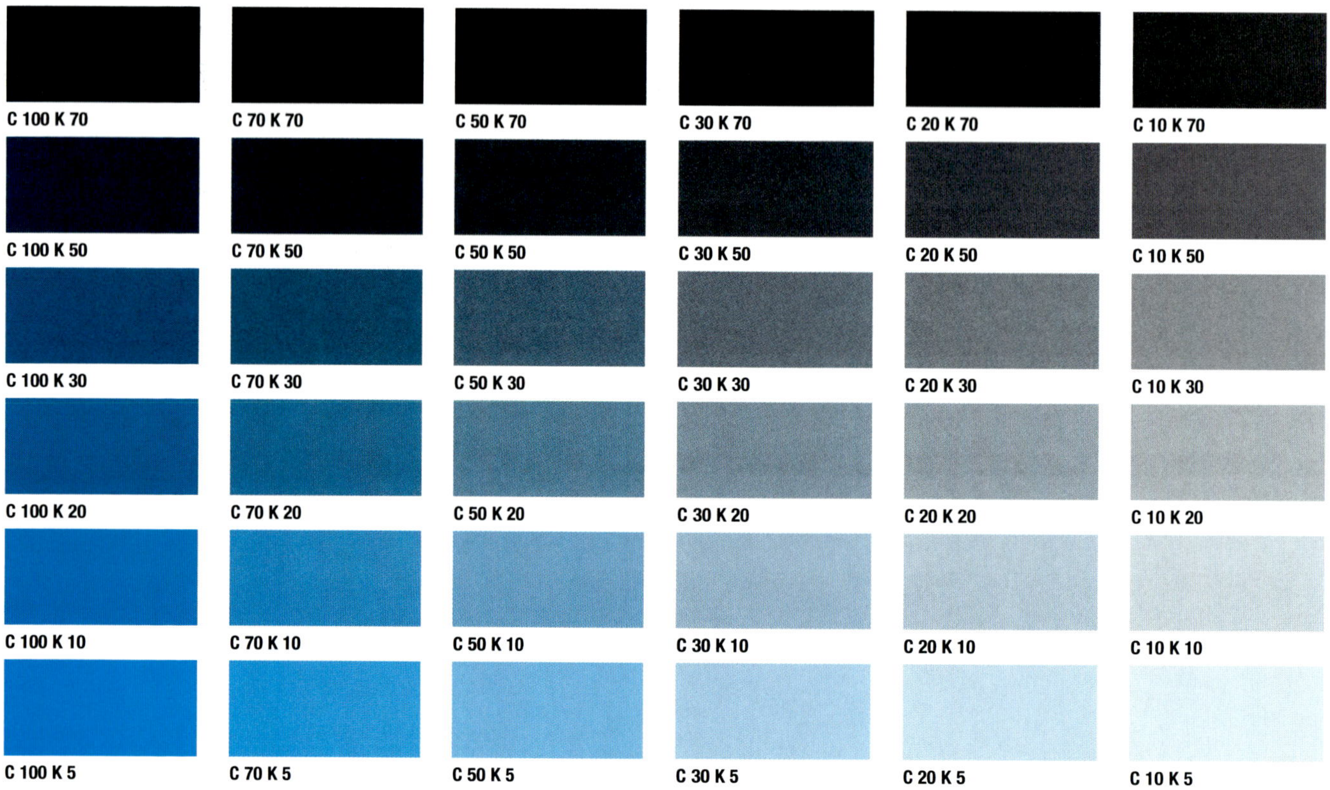

C 100 K 70 C 70 K 70 C 50 K 70 C 30 K 70 C 20 K 70 C 10 K 70

C 100 K 50 C 70 K 50 C 50 K 50 C 30 K 50 C 20 K 50 C 10 K 50

C 100 K 30 C 70 K 30 C 50 K 30 C 30 K 30 C 20 K 30 C 10 K 30

C 100 K 20 C 70 K 20 C 50 K 20 C 30 K 20 C 20 K 20 C 10 K 20

C 100 K 10 C 70 K 10 C 50 K 10 C 30 K 10 C 20 K 10 C 10 K 10

C 100 K 5 C 70 K 5 C 50 K 5 C 30 K 5 C 20 K 5 C 10 K 5

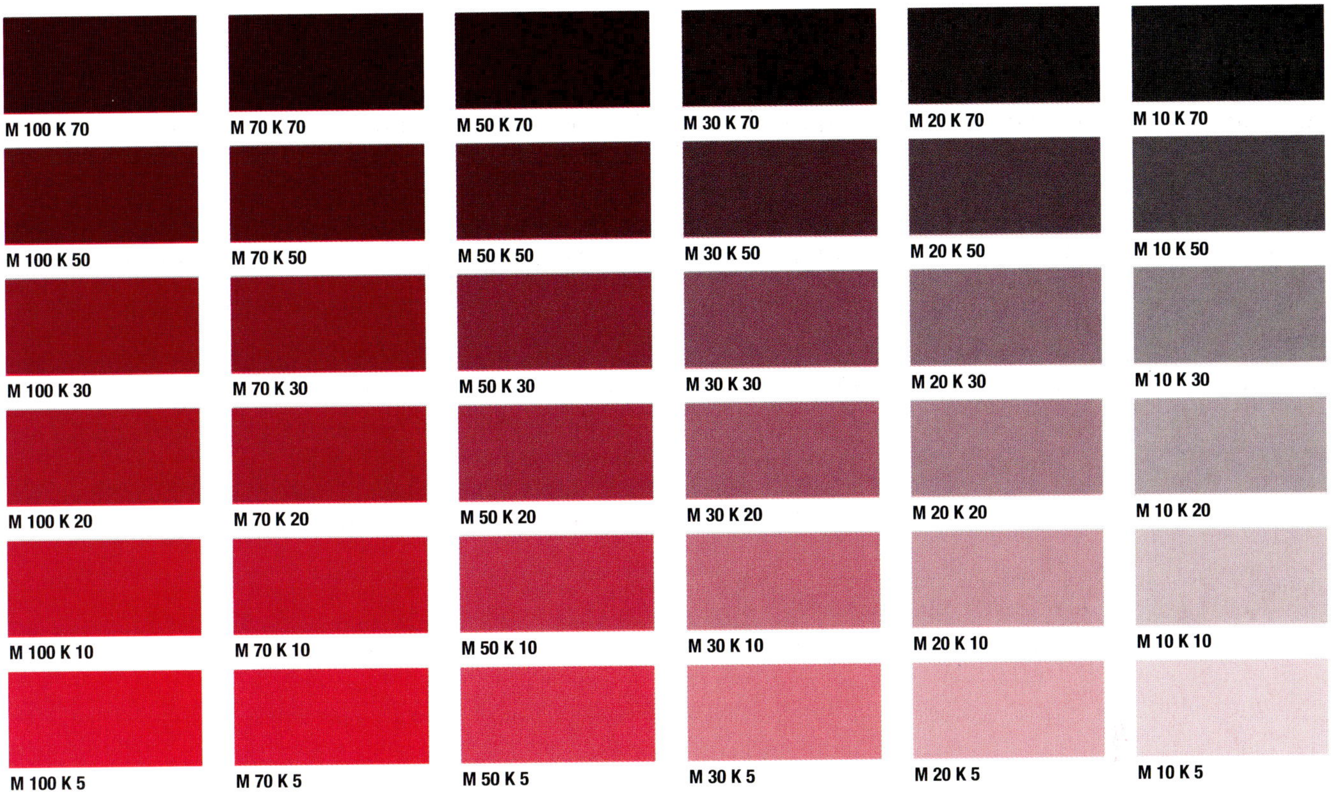

M 100 K 70 M 70 K 70 M 50 K 70 M 30 K 70 M 20 K 70 M 10 K 70

M 100 K 50 M 70 K 50 M 50 K 50 M 30 K 50 M 20 K 50 M 10 K 50

M 100 K 30 M 70 K 30 M 50 K 30 M 30 K 30 M 20 K 30 M 10 K 30

M 100 K 20 M 70 K 20 M 50 K 20 M 30 K 20 M 20 K 20 M 10 K 20

M 100 K 10 M 70 K 10 M 50 K 10 M 30 K 10 M 20 K 10 M 10 K 10

M 100 K 5 M 70 K 5 M 50 K 5 M 30 K 5 M 20 K 5 M 10 K 5

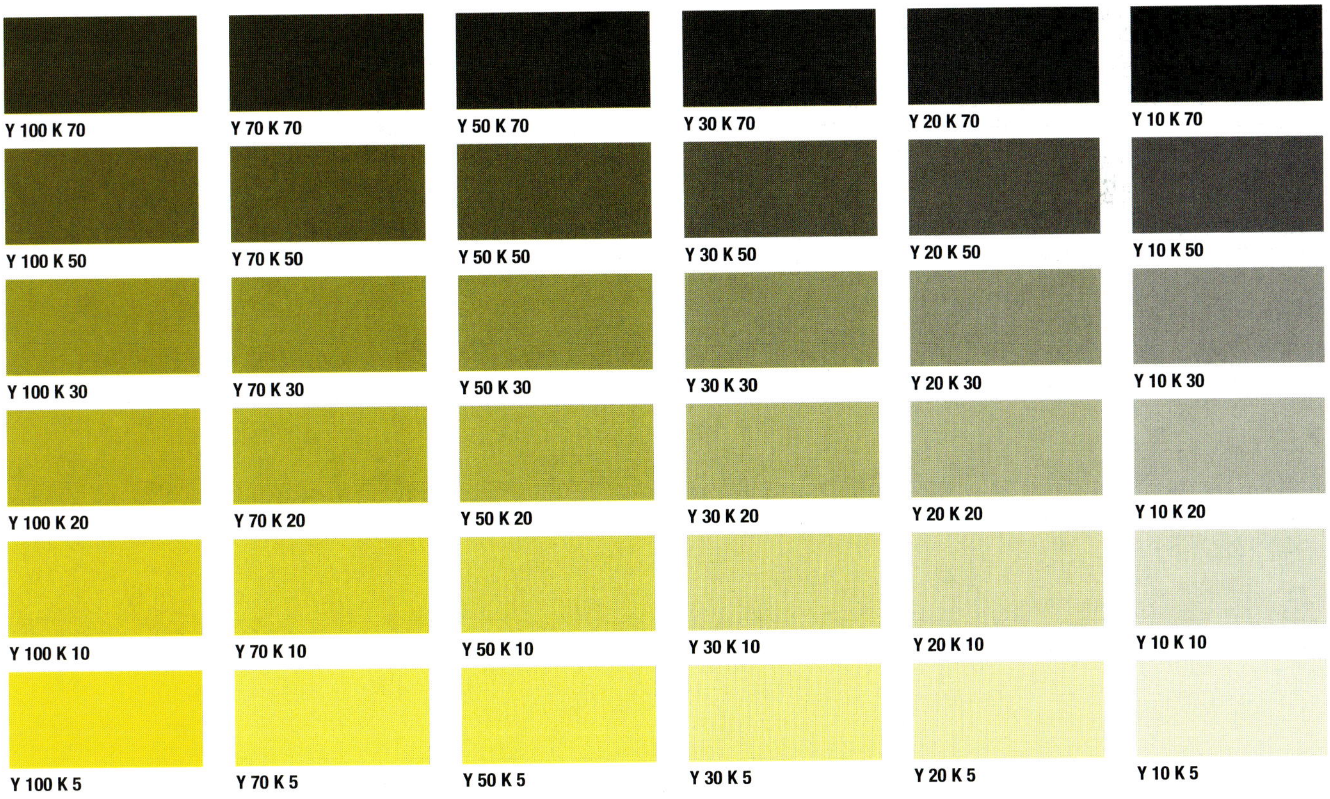

Y 100 K 70 Y 70 K 70 Y 50 K 70 Y 30 K 70 Y 20 K 70 Y 10 K 70

Y 100 K 50 Y 70 K 50 Y 50 K 50 Y 30 K 50 Y 20 K 50 Y 10 K 50

Y 100 K 30 Y 70 K 30 Y 50 K 30 Y 30 K 30 Y 20 K 30 Y 10 K 30

Y 100 K 20 Y 70 K 20 Y 50 K 20 Y 30 K 20 Y 20 K 20 Y 10 K 20

Y 100 K 10 Y 70 K 10 Y 50 K 10 Y 30 K 10 Y 20 K 10 Y 10 K 10

Y 100 K 5 Y 70 K 5 Y 50 K 5 Y 30 K 5 Y 20 K 5 Y 10 K 5

C 100 M 100 Y 100 C 70 M 100 Y 100 C 50 M 100 Y 100 C 30 M 100 Y 100 C 20 M 100 Y 100 C 10 M 100 Y 100

C 100 M 70 Y 100 C 70 M 70 Y 100 C 50 M 70 Y 100 C 30 M 70 Y 100 C 20 M 70 Y 100 C 10 M 70 Y 100

C 100 M 50 Y 100 C 70 M 50 Y 100 C 50 M 50 Y 100 C 30 M 50 Y 100 C 20 M 50 Y 100 C 10 M 50 Y 100

C 100 M 30 Y 100 C 70 M 30 Y 100 C 50 M 30 Y 100 C 30 M 30 Y 100 C 20 M 30 Y 100 C 10 M 30 Y 100

C 100 M 20 Y 100 C 70 M 20 Y 100 C 50 M 20 Y 100 C 30 M 20 Y 100 C 20 M 20 Y 100 C 10 M 20 Y 100

C 100 M 10 Y 100 C 70 M 10 Y 100 C 50 M 10 Y 100 C 30 M 10 Y 100 C 20 M 10 Y 100 C 10 M 10 Y 100

C 100 M 100 Y 70 C 70 M 100 Y 70 C 50 M 100 Y 70 C 30 M 100 Y 70 C 20 M 100 Y 70 C 10 M 100 Y 70

C 100 M 70 Y 70 C 70 M 70 Y 70 C 50 M 70 Y 70 C 30 M 70 Y 70 C 20 M 70 Y 70 C 10 M 70 Y 70

C 100 M 50 Y 70 C 70 M 50 Y 70 C 50 M 50 Y 70 C 30 M 50 Y 70 C 20 M 50 Y 70 C 10 M 50 Y 70

C 100 M 30 Y 70 C 70 M 30 Y 70 C 50 M 30 Y 70 C 30 M 30 Y 70 C 20 M 30 Y 70 C 10 M 30 Y 70

C 100 M 20 Y 70 C 70 M 20 Y 70 C 50 M 20 Y 70 C 30 M 20 Y 70 C 20 M 20 Y 70 C 10 M 20 Y 70

C 100 M 10 Y 70 C 70 M 10 Y 70 C 50 M 10 Y 70 C 30 M 10 Y 70 C 20 M 10 Y 70 C 10 M 10 Y 70

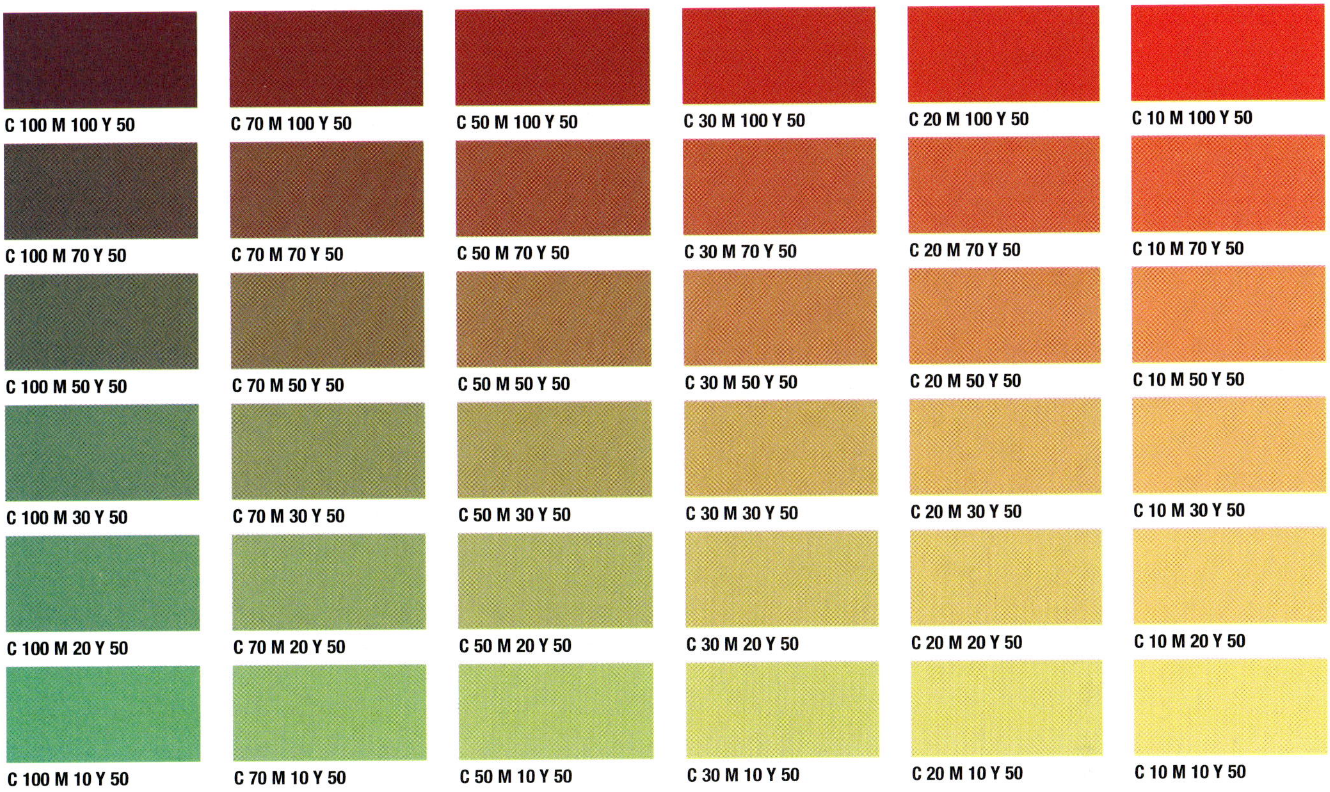

C 100 M 100 Y 50	C 70 M 100 Y 50	C 50 M 100 Y 50	C 30 M 100 Y 50	C 20 M 100 Y 50	C 10 M 100 Y 50
C 100 M 70 Y 50	C 70 M 70 Y 50	C 50 M 70 Y 50	C 30 M 70 Y 50	C 20 M 70 Y 50	C 10 M 70 Y 50
C 100 M 50 Y 50	C 70 M 50 Y 50	C 50 M 50 Y 50	C 30 M 50 Y 50	C 20 M 50 Y 50	C 10 M 50 Y 50
C 100 M 30 Y 50	C 70 M 30 Y 50	C 50 M 30 Y 50	C 30 M 30 Y 50	C 20 M 30 Y 50	C 10 M 30 Y 50
C 100 M 20 Y 50	C 70 M 20 Y 50	C 50 M 20 Y 50	C 30 M 20 Y 50	C 20 M 20 Y 50	C 10 M 20 Y 50
C 100 M 10 Y 50	C 70 M 10 Y 50	C 50 M 10 Y 50	C 30 M 10 Y 50	C 20 M 10 Y 50	C 10 M 10 Y 50

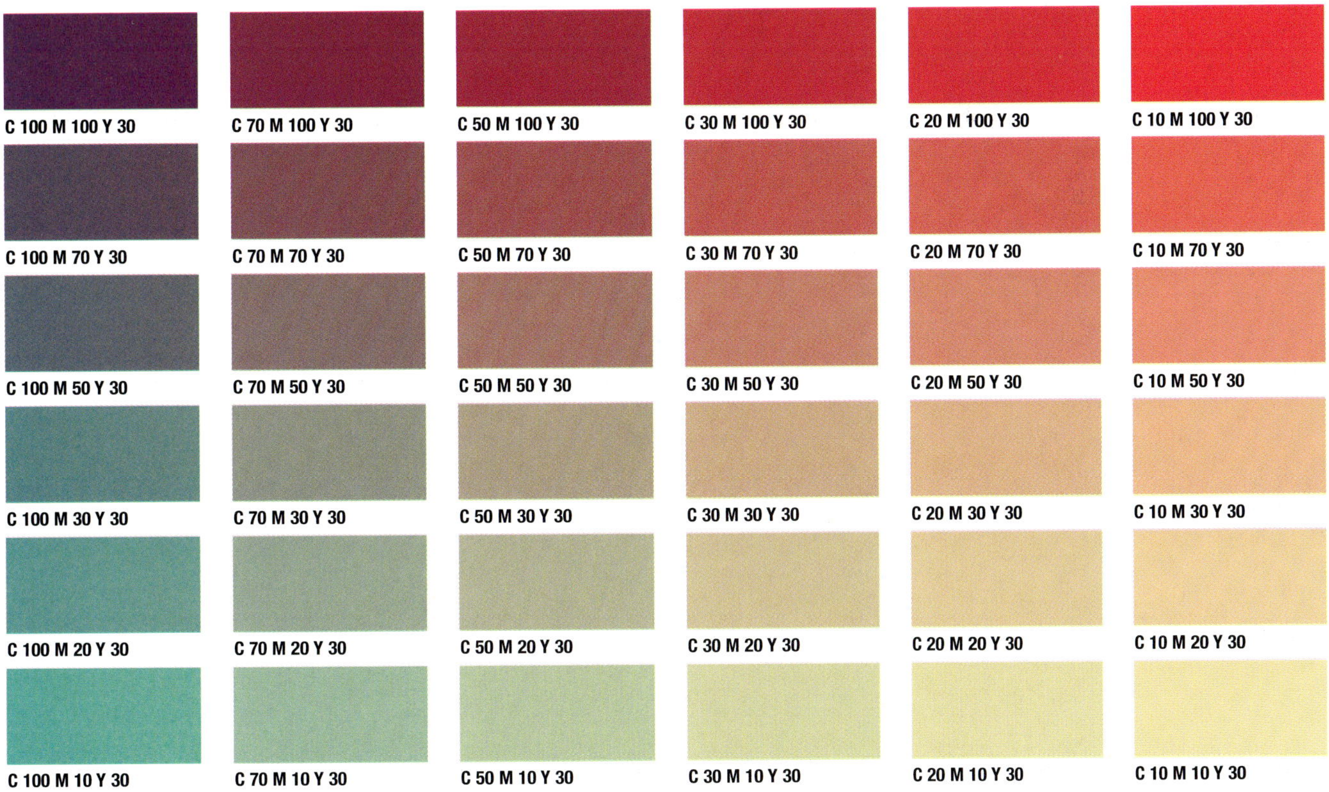

C 100 M 100 Y 30	C 70 M 100 Y 30	C 50 M 100 Y 30	C 30 M 100 Y 30	C 20 M 100 Y 30	C 10 M 100 Y 30
C 100 M 70 Y 30	C 70 M 70 Y 30	C 50 M 70 Y 30	C 30 M 70 Y 30	C 20 M 70 Y 30	C 10 M 70 Y 30
C 100 M 50 Y 30	C 70 M 50 Y 30	C 50 M 50 Y 30	C 30 M 50 Y 30	C 20 M 50 Y 30	C 10 M 50 Y 30
C 100 M 30 Y 30	C 70 M 30 Y 30	C 50 M 30 Y 30	C 30 M 30 Y 30	C 20 M 30 Y 30	C 10 M 30 Y 30
C 100 M 20 Y 30	C 70 M 20 Y 30	C 50 M 20 Y 30	C 30 M 20 Y 30	C 20 M 20 Y 30	C 10 M 20 Y 30
C 100 M 10 Y 30	C 70 M 10 Y 30	C 50 M 10 Y 30	C 30 M 10 Y 30	C 20 M 10 Y 30	C 10 M 10 Y 30

C 100 M 100 Y 20	C 70 M 100 Y 20	C 50 M 100 Y 20	C 30 M 100 Y 20	C 20 M 100 Y 20	C 10 M 100 Y 20
C 100 M 70 Y 20	C 70 M 70 Y 20	C 50 M 70 Y 20	C 30 M 70 Y 20	C 20 M 70 Y 20	C 10 M 70 Y 20
C 100 M 50 Y 20	C 70 M 50 Y 20	C 50 M 50 Y 20	C 30 M 50 Y 20	C 20 M 50 Y 20	C 10 M 50 Y 20
C 100 M 30 Y 20	C 70 M 30 Y 20	C 50 M 30 Y 20	C 30 M 30 Y 20	C 20 M 30 Y 20	C 10 M 30 Y 20
C 100 M 20 Y 20	C 70 M 20 Y 20	C 50 M 20 Y 20	C 30 M 20 Y 20	C 20 M 20 Y 20	C 10 M 20 Y 20
C 100 M 10 Y 20	C 70 M 10 Y 20	C 50 M 10 Y 20	C 30 M 10 Y 20	C 20 M 10 Y 20	C 10 M 10 Y 20

C 100 M 100 Y 10	C 70 M 100 Y 10	C 50 M 100 Y 10	C 30 M 100 Y 10	C 20 M 100 Y 10	C 10 M 100 Y 10
C 100 M 70 Y 10	C 70 M 70 Y 10	C 50 M 70 Y 10	C 30 M 70 Y 10	C 20 M 70 Y 10	C 10 M 70 Y 10
C 100 M 50 Y 10	C 70 M 50 Y 10	C 50 M 50 Y 10	C 30 M 50 Y 10	C 20 M 50 Y 10	C 10 M 50 Y 10
C 100 M 30 Y 10	C 70 M 30 Y 10	C 50 M 30 Y 10	C 30 M 30 Y 10	C 20 M 30 Y 10	C 10 M 30 Y 10
C 100 M 20 Y 10	C 70 M 20 Y 10	C 50 M 20 Y 10	C 30 M 20 Y 10	C 20 M 20 Y 10	C 10 M 20 Y 10
C 100 M 10 Y 10	C 70 M 10 Y 10	C 50 M 10 Y 10	C 30 M 10 Y 10	C 20 M 10 Y 10	C 10 M 10 Y 10

C 100 M 100 K 70	C 70 M 100 K 70	C 50 M 100 K 70	C 30 M 100 K 70	C 20 M 100 K 70	C 10 M 100 K 70
C 100 M 100 K 50	C 70 M 100 K 50	C 50 M 100 K 50	C 30 M 100 K 50	C 20 M 100 K 50	C 10 M 100 K 50
C 100 M 100 K 30	C 70 M 100 K 30	C 50 M 100 K 30	C 30 M 100 K 30	C 20 M 100 K 30	C 10 M 100 K 30
C 100 M 100 K 20	C 70 M 100 K 20	C 50 M 100 K 20	C 30 M 100 K 20	C 20 M 100 K 20	C 10 M 100 K 20
C 100 M 100 K 10	C 70 M 100 K 10	C 50 M 100 K 10	C 30 M 100 K 10	C 20 M 100 K 10	C 10 M 100 K 10
C 100 M 100 K 5	C 70 M 100 K 5	C 50 M 100 K 5	C 30 M 100 K 5	C 20 M 100 K 5	C 10 M 100 K 5

C 100 M 70 K 70	C 70 M 70 K 70	C 50 M 70 K 70	C 30 M 70 K 70	C 20 M 70 K 70	C 10 M 70 K 70
C 100 M 70 K 50	C 70 M 70 K 50	C 50 M 70 K 50	C 30 M 70 K 50	C 20 M 70 K 50	C 10 M 70 K 50
C 100 M 70 K 30	C 70 M 70 K 30	C 50 M 70 K 30	C 30 M 70 K 30	C 20 M 70 K 30	C 10 M 70 K 30
C 100 M 70 K 20	C 70 M 70 K 20	C 50 M 70 K 20	C 30 M 70 K 20	C 20 M 70 K 20	C 10 M 70 K 20
C 100 M 70 K 10	C 70 M 70 K 10	C 50 M 70 K 10	C 30 M 70 K 10	C 20 M 70 K 10	C 10 M 70 K 10
C 100 M 70 K 5	C 70 M 70 K 5	C 50 M 70 K 5	C 30 M 70 K 5	C 20 M 70 K 5	C 10 M 70 K 5

C 100 M 50 K 70	C 70 M 50 K 70	C 50 M 50 K 70	C 30 M 50 K 70	C 20 M 50 K 70	C 10 M 50 K 70
C 100 M 50 K 50	C 70 M 50 K 50	C 50 M 50 K 50	C 30 M 50 K 50	C 20 M 50 K 50	C 10 M 50 K 50
C 100 M 50 K 30	C 70 M 50 K 30	C 50 M 50 K 30	C 30 M 50 K 30	C 20 M 50 K 30	C 10 M 50 K 30
C 100 M 50 K 20	C 70 M 50 K 20	C 50 M 50 K 20	C 30 M 50 K 20	C 20 M 50 K 20	C 10 M 50 K 20
C 100 M 50 K 10	C 70 M 50 K 10	C 50 M 50 K 10	C 30 M 50 K 10	C 20 M 50 K 10	C 10 M 50 K 10
C 100 M 50 K 5	C 70 M 50 K 5	C 50 M 50 K 5	C 30 M 50 K 5	C 20 M 50 K 5	C 10 M 50 K 5

C 100 M 30 K 70	C 70 M 30 K 70	C 50 M 30 K 70	C 30 M 30 K 70	C 20 M 30 K 70	C 10 M 30 K 70
C 100 M 30 K 50	C 70 M 30 K 50	C 50 M 30 K 50	C 30 M 30 K 50	C 20 M 30 K 50	C 10 M 30 K 50
C 100 M 30 K 30	C 70 M 30 K 30	C 50 M 30 K 30	C 30 M 30 K 30	C 20 M 30 K 30	C 10 M 30 K 30
C 100 M 30 K 20	C 70 M 30 K 20	C 50 M 30 K 20	C 30 M 30 K 20	C 20 M 30 K 20	C 10 M 30 K 20
C 100 M 30 K 10	C 70 M 30 K 10	C 50 M 30 K 10	C 30 M 30 K 10	C 20 M 30 K 10	C 10 M 30 K 10
C 100 M 30 K 5	C 70 M 30 K 5	C 50 M 30 K 5	C 30 M 30 K 5	C 20 M 30 K 5	C 10 M 30 K 5

C 100 M 20 K 70	C 70 M 20 K 70	C 50 M 20 K 70	C 30 M 20 K 70	C 20 M 20 K 70	C 10 M 20 K 70
C 100 M 20 K 50	C 70 M 20 K 50	C 50 M 20 K 50	C 30 M 20 K 50	C 20 M 20 K 50	C 10 M 20 K 50
C 100 M 20 K 30	C 70 M 20 K 30	C 50 M 20 K 30	C 30 M 20 K 30	C 20 M 20 K 30	C 10 M 20 K 30
C 100 M 20 K 20	C 70 M 20 K 20	C 50 M 20 K 20	C 30 M 20 K 20	C 20 M 20 K 20	C 10 M 20 K 20
C 100 M 20 K 10	C 70 M 20 K 10	C 50 M 20 K 10	C 30 M 20 K 10	C 20 M 20 K 10	C 10 M 20 K 10
C 100 M 20 K 5	C 70 M 20 K 5	C 50 M 20 K 5	C 30 M 20 K 5	C 20 M 20 K 5	C 10 M 20 K 5

C 100 M 10 K 70	C 70 M 10 K 70	C 50 M 10 K 70	C 30 M 10 K 70	C 20 M 10 K 70	C 10 M 10 K 70
C 100 M 10 K 50	C 70 M 10 K 50	C 50 M 10 K 50	C 30 M 10 K 50	C 20 M 10 K 50	C 10 M 10 K 50
C 100 M 10 K 30	C 70 M 10 K 30	C 50 M 10 K 30	C 30 M 10 K 30	C 20 M 10 K 30	C 10 M 10 K 30
C 100 M 10 K 20	C 70 M 10 K 20	C 50 M 10 K 20	C 30 M 10 K 20	C 20 M 10 K 20	C 10 M 10 K 20
C 100 M 10 K 10	C 70 M 10 K 10	C 50 M 10 K 10	C 30 M 10 K 10	C 20 M 10 K 10	C 10 M 10 K 10
C 100 M 10 K 5	C 70 M 10 K 5	C 50 M 10 K 5	C 30 M 10 K 5	C 20 M 10 K 5	C 10 M 10 K 5

C 100 Y 100 K 70	C 70 Y 100 K 70	C 50 Y 100 K 70	C 30 Y 100 K 70	C 20 Y 100 K 70	C 10 Y 100 K 70
C 100 Y 100 K 50	C 70 Y 100 K 50	C 50 Y 100 K 50	C 30 Y 100 K 50	C 20 Y 100 K 50	C 10 Y 100 K 50
C 100 Y 100 K 30	C 70 Y 100 K 30	C 50 Y 100 K 30	C 30 Y 100 K 30	C 20 Y 100 K 30	C 10 Y 100 K 30
C 100 Y 100 K 20	C 70 Y 100 K 20	C 50 Y 100 K 20	C 30 Y 100 K 20	C 20 Y 100 K 20	C 10 Y 100 K 20
C 100 Y 100 K 10	C 70 Y 100 K 10	C 50 Y 100 K 10	C 30 Y 100 K 10	C 20 Y 100 K 10	C 10 Y 100 K 10
C 100 Y 100 K 5	C 70 Y 100 K 5	C 50 Y 100 K 5	C 30 Y 100 K 5	C 20 Y 100 K 5	C 10 Y 100 K 5

C 100 Y 70 K 70	C 70 Y 70 K 70	C 50 Y 70 K 70	C 30 Y 70 K 70	C 20 Y 70 K 70	C 10 Y 70 K 70
C 100 Y 70 K 50	C 70 Y 70 K 50	C 50 Y 70 K 50	C 30 Y 70 K 50	C 20 Y 70 K 50	C 10 Y 70 K 50
C 100 Y 70 K 30	C 70 Y 70 K 30	C 50 Y 70 K 30	C 30 Y 70 K 30	C 20 Y 70 K 30	C 10 Y 70 K 30
C 100 Y 70 K 20	C 70 Y 70 K 20	C 50 Y 70 K 20	C 30 Y 70 K 20	C 20 Y 70 K 20	C 10 Y 70 K 20
C 100 Y 70 K 10	C 70 Y 70 K 10	C 50 Y 70 K 10	C 30 Y 70 K 10	C 20 Y 70 K 10	C 10 Y 70 K 10
C 100 Y 70 K 5	C 70 Y 70 K 5	C 50 Y 70 K 5	C 30 Y 70 K 5	C 20 Y 70 K 5	C 10 Y 70 K 5

C 100 Y 50 K 70	C 70 Y 50 K 70	C 50 Y 50 K 70	C 30 Y 50 K 70	C 20 Y 50 K 70	C 10 Y 50 K 70
C 100 Y 50 K 50	C 70 Y 50 K 50	C 50 Y 50 K 50	C 30 Y 50 K 50	C 20 Y 50 K 50	C 10 Y 50 K 50
C 100 Y 50 K 30	C 70 Y 50 K 30	C 50 Y 50 K 30	C 30 Y 50 K 30	C 20 Y 50 K 30	C 10 Y 50 K 30
C 100 Y 50 K 20	C 70 Y 50 K 20	C 50 Y 50 K 20	C 30 Y 50 K 20	C 20 Y 50 K 20	C 10 Y 50 K 20
C 100 Y 50 K 10	C 70 Y 50 K 10	C 50 Y 50 K 10	C 30 Y 50 K 10	C 20 Y 50 K 10	C 10 Y 50 K 10
C 100 Y 50 K 5	C 70 Y 50 K 5	C 50 Y 50 K 5	C 30 Y 50 K 5	C 20 Y 50 K 5	C 10 Y 50 K 5

C 100 Y 30 K 70	C 70 Y 30 K 70	C 50 Y 30 K 70	C 30 Y 30 K 70	C 20 Y 30 K 70	C 10 Y 30 K 70
C 100 Y 30 K 50	C 70 Y 30 K 50	C 50 Y 30 K 50	C 30 Y 30 K 50	C 20 Y 30 K 50	C 10 Y 30 K 50
C 100 Y 30 K 30	C 70 Y 30 K 30	C 50 Y 30 K 30	C 30 Y 30 K 30	C 20 Y 30 K 30	C 10 Y 30 K 30
C 100 Y 30 K 20	C 70 Y 30 K 20	C 50 Y 30 K 20	C 30 Y 30 K 20	C 20 Y 30 K 20	C 10 Y 30 K 20
C 100 Y 30 K 10	C 70 Y 30 K 10	C 50 Y 30 K 10	C 30 Y 30 K 10	C 20 Y 30 K 10	C 10 Y 30 K 10
C 100 Y 30 K 5	C 70 Y 30 K 5	C 50 Y 30 K 5	C 30 Y 30 K 5	C 20 Y 30 K 5	C 10 Y 30 K 5

C 100 Y 20 K 70	C 70 Y 20 K 70	C 50 Y 20 K 70	C 30 Y 20 K 70	C 20 Y 20 K 70	C 10 Y 20 K 70
C 100 Y 20 K 50	C 70 Y 20 K 50	C 50 Y 20 K 50	C 30 Y 20 K 50	C 20 Y 20 K 50	C 10 Y 20 K 50
C 100 Y 20 K 30	C 70 Y 20 K 30	C 50 Y 20 K 30	C 30 Y 20 K 30	C 20 Y 20 K 30	C 10 Y 20 K 30
C 100 Y 20 K 20	C 70 Y 20 K 20	C 50 Y 20 K 20	C 30 Y 20 K 20	C 20 Y 20 K 20	C 10 Y 20 K 20
C 100 Y 20 K 10	C 70 Y 20 K 10	C 50 Y 20 K 10	C 30 Y 20 K 10	C 20 Y 20 K 10	C 10 Y 20 K 10
C 100 Y 20 K 5	C 70 Y 20 K 5	C 50 Y 20 K 5	C 30 Y 20 K 5	C 20 Y 20 K 5	C 10 Y 20 K 5

C 100 Y 10 K 70	C 70 Y 10 K 70	C 50 Y 10 K 70	C 30 Y 10 K 70	C 20 Y 10 K 70	C 10 Y 10 K 70
C 100 Y 10 K 50	C 70 Y 10 K 50	C 50 Y 10 K 50	C 30 Y 10 K 50	C 20 Y 10 K 50	C 10 Y 10 K 50
C 100 Y 10 K 30	C 70 Y 10 K 30	C 50 Y 10 K 30	C 30 Y 10 K 30	C 20 Y 10 K 30	C 10 Y 10 K 30
C 100 Y 10 K 20	C 70 Y 10 K 20	C 50 Y 10 K 20	C 30 Y 10 K 20	C 20 Y 10 K 20	C 10 Y 10 K 20
C 100 Y 10 K 10	C 70 Y 10 K 10	C 50 Y 10 K 10	C 30 Y 10 K 10	C 20 Y 10 K 10	C 10 Y 10 K 10
C 100 Y 10 K 5	C 70 Y 10 K 5	C 50 Y 10 K 5	C 30 Y 10 K 5	C 20 Y 10 K 5	C 10 Y 10 K 5

C 100 M 100 Y 100 K 70	C 70 M 100 Y 100 K 70	C 50 M 100 Y 100 K 70	C 30 M 100 Y 100 K 70	C 20 M 100 Y 100 K 70	C 10 M 100 Y 100 K 70
C 100 M 100 Y 100 K 50	C 70 M 100 Y 100 K 50	C 50 M 100 Y 100 K 50	C 30 M 100 Y 100 K 50	C 20 M 100 Y 100 K 50	C 10 M 100 Y 100 K 50
C 100 M 100 Y 100 K 30	C 70 M 100 Y 100 K 30	C 50 M 100 Y 100 K 30	C 30 M 100 Y 100 K 30	C 20 M 100 Y 100 K 30	C 10 M 100 Y 100 K 30
C 100 M 100 Y 100 K 20	C 70 M 100 Y 100 K 20	C 50 M 100 Y 100 K 20	C 30 M 100 Y 100 K 20	C 20 M 100 Y 100 K 20	C 10 M 100 Y 100 K 20
C 100 M 100 Y 100 K 10	C 70 M 100 Y 100 K 10	C 50 M 100 Y 100 K 10	C 30 M 100 Y 100 K 10	C 20 M 100 Y 100 K 10	C 10 M 100 Y 100 K 10
C 100 M 100 Y 100 K 5	C 70 M 100 Y 100 K 5	C 50 M 100 Y 100 K 5	C 30 M 100 Y 100 K 5	C 20 M 100 Y 100 K 5	C 10 M 100 Y 100 K 5

C 100 M 100 Y 70 K 70	C 70 M 100 Y 70 K 70	C 50 M 100 Y 70 K 70	C 30 M 100 Y 70 K 70	C 20 M 100 Y 70 K 70	C 10 M 100 Y 70 K 70
C 100 M 100 Y 70 K 50	C 70 M 100 Y 70 K 50	C 50 M 100 Y 70 K 50	C 30 M 100 Y 70 K 50	C 20 M 100 Y 70 K 50	C 10 M 100 Y 70 K 50
C 100 M 100 Y 70 K 30	C 70 M 100 Y 70 K 30	C 50 M 100 Y 70 K 30	C 30 M 100 Y 70 K 30	C 20 M 100 Y 70 K 30	C 10 M 100 Y 70 K 30
C 100 M 100 Y 70 K 20	C 70 M 100 Y 70 K 20	C 50 M 100 Y 70 K 20	C 30 M 100 Y 70 K 20	C 20 M 100 Y 70 K 20	C 10 M 100 Y 70 K 20
C 100 M 100 Y 70 K 10	C 70 M 100 Y 70 K 10	C 50 M 100 Y 70 K 10	C 30 M 100 Y 70 K 10	C 20 M 100 Y 70 K 10	C 10 M 100 Y 70 K 10
C 100 M 100 Y 70 K 5	C 70 M 100 Y 70 K 5	C 50 M 100 Y 70 K 5	C 30 M 100 Y 70 K 5	C 20 M 100 Y 70 K 5	C 10 M 100 Y 70 K 5

C 100 M 100 Y 50 K 70	C 70 M 100 Y 50 K 70	C 50 M 100 Y 50 K 70	C 30 M 100 Y 50 K 70	C 20 M 100 Y 50 K 70	C 10 M 100 Y 50 K 70
C 100 M 100 Y 50 K 50	C 70 M 100 Y 50 K 50	C 50 M 100 Y 50 K 50	C 30 M 100 Y 50 K 50	C 20 M 100 Y 50 K 50	C 10 M 100 Y 50 K 50
C 100 M 100 Y 50 K 30	C 70 M 100 Y 50 K 30	C 50 M 100 Y 50 K 30	C 30 M 100 Y 50 K 30	C 20 M 100 Y 50 K 30	C 10 M 100 Y 50 K 30
C 100 M 100 Y 50 K 20	C 70 M 100 Y 50 K 20	C 50 M 100 Y 50 K 20	C 30 M 100 Y 50 K 20	C 20 M 100 Y 50 K 20	C 10 M 100 Y 50 K 20
C 100 M 100 Y 50 K 10	C 70 M 100 Y 50 K 10	C 50 M 100 Y 50 K 10	C 30 M 100 Y 50 K 10	C 20 M 100 Y 50 K 10	C 10 M 100 Y 50 K 10
C 100 M 100 Y 50 K 5	C 70 M 100 Y 50 K 5	C 50 M 100 Y 50 K 5	C 30 M 100 Y 50 K 5	C 20 M 100 Y 50 K 5	C 10 M 100 Y 50 K 5

C 100 M 100 Y 30 K 70	C 70 M 100 Y 30 K 70	C 50 M 100 Y 30 K 70	C 30 M 100 Y 30 K 70	C 20 M 100 Y 30 K 70	C 10 M 100 Y 30 K 70
C 100 M 100 Y 30 K 50	C 70 M 100 Y 30 K 50	C 50 M 100 Y 30 K 50	C 30 M 100 Y 30 K 50	C 20 M 100 Y 30 K 50	C 10 M 100 Y 30 K 50
C 100 M 100 Y 30 K 30	C 70 M 100 Y 30 K 30	C 50 M 100 Y 30 K 30	C 30 M 100 Y 30 K 30	C 20 M 100 Y 30 K 30	C 10 M 100 Y 30 K 30
C 100 M 100 Y 30 K 20	C 70 M 100 Y 30 K 20	C 50 M 100 Y 30 K 20	C 30 M 100 Y 30 K 20	C 20 M 100 Y 30 K 20	C 10 M 100 Y 30 K 20
C 100 M 100 Y 30 K 10	C 70 M 100 Y 30 K 10	C 50 M 100 Y 30 K 10	C 30 M 100 Y 30 K 10	C 20 M 100 Y 30 K 10	C 10 M 100 Y 30 K 10
C 100 M 100 Y 30 K 5	C 70 M 100 Y 30 K 5	C 50 M 100 Y 30 K 5	C 30 M 100 Y 30 K 5	C 20 M 100 Y 30 K 5	C 10 M 100 Y 30 K 5

C 100 M 100 Y 20 K 70	C 70 M 100 Y 20 K 70	C 50 M 100 Y 20 K 70	C 30 M 100 Y 20 K 70	C 20 M 100 Y 20 K 70	C 10 M 100 Y 20 K 70
C 100 M 100 Y 20 K 50	C 70 M 100 Y 20 K 50	C 50 M 100 Y 20 K 50	C 30 M 100 Y 20 K 50	C 20 M 100 Y 20 K 50	C 10 M 100 Y 20 K 50
C 100 M 100 Y 20 K 30	C 70 M 100 Y 20 K 30	C 50 M 100 Y 20 K 30	C 30 M 100 Y 20 K 30	C 20 M 100 Y 20 K 30	C 10 M 100 Y 20 K 30
C 100 M 100 Y 20 K 20	C 70 M 100 Y 20 K 20	C 50 M 100 Y 20 K 20	C 30 M 100 Y 20 K 20	C 20 M 100 Y 20 K 20	C 10 M 100 Y 20 K 20
C 100 M 100 Y 20 K 10	C 70 M 100 Y 20 K 10	C 50 M 100 Y 20 K 10	C 30 M 100 Y 20 K 10	C 20 M 100 Y 20 K 10	C 10 M 100 Y 20 K 10
C 100 M 100 Y 20 K 5	C 70 M 100 Y 20 K 5	C 50 M 100 Y 20 K 5	C 30 M 100 Y 20 K 5	C 20 M 100 Y 20 K 5	C 10 M 100 Y 20 K 5

C 100 M 100 Y 10 K 70	C 70 M 100 Y 10 K 70	C 50 M 100 Y 10 K 70	C 30 M 100 Y 10 K 70	C 20 M 100 Y 10 K 70	C 10 M 100 Y 10 K 70
C 100 M 100 Y 10 K 50	C 70 M 100 Y 10 K 50	C 50 M 100 Y 10 K 50	C 30 M 100 Y 10 K 50	C 20 M 100 Y 10 K 50	C 10 M 100 Y 10 K 50
C 100 M 100 Y 10 K 30	C 70 M 100 Y 10 K 30	C 50 M 100 Y 10 K 30	C 30 M 100 Y 10 K 30	C 20 M 100 Y 10 K 30	C 10 M 100 Y 10 K 30
C 100 M 100 Y 10 K 20	C 70 M 100 Y 10 K 20	C 50 M 100 Y 10 K 20	C 30 M 100 Y 10 K 20	C 20 M 100 Y 10 K 20	C 10 M 100 Y 10 K 20
C 100 M 100 Y 10 K 10	C 70 M 100 Y 10 K 10	C 50 M 100 Y 10 K 10	C 30 M 100 Y 10 K 10	C 20 M 100 Y 10 K 10	C 10 M 100 Y 10 K 10
C 100 M 100 Y 10 K 5	C 70 M 100 Y 10 K 5	C 50 M 100 Y 10 K 5	C 30 M 100 Y 10 K 5	C 20 M 100 Y 10 K 5	C 10 M 100 Y 10 K 5

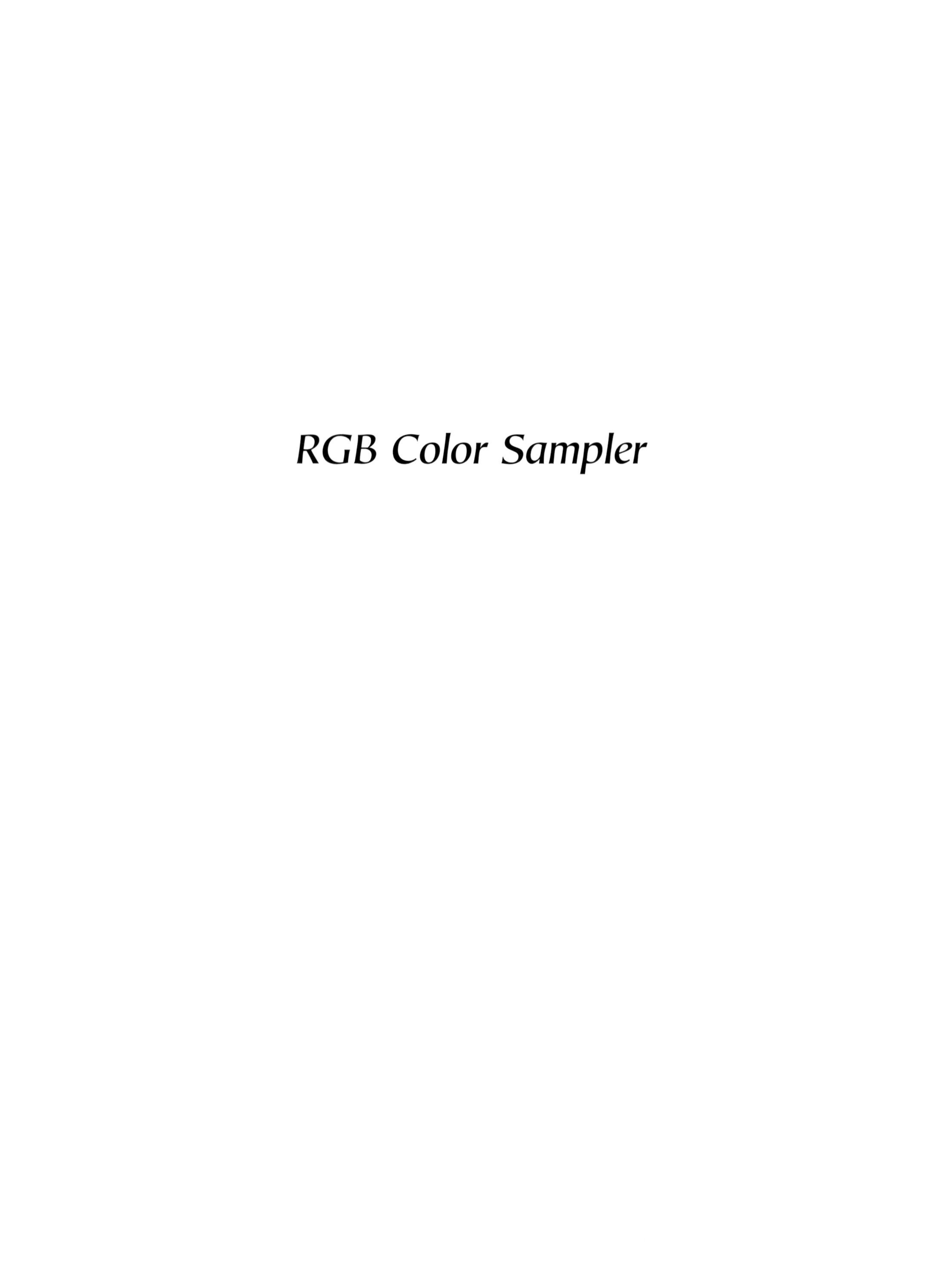

RGB Color Sampler

R 255 G 128 B 0 R 255 G 255 B 255

R 255 G 0 B 0 R 255 G 255 B 255

R 255 G 0 B 255 R 255 G 255 B 255

R 128 G 0 B 255 R 255 G 255 B 255

R 0 G 128 B 255 R 255 G 255 B 255

R 0 G 255 B 255 R 255 G 255 B 255

R 0 G 255 B 128 R 255 G 255 B 255

R 128 G 255 B 0 R 255 G 255 B 255

R 0 G 0 B 0

R 255 G 128 B 0

R 0 G 0 B 0

R 255 G 0 B 0

R 0 G 0 B 0

R 255 G 0 B 255

R 0 G 0 B 0

R 128 G 0 B 255

R 0 G 0 B 0

R 0 G 128 B 255

R 0 G 0 B 0

R 0 G 255 B 255

R 0 G 0 B 0

R 0 G 255 B 128

R 0 G 0 B 0

R 128 G 255 B 0

R 0 G 255 B 255
R 0 G 0 B 255

R 0 G 255 B 255
R 0 G 255 B 0

R 255 G 0 B 255
R 0 G 0 B 255

R 255 G 0 B 255
R 255 G 0 B 0

R 255 G 255 B 0
R 0 G 255 B 0

R 255 G 255 B 0
R 255 G 0 B 0

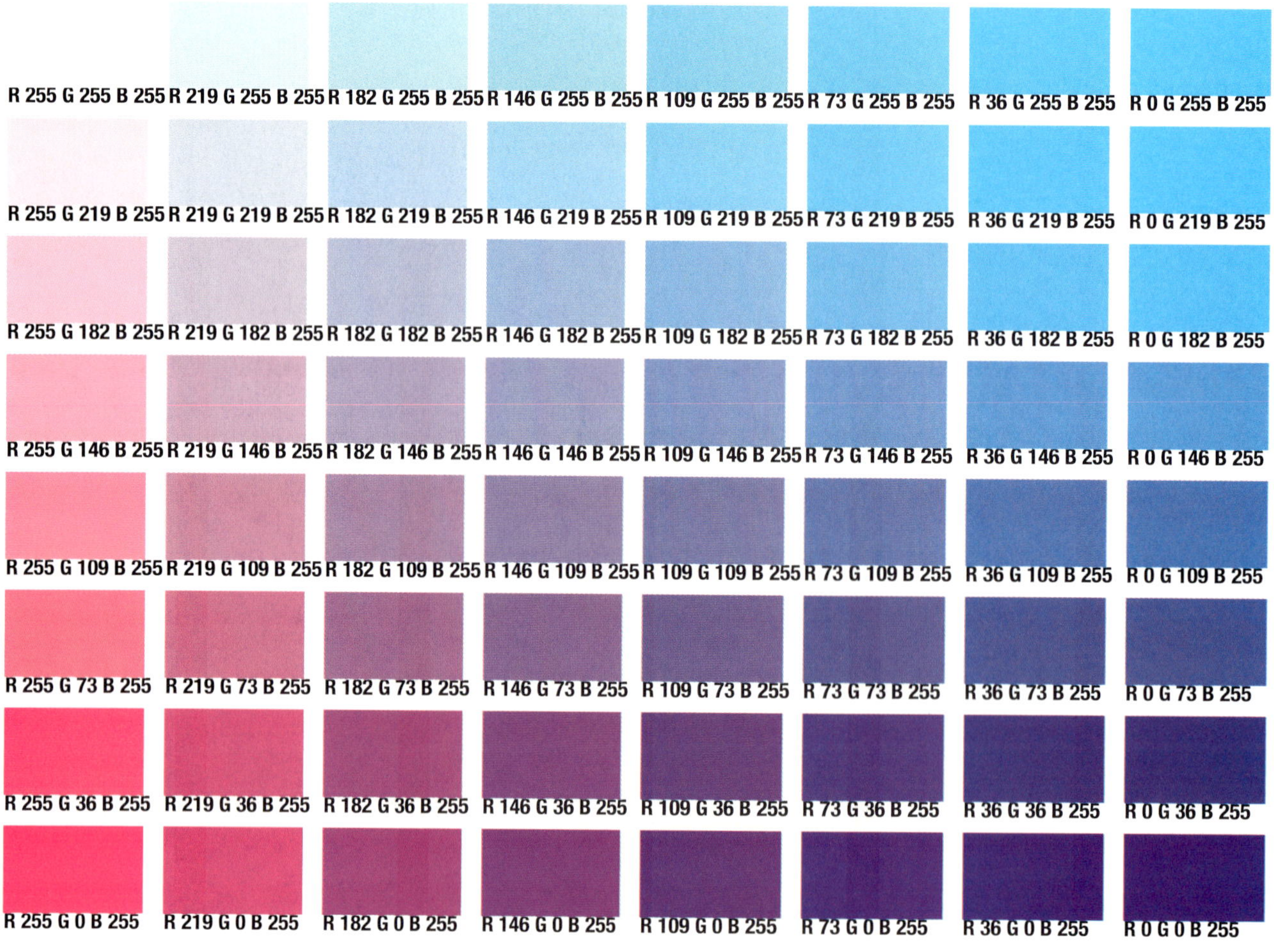

R 255 G 255 B 255	R 219 G 255 B 255	R 182 G 255 B 255	R 146 G 255 B 255	R 109 G 255 B 255	R 73 G 255 B 255	R 36 G 255 B 255	R 0 G 255 B 255
R 255 G 219 B 255	R 219 G 219 B 255	R 182 G 219 B 255	R 146 G 219 B 255	R 109 G 219 B 255	R 73 G 219 B 255	R 36 G 219 B 255	R 0 G 219 B 255
R 255 G 182 B 255	R 219 G 182 B 255	R 182 G 182 B 255	R 146 G 182 B 255	R 109 G 182 B 255	R 73 G 182 B 255	R 36 G 182 B 255	R 0 G 182 B 255
R 255 G 146 B 255	R 219 G 146 B 255	R 182 G 146 B 255	R 146 G 146 B 255	R 109 G 146 B 255	R 73 G 146 B 255	R 36 G 146 B 255	R 0 G 146 B 255
R 255 G 109 B 255	R 219 G 109 B 255	R 182 G 109 B 255	R 146 G 109 B 255	R 109 G 109 B 255	R 73 G 109 B 255	R 36 G 109 B 255	R 0 G 109 B 255
R 255 G 73 B 255	R 219 G 73 B 255	R 182 G 73 B 255	R 146 G 73 B 255	R 109 G 73 B 255	R 73 G 73 B 255	R 36 G 73 B 255	R 0 G 73 B 255
R 255 G 36 B 255	R 219 G 36 B 255	R 182 G 36 B 255	R 146 G 36 B 255	R 109 G 36 B 255	R 73 G 36 B 255	R 36 G 36 B 255	R 0 G 36 B 255
R 255 G 0 B 255	R 219 G 0 B 255	R 182 G 0 B 255	R 146 G 0 B 255	R 109 G 0 B 255	R 73 G 0 B 255	R 36 G 0 B 255	R 0 G 0 B 255

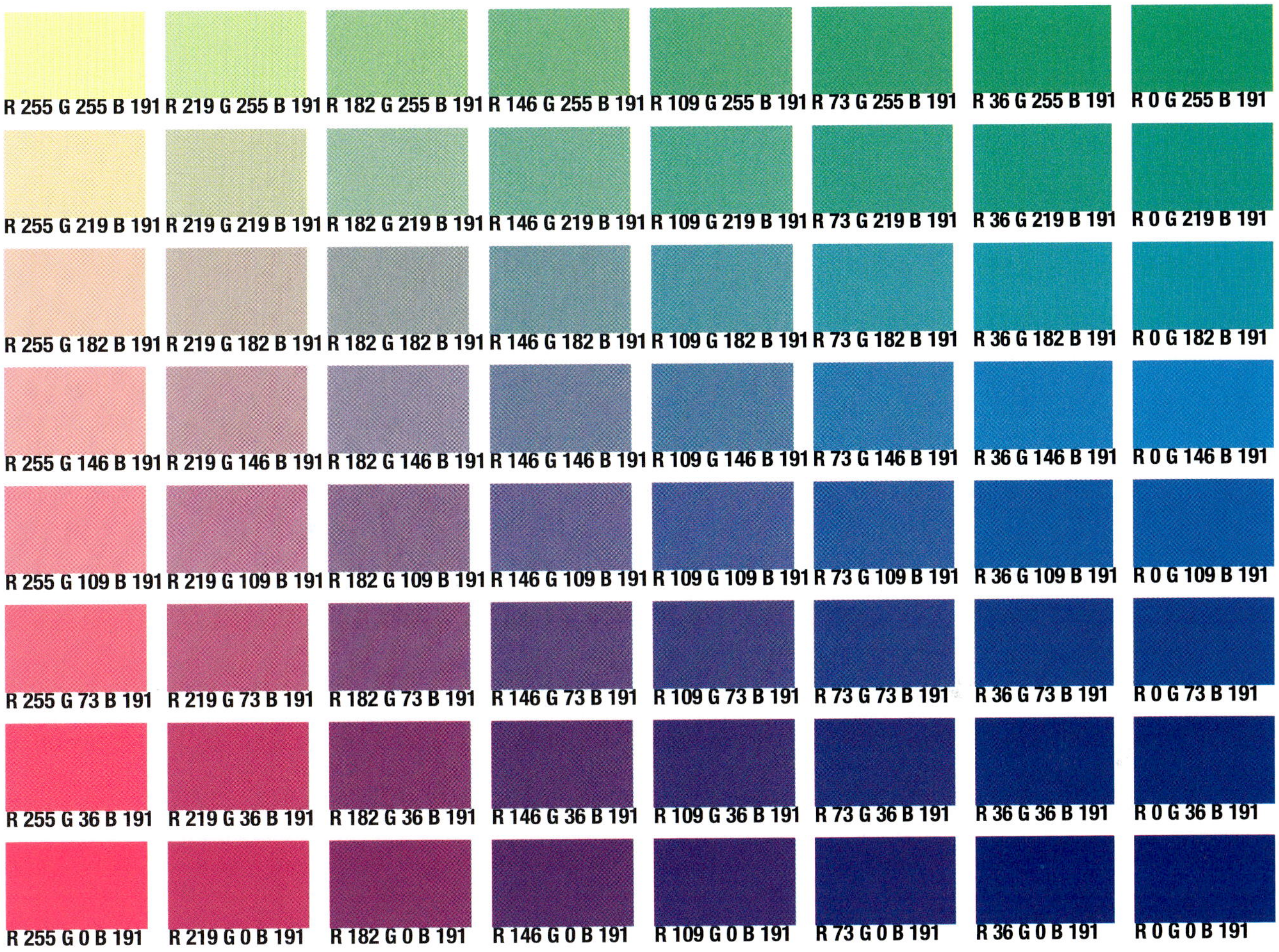

R 255 G 255 B 191	R 219 G 255 B 191	R 182 G 255 B 191	R 146 G 255 B 191	R 109 G 255 B 191	R 73 G 255 B 191	R 36 G 255 B 191	R 0 G 255 B 191
R 255 G 219 B 191	R 219 G 219 B 191	R 182 G 219 B 191	R 146 G 219 B 191	R 109 G 219 B 191	R 73 G 219 B 191	R 36 G 219 B 191	R 0 G 219 B 191
R 255 G 182 B 191	R 219 G 182 B 191	R 182 G 182 B 191	R 146 G 182 B 191	R 109 G 182 B 191	R 73 G 182 B 191	R 36 G 182 B 191	R 0 G 182 B 191
R 255 G 146 B 191	R 219 G 146 B 191	R 182 G 146 B 191	R 146 G 146 B 191	R 109 G 146 B 191	R 73 G 146 B 191	R 36 G 146 B 191	R 0 G 146 B 191
R 255 G 109 B 191	R 219 G 109 B 191	R 182 G 109 B 191	R 146 G 109 B 191	R 109 G 109 B 191	R 73 G 109 B 191	R 36 G 109 B 191	R 0 G 109 B 191
R 255 G 73 B 191	R 219 G 73 B 191	R 182 G 73 B 191	R 146 G 73 B 191	R 109 G 73 B 191	R 73 G 73 B 191	R 36 G 73 B 191	R 0 G 73 B 191
R 255 G 36 B 191	R 219 G 36 B 191	R 182 G 36 B 191	R 146 G 36 B 191	R 109 G 36 B 191	R 73 G 36 B 191	R 36 G 36 B 191	R 0 G 36 B 191
R 255 G 0 B 191	R 219 G 0 B 191	R 182 G 0 B 191	R 146 G 0 B 191	R 109 G 0 B 191	R 73 G 0 B 191	R 36 G 0 B 191	R 0 G 0 B 191

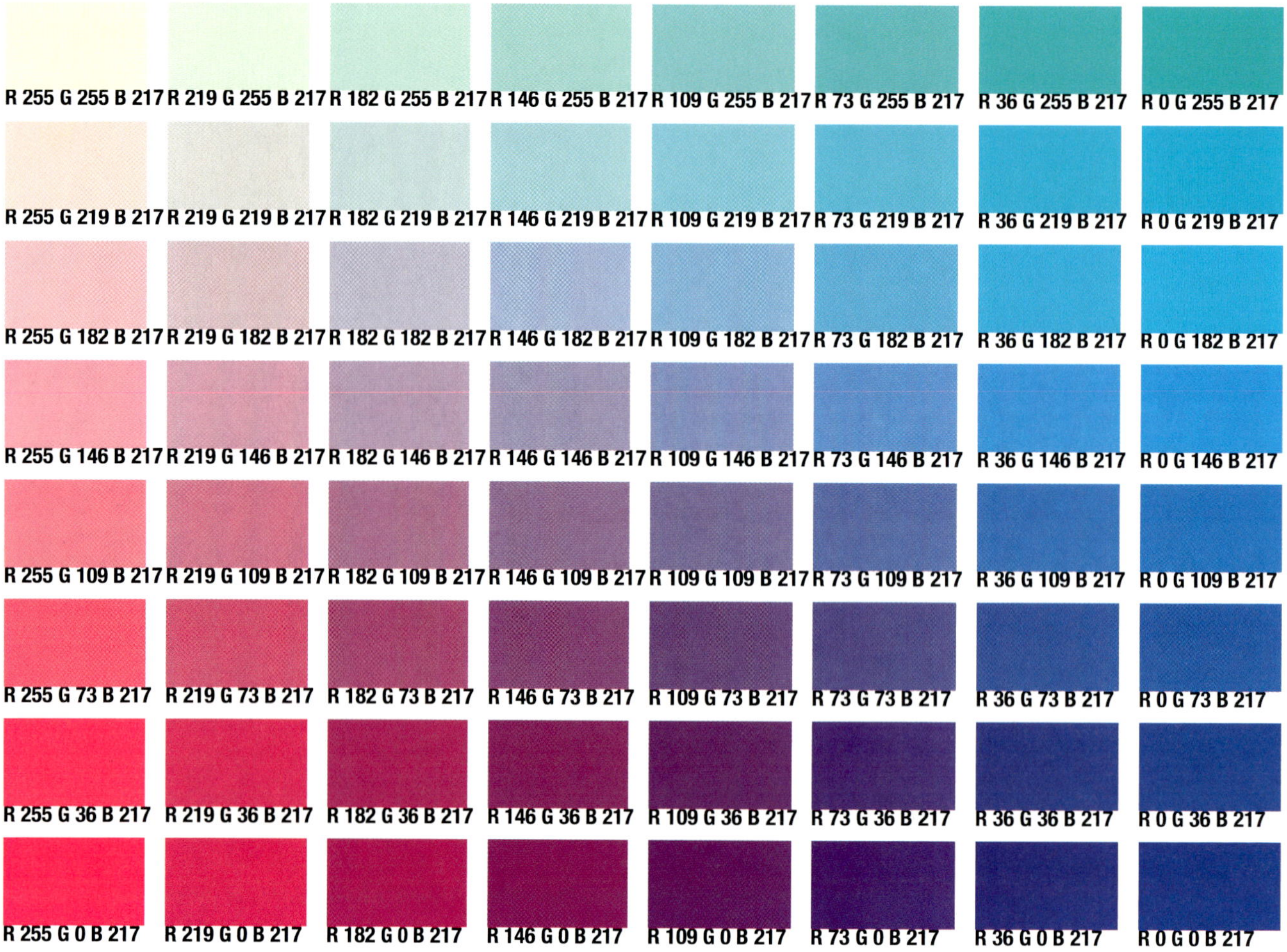

R 255 G 255 B 217 R 219 G 255 B 217 R 182 G 255 B 217 R 146 G 255 B 217 R 109 G 255 B 217 R 73 G 255 B 217 R 36 G 255 B 217 R 0 G 255 B 217

R 255 G 219 B 217 R 219 G 219 B 217 R 182 G 219 B 217 R 146 G 219 B 217 R 109 G 219 B 217 R 73 G 219 B 217 R 36 G 219 B 217 R 0 G 219 B 217

R 255 G 182 B 217 R 219 G 182 B 217 R 182 G 182 B 217 R 146 G 182 B 217 R 109 G 182 B 217 R 73 G 182 B 217 R 36 G 182 B 217 R 0 G 182 B 217

R 255 G 146 B 217 R 219 G 146 B 217 R 182 G 146 B 217 R 146 G 146 B 217 R 109 G 146 B 217 R 73 G 146 B 217 R 36 G 146 B 217 R 0 G 146 B 217

R 255 G 109 B 217 R 219 G 109 B 217 R 182 G 109 B 217 R 146 G 109 B 217 R 109 G 109 B 217 R 73 G 109 B 217 R 36 G 109 B 217 R 0 G 109 B 217

R 255 G 73 B 217 R 219 G 73 B 217 R 182 G 73 B 217 R 146 G 73 B 217 R 109 G 73 B 217 R 73 G 73 B 217 R 36 G 73 B 217 R 0 G 73 B 217

R 255 G 36 B 217 R 219 G 36 B 217 R 182 G 36 B 217 R 146 G 36 B 217 R 109 G 36 B 217 R 73 G 36 B 217 R 36 G 36 B 217 R 0 G 36 B 217

R 255 G 0 B 217 R 219 G 0 B 217 R 182 G 0 B 217 R 146 G 0 B 217 R 109 G 0 B 217 R 73 G 0 B 217 R 36 G 0 B 217 R 0 G 0 B 217

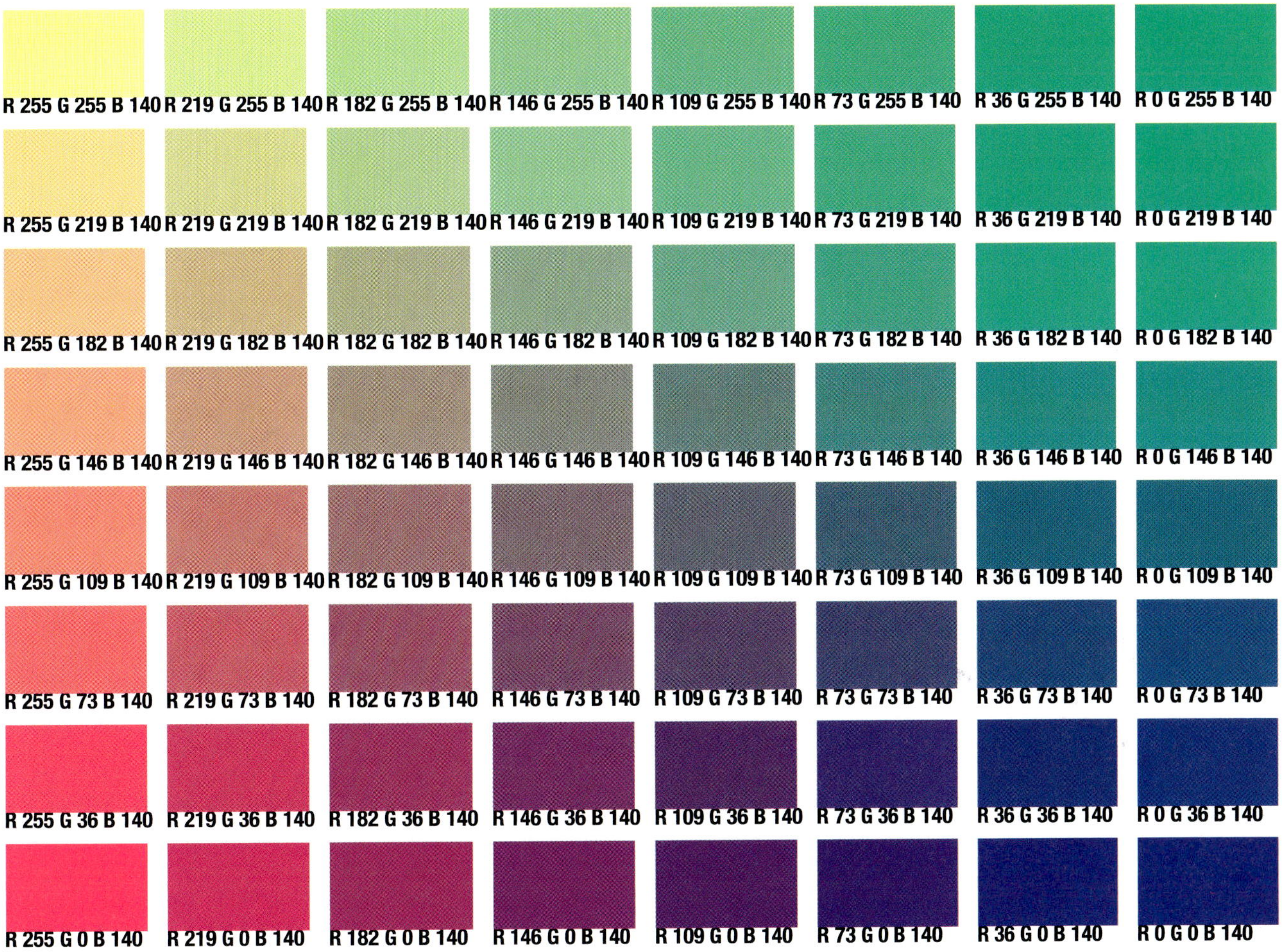

R 255 G 255 B 140	R 219 G 255 B 140	R 182 G 255 B 140	R 146 G 255 B 140	R 109 G 255 B 140	R 73 G 255 B 140	R 36 G 255 B 140	R 0 G 255 B 140
R 255 G 219 B 140	R 219 G 219 B 140	R 182 G 219 B 140	R 146 G 219 B 140	R 109 G 219 B 140	R 73 G 219 B 140	R 36 G 219 B 140	R 0 G 219 B 140
R 255 G 182 B 140	R 219 G 182 B 140	R 182 G 182 B 140	R 146 G 182 B 140	R 109 G 182 B 140	R 73 G 182 B 140	R 36 G 182 B 140	R 0 G 182 B 140
R 255 G 146 B 140	R 219 G 146 B 140	R 182 G 146 B 140	R 146 G 146 B 140	R 109 G 146 B 140	R 73 G 146 B 140	R 36 G 146 B 140	R 0 G 146 B 140
R 255 G 109 B 140	R 219 G 109 B 140	R 182 G 109 B 140	R 146 G 109 B 140	R 109 G 109 B 140	R 73 G 109 B 140	R 36 G 109 B 140	R 0 G 109 B 140
R 255 G 73 B 140	R 219 G 73 B 140	R 182 G 73 B 140	R 146 G 73 B 140	R 109 G 73 B 140	R 73 G 73 B 140	R 36 G 73 B 140	R 0 G 73 B 140
R 255 G 36 B 140	R 219 G 36 B 140	R 182 G 36 B 140	R 146 G 36 B 140	R 109 G 36 B 140	R 73 G 36 B 140	R 36 G 36 B 140	R 0 G 36 B 140
R 255 G 0 B 140	R 219 G 0 B 140	R 182 G 0 B 140	R 146 G 0 B 140	R 109 G 0 B 140	R 73 G 0 B 140	R 36 G 0 B 140	R 0 G 0 B 140

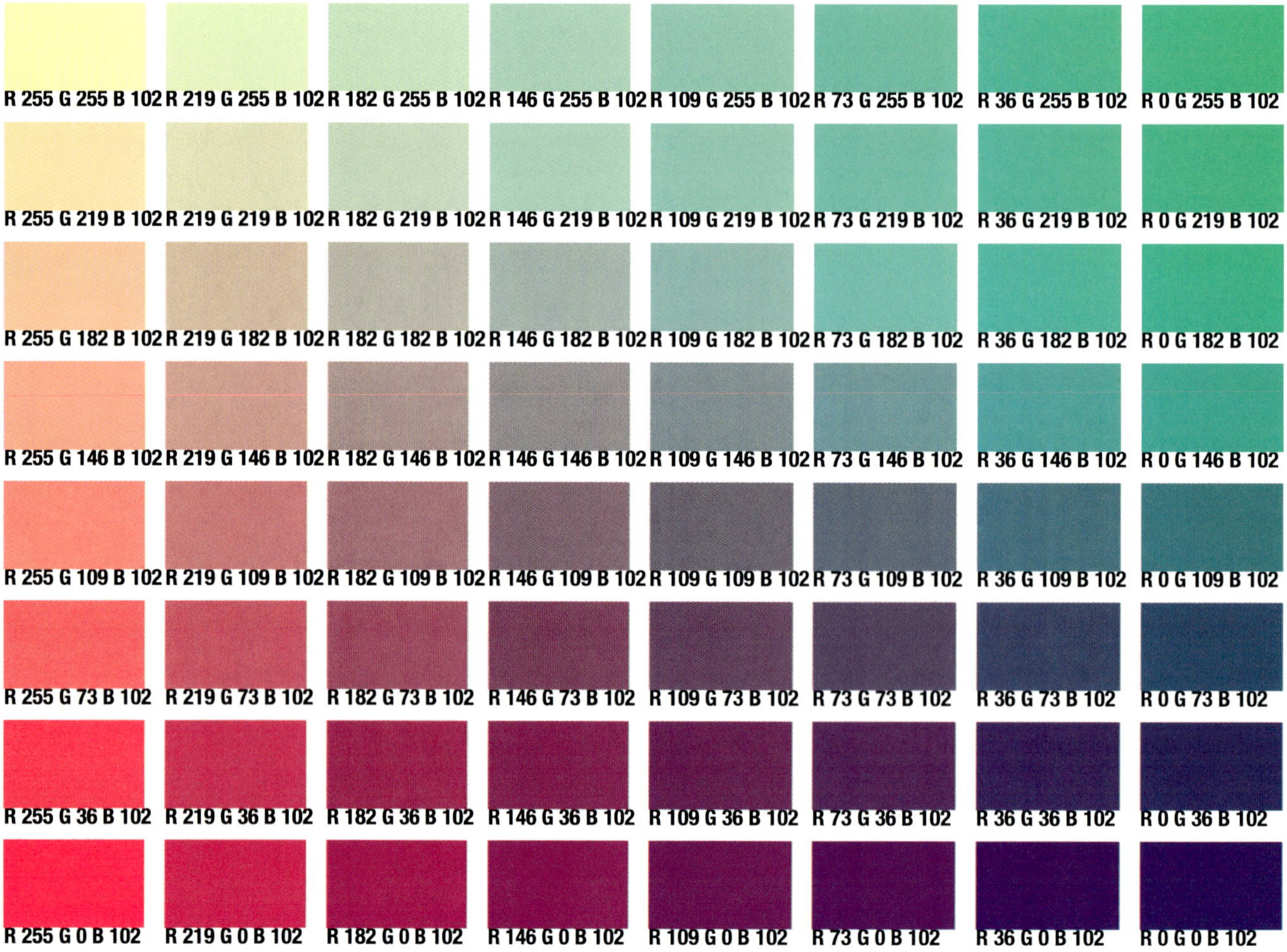

R 255 G 255 B 102	R 219 G 255 B 102	R 182 G 255 B 102	R 146 G 255 B 102	R 109 G 255 B 102	R 73 G 255 B 102	R 36 G 255 B 102	R 0 G 255 B 102
R 255 G 219 B 102	R 219 G 219 B 102	R 182 G 219 B 102	R 146 G 219 B 102	R 109 G 219 B 102	R 73 G 219 B 102	R 36 G 219 B 102	R 0 G 219 B 102
R 255 G 182 B 102	R 219 G 182 B 102	R 182 G 182 B 102	R 146 G 182 B 102	R 109 G 182 B 102	R 73 G 182 B 102	R 36 G 182 B 102	R 0 G 182 B 102
R 255 G 146 B 102	R 219 G 146 B 102	R 182 G 146 B 102	R 146 G 146 B 102	R 109 G 146 B 102	R 73 G 146 B 102	R 36 G 146 B 102	R 0 G 146 B 102
R 255 G 109 B 102	R 219 G 109 B 102	R 182 G 109 B 102	R 146 G 109 B 102	R 109 G 109 B 102	R 73 G 109 B 102	R 36 G 109 B 102	R 0 G 109 B 102
R 255 G 73 B 102	R 219 G 73 B 102	R 182 G 73 B 102	R 146 G 73 B 102	R 109 G 73 B 102	R 73 G 73 B 102	R 36 G 73 B 102	R 0 G 73 B 102
R 255 G 36 B 102	R 219 G 36 B 102	R 182 G 36 B 102	R 146 G 36 B 102	R 109 G 36 B 102	R 73 G 36 B 102	R 36 G 36 B 102	R 0 G 36 B 102
R 255 G 0 B 102	R 219 G 0 B 102	R 182 G 0 B 102	R 146 G 0 B 102	R 109 G 0 B 102	R 73 G 0 B 102	R 36 G 0 B 102	R 0 G 0 B 102

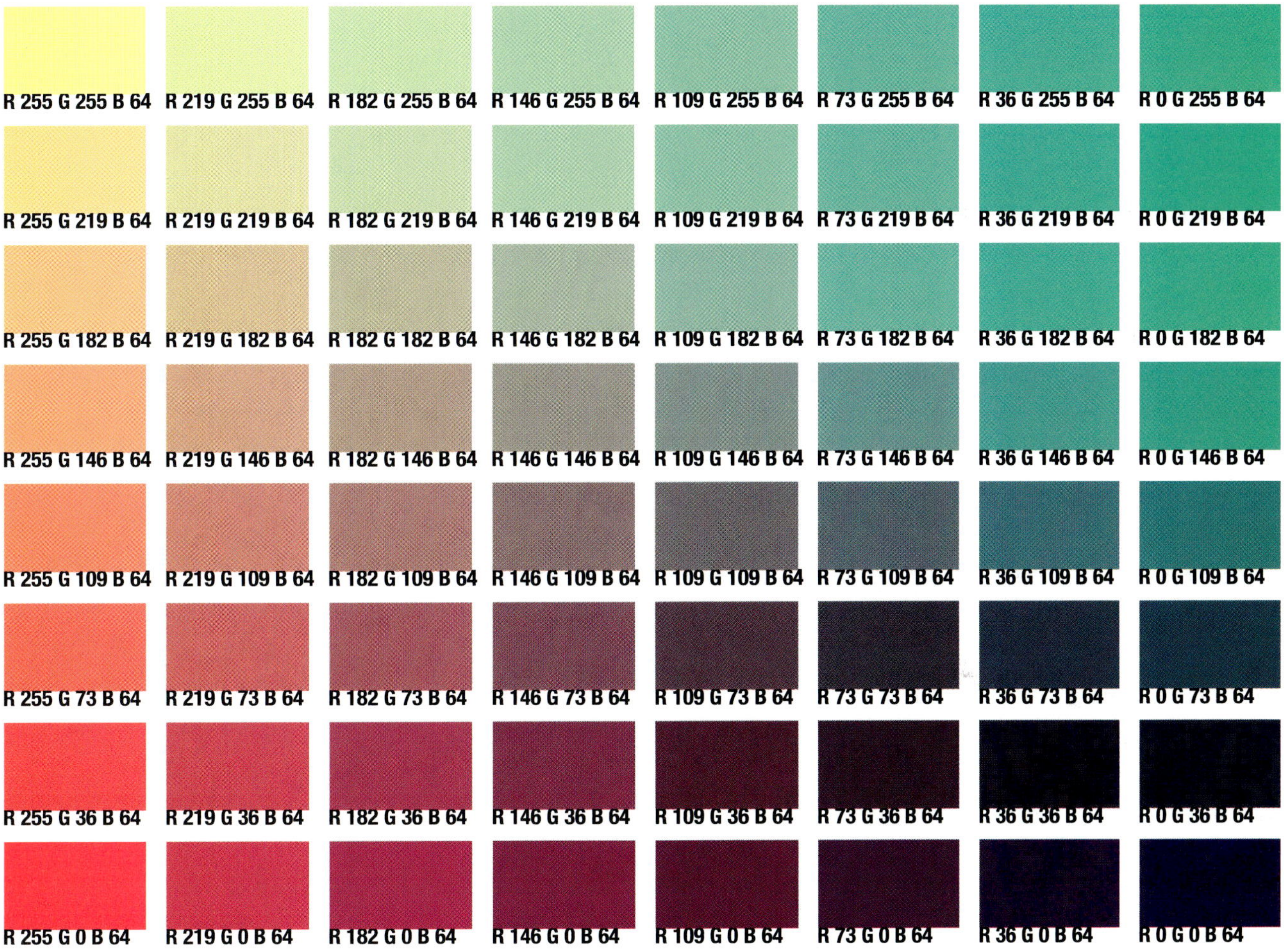

R 255 G 255 B 64	R 219 G 255 B 64	R 182 G 255 B 64	R 146 G 255 B 64	R 109 G 255 B 64	R 73 G 255 B 64	R 36 G 255 B 64	R 0 G 255 B 64
R 255 G 219 B 64	R 219 G 219 B 64	R 182 G 219 B 64	R 146 G 219 B 64	R 109 G 219 B 64	R 73 G 219 B 64	R 36 G 219 B 64	R 0 G 219 B 64
R 255 G 182 B 64	R 219 G 182 B 64	R 182 G 182 B 64	R 146 G 182 B 64	R 109 G 182 B 64	R 73 G 182 B 64	R 36 G 182 B 64	R 0 G 182 B 64
R 255 G 146 B 64	R 219 G 146 B 64	R 182 G 146 B 64	R 146 G 146 B 64	R 109 G 146 B 64	R 73 G 146 B 64	R 36 G 146 B 64	R 0 G 146 B 64
R 255 G 109 B 64	R 219 G 109 B 64	R 182 G 109 B 64	R 146 G 109 B 64	R 109 G 109 B 64	R 73 G 109 B 64	R 36 G 109 B 64	R 0 G 109 B 64
R 255 G 73 B 64	R 219 G 73 B 64	R 182 G 73 B 64	R 146 G 73 B 64	R 109 G 73 B 64	R 73 G 73 B 64	R 36 G 73 B 64	R 0 G 73 B 64
R 255 G 36 B 64	R 219 G 36 B 64	R 182 G 36 B 64	R 146 G 36 B 64	R 109 G 36 B 64	R 73 G 36 B 64	R 36 G 36 B 64	R 0 G 36 B 64
R 255 G 0 B 64	R 219 G 0 B 64	R 182 G 0 B 64	R 146 G 0 B 64	R 109 G 0 B 64	R 73 G 0 B 64	R 36 G 0 B 64	R 0 G 0 B 64

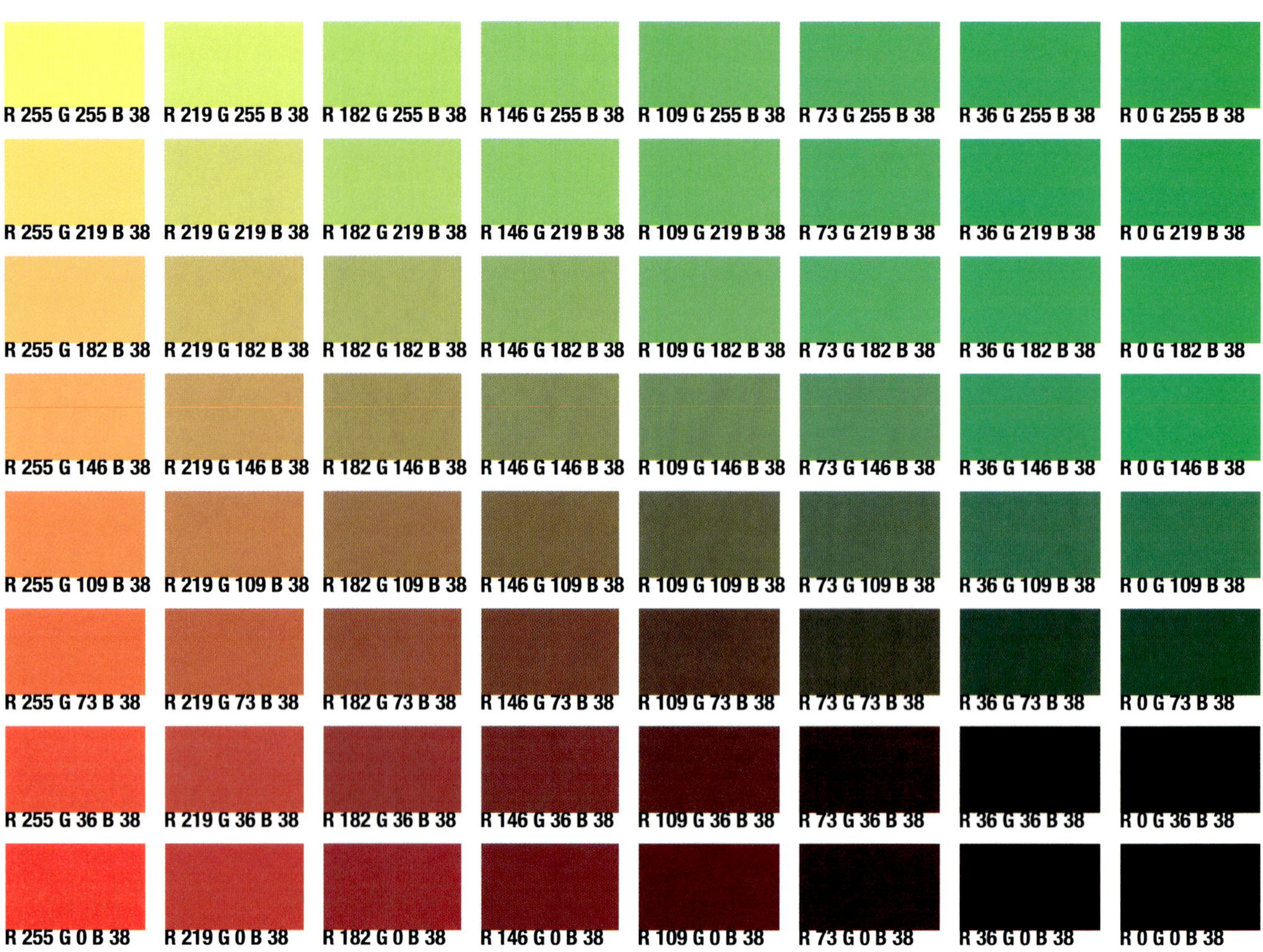
R 255 G 255 B 38
R 219 G 255 B 38
R 182 G 255 B 38
R 146 G 255 B 38
R 109 G 255 B 38
R 73 G 255 B 38
R 36 G 255 B 38
R 0 G 255 B 38
R 255 G 219 B 38
R 219 G 219 B 38
R 182 G 219 B 38
R 146 G 219 B 38
R 109 G 219 B 38
R 73 G 219 B 38
R 36 G 219 B 38
R 0 G 219 B 38
R 255 G 182 B 38
R 219 G 182 B 38
R 182 G 182 B 38
R 146 G 182 B 38
R 109 G 182 B 38
R 73 G 182 B 38
R 36 G 182 B 38
R 0 G 182 B 38
R 255 G 146 B 38
R 219 G 146 B 38
R 182 G 146 B 38
R 146 G 146 B 38
R 109 G 146 B 38
R 73 G 146 B 38
R 36 G 146 B 38
R 0 G 146 B 38
R 255 G 109 B 38
R 219 G 109 B 38
R 182 G 109 B 38
R 146 G 109 B 38
R 109 G 109 B 38
R 73 G 109 B 38
R 36 G 109 B 38
R 0 G 109 B 38
R 255 G 73 B 38
R 219 G 73 B 38
R 182 G 73 B 38
R 146 G 73 B 38
R 109 G 73 B 38
R 73 G 73 B 38
R 36 G 73 B 38
R 0 G 73 B 38
R 255 G 36 B 38
R 219 G 36 B 38
R 182 G 36 B 38
R 146 G 36 B 38
R 109 G 36 B 38
R 73 G 36 B 38
R 36 G 36 B 38
R 0 G 36 B 38
R 255 G 0 B 38
R 219 G 0 B 38
R 182 G 0 B 38
R 146 G 0 B 38
R 109 G 0 B 38
R 73 G 0 B 38
R 36 G 0 B 38
R 0 G 0 B 38

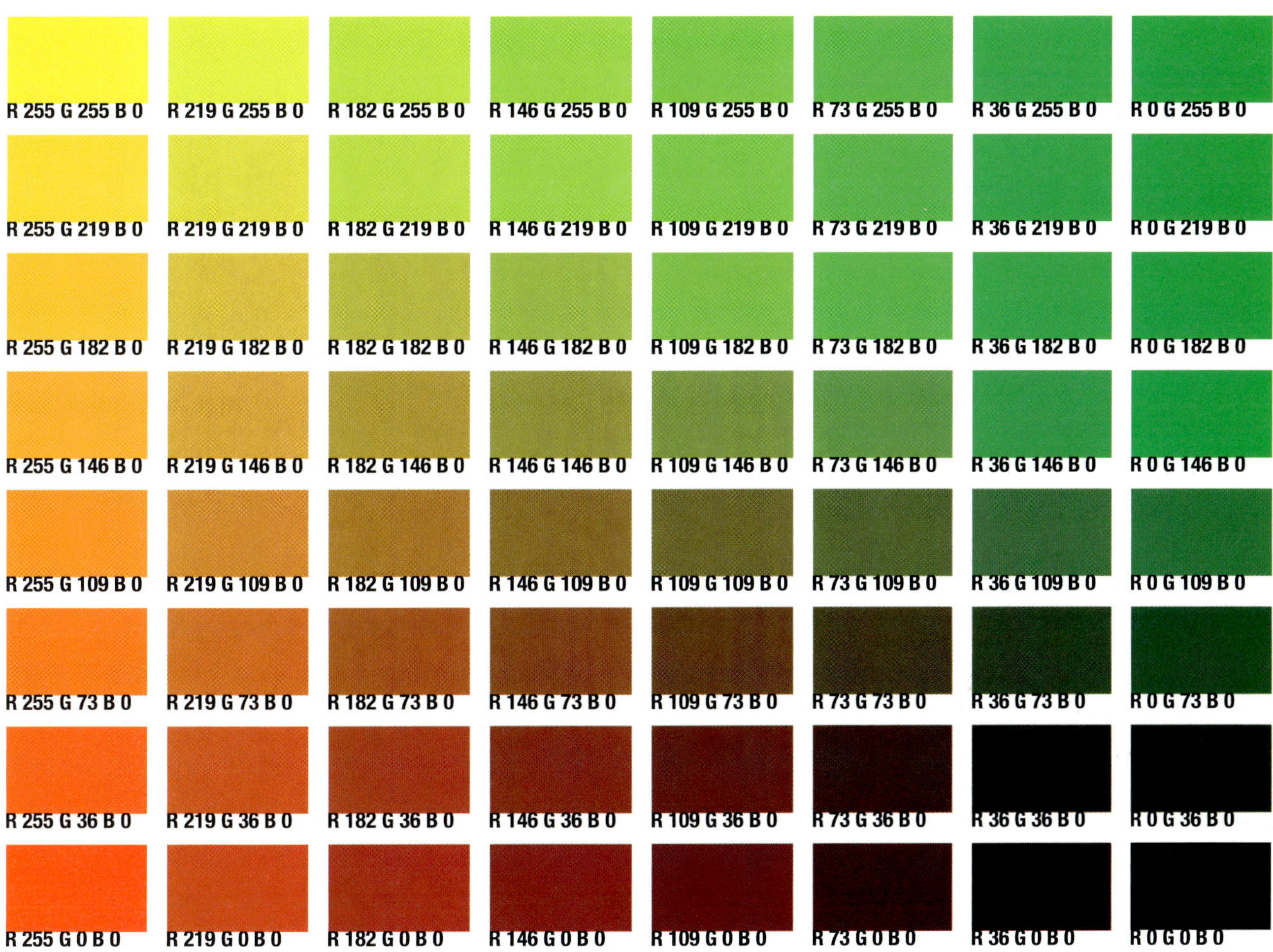
R 255 G 255 B 0
R 219 G 255 B 0
R 182 G 255 B 0
R 146 G 255 B 0
R 109 G 255 B 0
R 73 G 255 B 0
R 36 G 255 B 0
R 0 G 255 B 0
R 255 G 219 B 0
R 219 G 219 B 0
R 182 G 219 B 0
R 146 G 219 B 0
R 109 G 219 B 0
R 73 G 219 B 0
R 36 G 219 B 0
R 0 G 219 B 0
R 255 G 182 B 0
R 219 G 182 B 0
R 182 G 182 B 0
R 146 G 182 B 0
R 109 G 182 B 0
R 73 G 182 B 0
R 36 G 182 B 0
R 0 G 182 B 0
R 255 G 146 B 0
R 219 G 146 B 0
R 182 G 146 B 0
R 146 G 146 B 0
R 109 G 146 B 0
R 73 G 146 B 0
R 36 G 146 B 0
R 0 G 146 B 0
R 255 G 109 B 0
R 219 G 109 B 0
R 182 G 109 B 0
R 146 G 109 B 0
R 109 G 109 B 0
R 73 G 109 B 0
R 36 G 109 B 0
R 0 G 109 B 0
R 255 G 73 B 0
R 219 G 73 B 0
R 182 G 73 B 0
R 146 G 73 B 0
R 109 G 73 B 0
R 73 G 73 B 0
R 36 G 73 B 0
R 0 G 73 B 0
R 255 G 36 B 0
R 219 G 36 B 0
R 182 G 36 B 0
R 146 G 36 B 0
R 109 G 36 B 0
R 73 G 36 B 0
R 36 G 36 B 0
R 0 G 36 B 0
R 255 G 0 B 0
R 219 G 0 B 0
R 182 G 0 B 0
R 146 G 0 B 0
R 109 G 0 B 0
R 73 G 0 B 0
R 36 G 0 B 0
R 0 G 0 B 0

Color Vocabulary

Achromatic. The total absence of color: Comprised only of black, gray and white values.

Additive color. Color created by mixing the rays of white light, from which all color is derived. The spectrum of color exists within the rays of white light. Superimposing the three *additive* primaries (RGB), which when reversed will create white light.

Analogous Color. Colors that are closely related in hue. They are side-by-side on the color circle. Three to five colors in order constitute an analogous color harmony. They are basically a *family* of hues.

Atom. the smallest particle of an element that still retains the propertiesof any given element. The atom is the *mother-ship* with a cargo of smaller particles and units, including the all important color quark.

Brilliance. Same as the word intensity, which refers to the change in lightness in any given hue.

Chroma/Chromatic. Pertains specifically to the presence of color. The opposite of Achromatic.

Chiaroscuro. The average gradation of values from light to dark. A type of tonal shifting across a curved or variable surface, which is responsible for creating volume and mass. The skilled use of Chiaroscuro is to create believable space or the illusion of form, on a flat surface.

Color. Color is the visually revealed component of light. Color possesses certain physiological factors, which are accompanied by various psychological ramifications, and symbolical elements. The symbolical and psychological aspects of color are at variance, since they are determined by specific cultural perceptions.

Color Dyad. A color harmony consisting of two opposing colors on the color circle. Another definition for dyads is a *complementary* color scheme (see first page of chapter one).

Color Hexad. A color harmony comprised of six colors. A hexagon within the color circle determines specific color orders. The color order is designated by the points where each line meets. A hexad is made-up of three complementary pairs (see first page of chapter one).

Color Tetrad. A color harmony comprised of four colors. A tetrad can exist in two forms. The first is a perfect square inscribed within the color circle. Each point where lines connect will determine the harmony color order. The second form of a tetrad harmony can be determined by inscribing a rectangle in the color circle. The same method determines the color order as before. Tetrads contain two primary colors and their complements, or a complementary pair of intermediates (see first page of chapter one).

Color Triad. A color harmony containing three colors. A triad is an equilateral triangle inscribed within the color circle. Color harmony is determined by the point where each line meets. Primary and secondary triads are the most common (see first page of chapter one).

Color Quarks. Contained within the atom are *baryon* particles, each one containing three quarks. Each baryon bundle of three quarks contains one red, one green, and one blue quark. Together, these constitute the additive *primary* colors. Constantly colliding,these quarks form white light, the sum of all colors.

Mesons by comparison, carry a colored quark and a antiquark, which consist of *complementary* colors.

CMYK. An acronym for digital color: Cyan, magenta, yellow and black. They are the subtractive colors of inks in a printer.

Color while on the monitor is referred to as RGB *additive* color, but when printed, it becomes CMYK *subtractive* color.

Complementary Color. Two colors directly opposite of each other on the color circle.

The three basic complements are comprised of one primary and one secondary, such as Red and green, yellow and violet and blue and orange.

Electromagnetic Spectrum. A chart representing every possible radiation emitted from high energy gamma rays (shortest waves) to low energy radio waves (longest waves). *Visible light*, which equates to the spectrum of colors, is located in the center of the spectral chart between the gamma and radio waves spectrum.

Hue. Hue is the common *name* of a color and indicates it's position in the spectrum or color circle. Hue is determined by the specific wavelength of the color in a ray of white light.

Intensity. Intensity is the degree or amount of saturation strength, or purity in any particular hue. Intensity also refers to brightness, whereas it's cousin, which is *saturation* refers to purity. Intensity then, refers to a certain level of brightness in a given hue, as well as it's amount strength of purity in a given color.

Intermediate Color. A color produced by the mixture of one primary and one secondary color. In the color circle, it is located between any single primary and secondary color. It is also referred to as *tertiary* color. (see tertiary).

Key Color. When referring to key, we generally say that there are two states of existence for keys, that is to say high key and low key colors. High key is very bright, or think of a composition being very light, a tendency toward overall brightness or clarity. Low key is a dull state, or overall darker composition. Think of tints for high key and shades for low key. High key tends, at times to be somewhat radiant, where low key is not. Intermediate key is simply that; a means to be more specific.

Light. The revealed *source* of component colors within the electromagnetic system of wave lengths, known as the visible spectrum of color.

Local Color. Local, or objective color is the perceived notion about the color we see. It is what we *think we see*, as opposed to what the eye actually sees.

Monochromatic. Having only one hue with a complete range of values. So, a monochromatic blue composition will have a range or variable of values from light to dark blues.

Neutrals. *1.* The inclusion of all color wavelengths will produce white, and the absence of any wavelengths will be perceived as black. With neutrals, no single color is noticed—only a sense of light and dark, or the range from white through gray to black. *2.* A color altered by the addition of it's complement, so that the original sensation of hues is lost or grayed.

Neutralized Color. A color that has been grayed or reduced in intensity by being mixed with any of the neutrals, or with a complementary color.

Optical Color. A type of additive color when two or more colors are closely juxtaposed. When viewed from a distance these combinations of colors appear to blend optically to produce colors other than those seen as *local colors*. When positioned closely together, they are perceived as a new color. Optical color is what your eye *actually perceives*, as opposed to what you think you see.

Pigment. Physical color substances, both natural and synthetic, that can be mixed to cover a another tangible surface. Pigments are added to liquid vehicles, such as egg yolk or linseed oils to produce paints or inks, and are considered *subtractive* color. See *Sennelier Pigments* list of Pigment Properties in Chapter Two.

Primary Color. The preliminary hues that cannot be broken down in order to make other component colors. The basic hues in any *subtractive* color system that in theory may be used to mix all other colors (red, yellow and blue). In theory, all colors of subtractive pigments mixed produce black. *Additive primary* colors are the primaries of light (red, green and blue). All colors of the additive primary lights mixed produce white (light).

Reflected Color. The absolute truest color of any particular object is revealed by reflected color. It's true color is separated from the other spectral colors, when the remaining colors are absorbed into that object's surface. A red apple appears to be red because the red is reflected back into the viewer's eyes, while the remaining spectrum of colors are absorbed into the apple's surface. Basically, the molecular constitution of the apple's surface recognizes the ray of red light only.

Refracted Light. The bending of light as it travels from one transparent medium to another, such as when light travels through two pieces of glass, through a white diamond, or when light travels from air to water.

Saturation. In pigment, it is the absolute purity of a given hue. It is total freedom from black, gray or white; it is the pure state of a color, or full stregth. In additive color or prismatic hues, it is the color spectrum, which possesses the maximum saturation of a hue.

Secondary Color. A color produced by a mixture of two primary colors on the color circle, which are Orange, Green and Violet.

Shade. The addition of black to a given hue. Shading gradates from white to gray on the value scale, in that order.

Simultaneous Contrast. When two different colors, such as complements come into direct contact with one another, creating a neutral gray zone between. The contrast intensifies the difference between the two, and in many cases a thin gray line will appear at the point where the colors come together. This is particularly true when saturated red is joined to it's complement of green, which will produce a very obvious gray line between them. The two complements have visually cancelled each other at that juncture. Basically, the eye mixes the two complements, and cancels (neutralizes) them between.

Split-Complements. One specific color plus the two colors that exist on either side of it's complement. An example would be yellow and it's complement of violet. One half of violet would be added to red, producing a warm violet, and the other half of the violet would then be added to blue, which produces a cool violet. Therefore, the split complement is comprised of yellow, red-violet, and blue-violet. It is in effect a non-equilateral triangle of three colors. (see first page of chapter one)

Subjective Color. Color resulting from the mind, which demonstrates a personal viewpoint, particular bias, mood or emotion. Color combinations that tend to produce creative or original results.

Subtractive Color. The sensations of color that are produced by wavelengths of light, which are reflected back to the viewer's eyes after all other colors have been absorbed by the object. For example, the surface of a green leaf has a particular molecular constitution that is only recognized by green in the spectrum of visual light. All other colors are not accepted, and are absorbed into the leaf, rather than reflected back to the eye.

Temperature. The colors of the spectrum, which are observed in their warm to cool and cool to warm order. Warm colors are red, orange and yellow. Cool colors are green, blue, indigo and violet. Violet can be either warm or cool, depending on whether it is closer to the red side of the color wheel, or the blue side respectively.

Tertiary Color. Most refer to this as interchangeable with the word *intermediate*.

Tint. The addition of white to a given hue. Tinting is a gradient from gray to white on the value scale, in that order. Tinting tends to brighten a color.

Tone. Any hue with a combination of white and black, which reflects the overall values of a composition. The general tone of a composition can refer to the tints and shades throughout a given composition, which is responsible for it's overall ambiance.

Value. The relative degree of lightness or darkness, or light to dark gradations, which can be seen on a gray scale. *Chiaroscuro* is much the same in this respect.

Visible Spectrum. A band of seven individual colors that results when a beam of white light is broken into it's component wave lengths, which we can identify as particular hues (for example from the sun's white light). Located in the center of the electromagnetic spectrum in the form of *red, orange, yellow, green, blue, indigo (blue-green), and violet.*

Index

Note: page numbers in *italics* refer to illustrations; those followed by "n" refer to footnotes